MY TRUE NATURE
Volume Three

A Call for Me

MICHAEL JONES

Published in 2022 by FeedARead.com Publishing

A CIP catalogue record for this title is available from the British Library.

About the author

There are at least 15,000 Michael Joneses world-wide with an email account. The author is one of them.
mjmytruenature@gmail.com
To learn more about the background to the My True Nature series visit facebook.com/mytruenaturemichaeljones

Many thanks to Céline Nouzille for her artwork and cover design, and to Rose Simpson for her inspiration. And thank you to Rachel.

Once again, this book is dedicated to the memory of Professor Hazel Dewart, who introduced me to the work of John Bowlby, and Attachment Theory.

22nd November 1976

I'm nineteen now, and everything in my life feels like it's falling apart and out of control. When I was sixteen, I felt exactly the same, (was it really only three years ago?) All I wanted to do was write and draw, so my big notebooks were full of the story of my life. I didn't bother to hide my books anymore, and didn't care if anyone sneaked a look inside. After all, I didn't feel any sense of shame about what happened to me when I was little. Nobody can blame a child for the things that adults do.

Just after my sixteenth birthday, something terrible and shocking happened to me, and though my sense of shock gradually subsided, it was replaced by an awful feeling of dread. At the time, I was reading *Rebecca* by Daphne Du Maurier, and was fascinated by her description of the once-beautiful garden at Manderley, that was now derelict and completely overgrown. In my imagination, it was no longer a home for bunny rabbits, moles, squirrels, and other cute little animals, but was now inhabited by vicious creatures that were half-man and half goodness-knows-what, like the grotesque goblins of Arthur Rackham's illustrations for *Goblin Market*. For a while, I was haunted by that description of the abandoned garden, and my terrible feelings of loss and dread for the future felt like ivy that creeps up a tree, and gradually strangles the life out of it. I was desperate to talk to someone, to unburden myself of my grief and fear. I even wondered about writing to Stephen Hunter, my lovely Art Therapist, but had no idea how to contact him. So the only way I could stop the dread from choking me to death was to write all about myself.

This is the next part of my life story, which I wrote when I was sixteen.

○ ○ ○ ○ ○ ○

I want to write more about what happened six years ago, but I'm not ready yet, because it's still too painful. It will take me a little while to summon up the courage to do it, so for now I'm going to describe a painting. It's not something I've painted yet, but one day I will. Then I can finally get rid of the dreadful feelings that I have carried inside me, ever since that day when Muriel didn't come to collect me from school. The title of my painting is *Clouds Over the Estuary*.

Imagine that you are in an art gallery, just wandering around, when suddenly you see my huge painting. Unfortunately, there's no title or description on the wall next to the painting, so I'll have to help you try to make sense of this huge piece of Art. Let's walk back about fifteen feet (I told you it was big) and see what we can see.

I've decided to use a lot of blue, and some white and grey and silver, and light purple. It's one of what I call my 'big brush paintings', so you won't see very much when you are close up. It's a bit like one of Turner's paintings, except there is no shipwreck or warship on fire. The painting is dominated by the sky, and because I was inspired by Scotland, there's a lot of cloud. That's not so good for a family with children, who have planned a day out by the sea, but it's perfect for an artist like me, because clouds and sky in my paintings are where my feelings lie.

The sky is very interesting, because I've used a particular type of light blue that you will find in Vincent Van Gogh's *A Wheatfield, with Cypresses*. I saw that painting for the first time in a second hand shop in Ashbourne, and used three weeks' worth of pocket money to buy it. Muriel thought it would be fun to take me on the train up to London, to visit the National Gallery, to see the original painting. As you can imagine, I wanted to stand in front of that painting and examine it in minute detail. But, as usual, the painting was above my eye-level, and I couldn't get close enough. An attendant was watching me, and came over to talk to Muriel. Muriel said, 'Watch out, Pippa. I think we are about to be told off.' But the attendant smiled at me, reached into his pocket and said, 'Perhaps you might consider using these?' He handed me a small pair of gold binoculars. He said, 'These are opera glasses, and if you stand just here,' he pointed to a spot about ten feet away from the picture, 'I think you will get as good a view as if you were right up close to the painting.' And it was true! And of course, I lovingly examined every inch of that painting for half an hour. The blues in the sky excited me in a way that I can't describe. When we got home, I spent a long time trying to recreate the blues I had seen, and I was filled with the same excitement that I had felt in the Gallery. It excites me now, just to think about those colours.

I've put that blue in my painting, and the clouds I've painted suggest that it might be a nice day. But coming in from the right, from Scotland, we can see a huge dirty grey-black cloud. It has moved very fast, and at first you might think that it's ugly smoke, as if someone up on those Scottish hills is burning a huge pile of tyres and plastic. But these are rain clouds, so you can imagine that soon you will have to dash indoors.

Are there any people? If you look carefully, in the bottom right-hand corner you can just make out a figure by a low wall. You can't see any facial features, but from the long black hair, you might imagine she's a girl. Now, go up close to the picture and you'll see that I have painted this girl very carefully. It's a summer's day, but she's wearing a white woollen hat and a sensible Scottish jumper. She hasn't tucked her hair under her hat, so her hair is blowing in all directions. That's because in this part of lowland Scotland, and in this very wide estuary, there is always a lot of wind. During the day, the wind blows off the sea, and because it's a huge estuary, the breezes and strong winds blow in all directions. So you will always need a hat that you can pull down firmly, a sensible jumper to keep you warm, and an anorak close by, because it's bound to rain.

The girl is nearly ten. She has turned her head to the left, to look across the estuary, because she knows that's where England is. And that's where her mother and aunt are. She tries to stand there at a quarter past eight every morning, because

7

that was the exact time that she last saw her beloved aunt. The girl is convinced that at this time every morning, her mother and aunt will be looking towards Scotland, and thinking deeply about her. And hopefully, far away in the south of England, the aunt and the mother will be holding hands, to try to make their deep sorrow and longing bearable.

You can't see the girl's face, but I can tell you that she isn't crying. Instead, her face has a fixed blank expression, with a very slight smile. Her smile is her way of saying, 'I'm all right you know. Look, I'm smiling, so please leave me alone. Leave me alone to look at the mud and sand, and the lovely little black and white birds who fly about in groups, low over the mud, and peep-peep to each other all day long.'

I think I'm ready to write about what happened.

I knew that Muriel wouldn't come to collect me after school, and I think the adults in school knew that as well. Mr Wadeson, my headmaster, took me to the sick room and told me to lie down and have a rest. He asked his secretary to look after me, but she had jobs to do, so for a while I was on my own. Muriel's suitcase was in the corner of the room. It used to stay on top of the big wardrobe in Mummy and Muriel's bedroom. Sometimes, when I woke up in their bed, it would be the first thing that I saw. It used to be full of photos, and bits and pieces from when Muriel was younger, before she met us. And now it was in school, in the sick room, near me. I think I wasn't supposed to see it; but there it was, and that's how I knew that Muriel wouldn't be coming to collect me.

It was a Monday, and all weekend Mummy had been very nervous. I knew Muriel was nervous too, because she kept chewing the inside of her lips. Mummy had found it difficult to talk, and kept gazing out of the kitchen window, at nothing in particular. The telephone rang a lot, and once Mummy took the receiver off the hook, so that nobody could ring us. I wanted to go round to see Lucy, but Muriel said it would be best if I stayed at home. Nobody smiled, and both grown-ups sighed a lot. I knew that something terrible was going to happen. In the middle of the night I heard them both go downstairs, but I didn't dare go down to see them. I heard Mummy crying, and she said, 'That bastard,' and Muriel said, 'Shh, Ruth, shh.'

The terrible thing that we had all been waiting for was about to happen, but I didn't know what it was.

I heard all the children going to lunch. The secretary came in and said I must eat something, and that soon Lucy would bring me something nice. Lucy brought me a sandwich and two homemade biscuits. She said that one of the biscuits was hers, for her pudding, but she wanted me to have it. I looked at her, but couldn't open my mouth to say, 'Thank you, you are so kind, and I am so lucky to have a best friend like you.'

Lucy said, 'Pippa, please talk to me.' I wanted to talk, but I had lost the power to speak. She said, 'Mum says I must say goodbye to you. It's not fair.' Then she started crying.

I was lying on the bed and Lucy was sitting next to me, holding my hand. She wiped her nose on her sleeve and said, 'Sometimes when I'm in bed at night, Mum comes to tuck me in, and always asks me if I've said my prayers, and I say, "Of course I have!" But she knows it's not true, and she just looks in my eyes and smiles. But she isn't telling me off. She's really just reminding me, and then we say them together.

'But when I do remember to say my prayers, when I'm on my own in bed, I don't really say prayers like in church, where you say "Dear Lord" and "Amen". I just think of Jesus, and I thank him for all the nice things that I have, and the nice people I know, and the things I have done in the day. I used to ask him to make me read and write properly, and to make Mum and Dad have another baby. But I don't do that anymore, because some things just aren't possible. But I shall never forget to say my prayers now, because every night I'm going to pray for you. I have to be in bed at eight o'clock every night, so I'm going to pray for you then. I am going to pray that you are safe and happy, and that people are looking after you properly. I can't write you letters, because I know you wouldn't understand them.'

I supposed that Lucy's mum had told her that I was going away, and wouldn't be coming back. I didn't say anything to Lucy. I thought perhaps my heart was breaking, and I was dying from it. Lucy saw the suitcase and asked me if it was mine. I nodded. She said, 'Sit up Pippa, and let's look inside.' I think that was her idea of how to cheer me up. Perhaps she thought I was going on a lovely holiday. She opened it up and we saw my nice yellow pyjamas with the ladybird buttons, and my clothes for playing outdoors. And there was a big paper bag with some paintbrushes in it and some paints, and a box of pastels and a brand new sketchpad. And there was a dress that I liked, and some socks and knickers. Then we saw the yellow cloth bag, and I knew that Polish Teddy was inside.

Then the bell rang in the playground, to tell everyone that it was time to line up, ready to go back into class. Lucy said that Mr Wadeson had told her that she could stay with me for as long as she liked. She said I must eat my sandwich, because her mum had made it especially for me, and if I didn't eat it, then Lucy would get into trouble. I knew that wasn't true.
I did my best for her, because I didn't want her mum to think I had been ungrateful. I ate a few mouthfuls, but it all tasted like rubber, and I found it difficult to chew and swallow. Lucy said, 'Shall I help you?' and ate the rest.
Then she said she needed to do a wee very badly, and asked me to go to the toilets with her, because she was still scared of the spiders in there. I knew that she was just trying to cheer me up, and she picked up my Clarks sandals and begged me to put them on. They were almost destroyed by all the hard wear that I had put them through, and were becoming too tight, because I had grown so much recently. Muriel had promised to take me to the shoe shop to buy me a new pair, but I knew that wouldn't happen now. Lucy said, 'Come on, Pippa. Come with me. Please.'

It was a huge effort to get up off the bed, and Lucy held my hand as we walked to the toilets. I stood by the door while she did her wee, and then I realised that I needed to go too. Lucy stayed in the cubicle with me, which was the first time she had ever done that. As we walked back along the corridor, we passed our classroom. Our teacher, Mr Rooker, was standing up and telling the children to get out their exercise books. He saw us, opened the door, and said, 'Just a minute, girls...' but Mr Wadeson was outside the sick room with a lady, so we carried on walking towards him. Mr Wadeson had his back to us, and was talking to the lady. She pointed at me, and Mr Wadeson turned and said to us, 'Ah, there you are. Where have you been?'

I looked at the floor as we carried on walking towards them. Lucy explained that we had just been to the toilets, and Mr Wadeson crouched down next to me and held my hand. He said, 'Look at me Pippa.' I couldn't, so he put his fingers under my chin and very gently lifted my head up, so I was looking in his eyes. They were very shiny. He told me that the lady was called Miss Cornish, and that she had come to collect me. He said, 'Your Mummy and your Auntie Muriel are still in London. They have been to The Court, and The Judge has decided...' He coughed. 'The Judge has decided that you can't live with your mother and your aunt anymore. Miss Cornish has a piece of paper that explains that she is allowed to take you, and I have no choice but to let you go.'
He took his fingers away from my chin, and then stood up and put his hand gently on my shoulder. I put my head down again. I could see another pair of men's shoes next to his, and looked up and saw that it was Mr Rooker. June was there too, and she was holding Lucy's hand.

I looked up at Miss Cornish. She wasn't smiling, and I thought she looked very worried about something. Perhaps she thought I would scream and shout and kick her, or even try to bite her hand and run away. Perhaps she thought I'd shout 'I want my Mummy!' Or maybe she was worried that I would spit at her and yell, 'Keep away from me, you nasty fucking bitch!' But I didn't do any of those things. I could tell that she didn't like the job she was doing, so I knew it was best for me to go quietly, without a fuss. She took my hand and said, 'Come on Philippa, there's a good girl.'

We all went into the playground. A big shiny green car was parked outside the school gates. I wanted to say goodbye. I wanted to thank Mr Wadeson and Mr Rooker for being such kind and interesting teachers. I wanted to tell June that her school dinners were lovely, and to thank her for her sandwich, and to say I had eaten it all up. I wanted to say goodbye to Lucy. I wanted to tell her that she and Roger were my best friends in the whole world. But I didn't say anything to them, and I didn't even wave goodbye. I wanted to, but I couldn't open my mouth, because it felt like it was glued shut. And I couldn't move any of the muscles of my face, so it must have looked very blank. Even now, I worry sometimes that people in my lovely primary school thought I was a rude and ungrateful girl; after all they had done for me.

A big man was sitting in the driver's seat. He got out and opened the back door, then smiled at me and said, 'Hop in, there's a good girl.'

Mr Wadeson said to Miss Cornish, 'Don't forget this,' and passed her the suitcase. She took it without saying thank you. Then he said, 'And there's this too,' and held out my yellow cloth bag. Miss Cornish looked at it and said, 'That's all we can take.'

Mr Wadeson said, 'Goodbye, Pippa,' and bent down and kissed me on top of my head. I felt his arm around me and he was squeezing my shoulder very tightly, as if he didn't want to let me go. As I got in the car I heard June say, 'Oh dear,' and she sniffed very loudly. As the car moved away, I saw Lucy waving, gently. Mr Rooker had taken his glasses off and was wiping both his eyes with the back of his hand.

It was a very long drive. Once, Miss Cornish took a tube of Smarties out of her jacket pocket and offered them to me. I wanted to say, 'No thank you', but my mouth wouldn't work. I just looked ahead and fell asleep. There's not really much else to say about the journey. We stopped in a car park where there was a big café. Miss Cornish had some sandwiches and a flask full of tea for us all. She and the driver ate, but I didn't want anything, and just looked straight ahead. Miss Cornish took me into the café, to go to the toilet. I went into the cubicle and she said, 'Don't lock the door, there's a good girl.' I sat on the toilet, but no wee would come out. She said, 'Are you sure you've been?'

Then it was very dark, and when the car finally stopped, I was fast asleep. All I remember was a lady saying, 'Let's get you into bed. And what have you got in here?' She must have opened the yellow cloth bag, because she gave me Polish Teddy to cuddle.

The War begins

I was still asleep in the morning, when a lady came in and drew the curtains, and told me that she was Mrs Durkin, and it was a lovely sunny morning, and time for me to get up. She had a Scottish accent. I got out of bed straight away, and stood still. I was wearing a nightie that I had never seen before, and it was all wet at the back, and a bit at the front. Mrs Durkin saw it and pulled the bedclothes back, and there was a big damp patch that smelled of wee. She tutted and said, 'Goodness me! A big girl like you, doing a thing like that!' She went to a chest of drawers and took out some clothes. She said, 'I'll show you where the bathroom is, and then you can have a wash and put these on.'

I followed her to the bathroom, which was next to the bedroom. I thought I was going to have a bath, but Mrs Durkin said, 'There's no hot water for a bath. Baths are in the evening, so just wash yourself in the sink and make sure you dry yourself properly between your legs, so you don't get sore. When you've finished, I'll be in the bedroom and you can help me strip the bed.'

The soap had a horrible strong smell and the towel was old and rough. I was expecting to wear the clothes that Mummy and Muriel had packed, but instead there was a white vest, and a white blouse with a frilly collar and long sleeves with frilly cuffs. There was a pair of white knickers and a pair of long white socks. There was a kilt too, which was rather nice, but seemed a bit smart, and I worried that I might soon get the whole outfit dirty.

There were no slippers or shoes for me to wear. I went back in the bedroom and stood by my bed. I could see that all of the bed covers were wet, including the blankets and coverlet. Mrs Durkin must have forgotten to make me do a wee before she put me into bed. She was looking out of the big open windows. She said, with her back to me. 'Come here and look at the view.' I couldn't move, except to lower my head and look at the floor. She turned round, walked towards the bed, and said, 'Yes, you should be ashamed of yourself. This is not going to happen again. Do you hear me?' I didn't say anything. She pulled all the covers off my bed and we both saw a wet patch on the mattress. Mrs Durkin sighed and bundled up the wet sheets and held them out to me. My arms stayed at my sides. She put the sheets on the floor in front of me and said, 'Look, it was my fault that you wet the bed. I forgot to take you to the bathroom last night. Now, hold out your arms and you can carry the sheets downstairs. Then you can have breakfast. It's all ready for you in the dining room.' I did as I was told, and followed her out of the room.

Outside my room there was a big old grandfather clock, with a pendulum. It was a quarter past eight. That was the time, on the day before, that Muriel had said goodbye to me. I decided that every day, at exactly that time, I would think of Muriel. We were in a big house, and it reminded me of the hotel in Norfolk, where I had slept with Mummy. But this place was completely silent, so I wondered if there were any other guests staying there, apart from me. In the hall, there was a small table with a little gong and beater on it, and a big book with *visitors* written on the front. We went into a room that had

14

a dining table in it, covered with a white tablecloth, and places set for two people. In the middle of the table was a plate with some slices of funny-looking bread on it, and a little bowl of marmalade, and some butter in a small blue and white dish. There was a silver teapot and a little milk jug that matched the butter dish. Muriel would have said that the jug looked *charming*.

I could smell the bread, and realised that I was very hungry.
Mrs Durkin said, 'You'll need to eat a good hearty breakfast, because we have a busy day ahead of us. I'm going to show you around the park, and then we must go into town to buy you some new shoes. That'll be a nice adventure for you, won't it? Now help yourself to some bread and butter and marmalade, and make sure you use the wee spoon to scoop out the marmalade, because we don't want any butter getting in there.'
I could feel myself shutting down. I felt like a wasp had just stung me, and it was still there on my bare arm. If I moved, it would sting me again, and again, and again, and keep stinging me every time I moved, until it got tired, or ran out of its stingy poison, or just got bored. I wanted to know exactly what was happening to me. Where was I? Who was Mrs Durkin? How long was I going to stay there? Was this a boarding school? Were we here all on our own? Did Mummy know where I was? But all power of speech had vanished from my mouth.

Mrs Durkin took a slice of bread and put it on my plate, then spread some butter on it, very thinly, and took half a teaspoon of marmalade and spread that too. The bread was thick and long and only had a dark brown crust on the top and at the bottom. While she was spreading, Mrs Durkin said, 'This is good Scottish pan bread. I expect you've never seen the like of it before, when you lived in England. Now eat it up and I'll get your hot food ready. I'm sure you'll love that.'
As soon as she left the room, I helped myself to more marmalade and ate my slice of bread, and then another one. I heard Mrs Durkin clattering some pans and singing in a room

nearby, which I supposed was the kitchen. I went over to the window and looked out. It was lovely outside. There was a large stone terrace, with a beautiful lawn beyond, and I could smell roses. I saw a man with a noisy lawnmower, and he waved at me and came towards the terrace. He shouted, 'Hello there! You must be the wee lassie that's going to be living here!' Then he walked off behind his mower.

Where was I? Was it really possible that I had been taken all the way to Scotland? I knew from my atlas that Scotland was a long, long way from Ashbourne. Someone coughed behind me. It was Mrs Durkin, with a tea towel and a hot plate in her hand. She said, 'I don't remember saying you could leave the table. Go and sit back down and eat this lovely food, and mind you don't burn yourself, because the plate is very hot. I'm going to get mine ready. Make a start before it gets cold.'
There were two lovely fried eggs, with a slice of fried bread and some grilled tomatoes, and even a few mushrooms. Unfortunately, there were two very large slices of bacon on the plate. When Mrs Durkin came back in, I had my head down and my hands in my lap. I didn't dare look at her. She said, 'Come on now. You must be hungry after that long journey. You must have travelled about four hundred miles to get here.'
So I was in Scotland! We had driven all the way to Scotland!

I wanted to say, 'I'm very sorry Mrs Durkin, but I can't eat bacon, because I'm Jewish. Perhaps you don't know that, or perhaps you have forgotten that Jewish people don't eat pork. It's very kind of you, but I really can't eat it. And I mustn't eat anything else on the plate, in case it has touched the bacon. I'm sure you'll understand.' But I couldn't say any of those things.
She said, 'Eat it up.' I wanted to say, 'I really can't. Please don't make me,' but I couldn't.
She frowned. 'That's a perfectly good cooked breakfast. It mustn't go to waste.' I wanted to say, 'You have it. If it's so good, I don't mind you having it.' But my jaws were locked tight shut.

She scowled at me. 'But that's all there is. If you don't want it, then you can't be hungry. You may leave the table now, and go to your room. I will come up shortly, and we can have a wee talk about the rules here.'

I left the room and went upstairs. I wanted to clean my teeth, so I looked around for my suitcase. I felt sure that Mummy would have put a sponge bag in there, with my toothbrush and a tube of my favourite *Signal* toothpaste. She always wanted me to clean my teeth after breakfast, and used to say, 'I want everybody to see your lovely white teeth when you smile at them.' And if Muriel reminded me, I would run and clean my teeth really thoroughly, because she would always give me a kiss afterwards, on the lips. I couldn't find my suitcase anywhere, but I found Polish Teddy by the side of the bed. I picked him up and sniffed him all over, and was pleased that he didn't smell of my wee. I took him to the open window, and we both looked out. It was truly gorgeous outside. We could see across the lawn to some bushes, and two very tall pine trees that were swaying in the breeze, with a stone wall beneath them, that separated the garden from a small road, and beyond that a beach. I was somewhere by the seaside!

I said to Polish Teddy, 'Where are we, Teddy? Where is my suitcase? Where are my pyjamas and my clothes? Who is that horrible lady? How long are we going to be here? Is this a prison?' Then I realised that he might not understand me, because he had been made in Germany, and had lived with a Polish family. But he had been with me for a year, so I felt sure that he could understand a few basic words and everyday expressions in English. Roger once swore at Teddy, and he was certain that every time he walked past Teddy he could hear him telling Roger to fuck off. Roger only ever told that story to me, because he knew that Lucy got upset if she ever heard anyone swearing. Once Roger told me that he would rather have both his legs bitten off by a lion than upset Lucy. I think that was his way of telling me that he loved her, which I knew anyway. So I said in a very loud voice, (because that's how you speak to

17

foreigners), 'Me wish Muriel here. She go tell that stupid nasty lady that Pippa is Jewish, so don't eat pig meat! And me want nice soap, and me want dry my Lovely Place with soft towel. Me all itchy down there!'

I heard a cough down below, and looked down. Mrs Durkin was leaning out of the window and looking up at me. She said, 'Philippa! Who are you talking to?' I ran away from the window, but in my fright I left Polish Teddy on the window ledge. I rushed back to get him, but accidentally knocked him off the ledge. I heard him bounce on the terrace and Mrs Durkin said, 'This is just too bad!'

I heard Mrs Durkin marching upstairs, so I rushed to stand by my bed. She came in and said, 'So you *can* talk after all! We are not going to have any fun and games like that here! Now you can stay in here for the rest of the morning, and will only leave to go to the bathroom.'

She left the room and closed the door. I waited until I heard her footsteps on the stairs and on the tiled floor in the hallway, then I checked the door, to see if she had locked me in. I could open the door, but it made a squeaking noise, so I quickly shut it again.

I was very frightened, so I thought of Mummy and Muriel, and wondered what they would have done if they were a child like me. They had both suffered terribly when they were children, but were still alive and in love, and I knew that they were missing me very badly. But now Polish Teddy was gone, and I was truly on my own. I wanted to cry, and I could feel my eyes filling up with tears. But then I stopped myself. I thought, 'I know what Mummy and Muriel would do if they were me. They would say, "This is WAR!".'

There was nothing else to do except explore my room and look out of the window. It really was a lovely big room, and the view out onto the sea was delightful. I was very upset, and very hungry, but I wasn't going to show it. I just wished I could talk, because then I would be able to ask questions and explain myself, and defend myself against that beastly lady. Outside my room, the big clock was ticking. It chimed every hour, and once on the half hour. The man had stopped mowing the lawn and was standing, facing the bushes. I knew he was doing a wee. When he had finished, he did up the zip in his trousers, turned around and looked up at the house. I thought, 'If that were me, I would have checked to see if anyone was looking *before* I decided to have a wee, not afterwards.' Luckily, he was too far away for me to see anything. He saw me and waved. I wanted to wave back, but my arm wouldn't work. The man carried on trimming the bushes. There was something very large lying on the ground next to him. At first I thought it must be his coat, but then it stood up, squatted down, and started to do a poo on the lawn. The man shouted, 'Och no, Sinbad! Dinna do that here!' But it was too late. The man shook his head and laughed, and the huge dog walked away. I had never seen such an enormous dog in my whole life.

I soon got bored with looking out of the window, and was famished. I thought that if Mummy and Muriel were there with me, by now we would have eaten all our breakfast, and Mummy would have explained very politely to Mrs Durkin that we wouldn't like any bacon. Then we would have a quick look around the garden in the sunshine, before taking a walk down to the beach before lunch. We would be chatting and making plans for the rest of the day, and for the days that would follow. And if Mummy had seen the man doing a wee, she would have laughed and said something like 'That's men for you.' And I would have gone downstairs with Muriel, and laughed about me dropping Polish Teddy, and she would hope that sour-faced Mrs Durkin hadn't got too much of a fright, and we would all laugh. At first I would be shy, and hold Muriel's hand tightly, but I would soon get my confidence, and start laughing and skipping around in my bare feet on the lovely soft lawn. And I'd talk about the huge dog, and look at the trees and bushes and roses, and then stand still and slip into My Colour Dream. And Mummy and Muriel wouldn't mind about me being noisy and then suddenly dreaming, because they would know that I was happy. And they would have to explain to the other grown-ups that there was nothing wrong with me. I was just very sensitive to Nature and painting, and I used Art to express my feelings.

I knew I shouldn't have thought about Mummy and Muriel being with me. I had been trying all morning to stop myself from thinking about them. I started to feel as if I was drowning. I can't think of any other way to describe the awful feeling that started in my heart, and then seemed to take over my whole body. I wondered if my heart had broken, and all the blood was filling me up. I couldn't see anymore, because my eyes were full of tears, and I was gasping for breath, because I felt that my throat was full of thick liquid. I had the terrible feeling that I was going to wet myself, and I was terrified, because I thought that blood was trying to come out of my Lovely Place. I ran to the bathroom and sat on the toilet and cried and cried and cried. My wee seemed to go on forever, and I realised that I had been holding it in all morning. My loud weeping turned to a quiet whimper, and I could breathe a bit better. Then I stopped making a noise and I just felt completely empty.

Then the bathroom door opened, and Mrs Durkin came in. She looked straight at me and said, 'I thought it was you in here. When you have finished you can come and help us change the bed. And make sure you wash your hands.' She went out and left the door slightly open. Something happened inside me. She hadn't said anything about me crying. She didn't even think that I might be suffering, because I had been torn from my loving family, and driven in the night to a strange country. She didn't care that I was starving. And she didn't even bother to knock on the bathroom door, when she knew fine well that I was in there. I stopped feeling empty, and felt myself filling up with a completely different feeling. I was going to stay in that bathroom, and listen to her changing my bed. Then I was going to go downstairs and find Polish Teddy, and go in the kitchen and look in the cupboards, and help myself to any food that looked nice. And if Mrs Durkin tried to stop me, I would call her a fucking Scottish bitch, and throw plates and knives and forks at her, and she would have to call the police. And I would tell them that I had been treated terribly, and they would tell The Court, and then I would be taken back home again. I knew how I felt then; I was more than angry; I was furious and enraged.

Then I stopped feeling enraged, because other thoughts came into my mind. Who had told The Court that Mummy and Muriel weren't looking after me properly? Who were the people who had said that Mummy and Muriel were bad people, because they loved each other? Who had paid for the big shiny green car to come and take me away? Why was I so far away from home? Why was I in Scotland? Why was I in this big house? Who had decided that I should be kept here, and made to wear silly frilly clothes? Who did Mummy say was a bastard? It could only be one person. The person who always had to get what he wanted. The person who had so much money, that he owned factories, and bought and sold things all over the world. It had to be my father. That thought made me want to scream and yell terrible words at the top of my voice. I made my hands into fists and started to hit myself hard on the sides of my head. I tried to yell, but no sound came out.
Mrs Durkin came in again and said, 'Haven't you finished yet? Hurry up. We're waiting.' I ignored her. I didn't care that she saw me hitting myself. I didn't care that she saw me sitting on the toilet.

Then I had another thought. I thought about Mummy and Muriel, when they were children. Mummy had been taken away by strangers, and then the Germans killed her parents. Muriel's parents had been killed too, and she had been brought up by her grandparents, who had sent her to a boarding school, because they didn't want to look after her anymore. Now it was my turn to be taken away. But though Mummy and Muriel had suffered terribly, they had grown up to be nice people (apart from when Mummy became an alcoholic, but that was all my father's fault). Mummy and Muriel were both tough, and this had helped them to survive. So I had to be tough like them. But there was only one problem; I couldn't say anything. This seemed to happen to me whenever I was traumatised. I could talk to people who were kind to me, but became speechless in front of horrible people.

Jeanie
There was a quiet knock on the door, and a lady's voice said, 'Excuse me pet, but are you all right in there? Do you need any help with anything? I mean are you feeling sick, or something like that? Perhaps I can get you something? Mrs Durkin has gone up to the hotel now, and she's asked me to look after you for a wee while, and well, I know you must be feeling awful upset after everything that's happened to you, and I was thinking perhaps we could have a wee talk, and maybe go for a wee walk outside, and see Robbie and Sinbad. Robbie's one of the gardeners, and he works for my dad. My dad's in charge of the gardens and the golf course, so he's more important than anybody else who works here. At least that's what he says. He reckons that if the hotel ran out of beer and whisky, and food to eat, the guests wouldn't mind too much, because all they want to do is to play golf. But if one of the greens has a tiny lump in it, they go mad. That's why my dad doesn't care what Mrs Durkin thinks, and neither do I.

'Robbie's got your teddy. You see, Sinbad found it on the terrace, and Robbie took it off him. His face is a wee bit wet - I mean Teddy's face, not Robbie's - and he said he'd take good care of him for you. We can't change the bed anyway, because the mattress is still damp. I suppose they forgot to remind you to go to the toilet before you went to sleep last night. Mrs Durkin won't be back until lunchtime, so we have a good hour before she comes back. So you're quite safe. And what do you think about coming outside and saying hello to me? Robbie said he was doing a wee in the bushes this morning. He does it there just to annoy Mrs Durkin. And he saw someone at the window. He thought it was her, so he waved, but then he saw it was you, and now he's awful embarrassed.'

I didn't say anything. I couldn't. Then there was another knock and the voice said, 'I'm just going to pop my head round the door for a wee second, to make sure you're all right.' And she did. She wasn't a lady at all, but a big teenager. She had long ginger hair tied up in a bun at the back of her head, and was wearing a very short black dress with a white apron, and she had lipstick on. She said, 'Hello there. What's your name? They tell me you've come all the way from England. My name's Jeanette, but everyone calls me Jeanie, except Mrs Durkin, who's a bit of a dragon. Whenever she gets annoyed with me for not doing things properly, or if she's in one of her bad moods, I just say, "Yes, Mrs Durkin. No, Mrs Durkin. Three bags full Mrs Durkin," I'm not scared of her, and neither is my dad. He just ignores her. But she doesn't really like children, so it's bad luck that they chose her to look after you. But I'm always here, and you can come and see me whenever you like.'

I was still sitting on the toilet, and must have looked very strange, having just bashed myself round the head as hard as I could with my fists. But Jeanie didn't seem to bother about that. She asked me if I'd finished. I nodded my head and it ached a lot, and I realised I hadn't had anything to drink since the day before. She said, 'Well I'll just stand over here by the bath, while you get yourself ready, and then we'll go for a wee walk.'
I flushed the toilet and washed my hands, and Jeanie said, 'God, that soap really stinks! I'll bet it's that nasty Wright's Coal Tar Soap. We hate it, so my dad won't have it in the house. Now come and meet the biggest and gentlest doggie in the whole world.' Jeanie came towards me and held my hand, and we walked out together. As we reached the top of the stairs, I felt myself stopping. Once again, I had the feeling that I had lost control of my movements. Jeanie came back up to me and said, 'It's all right. I'll look after you.'

Those words had an instant effect on me, and I was able to walk down the stairs with her. I stopped at the front door. Jeanie said, 'What's the matter?' I looked at my feet. 'Oh heavens, you've got no shoes! Where are your shoes?'

By now, I think Jeanie had realised that I wasn't being silent on purpose. I supposed she thought I was just very shy. Or perhaps she thought that people from England couldn't understand Scottish people when they were talking, (which was true sometimes, because Jeanie spoke very quickly and her accent was very strong). But then Jeanie began to talk to herself, which is what most sensitive adults do when they are with a very quiet or unhappy child. 'Now what are we going to do? I don't know where Mrs Durkin has put your shoes. They must be somewhere, because I can't believe that you came all the way from England with just your socks on!'

We went through the kitchen and down a short flight of steps, into a dark area. There were lots of pairs of stout leather walking boots and wellies lined up, some coats hanging on pegs, and a stand full of walking sticks and umbrellas. Jeanie put one of the coats on. She looked ridiculous, and I laughed, even though I was a bit frightened. She said, 'These are for the visitors who want to go out walking on the golf course or on the beach, but don't realise how cold and wet it can be here in this part of Scotland!'

Again, I remembered that I was in Scotland, and I felt a dark shadow creeping all over me, like a big cloud passing in front of the sun. I reached out my hand and Jeanie took it and held it tight. She bent down and looked in my eyes. 'What is it my dear? Have I said something wrong?' I looked at her. 'Oh! Perhaps you didn't realise that you're in Scotland? Has nobody told you that?' I nodded my head 'Well then, we've got some explaining to do! But first let's find your shoes.'

Jeanie opened a door and there was a steep flight of steps, going down into the darkness. She switched on the light, and asked me if I wanted to wait at the top of the stairs, or go down with her. I just stood there. 'Do you want to stay here?' I shook my head. 'Or do you want to come down with me into the cellar, and help me find your shoes, and then come straight up again?' I nodded. We walked down carefully. The cellar was very big, and Jeanie said that it was probably almost as big as the whole of the ground floor of the house. It was very tidy, with rows of shelves and big wooden crates, and packing cases and metal trunks. There were so many interesting things to look at, but I just wanted to find my shoes. Right at the far end of the cellar, in a corner that was very dark, because the light from the lightbulbs could hardly reach it, was Muriel's suitcase. It looked like someone had thrown it there. I let go of Jeanie's hand and ran towards it. I opened it up and said a very quiet, 'Oh!' It was empty. Jeanie said, 'That's strange. I wonder what's going on. We can't have you walking around with no shoes on.'

I looked at my socks. The soles were already filthy from the dust on the cellar floor. I imagined Mrs Durkin looking at them and getting very angry with me, and I began to feel frightened. Jeanie said, 'Never you mind about your socks. I'll explain what happened. I don't care if she tells me off.'

Then I thought that Mrs Durkin had probably taken my shoes and put them somewhere safe, because we were going to the shoe shop in the afternoon. I wanted to explain this to Jeanie, but she said, 'I think I know where they are!'

We went back up to the kitchen, and Jeanie looked in a small cupboard full of all sorts of cleaning equipment, and a row of pegs with cloth bags hanging on them. Jeanie felt one of the bags and laughed. 'I think I've found them!'

She lifted out my battered old Clarks school sandals. I grabbed them from her and held them to my chest, as if they were long-lost friends. I put them on and Jeanie said, 'That's the first time I've seen you smile. What a bonnie lassie you are when you smile! I knew the shoes would be there, because that's the shopping bag that Mrs Durkin always takes into town. She's very forgetful, so she always fills up that bag with things that she needs to take on shopping trips. I should be a police detective!'

We went out of the front door and onto the terrace. There was a small metal table with four metal chairs round it, and Polish Teddy was sitting on one of the chairs. Jeanie told me to sit down with her, so that we could check that Teddy was all right. Immediately, the massive dog came up to us, sat next to Jeanie, and put his paw in her lap. He was so big that even though he was sitting down, his shoulders reached almost up to Jeanie's face. The dog put his paw in Jeanie's lap. She shook his paw, then took it away and folded her arms, but he put his paw in her lap again. Every time she took his paw away, he put it back, so she patted him on the head. Every time she stopped doing it, he nudged her hand with his nose. Jeanie said, 'Sinbad, will you stop it now? Och, he'll do that all morning if I let him. Why don't you have a go?'

I put my hand out, but Sinbad just looked at me. Jeanie said, 'You have to say, "Come here Sinbad" and make a noise with your lips like this, and then he'll come over.'

Miraculously, I heard myself say, 'Come here Sinbad,' and made a kissing noise, and he trotted over and sat down next to me, and put his paw in my lap.

Jeanie smiled at me and said, 'There you go! I knew all you needed was a little bit of kindness and you'd soon feel better. I know I shouldn't swear in front of children, but that Mrs Durkin is an awful d-i-t-s-h. She's in a foul mood today, because she only found out yesterday that you were coming, and it was going to be her job to look after you. So we had to open up The Lodge and get the rooms ready, and it was all rush, rush, rush, and very hush-hush too, because nobody knows who you are. But you must be very important, because only the very special visitors get to stay here in The Lodge.'

Jeanie took a breath. Her sentences were so long that it was quite difficult to follow what she was saying. But I didn't mind, because she was so full of joy, and it was obvious that she liked me. 'All the other guests stay up in the hotel, which is nice enough - don't get me wrong - but The Lodge is extra special. And don't you mind about not eating your breakfast, because I gave it to Sinbad, and I told him that it was a special present with love from you to him. And I almost forgot! I have something here especially for you.'

She stopped talking, and reached into the pocket of her apron and pulled out a Bounty Bar. I love Bounty. It's my favourite chocolate. When Muriel first came to live with us, we used to go to the shops every Saturday morning, to see if I wanted to spend the shilling pocket money that Mummy always gave me. And I would always ask Muriel if I could buy a Bounty, and every time she would answer, 'Of course you can, my love,' and then pay for it herself. Then we would walk to the Post Office and put my shilling into my savings account. On the way home, I would offer half of the Bounty to Muriel, but she would refuse to take a bite. But by the time we reached our house she would finally agree, and eat her half. It was our Saturday morning treat, and ever since, Bounty has always been a symbol of our love for each other.

I didn't know what was happening to me. The giant dog with his paw in my hand and the sight of the Bounty gave me the terrible flooded feeling again. But this time I let out a very loud wailing sound, and put my head on the table. Jeanie rushed to me and pulled me to her, and put me on her lap and said, 'There, there,' But I couldn't stop crying. She cradled me in her arms and rocked me, and this seemed to help. She said, 'Of course you're upset. This is the homesickness. All children get it when they leave home for the first time.' That made me cry even more. I wanted to speak. I wanted to tell her exactly what had happened to me; how I had been taken away from the people who I loved the most, and I had no idea where I was, or what was going to happen to me. I wasn't afraid of Jeanie, but I couldn't speak to her because I was crying so much.

Then Jeanie shouted, 'No Sinbad! You naughty dog! That's not yours! Oh no, little girl, Sinbad has just knocked the chocolate off the table and eaten it, with the wrapper and all! And by the way, what is your name?'

I wasn't crying so loudly now. I had to look at Sinbad. He was looking at me, and I thought he looked quite worried. I wasn't sure if he was worried about being told off, or because I was so upset. He coughed, and pieces of Bounty wrapper came out of his mouth. Then he leaned up against me. Jeanie said, 'He only does that to very special people. You're very lucky, because now he'll be your friend forever.'

I said, 'My name is Pippa and I'm nine years old, and I want my mummy.' Then I stuck my thumb in my mouth and Jeanie said, 'Of course you do my dear, of course you do.'

She took me into the kitchen to get me a drink of water. I drank the water down as if I was a thirsty man lost in the desert. Jeanie gave me another glassful, and another. 'She said, 'Jeez! Have you not had a drink since you've been here?'

I looked in her eyes. Jeanie whispered to herself, 'That woman is a prize bitch, and there's no mistaking.'

Then we went for a walk in the garden, and Sinbad walked along beside me. He was so big that his back came right up to my head. Jeanie explained that he was a Scottish deerhound, and he was the gentlest dog in the whole world. He never barked or got angry, and was the fastest runner you could imagine. He needed lots of exercise every day, otherwise he would get very frustrated and start chewing everything. The only problem was that if he saw a rabbit, or a deer, or a hare, he would chase it, and nine times out of twelve he would kill it, which was an awful thing. But it wasn't his fault, because God had made him that way, in the same way that God made us able to read and write and spell. Except Jeanie's dad said that God had perhaps been a bit tired when He was giving out the spelling skills, because Jeanie never had learned how to spell. But she didn't care, because she was good at lots of other things, and especially serving in the bar and the restaurant. And Mr Durkin the manager of the hotel said there were always double the men customers in the bar when she was serving the drinks, so she must have been extra talented at that.

I held Jeanie's hand, and Sinbad trotted beside me. Normally I would have been bursting with questions, and busy looking around. Muriel used to say that going for a walk with me was like walking with a toddler, because we always had to stop every few yards to look at something that I had noticed, and I was always falling over because I never looked where I was going. This thought made me cry again, though silently this time. Jeanie asked, 'Is it the homesickness again? Let's go into the hotel and get you some lemonade. That always cheers me up when I feel sad.'

The hotel

We reached the front of a very big house, and Jeanie explained that this was the hotel where Mr Durkin was the manager, and that he was a very cheerful man, and nothing like his wife, who as far as Jeanie was concerned, was an old battle-axe. I felt sure that if Mummy had been with us, she would have made a comment about Jeanie's colourful language.

I was just about to start crying again, when two men came towards us down the front steps, carrying big bags full of golf clubs. One of them had a large ginger moustache. He winked at Jeanie and said, 'Hello darling, are you working in the bar this afternoon?'

She said, 'I am that.'

The man said, 'Great! I'll be in the Nineteenth Hole as soon as I've finished beating Ron here.'

Ron laughed and patted Sinbad on the head. The man with the moustache said to him, 'Oh don't start patting the dog, or we'll never get started!'

We climbed the steps. Sinbad looked at the men, and then he looked at me. He followed me up the steps and sat down by the front door. The door was dark brown, with a huge pane of glass in it, so you could see right inside. Jeanie said, 'Sinbad's not allowed in the hotel. If he's still waiting here when we come out, then I'm sure that means he will be your friend forever!'

That thought made me feel much better, and I smiled.

The hotel lobby was wide, with a very shiny dark brown wooden floor. A man with a beard came up to us and said, 'There you are Jeanie! We'll be needing you to serve the lunches soon.' Then he looked at me and smiled a very big smile. He held out his hand towards me and, to my surprise, I took it and he shook it very hard. 'So you're our new guest! How lovely to meet you! And you've met Jeanie! Splendid! And have you met our very own special Sinbad yet?'

I put my head down. Jeanie said, 'Yes, Mr Durkin, we have. He's fallen in love with Pippa, and I'm sure he's waiting outside for us right now.'

Mr Durkin smiled and then looked at his watch. A man appeared with a big pile of papers and Mr Durkin said to us, 'Good, good,', then turned to the man and walked away with him.

Jeanie said, 'He's a very busy man. Those are the menus for this evening, and he's gone to talk to the chef.'

I was very hungry and thirsty. Jeanie said, 'You must be starving. I know I am. Let's go and find some lemonade and crisps!' She held my hand and took me into a room where there were lots of armchairs covered in tartan blankets, and with small round tables in front of them. Jeanie took me to a chair by the window, and told me to wait there while she went to get us a drink and something to eat. She could see that I was starting to panic so said, 'Dinna worry ma wee lassie. Bairns aren'y allowed in the bar. Ah'll be raight back.' I think she meant 'Don't worry my little girl. Children aren't allowed in the bar. I'll be back straight away.'

I thought to myself that if I were a guest in the hotel, and I knew that Jeanie was going to be serving the dinners, then I would choose to eat there every night of the week. She was one of those big girls that it was very easy to fall in love with. Despite myself, a tiny part of me was beginning to feel slightly warm inside.

I looked out of the window. There were groups of men everywhere, chatting and laughing and smoking, and carrying big golf bags, or pulling trolleys. Ginger Moustache Man and Ron were near the window, talking to another man. He said, 'Is Jeanie on tonight?'

Moustache Man grinned and said, 'She is indeed!'

The other man laughed and said, 'No need to guess where I'll be dining tonight then!'

We were on the edge of a huge golf course, and the hotel was specially designed for golfers. The walls were covered in pictures of men playing golf. They were drawings, old photos of groups of men, and a funny cartoon of a fat man whose tummy was so big he couldn't see that his golf ball had just landed by his feet, so he had a special contraption strapped round his waist, with a magnifying glass, to help him see where his golf ball was.

Jeanie came back in and said, 'Och, all the guests are just obsessed with golf. It's all they think about. And whisky. And beer.'

I almost said, 'And Jeanie,' but kept that thought to myself.

She had brought us two glasses of lemonade and three packets of crisps, on a round silver tray. She told me there was a drink and a packet of crisps for the both of us, and the third packet was for me to keep in my room, in case I got hungry in the night. Then she put her hand in her pocket and said, 'And this is for my new wee friend,' and pulled out a Bounty.

She grinned at me, wagged the Bounty in front of my face, and said, 'And don't take this out while Sinbad's around, because he'll just grab it off you!'

The lemonade was warm and very fizzy, and the bubbles went up my nose. The crisps were the old-fashioned Smiths Crisps, with the little dark-blue bag of salt inside, that you tore open and then sprinkled on your crisps. It was great fun to do that, but really the new type of *Ready-Salted* crisps were much tastier, because you would know that each crisp would taste salty. But with the blue bag of salt in the packet, you always had at least half a dozen crisps at the bottom with no salt on.

I was thinking this to myself and remembering that this was just the sort of thing that Lucy, Roger, and I would talk about.

This made me feel like crying, but Jeanie said, 'Och these crisps are okay, but I prefer the ready-salted ones, don't you?'

This made me wonder if people all over the world talked about the same things, which was a very comforting thought. Jeanie put her hand on my knee and said, 'That's a lovely wee smile you've got there.' My smile got bigger. She said, 'Is it true that you are Pippa Dunbar, and that your father is Mr Dunbar?' I nodded. 'And do you know that he owns this hotel?' I shook my head. Jeanie laughed. 'Well I never! He owns most of the properties around here, and quite a few of the hotels in town, as well as Pearson's, the big shop where you're going to get your shoes. Do you think that old cow Mrs Durkin knows that? Because if she did, then she wouldn't be treating you so unkind.'

So it was true! My father had taken Mummy to Court, and that was why I was here; stolen from Mummy and Muriel and everyone and everything that I loved! Jeanie said, 'Look at me Pippa. I want you to understand that I don't care who you are. You can be the richest girl in Scotland, or the poorest; I'd still treat you the same way. You are a bonnie wee lassie, and I like you for who you are, and that's all there is to it.'

Then a lady came and interrupted us. She was dressed like Jeanie, except her skirt wasn't quite so short, and her lipstick was a lighter shade of red. She said, 'Jeanie, we'll need you in exactly half an hour.' Then she looked at me and clapped her hands. 'Well hello! You must be our mysterious new guest. Jings! If you aren't the bonniest wee lassie I have ever seen! And wearing a bonnie wee kilt as well. You surely must be Scots?'

I put my head down. Jeanie whispered something to the lady. I could just about hear the words *the owner's daughter, old cow* and *terribly upset*.

The lady said, 'Och, I'm not surprised. You must come and see us here in the hotel whenever you like. But make sure that rascal Sinbad disnae follow you inside! I must be off now, hen, because I've tae get all the tables ready for lunch. There'll be extra golfers eating lunch tadae, now they've heard that our Jeanie's going to be serving! Bye, love!'

She went out, and Jeanie laughed and said, 'That's Auntie Morag. She's not my real auntie, but she has looked after me since I was a wee bairn.' Jeanie stopped smiling. I sensed there was a sad story about her mother. She looked me straight in the eyes, and I couldn't help looking back at her. Her eyes were light blue; like a faded misty blue. She really was very pretty. She said, 'I'm going to look after you as best I can. If you have any problems with Mrs Durkin, you just come and tell me. Do you promise?'
I kept looking in her eyes, and nodded my head. She kissed me on the end of my nose and said, 'Good. Now we must go back to The Lodge, so you can have your lunch.' I suddenly felt very stiff all over. Jeanie asked, 'What is it, Pippa? Are you scared?'
I put my head down and nodded. 'Then I'll have a word with Mr Durkin about that. He's in charge of everything here, and if something's not going right, then he likes to know about it straight away.'
Sinbad was waiting for me outside, and walked with us to The Lodge.

The fucking Scottish battle-axe and the horrible pie
I stood on the big mat inside the front door of The Lodge, and started to take off my shoes. Jeanie told me not to, in case I slipped over in my socks, on the shiny tiled floor. She led me into the kitchen, and Mrs Durkin was there, cooking. She ignored me, and started telling Jeanie off. 'Where have you been? You must ask me before you go anywhere with Philippa. Do you understand, Jeanette?
Jeanie nodded and said, 'Yes, Mrs Durkin.'
Mrs Durkin said, 'Now off you go and do your duties at the hotel.'
Jeanie tickled the back of my neck and then left. Mrs Durkin said to me, 'And you go and wash your hands and get ready for lunch. I'll bang the gong when it's ready.' She looked at my shoes. 'Where did you find those?'

I put my head down. 'Did Jeanette find them and give them to you?' I kept my head down. 'Take them off, right now, and go and put them back where you found them.' I didn't move. She took a step towards me. I felt that she wanted to hit me. 'You will obey me Philippa. I don't know what you were used to doing down in England, but here in Scotland, children respect their elders. And if they don't, then there are consequences. Do you understand?'

I didn't move. She turned back to the cooker, and continued making the lunch. It didn't smell very nice. I walked slowly along the hall, to the open front door. Sinbad was sitting on the terrace, waiting for me, so I patted him on the head for a few minutes, and then went back inside. I took off my shoes and left them by the front door, then went upstairs. My bed was still unmade, and the mattress was drying out. I went to the window to look at Sinbad. I saw my packet of crisps and the Bounty Bar on the dressing table. Jeanie must have put them there. I quickly opened the drawer and stuffed them inside. Sinbad was still on the terrace. I made a kissing noise and he looked up at me, then he walked off to the bushes and did a wee.

Lunchtime was horrible. Mrs Durkin banged the gong, so I walked downstairs and we sat together, like at breakfast. She had set two plates of food, each with boiled potatoes and carrots and a funny-looking pie. I was very, very hungry. She said, 'Now eat that all up. That's a delicious local Scotch pie, with fresh vegetables, and there's a banana and custard for your pudding.'

The Scotch pie was a small cylinder of greasy grey pastry, with a pastry lid that was hiding the meat that was inside. Dark brown gravy had seeped out through the lid.

Mummy had taught me that if ever there was meat for lunch at school, I should ask, very politely, what kind of meat it was. She told me to say, 'Excuse me, but do you mind if I might ask what kind of meat that is? You see, I'm not allowed to eat any

34

pork, or meat that has come from a pig. I hope you don't mind.'

The dinner ladies at school were always very pleased to tell me what the meat was, and if it was pork they would always say, 'Well, we'll just give you the vegetables, but we'll make sure you have an extra-large pudding, so you don't get hungry.' They never made a fuss about it, so I always smiled and said 'thank you', and June once told Mummy that everyone said how nice my manners were, so Mummy was very pleased with me. But Mummy said that if I was ever in a place where meat was served, and the people weren't sure what kind of meat it was, then I should politely say, 'No thank you very much.'

I ate all the vegetables that weren't touching the pie. Then I put my knife and fork together on my plate, to show that I had finished eating, just as Mummy had taught me. I didn't look at Mrs Durkin, who I knew was still eating. She said, 'What? You surely haven't finished? You haven't even touched your pie! Go on now, eat it all up.'

I put my hands in my lap and looked down at my plate. She sighed and tutted and said, 'Really, this is too bad!' She prised the lid off my pie with her knife. 'Look at that. That's perfectly fine Scottish mutton.'

I looked at it. It was a pinky light-brown blob of meat with some wobbly brown gravy on it. I had never heard the word *mutton* before. People in Scotland used strange words, so perhaps this was their word for pork. Anyway, I could tell from the smell that I wouldn't be able to eat it. I wanted to explain to Mrs Durkin exactly what the problem was, just as Mummy had taught me. I wanted to be a good girl, who was very polite and had lovely manners. But this lady, this dragon, this battle-axe, this bitch, this cow, was frightening the life out of me. Roger would have said that she was scaring the shit out of me. This reminded me that I hadn't done a poo for a long time, and my tummy was feeling funny.

I kept my head down. I knew what was going to happen next, because it had happened to me before. Sure enough, Mrs Durkin tutted and said, 'Well, if you won't eat it, then you can't be hungry. So there's no pudding for you until your plate is empty. Now you will sit there until you have eaten all of that pie.'

I wanted to call her a fucking Scottish battle-axe, but I knew that would be a very bad idea, so I just sat there with my head down. Mrs Durkin left the room. I jumped up from my chair and looked out of the window onto the terrace, to see if Sinbad was there, so I could throw the pie for him to eat. But he had gone for a walk.

I sat back down. Every five minutes or so, I heard Mrs Durkin walk to the door, look at me and then go away again. After doing this about five times she took my plate away and said, 'You will not defy me, Philippa. You will have this pie on your plate at teatime, and there will be no more food for you until you eat it. Do you understand?'

I kept very still. She said, 'You will come with me into town this afternoon, to buy some decent shoes, and then I will throw away those battered ones. Now go to your room and be ready to come down when you hear the gong.'

I didn't move. She said, 'Very well. Suit yourself. If you don't get ready, then I will go and buy the shoes on my own.'

She left the room and I went upstairs. I sat on the toilet, but nothing would come out. I sat there, thinking about what was happening to me. My father was to blame for all my problems. That was now very clear to me. He had made The Court take me away from Mummy and Muriel, and he had sent me here, to a big hotel on a golf course that he owned. That was bad enough, but being treated terribly by an awful lady was intolerable. But I didn't scream or hit my head, like I had done in the morning. Everything just went blank. I sat there and felt like a cheese soufflé Muriel and I had once cooked. We were very excited about it, but we took it out of the oven too soon, so it just collapsed in the middle. We laughed and laughed, and Mummy said it tasted delicious anyway. Now I felt as if the whole of my middle was collapsing. I didn't want to cry anymore, but I couldn't stop the awful feeling from flooding me again. I knew it was homesickness, so I told myself it was quite ordinary to feel like that. I wondered if people in prison felt homesickness more than children in hospital, or perhaps children in nasty boarding schools felt it worse than anyone else did.

The gong sounded. I stopped crying, jumped off the toilet and went downstairs. Mrs Durkin was standing by the front door, holding my Clarks sandals. She said, 'This is the last time you'll be wearing these.'
Mr Durkin was sitting in a car in front of The Lodge. He wasn't smiling. Mrs Durkin sat in the front and told me to get in the back. I looked out of the window. I saw the beach, briefly, and a red telephone box, and a sign that said *Sandyfoot*. Mr and Mrs Durkin didn't speak to each other until we reached the centre of the town, when Mrs Durkin said to her husband, 'You can drop us here. Meet us back here in three quarters of an hour.'

In Pearson's
Pearson's was a very big shop, and was lovely inside, because there seemed to be tartan everywhere. It was strange to think that my father owned this shop, and everything inside it, and paid the wages of everybody who worked there. Then I thought that he paid horrible Mrs Durkin's wages too, yet she was treating me so abominably.
We walked up a staircase to get to the children's clothing department. We were the only customers in that department, so I supposed that, at that moment, all the children in the town must have been in school. I wondered if Mrs Durkin was going to send me to school, and what it would be like. I would have to learn how to speak Scottish, that was for sure.

We went to a part of the room where all the shoes were on display. I was very pleased to see that there were lots of Clarks sandals, and some rather nice strong black shoes for girls. They looked like the sort of shoes that would be good to wear when I climbed trees. Mrs Durkin told me to follow her, and we sat down and waited to be served. Nobody came to see us, so Mrs

Durkin sighed and tutted and said under her breath, 'That's typical,' and went to the counter, where there was a bell. She hit it several times, very hard.

A lady came straight away, and Mrs Durkin told her that I needed a pair of sandals. Mrs Durkin was being very grumpy, but the lady smiled at her. She asked me how old I was and said, 'Goodness, your Clarks sandals have had a very good life! And surely you'll be needing another pair just the same, which we have in stock at a very reasonable price. And they are ideal for walking and playing in. And if you use the right polish, which we also have on sale, then they will last for a very long time.'

Mrs Durkin said, 'Just ordinary sandals. Nothing fancy. Measure her feet, and hurry up please, because we haven't got all day.'

The lady said, 'Very well, madam,' and winked at me. She asked me to take off my shoes, and we all noticed how dirty my socks were, from walking on the cellar floor. Mrs Durkin sighed. I wondered what I had done to her, to make her dislike me so much. It was probably because I didn't eat pork.

The lady said, 'What lovely feet! And big for your age too. In my experience, which is considerable, that means you are going to grow up tall.'

She went into a back room and came back with five boxes. There were four light-green boxes with lovely Clarks sandals inside, and a dirty white box with a nasty pair of open-toed sandals. Mummy had seen these in a shoe shop window once and said they reminded her of her stepfather, who was a Quaker, so always wore open-toed sandals. He had horrible toenails and Mummy didn't like to look at them, and he never wore socks with his sandals, even in winter. Muriel said that her grandmother had worn sandals like that too. Mummy always said it was terribly important for me to have the right shoes, so that my feet would be comfortable, and grow properly. She said that Clarks shoes were ideal. I loved my sandals, and one of my little pleasures was to clean them with Kiwi cherry blossom shoe polish. Mummy used to take great care of her feet, and Muriel said how lovely they looked, and often stroked them. Sometimes she even kissed Mummy's feet, and Mummy would laugh and tell Muriel that it was the loveliest feeling.

Mrs Durkin pointed to the open-toed sandals and said, 'These will be fine.'

The lady said, 'But surely madam would like to try some other shoes for her daughter? The pair you have chosen are from our budget range, so may not be as long-lasting or as comfortable as the Clarks shoes.'

Mrs Durkin ignored her and said, 'She's not my daughter. These are fine, and charge them to the Dunbar account.'

The lady looked very surprised. 'The Dunbar account?'

'Yes, and please hurry up, because my husband will be here shortly.'

The lady said, 'Really madam, if this is for the Dunbar account then I must have a very quick word with the manager.' She didn't wait for Mrs Durkin to say anything, but quickly walked downstairs. She came back almost straight away with a man wearing a very smart suit, and a tartan tie with a gold tiepin.

He said, 'Good afternoon madam. I understand you'd like to use the Dunbar account?'

Mrs Durkin sighed. 'Yes, that's correct. I am making a purchase on behalf of Mr Dunbar. It should have been authorised by his office in London.'

The manager looked at me. He said to Mrs Durkin, 'Oh it has been authorised, madam. It has indeed. But you see, that is a very special account and....'

I couldn't stand it anymore. I said, very loudly, 'Excuse me sir. I don't wish to butt in, but my name is Philippa Dunbar, and I think my father owns this shop. I'm staying at the golf hotel in Sandyfoot, and I think he owns that too. I'm sure he will be coming to see me soon, and he will want to see his daughter, his only daughter, wearing very smart Clarks sandals... that she has chosen herself. And a strong pair of shoes for when I play on the beach and climb trees.' Everyone looked at me, but I didn't stop. 'And he will not be pleased to see his daughter in a pair of budget range sandals, that make me look like an old granny, and a Quaker.' Then I put my head down. Mummy would have been very proud of me.

Mrs Durkin said, very crossly. 'I think we have spent enough time here for one day. My husband will call you tomorrow. Come on Philippa.'

I didn't move. Mrs Durkin took my hand, but my arm was floppy and my legs wouldn't move. The manager asked, 'Is everything all right, Mrs...'

'Durkin. Mrs Durkin. My husband is the manager of the hotel and golf course in Sandyfoot.'

The manager said, 'Ah yes, I know him well. How nice to meet you, at last. In fact, here he is now.'

Mr Durkin came in. He said to his wife, 'I've parked in the car park, so thought I'd come and tell you... oh, is everything all right?'

The manager shook Mr Durkin's hand and said, 'Well hello, Jamie. And how are you? How are things in Sandyfoot? I wonder if you could help us out here a wee bit. You see, your good lady wife wants to buy Mr Dunbar's daughter a pair of our cheapest sandals, and my assistant here, who just happens to be my wife, is recommending rather more appropriate items of footwear. They may be a wee bit more expensive, but are much more comfortable, and better for a child's growing feet. And, very importantly, better value in the long run, if you'll excuse my pun.'

I thought that was very funny, but only the manager's wife smiled. The manager continued, 'And as the young lady has pointed out, in the politest possible way, her father, who as we know owns both of our establishments, might be visiting her soon, and he will no doubt want his daughter to look as smart and comfortable as possible.'

Mr Durkin looked at his wife. She looked furious. He said to her, 'Well, that does seem to be a rather compelling argument, don't you think? And surely the price of the items we purchase is not as important as the quality?'

Mrs Durkin said, 'I really couldn't say. Give me the car keys. I'll be waiting in the car.'

Mr Durkin handed her the keys and she walked off. The manager looked at Mr Durkin. Mr Durkin looked at the manager. Mr Durkin asked the manager's wife what she would recommend. She smiled and said, 'Two pairs of Clarks sandals, chosen by the young lady, and fitted by me, and a good strong pair of shoes for running around in. And also a pair of smart black shiny shoes for wearing on special occasions, like going to Mass, or on special trips with her father.'

Mr Durkin said, 'Good, good. And can you fit her with a nice jacket as well, for when it rains and...' he winked at me, 'a pair of slacks or denim jeans or strong corduroys? Then put it all on the Dunbar account. I'll just pop downstairs and have a word with my good lady wife. Take as long as you like, and please could you do me a favour, and pop into the car park and give me a wave when you've finished?'

The lady assistant said to him, 'I'll do my best, Jamie.' She held her hand out to me and I took it. As she was taking me to try on my shoes, I heard the manager say to Mr Durkin, 'Thanks for that Jamie, that was an excellent decision, for all our sakes, wouldn't you say? If Mr Dunbar really is going to come here, then we'll need to do things properly for his daughter.'

Mr Durkin said, 'Do you sell dog houses here? Because I think I'll be sleeping in it tonight. Come over to the hotel one evening and bring *your* good lady wife and we can have a good laugh about it...once things have calmed down, that is.'

I left the shop with three big bags full of shoes and clothes, including a woolly hat that the manager's wife said I would need out there on the beach, seven pairs of nice ankle socks, a lovely pair of tartan slippers to keep my feet nice and warm indoors, and some pretty knickers that were a present from the manager and his wife. The manager's wife took me down to the carpark and rubbed my cheek with her fingers. She said that I was a very good girl, and one day I must come and meet her grandchildren, who were Day Girls at the Catholic boarding school. She felt sure that they would love to meet me, and perhaps she just might arrange for them to come up to the hotel and play with me.

Mr and Mrs Durkin didn't say anything to each other on the way back to the hotel, and when we arrived back at The Lodge, Sinbad was waiting for me on the terrace. Mrs Durkin took all my new shoes and clothes and told me to go up to my room. She went into the kitchen and I went to sit on the terrace with Sinbad. He rubbed himself against me and nearly knocked me over. I sat down, and patted him on the head, and held his paw. I started to count how many times he would make me take his paw and pat his head, but I lost count after sixty-two, because Mrs Durkin came and sat next to me. She said, 'I thought I told you to go to your room.' I put my head down. 'You will obey me, Philippa. That little display in Pearson's was a disgrace. Soon Mr Shepherd is going to telephone me, and ask me how you have been behaving. I will have to tell him that you have been very disobedient and insolent. Is that what you want?'

I didn't answer, or look at her. She said, 'Look at me Philippa;' She took my chin in her hand and forced my head up, until I had no choice but to look straight into her eyes. I wanted to scream in her face, so then she would try to hit me, but Sinbad would jump up and bite her, and then there would be a terrible row, and Mrs Durkin would have to leave me alone, and Jeanie would look after me instead. But I didn't scream. I just shut my eyes.

I heard her say, 'You will obey me. Your father wants you to be brought up properly. He may own this property, and many more besides, but he has asked me to care for you, and care for you I will.'

She let go of my chin, so I opened my eyes, but she was still looking at me. It felt like she hated me. She said, 'You will speak to me, and you will eat that pie. Do you understand?'

I kept looking at her eyes, but I didn't say anything.

Suddenly I needed to go to the toilet. I ran upstairs and sat on the loo. I was bursting to wee. I needed to do a poo as well, but nothing came out. I went to my room, and someone had made the bed, with clean sheets and new blankets. They had tucked Polish Teddy in, and turned him on his side, so he looked like he was asleep. I sat on my bed and felt a huge wave of sadness coming towards me, like the tidal wave in my Hokusai jigsaw. I was in the little boat, which was about to be smashed to pieces. I ran to the window and Sinbad looked up at me. The wave receded. Then I remembered the packet of crisps and the Bounty I had put in the drawer. I opened the drawer, and there were two Bounty bars! I took one out and opened the wrapper. It was a double Bounty, so had two small bars in it. I stuffed one in my mouth and the other I threw to Sinbad. He gobbled it up straight away, and then looked up at me, with his tail wagging.

Then I heard a wonderful sound. It was the engine of a Morris Traveller. I loved that sound, as much as I loved birds singing, or the sound of the stream, or the wind in the trees on a wet and windy night. It was the sound of Muriel's car. For a second, I thought that it must be Muriel coming to see me, but it was only the postman. He parked his car in front of The Lodge and honked his horn. Mrs Durkin came out and said, 'Why are you beeping your horn? Why don't you get out of your car and ring the bell, like all the other tradesmen?'

The postman put his hat on, which made him look rather important. He rolled down his window and shouted to Mrs Durkin, 'Two things, missus. This is a special delivery of a very heavy parcel, and there's no way I'm getting out of this car with that hound nearby. He'll have my leg off in no time!'

He was being very cheerful, but Mrs Durkin ignored him. 'What is it?'

'It's from doon sooth, and addressed to Miss Philippa Dunbar. Will you sign for it, and then take it inside? Or put the dog inside and I can leave the parcel here.'

Mrs Durkin said, 'Take it up to the hotel. You'll find no dogs there' The postman drove off.

I had a parcel! But now it was up at the hotel. And who was Doon Sooth? I thought that perhaps he was from India.

I heard the gong, and went into the dining room. Mrs Durkin was already sitting at the table. She had a plate of sandwiches in front of her, but the Scotch pie was sitting on a plate in my place. Mrs Durkin started eating one of her sandwiches, then she stopped and said, 'Heavens, I almost forgot, you haven't had a drink all afternoon. Here child, have some tea.'

She poured a cup of tea and put it next to my plate. There was a bowl of sugar lumps within reach and I helped myself to two. Mrs Durkin said, 'One, Philippa. Just one. That's all you need.'

Mummy always had two spoons of sugar in her tea. On the day we first met Muriel, we went to a café together and Mummy asked Muriel if she would like some sugar in her tea. Muriel smiled and said, 'No thanks, I'm sweet enough.'

Mummy laughed and said, 'Yes, I can imagine,' and Muriel went very red. But she smiled a huge smile and we both saw the gap between her beautiful white teeth for the very first time. I think it was then that I fell in love with Muriel. And Mummy did too, I'm sure.

Then I realised that I had forgotten to think about Muriel that morning. So much was happening to me, it was hard to think about anything. I started to feel very tired. I looked at the open windows and saw the wave rushing towards me again. I drank a sip of tea, and the wave receded. My tea didn't taste quite right with only one lump in it, but I drank it all, because I was so thirsty. But I wouldn't eat the pie. I put my hands in my lap and stared ahead of me, at the wave suspended in mid-air, like a huge blue and white plasticine sculpture. I thought about King Canute, trying to make the waves of the sea go backwards at his command. Mrs Durkin was Queen Canute, but she was not going to be able to control me, no matter what she did. Mummy and Muriel would never have given in when they were my age, and I was going to be strong, just like them.

Mrs Durkin had finished her sandwiches, and she said to me, 'No pie, so no more food for you. Now go to your room.' I wanted to say, 'I don't care about your pie, you fucking old witch!' But instead I just looked ahead. Mrs Durkin said, 'Suit yourself. It's you who will suffer in the end. When I bang the gong again, that will be time for you to have your bath and then to go to bed. I will fill the bath and you must not put in any more water. There is a clean towel for you, and a new toothbrush and toothpaste for you to use. And make sure you go to the toilet and say your prayers before you go to sleep.'

She put all the dishes on a big tray, including the nasty pie. I was relieved, because the smell was making me feel sick. She stopped by the door and said, 'There's another thing you must do. Here, in Scotland, children do their big job every morning, after breakfast. That is when you will do yours. And you must leave it, so that I can see that you have done it. Perhaps one day I will be able to trust you to be truthful, but for the time being you will leave it for me to see.' I had no idea what she was talking about. 'Oh, and there's one more important thing. Miss Grierson is coming to see you tomorrow morning. She is to be your school tutor, and she will come every morning to teach you everything you need to know. I will put your clothes out for you while you are having your bath, so you know what you must wear. Now off you go, up to your room.'
I didn't move. She went into the kitchen with the tray. I ran upstairs.

I threw myself onto the bed and put my head onto the pillow, but didn't cry. I banged my fists into the pillow and kicked my legs as hard as I could. I didn't stop until I accidentally bit my lip and it started to bleed. My tummy was hurting and I had a headache. I turned over, and Polish Teddy was looking at me. He said, 'She nasty woman. You good girl. You go and eat crisps.'
That was the very first time that my teddy had spoken to me. I whispered, 'Shh. Don't let her hear you. And anyway, she might come in and see me. I'll save the crisps until I know she has absolutely gone away.' Then a thought occurred to me; if Mrs Durkin left The Lodge, I would be all on my own in a very big house. I checked my bedroom door, to see if it had a key, so

I could lock myself in and be safe. But there was no key and no other way of locking the door. I thought that surely Jeanie would come and visit me, but remembered that she was going to be busy all evening, serving the golfers in the hotel restaurant.

I looked at the window. It was getting quite cold, and the wind was blowing the net curtains. I went to close the windows, and to take one last look at Sinbad. It wasn't dark, and I had forgotten to look at the clock to see exactly what time it was. I wanted to make sure that I was exactly on time to think about Lucy. I had only been away from home for a day and a bit, but already it seemed like an age. I wished I had a photo of Mummy and Muriel. Suddenly there was a very strong gust of wind, and the window banged and I got quite a fright. A voice said, 'I'm back!' and Ursula was sitting on my bed. She was dressed all in white, but had a lovely tartan sash draped over her shoulder, attached with a silver clasp. She said, 'Hello Pippa! What a fix you're in! But don't worry, because I've been watching over you. I've spoken to some other angels, and they all agree that you're doing a very good job here in Scotland.' And then she said, 'Brrr! It's cold in here! She fiddled with her sash, which actually was a very big piece of cloth that she wrapped round herself like a cloak. Ursula seemed quite a bit older than when I had seen her last. I wanted to cry; not with sadness this time, but with joy. She said, 'It was me that stopped the wave from drowning you. You're bound to feel sad. Who wouldn't, after all that's happened to you? But I'm not going away now. I'll always be here whenever you need me.'
I asked her if she had seen Mummy and Muriel. She said, 'Oh yes. It was them who sent me. Of course, they are terribly upset that The Court stopped you from living with them, but they will always be thinking of you. I imagine that Mr Shepherd will have told them that you are being well looked after.'
I said, 'Well, that's a lie, for a start!'

A loud voice from behind the door said, 'Philippa! Who are you talking to?' It was Mrs Durkin. She must have been listening at the door. Ursula put her fingers on her lips, but I was too frightened to say anything more. Mrs Durkin put her head round the door and told me my bath was ready. She said, 'And make sure you wash between your legs, and dry yourself properly down there.' Ursula made a funny face and I almost laughed. Mrs Durkin went away, and I whispered to Ursula, 'Will you come into the bathroom with me?' She said she would, but couldn't get in the bath with me, because she didn't want to get her feathers wet.

There was only a tiny amount of water in the bottom of the bath. That was what Mummy used to do when I was little and she was an alcoholic. I turned the hot tap on, but only warm water came out, and then it went cold. I wanted to cry, but Ursula said, 'Just have a quick wash all over and then get into bed and we can have a lovely long chat. Oh, and don't forget to wash and dry between your legs!'
I said, 'Silly old cow' and we both laughed.
While I was in the bath, I asked Ursula if she knew what a big job was. She said she had never heard of such a thing, but would ask the other angels, and see if they knew. I asked her if any of the angels spoke Scottish, and she said there was a Scottish angel called Mary who she was friends with, but sometimes it was hard to understand what she was talking about. I said I was frightened of Mrs Durkin, and didn't want her to lose her temper and start hitting me, like The Nasty Nun had done.
Ursula said I should talk to Jeanie about my worries, and tell her about all the bad things that were happening.

I got into bed, and Ursula said she would sit with me. I asked her to get into bed with me, but she said her wings were too big. I cuddled teddy, and Ursula said, 'Have you forgotten something?'
'Oh yes! My packet of crisps and the other Bounty!' Then I remembered that I had just cleaned my teeth.

47

Ursula said, 'Yes, but there's something much more important than that.' Of course, it was to pray with Lucy. Unfortunately, I had got into bed and turned off the light and didn't want to leave my room and look at the clock. Ursula said that she knew that now was the time to think hard about Lucy. I asked Ursula if Lucy had a Guardian Angel, because she never mentioned one. Ursula said that everyone had a Guardian Angel, but some people didn't know they had one, or didn't believe in them. So they weren't as lucky as me, because I could chat to mine a lot. I thought about all the nice things that Lucy and I had done, and especially about when we played in her garden and I taught her how to read. Ursula said she had been with me when I had broken my wrist, and she had been very surprised when Dorothy showed everyone her bosoms. She said I shouldn't be worried if I felt sad about being away from the people I loved. Those people loved me more than anything else in the world, and they would be thinking about me all the time. She said that everyone in Heaven was very pleased that I hadn't sworn at that horrible Mrs Durkin.

Some things were still bothering me. I had hardly eaten anything all day, my tummy was hurting, and I had a headache. I wanted to know what to do about not being able to talk to people who were being nasty to me. And when was Mrs Durkin going to give me something nice to eat? Ursula didn't think I should eat the pie, and told me give it to Sinbad, or tell Jeanie as soon as I could. Then Jeanie might talk to Mr Durkin, because he seemed very nice. Perhaps he would let me have my meals in the hotel. I stuck my thumb in my mouth and cuddled Polish Teddy. I felt Ursula stroking my hair and she kissed me goodnight.

The Parcel

In the night, I dreamed about playing with Lucy in her garden. When I woke up it was just getting light, but I wasn't quite sure where I was. For a minute I thought I was in my bed at home and that being in Scotland had been a horrible dream, but then I realised I was still in Scotland. I was bursting to do a wee, and had a quick feel to see if my bed was wet, but was very pleased to find out that it was dry. I rushed to the toilet and then ran back into my room. There was a dark shape by the dressing table. I drew the curtains and saw that it was the big parcel that had been delivered the day before. On the chair next to it were some clothes for me to wear. They were exactly the same as the day before, except for clean socks and knickers. They weren't the nice ankle socks and pretty knickers from the shop, but the boring ones that Mrs Durkin had given me. However, my super tartan slippers were under the chair. I put them on and they felt lovely. I felt I had won a battle. It was a small victory, but hopefully the first of many.

The parcel was addressed to 'Miss Philippa Dunbar, The Lodge, Sandyfoot Golf Hotel, Sandyfoot, Dumfriesshire, Scotland'. There were lots of nice stamps on it, and the postmark said 'London'. There was nothing on the brown wrapping paper that said who had sent it, and nothing about anyone called Doon Sooth. I went into the corridor and the clock said eight o'clock. I had fifteen minutes before I would have my deep think about Muriel. The parcel was wrapped up in strong brown wrapping paper that was stuck down with brown sticky tape, and it was securely fastened with hairy white string, tied in a tight knot. I would need a sharp knife or a pair of scissors to get into that huge parcel. I wanted to shake the parcel, to help me guess what was inside, but it was too heavy for me to lift. Then I wondered about how the parcel had got into my room. Someone must have come into my bedroom and put it there while I was sleeping. I didn't like the thought of Mrs Durkin seeing me asleep, so I told myself that it must have been Jeanie. That idea pleased me.

I closed my eyes and thought about Muriel. I told myself that I wasn't going to cry anymore. From now on, I was going to be a brave girl, like Mummy had been. I wondered what I was going to do about food. I wondered how long it takes for someone to die if they don't have anything to eat. Jesus had once said, 'Man cannot live on bread alone.' But he had been in the desert for forty days and forty nights, and only had honey and locusts to eat. All I had eaten was some toast and marmalade, some crisps, a Bounty and a few vegetables. Perhaps this was why I had a tummy ache. I hadn't done a poo for a long time, but had eaten next to nothing, so surely there was hardly anything to come out.

Then the gong sounded, so I jumped up and got dressed and went downstairs. I had spent my first Special Time with Muriel thinking about poo. She wouldn't have minded, because she was a nurse and used to say, 'What comes out of your body is just as important as what goes in.' That always made Mummy laugh.

Miss Grierson

I went into the dining room, and Mrs Durkin had already set my place. She had poured my cup of tea, and the Nasty Pie was on my plate. There was no other food on the table. I sipped my tea, but it didn't taste sweet enough, so I knew that the Old Battle-Axe had only put in one lump. There was no sugar bowl on the table. It was windy outside, so the windows were closed. I went over to see if Sinbad was on the terrace. He was lying there, waiting for me. I tapped on the window and he pricked up his ears. He looked at me and walked over to the window, wagging his tail. I ran back to get my plate and showed him the pie. He looked disappointed and walked away. He wasn't wagging his tail any more. This could mean only one thing; Scotch pies were so nasty that even dogs refused to eat them. I quickly sat back down and wondered if I had upset Sinbad so much that he would never trust me again.

Mrs Durkin came in and looked at my plate. She sighed and tutted and said, 'Still not hungry?' She took my plate away, and as she was leaving the room said to me, with her back turned, 'Go and get ready for Miss Grierson. She'll be here at nine o'clock. Come downstairs when you hear the sound of the gong. In the meantime, go and do your big job, and leave it there for me to look at.'

As soon as she left the room, I whispered to myself, 'Fucking old bag.' I went upstairs and cleaned my teeth. Perhaps that was my big job? I made my bed and thought that that surely must be my big job. I didn't want Mrs Durkin to see Polish Teddy, in case she decided to take him away from me as a punishment, so I decided that I would bring him downstairs with me when Miss Grierson came.

I didn't want to have someone coming to The Lodge to teach me. I wanted to go to school, so that I could be with other children. But I would probably need to have special Scottish lessons so that we could understand each other. Perhaps that was why I needed a tutor. I decided to do my best to be nice to Miss Grierson, and I hoped that I would be able to talk to her. I heard a car pull up outside, but it didn't sound like a Morris Traveller. The gong sounded and I went downstairs, with Polish Teddy under my arm. Mrs Durkin was in the dining room with another lady, who was short and quite large. Mrs Durkin said to me, 'Philippa, this is Miss Grierson, and she's going to be teaching you this morning. I've explained to her that you can speak when you want to, so let's have no more of your nonsense.' She looked at Polish Teddy. 'And what in heaven's name have you brought that thing down here for? Give him to me.' I held on to him tightly. Mrs Durkin said to Miss Grierson, 'You see what I mean? You've got your work cut out with this one.'

Miss Grierson said, 'Och, never you mind Mrs Durkin. I've taught in some of the finest schools in Edinburgh, and worked with thousands of young children. She'll be putty in my hands by the end of the morning, just you wait and see.'

Mrs Durkin said, 'Well I hope you have more success with her than I've had so far. Good luck to you.' She went out and shut the door behind her.

Miss Grierson took my hand and said, 'Well hello there young Philippa. And how are you this fine Scottish morning?' I looked at the window. She said, 'Och, it's only raining a wee bit. This is Scotland, after all.' She laughed to herself. 'And who's this that you've brought to show me?' She picked up Polish Teddy. 'And do you mind if I take a wee look at him?'

I felt like saying, 'Why are you asking me? You've already taken hold of him. I hope you've washed your hands.' But I just smiled.

She looked Polish Teddy all over, and said, 'My, but you are a lucky girl! This is a fine example of a German Steiff bear. I'd say he was probably made before The War, or perhaps just after. He must have cost a lot of money. Wherever did you get him? I have always wanted a big Steiff bear like that, but only had a very tiny one when I was a wee girl. Sadly, he was lost during The War. Just put him on the table, and he can watch us as we work. But mind he doesn't try and help you too much, because that would be cheating, eh?' I had to smile. 'Now, let me take a good look at you. My, that is a handsome kilt. And tartan slippers too! We'll make a fine wee Scottish lassie of you in no time! What do you think about that, eh?'

I looked at her. I even looked in her eyes. I did want to speak to her. I really did. What she was saying about my teddy and her teddy was going right into my heart.

I opened my mouth, but no sound came out, so I quickly shut it again. I felt myself putting my head down, but stopped myself. She smiled and said, 'Has the cat got your tongue this morning? You're probably just a wee bit shy. Anyway, let's get started. Let's do some nice sums.'

I stood beside her and she took an exercise book and a pencil out of her bag. She said, 'As a special treat, I'm going to let you write your name on the front cover.' The book was a light grey colour, and I could see that it was cheap and nasty, just like the ones you can buy in Woolworths. And I could tell that the pencil was just as cheap. It was one of those pencils that you got in Woolworths, where you could buy a pack of six for a shilling, and you thought you were getting a bargain, but when you wrote with them, the lead grated against the paper and your writing was very faint. And when you tried to sharpen them, the lead kept breaking. They were usually made in China.

Miss Grierson told me that children in Scotland always began writing with pencils, but if their handwriting was good enough, they could graduate to a fountain pen. However, Scottish children never used a fountain pen in their maths books, because maths was such a difficult subject, and especially for girls, so one would always find oneself needing to use an eraser to rub out one's mistakes.

I wrote my name, using my best handwriting. The writing was very faint and then the lead broke. Miss Grierson said, 'Fancy that! The girl in Woolworths assured me that these were the best quality pencils, and were specially made in China. Never mind, I can see that you have beautiful handwriting, so you can use a fountain pen.' She rummaged in her bag and pulled out a stubby navy blue fountain pen, and a small glass bottle of ink. The ink was *Stephens Quink,* which I knew was short for *quick ink.* I loved Quink. Mummy had bought me a bottle of turquoise Quink, to use with my gold fountain pen that Miss Cohn had given me. Miss Cohn's pen had a funny little rubber bladder inside it. When you had used up all the ink in your pen, you tipped the pen nib into the ink and squeezed the bladder, and when you let go it sucked up the ink, and hey presto, your pen was full of ink.

I rubbed my hands together and smiled. Miss Grierson said, 'Oh good, I thought you'd be pleased.' She showed me the pen. It was an *Osmiroid,* just like the ones that the older children were allowed to use in my last school. Miss Grierson ceremoniously opened the exercise book and said, 'It's always such a great pleasure when one opens a new exercise book, and writes on the first page.' She took the pen and said, 'I'm going to write something very beautiful here for you. It will show you exactly how we like children to write, here in Bonny Scotland.' There was a noise outside the window. The wind was howling and rain was lashing against the house. 'Well it's bonny sometimes, when the sun shines, I can assure you.' I was enjoying my lesson. She wrote
O WELL is me, my gay gos-hawk,

-That you can speak and flee;
For you can carry a love letter
-To my true love frae me.

Then she said, 'Oh dear! Oh dearie me!' The paper was so thin that the ink had soaked right through onto the back of the page, and even onto the third page. She said, 'Wait until I have a word with the manager of Woolworths about the quality of his materials. A teacher who has taught in some of the finest schools in Edinburgh can't possibly work with shoddy equipment, and neither can her pupils!'

I couldn't help smiling. I put my hand in hers. She looked at me and said, 'And what would you like to do Philippa? Miss Grierson is having a wee bit of a disastrous morning so far! Is it time for a wee drinky, do you think? Shall we go and see if we can make a wee coffee, and perhaps Mrs Durkin will give us a biscuit to go with it? If not, I've brought my own biscuits for us to share! Why not put your hand in my bag and fish around and see if you can find them?'

I put my hand in and pulled out a packet that said *Dr White's* on it. I said, 'Oh!' very loudly and quickly stuffed it back in her bag.

She said, 'Och no, not those!' She fanned her face with the exercise book and said, 'Is it me, or is it hot in here?' She laughed to herself and I couldn't help smiling. She said, 'No doubt you've seen those in your mummy's bag, you cheeky wee thing!'

That was true. Muriel used them too. Once we had been in a café, and Mummy said to Muriel, 'Oops! I think I'm starting! I'll just pop into the toilet, to sort myself out.' She looked in her bag and said, 'Muriel Standish! What am I always telling you? If you take my Doctor Whites without asking me, make sure you put them back!'

Muriel laughed and went out to the chemist and came back with two packets. She said, 'I love it when you start, because I know that your grumpiness is over, and my lovely Ruth has come back to me.' Mummy didn't say anything, but I knew that she was pleased. I was pleased too, because it's always nice to be around people who are in love.

I didn't want to put my hand back in Miss Grierson's bag, just in case I found something else that might cause embarrassment. I took her hand and whispered, 'Please come upstairs with me.' The shock had made me talk! I wondered if Miss Grierson was an expert in helping children who had been traumatised. She looked very surprised, but got up. I kept hold of her hand and led her upstairs. I couldn't hear Mrs Durkin anywhere, so supposed that she had gone out and left us alone. I took Miss Grierson into my bedroom and opened the dressing table drawer. The packet of crisps and the Bounty were still there, and I held out the Bounty to Miss Grierson.

She said, 'Och, would you believe it? A Bounty. If that isn't Miss Grierson's favourite. And do you think we could share it with our wee drinky?' Then she saw the parcel. 'Well, will you just look at that! Is it your birthday today? Well, we really must open it straight away, and see what's inside!'

She bent down and had the string undone in no time, and was ripping the paper off. She winked at me and said, 'Of course we must be careful not to tear these stamps. Do you collect them? Of course you don't, because that's a hobby for the boys. I have a wee nephew who just loves collecting stamps. Do you think Miss Grierson might have them to take to give him?'

I nodded. She squeezed my hand. 'Och, you are a wee lamb.' I smiled. I liked being called a lamb.

Inside was a box. Miss Grierson was very excited and said, 'Go on Philippa, you open it.' It was full of art materials. We took them all out and put them into big piles all over the floor, to see exactly what was there. There were paints and brushes, and pastels, and lots of sketchbooks, and paper of various thicknesses. Right at the bottom of the box there was a slip of paper, with the name of an art shop in London. Someone had typed on the paper, *To Miss Philippa Dunbar courtesy of Mr Andrew Dunbar.*

I felt a funny feeling start in my tummy and rise into my chest, but I forced it down again. I picked up a box of drawing pencils, a box of pastels and a big drawing pad, and held Miss Grierson's hand. She said, 'Let's go downstairs and you can spend a few minutes drawing me a nice wee picture. Perhaps a wee dog or a cat, or maybe even a house.' She went over to the dressing table and picked up the Bounty. 'And let's not forget this.'

We went back downstairs. I went into the dining room and started drawing, while Miss Grierson went into the kitchen to make some coffee and find some biscuits. How I had missed Art! With so many changes in my life, I hadn't felt at all like painting, or even looking at the beautiful things around me that might give me inspiration. Miss Grierson came in with a tray. She had made herself a cup of coffee and brought me a tall glass of milk and a plate full of biscuits. She looked at my drawing and said, 'My word!' I stopped to drink my milk and eat my half of the Bounty and when I had finished I said, 'Thank you very much Miss Grierson,' as if I had never had any problems with talking in all my life.

I carried on with my picture, drawing as fast and as furiously as I could. I was worried that Mrs Durkin might come in and stop me, but I was also directing all my fear and frustration and anger and sorrow into every stroke of my pencil. I said, 'Please excuse me Miss Grierson, but would you mind most awfully if I run upstairs to get some paints? It will make everything look so much better.'

'Of course not dearie, you go on ahead. I think we've finished our lessons for the morning anyway.'

I came back down with a lovely large box of CARAN d'ACHE aquarelle watercolour pencils. I said, 'Would you mind awfully getting me some water, so I can dip my pencils in?'

'Of course not pet. Just keep going. That's quite extraordinary.'

Just as Miss Grierson left the room, I heard the front door open. Mrs Durkin said, 'What's going on?'

Miss Grierson replied, 'I'm giving Philippa an art lesson, and I'm just getting her some water for her watercolour pencils. Go in and take a look if you like. I've always enjoyed teaching art.'

Mrs Durkin said, 'Call me when you have finished, and I might just have time to pop in and see how she has been getting on. Would you like a cup of a coffee, Miss Grierson?'

'Thank you no, Mrs Durkin, because I've just had one, and young Philippa has had a glass of milk and a few biscuits. Oh, and she's talking fine now; to me at least.'

'Really? I've had nothing but silence from her since she first set foot in this house.'

'Well, in my experience, you can never be too kind to children. Especially when they have had the terrible experience that this wee lassie's just had; being torn away from her mother's breast and driven half way across the country, and ending up here. No offence Mrs Durkin, but a wee girl like this needs lots of TLC. Not the cough mixture, but *tender, loving care*. It does wonders.'

'I'm only following orders.'

'Orders? Whose orders?'

'I have had instructions to prepare the child for a Good Catholic Education, and that's what I'm doing.'

Miss Grierson coughed and said, 'If you'll excuse me, Mrs Durkin, I'll just go and get the water for my pupil, so I can continue teaching her about art. She's very good, but even the best artists need a little tweaking of their technique. And we all know what happens if we don't put water on our aquarelle pencils, don't we?'

By the time Miss Grierson came back, I had finished the broad outline of what I wanted to do. Miss Grierson said, 'What a bold use of line! I think I can see something emerging. I can see what looks like Joan of Arc, but why is she standing on a big dog? Which reminds me, did you see the size of that dog out there this morning? I thought it was a horse. I nearly jumped back into my car!'

I said, 'Excuse me Miss Grierson, I don't wish to be rude, but I do my best art when there is absolute quiet around me.'

Miss Grierson said, 'Quite right. I'll just sit here and plan our next set of lessons.'

I knew that she was watching me, and I was very pleased.

I slipped into My Colour Dream. I was so excited about painting, and full of energy from the milk and biscuits, that I didn't notice anything else going on around me. I might have been working for an hour, or even more. When I had finished, I took in a deep breath, and breathed out noisily. I said, to myself, 'I love Art. All I need is for people to be kind to me and to let me paint, and then I am the happiest girl in the world.'

My eyes had gone a bit out of focus and I didn't really notice what was going on in the room. Miss Grierson was sitting next to me, looking a bit worried. She said, 'Is that so? And are you all right? I've been talking to you, but you've been ignoring me, which could be seen as being just a wee bit rude.'

I went red and said. 'Oh I'm really sorry. Has nobody told you anything about me? My father knows how important Art is for me, and that's why he sent me that huge box of art supplies. I usually do at least one painting a day.'

Miss Grierson said, 'And can you tell us something about your picture? It reminds me of Joan of Arc, but perhaps it's one of the Archangels? Possibly St Michael? The sword looks so sharp! And all that flaming orange hair! She's certainly very beautiful, but I wouldn't want to get on the wrong side of her! '

I said, 'Well, once I saw a painting by William Blake called *The Angel of Revelation* and that made a big impression on me, but I also love another painting of The Archangel Michael, mainly for the colours. I can't remember the name of the artist, but I think he was Italian. And the archangel in that painting is wearing such a wonderful blue breastplate that is practically transparent, so you can see his chest and his stomach muscles and even his tummy button. I've tried to show that here, because she really is so strong.'

A voice behind me said, 'Yes, yes, I think we can see that. We can see that very clearly.' It was Mrs Durkin. I didn't know that she had come into the room, so that gave me a terrible fright, and I couldn't talk any more. She asked, in a rather annoyed voice, 'And am I right in thinking that this angel is slaying a dragon?' I put my head down.

Miss Grierson didn't take any notice of Mrs Durkin, and asked me, 'And what might you call this work of art?'

I picked up an orange pastel and wrote in flowing letters, *My Guardian Angel will protect me.*

Miss Grierson said, 'Well there you are, Mrs Durkin. My work is done for this morning. Philippa, would you mind awfully if I took this picture with me? I promise to bring it back tomorrow.'

I nodded my head. Mrs Durkin said to me, 'Go and wash your hands, and then go and tidy your room.'

I took a deep breath and looked straight ahead of me. Ursula was sitting by the window and laughing. She had been there from the minute I had started painting. I said, 'Excuse me Miss Grierson, please can you tell me what is my big job? And why must I do it every morning after breakfast, and leave it for Mrs Durkin to look at? Really I have no idea what she means. And please can you teach me how to speak Scottish? Because it's awfully difficult for me to do as I'm told when I have no idea what someone is talking about. And thank you for teaching me this morning, and being so kind.'

I didn't wait for an answer, but went upstairs and washed my hands, and marvelled at all the art materials that covered the floor. Suddenly I remembered that I had forgotten Polish Teddy, so I ran down the stairs and walked into the dining room, took Teddy and walked out. Mrs Durkin said, 'The cheek of it!' Miss Grierson laughed.

I looked out of the window, and watched Miss Grierson get into her car. She looked up and saw me, and wound down her window and waved, so I waved back. She didn't drive out of the big gates and onto the road, but turned right and drove up the hill. I knew that she was going up to the hotel. I felt certain that she was going to have a wee drinky, and tell everyone that she had helped me to talk again, and improved my painting technique.

I had won another victory, but my head ached and my tummy was hurting.

I am irritable and going up the wall

Mummy and Muriel once had a long discussion about Mummy's bad moods. It was on the morning after Mummy had spent a whole day in her room. She said she had felt terribly irritable, and thought she was going mad, and driving herself and everyone around her up the wall. Muriel said, 'Ruth, you know how it is. It passes. Now you've woken up with a smile on your face and a spring in your step.' That was true. And we all knew what was best for Mummy when she felt a bad mood coming on. It was to go up to her bedroom, to sleep or read, or spend time up there talking with Muriel. And Muriel might do something nice to Mummy that would make her sigh and laugh. On days like that, Muriel and I would sit downstairs, and talk and draw, or do jigsaw puzzles, and we would cook together, and try not to make too much noise. Or we might have a nice walk on the Common, or go to the shops, and Muriel would be extra nice and kind to me, and almost certainly buy me a Bounty. I didn't feel lonely when Muriel went upstairs, because I knew that she was working her magic on Mummy, and that everything would soon be all right.

Mummy said, 'I know that, Muriel. I know that now, at this moment. But when I'm in it, I just don't know what to do with myself, and I can't imagine the awful feelings passing away. Sometimes I think you would both be better off without me.'

This shocked Muriel terribly. She said, 'Ruth! Please don't ever say that again! It's as if you have slapped me in the face.'

Mummy apologised and said, 'Sometimes I thank God that you are here.'

They could only really talk sensibly about Mummy's moods when Mummy was feeling fine. During the dark days, she was like a lioness in a cage. You had to be so careful when you were near her, or not go near her at all. Only Muriel could stand up to Mummy when she was in one of her desperate moods. I used to think of Muriel being a bit like a lion tamer, prepared to go into a cage with a dangerous beast.

As you read this, you might be thinking, 'Why on Earth did those two adults have such intimate conversations in front of their child? Why didn't they do what most parents did in those days: send me out of the room, or suggest I watch TV, or only talk about periods to each other when I wasn't around?' I think Muriel did it on purpose. I was a child who was full of questions, and was desperate to tell her all about my deepest fears. Those fears had developed precisely because the adults around me had talked in whispers, or they assumed that I wouldn't understand them, so they never tried to explain what was going on. Muriel once said to Mummy, 'Ruth, I want us always to have everything out in the open.' Mummy laughed at that, then looked serious and said that she agreed totally, but some things needed to be talked about when certain little ears weren't listening. This made Muriel frown so much that Mummy put her middle finger on Muriel's forehead, between her eyes, and gently rubbed it up and down. She said, 'Don't frown like that, my love, otherwise you'll grow up with a worry line.'

All these thoughts were passing through my mind one morning, as I stood at the garden wall, looking out across the road and at the beach. It was my special time for thinking about Muriel and Mummy. I went and stood at that wall whenever Mrs Durkin said I could play outside. On that particular morning, I had just had another breakfast of a glass of water and a slice of bread and margarine. Mrs Durkin had said that she was becoming very impatient with me, because I wouldn't speak to her. She kept asking me if I had done my Big Job, but I still didn't know what she meant. Sinbad was sitting next to me and I was patting his head. My arm was getting tired, because his head was quite high up and I had to stretch to get my hand onto the place that he really liked. I should have asked him to lie down, but I wanted to look over the wall, at the hills and the sea, and think about Mummy and Muriel.

I was feeling terribly blocked up, and my headache was getting worse. It was a dull ache, which never quite seemed to go away. It was exactly at that moment that I had the idea that My First Period was going to start. I was feeling irritable, and wondered if I was going to become like Mummy, and once a month drive myself and everybody else up the wall and round the bend. This thought frightened me a lot, and I wanted urgently to talk to Ursula about it. Miss Grierson only came to see me once, and Mrs Durkin told me that she was looking for another tutor, who was more suitable for my needs. I wasn't exactly sure what she meant, but I had a feeling that it would be someone who would be strict, and wouldn't give me milk and biscuits, or let me paint. I had been on my own for a few days, and spent my time reading and painting and walking around in front of The Lodge. Jeanie hadn't seen me since the first day, and I missed her. A taxi pulled up, and for a moment, I thought perhaps Mummy had come to see me. A lady got out of the taxi and went up the steps to The Lodge. Then Mrs Durkin called my name and told me to come indoors at once, so I raced indoors as fast as I could.

It wasn't Mummy. The lady and Mrs Durkin were standing in the hall and Mrs Durkin said, 'Here she is. Now Philippa, go upstairs and wash your hands before you work with Mrs Franklin. You don't know where that dog has been.'
After I washed my hands, I went into the dining room and Mrs Franklin said, 'Hello Philippa,' with an English accent. She shook my hand and smiled. She had brown hair that was going grey and smelled of cigarettes. I smiled back. She said, 'Well, let's get down to work, then we can go for a walk outside, and you can tell me all about that huge dog.'
I said, 'He's called Sinbad, and he's my friend.'

We did some sums and a spelling test and I found both of them quite easy. Mrs Franklin said that I was a clever girl, and next time she would have to make everything much harder for me. I wanted to tell her that I was very hungry and had a headache. Mrs Durkin brought in a tray with a cup of coffee and a biscuit and a glass of water on it. The biscuit was thick and round and light brown, with a thistle shape on it. It smelled lovely. Mrs Durkin said, 'The coffee and biscuit are for you Mrs Franklin,' and left the room.

Mrs Franklin said to me, 'You have my biscuit. You've earned it.'

I said thank you, and ate it as quickly as I could. Mrs Franklin looked surprised, but didn't say anything.

We went outside and stood by the wall. Mrs Franklin explained that if we had the most powerful telescope in the world, and looked straight ahead, then we would be looking west, and could see America. She said that to our right were some Scottish hills, and that was north. But to our left was a place called Cumbria. That was where the Lake District was, and she had lived there as a child. She said, 'That's to the south, and that's England. If you carried on walking for a few hundred miles, you'd find yourself in London.' She seemed very kind. I wanted to tell her that My First Period was about to start, but then Mrs Durkin came to see us. She said, 'Tell me Mrs Franklin, what would you do with a child who refused to talk to you, but would talk to other adults, and even to her teddy bear and the dog? Can you imagine such a child? Now, what would you do?'

Mrs Franklin looked at me. 'Well, I once heard of a girl who was like that. She wouldn't talk to any of the teachers in school, but would whisper to the other children in the playground. She was quite a wilful and manipulative girl. She talked to her parents and her brothers and sisters at home all right, but she refused point blank to talk to her grandfather. Her parents were at their wits' end and took their daughter to see a doctor. The doctor said that it would only be a matter of time before she spoke, and that everyone should leave her alone. Well, the teachers took this advice, but it didn't do any good. The child just became more and more stubborn, and refused to say anything to any adult in school. Then the mother became ill and the girl went to stay with her grandparents. The grandfather forbade her to leave her room unless she said, "Please may I leave my room?" And he wouldn't allow her to have anything to eat unless she said, "Please may I have some food?" '

I looked down at my shoes. Mrs Durkin said, 'Now tell us what happened then, Mrs Franklin.'

'Well, in no time at all, the girl did as she was told.'

'And did this cure her of her silence in front of adults?'

'Oh yes. I heard that she went back to school and talked to everyone, with no problems at all.'

'So would you say that she had learned her lesson?'

'Well yes, because I heard tell that from then on she was a perfect little girl, who always did exactly as she was told.'

'So would you say that in cases like this, with girls like this, you have to be cruel to be kind?'

'Oh, I don't see it as being cruel. It's more a question of adults helping a girl to learn the error of her ways.'

Mrs Durkin gave a horrible little laugh. It was obvious they were talking about me. She said, 'To learn the error of her ways. That's such a good way of putting it. You see, Philippa has a lot to learn. A lot. Her father has been extremely generous, and has sent her a huge box of beautiful paints and art materials. But what was the first thing that she did with them? She painted a most disgusting picture. It was of a lady who was practically naked! And to think that we paid good money to a tutor who allowed Philippa to do it! I'm sure that Mr Dunbar would be shocked if he ever heard of such a thing. So I agree with you. We would be failing in our duty if we were to allow that kind of thing to happen again.'

Mrs Franklin didn't say anything after that, and Mrs Durkin walked back to The Lodge. She said, 'Is that true Philippa? Have you done those things? Because if you have, it's really not the sort of thing that a nice girl like you should do. Take my advice and talk to Mrs Durkin. Tell her that you are sorry, and that you won't do it again. Then, like the girl in my story, you will have learned the error of your ways. Mrs

Durkin only wants the best for you. Children, and especially girls, must do as they are told, and understand that grown-ups know best. I'm sure that your father would agree with that.'

In *my story*! So it wasn't true, after all. She had made up a story about a girl like me, who had been treated terribly and made to talk, and somehow suddenly became a perfect girl. I wanted to scream at her and call her a fucking lying bitch, but my tongue was stuck to the top of my mouth and my head was hurting more than ever, and I thought I might be sick. It was windy and a leaf blew up in front of us. It was small and brown and dead, and spiralled upwards and over the wall and out of sight. Mrs Franklin took my hand and said, 'Let's go indoors now, and you can write a story. I'm sure you probably want to go to the toilet too.' We went back inside The Lodge, and I went upstairs to do a wee. I looked in the mirror. My face was very pale, and I had red blotches on my cheeks. My eyes had black rings around them, and the white parts of my eyes were full of tiny red veins. I looked like Mummy in the middle of one of her bad days. I went back downstairs and Mrs Franklin gave me a new exercise book and opened it at the first page. But I couldn't write anything. I just looked at the page and wanted to cry.

I am a prisoner

Mrs Franklin went away and I could smell cooking, so I knew that it was nearly lunchtime. Mrs Durkin told me to go upstairs and do my Big Job and leave it for her to look at. She said that I wasn't to come downstairs until I had done it. I went upstairs and looked out of the window. The wind was getting stronger, and huge towers of grey cloud were racing down from the Scottish mountain and heading across the sea, towards England. I went into the dining room and Mrs Durkin had set a place for me, with a plate of food that looked and smelled delicious. It was two sausages and mashed potato with onion gravy, and I thought that the sausages were probably made of beef.

Mrs Durkin went upstairs and I started eating as fast as I could. She came back down again and said, 'But you haven't done anything! There's nothing there! And I didn't say you could start eating.' She took the plate away from me and put it on the other side of the table. She said, 'You will ask for your food, and then you shall get it. Say, "Please may I eat, Mrs Durkin?" Say that, and you can have your lunch.' I put my head down. She said, 'I can wait.'

I kept my head down. I wanted to scream and shout at her, and call her every horrible name I had ever heard in my whole life. I wanted to punch her in the face, and kick and bite her. But I just kept my head down. My head was hurting very badly now. I wanted to cry, but wouldn't let myself. I heard a big flurry of wings, and Ursula was sitting by the window. She said, 'Say it Pippa. Just say it. Say it and then you can eat.'

I looked at Ursula and whispered, 'I can't. I can't say it.'

Mrs Durkin said, 'There you are. I knew you would talk sooner or later.' She handed me the plate of food and left the room. The mashed potato was cold, but I ate it anyway. It was very salty and not at all like Mummy's. I drank my water and went upstairs to my room.

Not long afterwards, Mrs Durkin came in and told me that Jeanie had asked to see me, but she had sent her away, because I had been wilful, stubborn, and defiant. Instead, I was to stay in my room until the gong sounded for tea. Then I would ask for my food, and after tea she would let me walk in the garden. I ignored her. As soon as she left the room, I went upstairs and opened my father's box, and took all the art materials out. Someone had taken away all of my sketchpads and paper.

What was the point of me having lots of the best paints, brushes, pastels and pencils if I had no paper? It was worse than having nothing to paint with at all. I thought that someone was playing a cruel trick on me, and I had no doubt who that person was. Ursula came and said she had seen Mrs Durkin take all the paper out of the box and had hidden it somewhere. She said I had to be very careful that I didn't make Mrs Durkin angry, because she could be quite dangerous. She might be someone who knew how to hit children but not leave a mark, so the police wouldn't believe me when I told them that she had beaten me. I told Ursula that this made me feel even more frightened, but she said that my father wouldn't allow anybody to hurt me, as long as he knew what was going on. I just had to find a way of telling him.

That gave me an idea. I looked at the wallpaper in my room. It was a cream colour, with small pink, lilac, and yellow flowers with light green leaves. I thought this design was very pretty, and looking at it made me feel calm. I had liked it so much that I had copied the pattern in one of my new notebooks. I knelt down and looked at where the wallpaper met the skirting board. Sure enough, just like in Muriel's old house in London, the paper had become unstuck at the bottom. My bed was next to the wall, so I crawled under it, and discovered that it was very easy to lift the wallpaper away from the wall without ripping it too much. I found some nice coloured pencils and crawled back under the bed. I pulled the paper a bit too hard and a large piece came off in my hand. That gave me a bit of a fright, but then I thought that this was a good idea, because then people would see the message I was about to write, and come and rescue me.

I wrote in red pencil, 'My name is Pippa Dunbar. I am a prisoner here. I am starving. My head hurts terribly. I want my Mummy.' I wanted to write the date, but didn't know what it was.

I was just about to move away from the wall, when I heard the door open and someone come in the room. I felt my heart jump. I saw Mrs Durkin's feet and heard her say, 'Philippa?' I heard her go into the bathroom and then she came back in the room again. I kept completely still. I heard her move around the room and tut to herself and sigh. She picked up the boxes of paint I had left on the floor and put them back in the big cardboard box.

She said, 'I know you are here. You are almost certainly under the bed. Tea will be ready when the gong sounds.'

I stayed under the bed for a long time. Nobody came back upstairs, so I decided to get into bed and try to go to sleep. It seemed better to be asleep and dream, rather than have nothing else to do except look out of the window. But I felt worse in bed, because all I could think about was how hungry and thirsty I was, and how much my head and tummy ached, and how I missed Mummy and Muriel. I was going to cry, but forced myself not to. Instead, I decided that I must escape. I spent a long time thinking about what to do, and then fell asleep.

A prisoner no more

I woke up when the gong sounded, but I didn't go down. I couldn't bear the thought of Mrs Durkin showing me food and forcing me to speak. I thought that it would be better to stay upstairs and not see the food at all. The gong sounded again. It sounded much louder, and I knew that an angry person was striking it. I walked to the top of the stairs. I wanted to shout, 'I'm not coming down! My father owns this house! If he knew how you were treating me, he would send someone straight away to tell you off, and make someone nice look after me, like Jeanie.'

Mrs Durkin saw me and said, 'Come down here straight away.' I had no choice. Some food was waiting for me. There were two fish paste sandwiches and a cup of tea. Mrs Durkin sat next to me and said, 'Ask for your food. Say, "Please may I eat, Mrs Durkin?" Say that and you may eat, and then I will tell Jeanie that she may come and see you. That's all you have to do. It's quite simple.'

I looked straight ahead, but Ursula wasn't there. I kept looking at the windows. It was raining very hard outside and the sky had gone very dark. As I stared at the windows, I could see little red and yellow spots, and there was a flash of light and I thought that a storm was starting. I kept staring, and more coloured lights flashed in front of my eyes, and I thought they looked quite beautiful, so I didn't want to stop looking at them.

But though there were more flashes of bright light, there was no thunder. I wondered if Ursula was behind the bright lights, but was having trouble finding a way through. Perhaps the other angels were talking to her and giving her ideas about how I might escape. Then suddenly I was by the window, looking at myself sitting at the table, with Mrs Durkin sitting next to me. I could see her mouth opening and closing, and I knew she was telling me, 'Say it. All you have to do is say it.' I saw Pippa's mouth answer and I could read her lips and she was saying, 'No. I won't say it. I want my mummy.' I saw Mrs Durkin say, 'You will do as I say. It's for your own good. One day you will thank me for this.' Then she left the room and suddenly I was back in my chair. I devoured the sandwiches and drank the tea, then went into the hall and opened the front door and ran in the pouring rain up to the hotel.

By the time I reached the hotel, I was soaking wet. I tried to push the front door open, but it was much too heavy. A man with a big umbrella came running up the steps and said, 'Allow me,' and opened the door for me. Everything inside was very bright and warm, but I just stood by the door, shivering. A man came over to me from behind the counter and said, 'Can I help you?' I told him I wanted to see Jeanie. He said, 'Come with me,' and took my hand. Then Mr Durkin was there and he asked the man, 'What's going on?'
The man said, 'I don't know. I just found her by the front door, and she says she wants Jeanie.'
Mr Durkin said, 'Then go and get her!'
Jeanie came in and said, 'Oh my goodness! She's soaking wet and shivering, and she has no shoes on!'
Mr Durkin said, 'Go and get her warm, and I'll see if I can find out what's going on.'

Jeanie found a tartan blanket and took me into Mr Durkin's office. He had a nice leather chair and Jeanie sat on it, and wrapped me in the blanket and put me on her lap. She asked me to tell her all about what had been happening, but I felt very cold and my teeth were chattering, so I couldn't say anything. She said that if she didn't change my clothes then I would catch my death of cold. I looked alarmed and she said, 'It's just an expression.' She said that she would ring down to The Lodge and ask Mr Durkin to bring some fresh clothes and a coat for me.

I shouted, 'No, no, no! I don't want to see *her* ever again!'

Jeanie said, 'OK. But do you feel all right?'

I told her I had a terrible headache and was very hungry. She said she was going to get me a drink, but I held onto her and wouldn't let her go. Then Mr Durkin came in and asked me to tell him all about what was wrong, but I wouldn't tell him and Jeanie said, 'She has an awful headache and she's starving.'

He said to Jeanie, 'Mrs Durkin is in an awful temper. Can you take the wee lassie upstairs to one of the spare rooms and give her a bath? Then I'll go back down to The Lodge and get her some warm clothes.'

I wish I could say that I have no memory of what happened next, but unfortunately I can remember everything. A man doctor came to see me in the bedroom, and Mr Durkin and Jeanie were there, and the doctor asked me lots of questions, but I couldn't talk to him. He asked me if I had a pain anywhere, so I pointed to my head and then my stomach. Actually that's not quite right, because I didn't know where my stomach was. At my age, you called everything between your chest and your Lovely Place *my tummy*.

Then the doctor said to Mr Durkin, 'It could be a number of things, including appendicitis, so I think we had better get her to hospital, just to be on the safe side.'

Mr Durkin said, 'Oh hell.'

My back passage

And he was right. It was hell. Mr Durkin drove me to the hospital in the town. All I can remember about the journey is Jeanie putting my suitcase in the boot of Mr Durkin's car and her sitting in the back with me, holding my hand. Seeing the suitcase made me think that, after all, someone had decided that I could go back home to Mummy and Muriel. Then Jeanie told me that the case had my pyjamas and slippers and Polish Teddy in it, and some clothes for when I was feeling better.

Mr Durkin took us into the hospital, but said he would need to get back to the hotel, to try to sort out the mess, and that Jeanie was to stay with me for as long as necessary. Jeanie told him that she couldn't possibly stay with me on her own, because she was too young, and she was afraid that the doctors might ask her questions that she couldn't answer, or perhaps ask her to make an important decision. Mr Durkin said, 'Of course not. What was I thinking of?'

This made me more frightened than ever. I wondered who was in control of my life, and I knew that I might have to have an operation.

A nurse showed us into a room, where a doctor told me to lie on a bed, and started talking to me. He said, 'Right my dear, you tell me all about what's wrong. But first let's see if I've got your name right. Is it Philippa Dunbar?'

Jeanie said, 'She likes to be called Pippa.'

He said to me, 'Is that so? That's a nice name.' I nodded. He had a kind face and a soft voice, and I thought that I would to be able to talk to him. He said, 'Let's talk about what you have had to eat, and if you've done your Big Job today.'

I whispered, 'I'm always hungry because I have to ask for food, and I can't speak when people make me do that, so I have only had bread and margarine to eat and water to drink.'

The doctor's eyebrows shot up and he asked Mr Durkin if that was true. Mr Durkin said, 'I can't imagine that that's the case.'

The doctor said to me, 'Pippa, that's a very serious thing to say about grown-ups. Let's talk about something else. Have you done your Big Job today?'

I whispered, 'I think so.'

He smiled and said, 'Well either you have or you haven't. Or perhaps you've forgotten?'

I whispered, 'Excuse me doctor, but people keep telling me to do my Big Job, and to leave it for them to look at, but I don't know what they mean.'

He smiled again, 'It means have you done a poo? Or perhaps it's called a Number Two in England? So have you done a poo today?'

I completely froze and couldn't say anything. I was too shocked. He said, 'Well, have you done a poo? It's very important that I know. It helps me to understand why your tummy hurts so much.'

I nodded. Obviously I was lying, but I wasn't going to talk to a complete stranger about something as private as that. He pressed my tummy and asked me if it hurt. It did. By chance, he had pressed me on exactly the spot where I knew my appendix was. I yelled. It wasn't really so painful, but ever since we got in the car, I had been hatching a plot. If I could convince the doctor to believe that I was ill, then perhaps I could explain to someone important that Mrs Durkin was torturing me. Then they would have to send me back home to Mummy.

The doctor said to Mr Durkin, 'I'm going to do a digital rectal examination.'

Mr Durkin said, 'I beg your pardon?'

'I need to insert my thumb in the patient's back passage.'

Mr Durkin looked very surprised and said, 'I'll just pop out. Call me when you've finished. Jeanie will stay and hold Philippa's hand.'

The doctor told me to turn over on my side. Jeanie came round to my side of the bed so that she could hold my hand. Her face was so close to mine that I could feel her warm breath. She was chewing Wrigley's Spearmint Chewing Gum. The doctor said, 'I'll just pull down your pants. You might feel a slight discomfort.' I went completely rigid. He had stuck his thumb up my bottom.

Jeanie said, 'Don't worry Pippa. My dad says that doctors are just like car mechanics. They ask a few questions, then have a good feel around. Then they know exactly what's wrong and how to fix the problem.'

72

The doctor laughed and said, 'Quite right, though I try not to make a habit of doing this sort of thing too often.' All the time they were talking, he was feeling around inside me. There was something in his voice that made me think of Muriel. Once a man in a café had spoken to her with just the same sort of voice, and had a cheeky smile on his face. Mummy said afterwards that the man had been a terrible flirt. Muriel told her that men could flirt with her as much as they liked, but they would never get anywhere. I closed my eyes and imagined that I was holding Muriel's hand. That was a very bad idea, because I started to cry. The doctor said, 'Does it really hurt that much?'

I whispered, 'I want my mummy.'

The doctor washed his hands and asked Jeanie to explain to him exactly what was going on. She told my story, as far as she knew it. She said that I had been brought to the hotel late one night, and I was the owner's daughter and, in her opinion, (and God could strike her down dead for saying it, and the doctor had to promise not to tell anyone that Jeanie had told him), but as far as she was concerned, I was not being looked after at all well.

The doctor went outside and I heard him talking to Mr Durkin. Then they both came in, and the doctor explained that he was going to keep me in hospital overnight, so that they could decide what was wrong with me, and what to do about it. He said to me, 'These two nice people will take you along to the children's ward. Then they will say goodbye to you, and the nurses will look after you.' The doctor was bending over me as he was talking. I wanted to hit him as hard as I could in the face. I wanted to bite his hand so hard that it bled. I wanted to yell 'Fuck off! Fuck off! Fuck off!' so loudly that everyone in the hospital would come running, to see what the noise was all about. I wanted to jump off the bed and run out of the door, and scream that someone was attacking me. But I didn't. I just did exactly as I was told.

Czesława Kwoka

Once someone showed me a book with the most horrific photos inside. It was a book about Auschwitz. Anyone looking at those pictures would feel sickened, but I am a Jew, and someone whose Jewish relatives had all disappeared in The War, and may even have been tortured and killed in a terrible death camp. So that made me feel ten times as shocked as anyone else. I don't think I have ever recovered from seeing those photos.

Recently I have been thinking more about Auschwitz, because in that book was a photograph that made me remember what I felt like at that moment in the hospital. It was a photograph of a Polish Catholic girl called Czesława Kwoka. She was fourteen years old, and had been arrested with her mother and brought to the camp. Like all the other prisoners, she was forced to go into a room to have her photograph taken; once from the side, once looking straight at the photographer, and once looking away from the camera. Someone had hacked all her hair off, and you could see that she had been crying, and that her lip and face had been bleeding. Apparently, she had no idea what was going on, and spoke no German, so didn't know what to do. A kapo yelled at her and struck her round the face, which made her lip and nose bleed. Czesława must have realised that if she didn't do exactly as she was told, then the kapo would beaten her again, or maybe even kill her. She dried the tears from her eyes and wiped the blood from her face, and did her best to follow the instructions.

I can't describe the look in Czesława's eyes. It pierced me. What must she have already seen? What must she have felt? I feel certain that she must have been thinking about her mother. All anyone knows for certain is that she died in the camp a month later. Nobody knows how she died.
I'm not saying that my experience was anywhere near as terrible as hers. Of course it wasn't. But seeing that photograph transported me back immediately to that moment in hospital, with the doctor feeling inside my bottom. That wasn't so bad;

after all, it was just an internal examination. But my mother wasn't with me, and I didn't know where she was, or what had happened to her. I had nobody to protect me. The only way I can describe the anguish I felt is to tell you about poor Czesława Kwoka, who was going to die in a prison camp, just because she was Polish.

Into the ward

A nurse came in and sat me in a wheelchair. She pushed me along a long corridor, while Jeanie and Mr Durkin followed behind, whispering to each other. We came to the door of the children's ward and Mr Durkin said he would wait outside, but that Jeanie would stay with me, until the nurses told her to go. The nurse said, 'It's better if the parents and family stay outside the ward, and only come in at Visiting Times, so say your goodbyes now.'

Jeanie said to the nurse, 'I'll do no such thing!' But Mr Durkin told her to do as she was told. Jeanie kissed me and told me I would be all right, and she would come and visit me as soon as she could. She said, 'Be sure and draw me a lovely picture, and I'll bring you a Bounty.'

I smiled inside when she said that, but outside I was completely frozen. It felt like the light inside me had completely gone out.

The nurse wheeled me into the ward, but halfway along she stopped to talk to another nurse. To my left, a baby with a big bandage on her head was standing in a cot, looking at me. She had a terrible look of sadness in her eyes. To my right, in a room all on his own, was a boy lying on his back in bed. He had a tube going into his nose and another one in his mouth. His eyes were closed, but he didn't look like he was asleep. I thought he was dead. I shut my eyes.

My bed was on the left-hand side, at the far end of the ward. Another nurse came and told me to take off my clothes and put on my pyjamas. There was a boy sitting up in the bed opposite, and I was sure that he was looking at me. Then the nurse told me to get into bed, and she took my temperature. Then she gave me a metal pan, and told me to put it under my bottom and do my business in it. I did as I was told, but nothing came out.

She said, 'If you don't do it here, then we'll have to walk you along to the toilets outside the ward.' I knew that would mean walking past the almost-dead boy and the sad baby, so I tried my best to do a wee. The nurse said I was a good girl, and told me that Visiting Time had just finished, and that in the morning a doctor would come to see me. Then they would know how long I was going to stay in hospital, and what would happen. She said I wasn't allowed to have anything to eat, but could drink water.

The nurse left me, and the boy opposite waved and smiled at me, so I smiled back, but couldn't wave. He said his name was Brian and that he had something called rheumatic fever. He said he felt fine, but wasn't allowed to go home, because his granny was too old to look after him, and because he kept being naughty. He was very cheerful and talked very loudly, so that I could hear him. Brian was the very first Scottish child I had spoken to. I wanted to speak to him, but my mouth wouldn't move. Then the nurses came and drew the curtains over the windows and told us to go to sleep, even though it was still light outside. There was nothing else to do, so I slept.

In the morning, a doctor came to see me. He said that lots of people had been ringing up about me, and a man called a social worker was going to come, and then they would decide what to do with me. I wanted to ask if he meant that people were talking to Mummy about taking me home, but my mouth wouldn't move. He felt my tummy, then called a nurse over and told her to take my temperature again, and to see if she could get me to do a bowel motion. When the doctor went away she said, 'Let's have a wee look in your cabinet and see if you've got anything interesting in there. Did anyone pack anything for you to play with, or perhaps a wee book to read?' She looked in the small cabinet beside my bed and said, 'Well hello there, young man!' She held up Polish Teddy, and I cried.

Mr Macmillan

A man came to see me, and he said he was Mr Macmillan, and that he was a social worker. He said that he was one of the people who were trying to decide what was going to happen to me. I think I hadn't opened my mouth all morning, except to drink some water. I wanted desperately to tell him about Mummy, and to beg him to let me go home. But the more I tried to force myself to talk, the more my words just seemed to disappear out of my head. Mr Macmillan asked me if I wanted to say anything, but I couldn't move at all. He said that if I didn't talk to him then it was going to be very difficult for him to know how to help me.

Then he saw Polish Teddy sitting on my bedside cabinet, and he said he was probably the nicest bear he had ever seen, and much more handsome than the one he had given his daughter. Then I cried without making a noise and he said, 'You really are a very unhappy girl, aren't you?' and I whispered, 'Yes.'

He asked me, 'Would it make you feel better if I explained what was happening?' I nodded, and he told me I was a very good girl. Then he explained that Mr Shepherd knew I was in hospital, and he had been trying to contact my father, but Daddy was in a foreign country and everyone was waiting to talk to him. I whispered, 'I want my mummy.'

Mr Macmillan said, 'Ah.' Then he was quiet for a while. Then he said, 'Shall I call you Philippa or Pippa? What do you like best?'

I whispered, 'Pippa, please.'

He smiled at me and told me that Mummy was all right, but that she wasn't allowed to see me.

Then he was quiet again. I liked him being quiet. Not because I wanted him to shut up, but I felt that all the time he was sitting there, thinking about me, he was somehow giving me the strength to say what I really wanted to say. He was a bit like my Art Therapist. He said, 'Mummy knows that you are in hospital, and that you are being looked after properly.'

I took a deep breath and closed my eyes. I hoped that when I opened them, Ursula would be there and would tell me what to say. I opened my eyes, but she wasn't there. All I saw was Brian doing a jigsaw puzzle with a lady. So I didn't say what I wanted to say. I didn't say that Mrs Durkin had been horrible to me, and that I never wanted to go back to The Lodge again.

But Mr Macmillan must have sensed something was wrong, or perhaps the doctor had told him what Jeanie had said about me being treated so badly. He patted my hand and said, 'I know that you're not able to talk right now. It was wrong of me to say that I can't help you. That was a silly thing to say. Of course you can write about how you feel, and you can even draw me a picture if you'd find that easier. Or when you feel a bit better, you can always talk to the nurses about yourself.'

I smiled for the first time. He said, 'Well, that's a nice smile. Let's see if we can find you some paper. Let's have a look in your cabinet, and see if anyone has left you anything to write or draw with. I know you are such a wonderful artist, so we mustn't stop you.' He looked inside my cabinet and said, 'Look at all these lovely new clothes!' He held up some of the clothes that had been packed for me. They were the new ones from my father's shop. Then he reached round the side of my cabinet and said, 'There's your suitcase here. Let's have a look inside and see if anyone has left anything.'

Suddenly I felt able to move, and leaned over to see what he was doing. Mr Macmillan opened the suitcase, but it was empty. But just the sight of something that had been touched by Mummy and Muriel seemed to warm me up inside. Mr Macmillan said, 'Hello, here's a piece of paper.' The suitcase had a cloth lining, which had a tear in it, and we could see the corner of a piece of paper sticking out. Mr Macmillan pulled at it and we saw that it was a white envelope. He gave the envelope to me and said, 'I wonder if there's anything inside?' I opened the envelope very carefully, and inside was a photograph. It was the photograph of me and Mummy and Muriel, sitting in the window in Canada.

Mr Macmillan said, 'What a lovely photograph. Is that Mummy?' He was pointing to Muriel. I shook my head. He smiled and put his finger on Mummy and said, 'Of course it isn't. I can see that she is your mummy. She looks just like you, and you look just like her.' Then he asked me, 'So that lady with you. Is she a friend of the family? Or perhaps an aunt?'

It felt like he was one of those grown-ups who knew how to work magic on sad and upset children like me. Big teardrops fell out of my eyes and one of them landed on Mummy's face. Mr Macmillan whipped his hanky out of his pocket and carefully dabbed my tear from the photo. He said, 'No harm done.' It was lovely to see Mummy and Muriel, and to remember that happy moment. But suddenly all my troubles just seemed to come rushing towards me, a bit like the tornado in The Wizard of Oz.

Brian shouted across, 'Hey, Mr Macmillan! Are you going to come and talk to me?' The lady sitting next to Brian told him to hush. Mr Macmillan started to get up and said, 'It's Brian's turn now.' But I grabbed him hard by the sleeve of his jacket and wouldn't let go. He said, 'It's all right, Pippa. I'm coming back.' But I still wouldn't let go. 'All right. I have an idea. I'll ask if Brian can come over here, or perhaps you can go over there.'

I let go of him, and he went over to talk to the lady with Brian. I heard her say, 'I don't see why not, but we had better ask a nurse.'

Mr Macmillan went over to speak to a nurse and she said, 'I'd better ask Matron.' The nurse went off, and as soon as she had gone, Mr Macmillan whispered something to Brian and the lady. He picked up the tray with the jigsaw on and brought it over to show me. Unfortunately, half way across the room, he dropped the tray, and all the pieces were scattered all over the floor.

The lady said, 'Oh no! We've been working on that puzzle for a long time!'

Brian laughed and said 'Good! I didn't really like it, anyway. Flowers in a vase is a bit boring.'

Then a new nurse came. She was older than the other nurses, and wore a dark blue uniform. She got cross with Mr Macmillan and said, 'Mr Macmillan, I see you are interfering again.'

He said, 'Sorry, Matron,' but he sounded like a naughty little boy who wasn't sorry at all. I looked at his face, and he was smiling to himself. He saw me looking at him and he winked at me.

Matron sighed, but I could see that she was only pretending to be cross. She said, 'Mr Macmillan, if you keep disrupting the smooth running of my ward, then I will have to keep you in my office every time you come and visit.'

Brian's lady helped Mr Macmillan pick up the pieces. She said, 'Now we'll have to count the pieces to make sure they're all there.' She said to me, 'Hello young lady, I'm Mrs Drew and I'm the hospital teacher. If I give you a pile of the pieces, will you count them for us, and Brian can count the rest? There should be three hundred and fifty pieces altogether. If there are any missing, then we'll have to search under the beds for them. There's nothing worse than a jigsaw puzzle with pieces missing, don't you think?'

I smiled at that. It seemed such a silly thing to say, but true. I felt like I was taking part in a funny television programme.

Mr Macmillan counted the pieces with Brian and I counted mine with Mrs Drew. There were five pieces missing. Mrs Drew said to me, 'Well I'm not going crawling under the beds to get them. I'm sure that they will turn up sooner or later. Perhaps you could make the puzzle for us and find out which pieces are missing?'

Flowers in a Vase by Renoir, c 1866

The puzzle was of a painting of beautiful flowers, and was called *Flowers in a Vase* by a painter called Renoir. I could see why Brian would find it boring. For a start, the background was grey, like a dirty grey wall. And the light brown pot, when you first looked at it, didn't seem very interesting at all. Even the surface that the pot was sitting on was a dull grey, like the slab of old marble I had seen in our neighbours' kitchen in Ashbourne. But that was the secret. The artist had chosen that dull and uninteresting background so that every colour he used for the flowers and leaves and stems would be eye-catching and exciting, even though half of the plants looked like weeds that he had pulled up from the garden and plonked in the pot. All the time I was looking at the pieces, I completely forgot where I was. I forgot I had a headache and that my tummy was hurting very badly. I forgot that I was far away from home and missing the people who loved me. Then a nurse came and said, 'Hurry up and put those away, because the doctor is coming to see you.'

Mr Macmillan said, 'Thank you nurse,' but didn't take any notice of her. He said to me, 'You carry on with the puzzle, and I'll go and have a word with the doctor.'

The doctor explains

I had just started the puzzle when Mr Macmillan returned with a doctor and Matron. The doctor was wearing a white coat and had a moustache. Mr Macmillan asked him if he'd like to sit down, but he said he'd prefer to stand, so Mr Macmillan sat on a chair. The doctor said to me, 'I'm going to examine you.' I went rigid. I didn't want him to do that horrible thing again, and especially with everyone being able to see what was happening. He said. 'It's all right. I'm just going to feel your tummy. I'll do my best to be as gentle as possible.'

Brian shouted, 'Hello doctor! When can I go home?' The doctor ignored him, and Matron went over and told Brian to be quiet. She came back and pulled down my pyjama bottoms and the doctor felt my tummy all over. He asked me where it hurt. I thought I'd better point to the same place as the day before, in case they thought I was making things up, and would send me back to The Lodge. The doctor's hands were very warm. He said, 'Hmm. Clearly there's chronic constipation, but...' He looked like he was thinking to himself. Then he said, 'We have parental permission now, so I think we should operate. I have a slot later this afternoon. So Matron, get everything ready please.' Then he went over to Brian, said a few words to him, and walked away.

Matron said to Mr Macmillan, 'Will you explain, Mr Macmillan, or shall I?'

He said, 'I'll explain as much as I can.' Matron went to get a chair for herself and sat down next to my bed. Mr Macmillan told me that he had spoken to Mr Shepherd on the phone. Mr Shepherd had spoken to my father, and Daddy had agreed that I should have an operation to remove my appendix, because that was what was causing me to have pains in my tummy and headaches.

I didn't say anything. I began to feel sick, even though I hadn't eaten anything for a long time. I always felt like that whenever anyone mentioned that my father had been talking about me.

Now Matron was talking, but I wasn't listening. I thought about the photo of me with Mummy and Muriel. I wondered who had put it in the envelope and hidden it in my case. And why did they have to hide it in the first place? Then I had the same idea that I often had when people talked about Mummy and Muriel. It was as if the two of them loving each other, and looking after me, was some sort of crime. And now The Judge had taken me away from them as a cruel punishment, except I was being punished as well.

Matron was saying to me, '... and so we will get you ready for your operation this afternoon. All being well, you can go home in a week's time. Now be a good girl and do exactly what the nurses tell you.' Then she walked away.

Mr Macmillan said, 'Pippa, do you understand what is going to happen to you?'

I shook my head. Mr Macmillan held my hand and said, 'I'll try and explain it as best I can. Things are a little bit of a mess at the moment, and it's my job to try to sort everything out. You're not going to go home, back to Mummy. Matron didn't mean that. What she meant was that you are going to leave the hospital. But we haven't sorted out yet *where* you are going to go. Lots of people have been talking about you. Where you have been staying has not been… it hasn't been quite right for you. We know that now. So your father must find a better way to look after you. The Court in London has put me in charge of making sure that you are looked after properly. So I'm going to go say goodbye now, and go back to my office, and speak to Mr Shepherd on the phone again.'

I started to feel sick again. I took a very deep breath and closed my eyes. There was a flutter of wings and I heard Ursula say, 'Ask him. You must ask him!'
I whispered, 'Please Mr Macmillan, will you talk to Mummy and tell her she mustn't worry about me? Will you tell her that I found the photograph, and now that makes me feel so much better? And will you tell her I am being very brave, just like she was when she was a little girl, so really she will know that I am going to be all right? Please will you tell her that?' He squeezed my hand and said yes, he would try to ring Mummy that afternoon. I cried again, but this time I didn't feel quite so desperate. A nurse was walking by and said, 'Whatever is the matter?' She gave me a hug, and told me that I was a good girl, and that everyone was very pleased with me for being so brave. She looked at my photo and said, 'I can see which one is your mum. Goodness, she looks just like you. She's a real beauty! She has lovely hair, just like yours, and the same eyebrows and nose. If you grow up to look like her, then all the boys will be chasing you!'

It was so nice to be able to talk about Mummy again, and funny to think about boys chasing me. So I stopped crying and Mr Macmillan squeezed my hand again, and said that he had to go. He said he would come back the next day and that I was a very good girl. After he left, I carried on doing the puzzle. Brian shouted over some jokes. I had heard some of them before, but they were still very funny. Someone had told him I was going to have an operation and I wasn't allowed to eat anything. He wanted to know if he could have my pudding, because it was going to be cake and custard, and that was his favourite. I nodded and he said, 'You'll be all right.'

The jigsaw was really fascinating. I looked at the picture on the box and wondered who Renoir was. I was looking forward to finding which five pieces were missing, because I had an idea that I could copy them from the box and try and make them look as much like the real missing pieces as I possibly could. I thought that wouldn't be too difficult. I had noticed that the colours on the box weren't the same as the colours on the actual jigsaw, but that made it even more interesting. I passed the time doing the puzzle and looking at my photo. I felt much better, because Mr Macmillan had squeezed my hand, and the nurse had hugged me and told me that everyone thought I was being brave. Perhaps all children do the same as I did, when in difficult situations and away from their parents. I took heart from even the smallest crumbs of physical comfort and praise. And I was burying myself in Art, to help me to block out all the bad things around me. But really all I wanted to do was to sit on Muriel's lap and suck my thumb. Not being allowed to do that was one of the things that was making me ill. I knew that, but I wondered if the doctors knew it. I suspected that Mr Macmillan and Jeanie knew all about how I was feeling, but I just wasn't able to tell them. I had an idea to write to them, to explain what I felt, but I still didn't trust anybody enough to do that. I wasn't going to let them take my letter and show it to The Judge. I wanted to talk to Ursula, but I knew she wouldn't show herself to me in hospital, because she didn't want the doctors to know about her. I had a desperate urge to do a painting of her and keep it close to me, but I knew that would be a bad idea.

All of these thoughts were passing round and round in my mind when two nurses came and told me it was time to get me ready for the operating theatre.

Scars

I knew what appendicitis was, and I knew that I didn't have it. I had seen Frances' red and purple scar on the right side of her tummy, just above her Lovely Place. Muriel had one too, though hers was now a reddy-pink. Sometimes I would see it when she was getting dressed or undressed, or in the bath, or in the changing room at the swimming pool. Whenever I saw it, I always wanted to touch it. It was such a strange thing to have. I had been used to seeing other children's scars, caused by falling over, or from burns. All children like to show each other these, and tell the stories of how they got them. But a scar from an operation was something completely different. A doctor had put you to sleep and then cut you open with a sharp knife. But you woke up feeling perfectly fine, with a nice neat scar, to remind you of how lucky you were that the doctors had made you better.

Both Frances and Muriel had told me how terrible they had felt before their operations, and how they soon got better, so I wasn't really frightened of what was going to happen to me. I knew I would be put to sleep and then wake up with a scar on my tummy, near my Lovely Place. To me, Frances and Muriel were the two most beautiful people in the whole world, so to look more like them didn't seem like such a bad idea. And the pain in my tummy and my headache were getting worse, so I didn't feel that I was telling lies. I knew what the appendix was, because Muriel had explained all about it, and even drawn pictures. It was a bit of our intestine that might have been useful millions of years ago, when humans ate grass, but now we eat meat, so it has shrunk and is useless. I wondered if it was a bit like nipples on boys, because they have them, but they aren't useful for anything. Muriel had said that the appendix was a bit annoying, because it was dangerous when it became infected, and it had to be cut out. She had never heard of a boy getting infected nipples. Muriel said that the two most common operations on children were removing their tonsils and removing their appendix. She told me that she was fourteen when hers had been removed. Then she whispered, 'They shaved all my hair off, down there.'
Mummy said, 'Muriel, that's going a bit too far, don't you think?'
Muriel said, 'Yes, Ruth, that's exactly what I thought when I woke up and saw that it had all gone! It had only just started to

grow nice and thick, and I was very proud of it. It's not as if it was getting in the surgeon's way or anything. I was more upset about that than being cut open!'

Mummy said, 'Really Muriel! The things you say!' But they both laughed.

Before my operation, everyone around me was very cheerful. The nurses all commented on my photograph, and how much progress I had made with the puzzle. I even thought that the operating theatre might be a grand place, with a stage and big curtains, but I hoped there wouldn't be an audience. I was actually feeling quite cheerful myself, and didn't even mind when the nurses told me that I couldn't wear my pyjamas anymore, but had to put on a funny-looking nightie. All I really remember about being in the theatre was a nurse talking to me nicely and asking me about myself. She kept hold of my hand and I found I was able to talk in a normal voice. I said, 'When I feel better I'm going to paint lots of pictures of a vase with flowers. I already know what colours I'm going to use. I'm going to start painting like Renoir, and then paint exactly in the way that I feel. I'm really looking forward to it.'

The nurse asked me if I could paint one for her, and I told her that I'd love to. The doctor with the moustache was there as well, and he said he'd like a painting too, and that a hospital was the best place to paint vases with flowers in, because all the patients had them. Then the nurse put a mask over my nose and mouth and said, 'Breathe in and count to ten.' I managed to reach just five.

Bonnie

Then I woke up back in the ward and it was morning, and I felt terribly sick and it was absolute agony to move. I was lying on my back, and turned my head to the side and sick went all over my pillow and onto the floor. Brian shouted that I had been sick, and a nurse came and told him to shush, because he might wake the new girl who was in the bed next to me. The nurse said I wasn't to worry about making a mess, and did I know that I had a new neighbour? She was a girl who had been climbing on a roof at school, trying to find a tennis ball, and had fallen off and broken her arm and ribs. She had had an emergency operation in the night, because her arm was very badly broken. Her name was Sheila Boniface, but everyone in school called her Bonnie.

This nurse was a chatterbox, and I knew that she was doing her best to make me feel better. Her name was Nurse Beattie. She gave me a wash, and every time she moved me, my tummy hurt and I cried, silently. She said that I would soon feel better, and that the doctor was going to see me very soon. I was very, very thirsty but couldn't tell anyone. The nurse gave me some water to drink and that made me feel a bit better.

Then I slept, and when I woke up it was lunchtime, but the smell of the food made me feel sick again. Brian shouted, 'Hello Pippa!' and told me that the doctors had been and looked at me while I was asleep. The girl next to me was awake, and she smiled at me and said her name was Bonnie and that she was eleven. She asked me what was wrong with me, so I pointed to my tummy. Bonnie looked puzzled and I wondered if she thought I was pointing to my Lovely Place. Then I felt dizzy and thought I was going to be sick, but nothing came out.

After lunch, Nurse Beattie came to see me, with a syringe in a small metal basin. She said it was full of penicillin, and she had to inject in my leg, so that I wouldn't become infected. As soon as I saw the big syringe and the long needle, I screamed and screamed and screamed. I grabbed hold of Nurse Beattie's hand and screamed some more. My tummy hurt every time I screamed, but once I had started, I couldn't stop myself. Nurse Beattie said, 'Oh dear,' and took the injection away. Bonnie was crying and said, 'Oh Pippa, please don't scream like that. Try and be brave.'

Then Matron came back with Nurse Beattie, and said I must have the injection, and that it didn't really hurt, and that I must be brave, and did I want to get all infected and then have to have another operation? 'And look,' she said, 'you've frightened Bonnie. She has injections and doesn't scream like that. And if you scream again, you'll frighten the baby and make her cry.'

Matron went away and came back with the metal dish. Nurse Beattie held onto my hand and said, 'Be a good girl. Just count to three and it will be all over.' I felt them lift up my bedclothes and move my nightie and then I felt a jab. I didn't scream out loud this time, but I felt myself screaming without making any noise. I must have looked horrible, because the nurse said, 'Oh you poor thing.'
Matron said, 'That wasn't so bad, was it?'
I whispered, 'I'm sorry. I'm sorry about not being brave. I just want my mummy.'
The nurse said, 'Of course you do, pet. Of course you do.' She put something hard in my hand. It was my photo, but someone had put it in a frame.

It all comes out
A little while later, Mr Macmillan came to see me, and said that the nurses had told him that I had been upset. I whispered, 'I still am, but I'm trying to keep it all inside.'
He patted my hand and asked me what had upset me, so I whispered that I didn't want any more injections. He said, 'Nobody likes injections. I hate them. I always eat a sweet after I've had one, to make me feel better. Once I ate a whole Mars Bar. I felt much better after that!' He was quiet, and so was I. Then he said, 'I've been very busy all morning, talking about you, and getting phone calls. I've spoken to Mr Shepherd, and he says you aren't going back to the hotel. We are all thinking about the best way for you to be looked after properly.'
Then he was quiet again. I could tell from looking at his face that he was thinking very carefully about what to say next. He said, 'And I've spoken to your mummy on the phone this afternoon. She told me to tell you that she loves you very much, and she is sure that you will feel better soon.'

I kept very still, but my heart started to beat very fast and I felt very hot. I whispered, 'Thank you, Mr Macmillan. I feel very happy now.'

I was very happy, but suddenly I had a terrible pain in my tummy and I said, 'Oh dear' and I felt a huge hot wave sweeping over me and then somehow it broke inside me. My tummy felt like it had suddenly caught fire. I felt wet, and there was a terrible smell in my bed, and Mr Macmillan rushed to get a nurse.

I had started to mess myself, and couldn't stop.

Just before the nurses came to clean me up, I turned to Bonnie in the bed next to me and whispered, 'I'm sorry.'

She smiled and said, 'Don't worry Pippa. I don't mind, really I don't.'

Three nurses washed me and changed my bed covers. I was terribly upset, but tried not to show it. The more I did as I was told, the more the nurses praised me and told me I was brave. But I didn't feel brave, and I didn't feel like I was a good girl. I had lied to the doctors and now I was suffering. Every time the nurses moved me, my tummy hurt terribly. Once, I looked down to see what they were doing and I saw I had a big bloody bandage stuck to my tummy.

I turned my head away and saw Bonnie looking at me. She said, 'You poor thing.'

I was terribly embarrassed by the smell, and the thought that she could see my Lovely Place, but she didn't seem to mind at all. Then the nurses had finished and I fell asleep.

Baby Theresa

The next day I was able to eat breakfast and drink properly; and the nurses said I should get out of bed and walk to the toilet. Nurse Beattie helped me out of bed, but it hurt every time I moved. She told me that the more I moved, then the better the wound inside me would heal. I shut my eyes and shuffled along, holding on to Nurse Beattie's arm. But then Matron called over to Nurse Beattie that I would be all right on my own. I opened my eyes, and to my horror I was standing in the middle of the ward, with the still, silent boy on one side and the baby on the other. The baby was standing still in her cot, holding onto the bars and looking at me with her sad eyes. I started to cry, but without making a noise.

Another nurse found me and said. 'Oh dear! I'm not going to leave you now.' She was true to her word, and took me outside the ward to the toilet, and stayed with me while I did a wee. She told me she was Nurse Fitzpatrick and said she was very pleased with me for going to the toilet properly. She told me that I had completely emptied my bowels the day before, and it would take a few days for my tummy to get back to normal. I didn't want to think about making a mess in my bed, and told Nurse Fitzpatrick that I was sorry. She said, 'Oh never you mind about that! I've had to clear up worse than that in my time!'

I wondered what could be worse than a bed full of diarrhoea.

The only bad thing about being in the toilet was that the toilet paper was that nasty shiny stuff.

I asked Nurse Fitzpatrick to tell me about the boy with the tubes. She explained that he was called Keith, and he was ten, and that he had run across the road without looking, and a car had run him over. He had been so badly injured that his brain wasn't working properly. He was in something called a coma, which was a very deep sleep, but he wasn't in any pain, and he had been like that for over a month.

How would you have reacted if you were nearly ten and had been told something like that? It felt like the nurse had just given me an injection of some frozen liquid. I sat on the toilet and shivered all over. I can still see poor Keith now. I was terrified of looking at him, but at the same time wanted to go and hold his hand and talk to him. I asked, 'Does he have any visitors?' The nurse said that his mother came to see him every day. Visitors were only allowed onto the ward for an hour each day in the late afternoon, at Visiting Time, but Keith's parents were allowed to see him whenever they wanted. I was pleased about that, at least, but I knew it meant that he was never going to get better again.

Then I asked her about the baby. She said, 'Oh That's Baby Theresa. Her mother was bathing her and she slipped and dropped the baby, and she banged her head so badly on the floor that it fractured her skull.'

'But why does she look so sad?'

'I suppose it's because she doesn't have any visitors.'

I was appalled. 'But what about her mummy and daddy? Why don't they come?'

'Oh, they did visit to start with, but the poor wee thing cried so much when they left, so Matron said it was better if the parents stopped coming.'

This was even more shocking. 'But do you pick her up and play with her, so she doesn't feel lonely?'

I was in for another shock. 'Oh no. Matron says we are nurses, and our job is to make children better. We don't really have time to play. We used to pick her up and give her a cuddle and sing to her, but she would cry when we put her down, so Matron and the doctors told us to leave her alone, except to feed and change her. She has got used to that now, and is a very good little girl. She never makes a sound.'

On the way back, near Keith and Baby Theresa, I pretended I had a terrible pain and needed to stop walking. I looked at Keith. His mother was there, holding his hand and talking to him. He stayed very still. I looked at Baby Theresa, and she looked at me. I smiled at her, but she just kept looking at me with her sad eyes. I asked the nurse if I could play with Baby Theresa. She said she would ask Matron, but she didn't think it was a good idea, in case it made Theresa cry again. I asked if she had any toys to play with, but she said no, because she had kept throwing them out of her cot, and the nurses had got tired of putting them back in again. I said I would be all right to walk back to my bed on my own, and would try to sit down on my chair. I wanted to talk to Bonnie.

I told Bonnie all about the baby, and she was as horrified as I was. She said it was cruel for a baby to be left all alone, especially as she would be missing her parents. Then Bonnie stopped talking. I thought she looked just as sad as the baby. I asked if everything was all right, and she said it was just her arm and her ribs hurting her. She asked me if I was going to have any visitors, and I said probably only Mr Macmillan. She asked me about him, and I told her my story. Well actually, I told her some of my story. I left out the bit about my mother becoming an alcoholic and then a lesbian, and my father being very rich, and an awful beast who had destroyed my life.

She asked me if my parents were divorced. It was the first time anyone had mentioned that idea to me. I said, 'Yes, and that's the whole problem.'
She said, 'I'm a Catholic, and they don't believe in divorce. But I do. I think if two parents really can't stand each other, then they should go and find someone new, and then the children will be happy again.' She said this with such force that she cried out, 'Ow! My ribs hurt.' I didn't want to talk any more about divorce and unhappy families. Bonnie said that she felt sad about being in hospital, because she missed her friends. Her parents lived in Africa, and they knew that she was in hospital, but of course they were too far away to come and see her. She looked sad and I wondered if she was going to cry. Then she said, 'At Visiting Time, will you talk to me and then we won't feel so lonely?' I said that would be a lovely idea. Then I had an idea of my own. I thought that perhaps we could ask Matron if she would let us play with the baby. Bonnie said that was a great idea, but thought we might be disappointed if Matron said no. Brian shouted across, 'Hey! What are you two talking about? Are you telling secrets about me?'
Mrs Drew was there and came over to see me, and to introduce herself to Bonnie. That was when I had another idea. I said, 'Excuse me Mrs Drew, please can you teach us how to sew? Because Bonnie and I want to make a toy for Baby Theresa over there.'
Mrs Drew said that this was the loveliest thing she had ever heard. Bonnie laughed and said, 'Ow!' because her ribs were hurting.

I laughed at her and said 'Ow!' too, because it was very painful. Then we both tried not to laugh, but it was impossible.

I am deeply humiliated

Then Nurse Beattie came and helped me get into bed, because the doctors were going to see us on their ward round. A group of men doctors and Matron came round to see all the children. They looked at Bonnie first. I was surprised to see that they didn't say hello to her, or even ask her how she was feeling. They all stood round and talked about her arm and ribs and how complicated the operation had been. Then it was my turn. Matron pulled back my bedclothes and lifted up my nightie so that everyone could look at me. The doctor in charge, the one with the moustache, said, 'Not a classic case of appendicitis by any means, but it was a straightforward job to remove it.'

I looked down at my tummy. There was a strip of thick bandage (I now know that this is called gauze). It was covered in dry blood and there were some lumps sticking out. A big shiver went through me, and I turned my head away towards Bonnie, who was looking at me. Then one of the men bent down, and his nose was practically touching me, so I could feel his breath on my Lovely Place. He said, 'And why have you used clips instead of stitches?'

The moustache doctor said, 'It's a new procedure, and I wanted to give it a go. It makes the scar more visible, and the clips can be a bit trickier to remove, but it saves time in the theatre, which is always a good thing.' The men laughed. The doctor said, 'The whole thing was probably brought on by chronic constipation. The patient hadn't passed a motion for at least ten days. But inserting a suppository up her back passage after the operation seems to have done the trick, by all accounts.'

Another doctor asked, 'And the reason for the constipation?'

'It's a fascinating story, but let's move on.' They walked away and left Nurse Beattie to pull down my nightie and tuck me into bed.

I felt like I was going red all over, and my face felt like it had little red-hot needles sticking into it. Nurse Beattie whispered, 'Good girl, Pippa. Do you like chocolate?'

That question took me completely by surprise, and I didn't feel hot anymore. I whispered back, 'Yes I do. I like Bounty the best of all.'

She said, 'Good. Everyone deserves a little treat sometimes.' She winked at me but didn't give me any chocolate.

Bonnie could see that I was very upset. Now, looking back, I can say that I felt a deep sense of having been humiliated. Bonnie said, 'Doctors can be so horrible sometimes. Fancy them talking like that about you.' I asked her if she had seen anything. She went red in the face and said, 'Well, I saw the bandage with blood on. But nothing else. Well, not very much really. Actually, I saw everything. But it doesn't matter, does it, because we're girls together?' She could see that it did matter. She tried to change the subject. 'Well fancy them talking about your poo in such loud voices. Did you really not go to the toilet for ten whole days? My mum says that you should go every day, otherwise you can get ill. But ten days? Do you think that might be a world record? You could tell everyone about it, and be in *The Guinness Book of Records* and be famous, and maybe get interviewed on The News, or even Blue Peter. Do you think they would send you a Blue Peter badge?'

This really was the funniest idea, and I laughed out loud, eve though my tummy hurt even more than usual. I whispered, 'You won't tell anyone, will you?'

She laughed and said, 'Ow! That hurt!' Then she smiled and whispered, 'Don't worry, I won't tell anyone. All girls have got one.'

'No, not that! I'm not so bothered about girls seeing that. Don't tell anyone about the other thing.'

She whispered, 'I promise. But do you think that Brian saw you?' I knew she was teasing me, but in the nicest possible way; as girls sometimes do when they are sharing an intimate moment. I was glad she was next to me. She asked if she could

play with Polish Teddy. I looked a bit surprised and she said, 'Well, he's so nice, and I feel like a baby at the moment.'
I knew that Bonnie was feeling lonely and frightened, and was missing her parents. Just like me. She hugged my teddy and went to sleep. I sucked my thumb, and didn't care if anyone saw me.

A blessing in disguise
I felt very tired in the afternoon. I was physically exhausted by the walk to the toilet and back, and emotionally drained by the doctors' behaviour, and thinking about the boy in the coma and the poor neglected baby. I was very up and down; I was very unhappy, then suddenly excited, and then finally exhausted. I wondered if the doctors had secretly given me some injections while I was asleep, to make me feel emotional. I didn't trust the doctors anymore. If they could shove something up my bottom while they were operating on me, they were capable of doing anything.

I must have dosed off, because suddenly I was aware of two adults sitting on either side of my bed. Mr Macmillan was there, with a new lady. I wondered if it was Mrs Macmillan, but she was much older. She had thick grey hair that might have been long once, but it looked like someone had cut it, so it was just long enough to reach the space in between her ears and her shoulders. It was a nice style, and suited her. She wore nice gold glasses, and had red lipstick. I liked the look of her. Mr Macmillan said, 'Hello Pippa. How are you? This is Mrs Pirie, Aileen Pirie.' He didn't say what she was doing there, so I supposed she was another social worker. I noticed that she was wearing a string of lovely turquoise beads, and had a diamond ring on her wedding finger. She smiled at me, but didn't say anything. I wondered what her voice would sound like, and I just knew that I would be able to talk to her.

Mr Macmillan asked me what I had been doing, and I told him, quietly, all about my trip to the toilet and seeing Keith and Baby Theresa, and how the doctors had upset me by looking at me down there, and talking about me in a horrible way. He said, 'Doctors are very important people, but sometimes they can forget that their patients have feelings. When doctors talk to the patients nicely and explain everything to them and their families, we say they have a good bedside manner. Some doctors don't think this is so important.'

I whispered, 'But he made a mistake. He said I hadn't done a poo for nearly ten days. But that wasn't right, because I have only been at The Lodge for three days, and then I was brought here.'

Mr Macmillan looked a bit surprised. He said, 'Well Pippa, it's true that someone has made a mistake. But I have been up to the hotel and talked to the grown-ups there, and they all say that you were there for ten days. And Mr Shepherd in London told me the same thing.' Hearing that man's name brought my mood down with a bump.

Mr Macmillan patted my hand, and said that he wanted me to listen to him very carefully. He explained that his job was to protect children. Sometimes families got into difficulties, so he helped them to care for their children properly. He knew all about Baby Theresa and Keith, and Brian, and now he had the job of making sure that I would be looked after properly. He said, 'You have definitely been at the hotel for ten days. During that time, the people who looked after you made some mistakes. They thought they knew how to look after children properly, but we now know that they didn't. You had hardly been out of your room, and you haven't eaten properly or been to the toilet properly. And if we count the day you were travelling, then that's eleven days. Not doing a poo for eleven days can make a person very ill, which is what happened to you. The doctors understood that, but they thought that you might have had appendicitis. They couldn't be sure, but it's very dangerous to leave someone with a bad appendix, so they decided to take it out.'

I wanted Mr Macmillan to stop talking. I didn't want him to know that I had been lying to the doctors about going to the toilet, and where my tummy hurt. I especially didn't want this new lady and Bonnie to know about that. Then Matron and all the nurses would know I was a liar, and would stop saying that I was a good girl, and might start to hurt me on purpose with the injections. Mr Macmillan held my hand. He said, 'Listen Pippa, none of what has happened to you has been your fault. People stop going to the toilet for all sorts of reasons, and in your case it's because you were deeply, deeply unhappy. That's probably why you can't remember half of what has happened. The doctors told me that when they took your appendix out, it was very infected, because you were what we call *constipated*. You hadn't done a poo for a very long time. So in one way it was a horrible thing for you, but in another way it's a blessing in disguise, because now we can all sit down together, and sort out how you are going to be looked after when you leave hospital.'

I could feel myself panic. He said, 'We'll talk about that in a minute, but let's talk a bit more about your illness. Sometimes being as constipated as you were, and being terribly unhappy, which you were; well it can make people see strange things. They might see flashing lights, and sometimes they see things that aren't really there. We say that they are hallucinating, and the things they think they see are called hallucinations. The same thing can happen to people who go for a long time without sleeping. When people are very upset, like you have been, then their minds can play tricks on them. That painting that you did...' I took in a deep breath and felt myself getting hot. 'That painting that you did; it's very lovely. I've seen it. But it upset some of the adults. They don't really understand you very well. I have read a lot about you and talked to quite a lot of people who know and understand you, including your mummy and your teachers at school. They all say what a wonderful artist you are. They told me about Ursula too.' I started to cry. The lady took my hand in both of hers. I turned to her and she looked right into my eyes and said, 'It's all right my dear.' Her voice was very soft and Scottish, and her hands were nice and warm.

I let go of Mr Macmillan's hand. I looked at him and said, 'Ursula's my Guardian Angel. There's nothing wrong with that.' I realised that I sounded very grumpy, so added, 'Is there?'

Mr Macmillan smiled. 'Not at all. But most people, well Catholics certainly, never see their Guardian Angel. They just believe that he is there with them.'

'Well I'm lucky then, because I can see mine. And she's a girl.'

It felt like we were having an argument, but I was trying not to. I looked at Mrs Aileen Pirie, and she was smiling at me. But it was more than a polite smile. It was a smile of kindness and understanding, like when my lovely teacher Miss Dawson used to smile at me. But she wasn't laughing at me either. I could see that she understood what I was talking about, so I said to her, 'You believe me Mrs Pirie, don't you?

She smiled even more, and now I could see her teeth. They were slightly yellow, and one of her front teeth was grey all over. She said, 'And I've read lots of things about you too. And everyone agrees that you are a lovely and charming child, and I can see that they are all telling the truth about that.'

She squeezed my hand and I squeezed hers back.

I asked Mr Macmillan, 'Please can you ask Matron if I can play with Baby Theresa?' I was feeling very tired and my tummy was hurting and I felt very thirsty.

He said, 'Let's talk about that another time. I won't forget. Perhaps you can talk to Mrs Pirie...Aileen... later. She's going to come and see you this evening at Visiting Time. But I imagine you need a drink. I know I do!'

Mrs Pirie lifted up a bag and said, 'I've brought you a present.' It was a bottle of *Tree Top Lime Juice Cordial*. I had always wanted to try that drink; not because of what it might taste like, but because I loved the shape of the bottle.

We all had a drink together, and Mr Macmillan offered one to Bonnie and she pretended that she hadn't been listening and said, 'Oh, I was just having a little sleep, but yes please!' She said she loved it. It had a very interesting taste, but more than anything I loved the colour and smell of the juice, and the shape of the bottle. I was looking forward to examining it closely.

Then I knew I had to go to the toilet again, and Mrs Aileen Pirie said she would take me. Mr Macmillan said that was a good idea, because he wanted to say hello to Brian, and to talk to Matron about me and the other children. I shuffled very slowly up the ward and we stopped to look at Keith and Baby Theresa. Keith's mum and a nurse were giving him a wash. Baby Theresa stood and looked at us. I waved at her, but she just looked. Mrs Pirie helped me in the toilet, and I wasn't shy at all. I remembered to say 'please' when I needed help, and she always said 'of course'. When I said 'thank you' she smiled and said, 'You're welcome.' She said, 'This toilet paper is really horrible. Fancy them using this awful shiny stuff in a hospital!' The paper wasn't in a roll, but there was a porcelain tray stuck to the wall where they put a little box of the nasty toilet paper. It said *medicated* on the box. Mrs Pirie said, 'I'm going to bring you a box of nice tissues that you can keep on top of your bedside cabinet. You can use them to blow your nose, and you can take some with you whenever you go to the toilet. Then you won't get sore in your special places.'

I said that I could use it to dry my tears as well. Then I asked her, 'Can I share some with Bonnie? She doesn't have any tissues, and she hates the shiny paper as much as I do. I think she might need it for her tears too.'
'Does she cry?'
'Well, I haven't seen her crying, but sometimes when she talks she almost does. I think underneath she is quite a sad girl, but she's trying to be brave.'
Then I remembered that she had cried when I had screamed so much before my first injection. I told Mrs Pirie, and she said, 'How shocking. You poor things.'

As we were talking, the terrible humiliation I had felt in front of the doctors just faded away and vanished. Once I was in the car with Mummy and Muriel, driving on the A3 to Guildford. Just as we came to a high part of the countryside called The Hog's Back, we were surrounded by a very heavy fog, so Muriel had to slow right down. But as soon as we started going down the hill into Guildford, the fog suddenly cleared, and we could see the huge red brick cathedral. Muriel said, 'Thank goodness we got through that awful fog, and it's behind us now.'

Mummy said, 'Yes, the fog has lifted, but now we have to look at that ghastly religious building in front of us.' They both laughed.

Mummy said, 'It's a bit of a metaphor, don't you think?' Muriel didn't say anything. I asked her what a metaphor was, and she said it was a very ugly building, like the Catholic cathedral in Westminster. Mummy laughed and said, 'That's a monstrosity!'

Muriel said she knew that, and that a metaphor was a huge giant rock that came hurtling out of space and smashed into The Earth, forming a huge crater, like The Devil's Punchbowl in Hindhead, not far from where we lived.

Mummy said, 'That's a *meteorite*. Muriel, do you really not know what a metaphor is?'

Muriel slowed the car right down and recited a poem

> Sunset and evening star,
> And one clear call for me!
> And may there be no moaning of the bar,
> When I put out to sea.

> But such a tide as moving seems asleep,
> Too full for sound and foam,
> When that which drew from out the boundless deep
> Turns again home.

> Twilight and evening bell,
> And after that the dark!
> And may there be no sadness of farewell,
> When I embark;

For tho' from out our bourne of Time and Place
The flood may bear me far,
I hope to see my Pilot face to face
When I have crost the bar.

Mummy said, 'Oh Muriel, that's so lovely, so perfect! Where did you learn it?'
Muriel looked very pleased with herself. 'We had a lovely English teacher at school. She taught us about metaphors, and told us that this poem was Tennyson's metaphor for his own death. I was terribly moved. The poem used to come into my mind every time someone in hospital passed away.' They both had tears in their eyes, so Mummy told Muriel to stop the car. Mummy held Muriel's hand and they were quiet together. Then Muriel said, 'Come on, whatever must Pippa think of us, behaving like a couple of old sillies?' I didn't think they were silly, or old.

It's funny how a memory as deep as that can suddenly enter your head. And just then, sitting on the toilet in a Scottish hospital, I could feel my own fog lifting. But instead of an ugly cathedral, I saw Mrs Aileen Pirie.

On the way back, we saw Nurse Fitzpatrick feed Baby Theresa with a spoon. I had always seen mothers talking to their babies when they fed them, and making jokes and telling the baby how good they were, and how much they loved them. But Nurse Fitzpatrick didn't say anything. I told Mrs Pirie that I called this part of the ward The Vale of Sadness.
She said, 'Yes, I know what you mean, Pippa. It is terribly sad, isn't it?' Then she said, 'Tell me about the huge dog at the hotel.' In the five minutes it took for me to shuffle back to my bed, I told her all about Sinbad. But I was completely exhausted and my wound hurt a lot, with a very strong pulsing feeling coming out of my scar, and I felt very itchy. Just before Mrs Pirie left, she tucked me in and squeezed my hand. She said, 'Am I allowed to give you a kiss and a cuddle, or will I

have to ask Matron and the doctors first?' That really was the funniest thing, though I tried very hard not to laugh. I said, 'Yes please,' and she kissed me on the forehead.

After Mrs Pirie left, Bonnie said that there was a slight mark of lipstick on my face. She said she wished that Mrs Pirie would kiss her. I felt warm in my tummy and wondered if I was going to have trouble again, but then I realised that it was one of my favourite feelings, and not diarrhoea. The lovely feeling made me think of Muriel and I cried. I tried to hide my tears from Bonnie, but she said, 'Are you homesick?'
I said, 'I don't have a home anymore.'
Bonnie said, 'That's how I feel sometimes.' I realised that she knew a lot about me, but I knew next to nothing about her.

Bonnie has visitors
After tea, it was Visiting Time. Mrs Aileen Pirie came to see me again, but this time on her own. She sat between Bonnie's bed and mine and talked to us both, so it seemed like we both had a visitor. She had been shopping, and had bought us each a box of Kleenex Man Size tissues. She said that the Man Size box didn't look as nice as the box designed for ladies, but the advert on the TV said that they were stronger, so were probably better for wiping our Special Places. I think at any other time I would have been embarrassed that a virtual stranger had been standing in a shop, thinking about how I was going to wipe my bottom and my Lovely Place. But at that moment, it was exactly what I needed from the grown-ups around me. Once again, I felt nice and warm inside. But there was more to come. She gave us a Bounty each! Normally Matron discouraged sweets on the children's ward, and nurses could get into serious trouble if they gave children chocolate, but Nurse Beattie had felt sorry for me after the doctors had treated me so badly. She had wanted to do something to make me feel better, so asked Mrs Pirie to buy me a Bounty. As if this kindness wasn't enough, Mrs Pirie gave me a box of pastels, a box of coloured pencils and a sketchpad. She had driven out to The Lodge and had collected all my clothes and

belongings, including my big box of art materials. It felt like Christmas.

Then a horrible thing happened to Bonnie. A nurse came to tidy her bed and told her that she was going to have some special visitors. Bonnie was very excited and asked in a loud voice, 'Is it Mum and Dad and my brother?'
The nurse said, 'I've been told it's your sister.' She looked very confused and disappointed. 'But I don't have a sister.' Then we looked up the ward and saw a wave of grey heading towards us. Bonnie said, 'Oh no!' and pretended she was asleep. It was a nun dressed in grey, and three girls wearing grey school uniforms. They were wearing thick grey coats, even though it was a sunny day and warm in the ward. Mrs Pirie moved her chair to my side of the bed, to allow them enough space to be near Bonnie, and we sat and watched what was going on. One of the girls was tall, one was chubby and round, and one was very small.

Bonnie was still pretending to be asleep. The girls looked at me, and the small girl smiled at me, so I smiled back. She said, 'Hello. What are you in here for?'
Another girl grabbed her arm and whispered, 'Shh Mary,' but it was too late.
The nun said, 'Mary. What did I tell you? We are here to see Sheila, and not to interfere with the other patients.' She smiled at Mrs Pirie and said, 'I do beg your pardon. I'm Sister Eugenie, and we are here just for a flying visit. We'll be out of your way soon.' Mrs Pirie didn't smile back.
The girls whispered, 'Poor Bonnie!' and 'Just look at her!'
Mary said 'Oh dear!' and tried to pull her hanky out of her coat pocket, but it was stuck.
I said to her, 'Here, have one of my Man Size tissues. The box is a bit ugly but they are extra strong.'
Sister Eugenie hissed, 'Mary! I have just told you! One more time and you will wait for us outside the ward.'
Mary wiped her eyes and said, 'Sorry Sister.'

Then Bonnie pretended to wake up. She groaned and said, 'Oh, my arm and ribs hurt! Where am I?' Then she shrieked, 'Oh my God! What are you lot doing here?'

The girls giggled. Sister Eugenie looked very cross. 'Sheila, we are here to see how you are progressing. These three girls have won a poetry competition in class, and the prize is to visit you.' The girls just stood there with their coats on. They were like sheep; too terrified to move, until the sheepdog barked at them. Sister barked, 'Well, come on girls, say something!'

The tall girl cleared her throat and said, 'How are you, Bonnie?'

Bonnie looked very pained. 'Well Juliet, I mustn't complain. The nurses are wonderful, of course. They try to make sure I don't suffer too much. I'm in such a lot of pain, as you can imagine, but my friend Pippa here is very kind and stops me from being lonely.'

Juliet said, 'Gosh!'

Sister Eugenie said, 'Now Mary, it's your turn.' Mary looked startled. Her face was very red. She said, 'Excuse me Sister, please may I take off my coat? I feel very hot, and my legs are a bit wobbly at seeing Bonnie like this.' Then she burst into tears.

Sister glared at her and sighed, 'Very well.'

Juliet helped Mary take off her coat. Mary just stood there, but eventually said, 'And I wanted to say...'

Sister cut her off, 'You've had your turn. Now Alice, you can read the winning poem.'

Alice was the round girl. She looked over at me and winked. I couldn't believe it. I tried to wink back at her, but I was no good at it, and just closed and opened my eyes quickly. Alice smiled an even bigger smile. Then she turned to Bonnie and ceremoniously took a piece of paper out of her coat pocket. She cleared her throat and read

'We didn't believe it was the truth,
When we heard you'd fallen off the roof.
Now you have got a broken arm,

And done yourself a lot of harm.

You fell and landed on your chest,
God knows you did not do your best.
If you had prayed for His advice,
He would have said, "It is not nice.
Do not go and get the ball,
Because you'll have a nasty fall.
You just might land upon your head,
And then you won't be alive, but dead."

But God forgives His lambs that stray,
So if you pray to Him,
Then you will live to be a better girl another day.'

She smiled and said, 'Those last three lines aren't so good,
but Sister told us to hurry up and finish.'
Mrs Pirie had her hand over her mouth, and I could see that she
was trying not to laugh. Juliet said, 'We hope you get better
soon.' Bonnie seemed overcome with emotion, and I had the
feeling that she wasn't acting anymore.
Mary said to me, 'Quick, give her one of those tissues, will
you? I mean, please. I think we have upset Bonnie!' I passed
her the whole box.
Sister said, 'We'll say a wee prayer together and then we'll be
on our way. What about my favourite? It seems very
appropriate, under the circumstances.'
They all made the Sign of the Cross. Bonnie made an
enormous effort to cross herself with her broken arm, but
yelled out in pain and sank back on her pillows. I thought she
had fainted. Sister said, 'You silly child. You'll do yourself
another injury. Use your other hand.' She looked at Juliet. 'You
begin, Juliet.'
Juliet blushed and mumbled, 'Hail, Holy Queen, Mother of
Mercy, hail, our life, our sweetness and our hope.'
The others joined in, 'To thee do we cry, poor banished
children of Eve: to thee do we send up our sighs, mourning and
weeping in this vale of tears. Turn then, most gracious

Advocate, thine eyes of mercy toward us, and after this our exile, show unto us the blessed fruit of thy womb, Jesus, O merciful, O loving, O sweet Virgin Mary! Amen.'

Brian shouted across, 'Well done! Now can you come and talk to me? I'm a poor orphan and never get any visitors. We can say prayers together if you like.'

Alice pleaded with Sister, 'Oh Sister please can we talk to him? He's poor and lonely!'

Sister scowled at Brian and said to Alice, 'Certainly not.'

Then Nurse Beattie came over and said, 'Excuse me Sister, but Matron would like a word.'

Sister looked annoyed, then smiled and said, 'Why of course.' She said to the girls. 'I will be gone for five minutes. You may talk quietly to Sheila, and then we will go back to school.'

As soon as she had gone, Juliet and Alice giggled. Mary looked at me and blushed. She thanked me for the tissues and said, 'I'm such a cry-baby, and I hate the sight of blood. Is your name short for Philippa?'

Bonnie said to her friends, 'Thank you for coming. But where's Émilie? Not being rude about you, of course, but I was hoping Émilie would come too.'

Juliet said, 'She didn't win the poetry competition, because her handwriting wasn't good enough. You know she has that lovely French handwriting; well Sister tried to get her to use school handwriting, but Émilie just refused. And anyway, she wrote her poem in French. Sister read it and said it wasn't a poem at all, so it didn't count. And she said that Good Catholic Girls shouldn't have feelings about other girls, like the ones Émilie had written about in her poem. Émilie was very upset, but she asked us to give you this.' She looked up the ward and then took an envelope out of her pocket.

Bonnie looked delighted and said, 'Quick, stick it under my pillow.'

Mary said, 'She told us to give you this as well.' She bent over and kissed Bonnie on both cheeks. 'She said it's a French kiss, and that's what best friends in France do to each other all the time.'

Bonnie went very red in the face and laughed, but then started to cry. Mary looked shocked. 'I'm sorry Bonnie; I didn't mean to upset you!'

'It's all right. I'm so glad that you could come. Your poem is lovely. But I just want Émilie here and not that...' she looked up the ward. Sister was coming back, '... and not that bloody awful penguin!'

Juliet and Mary gasped and told Bonnie to shush.

Alice was waving to Brian, and he blew her a kiss. She blew him one back. Bonnie wiped her eyes and said, 'I'm so lucky to have Pippa to talk to. Will you tell Émilie I'm thinking about her?'

Alice said, 'Shall I give her a French kiss?' Juliet laughed out loud.

Sister Eugenie arrived and told Mary to put her coat on, and then ordered the girls to say goodbye. She said to Mrs Pirie, 'I hope the girls behaved themselves while I was away. I hope we haven't disturbed you during your precious moments of Visiting Time.'

Mrs Pirie smiled and said, 'Not at all, Sister. They are perfect examples of how girls should be. You must be very proud of them, including poor, dear Bonnie, who really is in such agony sometimes. But she is so brave and never complains. She spends all her time thinking about the suffering of the other children, like a good Christian.'

Sister Eugenie said, 'Thank you. Thank you very much indeed,' but she wasn't smiling.

Alice asked, 'Please can we kiss Bonnie goodbye?'

Sister Eugenie scowled. 'Certainly not. Girls don't kiss each other, unless they are French.' She gave Bonnie a strange look. 'You may shake hands and say goodbye.'

They shook Bonnie's good hand and then they left. Sister didn't say goodbye to either Bonnie or us.

Mrs Pirie moved her chair back in between our beds. The three of us were quiet. Brian shouted over, 'Why have they all gone? I think the podgy one liked me!'

It was nearly time for the visitors to go home. Bonnie opened her envelope, took out a piece of paper, and smiled a very big smile. She said to Mrs Pirie, 'Excuse me Mrs Pirie, but can you read French? My friend Émilie has sent me her poem, but I don't understand what it says.' She handed Mrs Pirie the poem. Mrs Pirie looked at it. She said, 'What lovely handwriting. It's so… so French! Why don't we all write like that?'

Then she read

> J'adore Bonnie, plus que quiconque dans le monde entier.
> Elle est une sœur pour moi.
> Quand elle a sauté du toit
> Je pensais qu'elle était morte.
> J'aurais préféré que ce soit moi, et pas elle.
> Elle me manque terriblement.
> Je veux sentir sa douleur pour la lui enlever.
> Les mots ne peuvent décrire ce que je ressens
> Donc, je ne vais pas essayer de les écrire
> Bonnie comprendra
>
> Je m'en fiche de gagner le concours
> Je veux juste la voir.
> Si je ne gagne pas, elle saura quand même que
> Je veux désespérément la voir.

Mrs Pirie said to Bonnie, 'Oh it's lovely. So… so passionate! She really is your best friend, isn't she?'

Bonnie blushed and nodded. 'I feel like she's my twin sister. If she wasn't in school with me, I think I'd go crazy. Please can you translate it for me?'

Mrs Pirie smiled and said, 'I'll have a go.

> I love Bonnie more than anyone in the whole world.
> She is like my sister.
> When she jumped off the roof

I thought she was dead.
I wished it was me, but not her.
I miss her terribly.
I want to feel her pain, so it will be taken away from her.
Words cannot describe how I feel,
So I won't bother trying to write them.
Bonnie will understand

I don't care about winning the competition
I just want to see her.
If I don't win, she will still know that
I desperately want to see her.'

I said, 'Oh Bonnie, it's so lovely!' I thought about my best friend Lucy.
Bonnie said, 'I hate Sister Eugenie! Those three girls are my friends, but she knows my very best friend is Émilie. Sister organised that poetry competition so she could show all the girls in the class what happens when you break the rules. We were playing with a tennis ball and it went on the roof. If our balls go up there, then we're supposed to tell the caretaker, but he never bothers to get them down. I'm sure Sister tells him to leave them, so we won't be able to play anymore. She's like that; spiteful and always looking for a way to teach us a lesson. Émilie was going to climb up and get it. She's always getting into trouble. She speaks English perfectly well to me and understands everything, but when the teachers talk to her, she pretends she doesn't understand. She just says in her lovely French accent, "Repeat please?"

'I didn't want her to hurt herself, so I climbed up instead. I'm not very good at climbing, and I was quite frightened, but I didn't want to show it, in case Émilie tried to stop me, and climbed up herself. I just couldn't bear the thought of her hurting herself or getting into any more trouble. Oh, imagine if it was her here and not me! I just can't bear the thought of it! But she climbed up after me anyway!'

Bonnie was getting upset. Mrs Pirie said that she would have felt exactly the same. That cheered Bonnie up. She said, 'Would you? Would you really? I'm glad, because some of the older girls have said that I'm... that we... that Émilie and I are too... we are too friendly. Sister Eugenie said that to Émilie too. She said we are too close. But how can you be too friendly? I don't understand. My brother and I are so very close. He's at another boarding school, and I miss him so much. But nobody at home says I'm too close to him.'

I thought about Lucy. I asked, 'Is Émilie very pretty?'

'Oh yes. She's lovely.'

'Then perhaps the other girls are a bit jealous?' I thought that was a very grown up thing to say.

I was very pleased when Bonnie said, 'Yes, Pippa, you could be right. Perhaps that's it. I certainly feel jealous when she plays with other girls. I try not to be like that, but I just can't help it. You see, I don't want to share her. I can't bear the thought of her liking anyone else.'

When I think of Bonnie now, I think of Shakespeare's Antony and Cleopatra; with Bonnie as Cleopatra. When we studied the play, I used to smile and call it Émilie and Bonnie. I love the scene where the servant compares Antony to Caesar, and Cleopatra flies into a rage and shouts 'By Isis! I'll give thee bloody teeth!' I was fascinated by Bonnie, and was glad that she liked me. I wanted to meet Émilie, but I worried that Bonnie might become jealous and start to hate me.

Bonnie wanted to carry on telling her story. 'Anyway, to get onto the roof, I had to climb onto the top of a wall that was ten feet high, and about four feet from the back of the building. I was very frightened, but I jumped up, and at the same time grabbed onto the side of the roof and somehow managed to hold on and scramble up, even though it was extremely slippery. The roof was flat and there was a great big puddle in the middle, and it was just full of balls! Then I saw that Émilie had climbed up after me and we threw all the balls down, and all the girls were laughing, but then one of the nuns came and I ran to get down but slipped and fell right off.'

Mrs Pirie asked, 'Are there many foreign boarders at your school?'

'No. Émilie is the only one. Then there are girls like me, whose parents are Scottish but live in countries like Malawi or Kenya or Libya. They send us to board at the Convent because they say they want us to have a Good Scottish Catholic Education.'

I was taken aback. It hadn't occurred to me that the Convent was a boarding school! In my mind, boarding schools were just like prisons, with disgusting food and children with terrible haircuts. Bonnie's hair was a bit untidy, but it hadn't been horribly chopped about like Dominic's. I said, 'You poor thing!'

She started to cry and said, 'Oh please don't say that! I'm trying to be brave, but it's just not working!'

Mrs Pirie hugged Bonnie as best she could, without hurting her, and Bonnie stopped crying. Mrs Pirie said, 'Bonnie, there's an important difference between your story and what Émilie has written. You said you fell, but Émilie wrote that you jumped. Which one is right?'

Bonnie's face went bright red. She whispered something in Mrs Pirie's ear. I didn't hear what she said, but I knew what the truth was.

Nurse Beattie came and told Mrs Pirie it was nearly time for her to go. Mrs Pirie gave me a hug and a kiss, then asked Bonnie if she would like a hug and kiss as well. Bonnie stopped crying and said, 'Oh yes please!'

They hugged each other and Mrs Pirie said, 'You're a very good girl, Bonnie, and a wonderful actress and storyteller. It was just like watching television!'

'Really? Oh thank you for saying so! Do you think Sister believed I was unconscious?'

'Well, I think she wasn't entirely convinced, but your friends certainly believed it. I imagine they are at school now, and busy telling Émilie all about their visit, and how they woke you from a deep sleep, just like Sleeping Beauty! Now let me give you another kiss, and I'll see you both tomorrow afternoon, straight after lunch. Then Pippa, you and I and Mr Macmillan can have a good long talk.' She kissed Bonnie on both cheeks and said, 'By the way, that's how French people say hello and goodbye. Don't go round saying that you've been giving Émilie French Kisses. It means something completely different!' She laughed and put her chair away. Brian shouted goodbye and she blew him a kiss. After she had gone, he shouted over to us, 'Who's that? Is she your social worker?' I said that I didn't think so.

Bonnie said, 'What is she then?'

I said, 'I don't know.'

I can't sleep

The nurses came and washed our faces, and said that if we wanted to, we could both walk out to the toilets to do a wee and clean our teeth. You might think that would have been a boring thing to do, but to us it seemed like the most exciting adventure in the world. The nurses helped us out of bed and we set off, arm in arm. My tummy still hurt, but I found that if I was careful I could walk with longer steps, and didn't need to shuffle anymore. Poor Bonnie, on the other hand, was walking like an old lady, and every so often would have to stop, because her ribs were hurting. She had damaged her elbow, so her plaster cast went right up her arm, and she had to wear a sling. Bonnie complained that the weight of the plaster cast was hurting her shoulder. We stopped outside Keith's room, and we both agreed that it was a terrible shame. Baby Theresa was fast asleep. We whispered to each other that we would make her a special toy in the morning. I helped Bonnie in the toilet, and she asked me if I needed any help, and I said yes, even though I could easily manage on my own now. We both agreed that our soft toilet paper was marvellous.

On the way back, Bonnie told me that when Émilie first came to the school she used to kiss everyone on each cheek. She did it to all the girls in the dormitory first thing in the morning and last thing at night. She even tried to kiss the nuns and the teachers! Bonnie explained that in France everyone kisses everyone else. When you wake up at home and go downstairs to breakfast, you kiss your mum and dad on each cheek and your brothers and sisters too. When you go to school in France, you kiss all your friends, and your teacher might kiss all the children as well, if she felt like it. Then lots of the ten year olds in the school, who were the youngest girls, decided they would like to kiss each other in the mornings, and soon some of the older girls were doing it too. So Sister Winifred made an announcement in assembly that girls were not to kiss each other. In fact, she introduced a rule that there were to be no more what she called Public Displays of Affection. This included girls holding hands, walking arm-in-arm, or giving each other hugs. A lot of the older girls were very annoyed about this, and blamed Émilie. One girl even called Émilie a Stupid French Twat. Émilie didn't understand what the words meant, but slapped the girl anyway. Émilie got into terrible trouble, but just shrugged her shoulders and said to Bonnie, 'Je m'en fous'. Bonnie said that was French for 'I don't care'. But it was obvious that Émilie did care, because she cried bitterly, so Bonnie had to spend a long time hugging her in secret, to try to console her.

I thought that 'twat' meant the same as 'twit' and 'idiot'. I asked Bonnie what a twat was, and she pointed to her Lovely Place. She said it's a bit like the C Word. She said girls got into awful trouble in school if any of the nuns or prefects heard them swearing, and especially if they used words that sounded particularly vulgar and disgusting. But luckily all the other girls thought it meant idiot too, and most of the nuns were old and half-deaf, and probably thought you were saying twit, which wasn't a swear word. But Bonnie knew its real meaning because her brother, who went to a boys' boarding school, had told her.

Before we got into bed, we gave each other kisses on the cheeks. Bonnie said that she was worn out. She had another look at Émilie's poem and then kissed it and put it under her pillow. She went to sleep almost straight away. I had a warm feeling about Bonnie. Even though she was more than two years older than I was, she was treating me like an equal. I wondered if she knew how babies were made, and about periods. I was still worried about mine starting, but was too shy to talk to anyone about it.

I couldn't sleep. At night, as soon as it got dark outside, one of the nurses turned on the red light that hung in the middle of the ward. The switch was on the wall near my bed, and the red bulb cast a strange red glow over everything.

There had been so many things happening on the ward during the day, so I really hadn't had time to think about anything that might have been going on outside the hospital. The visit by the girls had been funny, but Sister Eugenie had frightened me. Luckily, Mrs Pirie had been there. I liked Mrs Pirie. She obviously liked Bonnie and me, because she told us how good we were. And it was obvious that she hadn't liked Sister one bit. But who was she, and why did she keep coming to see me? I was glad that Mrs Pirie had taken all my belongings away from The Lodge, but why did she still have them? And Mr Macmillan had said that lots of people had been talking about me, and he knew all about me because people had written about me. And if they knew all about me, then they must know all about Mummy and Muriel.

It was becoming easier for me to think about Mummy and Muriel, without getting terribly upset. I was in a hospital and was safe, even though I had injections, and doctors said nasty things when they were looking at me in my very private places. I knew that, sooner or later, I would have to leave hospital, but I had no idea what would happen to me. Then a terrible thought struck me. It came from nowhere. If The Judge had taken me away from Mummy and given me to my father, then where were Mummy and Muriel? What had The Judge decided to do to them? It was obvious; they had been sent to prison, because they were ladies who loved each other. I couldn't bear this thought, and I needed to find out immediately what had happened to them.

I waited for a nurse to come and switch the red light on. It was Nurse Fitzpatrick. I told her I couldn't sleep, because I was worried about something. She sat on a chair next to my bed. I lay on my side and she leaned forward, so that her face was very close to mine. She held my hand and whispered, 'What is it sweetie? What's bothering you?'

I whispered back, 'I miss my mummy. I think she's been sent to prison!' She looked very surprised. 'Prison? Whatever gave you that idea?'

I explained that The Judge in The Court had taken me away from Mummy, and I supposed that he had sent her to prison, because he thought that she had been a bad mother. Nurse Fitzpatrick said, 'Well, let's get this straight right now. Your mummy is not in prison, and she isn't a bad mother, and that's a fact.'

I was very pleased to hear that, so told her about my other worry: about what was going to happen to me when I left hospital. She said, 'Well I don't really know about that, but we do know that Mr Macmillan and your auntie have been very busy trying to sort things out. So why don't you ask your auntie when she comes to visit you tomorrow?'

I think my heart stopped. 'My auntie? Is Auntie Muriel coming?' 'I don't think her name's Muriel. It's that lady who comes with Mr Macmillan. I'm sure he told Matron that she's your aunt.'

I said, quite loudly, 'Oh no! That's a mistake.' I began to feel worse than ever.

Nurse said, 'I'm sorry Pippa. I don't understand. What's wrong with her being your auntie? She seems very nice to me.' I couldn't breathe. I sat up and felt myself gasping for air. Nurse grabbed hold of me and started rubbing my back. She gave me a drink of water and I choked on it, so she had to thump me on the back. Bonnie woke up and said, 'What's going on? Where am I?'

Nurse Fitzpatrick said, 'Pippa is a bit upset, but she's going to be all right now.'

Bonnie sat up and looked straight at us. She said, 'She's my friend and I wouldn't want anything bad to happen to her. I hope we can be friends forever.' Then she lay back down and closed her eyes.

Nurse Fitzpatrick laughed. 'She was talking in her sleep! The poor wee lassie is desperate to stay here, because she hates boarding school so much. Now tell me all about this auntie business.'

I didn't want to say anything, in case she told other people. She said, 'Let me guess. Is it something about your Mum and her... her friend?'

I was very surprised. But I desperately wanted to talk about Muriel, so it all came out. I told her everything. Well, obviously I left some details out. Actually, I left out most of the details of our family life. But I did tell her that The Judge in The Court had been told lots of lies, and the whole trial was a disgrace.

Nurse Fitzpatrick said, 'Well, Mr Macmillan is the one who told us about your mother and your auntie. We like to know everything about the children here, and especially about the ones he looks after. He's such a lovely man. We think that Matron is secretly in love with him. She's very grumpy and strict with us nurses, but Mr Macmillan can get away with murder! Matron says his heart is in the right place, and she listens very carefully to what he has to say. The doctors listen to him too.'

That gave me an idea. 'Well, would they listen to him if he told them that Baby Theresa was sad, because she has nobody to cuddle her or play with her, and because she has no toys to play with?'

The nurse knew exactly what I was doing. I was trying to ease my own pain by thinking about the pain of others. She whispered, 'You can ask him tomorrow. Now let's talk about your Scottish auntie.'

'I haven't got one. I only have my father.'

'Well obviously not. Doesn't your father have any brothers or sisters, or cousins? They would be your aunties.'

'I don't know anything about them. It's all a bit of a mystery.'

'Oh, I love mysteries. I've just got to do a wee job at the other end of the ward, but you can tell me all about it when I come back.'

I don't know if she came back or not. If she did, she would have found me fast asleep, and almost certainly with my thumb in my mouth.

Bonnie in red

The next morning, I woke up very early, and it was still dark. The nurses were still in their office at the other end of the ward, so I carefully got out of bed and found my pastels and coloured pencils and drawing pad. I looked closely at Bonnie, fast asleep in the red glow of the red light bulb, and slipped into My Colour Dream. After breakfast, Bonnie and I went to the toilet together. Keith was lying on his back with his eyes closed, and Baby Theresa looked at us with her big sad eyes. Bonnie said, 'Do you think if we prayed very hard, then Keith would wake up, and Baby Theresa will cheer up and start talking?'

I didn't know what to say about Keith. I said that we could try praying, but I thought that making a toy for Baby Theresa and playing with her would be more likely to work. Bonnie said that was a very funny thing to say. I was being quite serious, but thanked her anyway.

When we were back in bed, the nurses gave us a wash. I showed Bonnie my picture that I had done of her. She said, 'It's lovely, but it doesn't really look like me, does it?'

I was expecting her to say that, and was happy to explain the story. 'It's a bit smudgy, but I like it. I imagined you were dreaming about Émilie. I started by rubbing the red pastel gently across the page, and as I did it I knew exactly what to do with the black pencil. I quickly drew your outline and then tried to get your face and hair exactly as they were. I didn't

117

really worry about the small details, because I wanted to give the impression of a sleepy girl in the red glow. It was lovely how your hair had the red highlights in it. I think I captured that as best I could, because it was still quite dark! You can show it to Émilie when you go back to school.' I loved to talk about Art. I had discussed my paintings with so many grown-ups that I now had quite a good vocabulary.

Bonnie said, 'You sound so grown up! Now I understand. It's lovely, and very mysterious. What's that light brown and red bit? Is it Polish Teddy?' It was. She had taken a fancy to my teddy bear, so I let her sleep with him every night. She told me that Émilie had a funny cuddly rabbit thing that she called her *doudou,* and she couldn't possibly get to sleep unless she had it in bed with her. Émilie said that all French boys and girls had a doudou, and they only stopped taking it to bed when they got married. Another of Bonnie's school friends, Camilla, had a father who was an airline pilot, so was often away from home. When Camilla was little, she used to miss her father terribly. She used to cry at bedtime, and wouldn't go to sleep, even if she was in her mother's bed. Camilla's father had a smelly old flying jacket with a fleece lining, so one day her mother gave it to Camilla to look at. Camilla took it to bed with her every night and never cried in the night again, or had trouble with sleeping. She told Bonnie that her father smoked cigars and was a bit sweaty, and she loved the jacket so much because it smelled just like him!

After the ward round, Mrs Drew came to see us, and brought a big bag of material for us to make our toy for Baby Theresa. Brian wanted to join in too, so we let him choose what type of animal to make. He insisted that we make a duck out of yellow felt. We all sat at Brian's bed and happily sewed and talked, as if none of us had a care in the world. We had to help Bonnie, because she could only move one arm, but Brian was very happy to hold the material while I sewed the stitches. When Bonnie got tired, Brian took over the sewing, and he was very good and very quick. The nurses were very impressed with us, and even Matron said how nice it was to see us so busy together. She said to Brian, 'I can see that you are much better, so soon you'll be able to go home.'

Suddenly he started coughing, and lost interest in what we were doing. He said he didn't feel well, and needed to get back into bed. We all knew he didn't have a home to go to. Mrs Drew said that she would come back in the afternoon and help us finish off.

Just before Mrs Drew left, Bonnie showed her my painting. Mrs Drew thought that it was marvellous, and said that it gave her an idea. She whispered in my ear that she'd like me to draw a portrait of Brian, for him to keep, and paint a picture of flowers in a vase, as a way of saying thank you to the doctors and nurses.

The Plan

After lunch, Mr Macmillan and Mrs Pirie came to see me. I had been so busy with Baby Theresa's duck that I had completely forgotten about my worries of the night before. I was very excited, and talked in a loud voice about my painting and the toy for Baby Theresa, and what Mrs Drew wanted me to do. I don't think the grown-ups had seen me so excited before. Mr Macmillan said that he hadn't realised just how important Art was for me. I said, 'But didn't the people who wrote all about me write about that? And the people you spoke to you on the phone, didn't they tell you how much I love Art?' Mr Macmillan scratched his chin and said, 'Actually, they didn't really. I wish that they had. We've mostly been talking about where you should go when you leave here, and most importantly, who should look after you.' That brought me back down to earth with a bump. 'And we have to agree where you are going to go to school.'

Mrs Pirie made me a drink of lime juice cordial. Bonnie was with Mrs Drew and Brian, and they were stuffing the duck with kapok. Brian had cheered up, because he had eaten his favourite lunch of sausages, mashed potatoes, and peas, with spotted dick and custard for pudding.

I knew we were going to have a very important talk. I whispered that I felt very sorry for Brian, because he had nowhere to live. Mr Macmillan said, 'We're all doing our best for Brian, but Pippa, let's talk about you now.' I didn't want to talk about me now. He said that Matron had told him that I had been worried in the night. He told me that Mummy and Auntie Muriel were definitely not in prison. It was not a crime for people to love each other. Then he said, 'Don't worry, Pippa, Mummy and Muriel are both very well. I spoke to them both this morning. They are very pleased that you are getting better. Mummy says she feels certain that you are being a wonderful patient, and she is sure that you will have charmed all the doctors and nurses. I told her that both those things are true, and she was very pleased. Obviously they are both very sad not to be with you.'

He was very quiet after that, in his usual way.

I tried to stop myself from crying, but it was no use. Brian shouted over, 'What's going on?' I dried my tears on the Man Size tissues. Mr Macmillan said, 'Pippa, it's time to talk about what's going to happen to you when you leave hospital. That won't be long now. But we can't allow you to leave until we are all satisfied that you will be looked after properly. One thing is certain; you are not going back to the hotel. That arrangement didn't work out at all well. Everyone agrees about that. So, we have a plan.'

I didn't want to listen. I looked at what Bonnie and Brian were doing. They had finished stuffing the yellow duck, but there were pieces of white kapok all over the place. Brian was pretending to sneeze, and trying to make Bonnie laugh, and she was pretending to be cross with him.

Mrs Pirie said, 'Pippa, look at me.' She said it in the nicest possible way.

I said, 'Sorry. I was just looking at Bonnie and Brian. I always like to look at you, Mrs Pirie. You have such a nice face.'

She smiled and said, 'I know it's not easy for you to be here in Scotland, away from Mummy and Muriel. It must be awful for you. So I'm going to tell you a little bit about who I am. Then Mr Macmillan can talk about what we have planned for you.' She looked at him. 'And is it all right for me to say that Pippa's Mummy is pleased with the plans too?'

Mr Macmillan smiled. 'Yes. I have spoken to Mummy about what the plan is, and she thinks it's a lovely idea.' It was very difficult for me to accept that he could talk to Mummy whenever he wanted, but she wasn't allowed to talk to me. I cried again.

Mrs Pirie held my hand. She said, 'Listen Pippa. If I were you; if I were a little girl who had just been taken away from her Mummy, then I would be furious that Mr Macmillan had been allowed to speak to my mother, but I hadn't.' That really surprised me. I asked her, 'Do you get furious very often? I can't really imagine it.'

She smiled and said, 'Oh no. Perhaps I would, if I had to protect you from something horrible. Perhaps I might have felt furious with the rude doctors, but shouting at them wouldn't have got me anywhere. So perhaps I would have said something like, "Excuse me doctor, please can you explain to Pippa exactly what is happening, using words that are easy for her to understand?" But let's talk about exactly what is going to happen. The first thing you need to know is that I am not a complete stranger. I am related to your father, and I have known about you ever since you were born. I nearly went to your mother and father's wedding, but I was ill and couldn't go. You see, I'm your father's cousin. His father and my father were brothers. I say *were*, because my father is dead. Your father's father, who is my uncle and your grandfather, is very old. But he knows all about you, and lives in Scotland, and he would like to meet you one day.'

That was a bit of a surprise, but only in a small way, because after talking to Nurse Fitzpatrick in the night, I wanted Mrs Pirie to be my aunt. I knew that she liked me and understood me, and would protect me. What Mr Macmillan said next was more surprising. 'As you know, Pippa, lots of people have been talking about what is best for you, including your father. I haven't spoken to him, but I have spoken to Mr Shepherd, who speaks to your father on the telephone almost every day. Your father is very pleased that you are making good progress in hospital.'

I wanted to say, 'I don't care what he thinks.' They must have guessed what I was thinking, from the way I turned my head away. Mr Macmillan continued, 'So it has been decided that you will stay with Mrs Pirie. She is staying on a farm near a small town on the coast, not far from here, and I'm sure you will be very happy there.'

I was happy. I was very happy with that news. But how could I show it? How could I admit that I was happy, when all I wanted to do was to go home to Mummy and Muriel? Mrs Pirie said, 'What do you think about that, Pippa?'

I said, 'I think it's a very nice idea. But all I really want to do is to go home to Mummy.'

She said, 'I understand that. Of course I understand that. If I were you, then I would feel exactly the same.'

There; she had said it again; 'if I were you, then I would feel exactly the same'. Of course I had to trust her. I said, trying not to sound excited, 'What shall I call you?'

'Does *Auntie Aileen* sound all right to you? *Aunt* Aileen makes me sound a bit prim and proper.' She laughed at that idea, and I smiled. 'So, Pippa, what do you think? Or would you rather I called you Philippa?' That made me smile even more.

From that moment, she has always been Auntie Aileen to me. And to her I have always been Pippa. Not My Little Pipsqueak, or My Lovely Sausage, or Pumpkin, or Sweetheart, or My Lovely Girl, or Sweetie Pie, or My Darling Girl. Those were just some of the names that Muriel called me. To Auntie Aileen I was just plain Pippa. But that has always been enough for me, and always will be. Some people are very easy to love, and Auntie Aileen was one of them. I asked her, 'Do you have pigs on your farm? I love horses, of course, but I've been looking at them a lot, and I'd really like to take a close look at a pig.'

'Oh yes, we have a pig, and she's just about to have piglets.'

Piglets! I wanted to go there as soon as possible.

But I had to ask another question. To me, it was just as important as where I was going to live. Mr Macmillan said, 'And we must discuss where you are going to school. That hasn't been decided yet, but you must go to school as soon as possible. But I think that's enough thinking and planning for one day, don't you?'

I said, 'Yes it is, but can I ask you a question?'

'Of course you can.'

'Please can you tell Matron that Bonnie and I *must* play with Baby Theresa? Her toy is nearly finished and we want to give it to her as soon as possible, because we think it will make her happy.'

Mr Macmillan smiled. He said, 'It's a lovely idea. But I think that Theresa will be very happy very soon. Her parents are coming to take her home tomorrow. I can't *tell* Matron what to do, but I can certainly *ask* her.'

I was very disappointed. 'But we want to play with her. We want to be the ones to make her smile and talk.'

Auntie Aileen laughed. 'Well of course you do, but let's all be happy for Baby Theresa, now that she's finally going home. Perhaps you can give her your duck when her parents come and collect her. Then she will love it even more, because every time she plays with it, she will think of the happy time when she was reunited with her mummy and daddy. I know I would.'

I had to admit that was a good idea, but I wasn't sure that Bonnie would agree.

I think I was getting better. I hadn't thought about my tummy all day.

Brian farts very loudly

Bonnie and Brian were very pleased to hear that Baby Theresa would soon go home. Bonnie said that Mrs Pirie was right, and if we left the duck in Baby Theresa's cot, then her mum and dad could take it home with them. I told Brian and Bonnie that Mrs Pirie was really my auntie, and I was going to live with her, on her farm. I tried not to sound too pleased, because I thought of Brian not having a home, and Bonnie being imprisoned in a horrible boarding school. But they didn't mind at all, and they both asked if they could come and stay with me. I thought that was a wonderful idea.

At bedtime, we were supposed to read quietly, then the nurses came to say goodnight to each of us and tuck us in. Brian especially liked Nurse Fitzpatrick, who was usually there on night duty. During quiet time, Brian did a tremendous fart. Bonnie and I laughed out loud and then suffered terribly. Brian said that Baby Theresa had done it, and this made us laugh even more. Brian was very pleased with himself, but Nurse Fitzpatrick said to him, 'If you're able to behave like that, then it's a sign that you are well enough to go home.'
I think she was only joking, but it was something that Matron often said to Brian if he did something that she thought was bad behaviour; like being noisy or jumping around. I thought that really wasn't fair. When children are happy they make lots of noise and laugh, and sometimes jump about. It doesn't mean that they are being naughty. Once again, Brian was frightened, and didn't make another noise after that. But I think it was true about me; I felt ready to leave the hospital, and to start my new life.

After the nurses switched off the lights, Bonnie whispered to me for a long time. She said that everybody farts. At home, she and her brother farted all the time, and they had competitions to see whose farts were the loudest and smelliest. She said, 'But in our school, it's just not supposed to happen. Some girls do it and laugh their heads off. But if ever a nun hears us she usually says, "That's not very ladylike." One of the nuns in particular is a nasty cold-hearted bitch.'
I said, 'Bonnie, pleased don't use language like that!'
She looked sad. 'I can't help it. I don't like swearing, but when you are surrounded by cruel people, there's nothing else you

can do. Anyway, can I finish my story?' Bonnie may have been sad, but she loved to control an audience, even if it was only a nine-year old girl. I stuck my thumb in my mouth. 'Some of the prefects act as if they are even holier than the nuns. Once Juliet farted out loud and a prefect said, "Good Catholic Girls don't make noises like that." Émilie does the loudest and smelliest farts of all. I told her to do one in front of the nasty prefect, but the prefect just ignored her. I said to the prefect, "Excuse me, aren't you going to tell her off for doing that? It really stinks!"
The prefect said, "Oh no. She's French. I was on holiday in France once, and everyone there farts out loud all the time. It's part of their way of life. If a French person has a meal at your house and farts very loudly, you mustn't laugh or tell them off. To them it means that they have enjoyed their food and it has been well-digested."

'Émilie said that was nonsense. She said if she farted at the table then her father would get very angry, and send her to her room. She was frightened of her father. One of our friends who lives in Libya says that only Arabs are allowed to fart at the table. She told us that there are lots of French people in Libya, and maybe they taught the Arabs that it was good manners to let off during meals. But if you tell Émilie not to do something, then that just makes her want to do it even more. Once she farted very loudly during Mass, just to see what would happen. Lots of girls near us started giggling, and afterwards Sister Winifred, who is the Sister Superior, was very angry. She must have heard the fart coming from among our group. She made us all sit in our classroom, and told us that the girl who made the disgusting noise had to own up, or we would all have to stay indoors at playtime for a whole week. Of course Emilie immediately admitted that she had done it, and Sister made her stand outside her office and face the wall, every playtime for two weeks.'

This all sounded terribly unfair, and reminded me of the Nasty Nun who had beaten me. I wanted to tell Bonnie about that, but she seemed desperate to talk about herself. Her brother was two years older than her, and was the nicest boy in the whole world. She missed him a lot, and she knew that he missed her just as much. His name was Mark. He was at a horrible Catholic boys' boarding school near a place called Carlisle, which wasn't too far away from our town. But they weren't allowed to see each other, or even talk on the telephone, so he wouldn't even know that Bonnie was in hospital. This thought upset her terribly, and she had nobody to talk to about it.

She said I was lucky, because now I had a lovely auntie, and was going to live with her on a farm with lots of animals. I could have told her that I wasn't lucky at all, because I had been taken away from the people who loved me, just because they were lesbians. But I didn't know how to explain it. I didn't want to, because it was a secret, so instead I said, 'My mother and father are divorced.'

Bonnie was quite shocked. She said, 'But I thought you were a Catholic! Catholics aren't supposed to get divorced.'

I nearly said, 'But my mother's Jewish, and I'm Jewish too,' but I stopped myself. That was a secret too.

Bonnie said, 'If a boy farts out loud in Mark's school, then all the other boys laugh. Nobody says that he is *ungentlemanlike*. At lunch in his school, there is one monk in charge of about a hundred boys. He sits up on a high platform and eats his lunch at the same time as the boys. When he thinks that everyone has finished, he rings a small bell and all the boys have to be silent, while the monk says Grace After Meals. Well, one day it was completely silent and a boy did the most enormous fart. All the boys started laughing, and wouldn't stop. The monk kept ringing the bell, but the boys had gone out of control, and were laughing and clapping and shouting. So finally the monk sent every boy in the room upstairs to the dormitory. He made them all line up, and hit each one of them very hard on the hand with a leather belt. Mark waited at the back of the queue, because he thought that the monk's arm would be tired. But the monk said, "So Boniface, you thought you'd wait until the end, because you thought my arm would be tired? Well let's see exactly how tired I am!" He grabbed Mark by the ear and pulled down Mark's trousers and pants and hit him six times as hard as he could on the bare bottom.'

I had been laughing about the boy farting and the boys getting out of control, but this part of the story made me want to cry. It was so cruel. But there was worse to come. 'A terrible thing happened to Mark not long after he started school. He was only ten. He had written me a letter, but by accident he left it on his desk, and a boy picked it up and read it. In the letter, Mark said how much he missed me, and couldn't wait to see me again. The boy thought that Mark was writing to a girlfriend, and started running round with the letter, and reading it out loud to other boys. Mark told him that he was writing to me, his sister, but that just made it worse. The boy said things like, "Real boys don't love their sisters like that". So Mark grabbed the letter off the boy and pushed him. Mark said that he thought the other boy was just teasing him, and really they were quite good friends. But Mark was cross, because he loves me and felt embarrassed. Boys in that school have some very stupid ideas about girls.

'Then an even worse thing happened. Some other boys started shouting "Fight! Fight!" There's this place in the school, a sort of yard, where older boys go to smoke, because none of the monks can see them there. It's the place where boys fight each other too. So a crowd of boys grabbed Mark and his friend and marched them to the yard, and told them that they had to fight each other. By then there were about a hundred boys in a big circle, all pushing and shoving to get the best view, and shouting and swearing and trying to get Mark and his friend to hit each other. Mark told me that by then he and the other boy were both terrified, and didn't want to fight. The boy even said he was sorry, and Mark knew that he meant it. But the crowd were shouting and jeering, and wouldn't let Mark and his friend go until they had hurt each other. So they had to fight each other, and still the crowd weren't satisfied, and started shouting, "We want blood! We want blood!" So the boy hit Mark in the face and made his nose bleed. Then some prefects came and broke up the fight. Some boys in the crowd complained that it was the worst fight they had ever seen, and that it had been boring and a waste of time, and that it was like watching a pair of girls fighting.'

I said, 'Oh Bonnie! That's one of the most awful things I've ever heard.' Of course, I'd heard much worse than that, but it was a terrible story all the same. I felt myself shaking. I had a horrible picture in my mind of the crowd of boys yelling, and desperate to see two small boys hurt each other. I thought of the people who might have stood in the street and watched the Nazis beating my grandfather across the head with an iron bar. I thought of the soldiers laughing at Jesus, as they whipped him. I just didn't understand how people could get pleasure from watching other people being harmed and humiliated. I still can't understand it.

That was the moment when I realised I wanted to leave the hospital. The thought of being on a farm with Auntie Aileen was becoming more and more exciting. I wanted to talk to her.

Bonnie's secret
I wanted to go to sleep. I told Bonnie I was very upset for her and couldn't listen to any more. I asked her, 'Are boarding schools really so horrible?'

She said, 'Yes they are.'

A thought came into my mind. I said, 'Bonnie, would you like me to get into bed with you and comfort you?'

She said it was a lovely idea, but her bed was very narrow and I might bash her arm. Then she whispered, 'Can I tell you one more thing? It's a bit of a secret, and you really must promise never to tell anyone.' I didn't want to hear it, so didn't promise, but she told me anyway. 'Well, Émilie gets awfully homesick. She used to cry and cry in the night, so I felt terribly sorry for her. One night I got into her bed and we cuddled each other, and she went straight to sleep. Well, we liked it so much that we got into bed as often as we could. We waited until all the other girls were asleep, then I would creep into her bed, and we would whisper and cuddle each other. We only did it for a few minutes, then I would go back to my own bed.'

I said, 'There's nothing wrong with that. Why shouldn't you do it?' I had slept with Peter, so knew what I was talking about.

She said, 'That's what I think too, but last week we were in bed together, and fell fast asleep. And when Sister Carmel switched the dormitory lights on in the morning, she saw us in bed together, and was very angry. She told Sister Winifred, and she called us both into her office. She told us that Good Catholic Girls sleep in their own beds, and she has decided to split us up. She is going to put Émilie in another class, and we have to sleep in separate rooms, and we are not allowed to sit near each other at mealtimes. Some girls have been calling us names, but we can't complain to Sister Carmel about it, because I'm sure she will say that we deserve it. But what I really don't understand is that we haven't done anything wrong! My brother comforts me in the night, especially when my parents are arguing downstairs. In Malawi, whole families sleep in the same bed, including the Catholic families!'

She didn't say anything else. I heard her breathing very hard. I said, 'I do understand. If I were you and that happened to me, then I would feel exactly the same way.'

'Thank you Pippa. You won't tell anyone, will you?'

I said, 'Bonnie, did you jump off the roof?'

Bonnie paused. 'I did. It was a very silly thing to do. I wanted to kill myself, and I wanted those wicked nuns to get the blame. Everyone saw me jump, but they all said I fell. I shouldn't have done it. What shall I do? You won't tell anyone, will you?'

I said I wouldn't, but suggested she tell Mr Macmillan about it. I was going to tell her to talk to Auntie Aileen, but that thought suddenly seemed wrong. I wanted my new auntie all to myself. I went to sleep, thinking about Mummy and Muriel being so happy in bed together, and how Muriel jumped on the train in front of us, but perhaps she had gone to the station with the idea that she might throw herself in front of a train. We had saved her life, and she had saved ours.

129

I am an exceptional child

I woke up early again and wanted to see my Auntie straight away. I looked at Bonnie, still fast asleep in the red glow. I felt very sorry for her. Her parents lived in Africa, and I got the impression that they weren't very nice people. After all, what kind of parents would send their children thousands of miles away, because they wanted them to go to a Catholic school? And they argued downstairs in the night, which made the children so frightened and upset that they had to sleep together. And she was separated from the three people in the world who loved her so much. Actually, that was four people, if you included Émilie. But did her parents love her? No wonder she was so sad. I hoped I never had to go to a boarding school. After everything that I had been through in my short life, that would surely be enough to drive me mad.

The nurses drew the curtains and Bonnie woke up. She smiled at me and then she frowned. I knew that she was thinking about the secret that she had told me, but we never spoke about it again. It was very busy on the ward that morning. The doctors examined Bonnie and said that she could go back to school as soon as possible. She thanked the doctors, but she didn't sound pleased. I imagined that she was dreading going back to school, because she was going to suffer terribly. She would be able to see her best friend from a distance, but couldn't be near her.

The doctors examined me and I heard them say among themselves, 'This one can go as soon as she's had her clips removed. She's healing well, but it will be a few days yet.'
I felt like shouting at them, 'Hey! I'm here you know! Why not talk to me?' Then I realised that they were discussing whether I could go home or not. So I smiled politely and tried to be on my best behaviour, even though while they were talking amongst themselves they had forgotten to pull down my nightie, to cover my Lovely Place.

Mr Macmillan and Auntie Aileen arrived just after the ward round. Bonnie asked to talk to Mr Macmillan in private, and went with him into Matron's office. I wanted to tell my new auntie about what Bonnie had told me, but I decided not to, because I knew that this was what Bonnie was talking about to Mr Macmillan. I talked about my wound instead, and I realised that I was frightened that the doctors might hurt me, or when they took my clips out my wound might pop open, and they could see right inside me, all the way to my intestines, which might suddenly flop out with lots of blood. I felt dizzy and thought I was going to be sick. Auntie Aileen held my hand, and told me she was going to ask if she could come with me. As soon as she said that, my dizziness disappeared. I said, 'But only Keith's parents are allowed to come in the ward during the day.'

She said, 'Well, I think those rules are going to be changed soon. Mr Macmillan tells me that children get better much quicker if their parents can stay with them as long as they like. Perhaps one day parents will be able to sleep in the ward with their children. And anyway, we have decided to make an exception in your case, because you are an exceptional child.'

I said, 'Thank you Auntie Aileen.' She smiled. I liked saying her name.

Keith

I wanted to get out of bed and walk around, so asked Auntie Aileen if she would come with me to the toilet. It was still painful to walk, and we had to stop outside Keith's room. Baby Theresa was looking at us, as sad as ever. Mrs Drew had said that we could give Theresa our duck when her parents came to collect her in the afternoon. I waved at her, but she just looked at me.

Then I got a real fright. The door to Keith's room opened and his mother came out. I got even more of a fright when she talked to me. She said, 'Hello. I see you every day, walking up and down. It's nice to see that you are much better.'

I looked past her and could see Keith. He was as still as ever. Keith's mother saw me looking at him and said, 'Yes, Keith is still the same, but he's not suffering. Would you like to say hello to him?'

In stories I had read, the author sometimes wrote, 'She was so frightened that she nearly jumped out of her skin.' Well that's exactly how I felt. I tried my hardest not to show terror on my face. I think Keith's mum must have guessed from my hesitation that I didn't want to go in. She looked very disappointed, so I said, 'Yes please. I would love to. It's just that I feel so sad when I look at him.' I thought it was best to be honest, just in case I started screaming, or burst into tears and tried to run out of the room. Then I thought how silly I was being. He wasn't a monster. He was still alive, and looked just like he was sleeping peacefully, so it wouldn't be as bad as looking at a dead body.

We went to the toilet, and on the way back went inside Keith's room. Auntie Aileen closed the door quietly behind us, then held my hand. Keith's had a pipe going up his nose that was attached to his face by a piece of tape. His hair was very short, like a crew cut, and there was a very big dent on the side of his head, and a big purple scar. I felt sure that was the place where the car had hit him. I wanted to run out of the room, but I closed my eyes and thought, 'What if it was me lying there, and Peter came in and took one look at me and ran away? What would that do to Mummy, or Muriel?' I opened my eyes and saw a rubber pipe coming out from under his bedclothes and leading to a plastic bag near the floor. The bag was full of a yellow liquid. I knew that it was wee, so the pipe must have been attached to Keith's willy. Keith's mum asked me if I wanted to say hello. I didn't. I wanted to go back to my bed. But I knew that would make her terribly upset, so I said, 'Yes please, I'd love to. Would it be all right to hold his hand?' I didn't want to hold his hand at all. The thought of going near him and looking at his face was bad enough, so why had I offered to touch him? We moved round the bed to get closer to Keith's face, and Auntie Aileen kept hold of my hand. His mouth was wide open and his eyes were closed. He didn't look dead, but he didn't look like he was sleeping either. Auntie Aileen squeezed my hand. I looked at Keith's hand, and I reached out to touch it. His fingers were warm, but they didn't move. Keith's mum said, 'Keith! Keith! That very pretty girl has come to see you! You know; the one I've been telling you about, who walks up and down and is so brave, and sometimes looks at you. Well she's holding your hand right now. Aren't you a lucky boy?'

She asked me what my name was and I told her I was Pippa. She said that was such a pretty name, and she guessed from my accent that I was from England, and I told her I she was right. She asked me if I was on holiday in Scotland, or had I just moved here, or perhaps I was from the boarding school in the town? I looked at Auntie Aileen and she said to me, 'Do you want to tell Keith's mother your story?' I shook my head.

Keith's mother said to Auntie, 'I'm Janet Crisp. You can call me Janet.' Janet and Auntie Aileen shook hands and smiled at each other.

While they did that, I changed my mind, and thought of what to say. I said, 'My mother and father have just got divorced. My father owns Pearson's in the town and some of the hotels. I'm going to live with my auntie, and I'm very pleased about that. She has a pig, and soon it's going to have piglets.'

I didn't tell her how sad and upset and traumatised I had been. She had enough sadness in her life, and I felt sure that she didn't need to know about any of mine.

Janet said, 'Well fancy that. I mean fancy your father owning Pearson's! It's a lovely big shop, but a bit expensive for us. We bought Keith a pair of football boots there once, as a Christmas present. He was thrilled with them. Weren't you, love?'

Something moved inside me. It was a feeling just above my Lovely Place. It was like how I felt once when Peter and I found a young bird with a damaged wing. It looked like it had tried to fly away from its nest, but hadn't been ready, so had fallen to the ground. Its mother was flying around and chirping madly, because we were near her child. We both had the same funny feeling and ran away. Peter asked his dad if he could put the bird back in its nest, but he told Peter that it wouldn't be a good idea. He said we had to leave it, and let Nature take its course. We went back later and the baby bird and its mother had gone. I thought that the mother had been able to pick her baby up in her beak and fly back with him to the nest. Then she could look after him until he was ready to fly properly.

Peter thought that a cat had probably eaten it. I didn't like Peter for saying that. I told Mummy that I thought Peter could be quite horrible sometimes. She thought that he was probably right about the cat, but maybe he shouldn't have said out loud what he was thinking. She said, 'You won't stop liking him just because he said the wrong thing?'

I went red, but said, 'Of course not.'

Mummy said, 'Good. I'm glad. All lovers have little arguments. It doesn't mean anything.'

I must have gone into a little dream, standing there, holding Keith's hand. I heard his mum ask me, 'Do you like to sing? Keith loves singing.'

I asked, 'What songs did he like? I mean *does* he like?'

'Oh, he likes The Beatles and The Monkees. Do you know them?'

'Oh me too! I sang I'm a Believer in church once.' I told her about Peter and his sisters and how we sang along to The Beatles and danced The Twist.

She said that Keith loved to sing Can't Buy Me Love. She started singing it and I found myself joining in. I sang quietly at first and then sang louder and louder, because I wanted Keith to hear me. I patted his hand in time to the music. Janet said, 'Thank you Pippa. Thank you so much.' I wanted to ask, 'Do you think he heard us?' but it didn't feel right somehow. She said, 'I'm sure he heard you.'

I asked if we could sing Help. She said, 'Yes please. Keith and his dad and I watched the film together.'

I told her that my friend's uncle was one of the baddies in the film. She was very impressed. After we sang Help, Janet asked me if I had a favourite song.

I said, 'Yes I do. It's called *Colours*, and it's by Donovan. It's my auntie's favourite song. I miss her so much, and I sing it a lot in my head, and I hum it when I think of her, which is pretty much all the time.'

Janet looked a bit surprised. Auntie Aileen explained, 'Not me. Pippa means her auntie who lives with her mother down in England. They are very good friends, and her auntie loves Pippa very much.'

I sang *Colours*, and Janet blew her nose. I knew that I was making her cry, but didn't stop.

Auntie Aileen said it was time for us to go and have lunch, and Janet thanked me and said what a beautiful girl I was. I didn't know what to say, so patted Keith's hand and then we left.

Auntie Aileen kissed me, and said I was very special girl, and how lucky and proud she was to be able to look after me.

When we got back to my bed, Mr Macmillan was just leaving. He said that he would see me in the morning, but that Auntie Aileen would stay with me for the rest of the afternoon. He looked a bit worried about something, and went with Auntie Aileen to have a chat with Matron. I wanted to ask Bonnie what she had talked about, but she was very quiet. In fact, she was quiet for the rest of the day. I asked her if she was all right, and she said that she was just thinking about something important. I never discovered what it was.

Mrs Drew told us that Baby Theresa's parents had come to take their baby home. She took us over to Theresa's cot, where her mum and dad were getting her changed into some clean clothes. We had expected Theresa to be very happy and excited about seeing her parents, but she had exactly the same blank expression on her face, and looked at her parents with the same sad eyes. I think I had the same look on my face when I was taken away from Mummy and Muriel. I supposed that Baby Theresa was traumatised, just like me. But if I ever saw my mummy and Muriel again, I felt sure I would scream and shout and jump up and down and make the loudest noises I had ever made in my whole life. Bonnie asked Mrs Drew, in a whisper, 'Do you think the baby has forgotten who her mum and dad are?' That was a terrible, terrible thought.

Mrs Drew introduced us, and explained that we had made a cuddly toy for the baby. Theresa's mum was very pleased. Bonnie explained that if they gave it to Theresa in the car, or at home, then this might remind her of the happy time when they were all together again, and she could forget about being sad in hospital. The dad said that this was a wonderful idea, and that he had never met such kind and thoughtful children.

Brian was sitting in a wheelchair, because his joints were hurting him, and it was painful for him to walk. He said that nobody had ever called him kind and thoughtful before. The dad said that there was a first time for everything, and he was sure that lots of people would say the same thing in the future. Then the parents shook our hands and were gone.

We looked at Keith. I told Brian and Bonnie that I had held his hand and sung him some songs. I asked them if they would like to sing for Keith, but Bonnie said she couldn't, because it would be too upsetting for her, and Brian said that it wouldn't be worth it, because Keith couldn't hear them anyway. I was disappointed in both of them, but didn't say anything.

I've just re-read what I've just written a few minutes ago. I have written that I would jump up and down <u>if</u> I saw Mummy and Muriel again. If? If! I should have written <u>when</u>. <u>When</u> I saw them again. Was I beginning to give up believing that I would ever see my mother and Muriel again? On the surface, I seemed quite cheerful, but inside I'm sure I felt just like Baby Theresa. I was just more experienced than her at suffering, and had already become an expert in pushing my feelings deep down inside myself.

Goodbye Bonnie

A few days later, in the morning, Matron came to see Bonnie, and told her that after lunch a nun would come and take her back to school. Bonnie went with a nurse to have a bath and wash her hair. In the few days I had known her,

Bonnie had always had her long hair untied. When she came back, her hair was in a ponytail, and he looked completely different; not younger, not older, but like a completely different child. As we were eating lunch, Bonnie said, 'This will be my last decent meal for a long time. The food in our school is absolutely disgusting.' Then Sister Eugenie came to take Bonnie away. She smiled at me, but I didn't smile back. A nurse helped Bonnie get dressed. Bonnie still found lots of things very difficult. She wasn't able to do up her buttons or even put on her knickers without help, and her ribs still hurt. While the nurse was helping her, we saw Bonnie's bottom. Sister Eugenie was embarrassed and looked the other way. I didn't look away. I didn't want to be like that nun. Bonnie wasn't ashamed, and I wasn't embarrassed. I felt very sorry for Bonnie. She was so far away from home, and going to a place where nuns stopped you from having best friends.

I wondered who would help Bonnie at school. Really, it should have been Émilie's job. That would have been fun for both of them. But that wasn't going to happen now, because the nuns had banned them from being together. But who was going to help her now? It was obvious that the nuns wouldn't even touch her. I couldn't even be sure that her other friends would be allowed to help her, since it was against the rules for girls to touch each other. This made me so glad that I was going to be with Auntie Aileen. As long as I had her, then I would never feel alone. I thought about when I had fractured my wrist and smashed my face. Muriel and Mummy had been extra loving and caring, and I had enjoyed them loving me like that, even though I had been in the wars.

Bonnie looked terrible in her school uniform. It was all grey, and didn't suit her at all. She wasn't a pretty child anymore; that horrible nun had turned her into a Good Catholic Schoolgirl. Bonnie didn't cry when it was time to go. Sister Eugenie said, 'Sheila, say goodbye to your friend.'
I was sitting in bed and Bonnie leaned over to kiss me. Sister said, 'Not like that, Sheila. You can shake hands, or not at all.'

Bonnie put her hand forward, but I kissed her, on both cheeks. I whispered in her ear, 'Well, she can't boss me around.' I wanted to say, 'The silly bitch,' but stopped myself.

Brian shouted, 'What about me? Don't I get a kiss?'

Sister Eugenie said to Bonnie, 'It's time to go,' and led her up the ward. She looked like someone going back to prison.

I didn't want to be in hospital without Bonnie. Bonnie wasn't like any of my other friends. She wasn't pure and simple like Lucy. Bonnie's life was messy, and this had made her into a pickle. The biggest problem in our lives was LOVE. Bonnie thought that her parents didn't love each other, and she wasn't sure if they loved her either. If they did love her, then why did they send her so far away?

When I was little, I wasn't sure if Mummy loved me or not. That had been an awful feeling. But now I was sure that she did, but I wasn't allowed to be with her. I didn't like to think about my father. I knew I didn't love him. And while I was thinking about Bonnie being a pickle, I knew that I was one too. I didn't want to be a pickle. Now Bonnie had to survive on her own, with nobody to tuck her in or kiss her goodnight. It must have been hard for her to live with nuns who didn't like her, and were really quite cruel. They probably believed that they had to be cruel to children, because that would be good for them. I imagined that a child would have to be tough and strong to be able to live with adults like that. I had a feeling that every day at Bonnie's boarding school would be just like the days I spent in The Lodge. And Bonnie didn't even have a teddy bear to remind her of home, and the brother that she loved. Poor Bonnie; no wonder she jumped off the roof.

After Bonnie left, life on the ward was a bit dreary. It was nice to talk to Brian, and to have lessons with Mrs Drew, but I missed Bonnie. I told Auntie about that, and she thought that one of the main reasons I felt like that was because I was getting better. A few days later, Auntie Aileen and Matron told

me that it was time for me to have my clips removed and my wound dressed, and to have a nice warm bath. Auntie said, very quickly, 'And I'm coming with you, so you don't need to worry.'
That worked immediately. I didn't worry at all.

I didn't really know what my wound looked like. Every time the doctors examined my tummy, I turned my head away, and when I was sitting on the toilet, I closed my eyes so I wouldn't see it. I imagined that it would look just like Muriel's; a pinky-reddy line that would feel nice to run your finger along. We went into a small room with a bed in it. A new doctor was there with Nurse Beattie, and they both smiled at me. After I got onto the bed, the doctor explained that my scar would feel a bit delicate for a few weeks, and might not look very nice. He said, 'And don't go showing it to all your friends straight away. Wait for a while, until it looks more attractive.'
I thought that was a very funny thing to say. I laughed, but it didn't hurt so much.

My wound looked horrible. The gauze was stuck to it and covered in dry black blood. I was frightened that Nurse Beattie was going to yank the gauze off. Muriel had told me that most nurses believed in pulling a plaster off in one go, and didn't care how much it hurt the patient. She wasn't like that, and preferred to take the plaster off as slowly as possible. I was pleased that Nurse Beattie was just like Muriel, and the doctor wasn't at all in a hurry. He chatted to Auntie, and gave her instructions about how to look after me. He said, 'It's very important that Philippa avoids strenuous exercise, like running and climbing trees.' I was pleased that he didn't make a silly comment about me being a tomboy. Nurse Beattie bathed my wound with warm water. I closed my eyes and held Auntie's hand very tightly, and soon the gauze was off. There were six bloody light-grey metal clips holding my skin together. The doctor removed them with a pair of tweezers. I closed my eyes and it hurt, but I didn't call out, because I wanted to impress Auntie.

Then the doctor said, 'All done!' and I looked down and nearly cried. Instead of a nice neat line like Frances or Muriel's, there was a nasty red and bumpy line, with six tiny holes above it and six below.

Nurse Beattie said, 'Don't worry Pippa; soon it will look just as lovely as your Mummy's friend's scar.'

I had forgotten that I had once told her all about Muriel. Auntie Aileen smiled.

I went red, because I supposed she knew all about me being naked with Muriel a lot, and that this was one of the reasons why I had been taken away.

Nurse Beattie said, 'Now it's time for a nice bath. Who do you want to help you? Me or your Auntie?' That was another surprise. I had got used to the nurses doing things with my body. I was sure that, like Muriel, they had seen so many bodies in their lives that they were quite bored with them. But what would Auntie think? I said, 'Auntie please!'

Auntie said, 'How nice.' And it was nice. I was worried about getting water on my scar, but Auntie was very careful, and helped me get in the bath without hurting myself. She didn't mind me being in front of her with nothing on, and I didn't mind either. She said that God had made us all the same, except obviously boys and girls looked different.

I wondered if she was testing my knowledge of S-E-X. She had mentioned God for the first time. I hoped she wasn't a Catholic.

I have always felt that there is something special about taking your clothes off in front of someone else for the first time. I suppose people from Sweden and Finland, and nudists, and people living in the African countryside or Papua New Guinea, might not think about it, because they are used to being naked together. But for me, with my new Auntie, it had a very special significance. It was like a kind of test. Not a test for me, but a test of how we would live together. I knew enough about Catholics to know that for them, their naked bodies were very private, and perhaps even something to be ashamed of. I had learned that people have very different ideas about being naked, and you had to be very careful about what you said, in case someone got upset, or angry. I knew that Mummy's and Muriel's and my nakedness had been part of the problem for my father. Yet here I was, in front of his cousin, sitting in the bath with nothing on. And as I sat there, I thought, 'I don't know you. I don't know anything about you, except that you live on a farm and have a pregnant pig.'

But as she very carefully and very lovingly washed me all over, and as I sat wrapped in a big towel on her lap, sucking my thumb, I knew that as long as I lived with her, then I would be quite safe. And I was certain that Mummy and Muriel would be happy to know that at last I was with someone they could trust.

I felt certain that she would love me.

I said, 'Excuse me Auntie, I don't wish to be rude, but I'm worried my first period might start soon.'

She was very surprised, but laughed. 'And why do you think that?'

'Well, I was feeling all cross and irritable and blocked up, just like Mummy does.' I explained about Mummy's terrible moods, and how Muriel helped her to calm down and feel better.

Auntie Aileen said, 'Well, I think you might be a wee bit young for that. I don't see any signs of you being grown up enough just yet. Maybe it was just constipation. What do you think?'

I said, 'Oh, I'm still a big baby,' and stuck my thumb back in my mouth.

We had just passed another test.

It was such a relief

The next morning, it was my turn to leave. Brian was very quiet, and I knew he was feeling sad. The doctors came on their ward round and exposed my Lovely Place again, and said I could go home.

Auntie Aileen came after lunch and helped me to get dressed. I pretended that it was terribly painful for me to put my clothes on by myself, so that she would have to help me. My new clothes were lovely, and had that nice new smell that clothes have when you have just bought them, and you wear them for the first time.

Brian said, 'You look lovely! Not like Bonnie. Her school uniform was ugly.'

I kissed Brian on both cheeks, and gave him a drawing I had done of him making Theresa's duck with Mrs Drew. He was very pleased, but said he would give it to Mrs Drew, so that she wouldn't forget him. I told him that he must come and visit me on the farm. I knew he was trying to be brave, and he just managed to stop himself from crying. I kissed him again, and it was time to go. We walked past Keith's room, and his mum waved at me, and I went inside. Keith was as still as ever. I told his mum that I was leaving, and she kissed me and hoped that I would soon make a full recovery. Then she looked at Keith, and I knew that she was thinking that her son never would recover. I said goodbye, and went with Auntie into Matron's office, to say goodbye to Matron and all the nurses. I gave Matron my painting of Renoir's flowers in a vase, and all the nurses were astonished, and were delighted when Auntie gave them a big tin of Quality Street to share. Matron looked out of the window, and when she turned around, her face was pink and her eyes were shining. She held my hands and kissed me, and said, 'You are such a bonnie wee lassie. Thank you for going in to see our Keith. It made such a difference to his poor mother. And thank you for keeping an eye on Mr Macmillan, and stopping him getting into mischief.'

As I left the ward, I didn't feel like a prisoner going back to prison. It was such a relief. I held Auntie's hand, and once I was out of the ward, I felt like skipping down the corridor, but it would have hurt too much.

There was a shiny black car waiting for us outside the front of the hospital. I was holding onto Auntie Aileen's arm, but as soon as I saw the car, I went rigid and felt that I couldn't move. Auntie said, 'It's all right Pippa. It's all right. It's just a

142

taxi to take us to the farm.' As soon as Auntie said that, I could move again. But my tummy hurt and Auntie had to help me get into the back of the car. She said, 'It's a lovely drive, so let's look out of the window, and you can tell me what you think.'

And it was a lovely drive. After a few minutes, we crossed a wide river and were soon in the countryside. There seemed to be sheep and cows in every field that we passed. After about fifteen minutes, we could see the sea, and I forgot all about being frightened. We drove along the coast, and for a while the road was almost next to the beach. We saw a huge bay and passed several small rocky beaches. Auntie said that they were full of rock pools. I had read about rock pools and seen pictures of them, and had always wanted to see one for myself.

Then we drove through a small town with a church and several pubs and a sweet shop, and a park with swings, a roundabout and a tall slide. Auntie explained that this was the town of Kirkbrae, which was Scottish for 'church on the side of the hill'.

The taxi driver said, 'Aye, that's right, but when they first built the church, the people said it was too much effort to climb up the hill to worship the Lord in church every Sunday, so nobody went there. So they had to knock it doon and put it in the centre of the toon, which is very handy for the bar and the fish and chip shop as well!'

At least I think that's what he said. Auntie had a lovely Scottish accent and pronounced every letter in each word that she spoke, but this man sounded like he had never heard of a consonant in his life. Perhaps there was something wrong with his tongue. Anyway, I knew that he was joking. We drove up a hill outside the town and then down towards the sea again. Half way down we turned off the road and drove along a bumpy track until we came to a big metal gate. Auntie got out and opened the gate, and pointed to a sign that said, 'Brae Farm'.

The car drove through the gates and Auntie got in and said, 'Here we are, safe and sound in your new home.' We drove a very short way past some very large bushes, and a huge pine tree with a small lawn in front of it. The grass was covered in pinecones. We stopped in front of a house made out of red stone. It looked like The Lodge, but was much smaller.

Auntie got out of the car, but I couldn't move. I was gripped by more fear, which rose up through me and made my legs weak. I didn't know what the fear was, but as it passed into my tummy, I thought I was going to mess myself, just like when I was stuck on the branch, high up on Dominic's tree. Auntie opened the car door and said, 'Are you all right, Pippa? You've gone very pale.' I couldn't speak. She leaned into the car and said, 'Come on, Pippa. It's very nice inside the house.' But I still couldn't move. Auntie got back in the car and sat next to me, but left the car door open. She said, 'Listen Pippa. I forgot to tell you something very important. It was meant to be a surprise, but maybe it will just make things worse.'
The taxi driver switched off the engine and said, 'I'll just take a wee walk. Give me a shout when you're ready.' He walked towards the bushes.

Luna
Then a dog came running from around the side of the house and tried to jump into the car. I screamed. I don't like screaming, but sometimes it just comes out, like when I had my injections. The dog was frightened and tried to back away, but Auntie grabbed it by the collar and said, 'It's all right, Luna. This is Pippa, but she doesn't like silly dogs jumping all over her!' She said to me. 'I'm sorry Pippa, this is the surprise. This is Luna, and she's our dog, and I think she's the most wonderful creature in the world! I'm sure you'll be the best of friends. She's just excited to see us. She never jumps up at people.'
I looked at her. She was a beautiful border collie. She sat and panted, and looked at me with her big eyes. It was love at first sight, and suddenly I was able to walk out of the car. I patted Luna's head and she licked my hand. We walked to the front door of the house and Luna waited outside. Auntie said, 'She knows she's not allowed in, but she's expecting her walk.'
The bad spell cast on me in the car was suddenly broken.

We went in the house and Auntie said, 'Oh dear! I've forgotten to pay the driver! Wait here and I'll be back in a wee moment.' She ran outside and left me in the hall. I tried to run after her but it hurt too much, and the door suddenly slammed shut. I had the feeling that there was a man behind me, who wanted to grab me. I tried to open the front door but my hands must have been sweaty, and kept slipping on the big heavy doorknob. I banged and banged on the door with my fists and yelled, 'Let me out! Let me out!'

That made Luna bark, then Auntie opened the door and said, 'Pippa! Whatever is the matter?'

But I couldn't speak. I just sank to the floor and cried.

Auntie sat on the floor next to me and put her arm round me. She said, 'What's the matter? What is it my dear? Come on, let's sit in the kitchen and I'll put the kettle on. I've made us a special cake, and made your room up. I've tried to make it look as nice as possible, but you can change it around as much as you like. And shall I change my mind about Luna? Should we let her come in the house after all? Would that make you feel a bit better?'

My voice came back, 'Yes please.'

'Good girl, but please can you help me get up? Because I'm not as young as I used to be.'

That seemed like a very funny thing to say.

Tea, cake and a talk

In the kitchen, we had a nice cup of tea and I had two slices of delicious chocolate cake. Luna came in and sat next to me, and looked at me with her lovely big eyes, but Auntie said on no account was I to give the dog anything to eat; no matter how beseechingly she looked at me. She explained that dogs should only have one meal a day. Luna was a working dog by nature, and very intelligent, but needed lots of exercise and company. If she got bored, she would start to chew things, so it was going to be my job to keep her busy.

Then Auntie took my hand and said, 'Pippa, let's talk about what happened before you got in the car, and just before you got out. I think I know, but I just want to make sure that I've got it right.' I didn't want to talk about it, but Auntie squeezed my hand and said, 'Pippa, please try and tell me. What was it?' She smiled at me and looked in my eyes. I wondered how long it would be before she let me sit on her lap and suck my thumb. We both had to pass a few tests first.

It was always so much easier for me to relax and talk to adults if they said *Pippa* before they said something important. And if they looked in my eyes and smiled, and were quiet for a little while, it was easy to talk and discover what I was really feeling. I'm still the same now. I said, 'It felt just like when they took me away from school in the big shiny car, and when I was at The Lodge.'

She looked very serious. 'I thought it was that. But why did you get so frightened when I went out to pay the taxi driver?'

I didn't want to tell her, but knew I had to. 'I thought there was a man with big black gloves on and he was going to grab me and put me in a sack and then strangle the life out of me.'

'I understand.'

'Do you?' I didn't mean to say that. It sounded very cheeky and rude.

'Yes I do. I know that exact feeling. I'm sure lots of people do. I don't think about a man with black gloves, but sometimes, if I go outside the house in the dark, I suddenly panic and think there's someone out there, watching me. It's silly really, but you can't always control your fears.'

'So what do you do?'

'I run inside as fast as I can, and lock the door and draw the curtains.'

'But you're a grown-up!'

'I know. Isn't it silly? But inside every grown-up there's a little child, and sometimes that little child just pops up. But I'm here to look after you. And Luna will look after both of us, of course.'

I thought she was very nice. 'I know you're going to look after me, and I'm very pleased about it, but I don't really know who you are.'

I was surprised at myself. Now that I had started talking, I didn't want to stop. Now, I understand that all the people who loved me, including Mummy and Muriel, the teachers at school, Lucy's mum, and my Art Therapist, had all been working hard to build up my sense of security and trust in adults. But in the past few weeks this had all been completely stripped away. I had been crushed. I had felt safe in hospital, even though grown-ups did horrible things to me from time to time. It had been a very safe and secure place, but now, away from hospital I didn't feel safe at all.

I said, 'My light has gone out.'

'Your light?'

'There's a light inside me. M...' I stopped myself just in time. 'Someone used to say that I had a little light inside me, and when I was happy then she, that person, would say that she saw my light shining very brightly.'

'What a lovely idea. She must have been a very special person.'

I didn't say anything. Auntie was quiet, just like Mr Macmillan. She was waiting for me to say something. I said, 'I think my light has gone out.'

'Well, I'm here to get it shining again.'

Then it was my turn to be quiet. She didn't say anything, so I said exactly what was on my mind. 'Auntie Aileen, please don't be cross with me. I do want to talk to you. I think it will be lovely to talk to you. But I'm not sure I can.'

'Why not?'

'I don't know how to explain it'.

'Is it because you don't quite trust me yet? Is it because you're worried that I might tell other people? That I might tell Mr Shepherd, or even your father?'

147

I nodded. 'How did you know that? Is it because that's how you would feel if you were me?'

'Yes, that's right. And how did you know that?'

'You keep saying it. I like you saying it.'

She smiled and poured herself another cup of tea. She tasted it and said, 'It's horrible. I'll just boil some water and add it to the pot. Talking of pots, I haven't shown you where the toilet is, or anything!'

I knew what she was trying to do to me, and it was working. I smiled.

She said, 'You have such a lovely smile, Pippa. I'm here to look after you; to make sure that you feel safe and get better. Your father and Mr Macmillan have decided that.'

'But what if you die, or have a terrible accident, or get ill and can't look after me anymore? What will happen then? Or if they decide that you are not good enough, because you are too... too nice to me? Or they might think that you haven't made me into a Good Catholic? And what if my father decides to take me away, to live with him? He might take me to Malaysia, or South Africa or even Saudi Arabia, and nobody can stop him! It's bad enough being in Scotland and five hundred miles away from Mummy and M... but I'm not going to live in a foreign country!'

I was shouting. Auntie Aileen held my other hand. 'It's true, he might want to do that, because he is your father, and The Court has agreed that he is your Legal Guardian. That means that under The Law he is the person who can decide what is right for you, including whether you live with him or not. But...'

'See! I knew it was true!'

'Och, don't be so hasty! I was going to say that you can't live with your father, because he travels all over the world. And he wants you to live in Scotland. And, very importantly, he can't make big decisions like that unless he asks Mr Macmillan first.'

'But can't Mummy be my Legal Guardian?' 'I'm afraid not. The Court has said that she's not allowed, and she can't make decisions about you anymore.'

'Why not?'

She looked alarmed. I wished I hadn't asked that question. But I knew that she didn't agree with The Court, and that meant that she didn't agree with my father. She had passed another test.

My tummy felt very strange. I didn't know if it was because of the operation, or something else. I asked if I could lie down, so Auntie Aileen took me upstairs. I had a very big bedroom, with the sun shining through a window that looked out onto a small back garden. To my surprise, and huge pleasure, I could see the sea! I had a bookshelf full of books. One shelf was full of children's books, including *Five Children and It, The Railway Children,* and *Stig of the Dump.* Lots of my friends at school had read these books, but I had never had the time to read them, because I was always painting, or playing with Lucy and Roger.

There was a book about Sooty and Sweep, and another about Tom and Jerry, and an annual full of photos of pop stars, including The Beatles. There were several *Beano* and *Dandy* annuals and five very exciting *TinTin* books. I loved TinTin. I tried to watch *Hergé's Adventures of TinTin* whenever it was on TV, just before the BBC Six O'clock News. I used to be gripped with fear and excitement every time an episode finished, because it seemed impossible that TinTin could escape this time. (But at the back of my mind I knew that his dog, Snowy, would save him). Roger loved TinTin too, and used to pretend that he was Captain Haddock, just to make us laugh.

On another shelf there were books about Art and artists, and on the bottom shelf was the big box with all my art materials in it.

Auntie had somehow found out about the things that I liked, and had done her best to give them to me. All those new books must have cost so much money! I was so pleased, that I thought I might cry. Auntie asked me if I liked my room. Then I found that I was crying. It wasn't so much crying with happiness, but more a kind of relief, because I believed that at last I was safe. She said, 'It's all right, Pippa. I wanted to make your room look nice for you, so you can feel at home. But really I would prefer to have all these nice things downstairs, so that you won't be upstairs on your own for hours, making me feel lonely!'

As she said that, something huge moved inside me. I was being invited to stay downstairs, to play, and read and write, and paint, whenever I wanted, and for as long as I wanted. It felt like the very opposite of how life had been in Northumberland, when I was very young. Then I was banished to my cold bedroom, and was terrified of disturbing Mummy, downstairs in the warm kitchen.

I had a vision in my mind of the cave where Jesus was buried, and somehow the huge stone that was blocking it up was beginning to move away. But perhaps it was just wind. Since the operation, it felt like my tummy didn't belong to me anymore, because it was always doing strange things. And since they had taken me away from home, it felt like my eyes weren't my own, either. It seemed like I was always about to cry, trying to stop myself from crying, weeping buckets, or wiping away tears and snot. I always kept a large wad of Man-Size tissues stuffed up my sleeve, ready for the next time I was going to cry.

Does anybody actually like crying? I know I don't. Muriel used to say that it was good to cry, and that she usually felt better after 'a good cry.' But I never feel better after crying. It feels too emotional; like a huge stopper somewhere inside me has been forced out of place, so everything underneath it just bursts upwards. Then all the emotions that I have squeezed down, or tried to ignore, rise to the surface, and I have a horrible feeling of being completely overwhelmed and out of control.

Then afterwards I feel hot and exhausted. If I have been crying in front of someone, then I might feel embarrassed, or sometimes even ashamed. And I don't like how my face feels after I've been crying. The place on my face where my tears have been usually feels especially hot, and almost as if there have been marks left there. They feel like lines of raw skin after you have fallen over and scraped all the skin off, or where you have burnt yourself and it hasn't started to heal yet. So if I touch where the tears have been, it almost stings. And then I feel shaky all over and I try not to talk, because my voice will be wobbly, and I find it very difficult to get my eyes to focus. For me, crying is very emotionally, mentally, and physically distressing, and leaves me feeling all raw inside, and outside too.

So I have never ever had 'a good cry', and I try to avoid crying as much as I possibly can.

In my early days at Brae Farm, I seemed to cry all the time. I talked to Auntie about it, because I was worried about myself, and what she might think about me. She said that all the hurt that had been done to me was like a poison. The only way to make it come out was to rest, and do the things I liked, and to have lots of injections of love and comfort. Then the love would replace the poison. I thought she was talking about a big syringe, like in hospital. Auntie laughed and said that she was thinking about things like Bounty bars and porridge and chocolate cake, and walking by the sea, and painting, and playing with Luna, and generally having fun.

We unpacked my case and put Polish Teddy on my pillow. Auntie took out the photograph of me with Mummy and Muriel, and asked me if I would like to put it by my bed. She said, 'I expect that is your most treasured possession. I think it's a lovely picture. It's a lovely family photograph.' I didn't say anything, but since then have always called it 'My Family Photograph'.

I didn't want to go outside. I wanted to stay in my bedroom and do nothing, until I felt absolutely ready. But Auntie said that we would have to go out, because Luna needed her walk, and she didn't want to leave me in the house on my own.

Suddenly I didn't want to be in my room anymore.

I am overwhelmed and angry

We had to walk very slowly, because my wound had started to hurt quite a lot. Auntie told me to hold onto her arm, and we walked towards the farm. It was only just a few yards from the back of the house. I knew that, because as soon as we walked down the path there were all sorts of farmyard smells. There was another big metal gate, and beyond it some big sheds. There was mud and bits of straw everywhere. I told Auntie that the smells were making me feel a bit sick. I didn't want her to think I was ungrateful, so added, 'But usually I like farms.' This wasn't actually true, because I'd only ever been to a stables, and I loved the smell of horses.

She said, 'Don't worry, Pippa, I imagine that's because you're still not feeling quite well. Farms are dirty and smelly places, and they can take a bit of getting used to! This one is quite clean, but I'm sure it's not the best place to be if you're recovering from an operation. You can have a good look around once you feel fully better. In the meantime, I think that the beach will be the best place for us. I love the sea, don't you?'

We walked as quickly as we could across the farmyard and Auntie had to hold Luna by the scruff of the neck, to stop her running after the chickens and the geese. Auntie explained that Luna wasn't actually chasing the geese, but it was in her nature to want to control animals and to herd them around. Luna escaped from Auntie's grip and ran towards the geese, and started to make them run round the yard in a big group. Auntie laughed and said to me, 'It's no use, Pippa. I can't control her. You call her and see if she'll obey you.' She had to shout at me, because the geese were making so much noise. I thought the whole scene was wonderful, and I wasn't at all frightened of the geese. I called, 'Luna, come!' and she stopped bothering the geese and came to me straight away. I couldn't believe it.

Auntie laughed and said, 'There you are. I knew she would respond to you. I imagine you're one of those people who are wonderful with animals.'

That was a surprise. I had always thought that I was quite frightened of dogs.

We opened the gate and followed a path away from the farm, with small grassy fields on either side. The path was muddy and sloped downwards, and the fields on either side gradually became higher and higher above us. All the time we walked, the sound of the sea came nearer, and the smell of seawater became stronger. The mud beneath our feet became sand, and there were huge rocks on either side of the path. We turned a corner and there in front of us was the sea! The seawater was so close to us that we could only see a tiny patch of sand; before the water came swirling almost round our feet.

Auntie grabbed my hand and pulled me back, and explained that this was high tide, but the sea would soon start to go out again. We had to walk back for a short way along the path, until we could climb up the bank and into a grassy field. Then we walked towards the beach again, and stopped just above it. The wind was very strong now, and as I tried to talk it seemed to enter my mouth and whisk my words away. The sea was crashing on the huge boulders just below us, and the spray was splashing in our faces and whipping our hair against our cheeks, which made us laugh.

The sea was wild, and not at all like the calm sea in Norfolk. I wasn't frightened, but I was glad I wasn't on my own. I wondered if there was a cave down there. We walked to our right, and Auntie shouted that she knew a place where we could look out over the sea. We scrambled down a bank, and found a collection of enormous smooth grey rocks. One of them had a space that was like two seats that had been carved out by the sea. We sat on them, looking out to sea, with the water rushing in and out and splashing beneath us.

I had never had such an experience like that before, and could feel myself getting a bit dizzy with excitement.

Auntie said, 'As soon as I found this spot, I wanted to show it to you. I felt sure that you would love it. I named it Pippa's Seat.' I couldn't say anything. I closed my eyes, because I was becoming overwhelmed. Overwhelmed with excitement, with all my senses stretched; overwhelmed by the power of Nature; but most of all I was overwhelmed by a feeling deep inside that I couldn't put a name to. I think it might have been a mixture of relief and gratitude. Here, at last, was someone who I knew would love me. It was all becoming a bit too much for me to cope with. I was suddenly very warm, then very cold and then very warm again. The sound of the sea was getting louder and louder, and my whole body felt very light. I had the sensation that if there was a sudden strong gust of wind it might pick me up and blow me out to sea.

I jumped on Auntie's lap and shouted, 'Please hold me tight!' Auntie put her arms around me and squeezed me tight, and asked me if I was all right. I said, 'I'm a bit over-excited. It happens sometimes. If you talk to me, then I will calm down a bit.'

Auntie said, 'Do you know, Pippa, that you father owns this farm, and the house we are staying in, and he owns this beach too? It was your father's idea that I should come here and look after you. I'm not from here; not from this part of Scotland. I'm from way up north, near Aberdeen. I come from a wee town called Stranhaven. I've known about you ever since you were born. I've always wondered what you are like, and now I know!' I stopped being excited. Talking about my father had just ruined everything. The sea in front of me was suddenly like the dirty grey water that you see in the bottom of a bowl when you wash your socks by hand. I asked Auntie if we could go home. She said, 'In a wee while. But we have to talk about your father at some time, and now is as a good a time as any.'

I'm not usually someone who loses her temper, but I could feel myself getting very hot and bothered. I said the first thing that came into my head, just like Stephen Hunter had encouraged me to do. 'How can things that aren't alive be so lovely; like the sky and the clouds and the trees and sea and the rocks? But at the same time, how can people be so horrible? And this place is so lovely. I am so lucky. And my father owns all this, and wants me to know about it and enjoy it. But he is so cruel to Mummy and... And he hates them so much that he took me away from them! He knew I was happy, but he is so heartless; and he would rather make me an unhappy prisoner than allow me to live with... to live with Mummy. He hates Jews and he hates...' I couldn't say anything else. I cried and cried and couldn't stop.

Auntie held me closer and said, 'Pippa, stop for a minute. Listen to me.'

But I kept shouting. 'I try to be good. I try to be nice. But sometimes I feel so sad and I just can't hold it in anymore! I know you are a nice person. I know that one day soon I will love you. I feel it already. But really and truly, I just want to go home to my mummy. That's all I want in the whole world!'

Auntie took me off her lap, put me on my seat, and crouched down in front of me. 'Pippa, please listen. I understand, really I do. Anyone who had been hurt as much as you have would feel exactly the same way. I know I would. But I want to say something very important. It's perfectly all right for you to talk about Muriel. I know all about her. I know all about Mummy and Muriel, and I really don't mind at all. They sound like such lovely people. So please don't feel that you have to pretend that Muriel doesn't exist. I would like to know all about her.'

I shouted, 'It isn't fair! It isn't fair!' But then I realised that Auntie had mentioned Muriel's name for the first time, and all my anger just disappeared, like the air out of an untied balloon.

Auntie said, 'You have a good cry, Pippa. It all has to come out.'

'What has? What has to come out?' I wondered if I had been poisoned by all my injections in hospital, and it had to come out through all my tears and snot.

Auntie got up from crouching and said, 'Whoops! All the blood has just rushed to my head. People my age should get up slowly! Hold onto me in case I fall over!'

I was very surprised and asked her, without thinking, 'How old are you Auntie? If you don't mind me asking.'

She laughed. 'I'm going to be fifty in November. I'm the same age as your father.' I knew better than to comment on that. I knew she was old, but not that old. She took my hand and put it under her arm, and said, 'Come on Pippa. That's enough of the sea for the time being. Your father is a bit like King Canute. He might own the land, and think he can control what goes on there, but he doesn't own the sea that crashes on the shore, or the creatures that live in it, and he certainly can't control them! Let's go home and I'll make us a nice omelette with chips. Would you like baked beans as well? '

Obviously, I said, 'Yes please!'

Auntie put her fingers in her mouth and made a very loud whistle. I was very impressed. Luna came running towards us and was wet all over. She shook herself near me, which made me all wet, and I forgot I was angry. Auntie said, 'Luna is still exploring, but she always listens for my whistle.'

She asked me if I could whistle like her. I tried, but just made a blowing sound. She said, 'Would you like me to teach you?' I smiled and nodded. I felt Auntie's magic working on me.

We walked back to the house, and Auntie suggested I sit outside on the lawn and play with Luna, because we were desperate to get to know each other. Auntie propped the front door open and I went onto the lawn, under the pine tree. Luna loved me throwing the pinecones for her to catch. I couldn't throw very far, because it hurt my tummy, and she looked disappointed, so I just sat and stroked her. Close by I could hear a cock crowing and ducks quacking, and everywhere there was the sweet smell of cow manure. Usually I didn't mind that smell, but now it made me feel a bit sick.

Auntie came out and asked me if I would like some onions in my omelette, and perhaps some cheese too? I had only ever had plain omelettes. Auntie said, 'I'll cook two; one plain and one fancy, and we can share them, and you can tell me which one you like best.'

Small gestures like that have always made me feel warm inside. I could feel myself starting to cry again.

Both omelettes were delicious. Then I had a bath, and Auntie helped me, which made me feel much better. I wanted to go to sleep early, and was glad to be safe with Polish Teddy in a nice comfortable bed. My blanket was a deep red tartan, which made me think that while I was in Scotland, I would find out as much as I could about tartan. I was still feeling slightly shaky from being over-excited, and had a headache. Colours had lost their sharpness and objects seemed slightly blurred. When I closed my eyes, the room seemed to spin. I could smell and hear the sea, and even taste it, and feel the smooth but gritty rock against the palms of my hands, and see the glitter of the tiny specks of crystal in the rock, like grains of salt. And the greyness of the sea and blue patches of sky, as the clouds raced across it. And the *boom* of the waves as they hit the rocks, and the *sluck, sluck, sluck* of the water beneath us, and the rush of the water as it dragged back across the shingle before another wave crashed in. Auntie asked me what I was thinking about, but all I could say was, 'The Sea.'

The Man with the Black Gloves

Do you ever get the feeling, just before you go to sleep, that you are about to fall off a cliff? Then you fall, and in real life your leg gives a jerk? When I slept with Peter, he kicked me, and when we talked about it at breakfast, everyone said that they felt the same. That happens to me sometimes, but more often I have very strange thoughts, like a scrambled up cartoon, or like a silly Charlie Chaplin film. That's how I know I'm about to fall asleep. And if you have a nightmare that wakes you up, is it usually in the middle of the night, or just before it's time to wake up? I used to have mine in the middle of the night. Muriel once asked me, after one particularly horrible dream, if I could please have my nightmares just

157

before it was time for us all to wake up. That made me laugh, and I forget what had frightened me in the first place.

But on my first night with Auntie, I had one of the worst nightmares of my whole life, and it happened just before I dropped off to sleep. Auntie said that she'd like to read me *The Railway Children* before I went to sleep. I have to admit that I felt so exhausted that I wasn't really listening. I could see Auntie's lips moving and hear her voice, but it was coming from far away. I looked at the curtains and they seemed far away too. I wondered if Ursula would come and see me in this nice new house. Then Captain Haddock was shouting 'Blistering Barnacles, Pippa! Quick! Run away as fast as you can!' I had the feeling that someone was chasing me, but didn't want to look round. Then there was a big man in front of me, with huge black gloves on, and he had his arms raised and the fingers of his big black-gloved hands were getting ready to strangle me. I felt my legs kicking wildly and screamed as loudly as I could.

I sat up in bed, and Auntie was in front of me. She said, 'Goodness gracious Pippa, you gave me such a fright! Are you all right?' I thought I was still dreaming, so hid under the covers. I felt Auntie touch me and heard her say, 'It's all right. It's all right. It must have been a horrible dream.'
I put my head out from under the covers, and could see that it wasn't the middle of the night at all. There was still light coming through the curtains. Auntie was still sitting on my bed with *The Railway Children* in her lap. I must have fallen asleep while she was reading. I told her about the Man with the Black Gloves, and she looked very concerned. She said, 'It was a dream. But dreams are very important things, and tell us lots of things about what we are feeling.'
I remembered my Art Therapist, Stephen Hunter, saying exactly the same thing, and that made me feel much better. I said, 'I'm sorry for being naughty.'
Auntie looked very surprised. 'You haven't been naughty. You haven't done anything wrong.'

'I shouted at you today. I've never done that before. I'll try not to do it again.'

'But you didn't shout at me. You just expressed how you felt. What's wrong with that?'

'I'm worried that I might say something wrong, or do something that you don't like, then you might decide to give up your job, and then my father will get someone else to look after me.'

'What job?'

'You keep saying it's your job to look after me.'

'Oh, I see what you mean! Listen Pippa, I have an idea. Why don't you go back to sleep and then when you wake up we can have a nice breakfast together, and go down to the beach, and then we can talk some more? Would you like to do that?' I said I would. She said she would sit with me until I went to sleep, and would leave the landing light on, and the light on in the bathroom too. And if I needed anything in the night, all I had to do was call out for her, and she would hear me, and come and see what was the matter.

But for a long time, every night before I dropped off to sleep, I tried to run away from the Man with the Black Gloves, and screamed and fought with him. It worried Auntie so much that she said that she would like to talk to a doctor about it. I said that I needed to talk to someone like Stephen Hunter. Then I realised that Auntie was just like him. She was an expert in getting me to relax and talk about important things.

Porridge for breakfast, with syrup and milk

I slept very well in my new bed, and woke up with the sun on my face and the smell of the sea in my nose and the sound of a cockerel in my ears. It was only seven o'clock and Auntie was still asleep, so I began to read a TinTin book. I was happy on the outside, and excited about what new things I would discover during the day. I thought about Mummy and Muriel, and felt sad that they weren't with me to share this beautiful room and to meet Auntie. I felt sure that they would be friends with her and laugh a lot. I thought I was going to cry, but didn't. I heard some barking outside and saw Luna looking up at me. I knew she was calling for me to come outside to play with her.

I had always thought that porridge was some nasty slimy grey stuff that tasted of salt and reminded me of snot. But Auntie's breakfast porridge was creamy and golden looking, and tasted very sweet. She showed me how to make it, and it has been my favourite breakfast ever since. She said the secret was to think nice things about the person you were making the porridge for. If you were on your own then you had to think nice thoughts about yourself, which could be surprisingly difficult. If you did that, then you couldn't go wrong. Then she laughed and said that actually you could go badly wrong, like on the morning when she put the gas on too high and the doorbell rang, and she decided to have a nice long chat with the postman, because it would soon be her birthday and a parcel had arrived. But when she went into the kitchen, her pan was on fire, and she had to leave the kitchen window open all morning, to get rid of the awful smell. I laughed out loud at that and my tummy only hurt a little bit.

The other secret of making porridge is to soak the oats in milk during the night, and to add a tiny bit of salt while it is cooking. Then, when it was all ready, you add some fresh milk and a big spoonful of syrup, and close your eyes and think of all the nice things you are going to do during the coming day.

I was wearing my pyjamas and Auntie had on her nightie and dressing gown, and the sun was shining through the kitchen window, and Luna was outside, waiting for me. The porridge was warming me inside and I could feel it giving me energy. I wanted to go outside as soon as possible. I thought it might be nice to run on the beach with Luna, and throw a stick into the sea for her to collect and bring back to me, until both of us got bored. Then I looked at the clock and it was half past eight. I had forgotten to think about Mummy and Muriel, and it had been a long time since I had stopped and thought about Lucy at our special time. I stopped being happy, and put my spoon down. Auntie noticed, and asked me if anything was wrong. She said it was as if a little cloud had passed across my face.

I said, 'I feel happy. Thank you, Auntie, for helping me feel happy.'

She smiled and said, 'But... I think there is a *but*.'

'But I want to tell you lots of things, but I worry that I shouldn't.'

She looked serious and said, 'Don't worry, Pippa. I'm not going to tell anyone.'

'But what if I write something, or paint something and someone sees it, and starts to think that I'm not being looked after properly after all, and then I get taken away again?'

Auntie looked grave. 'I can tell you, Pippa, that that is just not going to happen. You can say and write and paint whatever you like.'

I decided to tell her about my special thinking times. I said, 'Every morning I try to stop and think about the last time I saw Mummy and...' I stopped myself.

'You can talk about your Auntie, you know. I imagine that you must miss her.'

'But can I really? If we hadn't met her, then I would still be with Mummy!' I still couldn't say *Muriel*. Just thinking about saying her name made me want to cry again, and I had decided that today was going to be a no-crying day.

Auntie said, 'That's true, in a way, but also not quite true.'

'I don't understand.'

Auntie was sitting opposite me. She smiled and said, 'Pippa, I know quite a lot about you. I've known about you for a long time. And Mr Macmillan has told me lots about you, and particularly about some of the painful things that have happened to you. From what I understand, your mummy wasn't well for a long time, and found it very difficult to look after you. There had been some very difficult incidents, and sometimes you were... I can't put it in any other way... you were left on your own, and were possibly in danger.'

I looked out of the window. Auntie said, 'Pippa, please listen to me. I know you don't like to think about the past, but it's very important. I know that some enormous damage has been done to you. I think to myself, "What can I, Aileen Pirie, possibly do to make you, Pippa Dunbar, feel better again?" And I asked Mr Macmillan the same question.'

I didn't look at her. I wanted to, but what she was saying was making me feel very nervous and uncomfortable. I touched the knife that was next to my plate. It was lovely and shiny, and when I moved it slightly, the sun shining on it made a tiny spot of light that moved on the wall facing me.

Actually, my hand was shaking and I couldn't stop it.

Auntie had stopped talking. I wouldn't look at her. Then she said, very quietly 'Pippa, please look at me.'

I whispered, 'I can't.'

She whispered back, 'Yes you can. What I'm going to say is very important.'

I looked in her eyes and she carried on talking to me. Her voice was slightly wobbly. I could tell that she was just as full of feeling as I was, and she looked like she was going to cry. I didn't want her to cry. 'We both, Mr Macmillan and I, we have both agreed that it is important to help you talk about the past, about what is happening now, and about what is going to happen in the future. We think it is very important that we help you to talk about Mummy, and especially about your Auntie Muriel, who we know loves you so very much. And I have the feeling that Muriel saved you and your Mummy.'

I was shocked to hear her say that she knew that Muriel loved me. I thought that the whole problem was Muriel's love for Mummy and me. Auntie said, 'There. I've said her name again. Your lovely Auntie Muriel. How does that feel?'

I felt all the delicious porridge start to rise up into my mouth. It tasted bitter and felt slimy. I didn't want to be sick, so swallowed hard, and coughed and stamped my foot, and hit myself on my knee with my fist, to try to force the porridge back down again. I wanted to run upstairs. I got up, but then sat back down again. I thought if I closed my eyes, then I might be able to say all the big important things that I had wanted to say to someone since I had been taken away from school. Then a picture of Stephen Hunter came into my mind. I never had any problems telling him everything. I opened my eyes and Auntie was looking right at me and smiling. She said, 'Tell me Pippa, what was it that Muriel did that made you feel better? If you fell over, or were feeling sad, or needed to talk about something, what did Muriel do to make it all better?'

I couldn't answer that question. I looked at Auntie, and her face was changing into Muriel's. The lines around Auntie's face were melting, and her pink lips were changing to a much deeper shade of red, and her blue-grey eyes were becoming lovely Muriel blue. And her neat grey hair was becoming blond and untidy, and curly strands were escaping from where she had tried to pin them in place, but were getting in her eyes, so that she had to push them away with her fists, or blow at them loudly, upwards through her lips, which was the thing that I most liked watching her do. And Auntie's smell of perfume was becoming the lovely smell of sweet sweat that Muriel always had, no matter how much she washed under her arms, or whatever strong soap she used. And I was floating back in time, to shortly after Muriel came to live with us, when I discovered that Mummy loved that smell as much as I did, because once, when she was sorting out the dirty laundry, I saw her pick up Muriel's blouse and breathe in the smell of it deeply. Then she sighed and whispered to herself, 'Muriel Standish, how is it possible that I can love you so very much?'

I heard Auntie talking to me, but she sounded just like Muriel. 'So, Pippa, how do you think I knew what books to buy you, to put in your bedroom? I didn't just guess. I phoned up your Mummy and Muriel's house and I spoke to Muriel. Your Mummy had gone up to London, so I told Muriel who I was, and all about what had happened to you, and how you were feeling, and that I had been chosen as the person who was going to look after you and make you feel better.'

I gasped. Auntie looked like herself again. 'You spoke to Muriel?'

'Yes I did. And she said that she was very happy to know that you were being cared for properly. I think that perhaps she used the word *delighted*, but it could have been *thrilled*. Anyway, she used a word that was very powerful, very *emotive,* to describe how she felt. I was very nervous about talking to her. She must have felt that in my voice. I thought I was going to cry, but I didn't want to do that. I wanted Muriel to feel that I was strong. Strong enough to care for you, and protect you, and heal you, and help you grow. I asked Muriel to tell me all about the things you liked, and she gave me a great long list. There were so many things on her list, so I had to run and get a piece of paper and a pen and write them all down. So I ordered as many books as I could about those subjects. She mentioned an Italian painter beginning with M, but she didn't know exactly how to spell his name, so I thought that perhaps it was Michelangelo. I knew it wasn't Mondrian, because he's Dutch, but I like him a lot, so wrote that down. I bought books about all the painters she mentioned. I have an idea that, like me, you might prefer Mondrian to Michelangelo.'

I said, 'It's Modigliani. We liked his paintings a lot, but I think I shouldn't look at them anymore.'

'Why not?'

I could feel myself going red. 'I just shouldn't.'

Auntie laughed. 'Ah! I think I know why.'

I said, 'I think liking Modigliani got us into trouble.'

Auntie smiled. 'Let's talk about all that another time. It's a very big subject, and very important.'

We didn't say anything for a little while. A big fat bee was buzzing by the window and Auntie got up. I thought perhaps she was going to kill it, but she opened the window and said, 'Come on now, out you go. Go outside where you belong, among the flowers.'

She sat down opposite me again. She said, 'I asked Muriel what I should do to make you feel better, and she said I should try to get you back to sleeping and eating well. And she said that they both missed you very much, but were being very strong. And now that we had talked together, she was sure that they could find it just a tiny bit easier to live their lives. I told Muriel, "I'm very sorry, but I am so full of emotion," and Muriel said that she was glad that I had called. She said that she knew that you would be all right, because you are a strong girl. I had to say goodbye and put the phone down quickly, because I was crying so much, just like I am now.'

I rushed towards Auntie, and she opened her arms and I turned round and she pulled me towards her. I said, 'When I was sad or upset, or just tired and a bit grumpy, Muriel used to put me on her lap and blow on my neck and kiss it, and I would sit there and suck my thumb, and then everything felt all right. And Mummy used to sit and watch us and smile, so then I knew that she was happy too. And Muriel used to tickle my tummy and call me funny names, and I knew that as long as she lived with us, then everything would be all right. And when I think about that, my heart just wants to burst, and I don't know if I am ever going to see them again.'
I didn't know what else to say. Auntie pulled me onto her lap and blew on my neck, and said, 'Just like that?'
And I said 'Yes, thank you very much' and she laughed.
She said, 'So you see, Pippa, I know a little bit about you, and I hope you might be able to tell me some more.'
I said, 'And please can you tell me something about yourself?'
She smiled and said, 'Of course I can. Just ask me some questions, and I'll do my best to answer. But please can we go down to the beach now? I can see some clouds heading our way, and the forecast is for rain later.'

Mrs Aileen Pirie
We sat on the beach together. During the night, the tide had gone out and was now coming back in again. I had to close my eyes, to stop myself from becoming overpowered by what I could see in front of me. I told Auntie about that and she said, 'You'll have plenty of time to get used to this beach. And one day, who knows, it might even belong to you.'

I couldn't imagine that I could possibly get used to this beach. There was sand and seaweed, and rocks and pebbles, and rock pools and my favourite little birds, and a sky that never seemed to keep still. I had to concentrate very hard to remember that I was there to find out all about my new auntie.

And this is what I discovered. Mrs Aileen Pirie was born Aileen Dunbar in 1917, during the First World War, in the small fishing port of Stranhaven, south of Aberdeen. She had two older brothers, so everyone always treated her as the baby in the family, which suited her just fine. Her father, Willie Dunbar, came from a long line of blacksmiths, who used to make things out of metal, and put shoes on horses and fix all kinds of machinery. He went away to The War, and when he came back he had two fingers missing. Aileen's father was also a Jack-Of-All-Trades, so when more people in the area bought cars and tractors, he opened a garage. He was a very generous man, and believed that education was a great gift. He was always telling his children to work as hard as they could in school, and was always very pleased when they had good school reports.

Auntie said that her father and mother were Socialists, and believed that you should share whatever you had with other people. When Willie came back from The War, he became more convinced than ever that Socialism was the only way to make sure that everyone was treated fairly. Most people in Stranhaven went to church and were honest God-fearing folk, but Willie disagreed with the Minister about religion. The two of them would meet in the evening and discuss religion and politics. Willie said that organised religion was just another way of keeping the poor people ignorant, and stopping them from rising up and taking what was their fair share of the wealth from the land and sea. Though Willie and the Minister would have heated debates about religion, they would always finish the evening with a few glasses of whisky. Then the Minister would laugh and say things like, 'If you look closely at The New Testament you will find that Christ was probably the very first Socialist.' Auntie said that their family was a happy one, and though they weren't rich, they never wanted for anything, and she always felt loved and content.

People in that part of Scotland had a very strong accent, and had so many unusual words that it was almost as if they spoke a foreign language. Even people from other parts of Scotland couldn't understand them. Just to prove it, Auntie said something to me, and I had no idea what she was saying. It sounded like Norwegian, or perhaps Spanish. (I had never heard either of those languages, but discovered later that I was right about the Norwegian, because lots of Vikings had lived in that part of Scotland).

She got married to a local man who worked on farms. His dream was to own his own farm, but he was very unlucky. One day he bought a piece of land without telling Auntie. It turned out to be useless for growing crops, and their animals always seemed to be sick. It took many years before they had a baby, but eventually they had a little boy called Callum. Callum was the love of Auntie's life, and the apple of his father's eye. Because they had been trying for a baby for so long, he was extra precious. One day, when he was seven years old, he went to school and was perfectly well, but his teacher sent him home because he had a bad headache. He became terribly ill in the night, and died suddenly. The shock was so great that Auntie never really recovered. She said that she became so sad that she thought she wouldn't be able to live anymore. On some days, she couldn't get out of bed, and when she did, her head felt like it was full of cotton wool. Her feet felt as if she was wearing diver's boots, so she could hardly lift them to walk. And then, for no good reason, she started to blame her husband for the death of their son. She knew that was ridiculous, because it really was nobody's fault that he became ill. But at the time, Auntie felt that she had to blame someone. She stopped believing in God, but that wasn't enough, so she turned against her poor husband. She told me that she couldn't *respond* to him anymore. So after a while he left her and went to live in a city called Aberdeen. There he worked in a shop, and because he was very good at his job, he was promoted to manager. But he met another woman, and didn't come back to Stranhaven. Auntie became very ill and went back to live with her parents, who were very happy to look after her. That was at the time that Mummy and Daddy got married.

Auntie didn't blame her husband for leaving her. She knew that she had become impossible to live with. It was the grief that was eating her up, like a huge worm inside her. But then a man moved into Stranhaven who became very friendly with Auntie. He worked for the local newspaper and was a Socialist. He met Auntie on the beach one day, and they got talking, and she suddenly told this man all her troubles. Auntie wept so much that the man took her back to his house and made her drink lots of tea, and cooked her a meal of fresh fish. Suddenly she felt that the terrible pain in her heart was beginning to ease. The man loved writing and he loved Art, and Auntie discovered that she was actually very good at painting, and the man encouraged her a lot. He was always writing, and wrote three very famous books about the area that they lived in. The first book was about a girl who lived on a farm, and about the local people, and their lives and personalities, and the arguments and friendships that they had before the First World War. His other books were about life after The First World War, and how the people's lives were changed forever.

Auntie spent a lot of time with this man, and soon they fell in love with each other. She didn't want to marry him, but he had three children to look after, because his wife had died. So, with time, Auntie became like a stepmother to them. She said that she and the man might just as well have got married, because they spent all their time together. She felt she had been given what she called 'a new lease of life'.

Auntie smiled when she talked about the man. She said that women loved to read his books, because he really understood women, and what made them tick. Soon the man became quite famous, and was asked to give a talk in Aberdeen. Auntie went with him, but she saw her husband in the audience, with his new lady friend. After the talk, Auntie's husband went to have a chat with the man, but Auntie was very embarrassed and left the room. Afterwards the man told her that her husband had said, 'Please let me shake your hand. Thank you for making Aileen happy again.' The man was very surprised, but pleased. Auntie's husband said that he should be proud of himself, because Auntie was a fine woman and deserved the best in life, and as far as he was concerned, the man was a great writer and a true Socialist, and that was good enough for him. Then he winked and said, 'Of course, everyone knows that Aileen is the heroine of your books. You can change her name and make her a teacher, but she's obviously Aileen.'

Then they both laughed and went to the bar and became very good friends. Aileen and her husband got divorced, and she and the man lived in the same house together. Both of those things caused a scandal in Stranhaven, because in those days, people didn't get divorced, and they certainly didn't live together without being married. That was known as 'living in sin'. And if a woman had a baby and she wasn't married, then that was even more of a sin, and as the child got older, people disliked the child as much as the mother, just because the mother wasn't married. So Auntie and the man decided to get married, but they never had any more children, even though they loved each other a lot. Her ex-husband married his new lady friend, and they had three children, one after the other. Auntie was surprised, and delighted, to discover that she liked the new wife very much, and was very happy that they had children. That was the last thing that Auntie said about her ex-husband and his wife, but it set off a question in my mind, that I knew I would have to ask Auntie about one day.

Auntie said that she still felt a sadness for Wee Callum, and she knew that it would never really go away, and that she would never forget him. But she had her man now, and a new family, and that was a great comfort to her. I said, 'So will I meet your new husband one day?'

She said, 'Oh yes, he's going to come to see us soon. He's really looking forward to meeting you.' I wasn't sure what to think about that. I didn't like men very much. Auntie said, 'His name is Tom; Tom Pirie, and his children... our children, are Maggie, Nicol and Jessie. If you like, you can call my husband Uncle Tom. I know that he would like that.'

'Would your children be like my cousins then?'

'I think so. Yes, that sounds right, though really you are not at all related. I think of them as being my own children, so it feels right that they should be your cousins.'

That sounded like an exciting idea, but Auntie changed the subject. 'Do you know, Pippa, I have to see the sea every day. Some people don't feel that they can face the day until they have had a cup of coffee or tea, or a cigarette, or have put their lipstick on. Some women I know have to do all those things before they feel good enough to leave the house. Well, I like all those things - not the cigarettes anymore, because they are very bad for you -but I feel that I must see the sea every day. Being by the sea is like... I don't know what it's like. I can't put it into words. It's a very special feeling.'

Then Auntie told me all about my father. Before she started, she said, 'I know you've only met your daddy a few times. And I have the feeling that he frightened you, and perhaps you don't feel very comfortable about thinking about him.' I didn't say anything. She said, 'Is that right, Pippa?' I nodded. Auntie sighed. 'But we have to talk about him. It's important that you know something about him. It will help you to understand what has happened to you. And I believe it will make you feel better.'

Something about the way she said the word *believe* made me listen very carefully, though I still felt very uncomfortable.

Auntie Aileen's father was called Willie, and he had a brother called Robert. Everyone called them Willie and Rab. Rab was my daddy's father, and my grandfather. He was the complete opposite of Aileen's father. Rab didn't like to get his hands dirty, and believed in God, and left Stranhaven as soon as he could. He became a shopkeeper in the same town where I had just been in hospital. He was always trying to get his brother Willie to earn more money. But Willie would laugh and say, 'We have enough. After all, we have a roof over our heads, and enough food to eat, and clothes to wear.'

And Rab would say, 'Aye, you have that, but your house is old and full of holes and your wife hasn't had a new coat for years, and when was the last time you ate something other than fish and tatties?'

That was actually quite a rude thing to say, even though he meant it as a joke. Willie's wife got angry and said that her coat might be old, but it was warm and would last her for at least another ten winters, and her food might be plain, but her children had never complained and would never go hungry.

Auntie smiled at me and said, 'That was quite true, though I did occasionally want to eat some chicken, and have a new dress and a pair of fine shoes, instead of wearing rough boots all the time. Rab had a son called Andrew, who is your father. Rab was determined that Andrew would go to a fine school and go to University, and perhaps become a doctor or a solicitor. Andrew was a quiet and sensitive boy, but good at sports and very good at arithmetic. But most of all he loved drawing and painting. Andrew's mother died suddenly when he was little, so he used to come up here for his holidays, because his father didn't have much time to look after him. We used to spend all our time together, and I would say that when we were young we were more like brother and sister. He was a very sweet boy, and liked exactly the same things as me, and had a lovely singing voice, and played the piano. But Andrew's father decided to send him away to boarding school. Rab was a Protestant but, for some reason, he thought that the Catholics were the best educated of all the Scots, so he sent Andrew to a Roman Catholic boarding school. Andrew hated it at first, because all the other boys came from wealthy Catholic families and Andrew was a Protestant boy. At first, the other boys were cruel to him and called him names, but Andrew was clever and good at sports, so soon he became very popular.

'The men who were in charge of the school were priests called *Jesuits*, and were very hard. They believed that it was good to be cruel to boys, and teach them to fear God. Surprisingly, Andrew enjoyed the hard life of the school. He didn't mind the horrible food, or playing sports outside in the freezing cold, or having only cold water to wash with, or being hit by the Jesuits every once in a while. He said it built his character and made him into a man, and he liked the Jesuits a lot. But when I met Andrew again, he seemed to have forced all the soft and gentle parts of himself deep down inside. It was as if he had squeezed all his goodness into a strong wooden box and hammered the lid down shut with strong nails.'
I thought of a coffin with love inside.

Auntie said that my father didn't want to dance with her anymore, or sing and play music, or talk about Art, or go for long walks with her and sit looking at the sea. He just talked about the power of money, and about how he was going to buy as much land as he possibly could. He said that Stranhaven and the town where he lived were one-horse towns, and he longed to see the world and make his fortune. That made me think of Puss in Boots and Dick Whittington. And my father did make his fortune. Once he boasted to Aileen that his aim in life was to own as much land and property as the Duke of Westminster, who is now the richest man in Britain, and even wealthier than the Queen. She said, 'And the strange thing is that Nicol, Uncle Tom's son, reminds me so much of your father, before he went to boarding school. He's kind, and thoughtful, and loves to talk and play with girls. Uncle Tom says that he will never send his children away to school. I'm very glad about that, because I love them all dearly, and want Nicol to stay just the way he is now.'

I said, 'Auntie, please! Please can you stop talking about my father? I'm getting a headache and my tummy's hurting.'

'There's just one more important thing that I need to tell you, and then I promise I'll stop for now. But we still must talk about him in the future, because he is such an important person in your life... and in my life too. It might be painful, but in the end it will be good for you, and for me,'

'Auntie, are you being cruel to be kind?'

She looked shocked and said, 'Oh no! I could never be cruel to you, Pippa! I would never want to be cruel to anyone, and especially not you!'

I was a bit taken aback by the force of her reaction. I said, 'I'm sorry Auntie, it was just a joke.'

She looked at me and smiled. She said, 'I knew it. Muriel was right of course. You are a big strong girl. Of course it's a funny joke. I can be a bit too serious sometimes.'

I said, 'So can Muriel.' I was surprised that I had said that, but it was true, because Muriel knew that I needed her to tell me the truth, and to help me understand about what was going on in my life. Now Auntie was doing the same.

Then Auntie said something that really bothered me, and has bothered me ever since. She said that my father became a man who wasn't very comfortable with girls and women. She said that he had loved to play and talk with her when they were children, but when he became a teenager he began to say rude things about girls and women. Once he said that the only reason he would ever marry and have children was so that he could have a boy. Then he would teach him all about business, so one day he would inherit his fortune. Auntie had asked him, 'But what if your wife has a girl? Why can't she run the business and then look after it after you die?' He had just laughed and told her not to be ridiculous.

After that, I didn't want to hear any more. But Auntie said that she had almost finished. She used the word *believe* again. 'You see, Pippa, I have never actually believed a word that your father has said since he went to that school. I can't believe that the quiet, sensitive, sweet cousin of mine could become a bitter and twisted businessman, who says silly things about girls and women. I believe that deep down inside he is still that

173

same sweet boy that I once knew. I don't know why I believe that, but I do. In the same way, I look at his lovely, sweet and sensitive daughter, who has exactly the same eyes as him, and the same walk, and the same way of moving her hands when she talks, and I believe that whatever happens to you, you will always be one of the sweetest girls in the whole world. And now I feel tired out and am desperate for a cup of tea and a little treat. Aren't you?'

I said, 'Auntie, did you have a crush on Daddy when you were growing up?'

Auntie went red. 'Whatever do you mean Pippa? Whatever gave you that idea?'

I smiled. It was the first time I had said *Daddy* for a long time. We shared a Bounty with our cup of tea.

What if I paint you a picture?

I was tired of listening, and a bit frightened of what I was going to hear next. I also had a question to ask that had been in my mind for a few years, and now I knew that Auntie had exactly the information I needed. I felt sure that she wouldn't mind answering my question, but I didn't quite know how to ask it. So instead I asked Auntie if I could paint a picture for her, and she said that would be a lovely idea. I said, 'But first, please can you tell me all about the sea?'

She said, 'I'll talk to you about it on the beach.' We walked back down to the beach again, and Auntie said, 'Once I took my paints down to the sea, because I had an idea. I asked myself, 'What would happen if instead of the sky being reflected in the sea, the land and the sea were reflected in the sky? I had seen the sky like that one sunset, but it was very hard to tell exactly what I had seen, because I had broken my glasses, so everything was a little blurred. It made the scene look like an Impressionist painting, if you know what I mean. Do you know about the Impressionists, Pippa?'

I said that I knew a lot about the Impressionists and that someone had once said that I was like one. I recited a long list of all the Impressionists I knew about. I left out Van Gogh, to see what Auntie would say, and asked me, 'And what about Vincent Van Gogh?'

'It's very strange, Auntie, because on some days I like his paintings, but on other days they make me feel uncomfortable inside.'

Auntie was impressed. 'That's a very grown up observation, if you don't mind me saying so.'

I explained that once I had spent a whole hour talking to Stephen Hunter about Van Gogh. Stephen explained that lots of people reacted like that. Van Gogh had experienced changes of mood, so his paintings appealed to you in different ways, depending on your own mood. I loved to talk with Stephen about moods, because Mummy's changing moods had been such a feature of my life. Sometimes I wondered if people looking at my paintings might feel the same.

I said, 'The only problem is that when I start to paint, I never quite know what is going to come out. And I know that some people don't like what I paint.' Auntie flicked through the pages in my painting pad, and looked closely at a painting I had done while I was in hospital. It was of a lady with an appendix scar. Auntie said, 'I think this might be Muriel.' I didn't say anything and went quite red. Auntie smiled. I said, 'You won't write down what I say, will you? You won't tell anyone?'

'No, I won't tell anyone.'

'Will you promise?'

'Well it depends what it is. It's not good to keep secrets. If it's something very serious, then I might have to tell Mr Macmillan, but I would always talk to you about it first.'

I told her about Frances in the bath, and how lovely she had looked, and how her loveliness had made me want to paint her. I told her about my paintings of Mummy and Muriel touching each other. And about how Daddy had taken photos of my pictures, and had sent someone to the house after we had left, to take photos of more of my paintings, so Daddy could use them as evidence against Mummy and Muriel in The Court.

I could see that Auntie was quite shocked about that. She said, 'I suppose that grown-ups and children might be surprised to know that you had been painting pictures of people in the nude. Some people might be worried that a little girl might be thinking about those things. I'm not one of those people though.'

I wanted to make absolutely sure that Auntie understood me, because I was desperate to paint again, but wouldn't do it unless I knew that I could completely trust her. 'But museums and art galleries and art books are full of pictures of people with no clothes on! Most of Henry Moore's sculptures, and lots of Matisse and Modigliani's paintings, are of people with nothing on! And in the church there are statues and paintings of Jesus on the cross, and he always has only a little piece of cloth covering his...you know.'

Auntie laughed. 'I never thought I'd be spending time talking to a child about Henry Moore and Matisse, or even Modigliani! It's wonderful! But let's think about this together. Let's imagine that I'm Mr Macmillan.' That was a funny idea. 'And let's suppose he comes to visit you and he sees lots of drawings and paintings of me in the nude. What is he going to think?'

'He's going to think that I like painting naked people.'

'That's true, Pippa, but I think he would be a bit surprised. He might wonder if I had been walking around naked in front of you, or swimming naked in the sea with you. He might not mind, but he might wonder if he could trust me, and I would have a lot of explaining to do. You see, in Scotland, most people don't like children to know about grown-ups' bodies and how they work.'

'You mean about S-E-X?'

'Yes, about that.'

The cork was now well and truly out of the bottle. I said, 'That's what all the trouble was about, I think. My daddy has got photos of Mummy and her lady friend and me with nothing on, in a swimming pool in Malaysia. He came to see us, and took the photos out of an envelope and sneered at Mummy, and said that Muriel was another pretty young nurse who Mummy had found to look after her and me. I didn't quite understand what he was saying, but I know that he was trying to hurt Mummy. And he said all those hurtful things in front of me. I used to have a bath with Mummy. There's nothing wrong with that. And we used to see each other when we were in the changing rooms at the swimming pool. And sometimes I had a bath with Muriel. I loved doing that.' Then I told her about when the Nasty Nun had beaten me, and how Muriel had sat in the bath with me, and kissed every single one of my cuts and bruises, to make them better.

Auntie was very quiet. We looked at the sea together. Seagulls were skimming the waves and crying and landing on the sand in front of us. They seemed to be solitary birds, who were always fighting each other. But the little black and white birds were having a lovely time together. They always seemed to be chatting and getting on with their business at the same time. I imagined them gossiping about each other and complaining about the seagulls, and laughing about them for not liking to eat all the delicious tiny worms in the sand. Auntie said, 'I didn't know about that.'

'About what?' I had stopped thinking about being beaten, and was busy concentrating on the birds.

'Pippa, I didn't know about the nun hitting you. It's not written down anywhere.'

'Well it's true. That's why Mummy took me away from Catholic schools. A doctor came to our house and saw all my cuts and bruises, and said it was a disgrace. He knew that I was traumatised and sent me to see Stephen Hunter.'

'You must have felt terrible.'

'I did. But I soon got better, because I knew that Mummy and Muriel wouldn't let it happen again. If I ever had to go to another Catholic school, I don't think I could learn anything. I'd be too frightened of being hit again.'

'Do you still have the marks on you?'

'I think so, but I never look at my bottom, so I'm not really sure. Perhaps the doctors saw them while they were operating on me and sticking things up inside me.'

'And I didn't know about Mummy's lady friend in Malaysia, or the photographs.'

'Well, that's true as well.' I told her about how the nasty guest had attacked Mummy's friend, and about Daddy sending Mummy and me back to England, which made Mummy become a lonely alcoholic. And I told her about Uncle Eric, and Lady Celia, and how we met Muriel and how, as far as I knew, Muriel had saved our lives.

Auntie looked out to sea. Finally, she said, 'There's nothing written about any of that. Nothing at all.'

I said, 'Well now you know.' I didn't want to talk about it anymore. I felt disgusted by the memory of my father sitting in our kitchen with Mr Shepherd. No matter how hard I concentrated on the lovely little birds, that picture wouldn't go away. I didn't want to sit on his beach anymore, even if it was the most beautiful place in the whole world.

Auntie looked at me and said, 'Pippa, what are you thinking about?'

I said, 'If I tell you, will you tell me what you are thinking about too?' That really was quite cheeky of me, because I still didn't know Auntie very well. That's exactly how I would have spoken to Muriel, though I would have been much more careful with Mummy. And anyway, I couldn't remember Mummy ever asking me a question like that.

Auntie laughed. She said, 'Is that how you talk to Muriel?'

'I used to. Yes.'

'Sorry. I was thinking that I would love to meet Muriel. Will you tell me more about her? And about Mummy?'

'I'd like to, but I think it might make me feel too sad.'

'Oh dear. But you can talk to me about them whenever you like. I'd really like to know all about them.'

'I think I might cry.'

'Is that a bad thing?' I explained why I didn't like crying. She said, 'But if you avoid talking about painful things because it

178

might make you cry, then your feelings can get all bottled up inside you. Sometimes people do that, and it makes them feel ill. That's what happened to me. It's probably what happened to your mummy too.'

'Is that what happened to me? Is that why I had a bad appendix?'

'Perhaps. I think I would need to know a bit more about what happened to you, before I could know what made you ill. But tell me, what were you thinking just now?'

'I was thinking that I'd like to paint again. I wanted to paint this beach. But then I thought about my father being so nasty to Mummy and to Muriel and to me, and now I don't want to be here anymore. It feels disgusting.'

'Well that's all the more reason to paint it. Is that what Stephen Hunter might have said?'

'Yes! He said the very same thing to me once. How did you know?'

'I read a very, very long report that he wrote about you. It was about twenty pages long! He really is a most fascinating man.'

'Daddy hated him. He called him a *shirt lifter*.'

Auntie said, 'Oh.'

I said, 'I'm sorry Auntie, I know it's wrong to use words like that. I don't know what it means. It sounded so horrible.'

'Where did you hear it? Did your father say it in front of you?'

'He said it to Mummy on the phone once. Mummy was terribly upset about it.'

You can paint whatever you like

I said, 'Please can I paint you a surprise picture?

'Will it be a naked lady?'

'Wait and see!' I knew I could completely trust Auntie, so started to play about, and she kept laughing at me. We had what I can only describe as a wonderful afternoon. I made several drawings of Luna. As I was sketching, I imagined that I was Matthew McCusker, or Henry Moore, preparing to make a grand work of Art. I was so absorbed in what I was doing, that I almost forgot that I hated my father so much. We had a picnic on the beach, and after we had eaten, Auntie said, 'You know,

Pippa, you can paint whatever you like. All I ask is that you show me what you have done, and talk to me about. It will be between you and me, just like Stephen Hunter. I won't show your paintings to anyone else, unless you want me to.'

'But Stephen Hunter wrote about me.'

'That's true, because it was part of his job to write something every time he saw you, and your mummy asked him to write a special report about you, to be read out in The Court. Mummy hoped that what Stephen wrote would help the Judge understand that she was a good mother, and was looking after you properly. Unfortunately, the Judge didn't agree.'

'What did Stephen Hunter say?'

'He said that you are a brilliant artist, and that your gift needs to be nurtured. That means it must be fed and cared for, so that it grows well; just like a child. He said that you don't realise it, but you use your Art to help you explore your feelings, and to tell people how you are feeling. He said that artists are honest people who must be allowed to paint whatever they like. He said that some people may find it difficult to understand how a young child could paint people with no clothes on, but he thought that this was perfectly natural. He also said that your parents, he meant Mummy and Muriel, were doing a wonderful job of looking after you.'

'So why didn't The Judge listen?'

'Because your father's barrister was very clever and persuasive. He made The Judge believe that you would be better off away from Mummy and Muriel.'

'And do you believe that?'

'I *believe* that mothers are the most important people in the world. Sometimes they need help to do their job well. That says everything about what I feel about what happened to you.'

She didn't say that she agreed with The Judge, or my father, so I supposed that she thought I should be with Mummy and Muriel. That was good enough for me, and after that, I always told her about everything that was worrying me.

And from that moment, I felt myself getting better. It was still painful to walk quickly, but as each day passed, I felt physically stronger. And I felt happier too. I laughed with Luna, and held Auntie's hand, and she let me sit on her lap, and I went back to sucking my thumb. The urge to paint and draw came back to me, as powerful as ever. I filled notebooks with drawings, and painted scenes from the beach as often as I could. The only thing I didn't do was explore the farm. Something happened there that upset me terribly. I still shudder when I think about it.

The piglets

One day, I asked Auntie if she would take me to have a look around the farm. She said, 'You must be feeling better now.'

'Not completely.'

'Don't worry. You're not going to go back to school. It's hardly worth it, and I can teach you lots of interesting things myself.'

That was true. I had been learning how to cook and sew and knit, and Auntie had a concertina, and was giving me lessons. I already knew about playing the piano, because Muriel had been teaching me, but the concertina was quite magical. It took me a while to get used to pulling and pushing the concertina in and out, and knowing exactly where to put my fingers, but Auntie said I was a very fast learner. She taught me a lovely Irish tune called 'Din Tarrant's Polka Number 2', and told me that once I had mastered that she would teach me how to play the theme tune to Captain Pugwash.

So we went for a walk around the farm, and saw the huge sow with her litter of twelve piglets. She was in a stall with a concrete floor, and was lying on her side, feeding them. I was delighted, fascinated and disgusted at the same time. All the piglets were fighting to get hold of the mother's teats, and all of them were successful, apart from one small one that his brothers and sisters kept pushing away. Auntie explained that he was the runt of the litter. She said that it wouldn't matter how much we tried to help him, he would never get enough milk.

181

I nearly cried, watching that poor creature being starved of his mother's milk. I told Auntie that I was too upset to watch anymore. She said that Nature is cruel, but there was nothing that we could do, because there was very likely something wrong with the piglet, and it would probably die anyway.

Watching the pig and her litter of piglets had convinced me that Mummy and all the Jews were right not to eat pork.

But the next day we saw something terrible. To get to the beach we had to walk past a great big pile of manure. After it rained and the sun came out, the heap would start to steam and give off a very strong smell. I didn't mind that at all; in fact, I found it quite fascinating to look at, with its mixture of strong colours and the dark brown oily liquid that oozed out of it. Auntie was walking slightly ahead of me and I was playing with Luna. Suddenly Auntie stopped at the manure heap and started to throw straw onto it. I went towards her and she said, 'Don't look, Pippa!'

But it was too late. I saw the small baby piglet thrown on the heap. It was dead and looked slightly squashed. Auntie said, 'The poor thing! The mother probably rolled over and squashed it. That happens all the time with pigs.'

I started to shake all over. Auntie told me to get her some more straw to cover up the piglet. I tried to pick up bits of straw but I just kept dropping them. Auntie said, 'Let's go back home. I'll ask Mr Ross to give the piglet a proper burial.'

Mr Ross and his wife ran the farm. He was always either getting on his tractor and driving away, or parking his tractor and getting off it. He always waved at me.

I was very upset, and the upset was so great that I didn't want to go outside at all. Auntie asked me to tell her exactly how I felt, but I didn't know. So she told me a story about when she was little and had seen a dead cat by the side of the road. She had been disgusted by it, but also felt sad that it was dead, and sorry for its owner. But I wasn't upset for any of those reasons, and suddenly I realised exactly what was going through my mind. It was about the poor piglet being abandoned by its mother, and then it's dead body being thrown onto a pile of manure and left to rot in the sunshine. How could a mother behave like that? Surely she should have seen that all the other piglets were getting enough milk, and she could have pushed one of them out of the way, so that the little one could have had his fair share? But really I was thinking about my own mother when I was little, and how I must have been like the poor little runt, upstairs in my freezing cold bedroom. All afternoon I felt covered by a terrible sadness, and it seemed as if the days of pleasure and fun with Auntie had never existed.

Father McGann

We had a telephone in the hall, and it used to ring quite a lot. I knew that it couldn't possibly be Mummy ringing, or anyone who wanted to talk to me. But I could now tell, from the tone of Auntie Aileen's voice, if it was a call from her husband, or her stepchildren, or from someone who was ringing to talk about me. If it was her husband, then she usually had a laugh in her voice, and afterwards she would smile and laugh with me and sing to herself. If it was from her stepchildren, then she would spend a long time trying to sort out squabbles between them, and often she would sigh afterwards and make herself a cup of tea. But if it was someone else, like Mr Shepherd or someone from his office, then she would have a serious voice, and afterwards she would frown.

One day, the phone rang and afterwards Auntie came to find me. I was under the pine tree with Luna. Auntie was frowning and said, 'Pippa, let's have a little chat.'
I have never liked anyone saying that to me. Nowadays it makes me feel guilty, and I imagine immediately that I have done something wrong. But in those days, it was always because someone had told Auntie to do something with me. I guessed it could be about one of two things; going to school or going to Mass. I had no wish to do either.
Auntie said, 'It's about being a Catholic. We have to think about your religion. That was Father McGann on the telephone. He's the local Catholic priest. He wants us to visit his church this afternoon and have a wee talk with you.'

I could tell that Auntie didn't think that was a good idea, but I wanted to make her life as easy as possible, so

I tried to sound cheerful. 'I suppose someone like Mr Shepherd has told him about me. I know The Court wants me to be a Good Catholic Girl.'

'Your father wants you to be brought up as a Catholic, and The Court agreed that he could do that. But whether you are a Good Catholic or not? Well, I don't quite know how you can measure that.'

I knew exactly how. 'It's easy, Auntie. You have to try not to sin, and obey the teachings of The Church. That means going to Mass every Sunday.'

'Ah. Is it as easy as that?'

'I think so.'

'And do you *want* to go to Mass every Sunday?'

'No. I'm Jewish. And churches frighten me. I can't look at the pictures of people beating Jesus. It reminds me of my grandfather.' I told Auntie all about Mummy's father being beaten to death in the street by the laughing Nazis, and how Mummy escaped in an armchair on the back of a lorry.

Auntie was shocked. I didn't like Auntie to be shocked, so I touched her on the arm and said, 'Don't worry Auntie, I'll go to the church and listen to the priest, and I will go to Mass every Sunday. But please will you promise never to leave me in the church on my own?'

I told her about the time I had wet myself and gone into shock. I did not tell her about Mummy almost attacking me, and the priest telling me in confession that I must have deserved it. She said, 'You poor lamb! It's a wonder that you are so happy and cheerful.' It wasn't a wonder to me. Muriel had saved my life, and now Auntie was doing the same.

So after lunch, we took a taxi into Kirkbrae, and went to see Father McGann in his church. Father McGann was a fat man with a red face. I imagined his housekeeper giving him a Full English Cooked Breakfast every morning, and a big meal in the evening. He reminded me of Friar Tuck. He said how much he'd like to show us round the church. It was very cold inside, and the first thing I saw was a carving of a skull and crossbones on the wall. Father McGann said, 'Ah, I see you've noticed the bones. There are no pirates buried here, as far as I know. That was a very common sign in churches here, to show us that death is ever-present. In those days there was far more disease and ill health than nowadays, and no proper doctors or hospitals. So people died very young. I imagine that they spent a lot of time thinking about death and the afterlife.'

I looked at Auntie. She looked very sad. I knew that she was thinking about Wee Callum. I held her hand and squeezed it. She squeezed mine back. Father asked me, 'Tell me Pippa, what do you know about Our Lord?'
I had decided to sound as happy as possible, and answer the questions as best I could. Then we could go back outside into the sunshine, and go home to see Luna. I said, 'My friend Lucy and her parents love Jesus. If they have a problem, they ask themselves, "What would Jesus have done?" Then they look in The Bible for answers, or they ask the vicar. I love the stories that Jesus told, especially about loving children. But some of the stories about Jesus are horrible, like the woman having stones thrown at her, and about Jesus on the cross. And I can't look at the Stations of the Cross, because they make me feel ill.'
Father didn't smile. 'Yes, it was cruel. But God loved us so much that he sent his only son to the world to be killed, so that we could all one day be free from sin.'

I thought it would be best if I asked a few questions. 'Please tell me Father, did the Jews really kill Jesus?'
'The Romans did, but the Jews helped them.'
'Please Father McGann, you are very kind. I know you are. But it makes me feel ill to talk about these things. I become very frightened, and start to shake and want to cry. It stops me sleeping properly in the night.' That was my way of telling him that I'd had enough.

He didn't take any notice, and asked me about the last time I'd received Communion and been to Confession. I told him that I had been terribly ill, so hadn't had time to go to Mass. I asked him, 'But do you believe in Guardian Angels?'

'Of course I do.'

'I'm glad, because lots of people don't. Have you got one?'

'Of course.'

'Have you ever seen him?'

'No.'

'Then how do you know that he's real?'

'Because I believe. I believe it.'

'Well that's nice. I'm so glad, because I believe it too.'

He seemed very pleased about that. He said, 'Shall we kneel in front of the altar and say a wee prayer together?'

I said, 'No thank you.'

'Well perhaps you would like me to hear your Confession.'

'No thank you.'

'Why not?'

'I haven't got anything to confess. I've never sinned.'

He laughed out loud, which made him wheezy and cough. I imagined him smoking big fat cigars after his evening meal. Once he got his breath back, he said, 'No child has ever spoken to me like that before! I see that we will have some work to do, to turn you back into a Good Catholic Lassie.'

I could feel myself getting very cross. I looked at Auntie. She wasn't smiling. I said, 'Excuse me Father, I don't wish to appear rude, but I don't want to be a Good Catholic Girl. I'm happy the way I am. Also, I have always wanted to light a candle, and think about Mummy and Daddy and all my friends I have left behind. And I'd like to think about Jesus at the same time. Please may I do that?' Father smiled. I looked at Auntie, and she was smiling too. We lit a candle each, and Auntie put half a crown in the moneybox. That was a lot of money, because the candles only cost thruppence each. Father smiled even more.

As we were looking at our candles, a very big thought occurred to me. Now that I was in my father's power, he would almost certainly want to send me to a Catholic school. Father McGann was mumbling prayers, so I waited until he had crossed himself, and then asked, 'Is there a Catholic school in this town?'

'There's a wee Catholic primary school, for children up to age eleven, then all the boys and girls go to non-Catholic high schools. Unless their parents can afford to send them to board at the Convent in the town.' Auntie was standing behind me. I saw Father look at her.

Oh Pippa!

Outside the church, Auntie asked me if I'd like to play on the swings in the playground. On any other day I would have answered, 'Yes please!' but suddenly I felt very tired and found it difficult to walk. My tummy felt much better, but it was as if my shoes were made of lead. Auntie must have guessed how I was feeling, because she said, 'Let's go to the café and have a nice cup of tea, and I'm going to buy you a treat!' The lead in my shoes suddenly became lighter.

In the café, Auntie bought me a lemon slice and a glass of lemonade. She said that everyone needs a treat once in a while. My lemon slice was full of thick fresh cream, and when I bit into it a dollop of cream stuck to the end of my nose. I thought that would make Auntie laugh, but she was frowning. I thought there could only be two reasons for her frown. I asked her, 'Excuse me Auntie, but are you thinking about Wee Callum?'
She smiled, but it was a sad smile. 'Yes, I was thinking about him in the church, when Father McGann was talking about death, and when I lit my candle. Why do you ask?'
I wanted to make it easy for her. 'Because you're frowning.'
'Oh, I frown a lot. Perhaps it's the sun in my eyes.'
'Can I ask you a question?' She looked startled. 'It's about Bonnie.' She frowned again. 'Please can I go and have a look outside Bonnie's school? I'd like to see where she is, and

perhaps we might even see her, and we could wave to each other.'

Auntie sighed. I knew I was right about what she was thinking. I said, 'And I know that's where Daddy's going to send me. Bonnie told me that girls can start there as soon as they are ten years old, and I'll be ten on the third of September. He's going to send me to board there, isn't he?'

My voice sounded very calm, but my tummy began to feel as if it was full of liquid.

Auntie said, 'Oh Pippa!' I knew that she didn't want me to go there. I was glad.

Auntie had silent tears running down her cheeks, and she sniffed and wiped them away with the back of her hand.

Something happened when I saw Auntie crying in front of me. If it had been a few years earlier, I would have been terrified, because I would have thought that the grown-up looking after me had lost control. But when Muriel joined us, she and Mummy cried a lot, and Muriel always talked to me about her feelings afterwards. She never apologised for crying, or felt embarrassed about it. I wanted to be like Muriel, in all sorts of ways, but perhaps without the crying. I couldn't put into words how I felt in that café in Kirkbrae, but I sensed that Auntie was crying because she felt like Muriel. She was crying because she understood my pain; and because she too had suffered a terrible loss. But I could feel that she was crying because she loved me, and felt pity and anger and deep sadness for me, and she could no longer hide it. I wasn't terrified that Auntie had lost control. I was glad that now we could be honest with each other. I felt I could tell her anything I wanted, and ask her about whatever I needed to know. I said, 'Please don't cry Auntie. Please don't be sad for me. I am a strong girl. Muriel said so. I know how lucky I am. I have a lovely house to live in, I have a farm, I have as much paint and paper as I could possibly want. I even have my own beach. But most importantly, I have you, and I can play with the loveliest dog in the whole world!'

Auntie dried her eyes. 'And never forget that you have a mother who loves you, and Muriel too. And, though you may not like to think about it, you have a father who loves you in his own way.'

From that moment on, whenever we went somewhere together, we held hands, or walked arm in arm. Whenever I wanted a cuddle, she would hug me, and let me to sit on her knee and suck my thumb, and she kissed me a lot and called me darling.

The Moon is calling me

That evening was very warm, so we decided to go to the beach. I wanted to swim, but I didn't have a swimming costume. Auntie said that we didn't need to worry about that, because nobody could see us, so we could swim in our underwear. But first she needed to look closely at my appendix scar, to see if it was fully healed. It looked very ugly to me. It was still very red and raised up and you could see the marks where the metal clips had been. Auntie asked if she could touch it. She ran her fingers gently along it, and I laughed because it tickled. Then she did it again, but this time she pressed a little. It didn't tickle, but it didn't hurt either. I felt my face go hot. Then she kissed her finger and touched my scar with it. She said, 'All better now.' She didn't say, '*It's* all better now.' She was talking to me as if I were a toddler who had just fallen over, and was crying because she had a tiny scratch on her leg. Muriel would have kissed me and spoken to me just like that; in the same way that she had kissed my bruised and battered bottom and legs.

I felt something moving in my chest. I said, 'Auntie, please can I tell you something?' She smiled. 'You call it my *Special Place*. I like that, but Muriel called it *My Lovely Place*.'
Auntie smiled again, 'Well it is special. And it's lovely at the same time. Some people call it their *Private Place*, and it is that too.'

189

'Please can I tell you something else?' I told her about the nasty man outside the shop, and especially about what he said about girls.

Auntie said, 'I knew nothing about that either. What a terrible story. Luckily you were with such nice people, who looked after you and protected you. Unfortunately, there are some men who just don't understand girls and women, and have some very strange ideas.'

I told her about Frances in the bath. She said it was a lovely story. I didn't tell her about being thrilled with Peter. Then Auntie's tummy rumbled very loudly. I asked her if she was hungry and she said, 'Not at all, but let's go down to the beach. The Moon is calling me.'

Auntie said that she wanted to look at the Moon shining on the sea, and that sometimes she could feel the Moon having a special effect on her. I wondered if she was going to change into a werewolf, but she said it was a special feeling in her tummy. She said, 'The light shining from the Moon is really reflected from the Sun, shining from the other side of the world. It's the Moon that controls the tides. It's not a Man in the Moon. I've always thought of it as a woman. The Moon influences us women, and we influence what happens on the Earth. When the Moon waxes and wanes in the sky, I feel something inside me waxing and waning too. The Moon has a very powerful force over me, and I'm sure that's true for all women, if only they knew it! For me, the Moon controls the ebb and flow in my body. I said that once to my husband, very soon after I met him. A short while later he made the main character in his book say exactly the same words! I was astonished, and slightly annoyed that he hadn't asked me, and I told him so. It was our first argument. But really I was delighted to know that he had been listening to me so carefully.

'A few years later, he told me that he had fallen in love with me at that moment, even though we had only met a few times. And I was falling for him too, so it wasn't a real argument, but more like two kittens play fighting. That's what

190

lovers often do in the early days of romance, when they are flirting with each other. So the Moon on the sea brings back all sorts of romantic memories. He's a very romantic man, and everyone feels that when they read his books. He's going to come and see us very soon. What do you think about that, Pippa?'

I said I was pleased. I didn't tell the truth; which was that I was slightly bothered, because I didn't want a man to come into our house, and especially not a man who was so in love with Auntie.

Auntie looked around her and said, 'There's no point in me getting my underwear all wet, so I'm going to strip off and have a quick dip. You can close your eyes if you don't want to look at me. And you can keep your knickers on if you like.' That seemed a bit silly, because she had seen me in the bath lots of times. We took our clothes off and held hands and walked into the sea. It was freezing! Auntie splashed around and then swam as fast as she could. I did the same. I felt thrilled. There is no other way to describe it; I was thrilled all over.

Afterwards, Auntie rubbed me down with a big towel. Then she wrapped us both up and we sat looking at the Moon. I told Auntie about my moment of bliss on the beach in Norfolk with Frances. Then Luna came running out of the water and shook herself all over us. Auntie's body was very pale, and her legs were hairy and she had big blue veins on her thighs. I asked her about them and she said, 'Those appeared after I had Wee Callum.'

Mummy's body was very smooth and quite hard, while Muriel's was soft and quite round in places. But Auntie's bottom was a bit lumpy and saggy, and the skin on her legs looked a bit like the peel of an orange. She saw me looking at her, but I could tell that she didn't care. I wanted to have what I call a *Ladies' Bodies Conversation,* and I knew this was absolutely the right time. 'Auntie, there's a question I've always wanted to ask. It's about the ladies in your family.'

191

She said, 'Ah' and laughed.' I think I know what's coming.'

'You see, Mummy has very small breasts. In fact, she doesn't really have any at all. I think she looks lovely.' 'And when she gets cold her nipples stick right out, and I like that too. I asked her once if I would have small breasts when I'm older. I wouldn't mind, but I think she's a bit embarrassed about it, especially as Muriel is...'

'Muriel has a fuller figure.'

'Yes. Everyone thinks she is George Harrison's wife. Anyway, Mummy said that it depends on what the ladies in Daddy's family are like. And...'

'And?'

'Well, you remind me of Mummy.'

'What a sweet girl you are. And yes, it's true; all the Dunbar women have *less-developed busts*.' She thought that was very funny.

That gave me courage to ask something else. 'And do your periods hurt you?'

'A little, but I've never had any problems. Not like some women.'

'I'm glad about that.' I told her about Mummy feeling blocked up and about her rages, but how Muriel had saved her. Auntie held my hand. 'This Muriel sounds like a very lovely person. You must miss her terribly.' Those words should have set me off crying, but they didn't. It was like talking to Stephen Hunter. You could say anything you liked to that man, and he seemed to understand everything.

We looked at the Moon a bit more. It was very bright, and I imagined it constantly pulling the sea back and then letting it go. Auntie's tummy was rumbling again. She said, 'Pippa, I understand why you are asking me these questions. .You're looking into the future, aren't you?'

'Yes I am. I like thinking about it, though I'm frightened of periods. Did you think about those things when you were a girl?'

'Oh yes! All the time! And especially when I found myself suddenly growing, and my body changing so quickly. It's all us

192

girls ever talked about, though we didn't really talk about periods in the family in those days.'

'So how did girls find out about them?'

'You might have found out from your big sister, or an older cousin, and your mother would tell you about it and help you. But you never let your father or your brothers know about it.'

I was having a very big think. The wind was beginning to blow and Auntie held me tighter. I could tell that she wasn't in a hurry to go home. Finally, I said it. 'There's something I don't quite understand. This is what caused the problems. I talked to Muriel and Mummy about periods and breasts and we were naked together sometimes. That's why I was taken away from them.'

'I don't think it was for that reason. Not really.'

'Then what was it then?'

'What do you think, Pippa?'

'Well I think I am allowed to talk to you about breasts and periods, and probably S-E-X if I wasn't so shy about it. And you can see me naked, and I can see you naked, and nobody will care. I think The Court took me away from Muriel and Mummy because they were ladies who loved each other.'

I could feel Auntie shudder. It might have been because she was cold. 'Pippa, I'm going to tell you something to help you understand what happened, and why everything was so messy for you when you first came to Scotland. Will you be a brave girl and listen very carefully? We are being very honest with each other, which is a grown up thing to do. So I hope we can talk about this a lot. It's just between you and me.'

I was a bit frightened about what I was going to hear. I said, 'OK Auntie. I'll do my best.'

'Good girl.' She kissed my hair. 'I want to talk about what happened in The Court. You see, until a little while ago, it was against the law in England for men to love other men and women to love other women. And two women who loved each other certainly wouldn't be allowed to look after children. But the law was going to change. Stephen Hunter and his colleagues at the hospital were very important. They think that there is nothing wrong with men loving men and women loving women. They say it's quite natural. The Government listened very carefully to what Stephen Hunter and other doctors had to say about that subject.'

She paused, to let that idea sink into my mind. 'Your father didn't like the idea of you being looked after by two ladies.' I tried to get up but Auntie held me tight. She kissed me again. 'I know it's difficult for you, Pippa, but I want you to know exactly what's happening. I love you very much. I think you know that, don't you?'

'Yes Auntie, I've always known it. And I love you too. Do you know that?'

'Yes, I do, you funny bunny.' I was ready to listen to what she had to say. 'I'm not saying your father was right to think that, but that's what he thought. The law in England was just about to change, so your father decided to rush through his divorce in The Court, and especially to arrange to have you taken away from your mummy and Muriel. It all happened so quickly that nobody had time to make proper arrangements for you.'

I wanted to cry. I said, 'I know you don't think it was a good idea. I'm glad about that. I think taking a child away from their mummy is the cruellest thing in the whole world.'

'But he thought it was the best thing for you. I don't think he meant to be cruel. He just has very strong ideas on that subject.'

'Is it because he's a Catholic?'

'Probably. I think that might have a lot to do with it, yes.'

'What do you think, Auntie? What do you think?'

'What do I think? I think that grown-ups must make decisions about their children because they love them. Your mummy and your daddy both love you, but they couldn't agree on how you should be brought up. So The Court had to decide.'

'But I think people told lies in The Court. I think Daddy's lawyer was very clever and The Judge believed him.'

Auntie didn't say anything about that. She said, 'What will you say to your daddy when you see him? Because one day you will see him again.'

'I don't know.'

'He's not a bad man, you know.'

'That's what Mummy said, but he has done some very bad things.'

'He has made some mistakes.'

'Well he can jolly well say sorry to me and put them right, and allow me to go back to Mummy and Muriel!'

'I'm glad we can talk about these things. It's very important to me.'

'And to me.' Then I said something that perhaps I didn't quite mean. 'I want to talk to Daddy on the telephone. I want him to come and see me here. I want him to know what a good job you are doing. I want him to know that you are making me very happy. I want to tell him that if I'm not allowed to live with Mummy, then I'd like to live with you.'

Auntie said, 'Oh Pippa!' She didn't cry this time, but she did kiss me on the top of my head.

When your time comes

It was getting cold, but I didn't want to go back to the house. I said, 'Auntie, can I ask you something?'

'Yes please, but we must go back soon.'

'Why? Are you cold?'

'A bit, but The Moon is doing her work on me.'

'What do you mean? Are you turning into a werewolf?'

'No, but I feel the Moon moving in me. She's working on my blood.'

'I don't understand.' Then I did understand. I said, 'Oh.' It was quite dark, so I hoped she couldn't see my red face. I felt something brush against my shoulder. I thought it was Luna, so I put my hand out to stroke her, but she wasn't there. I looked and saw Muriel sitting next to me. She was speaking to me, but suddenly the wind became very powerful and loud and I couldn't hear what she was saying. It looked like she was saying, 'Go to her. Go to her'.

I said, 'I will, I will!'

I heard Auntie say, 'Pippa are you all right? You've been quiet for five minutes and now you're shouting. Did you fall asleep?'

I said, 'What will happen to me at Christmas? Will I be here, with you? And can I tell you something? Something very important? I don't want to be on my own when my first period comes. I think it would be awful. Will you be able to come and see me, so you could show me what to do?'

'I don't know, my darling. That could be a long time from now. I can't promise, but I'll do my best to help you when your time comes.'

I stood up and shouted, 'But you must promise! Please promise me!'

She stood up and hugged me, but didn't promise. She said, 'We must go back now.'

I was her darling.

I am out of sorts

The next day, Auntie asked me if there was anything special I'd like to do. I must have been feeling better, because I wanted to be with other children again. I said, 'Actually Auntie, I have a list of things.'

She smiled and said, 'I hope it doesn't involve too much walking or swimming or climbing mountains.'

'No, no. But one day soon I would like to see The Convent. I don't want it to be a horrible secret.

And I'd like to see Bonnie and Juliet and the other girls again. And perhaps meet Émilie. It would be nice just to wave to them. And might they be able to come here and play with me?'

I saved the most important request for last. 'And I'd like to speak to Daddy on the telephone.' I took a deep breath. 'And I think it's about time he came to see his daughter, don't you?'

Auntie didn't smile. She said, 'I'll ring Mr Shepherd and Mr Macmillan, to see what can be done about that.'

'But why does Mr Macmillan need to know about Daddy coming? Does Daddy have to get his permission?'

'No darling, not permission, but I'm certain that both men will want to talk to each other. It will be easy for me to make the phone calls, but do you mind if we don't go out very far today, because I'm feeling a bit tired?' I understood.

I went upstairs to get my painting equipment. While I was there, I heard Auntie make a telephone call and laugh while she was talking. She was obviously talking to her husband. Then she made another call and she was very serious. She came to look for me and sat on my bed. She said, 'Pippa, I've just spoken to someone in Mr Shepherd's office, and he will pass on your message to your father about you wanting to speak to him.'
I felt my heart beating in a strange way and my throat was a little shaky. I said, 'Was that your husband on the phone as well?'
She smiled a very big smile and I saw her grey front tooth. 'Yes it was. How did you know?' I told her, and she started laughing. 'You really are a very observant child. My husband would love to meet you. In fact, he's coming here tomorrow. He's been in London, and was going to go straight home to Stranhaven, to sort out his children, but he said he misses me and would love to meet you, so I've suggested he stops off here for a few days. What do you think about that, Pippa?'
I said I was very pleased, but I wasn't.

I was very quiet for the rest of the day. I stayed upstairs and sometimes came down to the front room to read. I didn't want to play outside with Luna, and she looked very confused and disappointed. Auntie asked me if everything was all right, and I said I was fine. This wasn't true, but I didn't know what was wrong with me. I had started a painting of the sea the day before, with the beach and the rocks bathed in sunlight, and the little black and white birds pecking in the sand. It was my favourite subject, and I had made lots of sketches and several paintings that were variations on this theme. I decided to finish off the sky, but when I had finished, it looked like one of the most horrible pictures I had ever painted. I was about to tear it up when Auntie called me to come and eat supper. I didn't feel hungry and she asked me if I was feeling unwell. I wanted to

cry, but stopped myself. I went to bed early and Auntie stayed
with me. I screamed even louder than usual before I went into a
very deep sleep.

Mr Griffin

Auntie and I spent the morning tidying the house. I helped
her change our beds, and she was very impressed that I knew
how to make a bed. I told her that Muriel had shown me how to
do it, and I especially liked doing what Muriel called Hospital
Corners. I was trying my best to be cheerful, but really I was in
a very bad mood. I went outside to play with Luna, but she
kept looking at me as if she had done something wrong. It
seemed that she was my only friend in the whole world.

In the afternoon, a red car came into the drive. I supposed
it was the taxi coming to take us to the big town, to collect
Auntie's husband from the station. But it wasn't a taxi. The
man inside got out and said his name was Mr Griffin. He had
an English accent and Auntie shook hands with him. He smiled
at me and said, 'Good afternoon Pippa. How are you today?'
He was quite a big man, and wore glasses, and had a scar on
his chin.
I said, 'I'm very well thank you,' and he smiled and said,
'Good. This is a brand new car and you are the very first
passenger to ride in it. Isn't that exciting?' I didn't want to
smile, but couldn't help myself. Mummy would have said that
Mr Griffin was very charming.

It was a very interesting drive, because it was the first time
I had been to the big town since I had been in hospital. The
beaches we passed and the big bay looked lovely, even though
the day was overcast. Auntie sat next to me in the back of the
car and sometimes held my hand, and once kissed me, for no
reason at all. I was feeling very out of sorts. As we drove
across the bridge into town, Auntie asked me if I'd like to see
The Convent today. I started to cry. She held me close to her
and felt my forehead. She said, 'You really aren't right today,
are you, my little lamb?'

I wanted to say,' No I'm not at all right. I don't know what's wrong with me!' I wanted to tell her that I felt horrible inside, and wanted to go home and sit with Luna under the pine tree, and think about Muriel and Mummy and Lucy.

Then Auntie said, 'Look Pippa!' There was a group of about twenty girls, about my age, all dressed in grey, with straw hats on. They were walking in pairs, in a line, with a nun in front of them. The girls were all smiling and chatting and laughing, and each of them carried a rolled up towel under her arm.

Auntie said, 'They are Convent girls. They must be going off to the new swimming baths!' We stopped at the traffic lights and the girls crossed the road in front of our car. The last girl in the line slowed down to look at our car and I heard her say to her partner, 'Look at that lovely new Cortina!' But a gust of wind blew her hat off and then the lights changed. The girl and her partner didn't know what to do, so just stood there, right in front of our car.

Mr Griffin said, 'Now for some fun.' He got out of the car and the driver behind honked his horn, but Mr Griffin ignored him. We watched him say something to the girls, and helped them walk to the pavement. All the other girls were waiting, and the nun looked very cross. Mr Griffin reached down under our car and pulled out the hat. He brushed some dirt off it and handed it back to the girl. She was very red in the face, but laughing. She said, 'Thank you very much' in a very loud voice. Then she looked at me and waved. I waved back.

The traffic lights had changed back to red again and the girls moved off. Mr Griffin chuckled and said, 'What a drama!' I didn't feel out of sorts anymore. I was sitting in a brand new shiny red car, thinking about swimming with brand new friends, in a brand new swimming pool.

Mr Thomas Pirie

When we arrived at the station, a train was just arriving. Mr Griffin parked the car and Auntie asked him to wait. Mr Griffin opened the back door for us, and winked at me as I got out. Auntie held my hand and said to me, 'Quick, Pippa, we're just in time!' She practically pulled me into the station and onto the platform. People were getting off the train and Auntie said, 'There he is!' and pointed to a man with a ginger and grey beard and wearing a brown hat, and carrying a small suitcase in one hand and a large parcel under his arm. He put down his case and Auntie pulled me towards him. She said, 'Hello Tom!' He smiled at her and I could see he had a few teeth missing. He crouched down and said to me, 'Hello Pippa. I'm your new Uncle.' He looked in my eyes. 'Aileen said you were bonnie, and my goodness she was right. What bright blue eyes you have, and such dark hair! Have you recovered from your operation yet?'

I blushed bright red and completely lost the power of speech, but this time it was a very pleasant sensation. He straightened up and kissed Auntie on the lips. He said, 'God, I've missed you. London was awful.' Auntie went red too, and just smiled.

In the car, Uncle Tom sat in the front with Mr Griffin. I whispered to Auntie, 'Please can we drive past the swimming baths?'

She said, 'Of course we can.'

Mr Griffin didn't know where it was and we got slightly lost. We drove past a big red building surrounded by a grey wall. Auntie said, 'That's The Convent of Mary Immaculate.' Mr Griffin stopped the car in front of a set of tall metal gates, so we could have a look. The light-blue paint on the gates was peeling off in places, and I could see rust underneath. Through the gates, I saw a driveway, with a round island with some tall shrubs growing in it, and beyond it the big red school building. It looked old, and rather dirty. There was a big tree by the gates, and its branches were overhanging the wall. There was a long streak of white bird poo on the wall under the tree, stretching from the top of the wall right down to the pavement. It looked like hundreds of birds had sat in there, pooping away, but nobody had bothered to clean up their mess. I didn't see any schoolgirls. Auntie whispered, 'What do you think, Pippa? I whispered back, 'I don't know. Please can we go home now?'

Auntie said, 'Yes, of course.'

On the drive back everyone was quiet, and my new Uncle spent a lot of time looking out of the window. When we were passing the bay, he asked if we could stop the car, so he could get out and take a wee look. But Auntie said that she needed to get home as soon as possible. Uncle said, 'Of course. Silly me.' When we arrived at home, we got out of the car and Auntie tried to give Mr Griffin some money. He smiled and said, 'There's no need for that, thank you. It's my job.'

Auntie and Uncle went indoors and I stayed outside with Luna. I began to feel miserable again. I took hold of Luna's collar and led her to the open front door, put her in the hall and then closed the front door behind her. Then I ran as fast as I could down to the beach.

At the time, I didn't know why I did that. I felt like I wasn't me anymore, which was frightening. I sat on my favourite rock and looked at the beach. It was a very warm, sunny afternoon, but quite breezy, as usual. I knew the beach was beautiful, but it looked horrible. I didn't want to be there on my own, but I didn't want to go back to the house. I wanted Auntie to worry about me, and wonder where I was. Then I heard Luna running down the path, and she found me and licked my hand. I heard someone else coming and Auntie said, 'There you are!'

She was wearing a gold and orange headscarf. I didn't think it suited her, but kept that thought to myself. 'One day,' I thought, 'when it's her birthday, I will buy her a much nicer one'.

She sat down next to me and put her arm around me. She said, 'What is it Pippa? What's the matter? Tell Auntie.'

'It's nothing.' I wanted to sound quite normal, but my voice was grumpy.

'Pippa, I don't believe you. There is something. You never go anywhere on your own. I think I know what it is.'

'What is it then?' I was shocked with myself, because I sounded like Naomi when she was being very rude to her father. I said, 'I'm sorry Auntie! I didn't mean to be rude to you! It just came out! I don't know what's wrong!' I started crying again. I was fed up with crying, but seemed to be doing it all the time.

Auntie held me very tight and kissed my hair. She was quiet for a while. Then she said, 'Well, there is a word for how you feel, or how I think you might be feeling. It's because something has changed in our lives. Someone has come and it has... it has knocked you off balance. It's because my husband is here. And now you have to share me.'

Of course, she was right. I thought for a little while, then said, 'But when Muriel came to live with us, I didn't feel like that. I was glad. She and Mummy spent a lot of time on their own, but I was pleased about that. I never felt... I never felt left out.'

'So do you feel left out? Is that what it is?'

'I don't know!'

'You're still very delicate. Do you think you might be feeling jealous?

'I don't know. A girl at school once asked me about Peter, and I thought that perhaps she was his girlfriend instead of me. I just wanted to slap her.'

'Well *that* certainly sounds like jealousy. When I found out that my first husband had a lady friend I wanted to pull her hair out! But when Tom met her and told me how nice she was, I felt quite ashamed of myself. Why should I have been angry with her? I should have been angry with my husband. I suppose it's a normal reaction, but not a nice one.'

She stopped talking, to let that idea sink in. She said, 'The love that grown-ups have for each other is not the same as the love we have for children. I don't love you less because my grown-up love is here. I love you more.'

'Really?'

'Yes. I can't explain it, but I feel it is true.' Her voice was becoming very wobbly. 'Oh dear! Now I'm crying. We are such emotional people, you and I.'

I said, 'Please don't cry, Auntie.'

'Until recently, I haven't cried for a long time. And I haven't got a hanky!' I gave her mine and she started to laugh, but was crying at the same time. She said, 'I wish I could explain how I feel, but it's altogether too complicated!'

I said, 'I'm a bit frightened of men.'

Auntie stopped crying and blew her nose. 'Well, *my* man is very special. He's very quiet by nature, and really quite shy, but he's so excited about meeting you, and wants to ask you lots of questions.'

'What about? Hopefully not about Mummy.' I was appalled.

'Oh no. He wants to talk to you about Art. And he has a present for you. I can't wait for you to see it.'

'Is it the parcel he had under his arm?'

'Wait and see.'

I loved Auntie then, more than ever. I felt as if she was rescuing me from some awful sinking sand that I had stepped in by accident, and now it had me by the ankles, and was sucking me down.

I said, 'I don't like being jealous. I don't want to be jealous. I don't like it at all. How can I stop being jealous?'

'That's a very good question. I wonder if Tom might know the answer.'

'But I'm jealous of him. I want him to go away!'

'But then you'll never know what his present is!'

'I don't care!' I wanted to sound grumpy, but I was laughing.

'If I tell you that it's a painting, what would you say about that?' My jealousy disappeared, in a flash. I didn't want to talk about jealousy anymore. I felt embarrassed that I had even felt like that. And I wanted to see my painting. But Auntie hadn't quite finished. 'Nobody likes to feel jealous. It's an emotion that can be very difficult to live with. But it goes away, with time.'

'I think it's gone from me now. I don't want to think about it anymore.'

She laughed; 'You are a love! I'm so lucky to know you. You make me feel so happy, even if I do cry sometimes. Can you understand that?'

'Oh yes. Mummy and Muriel used to cry all the time. I used to get a bit fed up with it, if I'm honest. I told Stephen Hunter that, and he laughed. Then he said he was sorry, because Art Therapists weren't supposed to laugh at children. I said I wouldn't tell anyone and he laughed even more. I miss him. He wore the nicest jumpers you could imagine.'

Auntie smiled, but still wanted to talk about being jealous. 'But Pippa, what might happen if you start to love Tom more than me? I wonder how I might feel. I might feel jealous too. Imagine that!'

'That's a funny idea.'

'Pippa, seriously, you will promise not to run away and hide again? You can always talk to me about how you feel.'

'I promise. Sometimes I do things; and it feels like it's not me who is doing it. I knew it was wrong, but I couldn't stop myself.'

'Oh, all children are like that. And some grown-ups too; especially when they are feeling very strong emotions. It's quite normal, as long as you can talk about it afterwards, then it's all right. Just promise me that you, Pippa Dunbar, will never ever do that to me again.'

'But Auntie, I've already promised.'

'I know. But it's so important, I want to look in your eyes and hear you say it again.'

She cupped my face in her hands and moved her face right up close to mine. She looked very serious. I said, 'I promise, Auntie. I promise I won't run away from you again.' She closed her eyes and took in a very deep breath, then let it out again. She opened her eyes and kissed me on the nose, and then held me very tight, so that I couldn't breathe very well. She kissed me on the top of the head and said, 'I think you are one of the loveliest girls in the whole world.'

Then she let go of me and asked me, 'Do you want to come up to the house, or shall I get Tom to come and join us?'

'I'd like to stay here, but I don't want to be on my own anymore.'

She gave a piercing whistle, and we heard another whistle answering from near the house. A few minutes, later Uncle appeared. He had the parcel under his arm. It was a big rectangle, wrapped up in brown paper and tied with string. It was obviously a picture in a frame.

The Hunters in the Snow by **Pieter Bruegel the Elder**

Uncle Tom sat down beside me. He had changed his clothes and was wearing some trousers that were not quite white, and looked like they had been washed a lot. He still had his brown hat on, and his shirt was a very pale blue. I suspected that he had bought it a long time ago, and it had got quite faded. He said, 'Hello you two. Have you been having a good talk?'

I hoped Auntie wouldn't talk to him about emotions and jealousy or tell him about wanting to pull another woman's hair out. I never wanted to hear that story again. She said, 'Yes we have. And what's that you've got under your arm?'

Uncle winked at me. 'I'm so glad to be here. I didn't enjoy my trip to London at all. It was just awful. So many people rushing around, and the noise and smell of the traffic! I was down there to talk to a publisher, and all the time he was talking, my mind was on something else. I was thinking about meeting Pippa, and whether I had time to buy her a wee present. So when we had finished talking, and I had agreed to what my publisher wanted, and signed lots of pieces of paper, he put me in a taxi and told the driver to take me to a big shop. And I bought you this.' He handed me the parcel. 'I hope you like it.'

I wanted to open it, but I couldn't undo the knot in the string, so Auntie helped me. Then I realised that I had forgotten my manners and I said, 'Thank you. Thank you very much. You are very kind. But what should I call you?'

'You can call me Uncle Tom if you like. Does that sound all right to you?'

I nodded, and we carried on untying the string. Uncle Tom lit his pipe and sucked on it, and blew smoke into the air.

I knew what the painting was, even before we had taken all the wrapping paper off. I could hardly control my excitement, 'Oh! It's *The Hunters in the Snow*! I've only ever seen it in books!

Thank you Uncle Tom! Thank you!' Then I remembered when Muriel had shown me the painting of *The Blue Rider* that she had bought me. I had felt just the same then. Someone who didn't know me had gone to a lot of effort to find something to please me. I couldn't stop myself, and gave Uncle Tom a kiss on the beard. He looked very pleased. He clicked his fingers and said, 'I almost forgot. You're going to need this.' He reached into his jacket pocket and handed me a black velvet pouch. Inside was a small magnifying glass. He said, 'You'll need this to admire all the fine detail.'

Uncle took a pair of brown glasses out of his jacket pocket, and put them on. I don't know why he did that, because he spent most of his time peering over them. He said, 'This is my favourite painting. I used to spend a lot of time looking closely at it, just as you are now. You see that black bird there? He's sitting quite still on his branch. I'm sure Mr Bruegel spent a long time thinking about where exactly in the painting to put that bird. And here, his mate has just flown off, but our friend has decided to wait. He's there on purpose. He's looking forwards, and that tells us to look forwards too. The snow makes everything slow, and sometimes completely still. The trees are asleep; resting and waiting, but growing too. Their roots are pushing down, and growing outwards, and soon the force of the sun will bring the trees back into full life. I think that the black bird knows that. But he's waiting for something.'

Uncle was talking about me. I was the black bird. He didn't say so, but I could feel it. I understood why Auntie loved him so much. We looked quietly at the painting together, while he puffed on his pipe. I had never used a magnifying glass before. It was wonderful. Uncle Tom spoke again. 'I sometimes think I'm that bird. My friend has gone, but I'm waiting. What for? I'm not frightened of flying. Flying is what I do. It's something about being above everything, and looking down at all this activity. Everyone is moving, to keep warm. I could move if I wanted to, but not yet. What am I waiting for? What can I see? The frozen mill wheel, the people playing curling, and all the tiny details.'

He stroked his beard and puffed on his pipe. 'And all this...this idea, this image, this ... I can't think quite what to call it.' It felt like he was talking to himself now. 'It's all created by a man who decides to paint a bird on a branch. I used to stare at this painting and think, "If only I could be like that artist. If only I could have just a tiny fraction of his power. The power to make people stop and think, and ask themselves important questions. Well, what a wonderful thing that would be." So I wrote my books. And as I was writing, I thought of that bird, on his branch. And, to my surprise, someone liked my books and decided to publish them.'

I could feel that Uncle Tom was a kind man, and in that moment, my jealousy disappeared. Later, when we got to know each other better, he told me that he enjoyed being with me and Auntie, but liked to be on his own too. Like me, he liked to be still, and look at things very closely, or just absorb the atmosphere around him. At other times he would look at me, when he thought I wasn't looking. But he wasn't examining me, like a doctor might do, but he would look at me or other people with a dreamy look on his face.

The following day, when I was sitting with him and Luna on the beach, he asked me what I could see. He didn't say, 'What are you looking at, Pippa?' because it was obvious that I was looking at the sea and the sky. So I told him about the cloud I was particularly interested in at that moment, and especially the colours and shapes lower down, that were moving in a fascinating way.

He said, 'That wasn't what I was looking at. I was thinking about how everyone sees things differently. It's all about your point of view. You might see Luna, for example, as a playmate. A farmer would see her as a useful working dog. A goose might see her as a nuisance, who is going to boss it around.'

He was quiet. I knew that was giving me time to think about what he had just said. He was playing the same game as

Stephen Hunter. So I asked him, 'And what do you see when you look at Luna?'

Unlike Stephen Hunter, he was happy to give an answer. 'Well, I'm glad you asked me that. I see her as Aileen's dog, who is now your playmate as well. But I wonder what would happen if Aileen whistled for her now, but you wanted her to stay. What would Luna do?'

'I don't know. I suppose she would go with Auntie, because that's what she's been trained to do.'

'Good answer! I'm not saying you're right, but it's a very interesting idea. Shall we try it out this afternoon?'

I didn't want to, so didn't say anything. He said, 'Perhaps not.'

I trusted Uncle Tom enough now to tease him just a little bit. 'So will you put what we've just said into one of your stories?'

He smiled. 'If you give me your permission; yes, I'd like to very much. I have an idea to write a story from Luna's point of view. Do you think that might be interesting, Pippa?'

'Like *Black Beauty*?'

He laughed. 'Yes, I suppose so, I hadn't thought about *Black Beauty*. I think that was probably the first novel to look at life from an animal's point of view. So I will need to make my story sufficiently different, so that people won't think I'm copying Anna Sewell's ideas. Thank you, Pippa. If my story ever sees the light of day, you can tell your friends that you were present at its conception, if not its birth.'

I wasn't exactly sure what he meant, but it was nice to be thanked.

That night at bedtime, I screamed and screamed, and I was becoming frightened of going to sleep, because The Man with the Black Gloves was always coming towards me with his hands out, ready to strangle me. Auntie was getting very worried about me, and asked me what might make me feel better about going to sleep. She asked me if I thought seeing a doctor might help. I didn't want to see a doctor. I wanted to see Mummy and Muriel.

Talking with Uncle Tom

In the morning, I went down to the beach with Uncle Tom again. We sat on our rock and looked at the sea. Uncle Tom took out his pipe and started cleaning it. He didn't look at me, but cleared his throat, so I knew he was going to ask me an important question. But it wasn't a question; it was an order. 'Pippa, tell me what makes you scream so loudly and with such terror.'

The sun was shining, but I suddenly felt cold. 'Please Uncle Tom. I don't want to. I try to forget about him. Once the horrible man has seen me, then I don't think about him anymore.'

'That's not really true, is it?'

'No. It's not. I want it to be true.'

'Who is he?'

'I don't know. I can never see his face.' An idea occurred to me. 'Is he inside me? Because if I dream about him, is he inside me somewhere? Is there something wrong with me? Are other children like that?'

'Oh yes, other children are like that. My eldest one, Maggie, was fifteen when her mother died. She had terrible nightmares in the middle of the night. Perhaps she'll tell you about them one day. But I don't know anyone who has such powerful dreams as you do just before they drop off to sleep. From what I understand, people usually dream when they are deeply asleep, or just before they wake up. But I'm no expert. I'm a journalist, and we tend to know a little bit about lots of things!'

He smiled to himself and puffed on his pipe. I think he wanted me to say some more, just like Stephen Hunter and Mr Macmillan. But I didn't want to say anything, so kept quiet. He took a few more puffs and said, 'We all have something called a *subconscious*. Have you heard of that before?'

'I know what a submarine is. It goes under the sea. And when you faint, you are *unconscious*, so I guess it is something that is underneath you just before you go to sleep. Is it something under the bed, like a monster?'

He chuckled, so I knew he was laughing at me in a nice way; as kind adults do when children are trying hard to understand something, but say ridiculous things. I asked him, 'Was that a silly answer?'

'Not at all. I think you have almost hit the nail on the head! It's part of our mind. When you are awake and busy doing things during the day, then we say you are using the conscious part of your mind. But at the same time there is something else working in your mind, which truly starts to get busy when you are asleep.

'Some people say that your mind is a bit like an iceberg. We use the conscious part during the day, when we are learning and thinking and working, and talking with other people. But the large part, the subconscious, is always there, underneath.'

I thought about the Nasty Nun getting excited about The Titanic hitting an iceberg. 'Is it your soul? Catholics have souls, so do Non-Catholics have a subcontinent?'

'Do Non-Catholics have a subconscious, while Catholics don't have them, but have souls instead? What a fascinating idea! I imagine Catholics would like to think that! Well done, Pippa! Well done!'

I didn't know what I had done well, but it felt very nice to make a man laugh out loud like that.

Then he was serious again. 'You see, Pippa, when you are an artist, like a painter, or a writer, we are perhaps more in touch with our subconscious than other people, because we are always what I call 'up in our heads'. We are always looking closely at people and things, and we imagine how they feel. You have a strong imagination, and sometimes you let your imagination run wild. That's where inspiration comes into you. But it also comes from inside you. It comes out of your subconscious. So if you paint a picture, then it might be something you are looking at, but as you paint, ideas come from inside you, from your subconscious. They might be thoughts or feelings that you had forgotten about. Or they might be memories that you had pushed down into your subconscious, because they were too horrible to think about and talk about.'

I didn't like what Uncle Tom was saying. I wanted him to stop talking, and start smoking his pipe again. But he didn't take any notice of me. He was looking at the sea, and I wondered if he was talking to himself again. But then he turned himself round and looked at me, and our eyes met. 'Pippa, you have suffered a lot, and seen some terrible things, and things have happened to you that other children might never experience in their whole lives.'

I thought of Lucy. She had a mum and a dad who loved each other, and she was pure and her life was simple. If she had a subconscious, then she never mentioned it to me. She said she never dreamed about anything. Roger, on the other hand, was always dreaming about football and rugby. Once he told me that he had a nightmare about eating a giant marshmallow, and when he woke up, his pillow had disappeared, and he had feathers in his mouth. I told Mummy about that, and she explained that it was a funny joke. The next time I saw Roger, I punched him on the arm. That made him laugh even more, and after that he told us lots of jokes. Some of them were quite rude. Lucy said she didn't like it, so he stopped straight away. Roger was in love with Lucy. It was obvious to everybody, except to her, because she was pure and simple.
I was in love with Lucy too, but in a girls-can-like-other girls-and-that's-all right kind of way. I missed Lucy, and wanted to tell Uncle Tom about her.

But he said, 'There are things that happen, that you just don't understand. You want to understand them, but you can't. So you might try to push them down, to forget about them. But the more you push them down, the more they pop up. And they especially pop up in dreams. It's as if you have put a big piece of concrete on top of them. But writers and artists, we can't resist looking underneath that concrete. Or perhaps because we write and paint, the concrete quickly gets worn away by our pens and pencils, and those memories start to leak out.'

This seemed like a ridiculous idea to me, but I didn't like to say so.

Uncle Tom scratched his beard under his chin. I wondered if men grew beards just so they could spend a lot of time playing with them. Lucy used to play with her hair, twirling it round and round. And when she was worried about something in school (which was during most lessons) she would suck her hair. Perhaps it was her subconscious making her do it. I tried sucking my hair once, to be like Lucy, but didn't like the taste, so went back to sucking my thumb, which was much more satisfying. Lucy tried to suck her thumb, to be like me, but said it tasted horrible. When you are best friends with someone, you can talk about private things like that, and know that your friend won't tease you, or tell other people.

I wanted to talk about Lucy, but Uncle Tom was stroking his beard again. 'But you know, Pippa, most people think that your subconscious is full of bad thoughts and ideas and feelings and memories. But I believe there are nice things in there too. Perhaps you had a particularly lovely experience when you were a baby. Perhaps you were sitting on your mummy's knee and a bee was buzzing nearby. You can't remember it, because you were a baby. But now every time you hear a bee buzzing, you are pleased, but you don't know why. Or perhaps your mummy sang a particular lullaby to you just before you went to sleep, or you had a favourite blue blanket. So every time you see that shade of blue, you might suddenly find yourself humming that lullaby and smiling to yourself. You don't know why you do it, but it's a memory from deep down inside you, from a time when you were very happy.'

I was just about to tell him about Lucy, and how we had talked about fairy stories, and I had made her a book, and how we were running together and I looked at her and thought how lovely she looked, and how this made me fall and break my wrist. And how we had seen Roger's mother's breasts.

(Actually, I only wanted to talk about how beautiful Lucy's face and hair had been. I wasn't going to tell Uncle Tom about Dorothy's bosoms.) I tried to push Dorothy's breasts down into my subconscious, but they wouldn't go down there, probably because they were quite large. Obviously, they were bigger than Mummy's, but not as round as Muriel's, and Lucy and I had laughed so much whenever we thought about them. It made me completely forget that I had hurt myself. It was the only rude thing that Lucy and I ever talked about. Lucy said that when she got married, she was going to feed her babies with her breasts, and not use a bottle, like some mothers. I didn't say anything. I didn't like to think of Lucy being married. I pictured her living in a house with me. In my picture there was a baby, who was always outside sleeping nicely in a pram, and children playing happily in the garden, but there was never a man. I didn't dare tell Lucy about that, in case she thought it was silly.

Uncle Tom was saying, 'Or dreams can be your subconscious telling you to think about something. Perhaps it's a problem that you just can't sort out. Or it might be something bad that happened to you, but it hurts too much when you are reminded of it, or it's too frightening to think about it during the day, so it comes to visit you while you are asleep.'
I thought that Uncle Tom was remembering his wife. I was glad he was with Auntie. If they had dreams that frightened them the middle of the night, they could comfort each other.

Talking with Auntie
That night I didn't scream before I went to sleep. But in the middle of the night I dreamed of Lucy being Rapunzel and sucking her long hair, and me being the prince trying to save her: just like in the Ladybird book. But instead of the witch catching me and the birds pecking my eyes out, it was The Man with the Black Gloves, and he tried to strangle me. I woke up screaming, and Auntie came into my room, and stayed and talked to me. I told her that my subconscious was troubling me, but I had never known a man with black gloves. Auntie

wondered if I ought to talk to a special doctor about my dreams. I asked her if I could see an Art Therapist, like Stephen Hunter. She was feeling cold and asked me if she could climb into bed beside me. She said, 'I'm wide awake now. Are you wide awake, Pippa?' I was. I had wanted Auntie to get into bed with me ever since I had moved to that house. She said, 'Tell me, darling, what did you talk about with Stephen Hunter?'

'We talked about babies and dead animals. And a lot about blood. And Ursula. And Mummy on the ship.'

'Ursula? Oh yes, Stephen wrote a lot about her.'

'What did he say?' I was more wide-awake than ever.

'He said that all Catholics believe that they have a Guardian Angel, but that your belief was stronger than most. He also said it was quite common to have...'

She was thinking what words to use, so I said them for her, 'An Imaginary Friend. But Ursula is real! It makes me very cross indeed when people tell me that I have made her up.'

'Of course, of course. But tell me about Mummy on the ship. What happened to her?'

'She lost a baby.' I was glad we had changed the subject, because it was easier to talk about Mummy than about Ursula.

'Lost it?'

'The baby died. Actually, it was born dead, I think. No it wasn't. Mummy had terrible seasickness and pains in her tummy and started bleeding, and she rushed to sit on the toilet and the baby came out and it was only half-formed. And Mummy was ill afterwards and terribly upset, but the men wrapped the baby up in a sheet, and tied weights to it and threw into the sea. But they didn't tell Mummy they were going to do that. And Daddy wouldn't talk about it, and after that Mummy and Daddy didn't like each other in the same way.'

'How do you know all this?'

'Mummy told me and Muriel, and we all three talked about it with Stephen Hunter. Mummy cried a lot and she was sick in the street afterwards.'

'What did you think about that?'

'It was a horrible story and I didn't want to listen. But the more I heard these stories then the better I felt, because they were like Mummy's horrible secrets. But then they weren't secrets anymore. And then if I talked to Stephen about them I felt better.'

'Better?'

'Well, at first it had been horrible to hear about it, but Stephen said this horrible event, this thing that had happened, and Mummy's memory of it, was now out in the open. We could all see the problem clearly, so now it was easier to think about it and talk about it. Then we wouldn't be frightened of it anymore.'

Auntie didn't say anything for a little while. She sighed and said, 'I suppose such an awful memory would frighten anybody. It could come back as a dream in the night and frighten you; in the same way that you might be frightened if you see a big dog, or a lion. You want to run away from it and hide. And if you can't do that, then you might want to close your eyes and pretend it's not there. Or you might stand perfectly still and tell yourself that it's not really happening to you, and you secretly hope that if you tell yourself that enough times, then it might turn out to be true.'

We couldn't see each other. She had her arm around me and I was sucking my thumb. I could feel her heart beating. She let out another sigh, and I knew she was thinking about Wee Callum. I whispered, 'Or perhaps a wolf. You might be frightened of a wolf. I used to be terrified of wolves. Now it's a man with black gloves.'

Auntie said, 'Hmm.'

Uncle Tom said *Hmm* a lot, and especially when I talked to him about important subjects like Art. He didn't say *Ah* like some grown-ups. And he never said, 'I understand'. Once I asked him if he believed in God, and about what happened when we die. He said that sometimes it was a big worry. He said, 'I think about it, but I don't really know the answer. But sometimes just talking about things that worry us, or writing about it, or drawing or painting, can help us.'

I said, 'Help us to do what?'

'I don't know. It just helps.' I wanted to kiss his beard. He lit his pipe.

Auntie and I were quiet again. I was enjoying having her so close to me. I said, 'I like to talk about Stephen Hunter. It helps me remember how I felt. I felt... better. And not so terrified. And he loved Art as much as I do. And what was so nice was that Mummy and Muriel liked him too. Mummy once said that Stephen knew exactly which button to press, but sometimes he pushed the wrong button, on purpose. Muriel said she'd like to push Mummy's button. That made them both laugh a lot. When I asked them why they were laughing, they wouldn't tell me. I didn't mind, because they were making each other happy. That's how I knew that it was good to talk to Stephen Hunter, even though we cried a lot. And sometimes Muriel was quiet for a long time afterwards. Then they both went to see a lady on their own, every Thursday. That was their private time for themselves. I loved it, because they always left me for the evening at Lucy's house. I hope they keep going to see her, so they can stay happy, even though I was taken away from them.'

Auntie kissed me.

Talking with Uncle Tom again

In the morning, the phone rang, and Uncle Tom answered it and spoke to someone for a long time. I supposed it was his publisher. Then he said, 'Goodbye Mr Shepherd. That was a very useful conversation,' and put the phone down.

He asked me if we could go and sit outside, under the pine tree. He said I could do some painting outside. I went to get my painting things, but was feeling wobbly on my legs, so sat down on the grass. Uncle Tom sat on a chair. He said, 'I was feeling very pleased with myself last night, because you went off to sleep like a lamb. But then in the middle of the night you started screaming. Did Auntie help you settle down again?'

'Yes, she did.'

'What did you talk about?'

'Didn't Auntie tell you?' I hoped that she hadn't. I didn't want Uncle Tom to know about Mummy bleeding and losing her baby. If the baby had lived, then I would have had a big sister or brother. I tried to push that thought down. The concrete seemed to melt and the baby just slipped beneath it. Then the concrete sealed itself up again. I asked him, 'Doesn't Auntie tell you things about me?'

'Not really.'

'Why not?'

'Because you told her not to.'

'I didn't.'

'Yes you did. You made her promise not to tell anyone about things you said, or to let anyone look at your pictures. I'm dying to look at them!'

'But I meant she was not to tell horrible people, like doctors. And…'

I couldn't say the next name. He said it for me. 'And other horrible people like Mr Shepherd?' I nodded. I shivered as well. He said, 'Horrible people? Horrible men and women?'

'Well, not ladies. Horrible men. I've only known two really horrible ladies in my life. Actually three.' I told him about the nasty dinner lady and the nun who beat me, and Mrs Durkin.

He looked shocked. 'What sort of men? What sort of horrible men?'

Something came into my head. I think it came from my subconscious. 'Can I tell you something very private?'

'As long as you don't mind me telling Auntie. We have both agreed that we have to share things that people tell us, if it's something very important. It's a very good rule.'

'A doctor stuck his thumb up my bottom in the hospital.' I really didn't know why I told him that.

'That must have been awful.'

'Yes it was. He didn't even tell me he was going to do it!'

'Some doctors can be like that. It's very annoying. They don't mean to be horrible. To them we are just problems to be solved as quickly as possible. One of my children had that done to her. She swore at the doctor!'

I couldn't believe it. 'And what did you say to her about that? Did you tell her off?'

'No I didn't. But I was a bit surprised that she knew such rude words. But tell me Pippa, is your father one of those nasty men?'

'Yes. Yes he is. He is the nastiest of them all. I don't want to think about him.'

'What did he look like?'

I thought that perhaps Uncle Tom hadn't heard me. So I said, a bit louder, 'I said I don't want to think about him!'

Uncle Tom didn't take any notice. 'What was he wearing?'

I didn't want to talk about my father, so I told Uncle Tom about Mummy losing her baby. He scratched his beard. 'Did you mind Mummy telling you about that?' I told him what I had told Auntie in the night, but added a new thought, 'And I know that Mummy really wanted to have me, and was thrilled when I was born, and she loved me twice as much because I was a good baby.'

'What's a *good baby*?'

'One that doesn't cry much, and sleeps all through the night. And drinks her mummy's milk and eats her food and is happy.'

'So a good baby is really the same as a good girl?' He was talking to himself again.

'I don't know what you mean.'

'Neither do I, but it sounds quite clever. I'll have to think about what I've just said. Thank you Pippa.'

'What for?'

'I'm not sure. For giving me that idea. I love talking to you! And will you think about that idea too?'

'What idea was that?' I was getting a bit confused. I sucked my thumb and patted Luna's head at the same time. That was becoming one of my favourite habits. I found it very comforting, and I was sure that Luna was comforted too. I said, 'Yes, I will!' I hadn't lost interest, but I didn't want to talk anymore.

We both laughed, though I wasn't sure exactly what I was laughing about. Uncle Tom took his notebook and pen out of his jacket pocket. He said, 'It's time for me to do some writing. Would you like to draw or paint something? We could sit here and be creative together.'

After about an hour of painting and writing together, Uncle said, 'You know, Pippa, being brave is not just about jumping in the sea to rescue someone. It's about facing up to the things that terrify us.'

I was painting Ursula killing a man with black gloves. I knew it was my father. I didn't want Ursula to kill him, but just to frighten him away. Then he would know that the next time he saw me he would have to be nice to me. Then perhaps we could become friends again, and he would understand how much I had been hurt inside. And then he would send me back to Mummy and Muriel.

Mr Macmillan visits

The next day Mr Macmillan came to see us. Auntie told me at breakfast time that he wanted to talk to us about what was going to happen to me next. I asked her if I was going to be a boarder at the Roman Catholic school and she said I was. I felt a terrible wave of seawater come towards me. It was my sadness, like the great wave that Hokusai painted. So I asked Auntie if I could stay with her at Christmas and she said, 'That's one of the things we are going to talk about. And yes, that is what I want to happen.'

The wave didn't wash me away. It flowed over me, without making me wet.

Auntie said that we should go down to the beach, and Mr Macmillan could meet us there. She said that people with jobs like his didn't get many treats, and she thought that being on the beach on a sunny day was one of the nicest treats in the world. That, and eating chocolate cake. So we made a cake for us to eat on the beach together.

When Mr Macmillan saw me he said, 'My goodness, Pippa, you do look well! The last time I saw you, you were as white as a sheet and had big black rings under your eyes, and could hardly walk!'

I had done my best to forget about being in hospital. I was beginning to think that if I wasn't careful, I would stuff too many things into my subconscious, and everything would come bursting to the surface, like when I had made a terrible mess in my hospital bed.

I asked Mr Macmillan about the children who had been in hospital with me. He told me that Brian was now with a new family, and he seemed to be happy with them. I asked him about Bonnie and he said that Bonnie had left the boarding school and gone back to Africa. He didn't know about Émilie. I didn't want to ask him about Keith, but he told me that unfortunately Keith had died. One morning the nurses went in to see him, but he had died in the night. Everyone had been very upset, and especially his mother and father and all his family. But he had had a lovely funeral, and he was buried in the cemetery in the town.

I didn't cry when I heard that, because I could tell that Keith was never going to be a normal boy again. And when I had sung to him, and held his hand, it felt like he was almost dead, and if the doctors had pulled the tubes out of him, then he would have died straight away.

We were all quiet. Uncle Tom asked to be excused, because he needed to do some more writing, so Auntie and Mr Macmillan and I sat and looked out to sea. Luna lay next to me, and I stroked her back. Then Mr Macmillan cleared his throat and said, 'Pippa, I have some important news for you. Your father is coming to London and he wants to meet you.'

I knew that was coming. I said, 'Well I don't want to go to London. It's too far.' I tried to sound as grumpy as possible.

'But would you like to meet him?'

'I have to.'

'Why? Why do you have to?'

'To tell him how happy I am.'

'And are you happy?'

'Well, yes I am. I know I'm very lucky to be with Auntie. She loves me, and that makes me feel so much better. And of course I love her.' Auntie smiled. 'But deep down, I'm deeply unhappy. I think I've been wounded, and it's never going to heal up properly unless I go back to Mummy. I've tried to push it all into my subconscious, but I'm worried that it's almost full up.'

Mr Macmillan smiled. This made me feel cross. I wanted to tell him that being wounded deep down was no laughing matter. He said, 'I'm sorry. I shouldn't have smiled. Is that annoying?'

'Yes it is, but I'm far too polite to say so.'

He smiled again. I was glad, because when he smiled he looked like when he had dropped the jigsaw puzzle, and Matron had told him off. 'I'm sorry, Pippa. The reason why I was smiling was because... because you are quite an extraordinary little girl. Actually, you are quite a big girl. Lots of children I know who have had terrible experiences aren't able to talk about their feelings. This is because they don't know how they feel, or don't have the words to express themselves properly. But you do. I wish all children could have a grown-up they can talk to, who really understands how they feel.'

This gave me an idea. 'Please can you find me someone to paint with? Another Art Therapist, like Stephen Hunter.'

'I can try. I can certainly try. But please tell me Pippa, why do you want to tell your daddy that you are happy, when really you are not?'

'I can't say.'

'Yes you can'.

'Because then he won't make me go and live with him in a foreign country.'

'And...'

'And then I can stay with Auntie, and one day go back to Mummy.'

Mr Macmillan didn't say anything for a while. Then he asked, 'Could you talk to your father on the telephone?'

I thought about this. 'Yes I could. He could ask me questions, and I could answer either *yes* or *no*.'

Mr Macmillan said, 'Good. Well done, Pippa. I know it's a very important thing to do. Now can we talk about something else?'

I don't know why he asked me that, because he was going to talk about it anyway. He looked at Auntie. She said, 'Mr Macmillan and I have been talking together. And Mr Macmillan has been talking to your daddy. The school holidays are going to start soon, and when they do, we think it would be nice if you could spend them with us in Stranhaven. Then you can meet Tom's family, and make friends with his children. And of course, Luna will come with us too. What do you think about that idea?'

I said, 'That sounds like a nice idea.' But really, I wasn't very happy about it. I knew it was a long way away, and would take me further away from Mummy and Muriel.

I said, 'When can I see Mummy and Muriel? And when can I talk to them on the phone?'

I was trying very hard to be a good girl, but I couldn't manage it anymore. I started crying. Auntie put her arms around me. Mr Macmillan didn't say anything. He waited until I had stopped crying, then said, 'Talk to your daddy first. You can ask him. He needs to know how you feel.'

'But I want him to think I'm a good girl. I don't want to make him angry.'

Mr Macmillan and Auntie looked at each other. Auntie said, 'I will talk to Daddy as well. I'm sure that will help.' Then we talked about my new school. Mr Macmillan had talked to the nun in charge, Sister Winifred, and had arranged for me to visit with Auntie in the next few days.

I felt myself closing up inside. My mouth felt dry and my throat felt sore, as if I had been shouting a lot. My head started to ache, and Auntie said that we ought to go back to the house, so we walked back together. I needed to do a wee, but sat on the toilet and nothing would come out. Auntie came in to see if I was all right, and I just cried and cried. I was so upset and no words would come out.

For the rest of the day I did a jigsaw puzzle in the front room.

A phone call

That evening the phone rang. Auntie answered it and I knew it was my father. Auntie passed me the receiver and a Scottish man's voice said, 'Hello Pippa, is that you?'

I stood very still, trying to stop my voice from shaking. 'Hello Daddy, yes it's me here. It's Pippa. How are you?'

'I'm very well, thank you. And how are you enjoying being in Scotland? How is the beach? I imagine it's glorious in this weather?'

'Yes thank you, Daddy. I'm enjoying myself very much, and Auntie has a lovely dog called Luna.'

'Good, good. 'He had a smile in his voice.

I wasn't going to ask him, but it just came out. 'Excuse me for asking you Daddy, but when you came to our house last time, were you wearing gloves?'

'Yes I was. As a matter of fact, I left my gloves in your house. Your mother kindly posted them to my office for me.'

'What colour were they?'

'Black. Why do you ask?'

I started to cough, but managed to say, 'I was just wondering.'

'It seems like a strange question.' I was quiet. 'Hello Pippa, are you still there?'

'Yes I am.'

'Did you like the paints I sent you?'

'Oh yes! They are lovely. I'm very sorry, Daddy, I forgot to thank you. You see, so much has changed in my life, and then I was ill and everything is like being in a strange dream.' I had no idea what I was talking about. I think I was quite frightened, as if there was a wild animal in front of me, like a giant snake. It could talk and I had to trick it, to stop it from attacking me.

Daddy asked, 'Would you like some more?'

'Oh, yes please! That would be very kind of you.' I forgot I was talking to a wild beast and, just for a few moments, I was a little girl talking to her daddy. 'Daddy, do you mind if I ask you something? I hope you won't get cross with me. Please can I talk to Mummy on the phone? 'He didn't hesitate. 'Of course you can. Of course you can.'

'Thank you Daddy. I feel much better now. Really I do.'

'I'm glad.'

We were both quiet. I think he had run out of things to say to me. I said, 'I hope one day I'll be able to come and see you, but at the moment I'm very busy.'

He laughed. 'That would be nice. I'm very busy too.' There was another silence. Finally, he said, 'Well goodbye then, Pippa. I hope you enjoy your time in Stranhaven. They have a very special swimming baths there. Be sure and write to me.'

'I will Daddy. I promise. I'll write to you about my opinion.'

'That will be nice. Well, goodbye then.'

'Goodbye.' I put the phone down. I didn't know what my opinion was, but it sounded very important.

At last

All the time that I had been on the phone, Auntie had been sitting by my side. I was shaking all over, so she put me on her knee and we sat there quietly, not saying anything. Then the phone rang again. Auntie answered it and said, 'Yes, she's here.' I supposed it was Daddy. Perhaps he had forgotten to tell me something. But it was Mummy.

Mummy sounded very far away, and I had to press the phone receiver hard against my ear to make sure that I could hear her properly. She asked me how I was, but her voice sounded very shaky, so I decided to say everything I wanted to say, so that she could just listen, and when she was ready she could tell me about herself. I told her that Auntie was looking after me, and that I had been a bit ill, but that now I was fine, and could run around like normal. And I had a lovely dog to play with, and I was staying on a farm, and just down a path there was a lovely beach. And I hadn't been to school, but that didn't matter, because Auntie was teaching me lots of interesting things, and it had just been decided that I was going to a place called Stranhaven for my summer holidays.

All the time I was telling Mummy these things she was saying, 'Lovely' and 'That's nice' and 'Aren't you a lucky girl?' But really, all I wanted to do was to tell her how much I missed her, and beg her to please go back to The Court, and tell The Judge that he had made a terrible mistake. But I knew not to say things like that, because every time she said, 'That's lovely' I could hear her voice getting more and more wobbly, and I knew she was in terrible pain. I wanted to ask her about Muriel, and to tell her to explain to Muriel that I understood why she didn't say goodbye to me on the day that they took me away from school. But instead I told her that I had a lovely big box of paints, and I had done lots of pictures, and spent time on the beach; collecting stones and shells and bits of driftwood and making patterns with them. Then I said, 'Mummy. I've just been speaking to Daddy, and he said a very strange thing. He said that he left his black gloves in our house, and that you sent them to him. Why did you do that?'

Mummy sounded taken aback. 'Why did you talk about his gloves? It was Muriel's idea. I was so cross, I wanted to throw them on the fire! But I'm glad I didn't. Was he pleased?'

'He sounded very pleased.'

'Good. I shall tell Muriel, because she said it was a very important thing to do.'

Then I heard a hissing sound and lots of crackling and Mummy's voice was very difficult to hear. I shouted, 'Are you still there, Mummy?'

But all I could hear was crackling. I quickly passed the receiver to Auntie and she said, 'Hello? Hello Ruth? Are you still there? I hope you can hear me. I'll call you back in a few minutes. Hello? Hello?'

But the only thing that Auntie could hear was a fuzzy noise and lots of crackles, so she put the receiver back on its cradle. Auntie told me not to worry, because she had written Mummy's telephone number down somewhere. She said, 'I don't want to move, Pippa. I want you to stay on my knee. What's your telephone number at home?' I couldn't remember. I felt Hokusai's wave coming towards me. Then I remembered the number, and the wave shrank back. Auntie rang the operator and asked her to make a trunk call to Ashbourne. The operator put the call through and Auntie said, 'Hello Ruth? Can you hear me now?'

I heard Mummy say, 'Yes, thank you. That's much better.' Then she said, 'Before you pass me to Pippa, I just want to say how grateful I am to you for being so kind and loving to my daughter. We are both very, very grateful. It means the world to us to know that Pippa is, how can I put it, as happy as she could be.'

Auntie said, 'Och, it's a pleasure. It's one of the greatest pleasures, if I'm honest. She's a bonnie lassie, with the loveliest nature. She's obviously been very well brought up. But I'll pass you over now, and you two can talk for as long as you like. And don't you worry about the cost of the call.'

Then she gave me the receiver.

I shouted, 'Hello Mummy. I'm back again! What have you been doing?' Mummy told me that she and Muriel had been very busy. Mummy had been going up to London, and all the tenants in Muriel's house were very nice. Muriel and Mummy went to church every Sunday, and everyone asked about me and said prayers for me. And they had seen Lucy and her parents in church, and Lucy sent a big *hello*, and she would be thrilled to know that Mummy had finally spoken to me. And Roger always asked about me, and Little Willie was much less of a handful now, and was really quite clever, once you could understand what he was saying.

All the time that Mummy was talking, there were tears running down my cheeks. I didn't want to say anything, because I didn't want her to know that I was upset. Mummy said, 'Hello Pippa? Are you still there?' But I couldn't say anything, so Auntie took the receiver out of my hand.

Auntie said, 'Hello Ruth. Pippa's upset, as you can imagine. She's here now. I have her sitting with me, on my knee. She's becoming a very big strong girl, and you need have no worries about her health.'

Then Mummy talked for a while. I couldn't hear her words, but suddenly she stopped and I could hear her crying. Then she started talking again and Auntie said, 'Yes Ruth, I heard everything you said, and I'll tell Pippa everything. And yes, we'll ring you as soon as we get to Stranhaven, and yes, Mr Macmillan is a lovely man. But as tough as old boots. You won't find a social worker better than him. He's the velvet fist in the iron glove. Or is it the other way round? You two can say your goodbyes now, and we'll speak again soon. You take care now, Ruth.'

She passed the receiver to me. Mummy said, 'Goodbye now, Pippa. You know that Mummy loves you, don't you?'

I said, 'Yes Mummy. Of course I know that. I won't forget that.'

'Goodbye my love, and have a lovely summer holiday with Auntie Aileen, and I'm sure you'll have lots of fun with your cousins.'

Then I could hear her starting to cry again. I said, 'It's all right Mummy. You don't need to worry about me. I'm like you. Byebye Mummy.' I passed the phone to Auntie and she listened, but all she could hear was the dialling tone. Mummy had gone.

We didn't say anything to each other for a few minutes. I just sat and sucked my thumb. Then Auntie said, 'Your Mummy told me that she's been talking to your daddy on the phone. He has apologised to her about some of the harsh things that were said in The Court. He had no idea that his legal counsel was going to be so... so horrible and cruel. But your daddy is very clear in his mind that you must go to a Catholic boarding school.'

I spent the rest of the evening in my bedroom. I painted a picture for Keith. It was of a lovely sunset that I had seen once in Ashbourne. I pretended it was on my beach, with lots of pink, purple, and red, and even some green. When I first saw a sunset as spectacular as that, I told myself that no matter how much anyone tried, they would never be able to find the colours to make that sky. But I was very pleased with what I had done. When Auntie came up to see me, I asked her if we could put some flowers on Keith's grave, and find some way of giving my picture to his mother and father.

I didn't dream about the Man with the Black Gloves again. Once, Uncle Tom asked me why I had stopped having nightmares, and I told him about my conversations with Daddy and Mummy. He stroked his beard and smiled to himself and said, 'Well, well.'

I was feeling a bit cheeky and said, 'I hope you won't write a story about that one day.'

He laughed and said, 'I see you are getting to know me and my ways.' Then he looked serious and said, 'No, Pippa, I won't do that, no matter how tempting it might be.' Then he smiled again and said, 'I'll make the gloves brown; then nobody will guess that it was your story.' That was funny.

Sister Winifred

The next day, after breakfast, Auntie rang my new school, to ask if we could visit. The secretary said that the Sister Principal, Sister Winifred, was the only one who could arrange visits, and at the moment she was very busy. She told Auntie to ring back later in the morning. Auntie explained that my father had already arranged a place for me, to start in September, but it would be very important for me to see what the school looked like, so that I could look forward to it.

When Auntie finished the call, I told her that the only things I was looking forward to when I started school were meeting the girls I had spoken to in hospital, perhaps getting to know Émilie, going swimming, and wearing a nice straw hat. I had always wanted to wear a straw hat.

Auntie explained that we only had two days left on the farm, because after that we were going to go to Stranhaven on the train. That meant that we only had one day to visit the school, and then go to Pearson's to order all my school clothes.

By lunchtime, nobody from the school had rung back, so Auntie rang again. The secretary was very embarrassed and said that Sister Winifred had told her that there was no need for us to visit, because my father had already arranged my place. Auntie said, 'But surely we can look round, to help the child to understand what her school will be like?'

Auntie heard the secretary talking to someone and then she said to Auntie, 'You can come this afternoon and collect the list of compulsory clothing, but Sister will be too busy to see you.'

Auntie put the phone down. She said to me, 'Pippa, there's no use me trying to hide how I feel. I am very cross. We will go to the school this afternoon, and I will insist that someone shows us round. And really there's no need for us to go to Pearson's, because I can just phone them up and order everything for you. They will know your size from the last time you went there to get clothes.'

I didn't usually like to argue with grown-ups, because I had been brought up to believe that they knew what was best for me. However, I must have come to trust Auntie, because I said, 'Excuse me Auntie Aileen...'

She laughed and said, 'Oh Pippa! I just know you are going to tell me that I have made a mistake, and that you have a better suggestion. I'm just a bit cross with Sister, that's all.'

I said, 'Well, now you mention it, perhaps it would be a good idea for me to try the clothes on, in case I've grown, and to see what everything really looks like. And I might need to try on the hat as well.'

Auntie said that would be a very good idea, so I added, 'And it would be fun to go back to Pearson's. Could we buy a small present for each of Uncle Tom's children?' Auntie said that was a lovely idea, and gave me a big kiss.

I was being cheerful, but at the same time I wondered how I would be able to say goodbye to Auntie, and how I was going to survive on my own in boarding school.

Auntie made a phone call, and soon afterwards Mr Griffin arrived in his car. He was very pleased to see us again. When we got to the school, Mr Griffin drove his car through the school gates and parked in front of the main school building. Auntie told him that he could meet us at Pearson's, but he was very insistent that he would wait. He took out a newspaper and started reading it. We walked up the steps towards a big wooden door that had a very big and shiny pane of glass in it. We had just gone through the door when Sister Eugenie came towards us. I thought she was going to say hello to us, but instead she said to Auntie, 'Is that your husband sitting in that car? If so, please tell him that he can't park there. He will have to park in the street.'

Auntie said, 'I'm awfully sorry, but we are in a hurry. Perhaps you could tell him yourself?'

Sister Eugenie tutted and went outside and knocked on Mr Griffin's car window. He slowly wound it down, and she said something to him. Mr Griffin said something back to her and then wound his window back up again. Sister Eugenie turned round and came up the steps towards the front door, and walked straight past us. We could see that she was very annoyed. Mr Griffin waved at me and winked, then carried on reading his newspaper.

We were in a lobby, with very shiny tiles on the floor and a large crucifix on one of the walls, and a table with a statue of Our Lady on it. We went through a set of doors with shiny glass in them, and into a tiled passage. We heard some hurried footsteps, and two big girls, dressed all in grey, walked quickly past us. Then we heard a loud voice from along the passage say, 'Slowly, girls, slowly!'

I gripped Auntie's hand tightly. The girls immediately stopped and turned round. They both said, 'Sorry, Sister Winifred,' and walked slowly away. There was a shiny wooden seat in the lobby, and Auntie told me to sit on it. I didn't want her to leave me, but she told me she would be back in a few minutes. I heard her say, 'Excuse me Sister Winifred!'

Sister said, 'Yes?' and I heard her hard shoes walking towards Auntie. They were just round the corner from me, and the door was open, so I could hear what they were saying.

Auntie said, 'I have come to collect a school clothing and equipment list, and to show a child around the school. She will be starting in September.'

'Are you the lady who telephoned this morning, asking to be shown around the school?'

'That's correct.'

'And did my secretary not make it clear to you that a visit today would be out of the question?'

'She did. However, we will be leaving for Stranhaven soon, and all I am asking for is a short visit round the school.'

'No. I repeat, that is out of the question. Visit days for prospective pupils are held three times a year. In exceptional circumstances, visits can be arranged two weeks in advance, and can take place on a Tuesday morning.' I could hear that Sister Winifred was beginning to get annoyed.

Auntie didn't sound cross at all. 'I have with me the daughter of Mr Andrew Dunbar.'

'And you are?'

'I'm her aunt. I have legal responsibility to look after her on Mr Dunbar's behalf. But surely you know that, because I believe that Mr Macmillan spoke to you on the telephone and arranged for us to visit.'

Sister said, 'Be that as it may, as I have just said, a visit is not possible today. We make no exceptions here, whoever the girl's father might be.' There was a pause. I wondered if Auntie was thinking of what to say next, but she kept quiet. Sister said, 'You may go to the school office and collect the clothing list from the school secretary, and ask her to book you in for a visit in a few weeks' time. Now I really must be going.'

I heard her loud footsteps walking away.

Auntie came back into the lobby. I stood up and told her that I was frightened, and wanted to sit in the car with Mr Griffin. She said, 'Certainly not. We are going to have a quick look round. I've no idea where the office is, and until someone tells me where to find it, then we are perfectly entitled to wander around.' She smiled at me and took my hand and said, 'Don't you think so, Pippa?' She had a naughty look on her face, just like Mr Macmillan.

231

There was a sign in front of us with OFFICE written on it, and an arrow pointing up a very big flight of stairs. There were shiny metal rails at the side of the stairs, with a dark-brown polished wooden bannister, with rounded brass knobs at regular intervals all the way along the top. Auntie touched one and said, 'These have no doubt been put here to stop the girls from sliding down the bannisters.' She didn't seem to see the sign, so we walked along a long corridor. At the end of it was a big room, with lots of long tables and wooden benches. A nun was laying the tables with a huge pile of plates and knives and forks. There was an unpleasant smell of cooking everywhere. The nun looked up, and Auntie quickly turned me round and we walked to the other end of the corridor. There were classrooms on either side. Every classroom door had a big shiny pane of glass in it, so we could quickly peek in. In the first class, an old nun was sitting at a big desk in front of rows of girls about the same age as Bonnie. The nun looked like she was asleep. The girls were all busy reading. In the next class, another nun was writing on a big blackboard. She called out, without looking round, 'Who's that talking? Parker, is it you again?'

Sister Anne

In the third class, another nun was sitting at her desk, surrounded by a group of girls. She was looking at their exercise books. One of the girls looked at us and smiled. It was Juliet! I waved at her, and then she recognised me and gave me a big wave back. She nudged a girl next to her, pointed at me and whispered something. The nun looked up and I hid behind Auntie. Then I heard the classroom door open and a voice said, 'Hello. Are you lost? Can I help you?'

Auntie said, 'Oh no. We're fine thank you. We're just on a walk round the school, because Pippa is going to start here in September. She's Pippa Dunbar.'

The nun said, 'Ah yes. I was hoping that you'd both visit. I'm so glad to meet you both.'

I tried to hide even further behind Auntie, but the nun said, 'There's no need to hide. I imagine that you're a little bit shy.

Come in and see what we're doing. Some of the girls are a bit sleepy this afternoon, and could do with something exciting to wake them up!'

I couldn't stop myself from looking right in her face. She looked in my eyes and smiled at me. She said, 'And what beautiful blue eyes, and such dark hair. Are you Irish, by any chance?'

I couldn't quite believe what was happening, but found myself standing in front of the class, still holding Auntie's hand. The nun told the girls crowding round her desk to go and sit down. Then she said, 'Juliet, you seem to know who this young lady is. Please can you tell us how you know her?'

I went bright red and some of the girls said, 'Aah.'

Juliet said, 'Well Sister, we met Pippa while we were visiting Bonnie, I mean Sheila, in hospital. She was in the bed next to Bonnie, and she was very kind to Bonnie, I mean Sheila.'

The nun smiled and said to me, 'I'm glad you are better. And are you really starting with us in September?'

I put my head down. She said to the class, 'Who would like to explain to Pippa and her aunt what we are studying today?'

Several girls put their hands up, and the nun chose a girl with skin like mine, and very big brown eyes. The nun said, 'Yes Émilie? What are we doing?'

It was Émilie! She stood up and said, 'We are stoodying ow to bisect a ciercool, Seestair.' She had the most adorable French accent.

The nun smiled. 'Bravo Émilie, très bien!'

Émilie smiled a very big smile.

Sister said, 'Juliet, please will you show Pippa what you have been doing with Émilie? The rest of you girls carry on with your work.' There was some giggling going on, and the nun said, 'Come on girls. We want to give Pippa a good impression, otherwise she might change her mind and go to another school. And that would be an awful shame, wouldn't it?' The girls laughed, quietly.

Émilie and Julia came out to the front of the class with Émilie's exercise book. Émilie said to me. 'Allo Peepa. Ah ope you coam to zis school.'

The nun smiled again. Émilie's book was full of very neat diagrams and lovely writing. Juliet told me that Sister Anne was a super maths teacher, and especially loved geometry, which was why they were learning so much about it. Then she whispered, 'Bonnie's not here anymore.'

I whispered back, 'I know. Mr Macmillan told me.'

Émilie whispered, 'Ee iz ze nars man oo say Bonnie muzzer and fahzer zat Bonnie she jump off ze beeg roof?

I nodded. The nun was busy telling Auntie about how much she enjoyed teaching maths. Émilie whispered, 'You curm 'ere soon?'

I whispered, 'I think so.'

Julia said, 'How lovely! I'll tell the other girls, and we'll all look after you.'

Émilie looked sad. Then the nun came over to us and said, 'Well done girls. I hope you've done a good job, and convinced Pippa to join us!' She put a hand on each of their shoulders, 'Now back you go to your desks, because it's nearly time for us to finish our lesson.'

The girls went to sit down. Sister said to them, 'Manners, girls! Manners! Don't forget to say goodbye!'

The two girls came back and Juliet shook Auntie's hand and said, 'Goodbye. It was lovely to meet you again.'

Auntie smiled and said it had been a pleasure. Then Juliet shook my hand. She looked in my eyes and smiled. I felt warm inside.

Then Auntie did something unexpected. She hugged Émilie and kissed her on both cheeks. Émilie looked very surprised, and then smiled an enormous smile. She looked beautiful. I decided to do the same. I put my face towards Émilie's and she gave me a kiss on each cheek. Then she looked in my eyes again and gave me two more kisses.

Some girls giggled, but Sister Anne said, 'Don't be silly, girls, that's how French people say *hello* and *goodbye* to each other. I think it's rather charming.' She took my hand in both of hers. She looked right into my eyes and said to me, 'Goodbye my dear, and I do hope we'll see you in September!'

I went bright red, and she smiled again. I think she wanted to kiss me, but was stopping herself. Some of the girls said, 'Aah,' again, and Sister Anne smiled at them.

As we were leaving the classroom, she said to the class, 'Well done girls. I'm very proud of you. That's exactly the sort of excellent behaviour I know I can expect from you all. Well done.'

I looked at Émilie once more. She waved at me. I had a warm feeling just above my Lovely Place, like I was melting. Auntie said, 'Come on Pippa, let's go to the office and find that list. What an extraordinary woman.'

Émilie

Then we heard a girl's voice behind us say 'Excusez-moi!' It was Émilie. She said to us, 'Seestair Anne, she say me to show to you ze office.'

Auntie looked and sounded delighted. She said to Émilie, 'Je parle français. Pas parfaitement, mais suffisamment pour comprendre des choses importantes que tu veux peut-être nous dire.'

Émilie looked very surprised, then smiled and went red. I thought she was going to cry with happiness. She put her hand in Auntie's. She said, 'I show you le dortoir.'

Émilie pulled Auntie's hand and said, 'Come, come. Zis way. It up high en haut ze stairs.'

So up the stairs we went, with Émilie pulling Auntie, and me following one step behind, holding Auntie's other hand. Each stair was made of shiny grey stone and was very worn; probably from the thousands of girls' and nuns' feet that had climbed them every day over the years. I counted fifteen stairs, and looked up and saw a huge stained glass window of Our Lady. The sunlight was shining through. I had never seen a stained glass window close up and wanted to stop to see how it was made, but I noticed that next to the window was a toilet. A nun was on her hands and knees with her back to us, scrubbing the floor. On the first floor we paused, and Émilie pointed to the office. She said, 'Vite, vite!' and pulled us up another flight of stairs.

We walked quickly up onto another floor, and to our left saw an open door into a room with beds in. In front of us was a washroom with rows of sinks. A nun was mopping the floor. We turned to go up more stairs, but just before we climbed, I looked to my left, down a long corridor with a huge set of windows at the end. I saw a little old lady dressed in a nurse's uniform. Émilie whispered, 'Vite! She nurse. She horrible. She sorcière!'

At the top of fifteen steps there was a narrow landing with five doors. I could smell very strong bleach and guessed that they were toilets. Then we went up another flight and came to a big landing with a floor that was made up of small white and dark blue mosaic tiles. I wanted to look at the pattern, but Émilie wouldn't let me stop. She put her finger to her lips and gently opened a door, and took us into a long room with beds on either side. The beds were made of iron and all very carefully made up, with a thin light blue-grey cover on each one. As Émilie led us to the far end of the room, the wooden floor creaked under our feet. They were floorboards that had once been very carefully polished, but now seemed a bit worn. I imagined that if you walked on them with bare feet you would get a splinter.

There was a wooden cabinet next to each bed, and I supposed that was where the girls kept their belongings. There were small rooms off the main room, and each one had four beds in it. At the far end of the main room was a row of sinks, and above them a mantelpiece with a very large statue of Our Lady on it. On either side of the statue were two vases full of brightly coloured plastic flowers. Émilie pressed a light switch and suddenly the whole wall was lit up by bright coloured lights. She whispered, 'Oh là là!' and switched them off.

Round the corner from Our Lady was a room full of sinks and a row of low basins, that I supposed you washed your feet in.

Émilie gestured for us to follow her into a small room next to the washroom. There were three very tidy beds and another with just a mattress on it. The mattress looked very old and lumpy. Émilie pointed at it and whispered 'That was Bonnie bed.' She opened the cupboard next to her bed and a jumble of clothes fell onto the floor. She giggled and said, 'Oh là là!' and shoved the clothes back in again. She whispered, 'Zat my locker.'

Then Émilie and Auntie had a whispered conversation in French and English.

Auntie: Où est Bonnie?

Émilie: Elle est en Afrique. Elle est rentrée chez elle.

Auntie: Monsieur Macmillan a-t-il dit à Sister Winifred que Bonnie était très malheureuse?

Émilie: She jermp off ze roof. She kees me on ze leeps, zen she jermp. She not fall. She won keel 'erself.

Auntie: So Mr Macmillan told Bonnie's parents she was very unhappy?

Émilie: Oui. Now I vayree un'appy. My eeyurt eez gon burst!

So it was true; Bonnie had tried to kill herself. I felt myself tremble all over. I suddenly felt very frightened, and wanted to run away from this horrible school and never come back again. Then Émilie pointed to Bonnie's bed, and then her own, and said something to Auntie in French and burst into tears. She had explained that this was the bed that Bonnie used to sleep in, and the two girls had been caught fast asleep in Émilie's bed. Auntie put her arm round Émilie and hugged her tightly, and kissed her. I took my hanky out of my sleeve and gave it to Émilie, to blow her nose on. It was my favourite hanky, with pretty embroidered dark yellow and blue flowers at each corner. Émilie looked at it and cried even more.

Auntie opened her handbag and took out two sweets. She gave one to Émilie and the other to me. If Auntie had thought that this would calm Émilie down, then she had made a big mistake. Émilie started wailing even louder. Auntie sat on Émilie's bed and pulled Émilie towards her. She hugged her again and kissed her soaking wet cheeks and said, 'Shh, shh. It's all right. It's all right.'

I stood looking at them both.

Then we heard footsteps on the creaky floorboards in the main part of the dormitory. They were coming slowly towards us. Émilie immediately stopped crying, stood up, and whispered, 'Oh la vache! C'est Sister Carmel. Je déteste cette bonne sœur! Elle me frappe.'

She blew her nose on my hanky and stuffed it up her sleeve. Then an old nun was in the doorway, holding a walking stick. She said, 'Émilie! What in heaven's name are you doing here?' She said to Auntie, 'And who are you? And why are you in here with one of the girls?' She had an Irish accent, and when she looked at Auntie, one of her eyes looked at Auntie's face, but the other one looked at me. I was very frightened. Émilie let go of Auntie and put her hands by her sides. She looked at the floor and was silent. Auntie didn't seem at all frightened. She stood up and I tried to hide behind her. She said to the nun, 'I am this girl's aunt.' She moved so that the nun could see me. 'Her name is Pippa Dunbar. This charming girl, Émilie, is very kindly showing us round the school. Sister Anne asked her to.'

The nun didn't smile. She said, 'Émilie, go back to your class.' Émilie didn't move. The nun tutted and said to Auntie, 'The little minx pretends that she doesn't know what I'm talking about, but she understands every word.'

Auntie spoke to Émilie in French and Émilie said, 'Merci beaucoup, Madame,' and put her face up towards Auntie. Auntie kissed her on the cheeks, three times. Then Émilie winked at me and kissed me three times. She whispered in my ear 'A bientôt, ma belle amie,' then left the room.

The nun said, 'So Sister Anne told that girl to show you round the school? That seems a little unlikely to me.'

Auntie ignored that remark and said, 'As I was saying, I'm Pippa's aunt. She's due to start at this school in September.'

The nun gave Auntie a very strange look, as if Auntie was dirty, or smelled. Auntie ignored that look too. I tried not to look at the nun's eyes. They were like searchlights, moving in different directions. They disgusted me. Auntie said, 'I imagine you know Pippa's story. I am the Aunt who cares for her while she lives in Scotland.'

The nun gave an odd smile. She said, 'Oh *that* aunt. For a moment I thought you were the one...' then she stopped herself. I knew what she was thinking. She thought that Auntie Aileen was Muriel. Someone must have told her all about me. I wanted to kick her walking stick away from her, so that she would fall on the floor, and then we could run away.

Auntie said, 'We have thoroughly enjoyed our little tour. Now we really must go to the office. We are in a hurry to catch Pearson's before it closes.'

The nun didn't smile. One of her eyes looked at me and she said, 'Rich or poor, we are all equal in the eyes of the Good Lord. All the girls here are treated in the same way.'

I wanted to say, 'Yes, they are all treated terribly badly; sleeping on lumpy beds with thin blankets and having to wash all over in a sink and eat smelly food!' Instead, I looked away from her eye.

Auntie said, 'Thank you Sister, we will find the office on our own.'

She led me out of the dormitory and down to the office.

The secretary in the office was a very young lady. She smiled at me and said, 'And you must be Pippa. How nice to meet you.' Behind her was another office. The door was closed, and we could hear a lady talking on the telephone. The secretary whispered to Auntie, 'I understand you've just met Sister Winifred in the corridor downstairs.'

Auntie smiled. 'Yes. We got a little lost, but have just been talking to an extremely charming nun who was teaching the children mathematics.'

The secretary stopped looking worried and smiled. 'Ah, so you've met Sister Anne.'

Auntie said, 'Her and Sister Winifred are like chalk and cheese.'

The secretary laughed nervously and looked over her shoulder. She thrust an envelope at Auntie and said, 'It's best if you go now, so you can catch Pearson's before it closes.' Then she cleared her throat. 'Excuse me for asking, but is it true that Pippa's father owns Pearson's, and most of the hotels in the town, and the golf course out at Sandyfoot, and most of the land around Kirkbrae?'

Auntie whispered, 'Yes. But please promise me that you won't tell anyone. We want Pippa to be just the same as everyone else.'

The young secretary said, 'Oh yes, of course. I promise not to say anything.'

In the car, Auntie said to Mr Griffin, 'What a strange way to behave! The nun in charge clearly wasn't going to be told what to do by me. She knew she had to allow us to look around, but wasn't going to admit it.'

Mr Griffin just smiled and asked, 'Where to now?'

Auntie sighed. 'Let's go shopping, and then home.'

I liked Sister Anne. Some of my fear about going to that school had gone away. I wondered if I would have nightmares about the old nun with the horrible eyes.

In Pearson's

I liked Pearson's. Daddy owned it and so, in a way, I imagined it belonged to me. The staff were very friendly too. I asked Auntie if they were so nice to us because they knew that Daddy was the owner. She said, 'Och no, they're like that with everyone. They bend over backwards to make sure the customers are happy.' I hadn't heard that expression before, and it made me smile.

The manager's wife remembered me and asked me if all the clothes we had chosen together had fitted me. She said I looked so much happier, and I seemed like a completely different child. She said she loved the colour of my skin, which she described as *olive*. She said, 'There's no way anyone could mistake you for a wee Scottish lassie. You look like one of the Italian lassies at the Convent. They're not real Italians, but their parents are. They came here after The War, and usually own restaurants and cafés, and even make ice cream! But your

240

father's Scottish, so I wonder where you get your dark looks from? Is your mother Italian?'

I looked at Auntie, who said, 'We haven't got long before the shop closes.'

The lady said, 'Of course.' Then she poked me in the tummy and said, 'And it looks like you've had a few decent meals since I saw you last!'

I had no idea how long I had been in Scotland. The terrible imprisonment at The Lodge and my time in hospital seemed so long ago. The grown-ups agreed that the best thing to do would be to take my measurements, then we could leave the list in the shop and the staff would get all my clothes ready. That was the first time I fully realised that once I had my uniform on, and went to the Convent, I would be just another boarding school girl, and wouldn't be special anymore.

Auntie reminded the manager's wife to make sure that all the clothes we ordered were a size larger, to allow for growth. They both agreed that girls my age grew a lot, and some of them very quickly. The manager's wife said, 'To make things easier for you, just take one set of uniform with you, to wear on your first day, and we can arrange for the rest of your clothes to be put in a trunk and sent on to the school, so they are ready for you on the day that you arrive.'

Auntie asked if that was usual, and the manager's wife said, 'For some of the girls, yes. Particularly those whose parents live overseas or who are... who are very well off. The girls usually have a trunk that their parents bring in the car or on the train. It's quite a sight to see them arrive on the trains the day before school starts.

I asked, 'But what if your family only have a small car, and the trunk won't fit in it?'

'Then they can send the trunk on the train, in advance, and you can arrange for it to be collected from the station and taken to the school.'

Auntie said, 'That all seems very complicated.'

'We have all the details here. You call the taxi service, or arrange it all by letter. It's surprising what having a private school in the town does for the local economy!'

While this conversation was going on, I was doing my best to fight a growing feeling of desperation. Every detail they discussed was like a slap in the face, because I knew that once again I was going to be separated from people who loved me. Some girls might have been excited at the thought of leaving home and going to a new school, but I was filling up with despair. I tried to smile.

The lady handed Auntie a pile of grey clothes, and took us to the changing room. I wasn't at all excited, like when I usually tried on new clothes. The uniform didn't even have the nice new smell. We went to the big mirror in the middle of the department. I thought I looked awful, and wanted to cry. I was wearing a white blouse with long sleeves, a grey pinafore dress and some very baggy tights that made me feel itchy and hot. I had a grey blazer with a light green and yellow trim, but no pockets. It was very thick, and the sleeves were too long. Auntie saw that I was becoming upset and said, 'You know, Pippa, it doesn't really matter what you look like. It's very cold in Scotland, so you will be very pleased to have all these woollen clothes on.'

The lady agreed. 'That's very true. And for that reason, I've chosen some nice thick vests, and a pile of short socks for you to wear before you put your tights on. I'm afraid that the shoes you have to wear aren't really going to keep you as warm as they should.'

The shoes were a dull black, and looked and felt what I would call *clumpy*. They were plain and ugly and had a big buckle, and looked like the kind of summer shoes that girls used to wear during The War. I asked if those were shoes that you only wore inside the buildings. Auntie said that there was no other footwear on the list; no outdoor shoes or boots, or even wellies. I didn't understand, and neither did she. And there was no PE kit either.

The lady said, 'I don't think they do PE, or if they do then they don't get changed for it.' She could see how unhappy I was. She patted my arm and said, 'Never mind, my dear, I'm going to choose two very bright bath towels for you, and another smaller one for when you go swimming. And would you let me choose some nice underwear for you?'

I said, 'Yes please,' because she had made such good choices the last time.

There were two more things to think about. First, we had to try on a coat. I wasn't surprised to see it was grey. It was very thick and very warm, and I told myself that this was a good thing, because I wouldn't be too cold. The lady explained that the school had a rule that on Sundays you were allowed to wear another coat, of any colour you liked. And you could wear the same coat every time you went to Mass. She said, 'You'll need to make sure it's as thick as possible, because I have been in that church, and it's freezing all year round. But it is lovely to see the girls wearing something that really reflects their personality.' This piece of information had two sides to it; the horrible thought of having to go to Mass, but the nice thought of wearing my own coat. The duffel coat that Mummy and Muriel had bought me in Gamages was very, very precious to me. I wanted to tell the lady that my duffel coat would always remind me of the day I realised that Mummy and Muriel were deeply in love, and that their love included me. But I knew not to. In the hurry to take me away to Scotland, Mummy had only packed summer clothes, so I supposed that Auntie would have to ring Mummy and ask her to post my duffel coat to us. Then I thought that it was now probably too small.

The last thing we tried on was my straw hat. I loved it, and putting it on and seeing myself in the mirror helped me to feel better about wearing school uniform. But there was a slight disappointment. Convent girls were only allowed to wear a straw hat in summer. For all the other seasons I had to wear a navy blue beret. Auntie asked me to try it on and said it really suited me, and that I looked very French, just like Émilie. This brought a smile to my face. The lady said, 'But I've been to the school in the winter and seen some girls wearing all sorts of hats in the school grounds. I think it's only when they go out into the town that they have to wear exactly the same thing on their head. But they look bonnie all the same, and you my dear, will be the bonniest of all!'

A bell rang downstairs and the lady said there was ten minutes until the shop closed, but we wouldn't have to worry about the time. The two adults looked at each other, and I knew they were making this special exception for me, because my daddy was the owner of the shop. But I didn't want to stay any longer. There was only one more thing I wanted to know, 'What do I wear in bed? Are there rules about that?'

The lady smiled and said, 'Nobody ever orders nightwear, and it's not on the list, so I suppose you can wear what you like!'

I said, 'I like pyjamas, really. Thick ones.'

Auntie said, 'Good idea.'

I already had a pair of pyjamas, that Mummy had packed. They were yellow with teddy bears on, and I loved wearing them. We hurried over to the nightwear section and straight away found exactly what I wanted. Two pairs of yellow pyjamas with puppies on. Auntie said to the lady, 'Don't put those on the account. I want to pay for them myself, if you don't mind.'

There was one more thing. The lady asked me what my number was. I didn't know what she meant. She explained that all of the girls had a number. It had to be sewn into every item of clothing, and we had to find a cobbler who could hammer some small nails into the bottom of my shoes, in the shape of my number, so they wouldn't get mixed up in school.

My number was at the top of the official piece of paper. It was 69.

Buying the uniform made me realise that my school life was going to be unlike anything I had experienced before. It felt like I was being sent to an expensive prison. The whole experience cast a huge shadow over me, as if every nice thing I had done with Auntie had been made dirty. It was as if Auntie had woven a lovely carpet for me to walk on, and someone had stepped on dog poo and walked all over it, on purpose. I know Auntie felt the same as me. In the car she sighed and said, 'Well, now that's that over and done with, let's have a nice evening together.'

The next day we tidied up the house, and Uncle Tom joined in with the cleaning. I was a bit surprised about that. He said that he had got used to being both a mother and a father in the time between his wife's death and meeting Auntie. And he laughed and said, 'And why shouldn't men and women share the jobs?' Auntie kissed him, and he winked at me and said, 'You see Pippa, if you share the chores, then that makes for a happy marriage.'
That evening, we said goodbye to the beach and the fields that I had come to love. Auntie explained that the house would be rented out to families who came to stay there on holiday. I was sad to go, but I wanted to be with other children. I just hoped that they were nice, and easy to get on with, but somehow I doubted it.

On the train to Stranhaven
After breakfast, Mr Griffin put our big bags and my art materials in the boot of his car, and drove us, with Luna, to the station in the town. He said to Auntie, 'Have a safe journey and I'll see you in Stranhaven.' It was cold and pouring with rain, even though it was the day before the start of the summer holidays. On the train, I sat next to Auntie, and Uncle Tom sat opposite. I was very pleased that Luna chose to sit on the floor next to me. I had felt sad to leave the house, and this feeling increased as the train left the town. I thought about poor dead Keith, and realised that we hadn't been to put flowers on his grave, or sent my picture to his parents. I told Auntie, and she said that she was sure the nuns in school would allow me to visit the grave, because the cemetery was right next to my

school. And she would ask Mr Macmillan to send my picture to Keith's parents.

Then I told Auntie that I didn't want to be so far away from Mummy, and the further we went on the train the sadder I was becoming. She said, 'I can imagine, but let's all have a lovely holiday together.'

I said, 'Auntie, can I tell you something?' That was my way of letting her know I was about to say something important about my feelings.

She smiled and said, 'Of course you can.'

A lady sitting by the door in our compartment was doing her knitting, but I didn't care if she was listening or not. I said, 'I think I might be jealous in Stranhaven. I think I'm feeling it right now. I don't want to share you with other people.'

Auntie smiled, and I knew exactly what she was going to say. She said it, 'I'm sure that I would feel exactly the same if I were you.'

I said, 'I knew you were going to say that.' The lady stopped her knitting.

Auntie said, 'That's such a grown up thing to say, Pippa. I wish the others could talk about their feelings like that. I have to warn you, Pippa, it's quite a struggle at times in our house, isn't it Tom?'

Uncle Tom had been looking out of the window. I thought his mind was miles away, and I supposed that he was thinking about something that he was going to write. But he had been listening, after all. I thought that it would take me a long time to get used to Uncle Tom and his ways. He was a nice man, but Auntie was much easier to talk to. He said, 'After her mother died, Maggie used to think that she had to be the woman of the house. Then your Auntie came along, and Maggie could go back to being herself again. Now she's grown up, but sometimes I think she's like a referee between the warring factions. And Jessie is... how to describe Jessie? It's hard to know what's going on in her pretty little head. And Nicol? Well, where shall we start? Let's just say that we're having a holiday from each other. Nicol gets on best with Maggie, and our dear friend Mrs Alderson, who are both at home at the moment, looking after everyone. Mrs Alderson is like a grandmother to Nicol, and he likes to spend time with her and her husband. He's always very well-behaved for them. But unfortunately, Jessie is… I'm not sure how to describe Jessie, and I'm a writer, so that might give you an idea of the magnitude of the problem!'

This was all news to me. Auntie had told me a little bit about the family I was going to stay with, but I hadn't asked about them, even though Auntie had spoken to them on the telephone on most evenings. Perhaps it was jealousy that had stopped me from being curious.

For a long time after that, Auntie and Uncle Tom talked about Nicol. He was rude to Auntie, and sulked. He provoked his father and little sister, and seemed to enjoy his father telling him off. He was particularly rude and aggressive towards Jessie at mealtimes. They used phrases like, *lost soul, he has lost his way*, and *argumentative*, and Uncle admitted that sometimes he wanted to knock Nicol's block off. Auntie said that the family had all been through a terrible tragedy, and everyone had had to make a lot of adjustments when she came to live with them. Uncle Tom said, 'That's very true Aileen, but it's been a long time.'

She said, 'But these things can take years, Tom.'

He leaned over and patted her hand and said, 'Sorry, my dear. That was very insensitive of me. I do apologise.'

I didn't like the idea of living with children who were at war with each other.

What I also learned about Nicol was that he liked girls, and for some reason this was a problem. Apparently, he liked talking to girls more than playing with boys, and some of the boys at school had been calling him nasty names. I didn't understand that at all. I told Uncle Tom about Roger, and how he played with Lucy and me all the time. I didn't mention that Roger probably did it because he was in love with Lucy, but I did tell him that Roger solved the name-calling problem by hitting a few big boys. I told them I didn't think that Nicol would like me, because he was a lot older than me. Uncle Tom said, 'Oh I'm sure he will. He has been asking me all about you.'

He saw me panicking and added, 'But naturally I haven't told him anything. Well just the bare bones.'

I asked Auntie about what I should say about myself. She said I could tell the children as little or as much as I liked. I didn't want them to know anything. I never knew how to explain about my family.

Uncle Tom said, 'I wish I wasn't banned from writing about people I know, because Pippa, I'd certainly put you in one of my books! You are such a wise and thoughtful girl!'

Auntie said, 'And that's the greatest praise you can possibly get from a Highland man like Uncle Tom! They are not the most open men in the world about their feelings, are they Tom?'

Uncle laughed, and I thought he was blushing under his grey and ginger beard. 'Well in a way that's true. We're a dour bunch, us Heelanders, and we dinna laik aways goin' on aboot oor feelings like the womenfolk, or the pansies frae doon sooth.' He was putting on a very strong Stranhaven accent, to make us laugh, but I knew he was being serious.

I imagined men from the north of Scotland being very tough and dangerous, and wearing kilts and carrying huge swords, and growing thick ginger beards, and not liking boys who they thought were sissies. I had seen pictures of Scotsmen like that in my comics. Uncle Tom said to me, 'I'm going to tell a joke. See if you get it.'

Auntie said, 'Tom, that's not fair!'

'I just want to show Pippa that Highlanders are not all pessimistic and hard-bitten.'

This was his joke. 'A Highland man loved his wife so much that he told her.'

The lady with the knitting roared with laughter and said, 'Wait until I tell that one to my husband!'

We all looked at her. She coughed and said to Uncle Tom, 'I'm awful sorry. I couldn't help listening. Are you by any chance Thomas Pirie, the famous author?'

Uncle Tom smiled at her and said, 'I am that, madam.'

'I thought so. I'm a great admirer of your work. It's so... so, dare I say it, *lusty*. I don't mean that in the Biblical sense, shall we say. Perhaps *earthy* might be a better word. My husband hates your writing, I'm afraid to say, but then he detests Socialists. All my lady friends have copies of your trilogy. They will be so jealous to know that I have met you!'

Uncle Tom seemed very pleased, and said, 'And you will be making my dear wife jealous by saying such things, madam.'

The three adults laughed out loud. The lady said, 'And I really enjoyed your recent radio interview. It's wonderful to think that a Scottish author is finally getting the recognition he deserves. And what was it like being on *Desert Island Discs*? I loved your choice of music. *Lark Ascending* is my favourite too. And it's wonderful to know,' she looked at Auntie, 'that I have met Mr Pirie's... how shall I put it? His *muse*, and inspiration for the heroine of your trilogy.'

Auntie's cheeks were pink. I think she was pleased. She said, 'How do you know that, if you don't mind me asking? Tom, have you been talking to journalists about that? You promised me!' I thought that she was telling him off, but she was laughing.'

The lady looked a bit worried. 'No dear, it's just that looking at you; your face, your hair, your smile, and listening to your voice, it's obvious that you are Winnie.'

Uncle Tom said, 'Thank you. Thank you very much. I'm delighted that your husband hates my work!'

The adults laughed again, and then were quiet. The lady carried on knitting. I hadn't understood Uncle's joke at all.

I wasn't sure I wanted to meet Nicol. I wondered if he was like Naomi, and had seen Uncle Tom and his wife having S-E-X when he was a little boy. I didn't like myself for thinking that. But then I thought that it could be quite nice to meet him, after all. Auntie had said that he was just like my daddy, when he was the same age. It was obvious that Auntie had been very fond of my father, and it was his school's fault for making him become horrible and not like girls anymore. I wondered if Nicol might be like Peter, except Nicol sounded like a pickle, and Peter was not at all a pickle, except when he got jealous once, because he thought that I might like to spend time with his big sister. Then I remembered that being jealous was an emotion, a feeling, and it didn't always mean you were a pickle. Lots of people feel jealous, sometimes. Even Jesus must have felt jealous, and He probably made up a parable about it. Perhaps it was called, *The Woman at the Well who was Jealous*. But perhaps St Peter didn't think it was one of Jesus' better stories, so he told Matthew, Mark, Luke and John not to bother writing it down in The Gospels. I thought that was a shame, because it would have been helpful to know what Jesus had to say about our feelings.

I stopped thinking about feelings, but couldn't stop thinking about Nicol, which was a bit annoying. So I concentrated on looking out of the window, and looking at the reflection of me wearing my beret. We had decided not to bring my straw hat, because Auntie was worried that the wind might blow it away, or the Stranhaven rain might ruin it forever. I practised wearing my beret in different ways and wondered if I looked French, like Émilie. She really was a fascinating girl.

Stranhaven
When we got to the station at Stranhaven, there was a grown up lady and a boy and a girl waiting for us. The lady was tall and had very short hair, but she didn't look like a man. Her hairstyle made her look very pretty; like Audrey Hepburn, but ginger. She threw herself at Auntie and kissed her and said, 'Don't ever leave us like that again!' But she was laughing. She was Maggie. She said, 'Hello Dad,' to Uncle Tom and then turned her attention to me. She picked me up and kissed me and said, 'And you must be the lovely Pippa! I've been waiting for such a long time to meet you. You can be my long-lost little

cousin, if you like!' While Maggie was kissing and shouting at me, the girl, who I knew was Jessie, had jumped into her father's arms and wouldn't allow him to put her down. The boy, who must have been Nicol, just stood still and watched everybody. I looked at him and he looked away. I had been expecting some big ugly boy, covered in spots and with a terrible haircut and a horrible temper, but he was quite the opposite. He was the same height as me and his hair looked lovely. His face was quite beautiful. That's really the only way to describe him. I was very disappointed that he didn't look at me, but I supposed that he was very shy.

Luna jumped up at Nicol and tried to lick his face, and Nicol said, 'Hello Luna, did you miss me?' Auntie went towards him and said, 'Hello Nicol. I missed you,' and kissed him on the cheek. He didn't smile, but went slightly red. His father came over, still holding Jessie, and ruffled his hair and said, 'Hello Son. Have you been looking after Mrs Alderson, like you promised?' Nicol frowned and moved his head slightly backwards.

Uncle Tom took his hand away and frowned as well. He said to Nicol, 'Come and say hello to Pippa. She's going to be with us for the whole of the summer, so we're hoping that you'll all have a wonderful time together.'

Nicol didn't move. I didn't know what to do, so just stood still. I wanted to say, 'Hello Nicol. Are you really a lost soul? I'm a lost soul too, so can we be friends?' I knew not to say that, but instead I did something quite surprising. I kissed him on each cheek. His eyes opened wide. I said, 'That's what French people do. I've only been in Scotland for a little while, so I don't know how you say hello here.'

Nicol laughed. I heard Jessie behind me say, 'That girl kissed Nicol.'

Uncle Tom said, 'I know. And her name's Pippa. Would you like her to kiss you too?'

Jessie said, 'Yes please.' Her father leaned over so that Jessie's face was near mine and I kissed her on each cheek. She said, 'Thank you very much.'

251

Everyone laughed, including Nicol.

And so began a lovely, unforgettable summer holiday. It wasn't always easy, but it was certainly unforgettable.

Uncle Tom's house was on the other side of the town, and halfway up a hill, so the plan was for as many of us as possible to squeeze into a taxi. There wasn't enough room, so Maggie said that she would walk back to the house with Nicol, Jessie, and Luna. Nicol frowned, Jessie started whinging, and Luna barked. Then Mr Griffin appeared in his shiny red Cortina and waved at us. Uncle Tom got out of the taxi and spoke to him, then came back and said that Auntie and I should go with Mr Griffin.

Nicol coughed and said, 'Can I go with them? That looks like a brand new Cortina.'

His father agreed, so Nicol sat in the back with me. I was so busy thinking about sitting next to him, that I didn't even look out of the window. He was wearing shorts and had a big bruise on his leg. He saw me looking at it and covered it with his hand. He said to me, 'Are you French?' He had the loveliest Scottish accent.

I told him I wasn't, but had a friend who was. He coughed and fluttered his eyelashes, 'Are you from England then?' I said I was. He coughed and fluttered his eyelashes. 'So how do people in England say hello to each other then?'

'Well, usually they shake hands or just say hello.'

'The same as in Scotland then.'

'Yes, I think so.'

We didn't say anything else after that. Scotland felt like a foreign country to me. Nicol's accent was almost as strong as Émilie's.

Uncle Tom's house was quite big, with a rusty metal front gate that was hanging off its hinges, and a very untidy front garden. But although everything in the garden was untidy, it looked like a very friendly place. The front door was red and all the window frames were painted light blue. An old lady came out and walked straight towards me. She grabbed my cheeks, gave me a kiss, and said, 'And you must be Pippa. What a bonnie lassie you are! Let me take a good look at you! Thank goodness you are here, because you can play with Nicol and Jessie, and get them out from under my feet! Poor Nicol's been talking non-stop about you!' I didn't believe that was true for one minute, but I went red anyway. He really was a most handsome boy, and I couldn't wait to get to know him better. But I was worried that he might be one of those boys who Roger said were very boring, because all they did was talk about trains and cars, and spent lots of time making *Airfix* model aeroplanes, and arguing about who was the best fighter in the school.

Everything in the house looked old and dusty and a bit battered, but it seemed like the sort of house where if you ran around and broke something, then nobody would mind. Mrs Alderson had cooked us a big meal and the table had been laid, and I suddenly felt very shy. I suppose that's quite natural, because even now that still happens to me when I am with new people. But this was something much more powerful. I felt flooded with an overwhelming feeling that I needed to be with Mummy and Muriel. I could hear people talking to me, but didn't know what they were saying, and my eyes went blurred. Auntie must have noticed, because she said, 'Quick Nicol, get Pippa a glass of water, and I'll help her to sit down.' She sat me on the sofa and I could feel Nicol sit next to me and hear him say, 'Here, drink some water,' but I couldn't take the glass from him. Then the feeling went away, but it was too late because everyone was looking at me. I felt very embarrassed and wanted to run out of the house.

Nicol in the garden

It was time to sit round the table. Nicol coughed and said, 'Can Pippa sit next to me?' Everyone looked at him. He fluttered his eyelashes and said, 'What? What's the matter? I'm only trying to be friendly.'

Auntie said, 'Of course you are. What a good idea. Would you like that, Pippa?'

I started crying and said, 'I'm very sorry, but I want to go home.'

Mrs Alderson said, 'Poor wee love. What she needs is some soup.'

Auntie said, 'I've got an idea. You all eat your food, while I take Pippa for a wee walk in the garden' She helped me to stand up, and led me through the kitchen and into the back garden. We sat on rusty chairs, next to an even rustier table.

Nicol came out. He coughed and said, 'You forgot your water.' I felt very hot all over and then I thought I was going to be sick. My eyes were full of water and I heard Nicol shout, 'Watch out!' And I was sick.

Auntie said, 'Quick Nicol, run and get a cloth and tell your father that Pippa has been sick.'

He did as he was told, and came back with a tea towel. I thought Auntie was going to tell him to go and get something else to wipe my mouth with, but she said, 'Good boy. That's just the thing. Would you mind staying out here with Pippa for a wee while? Then you can both come in and have some food when she feels better.'

Nicol didn't say anything. He looked a bit frightened. Finally, he said, 'Wwwwhere is your home?'

I cried a bit more and said, 'That's the problem, Nicol, I don't think I have one anymore. I'm a lost soul.' He gave me my glass of water. I said, 'Thank you Peter.'

He said, 'My name's Nicol.' I went red. He said, 'Yyyou're not looking pale anymore, so are you feeling better now?' I nodded. He said, 'I don't like to see people being sick.'

'Why not?'

'It makes me think of my mum.'

'Was she ill for a long time?'

'No, she died giving birth to Jessie. I don't really like to talk about it.' That was very surprising, and shocking. Surprising because this was our first chat, and straight away he was talking about his dead mother; and shocking because I didn't know that ladies could die giving birth. I supposed that the baby just slid out, like a puppy or a kitten, or a piglet. I felt sick again, but forced it down and drank some water.

I said, 'Oh.' I didn't know what else to say.

Nicol looked disappointed. I thought he was going to get up and walk away, so I said, 'I went to a special person who helped me to talk about my problems.'

He said, 'I have someone like that. I have Rhona. She's one of the musicians who live in the cottages near the top of the hill. I look after her cat. Is your mother dead as well?'

I told him that she was alive, but I wasn't allowed to see her. He looked puzzled, but didn't say anything. I supposed he was thinking of what to say about that, or about asking another question, but all he said was, 'Oh!'

I don't know why, but that seemed very funny, so I laughed, and Nicol smiled. I had thought that I might have to talk to Nicol in a grown-up way, so that he would be interested in me. But I suddenly knew that he liked me and I could say whatever I wanted. So I said, 'I feel better now, but I'm bursting for a wee,' which was how I used to talk to Peter and Roger.

He said, 'Good.'

'What's good?'

'Mrs Alderson keeps telling me I have to be on my best behaviour with you, because you are a very polite wee girl. So I was worried about how to talk to you.'

'But I *am* polite. I always say please and thank you.'

'But polite girls don't tell boys that they need to do a wee. That's how Jessie talks.'

'Well I don't like people who swear and talk about rude things, if that's what you mean'

He looked worried, 'Och no. I didna mean that. It's just... it's just...'

I said, 'It's just that if I don't do a wee right now then...' We laughed. We got up to go indoors and Luna smelled my sick. Thankfully, she didn't eat it.

When we went back inside, Mrs Alderson kissed me and told us that she had kept our food warm. I didn't know where everyone else had gone. Mrs Alderson said, 'Right Nicol, I'm away now. You be a good boy and look after your bonnie wee cousin. And try not to fight with Jessie. It's not her fault that she's the way she is.'

Nicol got up and put his arms around Mrs Alderson. She held him tight and kissed him on the top of his head. He said, 'Byebye Mrs Alderson. Thank you for looking after us.'

She ruffled his hair and said, 'You look just like your mother, but you're your father's son. That's why you both fight so much.'

It was the first time I had seen a boy behave like that. If Roger's mum ever tried to kiss him in front of Lucy and me, he squirmed and tried to push his mother away, and told her to stop being so soppy.

What's wrong with Nicol?

I couldn't understand what Nicol saw in me. I was still not quite ten, and he was twelve. He should have been spending time with boys and girls of his own age. But then something happened that made me understand him. A little while after our meal, Nicol asked his dad if we could both go to see Rhona's garden, to check if her cat was all right. Uncle Tom said, 'Of course you can, Nicol. What a good idea. But take Jessie with you as well.' Nicol didn't say anything else to his dad, which seemed a bit rude, so I said, 'Thank you, Uncle Tom.'

He said, 'You're welcome, Pippa,' and then looked at Nicol, who looked away.

The three of us walked up the hill, and after a few minutes Jessie saw a cat and stopped to stroke it. Nicol tutted at her and said, 'Come on Jessie. Stop dawdling! It's just a silly old cat!'

I stopped walking and went to stroke the cat. Nicol was a few paces up the hill. I looked up at him and he looked very annoyed, but he didn't say anything else. I said, 'Come on Jessie, would you like to hold my hand?' She left the cat and smiled at me. When we reached Nicol, he said, 'She's such a baby! You'll only make her worse.'

I don't know what got into me. I'd only known this boy for a few hours. I said, 'No she's not. Don't speak like that! If you are going to be nasty, then I won't come with you. I don't have to come with you, you know.'

Nicol looked shocked. He said, 'I'm sssssorry. I didn't mean it.' He looked like I had hit him.

But I wasn't going to stop. 'Yes you did. You did mean it.'

He wouldn't look at me. He said, 'IIIIIIIIII…. IIIIIIII….' He made a fist and banged his leg with it. 'IIII'm sorry for being…. III'm sorry for being nasty to Jessie.'

'Will you do your best to try not to do it again?'

'Yyyyyyyyes. I wwwwill.'

The little sister stood next to me. She didn't seem to be taking any notice of what was going on between us, but I could tell that she was drinking it all in. Nicol didn't say anything. We walked up the hill and I tried to look in his face, but he kept it turned away from me. I held Jessie's hand, and she looked very pleased.

We walked up the hill, in silence. We were almost in the countryside. A short way up ahead a man was fixing a stone wall. As we passed him he said something in Scottish to Nicol, and Nicol laughed. I asked Nicol what the man said, but he wouldn't say anything. Then I understood what was wrong with Nicol. I wanted to talk to him about it.

After about a hundred yards, we came to another wall with a rusty iron gate. I wondered if everything around here was either made of stone or rusty metal. Nicol pushed the gate open and smiled as he showed me his hand. It was covered in light brown rust. Then a big black cat with a white face and white paws jumped up onto the wall. Nicol said, 'Hello William,' and stroked him.

Jessie said, 'You see how horrible Nicol is? He tells me off for stroking a cat and calls me a baby, but then he strokes William and that's all right.'

I said, 'But Nicol has already said he was sorry about being nasty, and is going to try not to do it again. So you should forgive him, and stop going on about it.'

Now it was her turn to look as if she had been hit. She said, 'I don't like it here. I want to go home.'

I said, 'Why don't you stroke William?'

She said, 'He's just a silly old cat.' But she was laughing.

I thought, 'There's nothing sweet and babyish about Jessie. She's a clever one.' Nicol said, 'Dddddooo you want to look in the garden?' Jessie said she didn't want to go in, because it was haunted. But she said it in a playful way; not like when Lucy and I had been terrified in front of the cemetery.

Rhona's garden

There was a gravel path, and the grass on either side of it was very high and full of tall yellow and lilac flowers. In front of us was a row of four cottages, all joined together, and each with a very brightly coloured front door. All the window frames were painted light blue. We walked towards the cottages and William the cat followed us. Jessie gripped my hand tightly and said, 'I'm scared!'

I said, 'I'm not frightened; at least not if we hold hands.' But I was, a little.

Nicol led us to the front of the cottage on the left hand side, at the end of the row. There was a big flowerpot by the door, with a bushy plant in it, with tiny purple flowers. Nicol touched the plant and dragged his hand through it. He put his hand up to my nose and said, 'Smell that.' I did. It was the most gorgeous smell, like soap. He said, 'That's rosemary.' I've loved the smell of rosemary, and the name, ever since. Nicol knocked on the door, but there was no answer. We went into the garden by the side of the house. A rusty bicycle was leaning up against the wall. I asked Nicol if he had a bike. He said, 'I do, but I don't ride it much. It's a girl's bike. The boys tease me. They call me a girl.'

'Well you're not a girl.'

'I know that, but....'

I couldn't get him to say any more about it.

Nicol told me to look through the window. There was a room with white walls, with big pieces of brightly coloured cloth hanging here and there. The only furniture was a table propped against the wall by the door, and some very big bright cushions scattered on the floor. An enormous canvas was propped up against one of the walls. I couldn't see it very clearly, but there some very interesting shapes painted on it. I had never seen anything like it. Nicol said, 'This is their studio. This is where they write songs and rehearse. Maggie is going to decorate it before they come back. '

Jessie asked him, 'Where have all the musical instruments gone?'

'Oh, they've taken them with them to Europe. I suppose they'll bring them all back again.'

I asked Nicol when they would come back. He said, 'Towards the end of the holidays. They're going to most of the countries in Europe.'

I wanted to look at the painting for a bit longer, but Nicol insisted on showing me the garden.

I imagined that the garden would be full of long grass and weeds, but it was actually very tidy. Nicol explained that he went up there on most days and tried to keep the garden as tidy as possible. There were some small trees too, and each one had interesting things hanging from its branches. The first tree we looked at was small and old and very twisted, as if it had been struggling to grow all its life. Someone had tied a mobile to one of the lower branches, made out of a wooden hoop with lots of small white bones and shells hanging from it. Nicol explained that these were sheep bones that the musicians had found up on the hills, and shells from the beach. Rhona and Nicol had made the mobile together, and as the wind blew, it knocked the bones and shells together. I didn't like the idea of a musical instrument made from bones, but had to admit that they made a nice sound when the wind blew, and knocked them together. There was something quite fascinating hanging from another tree. It was a big circle made of thin branches woven together, with coloured strings woven across the circle, so it looked like a spider's web. The strings had feathers, wooden beads, shells, and pieces of ribbon and wool hanging from them, and in the centre of the circle was a stone with a hole in it.

Nicol explained that this was a dreamcatcher, and he had helped Rhona and the other musicians to make it. He explained that the Red Indians made them to hang in their wigwams, near the children's beds. When the children dreamed, the bad dreams passed through web, but the spider in the middle would catch the good dreams. Jessie said it was the other way round; that the spider caught the bad dreams, so that only the good dreams went into the children's minds while they were sleeping. Nicol said he wasn't sure about that, but he liked making them anyway. I agreed that they were lovely, and asked Nicol if they were difficult to make. He said that one day he would help me make one. I secretly hoped it would be very complicated, so we would have to spend hours and hours together. I asked Nicol if he had lots of dreams, and he said that he often had nightmares. I told him that I had a nightmare every night. Jessie said, 'I never have nightmares.'
Nicol said, 'That's because you are a nightmare.'
Jessie said we should go home, because Nicol was being horrible again. Nicol said that he was only joking, and that Maggie had said the same thing once. I must admit that I was thinking the same thing, about Jessie being a nightmare, but had decided not to say it.

I asked Nicol if we could have another look at the painting. While I was looking he said, 'Rhona taught me to play the tin whistle. She thinks that wind instruments will be best for me.' I didn't know what a wind instrument was. I thought it might be like the mobile of bones and shells that knocked together in the wind. I wondered if Rhona was a witch.
He said, 'It's an instrument that you blow. One of their friends came here with a whole load of wind instruments. He showed

me how to play the clarinet and the saxophone. Of course, I could only get a few notes out of each instrument, but he thought I would make a promising musician.'

I was trying to think of something else to say about music, so that Nicol would fall in love with me. He said, 'The man thought that playing the saxophone and the clarinet would help me...'

Jessie said, 'Help you do what? Ride a bicycle properly?'

We ignored her, but she carried on, 'Help you do your laces up? Help you tidy your room?'

I said, 'Jessie, have you got a boyfriend?'

She looked surprised, 'Of course I have.' But I knew that she hadn't. That shut her up.

Nicol said, 'To help me t...t...t... 'He hit his leg hard with his fist and took a deep breath. 'Talk properly!' He almost shouted the words.

I knew what was wrong with Nicol. He had a stutter. I had seen boys like that in schools I had been to. It was horrible to listen to them talking, and to watch them being upset when their words got stuck, and when other boys teased them and copied how they talked.

Someone had built a large circle of big flat stones under some of the trees. In the middle was a burnt patch of grass. Nicol told me that Maggie and Rhona had built the circle, and on fine evenings the musicians would light a fire in the middle and sit around smoking and drinking beer, and playing music together. Maggie would join them on most evenings. Nicol said that his dad had told the musicians that he was happy for his children to be there, but the grown-ups were not to smoke in front of them. Nicol said, 'That doesn't make any sense, because Dad is always puffing away on his pipe in front of us.'

Jessie changed the subject, and said that she thought that Rhona was a witch. She was very pretty, but sometimes wore a long black dress, and a purple cape instead of a coat. And she had a black cat. And she sang songs about fairies and the Moon. And sometimes when she was cold she wrapped a very colourful blanket thing around her, instead of wearing a jumper like normal people. I asked her if Rhona had a broomstick. Jessie said, 'Don't be silly. She has a bike.' That was very funny, and Jessie looked pleased that she had made me laugh.

Nicol smiled, but didn't say anything. Jessie added, 'Maggie gave her old bike to Nicol, because he had an accident on his. He banged his balls on the crossbar. He couldn't breathe and then he cried and his balls were all bruised, and Mummy and Maggie took turns to rub cream on them. And I saw them. They were purple, like plums.'

I felt embarrassed at hearing that piece of information. But if Jessie was expecting Nicol to get angry with her, she was in for a big surprise. He just laughed and said, 'I had to stay off school for two days, because it hurt so much, I could hardly walk!'

Nicol looked at my hands. He said, 'Your fingers are very long, just like mine. Do you play music?'

I thought of Naomi and Dominic, who had fallen in love with each other at first sight, because they both loved music. I said, 'I play the piano a little bit, and Auntie is teaching me how to play the concertina. I'm hoping to learn *Captain Pugwash*.'

Nicol looked very pleased. 'I can play that on the tin whistle. And Jessie can play it on the concertina already, can't you Jessie? We can teach you. It's really called *The Trumpet Hornpipe*.'

Jessie said, 'I've got long fingers too. Look! And the concertina is so easy, and one day I'm going to learn the accordion, but Dad has got to sell lots more books before he will have enough money to buy me one.'

Jessie started dancing around and said she needed a poo. Nicol pointed to a small shed at the top of the garden and said that she could use the dry toilet. She said, 'I'm not going in there! It's full of spiders, and there's nowhere to wash your hands!'

Nicol offered to help her, but Jessie wanted me to do it. I thought that she was old enough to sort herself out, and almost said so, but Nicol asked me, 'What shall we do?'

So I said, 'I'll do it.'

I got a big surprise when I entered the shed. It wasn't full of spiders at all. It was clean and tidy. There was a little cabinet with a drawer full of sawdust and dry leaves, and a metal scoop. Jessie explained what she had to do. 'You lift the lid, just like an ordinary toilet, and underneath there's a big bucket. When you've finished, you wipe yourself with this newspaper here,' She pointed to some strips of newspaper, hanging on a nail, 'Then you take a scoop of sawdust and leaves and put that on top, so it's all nice and covered up and won't smell, and then you close the lid. And then if the grass is wet outside, you wipe your hands on the grass, and then give your hands a good wash when you go indoors.'

I couldn't understand why Jessie had made such a fuss about needing help, when she clearly enjoyed being in there. She made me stay with her while she went to the toilet. Thankfully, she only did a wee, because I was sure that she would have asked me to wipe her bottom.

While she was weeing, I had a look around. On our right was a window with a curtain covering it. The pattern on the curtain was similar to the wall hangings in the studio. I would have liked a piece of cloth like that, perhaps to put on my bed. There was a big poster tacked on the wall opposite the curtains. It had a drawing of a caterpillar sitting on a toadstool, smoking a strange pipe, just like in *Alice in Wonderland.* He was surrounded by billowing green smoke and there was lots of purple swirly writing in it. The writing said, *Experience the GROOVE! Trailing Clouds of Glory live!!! March 10 1967* and it gave the name and address in Cambridge, where you could experience the GROOVE.

On the back wall of the toilet was a smaller, black and white poster, with a photo of two men and two ladies sitting under a tree. It said *Trailing Clouds of Glory, April 3rd 1967.* At the bottom of the poster was something that made me feel cold all over and shiver. It said, *GUILDFORD CIVIC HALL.* I knew exactly where that was. Mummy and Muriel had taken me there once, by accident. Muriel had bought tickets to go to a pantomime, and thought it was at the Civic Hall, when it was really at the theatre. Seeing the word *Guildford* gave me a very strange feeling. All the time I was in the garden I felt as if I was in another world, in another life. I was with foreigners, who were like me, but also different. And we were in a wild garden that, despite Jessie's complaints, was enchanting. It was as if I had jumped in Doctor Who's Tardis and landed in the North of Scotland. But seeing the poster made me feel as if I had suddenly gone flying back in time to a freezing cold day in Guildford.

I urgently needed to do a poo. I told Jessie and she said, 'Oh, I'll just wait in here for you.'

I said, 'No you won't. Go and wait outside with Nicol. And don't tell him what I'm doing!'

She went outside, but I knew I had made a mistake. I had already realised that if Nicol or I told Jessie not to do something, she would just go ahead and do it.

As soon as I sat on the toilet, I felt much better. I didn't need to go after all. It was just the shock caused by seeing that word, *Guildford*. I heard Jessie outside, telling Nicol that I had almost pooed my knickers and it smelled terrible. For a second, I wanted to slap her. But then I didn't, because I knew that Nicol wouldn't mind about knowing that. He had been brought up with girls, and he hadn't cared that I knew about his bruised privates. And anyway, I was sure he knew that his sister was a little liar. What I couldn't understand was why she was like that. I went into a little dream, as I often still do when I'm on the toilet. In that dream I saw a little baby, with her mother lying dead next to her, with no milk in her breasts, and everyone around her weeping. The baby was screaming, but Maggie was the only person who took any notice of her. Maggie ran down the hill and begged the shopkeeper to give her some baby milk powder, because her mother had just died. When she finally got back home, the baby was screaming louder than ever. Then Maggie realised that they didn't have a baby bottle, so she had to run back down to the shop to get one.

By the time she got back again, the baby had been put in another room, but wasn't screaming anymore. She had gone silent, and stared at Maggie with sad eyes, just like Baby Theresa in the hospital. And finally Maggie fed her and she was quiet after that, and only cried when she was hungry. Then I realised that it didn't matter how much attention you gave Jessie, it could never be enough. Her mother was dead, and everyone blamed her for it.

I decided to be Jessie's friend. I looked up, and there was a small dreamcatcher hanging above me. There was a little black spider in the middle. I looked at it closely, and saw that it was made of plastic. That made me smile. I looked at the two ladies in the poster. They both had long black hair that was blowing in the wind, and were smiling. One had a tooth missing. I had to agree with Jessie, she did look a bit like a witch. I hoped Rhona was the one with all her teeth. Both of the ladies had wrapped patterned blankets round themselves, and the men had funny thick coats on, and one was wearing a big pointy hat. I was sure that they were hippies, just like The Wizard and Noelle.

Someone knocked on the door, and that made me jump. It was Nicol, asking me if I was all right. I pulled my knickers up and my dress down and opened the door. Nicol looked a bit embarrassed, so I said, 'Don't worry. I didn't do anything. It was a false alarm.' Jessie appeared and the three of us crowded into the toilet. I showed them the poster from Guildford, and told them that it was near where I used to live. Nicol thought that was a very mysterious sign. He said that the lady with the tooth missing was called Etsy, and he agreed that she did look a bit witchy sometimes.

I was very quiet on the way back down the hill. Nicol asked me if I was all right, so I told him I was thinking about Mummy, and wanted to talk to her. Jessie said, 'Is it true that your mum and dad don't like each other?'
I thought, 'You little stirrer!' but said, 'They used to be like that, but they're divorced now, so I hope they're going to be friends again.' That was true.
Jessie said, 'Like Mummy and her other husband then?'

Nicol said, 'You mean Aileen and her ex-husband.'
'No I don't. I think she's my mummy. That's how I like it.'

Nicol didn't say anything else. I looked in his face, but he looked over my shoulder. When we got back to the house, Auntie asked me to go upstairs and unpack my night things, and told me that I was going to sleep with Jessie. Nicol and Jessie came up with me and admired my pyjamas. I asked to see Nicol's room, but he said it was very untidy and he would feel ashamed if I saw it. Jessie said that their dad was always getting cross with Nicol about the state of his room. Nicol said, 'Well, I've turned over a new leaf now.'
I took out Polish Teddy and Jessie was very impressed, and told me that that she liked to have all her dolls in bed with her. She said, 'Nicol's got a woollen dog that he's had ever since he was a baby.'
Nicol went red. I knew that he was trying to stop himself from saying something rude to Jessie. I said, 'That's lovely.' I meant it. I liked boys who were soft.

I wanted to be on my own, but at the same time I wanted to be with Nicol. I thought I should always tell Nicol exactly what I was thinking, so I said, 'Nicol, when you are an artist, like me, you feel inspired. This means that things happen to you and this gives you ideas. And then sometimes you need to be on your own, so you can think about them. I want to paint something, but I don't think there's time.' It was starting to get dark.
He said, 'Do you want me to leave you alone then?'
'No I don't. I want you to be with me. But would you mind if we didn't talk?'
'Of course not. Talking makes me tired.' I hadn't thought about that. Jessie said that she wanted to stay with us.

In the night
Later, when Jessie and I were both in bed, Auntie came to kiss us goodnight. Jessie said she wanted her dad to come up and kiss her, but Auntie told her that he had gone out for a wee

walk. Jessie said that he'd probably gone to the bar to have a drink with his friends, and that she couldn't possibly go to sleep until he came back. Auntie told Jessie how lucky she was to have me to keep her company.

Nicol knocked on the door and sat on my bed. He had his pyjamas on too. He asked Auntie if we could go to the swimming pool in the morning. Auntie thought that was an excellent idea, and Nicol looked very pleased.

Jessie said, 'Aren't you going to kiss me goodnight, Nicol?'

Nicol said, 'But I never do. That's Dad and Aileen's job. Or you can ask Maggie.'

Jessie made a face and said, 'Please Nicol. Just this once?' He kissed her on the cheek. She said, 'Now, what about Pippa? She needs a kiss too.'

I didn't say anything, because secretly I had been hoping that in this house everyone might kiss everybody else goodnight.

Nicol said 'Goodnight everybody,' and went back to his bedroom.

Auntie said, 'Now Pippa, you have a good night's sleep, but if you need anything in the night, come and knock on our bedroom door, and I'll get up straight away.' I knew she was talking about my nightmares.

Jessie asked where Maggie was and Auntie told her that she had gone out too. Jessie said, 'Is she off to see her boyfriend?' Auntie just smiled and said she'd like to brush our hair.

After Auntie had gone, Jessie and I lay in our beds looking at each other. I had Polish Teddy and she had Mr Blanket, who was really just an old piece of pink rag that had once been part of a blanket in her cot when she was a baby. I thought about how nice it would be to find out about everyone in this family, but not to let them know about me. I was very pleased to be in my bed, in Stranhaven.

Jessie whispered to me. 'You suck your thumb.'

'I know. I like doing it.'

'But you're a big girl.'

'Well perhaps I have a baby inside me.' I knew that was a mistake as soon as the words left my lips.

'Inside you? In your tummy?' It didn't matter what I said, Jessie was convinced I was pregnant. 'Is your baby going to come in the night? Will it cry and wake me up? Is that why Mummy said you should knock on her door? What will you call it if it's a boy?'

I lay on my back and thought about what to say next. How could I explain that everyone has a little baby inside them, that one day grows into a little child, but always stays with you, even when you are a grown up? Jessie was a serious pickle, and was obviously trying to get Nicol into trouble as often as she could. But then, I thought, it must be awful to be born and your mother dies, and you have to live with everyone being terribly upset. But Jessie had gone fast asleep. I got out of bed and kissed her. She muttered, 'Night night.' I looked out of the window. Everything was dark outside. I heard the gate squeak as it opened, and saw a red point of light as someone puffed on a cigarette. I hurried away from the window and into bed, and hid under the covers.

I went to sleep straight away, but I woke up in the night with a feeling that I must speak to Mummy urgently. I couldn't get back to sleep, and wondered what to do. The feeling was getting bigger and bigger inside me, and I found it difficult to breathe. I thought I should go to the toilet. Our bedroom door was open slightly and I could see a faint light shining. I picked up Polish Teddy and went out into the corridor. There was a light shining under one of the doors. I wasn't sure exactly where I was, or if that was Uncle Tom and Auntie's bedroom. I knocked on the door, and Maggie opened it. She was in her nightie. She didn't look surprised, and said, 'Hello Pippa, are you all right?' I didn't know what to say, so Maggie told me to come into her room and sit on her bed. Her bedside light was on, and she had been reading a book called The Hobbit, and the illustration on the cover caught my eye. It was mainly green, with some mysterious-looking mountains. Maggie said, 'I love this book. Rhona gave it to me.'

She had a glass of water by her bed and gave me some to drink. I immediately felt better, but wide-awake. Maggie's clock said half past midnight. She said, 'What is it, Pippa? What's bothering you?' I told her I was too happy. I told her that being happy made me feel something that I didn't have a word for. I said that I shouldn't be happy when Mummy was so far away and missing me. It didn't feel right.

Maggie didn't say anything, so I told her about Muriel. I don't know why I did that. She said, 'I wonder if you feel *guilty*. It's a strange feeling. I felt guilty after my mum died. Everybody was still very sad, and the house always felt gloomy and miserable. One day a friend asked me if I would like to go with her to Aberdeen, to watch a film. It was a silly film called *Roman Holiday* with Audrey Hepburn and Gregory Peck. I loved it and we laughed a lot. Afterwards, my friend treated me to an ice cream and we talked about how silly the film had been. In the middle of laughing, I started crying. I didn't know why. Then we talked about it, and my friend helped me to understand that I felt guilty about having fun, when my mum was dead in her grave. My friend's grandfather had died and she had loved him dearly. When he was dying, he had said to her, "I don't want you to be sad when I'm gone. Just enjoy yourself and know that I'm pleased that you are happy." Of course she was sad that he was dead, but she didn't feel guilty, like me.' All of that made perfect sense. It was exactly what I was feeling. She said, 'So do you think you'd like to talk to Muriel? Is that what's bothering you so much?'
I said, 'One of the things, yes.'
'Are lots of things bothering you?'
'Oh yes. I'm afraid that my subconscious is quite full up, and I don't know what to do about it. I thinks that's why sometimes I can't breathe properly, and my heart beats very fast, and I can't see properly, so everything is a blur, and I can't hear properly when people talk to me, and I feel sick.'
Maggie smiled and said, 'So it's your subconscious? Have you been talking to my dad about that, by any chance?'

She ran her hands through my hair. She said, 'I must go to sleep now. You have such lovely thick hair, but it needs a bit of looking after. Can I style it for you? I cut Nicol's hair the other day. What do you think about it?'

I said, 'He's lovely. I mean his hair looks lovely.'

Maggie smiled. 'I love cutting hair. I've done everyone's in the family. You can be next, if you like.' While she was telling me this, she was rubbing the top of my head and pressing with her fingers, and squeezing my neck gently. It was a lovely feeling. I now know it was my very first Indian Head Massage. Nicol told me that Maggie always washed his hair and did the same thing to him too. She had learned it from Rhona, who had been taught it by an Indian lady who lived in Glasgow.

She took me to the toilet, and then to my bed, and tucked me in and kissed me goodnight. She had a very interesting smell.

I slept very peacefully. Muriel would have said that I had slept like a lamb.

Who can I talk to?

In the morning, I woke up very early. It was light, but Jessie was still fast asleep, so I went downstairs. I looked out of the kitchen window and Luna saw me and wagged her tail. She wasn't allowed in the house, but I thought I could let her in and pretend that I didn't know that rule. But then I thought I would be behaving just like Jessie. And anyway, Luna knew the rules, so probably wouldn't come in. While I was thinking about that, I felt someone squeeze my waist. I got a bit of a fright, but it was only Nicol. I say it was *only Nicol*, but that is ridiculous. I had hovered outside his bedroom door and thought very hard about tapping on it, very gently, and then sneaking in to talk to him. I was very pleased he had touched me, but pretended to be frightened.

Muriel used to creep up behind Mummy sometimes and tickle her, and Mummy would laugh and say, 'Muriel Standish! You'll give me a heart attack one day!' Then they would hug and kiss each other, and laugh and look in each other's eyes. I loved that. I didn't feel at all jealous or left out, because I knew that they loved me too. I had thought that the three of us would be together forever.

Nicol looked a bit embarrassed. I suppose he had crept up on me and touched me, and now didn't know what to do or say. So I told him that I had woken up and felt worried. He asked me what I was worried about, but for some reason I couldn't tell him. He said, 'You can talk to Maggie then. She understands everything, and never tells.'

I told him that I thought Maggie was asleep. He said, 'Tell me then. I won't tell anyone.'

I said, 'But I don't want to tell you my worries, Nicol, because then you will carry them around. And anyway, they are really just my silly problems and things I don't understand.'

'But you have to tell someone; otherwise you will go off pop, like me.'

Then Jessie came in and asked what the two of us were talking about. I could feel that Nicol didn't want her there. I didn't want her there either, and I didn't like myself for thinking that. We all sat round the dining room table, and Jessie sat quietly and picked her nose.

I wanted Nicol to keep talking, but I knew that we couldn't trust Jessie with anything that was a bit private. So I asked him, 'You went off pop?'

'Yes. I smashed a window.'

All I could say was, 'Oh.'

He frowned. 'Do you not want me to tell you about it?'

'Well I do, and I don't.'

'Why do you?'

'Because I want to know what happened.'

'And why don't you?'

'I have a funny feeling about it.' Just then I felt that I was a very little girl, and he was a big clever boy, and much too clever for me. He didn't say anything. I thought about how talking made him feel tired.

He said, 'I'll tell you anyway.'

271

Nicol told me that it happened soon after Aileen came to live with them. Uncle Tom had told Nicol that he couldn't go out on his bike. It was just a small thing, really, and he wasn't that bothered about going, but his father telling him he couldn't do it made Nicol fly into a rage. He went out into the garden and picked up a stone. His father was in the kitchen, by the window. Nicol threw the stone. He had meant the stone to hit the wall, to make a bang, so that his father would come out and see what was going on, and then they would talk together, and hopefully Uncle Tom would put his arm around him and tell him, 'Nicol, I'm sorry. I made a mistake. You go out on your bike, and when you come back we can have a nice cup of tea and a piece of cake, and you and me can have a nice chat together, and maybe play a game of cards, and you will win, and we will laugh together.'

Nicol was breathing in and out quite loudly, through his nose and out of his mouth. I asked him if he was all right. He said that he used to get very upset, but Rhona had taught him how to breathe slowly and deeply, to help calm himself down. 'So I threw the stone as hard as I could, but it hit the window and the glass shattered and went all over Dad, and he ran outside and walloped me.'
'And did you tell him that it was a mistake?'
'No.'
'Why not?'
'We were very angry with each other.'
'What did Auntie say?'
'She said that Dad shouldn't have hit me.'
'Did she say anything else?'
'She sent Dad out, and I helped her clear up all the glass. I was very... I was very frightened. I was frightened of a horrible feeling inside me. I was frightened that I might kill someone.'
'Did you tell Auntie that?'
'No. Not really.'
'Then what happened?'
'She put me on her knee, and she cried.'
'Auntie cried? Not you?' I couldn't believe it.

'No. She cried and cried. And she told me that if Wee Callum had been alive, she was certain that he would have been as bonnie as me.'

'Did Auntie tell you that she felt the same as you sometimes, and knew how you felt inside?'

'How did you know that?'

'That's what she says to me when I'm upset.'

'Do you get upset a lot?'

'Yes I do. But I think I feel a lot better now. I miss my mummy and... and my auntie terribly.'

Suddenly I was glad that Jessie was there. I said to her, 'Jessie, you will promise not to tell Maggie anything about this?'

She didn't say anything, so I made her promise. I knew that she would tell Maggie as soon as she could, and then Maggie would tell Auntie, and finally Auntie would tell Uncle Tom. And then Uncle Tom would know all about the smashed window. I hoped that then he might hug his son and tell him how much he loved him. I wondered to myself if I was becoming a bit of a *stirrer*.

Nicol laughed. Jessie looked confused.

Then Auntie came downstairs and helped us to get breakfast ready. She asked us if we wanted to go swimming. I shouted, 'Yes please! Yes please!'

Nicol said, 'Does Jessie have to come too?'

I didn't think that was a nice thing to say, so gave Nicol what I called my *Dirty Look*. Sometimes teachers did that if someone was being naughty on the other side of the classroom. I liked to practice it in the mirror. It was a frown and a stare mixed together. Nicol laughed and said, 'What's that look supposed to mean?' I told him it was my *Dirty Look* and he thought that was even funnier.

Jessie said, 'Nicol never wants me to go. He says I slow him down.'

I asked Jessie if she could swim and she shook her head. 'Would you like me to teach you?'

She smiled and nodded. Nicol looked annoyed.

Stranhaven swimming baths

I have to say here and now that Stranhaven Swimming Baths is the most wonderful swimming pool in the whole world. It's huge, and no matter how busy it is, there is always space to move around. But the most remarkable thing is that it is full of seawater. I don't know how they do it, but it is always lovely and clean and fresh, and doesn't make your skin go all dry and make your hair feel horrible, like pools that have chlorine in the water. And your eyes don't sting either, when the water gets in them. But if I could change just one thing, I would put a roof on it. We went there at ten o'clock in the morning. The sun was shining and the wind was blowing, (the wind always blows in Stranhaven), but the water was freezing! Apparently, the pool is heated, but every time I went there it was quite cold. But as Muriel always used to say, 'As long as you keep moving, then you won't get cold.'

I said that to Jessie after we had been in the water for about ten minutes, because she decided that she didn't want me to teach her how to swim, because it was too difficult, and she was too cold. I knew what the problem was; I wanted to be with Nicol, and Jessie realised that I wasn't giving her my full attention. Nicol was a very good swimmer, and I just wanted to be near him all the time. I think he wanted to be near me too, because he kept waving. I wanted to show him all the things I could do, like the breaststroke and the butterfly, and how good I was at diving, and how long I could hold my breath under the water. But I was stuck in the shallow end with Jessie. I knew it was unkind of me to think like that, so I forced myself to turn my back on Nicol, and splashed about with Jessie instead. That cheered her up, and I kept telling her that she was a good girl, so in no time at all she was showing me exactly what she could do.

Then Nicol came to join us and we both showed Jessie how to dive off the side. She was delighted to have attention from both of us, and she particularly liked her big brother telling her how pleased he was with her.

I could feel the salty water working a kind of healing magic on me. I hadn't had a proper wash since I had been in Stranhaven, and it was as if the seawater was cleaning me, and finally removing the last of the horrors that I had suffered at The Lodge and in hospital. We were in the shallow end and I had a funny, lovely feeling whenever Nicol came near me. He swam around us, like a shark, and every so often would grab us by our waists, to make us shriek, and he opened his legs wide and made us swim between them.

Then suddenly he said, 'Llllets ggget out.'

He didn't say why, but looked over towards the deep end. Three big boys were walking towards us. Nicol made us swim to the other side of the shallow end, so we could climb out and go to the changing rooms, but by the time we reached the side, the boys were standing there.

Nicol said to me, 'Don't say anything. They don't like people from England. And they don't like me.'

The boys were looking down on us. The biggest one said, 'Hello Nnnnicol. Is that your new g…g…g.. girlf…f… f..friend?'

Nicol told us to go and get changed, and that he would meet us outside the swimming baths. I didn't want to leave him, but I did as he said. I turned round just before we went through the door into the changing rooms. Nicol was trying to climb up the steps to get out, but the boys were stopping him. Jessie held my hand and said that we should tell a lifeguard that some nasty big boys were picking on Nicol. But just then, a man on the other side of the pool blew a whistle and pointed at the boys, and they let Nicol get out of the pool. Unfortunately, they followed him into the changing rooms.

The nasty boys

Jessie and I got changed very quickly and went into the lobby at the front of the building. Nicol was waiting there, but so were the nasty boys. Nicol came over to us. He looked very frightened and said we had to go into the car park as soon as possible.

The boys followed us into the car park and stood in front of us, blocking our way past them. Every time we tried to walk past them, they moved and blocked our way again. The shortest of them was taller than me. He was the one that started to say rude things. He stepped forward and said to Nicol. 'Is that your new girlfriend, Nnnnicol? She looks a bit young. I bet she hasn't even got any hair on her fanny yet!'

I moved towards the boy. Nicol held my arm and tried to pull me back. I said to the boy, in a very low voice, 'Say that again.' He laughed at me and said, 'Say what again? His cock is so small; it wouldn't even fit inside your hole.'

I said, 'You heard. If you say it again, I'll punch you. If you don't say it again, I'll punch you even harder. And if I punch you, you won't fucking get up again. So you'd better hurry up and make up your mind, you fucking Scottish bastard.' I didn't shout the words; I just said them. I had put on a London accent, so I sounded like one of the tough children from my Catholic school in Rayners Park, who were always getting into trouble for swearing and fighting.

It was my swearing that changed the look on the boy's face. He wasn't smiling anymore. I made my hands into fists. He said, 'I don't fight girls.'

I said, 'But I fight boys' and I jumped in the air and punched him as hard as I could, right on the nose. It started to bleed. The boy dropped to his knees and put his hands to his face. I felt an arm on my shoulder and a lady's voice saying, 'That's enough. Stop fighting.' I shrugged my shoulder, to try to make her take her hand off me. I swung my leg, to kick the boy as hard as I could, but the lady pulled me back. My foot missed, and I lost my balance and fell over. Nobody else said anything. The lady helped the boy get up, so I jumped up and tried to hit him again. But the lady put her arm out and said to me, 'You've made your point. Now stop trying to hit him.'

I think I was completely out of control, because I was just getting ready to hit one of the other boys when a man's voice said, 'Pippa! Stop trying to hurt them. It's not worth it.'

I turned round. It was Mr Griffin. He had driven up by the side of us and had rolled down his window. He got out of his car and said, 'What's going on?'

I was shaking all over, and couldn't say anything. I had a quick look around. Everyone was very still. There was a small crowd of grown-ups standing near us. Jessie started to cry and Nicol put his arm round her. The lady said to Mr Griffin, 'I saw those boys picking on her, so she punched one of them.'
I said, 'He said something about me having...' My voice was very shaky, but I was determined not to cry. I still wanted to do some punching.
The boy with the bloody nose said, 'My dad's a policeman.'
Mr Griffin smiled. He said, 'Good. Because I was just on my way down to the police station. Isn't that lucky? Now I can tell your father that you've been... you've been what? Saying disgusting things to little girls?' He looked at the other two boys. 'Shall I do that, boys?' They didn't say anything. Mr Griffin spoke very quietly to the lady, 'Are you a witness madam? Do you mind if I take your name and address, just in case the police want to take this further?'
The lady looked very pleased. 'Certainly. Such dreadful language to use to a wee lassie. No wonder she swore at him and punched him.' She patted me on the shoulder and said, 'Well done, dearie.'

Mr Griffin took a step towards the boys. They took a step back. Nicol held my hand. He was shaking. Jessie had stopped crying. She said, 'I want to go home.'
Mr Griffin smiled at her. 'You will Jessie, you will. But I want to talk to these boys first. You see, they've made a mistake, and we need to sort them out.' He took another step forwards. The two boys without bloody noses tried to run away, but some grown-ups behind them blocked their escape.
Mr Griffin carried on. His voice was very steady, but menacing. He took a hanky out of his pocket, took his glasses off and wiped them, then put his glasses back on again. 'You see, boys, I have a bit of a st.. st... stutter. Did you hear it? It's

not a good sign. It means that if anyone says something nasty about the way I speak, then there will be, how can I put it, very serious consequences.' The boys looked terrified. Mr Griffin said, 'You see, boys, I'm always telling Nicol to avoid getting into the *Red Mist*. Have you heard of the Red Mist, boys?' They shook their heads. 'Well, if you see the Red Mist in front of your eyes, it means that very shortly you will become very angry, and probably very dangerous. Now Nicol's a good boy, and knows how to control himself. Don't you Nicol?'

Nicol got a shock. He nodded. 'Good boy. But Pippa here, she's very... how can I put it? Headstrong? No, that's not the right word. Help me boys, find a good word to describe Pippa.' The boys didn't say anything. They looked very frightened. Mr Griffin looked them straight in the eyes. 'I know. What about, *excitable?* Or perhaps *hot-headed*? But what makes Pippa dangerous; what you should be really scared of, is that she doesn't see the Red Mist. If she decides to hit someone, she just does it. Or maybe, like all girls, she doesn't like to be insulted about her... about things that are very private. What do you think, boys?' They looked even more terrified. Mr Griffin smiled again. 'Come on boys. Nod if you agree with me.'
They nodded their heads. They looked like those toy nodding dogs that some people have on the shelf at the back of their cars.

He put his arm on the bleeding boy's shoulder, and held out his hanky. The boy didn't know what to do with it. Mr Griffin smiled and said, 'Put the hanky up to your nose, and breathe through your mouth. That should stop the bleeding. Unless, of course, Pippa has broken your nose, in which case you'll need a trip to the hospital.' The boy did as he was told. Mr Griffin turned to me, 'Tell me, Pippa, when you hit him, did you hear a cracking sound, like when a hammer hits a nut, and smashes it into tiny pieces?'
I rushed towards the boy again, but Mr Griffin grabbed me by the shoulder. 'Easy now, Pippa. This poor lad has had enough. He won't bother you again.' He turned to the bleeding boy,

'Your nose will stop bleeding, soon, but it looks to me like Pippa didn't hit you half as hard as she could have. If she'd hit you twice, she'd have snapped your nose in two.' He clicked his fingers in front of the nasty boy's face. 'I've just arrived in town, and as I say, I'm on my way to the police station. I always like to tell my friends in the police that I'm in town. It's a shame, but trouble seems to follow men like me around.'

He laced the fingers of both hands together and pushed his hands towards the boys, and cracked his knuckles. Jessie gasped. Mr Griffin smiled at her, then looked at the boys. 'Maybe it's because of what I did in The War. That, and me being such a big fella.'

He paused. It was like watching someone on television. I had seen a gangster on *Dixon of Dock Green* behaving just like that, and I had been terrified of him, and Muriel had to calm me down and remind me that it wasn't real. But this was real, and my hand hurt too, and that was very real. Mr Griffin's voice got even lower, so we could hardly hear him. 'Now what shall I tell the police? That there's been a gang of boys insulting a little girl and her friend? Shall I tell them exactly what was said? I can't imagine they would come running up here to put young Pippa in handcuffs.'

The lady said, 'It's a disgrace, really it is. And in Stranhaven of all places! I'm ashamed! If this man hadn't arrived, I'd have given these boys a good seeing too myself!'

'Thank you, madam. But there's been enough blood spilt for one day. I think that these boys should go for a wee walk up the road with Nicol. They should make their peace with him. They should invite him to go swimming with them one day. And if ever anyone dares to call Nicol names in school, they should stick up for him. That seems like a good way for me to end things. Don't you think?' The boys were speechless. 'Do we understand each other?'

They whispered, 'Yes.'

'Yes sir. You will call me *sir* from now on. Let's try again.'

The boys all said, 'Yes, sir.' The boy with the bloody nose was crying, and the runny snot coming out of his nose was mixed with blood.

'Good. Everyone makes mistakes. You've made a big one. Now learn from it. Be wise, boys. Stay on Nicol's good side.'

Jessie was standing behind Mr Griffin, and Nicol and I were standing together, by his side. He turned his head towards us. 'Now, Pippa and Jessie, get in the car.' He said to Nicol, 'Nicol, these boys are now officially your friends. Do you want to stay with them, or come with me?'

Nicol tried to say something, but his words wouldn't come out.

'Oh dear, boys, I think Nicol's getting angry. He'd better come with me; so you'll be safe. Get in the car, boy.'

Nicol did as he was told, and sat in the front. Mr Griffin got in, and said to the boy I had hit, 'Take my hanky. But make sure you give it a good wash, and then drop it off at the police station, and I'll collect it from there. There's no hurry. I'll be in town for a while.' He wound up his window and waved to the nasty boys. They just stood there, gawping.

On the way back to Nicol's house, Mr Griffin said, 'Well done Pippa. That taught them a lesson. But please, no more fighting while you're in Stranhaven. If there's any more trouble, then I won't be far away. But somehow, I don't think anyone will trouble you again. Nicol, what do you think?'

Nicol said, 'I'm sorry.'

Mr Griffin patted Nicol's knee. 'Sorry for what? You've got nothing to be sorry about. Those boys are the sorry ones.'

Nicol asked him, 'Who are you? And what did you do in The War?'

'Let's just say that I protected people. Important people.'

Jessie asked him, 'Are you Pippa's bodyguard?'

Mr Griffin smiled. 'Yes Jessie, clever girl. You could say that. Yes, you could say that.'

Jessie smiled. She looked at my hand. The boy's blood was still on my knuckles. I was quite shaken. I wondered if there was something nasty inside me, that made me want to swear at people and hit them.

When we got home, Mr Griffin spoke to Uncle Tom and Auntie, while we sat in the garden. Nicol said to Jessie, 'You will tell the truth about what happened, won't you? But please don't repeat what the boys said to Pippa.'

'Well what shall I say then?'

'Och, I don't know.'

I said, 'I think she should tell them. Otherwise they might not understand why I had to hit them.'

For once, Jessie didn't look as if she was going to cause trouble. She said, 'I don't want to say those words. Nicol, you say them.'

Nicol looked horrified. 'I'm not saying that.'

I thought about Peter and the Nasty Man outside the shops, who had shown us his willy.

Maggie came out to see us, and Nicol told her that he wanted to talk to her indoors, on his own. I didn't mind, because I knew that he would tell her about the horrible words that the boys had used. He didn't seem at all bothered that I had punched a nasty boy from his school and called him a *fucking Scottish bastard.* He was just worried about his parents hearing the words *fanny* and *cock.*

Jessie and I sat in the garden. She said, 'I don't feel very well. I want to go to bed.' After a few minutes, Maggie came to talk to us. She told us to tell her exactly what had happened. I let Jessie tell the story, but she didn't want to say the rude words, so I whispered them in Maggie's ear.

She said, 'Well done Pippa. I'd have done exactly the same thing. That's the only way to deal with boys who are rude about girls like that.'

Jessie looked very surprised, then she started to cry. It was then that I realised how frightened and upset she had been by the whole incident. I didn't quite know how I was feeling. Outside the swimming baths, I had put on a tough voice and it didn't feel like it was me who was swearing and hitting. Now my hand hurt, but I didn't want to tell anybody. I hoped that the grown-ups weren't talking about sending me away. I hoped that they didn't have to tell my father.

Auntie Aileen called us indoors. She was laying the table for lunch. Mr Griffin had left, and Nicol was upstairs in his room. Uncle Tom said hello to us and then went outside in the garden to smoke his pipe. I wondered if he had told Nicol off and sent him to his room.

○ ○ ○ ○ ○ ○

25th November 1976

Now, nine years later, having witnessed violence, and broken up a few fights myself, I can think clearly about what happened. I hadn't lost control. I didn't see the Red Mist. I knew that the only way to deal with those boys was to frighten them. I didn't want Nicol to try to do that. I knew that those boys were going to try to make him angry and lose his temper, and then they would hit him and humiliate him. I didn't want that to happen.

I hate people fighting, but what I hate most is the crowd who are watching. It's not the fighting that makes me shake; it's the deep humiliation inflicted on the loser. It reminds me of Jesus, because the whole point of the Crucifixion was to humiliate him. And very deep down, it reminded me of my Grandfather, who had been beaten to death in the street.

I had been in total control of myself. People often think that Roman Catholic schools as places where nice boys and girls get educated. That might be true of the posh schools, where the parents pay to have their nice children indoctrinated with the Catholic Faith. But any Catholic child can go to a Roman Catholic state school. So you get the full range going there: the wealthy and middle class children, who are often very sweet, and have been brought up to be very prim and proper, and then you get the dirt poor. And in my primary schools, it was the dirt poor boys who did all the fighting.

Sometimes it was fighting because of an argument, but often it was fighting for the pleasure that it gave them. They loved to be in the middle of a ring of yelling boys, (and sometimes girls,) and doing their best to knock seven bells out of their opponent. I hated the crowds who used to watch the fights, and the children walking away afterwards, discussing who had been the best fighter. Sometimes on the bus, or on the way home from school, I might overhear older schoolboys discussing who were the toughest boys in their school, and imagining what would happen if they both got into a big fight. That type of talk made me shiver with revulsion.

So when I saw the three boys, and how frightened Nicol was, I planned what I was going to do. I imagined I was one of the tough Catholic boys from my primary school in Rayners Park. The fights always started with insults and swearing, and then suddenly flared up into extreme violence. They began with punching and kicking, and then the boys grappling with each other on the ground, until the best fighter got in the most punches and kicks. So I knew, as I helped Jessie in the changing rooms, that I would probably have to fight in the car park. And I knew that slapping would be no good. I had seen girls slapping boys, but that just made the boys laugh. I had seen girls slapping each other, but they didn't really hurt themselves. So I knew that I would have to punch, and punch very hard. And I would have to aim for the nose. I would have to get my punch in first, and make an example of one of the boys, by making him bleed.

Now I am writing about it, I feel cold. Not physically cold, but emotionally; as if I have flicked a switch and blocked off the love that usually flows from my heart. It makes me feel ruthless, so that I am able to deal with danger. That's how I felt before and during the fight. I hadn't seen any Red Mist. I hadn't lost control. That's what the boys had wanted. They were going to insult Nicol and me until Nicol saw the Red Mist in front of his eyes and started fighting. And then afterwards the nasty boys could say what all nasty boys say: 'But he started it!'

I have always thought that girls should be taught how to defend themselves properly. If you really have to hit somebody, slapping gets you nowhere.

○ ○ ○ ○ ○ ○

Afterwards, in the garden, and in the kitchen, and for the rest of the day, my emotions were turned back on again. As we all sat at the dining table, I was very frightened. Not of the nasty boys; I was sure that, because of my violence and Mr Griffin's terrifying intimidation, they would never bother us again. No, I was terrified that all the love I had felt around me; from Auntie and Uncle Tom, and the love I could feel growing from Nicol and Maggie, and even from annoying little Jessie, would disappear. I was terrified that they might even turn against me, and decide to send me back to my father. And it was this terror that made me feel as if I was going to explode with desperation. Nicol was sitting next to me, while Maggie and Jessie sat opposite. Auntie said, 'Before we have our lunch together, let's talk about what happened.'

Nicol said, 'It was all my fffffault!'

Maggie said, 'Shh, Nicol. You know that's not true.'

I was looking at the pattern on my plate, but I took a quick look at Nicol. He was crying. It hurt me, in my chest, to see him upset. I didn't want him to talk and start stuttering, so I decided that I would explain what happened. I didn't mention exactly what the nasty boys had said; I knew that Maggie would do that, but I told Auntie that they had been going to hit Nicol, so I decided to stop them by hitting one of them first.

I expected Jessie to say something; perhaps to exaggerate or tell a lie, to get her brother into trouble, but she was silent. I think that the poor little girl had been terrified and shocked by my violence, and the blood. And I think she was terrified of Mr Griffin too. Auntie said, 'Well, I don't really know what to say. It wasn't your fault. It was the big boys' fault for being so horrible.'

284

Uncle Tom said, 'But violence has never solved any problems. But let's not worry about it anymore. I'm more interested in who's hungry.'

None of us wanted to eat anything. Usually swimming made me feel absolutely famished, but the thought of eating made me feel slightly sick. Maggie said, 'I'm starving! Nicol, if you don't want your sausages, then I'd better help you!' She reached over to Nicol's plate with her fork.
He said, 'Oi, Maggie! Get away with you!' Then he said to me, 'Well Pippa, if you don't want to eat, then I'd better help you,' and started to take some food off my plate. He smiled at me, and suddenly all my bad feelings just vanished. The only one who wasn't eating was poor Jessie. She asked to leave the table and went upstairs. I felt very, very sorry for her. I hoped that she would come into my bed in the night, and tell me all her troubles.

Something very personal

Nicol asked if we could go up to Rhona's garden again. Jessie said she didn't want to come with us, because she didn't feel very well. She still looked very shocked, and I thought she was probably worried that she might see the nasty boys again. Maggie offered to stay at home, to play with her, and read her stories. So Nicol, Luna, and I set off up the hill. I had more or less ignored Luna since I'd been in Stranhaven. She didn't seem to mind, because she obviously liked Nicol the most.

On the way up the hill, Nicol told me about the huge standing stone outside the town. It was a mysterious lump of rock, called The Lang Stane, which stuck straight out of the ground. Some people said it had been put there by giants before The Great Flood. Uncle Tom thought that a strange group called The Beaker People had dragged it there, and used it to worship the Sun, or perhaps the Moon, or maybe both. But nobody really knew who had put it there, or what it was for. Maggie said that the menfolk put it there, to show everyone how powerful they were, but the men didn't like to admit that it was the women who were really in charge. The only thing that anybody knew for sure was that Lang Stane was put there before Jesus became a Christian, so that was at least 1,967 years ago.

Then Nicol told me something that upset me. He said that Jessie was frightened of me and didn't want me to sleep in her room anymore. She hadn't liked me swearing and making the boy's nose bleed. That was a shock. I had imagined that she would think that I was someone who would protect her.

We went into the garden again and sat under the dreamcatcher. We were both very quiet. I asked Nicol, 'Do you hate me as well?' He shook his head.

'Are you unhappy with me because I swore and hit the boy on the nose?' Shake.

'Is it because I'm a better swimmer than you?' He laughed and shook his head.

Then he looked very serious. He took a deep breath and hit his leg. I didn't want him to do that. There was always a bruise there. I would have preferred him to stay quiet, rather than do that to himself. The words exploded out of his mouth. 'I can't say it!'

'Please say it. You are making me very unhappy. I have lots of unhappiness in my life, so I don't want any more.'

'It's what the boy said. Don't you feel disgusted by it?'

'Yes, but then I punched him, so I've sort of forgotten about it. I'm more worried about Jessie being frightened of me. And perhaps your Dad will speak to my Daddy on the phone, and they will decide to send me away again.'

Nicol ignored that. 'But what did they mean?'

I said, 'Oh, well, if you don't know, then I can't tell you.' As soon as I said it, I knew it was a stupid thing to say.

Nicol looked hurt. I didn't want to be the one who told him about S-E-X. Everyone might be furious with me for telling him, and causing more problems in the family. Also, I was very embarrassed. I didn't want to talk about those things. It was too private. He asked me, 'So you know what it means?'

'Yes I do. It's very private.'

'I don't know what to do. I want to know, but don't know who to ask.'

'You could ask Auntie, or Maggie, or perhaps your dad. He really is the best person because he knows about...he knows about boys. I suppose they must be very different to girls.'

I could tell that this wasn't enough for him. I could also tell that we weren't going to talk about S-E-X in a rude and nasty way. Not like Michelle at school, who had been rude about it, and stopped me from wanting to be her friend. It wasn't like that at all, but I still felt very shy.

I said, 'Do you still like me?'

He didn't say anything. I wanted to cry. My voice was wobbly, but I managed to say, 'I want to go home now.'

He put his hand on mine. 'Please don't. I don't want to go home. I want you to stay here, with me.'

Luna came to sit next to me. I smiled. 'At least Luna likes me.'

'Of course she likes you. Everyone likes you.' Then he said the thing that I most wanted to hear, 'And I like you very much.'

'Are you sure?' Those words just came out of me.

He said, straight away, 'Yes. I'm sure.'

'That's all right then. So if I tell you, I might get some things wrong, so please will you promise me you will ask someone to tell you all about it properly? Some things I don't quite understand. It sounds a bit horrible, and I can't believe it's true. Grown-ups say that it feels nice, but I can't imagine it.'

So I told him. When I had finished, I didn't know what Nicol was thinking, so I asked him, 'Do you think it's disgusting? I can't imagine how anyone could like doing that to each other.'

He looked down at the ground. 'I don't like to think about my mum and dad doing that. Do you think he still does it, to Aileen?'

I hadn't thought about that, so said the first thing that came into my head, 'I don't think so. They look too old for that.'

'Are you sure?'

'No. And you must promise one more thing. You must promise not to tell anyone that I told you.'

'Why not?'

'I don't think I'm supposed to know.'

'But who told you?'

'My Auntie.'

'Who, Aileen?'

'No, my Auntie Muriel.' It was the first time I had said her name to Nicol. It sounded strange, as if she was someone who I had read about in a book, and wasn't real. I wanted to tell him everything about me, but I didn't know where to start.

Nicol looked up at the dreamcatcher above our heads, and said, 'Thank you very much, Pippa.'

'For telling you about S-E-X?'

'Yes, and for hitting the boy in the face. Do you think I'm a coward?'

'Oh no!'

'But I'm a boy. I should have done it myself. They will go around saying things like, "You need a girl to fight your battles for you." And they might start calling me a *poof* again.'

'A poof? What does that mean?' I had an idea that I had heard that word somewhere before.

'It means a boy who is like a girl. They call me that a lot at school. It's because I don't play football, and like to talk to girls.'

'Well I think you are a very nice poof then. I wish more boys could be poofs. Peter liked to talk to me a lot, but he liked to play football too. I think it's silly to go round calling people names, just because they like to do things that are a bit different.'

We didn't say anything else. A big fat bumblebee flew over our heads and landed on a tall yellow wildflower. I kept looking at it. I knew that Nicol was looking at me, but I didn't want to look at him. I was feeling a little bit shaky, like I used to feel at The Lodge when I hadn't had enough to eat. I wanted some chocolate. I said, without looking at him, 'I like being here, but I feel a bit funny, in my tummy.'

He didn't take any notice. 'I wanted to ask you something.'

All I could say was, 'Oh.' I didn't want to talk about S-E-X anymore. I wished we hadn't started in the first place.

'There are lots of things I don't understand.'

'Well I don't know anything else. I've told you everything that Muriel said to me about it.' That, of course, wasn't true. I hadn't told him that Mummy and Muriel loved each other in the night.

I looked at Nicol. He said, 'Are you cross with me about something? Is it because we talked about that?'

'No. I'm not cross. I don't know what I am. I'm still only nine, and you are such a big boy.'

'I'm not big. You are almost as tall as me. I don't think you are a little girl.'

'Well I am. I still have a teddy bear and I like to suck my thumb!' He didn't say anything, so I said, 'Sometimes it feels like my tummy has a big hole in it, so I always feel empty. I miss my Mummy and my Auntie so much. I like being here with you, really I do, but sometimes I think I'm just going to die with sadness.' I didn't know I was feeling like that until I said it. I started to cry.

Nicol put his arm round me and said, 'Please don't cry. I feel like that too. Well I used to, until Aileen came along. I just want to tell you something about Mum and Dad, that's all.'

He took his arm away from my shoulders, but I took his hand and made him put his arm back around me. He smiled. 'I think I understand a bit better. One day Maggie and Dad had an awful argument. It was all about nothing. Dad was doing the washing up and Maggie was drying the dishes. It wasn't long after Aileen came to live with us. For a wee while we were all on our best behaviour, but this was the first big argument. Maggie has this annoying habit of not putting the knives and forks back in the right place in the drawer. She just slings them in any old how. So Dad said, "I wish to God you'd put those things back in the right place!" Maggie yelled back, "And I wish to God you could have kept your dirty hands off Mum, then perhaps she might still be alive!" Then she threw the knives and forks at Dad, and ran out of the room, and slammed the door.

'It was horrible, because Dad started to cry, and I was very frightened, and then Jessie started to cry as well. Aileen hugged Dad and told him to go outside and smoke his pipe and calm down, and she went upstairs to talk to Maggie. When she was inside Maggie's room, I crept upstairs with Jessie and we went into my room and sat by the wall. It's very thin, so we could hear most of what they were saying. I don't know why I did that, and ever since I've wished that I hadn't. I just wanted to understand what Maggie had shouted.

'Aileen told Maggie that when someone dies we feel a thing called *grief,* and as well as feeling very sad, you can feel very angry. Maggie said, "Good. Because I'm very angry. I'm very angry with Dad. If he hadn't had sex with Mum then she wouldn't have got pregnant, then she wouldn't have died." I didn't know what that meant. I thought she said *six or sax.* I didn't want to hear any more, but couldn't stop myself from listening. I tried to make Jessie go away, but she said that she wanted to hear it too. Aileen said that six wasn't just about making babies. She said that it's about love. And you didn't always have a baby each time you had six. Maggie said that she didn't know that. So then Aileen said that sometimes when people loved each other as much as Dad and Mum did, then they liked to show it through six. And then it can be the loveliest feeling in the world. And when you start doing it with each other, then you just don't want to stop. And it can be the woman who wants to do it just as much as the man, and sometimes more. And Aileen said she knew that because she had felt like that with her husband, and Wee Callum had been a child of love, just like Jessie. And she said that some people can have six all the time and never have a baby, while others seem to have babies all the time. It could be luck, or bad luck, depending on whether you wanted a baby or not. Then Maggie cried and said that she was sorry, and hadn't really understood about six. Aileen helped her go downstairs and say sorry to Dad. Then Dad and Maggie went for a drive up to the Lang Stane, where they had a long chat, and they've been the best of friends ever since.'

Nicol looked at me. I think he wanted me to say something, but I didn't know what to say. I had never shouted at Mummy, let alone thrown something at her. I saw a shocking picture of Maggie yelling and throwing the cutlery. But it was Maggie and Aileen talking about S-E-X that had really upset Nicol. He hadn't known know what it was, but he supposed that it was something that his Dad had done to his mother. And because of that, Jessie had been born, and that was what had killed his mum. He had wanted to ask Aileen all sorts of questions, but didn't want to tell Aileen that he and Jessie had been listening. I suppose he had been worried that if Aileen found out, then she might decide to leave them. Children think like that. I knew that, because I still was one. And Nicol had carried that upset with him for a long time. And he hated his father for doing something to his mother that had killed her.

Then Nicol started to cry. He didn't cry very loudly, and he tried to hide it from me. It upset me to see him crying. So I said, 'Would you like to see my appendix scar?'
It seemed like a perfectly natural thing to do at the time. I didn't give him a chance to think about it. I stood up, lifted up my dress and showed him. It certainly stopped him from crying.
He said, 'Oh my goodness. What did they do to you?'
I hadn't really looked at my scar closely since I had been to Stranhaven, because there wasn't really anywhere to be private. And usually you had to be as quick as possible in the toilet, because there was always someone else who wanted to use it. Jessie had seen it and thought it looked horrible. I was quite proud of it. I looked down, and Nicol was examining it very closely; just as I used to with Muriel's.

I pulled my dress down, and asked him, 'Do you think it looks ugly?'

He whispered, 'No. Not at all. It's not ugly at all.' After that, we didn't say anything for a long time. The bee was still buzzing away. I looked up at the sky. There were some very dark clouds moving in front of the sun, and a shadow swept over the garden. But I didn't care. I could have stayed there, in that garden, forever.

On the way home, Nicol asked me if one day he could look at my scar again, and I told him that he could. Then I thought about it, 'But please Nicol, you will promise not to tell anyone that I showed it to you?'

He said, straight away, without thinking, 'Of course not. I promise. And will you promise, Pippa, to keep it a secret too?'

Half of me didn't want to have a secret with Nicol, but the other half did, and I found it very exciting.

In bed with Maggie

That night I woke up to find Jessie in bed with me. She was snoring and dribbling and her breath smelled very strong. I knew what that smell was. It was tonsillitis. I knew that because Lucy used to get tonsillitis a lot, and her breath always had that very strong smell that makes you want to turn your head away. Muriel once told me that it was a warning sign, to let everyone know that her breath was full of infectious germs. Jessie's face was very hot. I didn't want to get tonsillitis, so I got out of bed. I hoped that Maggie would still be awake, so I knocked on her door and she told me to come in. She was reading *The Hobbit* again. She said, 'Hello Pippa! I had an idea that I might see you in here again.'

I explained about Jessie having tonsillitis, so Maggie told me to wait, while she went to see Jessie. Maggie's bed was warm, so I got in. The covers had Maggie's interesting smell on them.

There was some noise in the passage, and Maggie came back and explained that Jessie was burning hot. She had woken up Auntie Aileen, who was now busy giving Jessie some medicine. I asked Maggie if I could sleep in her bed, because my bedroom was full of tonsillitis germs. She laughed. 'It's a lovely idea, but we've just spent the last four years trying to get Jessie out of my bed. Why does everyone want to sleep with me? She has gone in with Aileen and Dad, and you can go back to your own room.' She saw my disappointed expression, 'But before I turf you out, tell me about Muriel. What does she look like?'

Without thinking, I said, 'People say that she looks like Pattie Harrison; George Harrison's wife. I think she's lovely. Sometimes when she and Mummy are walking along the street, men whistle at them. Especially in Islington, where there are lots of builders working.'

Maggie gave a long whistle, but very quietly. 'Is it like that? That's called a wolf whistle.'

'I know. Mummy used to say, "Some men are like bloody wolves." I was a bit shocked to hear her swear like that, but she told me that sometimes men made her so angry that she had to swear. And anyway, she told me that The Pope had said that bloody wasn't a swear word anymore. Muriel had thought that was a very funny thing to say. I loved it when they are like that. I loved to hear Mummy laughing.'

Maggie said, 'I can imagine. And what is her hair like? I suppose it's short?'

'Oh no! It's long and fair. She likes to wear it in a French plait. Shall I get my photo?'

'You have a photo?'

I went to get it out from where I had hidden it in my suitcase. I was very excited, and almost ran back to Maggie's room. She said, 'Jump into bed with me, and we can look at it. But you must promise not to go to sleep.' She ran her fingers over the photo. 'She's not at all how I imagined her. I thought she would have short hair and be quite mannish. But she's very feminine!'

We looked at Muriel. She was leaning forward on the window ledge and had her arms folded under her chest. She was wearing her old white blouse with the missing top buttons.

293

When Roger's mum gave us the photo, she said that Muriel had posed like that on purpose, to expose her *décolletage*. She had talked in French so I wouldn't know what she was talking about. Of course, afterwards I asked Muriel about it and she said, 'It's so that everyone can see my friends.' Then she laughed and added, 'Which is not true, of course!'

Maggie took me back to bed, gave me a big loud kiss and tucked me in. She said, 'I liked talking about Muriel.'
'I did too.'
'It didn't upset you?'
'No. Not at all.' That thought gave me a nice feeling, though I wasn't sure why. I didn't want to let Maggie go. I held her hand. 'What is Rhona like?'
Maggie sat on my bed. 'Oh she's very special. All the musicians are. Etsy is a bit... a bit spiky. You never know quite what she's thinking. They call her Etsy because her French fans say she is *une étoile*. It means star, and I suppose in many ways she thinks that she's the star of the group. But I think that Rhona is the true star. She has a lot of fans too. I've been told that she gets a huge amount of applause after she has sung a song. Alec and Jerry complain that since the girls joined the group, nobody in the audience pays much attention to them anymore. And Rhona is sunny and very positive, and has been very good for Nicol. He adores her.'
Suddenly a terrible sheet of jealousy covered me. I didn't want to talk about Rhona anymore. But Maggie didn't notice. 'She's four years older than me. I'd love to be like her; travelling all over the world and singing in front of such big audiences.'

I noticed a small desk with an old typewriter on it. Maggie saw me looking at a dreamcatcher that was hanging above the desk. She said, 'Rhona made me that. She's such a lovely person. Shall I tell you what she looks like?'
'No thank you. I want to go to sleep now, if you don't mind.' I sounded very grumpy and ungrateful. Maggie looked very surprised, then she laughed. She tweaked my nose, 'Oh, I get it!'

'No you don't. It's a secret.'

'Well it's not a secret from me! It's because I said that Nicol adores Rhona, isn't it?' My face was burning. I wondered if I had caught tonsillitis. 'But your secret's safe with me. I'm not like Jessie. And anyway, we've all noticed something very important, that makes us all very happy.'

'What's that?' I was still grumpy.

'Nicol loves talking to you. He hardly stutters at all when he's with you. You are such a clever girl for helping him like that.'

I wasn't grumpy anymore. 'So what does Rhona look like?'

'Well, she has very long dark hair, but in my opinion she doesn't look after it. She washes it too often and blow-dries it, so all the natural oils are getting destroyed. And she needs someone like me to sort out her split ends. Etsy doesn't care about her hair, and neither do the boys. They should, because if you are going to grow your hair long, then you need to have it styled in a special way. Alec looks like he's wearing a German soldier's helmet, and Jerry's hair needs to be cut very short, so that we can start all over again. When they come back, I'm going to offer to style their hair for them. Rhona has promised me that I can style her hair, because she wants to make a record of her own, and she wants to look nice in the photo on the front cover. She has a lovely face, and lovely brown eyes. They are travelling all over Europe now, so you won't meet her until near the end of the school holidays.'

Thomas Hardy

I fell asleep, and when I woke up, I remembered that Maggie hadn't given me back my photo. This made me panic, but then Nicol knocked on my door and asked me to come downstairs with him. Uncle Tom and Auntie were eating breakfast, but Maggie had gone out. Jessie was upstairs, ill in bed. My photo was on the table, in front of the place set for me. Nicol asked me who it was, but I didn't want to say. He said, 'It's obvious who that is.' He pointed to Mummy. 'You look exactly like her.' That was true. He pointed to Muriel. I didn't want him to say anything else. 'And is that your Auntie?'

I mumbled, 'Yes it is.' He didn't say any more, thank goodness.

Uncle Tom said, 'I love old family photographs. You can learn so much about yourself from looking at them. It's one of my favourite subjects.'

Nicol said, 'Is that why you write about them in your novels?'

Uncle Tom looked surprised, and very pleased. 'Exactly for that reason. It's a good way to describe a character, and to let the reader know something about his personality and history.'

Nicol asked, 'So is that why in your first novel it begins with Winnie looking at a photo of her father and mother, before she was born? And because of that we know exactly what she looks like, because she tells us that her nose and hair are like her father's, but her mouth and eyes are like her mother's. But she doesn't have her father's temper at all.'

'Exactly. Well done Nicol!'

Auntie said, 'Like father, like son.'

Nicol smiled.

Then it was my turn to get some praise. Auntie said, 'And how did you know, Pippa, that Jessie had tonsillitis?' I explained about her breath and that Lucy was the same.

Uncle Tom said, 'It's extraordinary that such a young child should know so many things about life.'

I said, without thinking, 'I suppose it's because so many things have happened to me.'

Uncle Tom said, 'Thomas Hardy wrote, "Experience is as to intensity, and not as to duration." It's about a young woman called Tess, who is suffering terribly, but only for a short time. But the feeling is so strong, it is just as painful as someone who has a similar ache, but for longer;'

Auntie said, 'Are you sure Tom? I thought Tess was blissfully happy, but only for a brief time.'

Uncle Tom laughed. 'You can look it up if you like. As you know, I'm a huge fan of Hardy, but I can't read him anymore, not since someone in an English newspaper described me as being a Scottish Thomas Hardy. If I read one of his novels, I might be influenced or inspired by him, and then I'll be accused of plagiarism. So you'll have to check it for me, my dear!'

They both thought that was very funny. Nicol looked at me and tutted, and rolled his eyes. Everyone laughed at him. He could see that I had no idea about what Uncle Tom was talking about. Nicol said, 'Plagiarism is stealing someone else's ideas, and pretending they are your own. Rhona says it's something that singers do all the time. She said that some American singers come over here and listen to old Scottish songs, and then go back to America and write songs that they say came out of their heads, but are really just old Scottish folk songs.'

That was the most I had ever heard Nicol say at the table. I wondered if artists stole other artists' ideas. I didn't think I had done that; well not on purpose, anyway.

Then Auntie talked about what was going to happen during the day. She explained that Maggie had received a letter from Rhona, and was very excited because the group's tour was going very well, and they had a date for when they would come back to Stranhaven, towards the end of August. Maggie had gone up to the cottages to do some more decorating. Nicol had wanted to go with her, but Uncle Tom had reminded him that I would probably want to go as well.

Why did my feelings change so suddenly? One minute I was smiling at Nicol and feeling warm inside, but the next second I felt as if a wasp had stung me. Nicol had forgotten about me, because he wanted to go running off to his beloved Rhona's cottage! I said I thought I might have tonsillitis, and wanted to stay at home and do some painting. Nicol looked very disappointed and said, Bbbb...' I felt him bang his leg. 'But I want you to come with me! If you don't go then I won't go either!' I thought he was going to cry.

Auntie said, 'It's all right my love. Pippa, are you really feeling unwell?'

I put my head down. I felt ashamed of myself. Now it was my turn to want to cry. Uncle Tom said, 'Come here, Pippa. Let me feel your temperature.'

Then I did cry. I cried a lot, and my tears dripped onto the photograph, onto Mummy and Muriel and me. I said, 'I've told a lie. I don't know why I said it. I've never told a lie in my whole life!'

Auntie said, 'My poor love. Come here and let me give you a cuddle.' But I couldn't go to her. My whole body felt like a stone, and there was so much water coming out of my eyes that I was worried that my photo would be ruined. Auntie came over to me and said, 'Come outside with me. I want to talk to you about something.'

Nicol's face was red, and I didn't know if he felt embarrassed or frightened. Auntie said, 'Shh, shhh, you'll wake Jessie. She needs to sleep for as long as possible, so she'll feel better.'

That stopped me crying, straight away.

We sat in the garden, and I climbed onto Auntie's lap and sucked my thumb. Auntie asked me what was wrong, but I couldn't say anything, so she asked me some questions.

'Have you had a bad dream?' Shake head.

'Are you missing Mummy and Muriel?' Shake head, then nod.

'Is that's what's upsetting you?' Shake head.

Is it Jessie? I know she can be very difficult. I think you're finding that out.' Shake head.

'Is it Nicol?' Nod.

'Has he been unkind to you?' Very big shake of the head.

'Is it something to do with Rhona?' No nod and no shake.

'Ah! I know what it is. It's about Nicol and Rhona, isn't it?'

Finally, I could talk. I took my thumb out of my mouth and looked towards the kitchen. I said, 'I'm feeling jealous. I'm jealous of Rhona, because Nicol likes her, and I think he might like her more than me.'

Auntie laughed. It was her lovely laugh, just like Muriel. That laugh said to me, 'You are a funny girl and I love you'. She said, 'You don't have to worry about Rhona. She's a grown-up. She's just like an Auntie to Nicol. We like her very much. Nicol used to be such an upset little boy, but now he's growing up very fast, and Rhona helps him to understand himself. So you don't need to feel jealous.'

I understood that perfectly, and my jealousy vanished.

Auntie said, 'We hoped that you and Nicol would get on well together, but we didn't think you would become such good friends so quickly.' I wanted to say something about that, but Auntie stopped me. She said very quietly, 'Shh. Shh. I want to tell you something very important. It's about feelings, about emotions. You see, Nicol and Maggie and yourself all had a good start in life. I know things went very wrong for you for a while, just like Maggie and Nicol. But I know that for the first three years of your life you had a lovely time with your mummy, and this made you both very close to each other. It was the same with Maggie and Nicol, until their mother became ill and died. But you are lucky, because you are someone who can talk about her feelings. I know you get upset, but that's your feelings telling you something important. Maggie is just the same. She's what I would call, "in touch with her emotions". It can make life a bit difficult sometimes, because she can get quite upset, and tells people exactly how she feels. But she calms down afterwards, and usually says sorry if she's been angry and was shouting. But Nicol's not like that. He doesn't know how he feels, and he gets all tied up in knots.'

'Just like his talking?'

'Yes, I believe you're right; just like his talking. But Jessie? Well she's a completely different story. She had a very bad start to life. Her mother died and then Jessie was ill and everyone around her was upset. I think, in some way, everyone blames Jessie for her mother's death. So she's very attention-seeking and annoying, and tells terrible lies, and tells tales to get other children into trouble. But it's all to get her father's attention. Maggie understands that now, but Jessie drives Nicol mad, as you've found out.'

'Yes I have, but I feel sorry for her. But I think I understand. I think I would feel like that if I were her.'

'Do you? Would you? I'm glad, because she has no friends at school. She's always causing trouble between children, so they all leave her alone.'

'What about Nicol? What about his feelings and his emotions?'

'Well that's why I think you are going to be so good for each other. I know he's older than you are, but he hasn't really had anyone to talk to about how he feels. He's very close to Maggie, and he tells her some things, but he's worried that his father will find out. I'm not sure why, but he's scared of his father, and quite angry with him too. It's caused us quite a few problems in the past. But then the young musicians came to live up the road, and he met Rhona. For some reason, she has taken a shine to Nicol and has taken him under her wing. I'm sure that he tells her all of his troubles. He spends all his time up there when Rhona is at home.'

I started to feel sorry that I had been jealous. I wondered if Nicol would one day feel jealous of Muriel, if he ever met her. At first that was an exciting thought, but then it started to bother me. Auntie said, 'The one thing that Jessie and Nicol agree on is music. Jessie is very musical. Nicol is too, but he has to think about it, while Jessie is… well you just ask her to play the concertina and see what happens.'

'I wonder if she's like me; she expresses her feelings through music, like I do through my Art?'

'It's possible. Yes, you could be right.'

She scratched her head. 'Talking of painting, why don't you and Nicol go up to see Maggie at Rhona's house? You could take your paints along with you.'

I couldn't think of a nicer thing to do. I wanted to ask one more thing. 'Does Maggie like to play an instrument?'

'Well not really. She likes to sing, especially with Rhona and the others. She can play the harmonica quite well. But she prefers to help her father with his writing. She types up all his work and they talk together for hours.'

I thought of something. 'What about you, Auntie? Do you do something for yourself?'

300

'Oh, that's such a nice question! I like to knit, and walk with Luna by the sea. And of course I like to make cakes. And I used to paint a lot, but I don't really have time anymore.'

Then she changed the subject. 'Now we really must think about Jessie. She gets ill quite often and it's a real drama, as I think you can imagine. The best thing for us all would be if you and Nicol could go and have fun and be happy together. Is that possible?'

'I'll try.'

Auntie said, 'You are such an emotional girl. That's a very good thing, but it can be painful sometimes.'

I said, 'I'm sorry Auntie.'

'What for?'

'For being an emotional girl.'

She laughed. I looked towards the kitchen. Nicol was at the window, looking at us. I waved at him, and he waved back. I climbed off Auntie's lap and walked towards the house.

In Rhona's Garden, again

Nicol and I walked up the hill to the Musicians' cottages. Nicol said that he was sorry that his little sister was ill, but sometimes it was nice to be without her. She liked to tell tales about him and this made him angry, so they were always fighting, and then his father told him off. I didn't say anything about that. I was thinking that sometimes it's better not to talk about other people when they are not there. Lucy once told Roger off, because he was saying something nasty about a boy at school. Lucy said, 'Roger, you really mustn't talk about people behind their backs. If you've got something to say to them, you must say it to their face.'

Roger's face went red and he said, 'I'm sorry, Lucy. I'll try not to do it again.'

Lucy, said, 'Good. I'm glad.' Sometimes I wondered if Lucy really did know that Roger was secretly in love with her. Jessie talked about Nicol a lot behind his back. I think she did it to try to get me to say something, and then she would tell Nicol, behind *my* back.

Whenever we passed a wall, Nicol told me about the stones. There were lots of different types of stone walls in the area, and he had learned all about them from the man who had been fixing the wall. He was Mrs Alderson's husband, and was a dry stone dyker, who fixed people's stone walls, and built new ones. Nicol said he was very lucky, because Mr Alderson let Nicol help him. I hadn't really looked at the walls properly, but now I was suddenly interested in all the different patterns and shapes and their names. And I could see that Nicol was pleased that I was taking an interest. He really was a very nice boy. I asked him if he got all his muscles from picking up heavy stones. He just laughed and his face went a bit red. I thought about how nice it can be to make things together. I wanted to learn how to build a wall.

Nicol said that Maggie was probably busy inside the house, so he didn't want to disturb her. I had been hoping to have a look at some of the other rooms, in case they had more interesting paintings and pieces of cloth in them. I wanted to say hello to Maggie as well, but didn't feel that I could ask Nicol. We sat in the stone circle again. Nicol whispered, 'Listen! What can you hear?'
'A bee buzzing, me breathing, and some birds singing.'
'There it is again! It's the bird I've been listening for!'
A bird was singing in a tall tree at the back of the garden. We could hear his voice louder than all the others. Sometimes there were six notes, sometimes five, and once I think there were seven. Sometimes he sang the same tune, but there were also little variations. Each time the bird sang, Nicol whistled back, loudly. He thought that the bird was responding to him, but when he stopped whistling, the bird just carried on singing.

Nicol explained that the first time he heard the bird he ran into the house and told Rhona about it. They both listened very carefully and Rhona tried to copy the birdsong on her piano. There were three or four different tunes, and she kept repeating them and then swapping the notes around. He said it was a kind of an improvisation, but then she made it into her own tune. She made him sit next to her and every time she played her notes, he had to respond with his own set of notes. They sat for a long time, and Rhona was very excited and kissed Nicol and said what a wonderful inspiration he was. Over the next few days, she sat in the garden and at the piano, and finally made a complete melody and called it 'The Call'.

I said, 'Like *Lark Ascending* by Vaughan Williams.'

Nicol looked very surprised. 'How did you know that?'

I told him about my friend Naomi and her passion for music, and how she was determined to play it one day. Nicol was very impressed, and told me that his dad had told him about Lark Ascending, and that Rhona had had the same idea.

I was busy thinking about Nicol and Rhona playing the piano, and when Naomi met Dominic and fell in love with him. Nicol said, 'I just wish it was a different bird singing.'

I didn't know what he meant, but he wouldn't explain. He ran over to a big shed and came back with a bag made from bits of coloured cloth sewn together, and the cloth had tiny round mirrors sewn into it. It must have taken someone ages to make that. Nicol said that Rhona had given it to him, and he kept all his special dreamcatcher materials in it. He had to keep it hidden, because Jessie liked to take everything out, and usually left it lying around. He showed me a small circle of branches, and some wool, and a collection of feathers and stones. He said, 'I'm going to make a dreamcatcher for Jessie, to help her get better.'

I was beginning to like Nicol more and more. A boy who could be nice to his sister, even though she was a nightmare and a stirrer, must be a very nice boy indeed. I wondered if we could become boyfriend and girlfriend. Then I remembered that Peter and I had never stopped being in love with each other. I wondered if you were allowed to have two boyfriends at the same time.

I watched Nicol making his dreamcatcher. As he was weaving the wool in and out, I felt myself floating up into the tree that we were sitting under. I was a bird in the tree up above, looking down on two children, through the dreamcatcher hanging on the branch. Mixed in with my thoughts was the picture of Peter and me up high in the tree in his garden, just before we kissed each other on the lips, and Ursula, in an orange glow, watching us.

Nicol said something that jolted me out of my trance. 'It was a great tit!' He almost shouted the words. 'I asked Mr Alderson what bird he thought it was that was singing our song. I wish it could have been any other bird but that, because I get stuck on those two sounds, *g* and *t*. And because people will laugh when I tell them.'

I didn't laugh, or even smile. 'Why will they laugh?' I knew why. Half of me didn't want to talk about it anymore, but half of me knew why it was so funny.

Nicol looked cross. 'Why will they laugh? Are you teasing me? Because if you are, I don't like it.' Nicol was trying to sound cross, but his cheeky smile told me that he thought it was funny.

I tried to sound serious. 'Please don't be cross. Is it because people call ladies' breasts *tits*?'

'Yes it is.'

'Well I think that's silly. But it is quite funny at the same time. I'll try not to laugh or smile if we talk about it again. It's a very serious matter.' Then we both laughed.

Nicol said, 'Maggie laughed her head off when I told her. Rhona thought it was very funny too. She said to Maggie, "I can already see a pair of great tits in this garden." '

Nicol tried to say something else, but his words got stuck. He hit himself on the leg. I said, 'Please don't hit yourself.'

'I don't know what else to do! It helps me get the words out.'

'But you have a big bruise on your leg. It must hurt.' He didn't say anything. He just looked sad. I said, 'What if you held my hand and squeezed it, instead of banging yourself like that?'

'Well I think I would probably squeeze your hand off!' He was laughing, but I thought he might start to cry.

I said, 'I don't mind how you talk. I don't mind if we don't talk at all!' I really meant it. I didn't want him to suffer.

He said, very loudly, 'But I want to talk!'

Then we sat quietly while he made his dreamcatcher and I did some drawing. I floated off again, and heard Nicol tell me a story.

The King Who Believed He Owned the Sea

'It was a long time ago, when Mummy was still alive. We went to The Castle. We always went there, to play on the beach. You could look up and see the castle on top of the cliff. One day, Dad had heard that someone had bought the castle, so we went for a walk there. We wanted to go down to the beach as usual, but someone had put up a fence, to block the way. We looked for a gate to let us in, but there was no gate, just a sign saying *Private Property,* and telling people that they could pay to go inside the castle. I wanted to go inside, but Dad was very angry and said he wasn't going to pay. We looked down and could see people on the beach, because they had paid to go down there. Maggie really wanted to go inside the castle and onto the beach, but Dad said, "I'm damned if I'll pay to touch the sea!" Then a man walked towards us from inside the fence. I think he was there to check that we weren't going to climb over and get in for free. Dad said to him, "And will you be making us pay to look at the sea, and to smell it? I imagine the new owner is some damned Englishman, come to take away more land from the Scots?"

The man said, "Och no. He's a Scot. He lives in Edinburgh. You'll know who he is. He's awful big in the films."

Dad was furious. Mum said, "Hush Tom, don't curse and shout in front of the baby."

Maggie said, "What baby?" Then Mum explained that she had a baby inside her.

'Dad said he was going to write a story about the castle, but he never did. So I've written one instead. It's only very short. I showed it to Rhona and she's made it into a song. She's read all my stories and poems and has made a long song, with the tune of the great tit. It lasts twenty minutes! She played some of the tunes from it and it sounds a little bit like *Sing a Song of Sixpence.* But then the tune becomes quite complicated, and mixed up with a song called *Jamaica Farewell* by Harry Belafonte, and she sings about my story. I'll tell it to you. A king has a terror that one night a huge storm will make the sea smash against the cliffs, and bring his castle crashing down and kill his wife and baby. So he decides to build a huge wall, to stop the sea from crashing onto the cliff below his castle. But no matter how long the wall was, the sea just came creeping round it. And no matter how high the wall was, the sea made the sand wet and the wall came crashing down. The King was full of anger, and all he could think about was building the wall stronger and higher. The Queen stopped loving him and his children grew up to hate their father. But all the time the sea kept coming, until one day the king died of anger. Sometimes I think of him jumping off the cliff into the sea, or falling over by accident. But Rhona says it doesn't really matter how he died, because he wasn't really angry, just full of sadness, for some unknown reason.'

While Nicol was talking, I was busy drawing. In my drawing it was spring; the time for pink buds and white apple blossom. I felt Nicol touching my hand and heard him asking me if I was all right. I slid out of My Colour Dream and said the first thing that came into my mind, 'Please can we go to Jessie?'

'Why?'

'I don't know. I just think we should be with her.'

'Why should we?' He wasn't asking in a nasty way. These days, Nicol was trying very hard to be nice to his little sister. I think he really wanted to know what I was thinking. But I was only nine, and sometimes my head hurt from thinking too much and explaining everything. But I would do anything for Nicol, so said, 'I think I just want to. It's not her fault.'

'What do you mean?'

'I don't know what I mean. She can't help it. She's only a little girl. I'm only a little girl!'

306

Nicol looked at me, and looked a bit worried. I knew he liked me. He liked me enough not to want to upset me. That gave me a lovely feeling in my heart. I held his hand again.

Then Maggie came out of the house. I tried to take my hand out of Nicol's, but he held onto it. Maggie smiled at us and asked what we had been doing. I told her, doing my best not to smile, 'We've been talking about the great tits.'
Maggie tried not to smile too, but couldn't stop herself. The three of us laughed. Maggie said, 'Let's go home.'
I told Maggie that we had been making a dreamcatcher for Jessie. I didn't want to show her my drawing. I suddenly became shy about being an artist. She looked at it and said, 'Goodness gracious!'

Jessie was still asleep, so we crept upstairs and put the dreamcatcher on her bed. I gave my drawing to Nicol and he put it on his bedroom wall straight away, next to his Trailing Clouds of Glory poster. The poster was another brightly coloured painting, with lots of swirling lines. I could just make out some fairies, and what looked like an angel. It was advertising the group playing in San Francisco. Rhona had written on it, 'To Nicol, my lovely storyteller and Wise Old Man.'

A day with Jessie
A few days later, Jessie was better, but on that same day Nicol went with his father to visit The Lang Stane. They were going to walk there and back, and were taking some food for lunch. I wanted to go too, but didn't like to ask. Nicol told me that he didn't really want to go, but he wouldn't say why. I was hoping it was because he wanted to be with me instead, but he didn't say that. They set off after breakfast and took Luna with them. Maggie had gone to Aberdeen, so I stayed with Auntie Aileen and Jessie.

Jessie wanted to play with her dolls in the garden. She had decided to make a house for them, out of old bits of wood and

307

junk from the shed, and wanted me to help her. As soon as we were in the garden on our own she said, 'You love Nicol, don't you? I know you do. I can tell.'

I didn't deny it, so that was as good as agreeing with her. She had trapped me again. I said, 'How do you know then?'

'You're always looking at him. And he looks at you a lot. And you hate it when he's not with you. And you hold hands under the table. I've seen you do it.'

There was no point in denying it, so I thought I'd turn the tables on her. 'Have you ever loved a boy?'

'Oh no! Boys are disgusting.'

Then I changed the subject, to get her away from talking about Nicol and me. 'Has Maggie got a boyfriend?'

'I don't think so. She used to, but he dumped her for another girl. Maggie was very upset, and stayed in her room for days. Now she spends all her time with the Musicians. She loves cutting hair. She's really good at it. Her and Dad spend ages together, writing his books.'

I thought I'd change the subject completely. 'Auntie Aileen says you're a brilliant musician.'

'Really?'

'Will you teach me how to play something?'

'Only if you'll show me how to draw.'

Then I thought of something that might get her on my side, so she would stop thinking about Nicol and me altogether. I said, 'Do you like Sooty and Sweep? I love them. I especially love Sweep, because Sooty is always getting him into trouble. I think you're a bit like Sooty.'

This did the trick. In no time, Jessie and I were talking about our favourite Sooty and Sweep episodes. I drew a picture of the puppets for her to colour in, and she promised me that she would show me how to play *Captain Pugwash* on the concertina. And after that, she forgot about trying to trick me, and became completely absorbed in playing with her dolls. I say *absorbed* because that's the only word I can think of to describe Jessie. She was like me when I was painting; she seemed to completely forget about what was going on around her.

Each of the dolls had a complicated life story. Jenny had been found wandering on the hills, starving and weeping and dressed in rags. She spoke a strange language that nobody but Jessie could understand. Her real name was Genevieve, and she was from Hong Kong (this was true, because she was made of plastic and there was writing on her neck that said 'Made in Hong Kong'). Aggie's mother and father were lazy and had allowed her to play near a busy main road, and a car ran her over. The police took Aggie away from her parents, and gave her to Jessie, and everyone agreed that Aggie was much happier now. Jock was simple in the head and all the other dolls teased him, but in the night he got out of bed and pinched them hard, so they were scared of him. Karen ate too many sweets, so the dentist had to take all her teeth out. Cathy had fallen in love with a boy at school, but he had dumped her and she was heartbroken and had gone mad. Dolly had lived with a beautiful woman, who turned into a witch and cast a spell on her, so she was invisible, but only clever people could see her.

In all the stories, Jessie was the only one who listened to their problems, stopped them from fighting each other, and saved them from danger. Each doll had a special voice and accent. One of them was French and ate snails, which we had to find in the garden. Heidi was Swiss, but was handicapped, because a goat had found her sleeping in a field in The Alps, and had eaten half her leg, and it had to be amputated. Jessie took great pleasure in cutting Heidi's leg off and sewing it back on again. I told Jessie that before my operation the nurse had given me gas to make me go to sleep. Jessie said, 'Swiss people don't need things like that. They eat cheese with holes in.' She often said things that seemed sensible to her, but made other people laugh out loud.

And I was delighted when Jessie allowed me to join in the dramas surrounding each of her dolls. We spent a long time building the big house for them, and she shrieked with laughter when it collapsed, causing several of her dolls to have major injuries that required hospital treatment. Of course, Jessie was a famous surgeon, and she let me be the nurse who obeyed her orders. Jessie bathed and dressed their wounds (they were always having accidents) and fed them (for some strange reason they all only ate grass with Heinz Salad Cream) and kissed them, and read them a bedtime story and tucked them in.

○ ○ ○ ○ ○ ○

28th November 1976

I can picture us now. There we were, two little girls playing nicely together with dollies. I was, after all, still only nine and she was just eight. Even after all the things that had happened to me, and all the things that were going on inside me, I was still just a little girl, who liked to do little girl things. But, if you had been able to look closely at what we were doing and saying, it was deeply sinister, and a reflection of all the twists and turns our lives had taken.

As we played and laughed and sang, I thought of Lucy; Lucy pure and simple. Jessie was neither pure nor simple. She was a very complicated little girl. And being complicated like that sometimes made her nasty to everyone around her.

And me? What was I? I wasn't pure. I wasn't simple. I had seen the horrors of the forest at night, and felt the wolf waiting for me. I had been taken from my parents, (in my mind, Muriel was one of my true parents), and I had been locked in the tower with only a witch to visit me. I knew how it felt to be abandoned in the forest, with the wolf searching for me, then finding me, and watching my every move.

Jessie and I were playing in the world of horror that is the stuff of Grimm's fairy tales. A strange forest where beautiful, innocent children are exposed to the horrors of adult life, then punished for their parents' misdemeanours and thwarted urges. We children were innocent, like Hansel and Gretel, or Rapunzel. None of this was our fault.

310

While we were kissing the dolls goodnight, I asked, 'Jessie, do you miss your mummy?'

Quick as a flash, she answered, 'Aileen is my mummy.'

I said, 'I miss mine terribly.'

She said, 'My real mummy is a skeleton under the ground.'

I shivered.

Goblin Market

Jessie wanted to read the dolls a bedtime story. I thought that we could just tell a story, like The Three Bears, or The Gingerbread Man, but Jessie said that those were stories for babies, and her children needed something more grown up. She told me that Maggie had a book in her room, and Jessie was allowed to read it. She said that I should go into Maggie's room and get it. I had never been into Maggie's room without her permission, but Jessie said that Maggie always let her go in there, so she was sure it would be all right for me too. She said that Maggie always kept the book by her bed. I didn't want to go, but Jessie said that the dolls would be very upset if I didn't do it. She started talking in strange voices, pretending to be the dolls getting upset. She was making me feel uncomfortable, so I said I would go, just to shut her up.

I went into the house through the kitchen door, and as I walked quietly to the stairs, I could see the front door wide open, and the back of Auntie Aileen, bending over and pulling out some weeds. Usually I would have said hello to her, but I just went straight up the stairs, making sure that she didn't see or hear me. I knew that what I was doing was wrong. I knocked on Maggie's bedroom door. That was a silly thing to do, because I knew that she wasn't in the house. It was the first time in my life that I had sneaked into anyone's room. Roger told Lucy and me that once he had gone into his Mum's bedroom and looked through all her drawers and in her wardrobe. Lucy had been shocked, so Roger promised her that he would never do it again. But Lucy asked him if he had found anything interesting, and he said, 'Not really'. He told me afterwards that he had found an envelope in his mum's underwear drawer. Inside were photographs. That's all he would tell me, which made me think that they were photos of something a bit rude, like the ones that poor Vincent had found in the stream. I didn't dare ask Roger if I was right, in case he thought I was a girl who wanted to know about rude things. And then he might tell Lucy that I had been interested in rudeness. I had never ever wanted Lucy to think about me like that.

Thinking about lovely, good and honest Lucy made me want to turn around and go back outside, and tell Jessie that I hadn't found anything. But that would have been telling a lie. So I opened the door and went in. It was the first time I had seen Maggie's room in the daytime. It was a bit untidy. She hadn't bothered to make her bed, and had thrown her dirty clothes on the floor. The room had the same very interesting smell that I noticed whenever I was near Maggie. I had a secret and powerful urge to look in all her drawers and in her wardrobe, but I forced it away. I looked at her walls instead.

Maggie had the same poster on her wall of Trailing Clouds of Glory as Nicol had in his room. At the top, someone had written on it, *To Maggie, My Fiery Antidote.* At the bottom was a strange poem:

> For there is no friend like a sister
> In calm or stormy weather;
> To cheer one on the tedious way,
> To fetch one if one goes astray,
> To lift one if one totters down,
> To strengthen while one stands.

Under these lines were three red splodges. I looked at them very closely. Someone had put bright red lipstick on their lips and kissed the poster. On the wall below the poster, there was a black and white photograph in a frame. It was of a woman with long dark hair, singing into a microphone. She was wearing a T-shirt that had *San Francisco* written on it, in swirly letters.

I have no idea why I did what I did next. I looked under her pillow. There was a yellow T-shirt with *San Francisco* written on it, in swirly letters. Then I did another odd thing. I smelled the shirt. It had a faint smell of Maggie and sweat on it. I quickly stuffed it back under her pillow and looked for the book. There it was, on her bedside table. It was a big book, called *Goblin Market* with a very strange illustration on the front. It showed a young lady dressed in white, with nasty goblins crawling all over her and pulling at her dress and trying to force her to eat fruit. Next to the book was a little blue bottle. I picked it up and it was sticky. I put it down, but the stickiness stayed on my fingers. I smelled them, and it was the same smell as Maggie, and the smell on the T-shirt. It was a strong smell that reminded me of dust and old dry oil paint, but also of lemons and oranges, and perhaps pepper as well.

I really didn't want to look inside the book, but couldn't stop myself. Inside the front cover, someone had written in purple ink,

To my Lizzie. Thank you for rescuing me from The Goblin Men.

Your Laura xxx

I closed the book and stuffed it up my jumper, then quickly and quietly went downstairs. Just as I was on the bottom step of the stairs, Auntie saw me and waved. I waved back. In the garden, Jessie grabbed the book off me. She had a very mischievous look on her face, and I knew that she had tricked me. I said, 'We're not supposed to have this book, are we?'
Jessie didn't answer, and opened the book. She looked at the purple writing and said, 'What do you think that means?' I said I had no idea and didn't want to play anymore.
She said, 'Of course you do. Come and look at these pictures and read the story to the dolls. They won't go to sleep until

they've had their story. And anyway, if you don't read it, I'll tell Maggie that you've been in her room.'

I said, 'Tell her then. I don't care. As soon as she comes home I'm going to tell her myself, and I'll say that you tricked me into doing it.'

Jessie looked frightened. 'No Pippa. Please don't do that. I'm sorry. We'll just have a quick look at it and then you can put it back.'

I wasn't going to stand for her nonsense anymore. 'No. I don't want to look at it. I think it's Maggie's precious book. I think that Rhona gave it to her, and she would be very upset if anything happened to it. Give it back to me now, or I'll tell Auntie, and then you will be in big trouble.'

She gave me a sly look. 'I won't be in trouble. You will be though, for going into Maggie's room without her permission.'

I put my hands on my hips and tried to look as old as possible. Really, I was quite frightened of Jessie. I said, 'I'm going to tell Auntie myself. She'll know that you tricked me and she'll forgive me, but you'll get a big telling off. And your Dad will be very cross when he comes home, and Maggie will be too.' That completely shut her up. She thrust the book into my hands, but I didn't want to touch it.

She whispered, 'Please, Pippa. I'm sorry. Please put it back. I do such stupid things sometimes. I'm really very sorry.' She started to cry. That gave me quite a shock. At first I thought that she was just pretending to cry, but there were real tears running down her cheeks, and her face was all red.

I rushed towards her and held her and said, 'You're not stupid. You're very clever. But you're just like me; a bit of a pickle. It's not your fault. I think we should both try and put it back, right now.'

But Auntie was walking towards us and said, 'Hello you two. What are you up to? Come and have a nice cup of tea.' I stupidly tried to hide the book behind my back. Auntie saw it and said, 'Pippa. What's that? Show me.'

I put my head down and held out the book for her to look at. She said, 'Where did you get this? It's Maggie's precious book.' I kept my head down. I felt thoroughly ashamed of myself, as if I was a thief.

Jessie said, 'I'm sorry Mummy. It's all my fault. Please don't be cross with Pippa.' Then she told Auntie about how she had tricked me into going into Maggie's room.

I wanted to kiss Jessie for being so honest, but was still terrified that Auntie would tell me off. I was going to cry, but tried to control myself. Perhaps it was the pressure of my tears building up, or just sheer panic, but suddenly I felt as if I was going to wet myself. I ran as fast as I could into the house, and raced up the stairs and got into the toilet just in time. I heard footsteps on the stairs and Auntie called out, 'Pippa, where are you? Are you all right?'

But I wasn't all right at all. I was very, very upset. I was convinced that Auntie was going to ring Mr Shepherd and tell him to take me away. Auntie opened the door, and must have got quite a shock, because I had squeezed myself into a corner and curled up in a ball, and was shaking all over. I felt Auntie's hand stroking my back and heard her say, 'Pippa, whatever is the matter? You haven't done anything wrong. Jessie has just tricked you into doing something. Auntie's not cross with you.'

I felt terrible, as if I was going to be sick. Auntie made me stand up and said, 'Come and lie down. Jessie's outside, putting away her dolls and tidying up the garden. I'll just go and put Maggie's book back and then we can have a wee chat together.'

And that's what we did. Jessie stayed outside and left us alone. I imagine that she had been frightened by me running away, and was doing her best to try to make everything better again between us. Auntie explained that Jessie was a very mixed up little girl, and that I was doing very well to put up with her nonsense. It was such a shame that none of the children at school wanted to play with her, but she had upset so many of them, which made them very wary of her.

I didn't know what to say. I tried to say, 'I'm very sorry Auntie', but the words just wouldn't come out. Auntie just sat quietly next to me, while I lay on the bed, looking at the ceiling. Then there was a knock on the door and Jessie's voice said, 'Please can I come in? I've tidied everything away and I'm worried about Pippa. Is she in there?'

Auntie told Jessie to come in. She looked at me and burst into tears. She said, through her sobs, 'Oh no! Is Pippa dead? Have I killed her with my wickedness?'

Auntie said to Jessie, 'Don't be so silly. She's just upset, because you made her do something wrong. That's quite a normal reaction. Now please stop behaving as if you are the queen of the stage and in the middle of a huge drama. Then come here and let me give you a big hug, you silly girl!' Jessie stopped crying straight away, and jumped onto Auntie's lap and practically knocked her over. I stopped looking dead, and sat up. Jessie winked at me. She really was a strange girl. I asked Auntie if I should tell Maggie about what we had done. Auntie said that wouldn't be necessary. I didn't tell her that I had seen the T-shirt under Maggie's pillow, or that I had smelled it.

Mist on the field

I stayed indoors for the rest of the day. I needed to calm myself down, so did some painting. Jessie went outside and helped Auntie in the garden. I had thought that all my shocks would be over, but I realised that even the smallest problem became a huge upset for me. Jessie, on the other hand, didn't seem to care about causing problems. While I was painting, I thought about Mummy, and how I had been very frightened of upsetting her. I thought about going to boarding school, and wondered if I would be able to cope on my own with those horrible cold nuns. I couldn't imagine any of them putting me on their knee. The thought of touching them, or them touching me, was repulsive. It would be like touching a slug, or a dead animal. But then I thought about Sister Anne, and how kind she had been to us, and suddenly the thought of boarding school didn't seem quite so bad.

Then I thought about Nicol. He really was my best Scottish friend now. Nobody could replace Lucy, of course, but I felt myself missing him, and wanted him to hurry up and come back from the Lang Stane. I hoped he would have a good chat with his dad, and then they would be the best of friends forever. And I really didn't like myself for getting so upset all the time. I hated feeling shaky if I thought someone might tell me off. I didn't like the feeling that I had disappointed the people who loved me, and that I had let them down. But I didn't know what to do about it. I wanted to explain this to someone, so that they could tell me what to think and what to do. I didn't want any more tears. I didn't want to be the queen of the stage and in the middle of a big drama. It was all too hard for me to think about, but painting helped to soothe my brain. When I had finished, I had painted mist on a field in the early morning, with shapes in the distance that could be cows, or sheep, or tree stumps, or part of a hedge. In the foreground was a dry stone wall with little purple and yellow flowers growing between the stones. A cat was sitting on top.

I was very pleased with it, and thought about giving it to Maggie. I wanted to tell her all about borrowing her book. And I wanted her to explain it to me too, because I wanted to know why such a nice lady had such a horrible book by her bedside. Then I changed my mind, and decided to give the painting to Nicol. It was obvious to me that Nicol was a very special boy. I think everyone who knew him felt the same. But it was something that Auntie had told me that made him feel extra special to me. Auntie had obviously been in love with Daddy, when they were children. If she had had the same feeling in her heart, and all over, as I felt for Nicol, then she must have missed him terribly when he went away to boarding school. And then, when he came back, he was completely changed, and didn't want to play with her anymore! But it was me who was going away to school, and Nicol who was staying at home. Would I change, and perhaps become a girl who only cared about being a Good Catholic Girl, and thought that boys were stupid, and that falling in love was a Sin? It was a terrible thought, and that's why I wanted Nicol to have my painting. I wanted him to like me as much as I liked him. And then I thought about Daddy. But I wasn't at all sure what I felt about him. Auntie had said that he was still a lovely person, just like he had been before he went away and fell in love with money. And if, underneath everything, he was just like Nicol, then he must be a very nice man. And if I could make him fall in love with me, as his daughter, then maybe he would realise that he had made a terrible mistake, and allow me to go back to Mummy and Muriel.

Nicol comes back

Then Nicol came back and went upstairs to his room, and shut the door, without saying hello to me. At teatime, he sat next to me, as usual, but wouldn't look at me. I looked at him again, but he was looking at his dad. He was doing that on purpose, so that he wouldn't have to look at me. That was horrible. I wanted to ask him what I had done wrong, but of course we were at the dining table with all the family, so I had to pretend that nothing strange was happening. I made a tremendous effort to pretend that everything was just like normal. We were eating fish fingers with mashed potatoes and baked beans, which I usually loved, but somehow it all tasted like cardboard and felt like mud in my mouth. Uncle Tom asked me what I had been doing while they were away. I mumbled, 'I played with Jessie,' but that was all I could manage to say.

After tea, Nicol went back up to his room and Jessie sat with Uncle Tom. Maggie came in and said that she was starving. There was some food left over, and she took it out into the garden. I offered to help Auntie with the washing up, but she said, 'Why don't you go and talk to Maggie?' Auntie must have felt that there was something wrong between Nicol and me. I went upstairs and got Polish Teddy from my room. I put him on the floor outside Nicol's room, knocked on the door and ran as quickly as I could down the stairs, and went outside to talk to Maggie. She asked me what we had been doing during the day. I don't know why, but I felt the urge to tell her that I had been in her room. When I explained what I had done, she laughed and said that we were naughty girls, and mustn't do it again. She said, 'I know my little sister. She's full of mischief. I imagine she was trying to get you into trouble. She's a little monkey.'

I didn't tell her about the T-shirt under her pillow. I asked her about *Goblin Market*. She said, 'Rhona gave it to me as a present. She writes a lot of poetry and songs, as you can imagine, but the boys in the group don't really like them. Yes, it's a very strange poem. At first, I really didn't like it. I especially didn't like the horrible illustrations by Arthur Rackham. But then Rhona explained what the poem meant to her, and now I could never be apart from it. It's a good job you didn't spoil it, because it's one of my most treasured possessions.'

I said, 'I'm very sorry, Maggie. I promise not to do anything like that again.'

She said, 'Oh that's all right. But I'm sure that monkey of a little sister of mine will try to get you to do more of her mischief. I'm surprised that she didn't ask you to get my favourite T-shirt. That really would have been the end!'

I had to tell her. 'Maggie, I saw a T-shirt sticking out from under your pillow. I don't know why, but I just had to look at it.'

She finished eating her tea. All the time that she was eating, I was convinced that I was going to get the telling off that I deserved. She put down her knife and fork, looked at me, and smiled. 'What do you think about it? Tell me, honestly.'

That seemed like a very strange question. I didn't want to say any more about it, but Maggie had forgiven me, and I wanted to please her. 'I think it's the same one that Rhona wore in the photograph underneath your poster.' I should have stopped there. 'And you like each other so much that she gave it to you. Perhaps you might like to wear it in bed, or hold it in the night.'

Maggie's face went bright red. 'And how do you know that?' She didn't ask it in a nasty way, but she said it very quietly, as if we were talking about a secret.

'Well that's what I would do if I liked someone a lot. It's like Polish Teddy. Mummy loved Muriel the minute she saw her. They have never told me that, but I know she did. And I loved Muriel as well. So when she gave me Polish Teddy to keep, I fell in love with him too. So every time I touch him, I think of Muriel. And when I first got him, he smelled of Muriel's old house, so I used to sniff him a lot. So I suppose it's the same for you with Rhona's T-shirt.' Then I told her about Mummy smelling Muriel's dirty blouse, and what Mummy said.

Maggie said, 'If only I could meet them! We would have so much to talk about! Would you mind if I tell Rhona about that?'

I was so relieved that Maggie still liked me, that I would have promised her anything.

Then Jessie came running outside, and Maggie told her off for sending me into her room. She didn't joke with Jessie, like she had done with me, but was quite cross with her. Jessie said she was sorry, but I could tell that she didn't care at all.

Then it became very cloudy and started to rain. I wanted to go to bed, even though it was quite early. I went upstairs to have a wash and clean my teeth. Polish Teddy had gone from outside Nicol's room. I hoped Nicol had taken him, to keep in his bed during the night. But when I went into my room, Teddy was in my bed, on his side, as if he were asleep. I looked at my photo of Muriel and Mummy, and wanted to go home. I had the same feeling I always felt when things were going wrong. All the happiness that had landed like coloured dust on my surface had been blown away by the wind. And I was left with exactly the same feeling that had overwhelmed me in the shiny car, as it took me away from school. Auntie came up and was surprised to see me already in bed and trying to go to sleep. She asked me if everything was all right, so I told her I had a headache and a tummy ache. I could tell that she didn't believe me. She said, 'And what else?'

320

I whispered, 'I don't think Nicol likes me anymore.'

She said, 'Of course he does. He's just a complicated boy. He'll sort himself out soon. You just need to be patient with him. He's just like his dad. When Uncle Tom has a problem, he goes quiet, and you have to wait for him to sort it all out in his head.' She kissed me and said, 'Don't worry, my love.'

The next morning when I went down to breakfast, Jessie and Maggie were already eating and talking quietly to each other. Jessie saw me and told Maggie to shush. Nicol came in and said, 'Hello everybbbbbbbbbb...everyone.' But he still wouldn't look at me. Auntie asked us if we would like to go swimming. I wanted to go, but Nicol said he didn't feel very well, so wanted to stay at home.

I said, 'I don't want to go if Nicol isn't coming.' He didn't look at me.

Jessie wailed, 'That's not fair I want to go!'

Maggie said that she would be happy to take us. Nicol asked to leave the table and left the room. Maggie went after him. I didn't want to have any breakfast, but forced myself to eat some toast and marmalade.

Maggie came back in and said that she had persuaded Nicol to change his mind.

Our walk to the to the swimming baths felt horrible. I tried to walk next to Nicol, but each time I went near him he moved, so that Maggie would be in-between us, and I ended up holding Jessie's hand most of the way there. In the pool, Nicol swam up and down, while I stayed with Jessie in the shallow end. Every so often Maggie would swim over to him and talk, and then swim away again. Sometimes he got out of the water, but never waved to me. I felt horribly cold outside and inside and wanted to get out. After about half an hour, we went into the changing rooms. Nicol hadn't looked at me once.

In the changing rooms, Maggie told me to go into the same cubicle as Jessie, to help her to get dried and dressed. Jessie was perfectly capable of doing it herself, but always took a long time, and made us wait for ages. There was a puddle of dirty water on the floor in our cubicle. As soon as we had taken off our costumes, Jessie dropped her towel in the puddle, so had to use mine. Maggie was in the cubicle next door and heard me telling Jessie to hurry up because I was freezing. Maggie came in and started to rub me down with her towel, to keep me warm. We were all squashed together, and I whispered, 'What's the matter with Nicol? He won't talk to me, and I think he doesn't like me anymore.'

Maggie said, 'Nicol is worried that he likes you too much. He's not sure if he's supposed to, because you're like our cousin, or even our sister. He thinks that you might be very upset when you go away to school, so he says it's better if he isn't friendly with you anymore. He thinks he shouldn't hold hands with you, and says it's better if he goes to find some new friends.'

I had been freezing cold, but suddenly felt hot all over. I wanted to get out of that cubicle and tell Nicol that I wouldn't be very upset when I went to school. Maggie looked at me. I don't know why, but she said, 'Can I look at your scar?'

She touched it, but it felt just like she was one of the doctors. She touched me under the chin and kissed me on the cheek and said, 'I think you're the loveliest girl in the world. Along with Jessie, of course. I think that Nicol's just a bit mixed up. He's only twelve, after all, so he's still a boy. And boys take a lot longer to grow up than us girls. They often have very silly ideas and do very silly things, while we are so sensible. Aren't we Jessie?'

I didn't like to disagree with Maggie, but Jessie was one of the silliest girls I had ever met.

Nicol was waiting for us in the foyer. He said to Maggie, 'What took you so long?'

Jessie said, 'We were talking about you. You've upset Pippa. And Maggie was looking at Pippa's scar.'

Nicol went red.

Mr Griffin was sitting in his car in the car park. He waved at us, so Maggie went over to talk to him. She came back and told us that she and Jessie were going to buy some sweets, while

Nicol and I could have a lift with Mr Griffin, or walk home on our own. Nicol said that he would like to walk home. I didn't know if he wanted me to come with him or not, so I said, 'What shall I do?'

He said, 'Do what you like.' He said it in a horrible way, so I told him I wanted to go home with Mr Griffin. Then Nicol said, 'Nnnnno. Walk with me, ppppppplease.'

I couldn't bear to hear him stuttering like that. I knew that he was very unhappy.

We walked up through the town, without saying anything. As we reached the hill, my appendix scar started to hurt and my tummy started aching. I just knew that I had to say something, so I said, 'Nicol, have I done something wrong? Why are you being so horrible to me? Why won't you talk to me?'

In my head, The Beatles were singing *Hold Your Hand*. Nicol looked straight ahead, but I could see that his face and neck had gone red all over. I said, 'I don't mind if you don't hold my hand, but when I touch you I feel joy inside. I forget all about missing my mummy. My life has been horrible sometimes, but I love being with you. And if you don't talk to me, I think it will be another sadness in my life. That's all I want to say, really. Now I think I want Mr Griffin to give me a lift home.' I wanted to cry.

Nicol stopped walking. He looked at me, at last. He said, 'Please don't. It's true what you said. Dad told me all about it.'

'About what?'

'It's called 'The Birds and the Bees'. It's about what married people do. But you got something wrong. It's not liquid that comes out of the man. It's something else. It's the man's seeds.'

I said, 'Well maybe people in Scotland do it differently than in England.'

Nicol said, 'That makes sense.'

We walked together. I didn't dare look at him. Once I felt his hand knock against mine, but it might have been an accident. I was thinking about what to say. The Beatles were now singing *Can't Buy Me Love.*

Then I said what I wanted to say, 'Nicol, I want to say one more thing about that, then I don't want to talk about it ever again, because I don't like to talk about it.' I took a deep breath. 'When two grown-ups who you love, and who love you as well, are in bed together in the night, and you hear them making noises and laughing; I think that's one of the happiest sounds in the world. It means that they really love each other, and then I feel safe and sound, and can go to sleep knowing that they will love me too.'

We didn't say anything for a while. There was a low wall outside a church and we sat on it. Nicol said, 'We had our mum's funeral in a church. Her grave is very messy. The deer eat all the flowers and grass, and the rabbits dig holes. I used to think that they would dig all the way down to her coffin.'

That was a horrible idea, but I could feel chocolate melting in my tummy, because Nicol was coming back to me, at last. I said, 'Well we could make some decorations out of stones and shells, if you like.'

'Yes I would like that. That's a very nice idea.'

He touched my hand and said, 'I'm sorry for being horrible. Did Jessie tell you all about it?'

'Jessie? No. She didn't say anything. It was Maggie who told me.'

'But Jessie came to see me in the night. I told her that I didn't want to upset you, and told her to tell you.' That was an odd thing. I didn't understand Jessie at all. I thought she would have loved to tell me something like that, but instead she kept it a secret.

Then someone shouted Nicol's name from across the road, and I saw two boys waving at us. They were wearing identical red football shirts, white shorts and red socks, and one of them was holding a football. I supposed that they were twins, except that the one who spoke was slightly taller than the other. They crossed the road, and the taller one said something to Nicol that

I didn't understand. The boy pointed at me, said something else, and smiled at me. He had a front tooth missing.

Nicol said, 'This is my new friend Pippa. She's staying with us. She's from England.'

The twins looked at Nicol. They both looked very surprised about something. Nicol said, 'What? What are you gawping at? Do you think I'm a daftie or something?'

The slightly shorter one said, 'Well no, but...'

Then Mr Griffin's car stopped next to us, with Maggie and Jessie in the back. Maggie said, 'Come on you two, come home with us.' She said to the twins, 'Hello Kenny, hello Kirsty. Do you want to come as well?'

The one with the tooth missing said, 'We'll need to ask our dad.'

Maggie said, 'Well run along home, and then come and see us, and bring your fiddle won't you, Kirsty?'

The boy with the tooth missing said, 'I can't, it's got a string missing, and anyway it's too small.'

I didn't understand why everyone was calling him Kirsty.

A girl boy

Maggie got in the front, and Nicol and I sat in the back with Jessie. Nicol's leg touched mine, but he didn't move it away. Jessie asked Nicol, 'Have you two made up?' Nicol didn't say anything. I wanted to punch Jessie. She was such a shit stirrer. Jessie said, 'That's Kirsty and Kenny. They're our cousins. They've just been on holiday. Kirsty is such a tomboy. Their father is our Uncle Jimmy. He's big friends with dad. Their mum is my dead mum's sister. She's called Auntie Màiri. She's a daftie and drinks all the time.'

Maggie turned round and said, 'Jessie, don't you ever say anything like that again!'

Jessie said, 'But it's true. She's always getting drunk.'

Nicol said, 'It's not her fault. And you had better shut up, Jessie.'

Jessie was enjoying herself. Maggie said, 'Please Jessie, their mum has just gone back into hospital again. I know they looked happy, but they're just putting a brave face on it, as usual. And if you say anything about Auntie Màiri, I'll tell them not to play music with you.'

When we got home, the front room floor was covered in big brown cardboard boxes. I supposed that they were something to do with Uncle Tom's writing. I was starving, and luckily Auntie had prepared a very big lunch. She said that the twins' mother was in hospital and they were going to eat with us. Almost as soon as she had said it, there was a knock at the front door and they came in. We all squeezed together around the table and the twins ate as if they had never seen food before. I couldn't take my eyes off Kirsty. She was just like a boy. She looked even more like a boy than her twin brother. She kept looking at me and smiling. I wanted to talk to her and ask her all sorts of questions. I noticed that the twins had the same haircuts as Nicol, and I was sure that Maggie had cut their hair.

Auntie Aileen went into the kitchen and Kirsty whispered, 'Are the hairy people back yet?'
Jessie said, 'They're not hairy people. They're called *beatniks*.'
Maggie said, 'If you are talking about Rhona and her friends, then I think you'll find that the correct way to describe them is *hippies*. And they won't be back until the end of August.'
I said, 'I've met some hippies before.' I told them how I had got stuck up the tree, and how The Wizard had saved my life. I described him and his girlfriend and finished by saying, 'And Noelle smelled just like Maggie. It was the same perfume, I mean.'
I went red and looked at my plate. I felt everyone looking at me. Maggie said, 'It's called Patchouli Oil. Rhona gave me a bottle of it.'

I wanted to leave the table and talk to the strange girl-boy sitting opposite me. After pudding, the four of us children went into the garden. I said to Kirsty, 'Would you like to come with me and help Maggie do the washing up?'

She said, 'Good idea,' and she came back inside with me. Jessie followed us. Kirsty said, 'Go away Jessie, you are such a Nosey Parker.'

I was shocked. I said, 'Don't be like that to Jessie. If you don't want her to know something, then don't say it. It's not her fault. She's only young.'

Kirsty looked very surprised. I thought she was going to walk away, but she didn't. She said, 'Sorry, Jessie. It's just that my mum's in hospital again, and me and my brother are all over the place, again.'

I liked this girl-boy. I liked her very much. Maggie had her back to us, but I knew that she was listening. I said, 'My mummy used to drink lots of whisky and leave me on my own. But then she went to a special hospital and saw a special doctor every week, and she's all right now.'

Kirsty looked very impressed, 'But didn't your dad look after you?'

'Oh no, my parents are divorced.' It was strange. I was boasting about my problems, to make Kirsty feel better.

Maggie gave us a tea towel each and said, 'Come on you three, do the drying up and then we can all go in the front room and open those boxes. Aren't you desperate to see what's inside?'

Jessie whispered in my ear, 'I love you, Pippa.'

I said, 'Well if that's true, then why didn't you tell me about what Nicol told you in the night?'

She smiled and said, 'I forgot.' I pinched her arm and she squealed and said, 'Maggie, Pippa's hurting me!'

After drying up, we went into the front room. There were so many boxes! The three of us sat on the sofa, looking at them. I said to Kirsty, 'I hope you didn't mind me looking at you all the time. It's just that you look just like a boy, but you are really a girl. How do you do it?'

I wondered if she was going to be annoyed with me for asking such a personal question, but she just laughed and said, 'Boys have more fun than girls.'

I said, 'Well I like being a girl. I think it's fun.'

'Do you play football and climb trees, and have a penknife?'

'I used to climb trees, and I'm good at throwing and catching. I used to do that with my friend Lucy.' Actually, Kirsty was right. Lucy had been a real girl until she met me, and then she became a bit more active and got dirty quite a lot. And her parents had to buy her trousers, to wear whenever I came to play with her.

Kirsty said, 'I like you. How did you get Nicol to speak properly? We all like him, but he's a very sad boy. And he's more like a lassie than a boy. I suppose it's because he spends so much time with his sisters and playing with us girls. The boys tease him because of his stutter, so I hit them.'

I said, 'I hit a boy down at the swimming baths the other day, and made his nose bleed. He said his dad's a policeman.'

Kirsty looked astonished. 'It was you? I know that boy. We played football in the park with him this morning. His nose is still sore, but he told me it was a boy who did it.'

'Well it was me, and I'm a girl.'

Jessie said, 'They were teasing Nicol about his stutter, so Pippa called him *a fucking Scottish bastard*, and hit him so hard he fell over.'

Kirsty was hugely impressed. She looked at me, 'But you don't look rough and tough!'

'I'm not, but I've seen lots of fights, so just know what to do'

She asked me to tell her exactly what I had done. I said, 'Well, boys expect you to slap them, but they know that won't hurt. So you have to punch them in the face, and it's best if you can hit them in the eye or the nose, because that hurts the most, so then they might bleed and stop, or run away. I didn't want him to fall over, but when he did, I thought I should kick him very hard where it really hurts. But a lady stopped me from doing that.'

Kirsty said, 'That's exactly what I'd like to do. Are you Nicol's girlfriend?'

I wanted to deny it, but went red instead. Jessie said, 'They broke up, but now they're back together again.'

I said, 'I wonder what's in the boxes?'

Black Jack David

Luckily, Auntie and Maggie came in the room with Kenny and Nicol, and saved me from any more embarrassing questions. But I felt very pleased with myself, because I knew that I had made a new friend, and had finally got Jessie on my side.

The front room was full of people, and then Uncle Tom came in, with a man I'd never seen before. I could tell straight away that he was Kenny and Kirsty's father, because they had the same nose and ears. He said, 'Hello everybody.' He was smiling, but his voice sounded a bit shaky, probably because his wife was in hospital again. Auntie told us children to sit on the floor and let the grown-ups sit on the sofa. Kirsty's father said, 'It's OK. I'll just stand here by the door.' I felt sorry for him, because his wife had just been taken away and put in a hospital, because she was an alcoholic.

Uncle Tom said, 'You're probably wondering what all these boxes are. Well, you have Pippa to thank for all this. Actually, it's Pippa's father really. You see, Aileen has been looking after Pippa for quite a few weeks now. Pippa's father, Mr Dunbar, wanted to pay Aileen, but of course she refused. So to show his appreciation, he arranged for Mr Griffin to collect these packages. I'm not exactly sure what's inside, but I hope you'll all be pleased with what he has given you.'

It felt like Uncle Tom had just hit me in the face. I had hardly thought about my father since I had been in Stranhaven. And now Uncle Tom was mentioning his name in front of everyone. But I didn't have time to think, because Uncle Tom got down on the floor and opened the first box. Auntie Aileen said, 'Oh my goodness!' It was an accordion. Uncle Tom gave it to Jessie. It was very heavy, so he just put it in front of Jessie, who sat and stroked all its buttons and shiny metal surfaces. It really was a thing of beauty. The next box was for Nicol. It was a saxophone! It said 'Alto Saxophone' on the box, and Nicol picked it up and started blowing into it. He was very, very excited, and tried to speak, but no words would come out.

329

Everyone clapped. Uncle Tom put his arm around Nicol's shoulder, and Nicol looked very pleased about that.

There were four boxes left. Uncle Tom gave a huge box to Maggie. Her hands were shaking and she took a long time to undo the knot in the string. There were three boxes inside, two big ones and a very small one. She opened the small box first and it was a harmonica. She blew into it and said, 'How wonderful! I lost my other one somewhere up at Rhona's,' and then she went red in the face. In the other box was a brand new shiny typewriter. Uncle Tom said, 'Mr Dunbar – well, really you could call him your Uncle Andrew 'was very keen that you should have that. He thought you should stop typing up my books and articles and start to concentrate on your own work!'
I thought she was going to cry. The third box had a black leather case inside. Maggie opened it and drew in her breath in astonishment. It was a hairdressing kit, with all sorts of different types of scissors and combs. Maggie said, 'But this is the best kit you can get. How did he know?' Then she did start to cry, which started to upset me, even though she was very happy.

But I stopped feeling worried about Maggie, because there was something for me. I asked Nicol to help me open the box. It was a concertina! It was the same make as Auntie and Jessie's, but wasn't at all new or shiny, but looked quite old. Auntie said, 'Oh, it's beautiful. I bet it sounds beautiful too!' She asked me if she could play a few notes, and sure enough, it had a beautiful tone. She said, 'This is a really well-loved instrument. Your father really is a very generous man!'
I said, 'Yes, he is. He's very generous.' But I wasn't really thinking about what I was saying; because I was too busy running my hands over my concertina.

There were still two boxes left on the floor. Uncle Tom got up and asked Kirsty and Kenny's dad to go outside with him. Then Auntie Aileen gave a box to each of the twins. Everyone looked at them. Auntie said, 'And these are special presents, just for you. You are family, and it wouldn't be right if you didn't have something.' Kenny had a small guitar and Kirsty a fiddle. Kenny was absolutely delighted and kissed Auntie. She said, 'It's not me you should be kissing, but Pippa.'

He didn't want to do that, but said, 'Thank you very much Pippa.'

Auntie helped Kenny and Kirsty to tune their instruments, while everyone else started to experiment with theirs. I could play one tune already and had almost mastered Captain Pugwash, so I played both my tunes. Jessie joined in and seemed to know exactly what to do with her accordion. She didn't play it perfectly, by any means, but it was obvious that she had played one before. Nicol played a tune that Rhona's friend had taught him, called *Hit the Road Jack*.

I was very surprised when Jessie said, 'Right everybody, listen to me.' She was the youngest person in the room, but everyone, including Maggie, did as they were told. And it soon became clear why: Jessie was very talented. She said, 'Let's start with Black Jack David. Maggie, you can sing and then when I say Go! Nicol, you can play Hit the Road Jack, and then we can all do Captain Pugwash.

Kirsty did an introduction on the fiddle and then Maggie started singing

Oh Black Jack David is the name that I bear,

Been alone in the forest a long time,

But the time is coming when a lady I'll find

And then all the instruments joined in and everyone sang

I will love her, hold her

Singing through the green, green trees!

It sounded just wonderful. Really, we were just a bunch of children bashing around, but I had never heard anything like it. I sat with my concertina on my lap and felt I was in heaven. How had these children all learned to play so well? They all looked so happy, and joined in shouting, 'Singing through the green, green trees!' as if they didn't have a care in the world. I looked at Jessie, leading everyone, including Maggie. She was

331

still only eight, but knew exactly what she was doing. What I didn't know is that everyone in this family, including Auntie, was very musical, and they played regularly with Kirsty and Kenny. Then it was time to play Captain Pugwash, and I was able to join in with everybody else.

We sang Black Jack David again and I listened to the words. Maggie told me that it was a very old song, about a Gypsy man who lived deep in the woods, and charmed a teenage girl called Heloise away from her father.

Jessie insisted that we play the songs over and over again. The more we played, the more comfortable we became with our new instruments. I felt myself becoming a bit overwhelmed, so I put my concertina down, and said I wanted to go to the toilet. Auntie smiled and nodded, but the others just ignored me and kept on playing. I went into the garden, where Uncle Tom, Mr Griffin, and Kirsty's father were sitting at the table, smoking funny black cigarettes with gold filters. The smoke had a very strong smell, and was quite different to any other cigarette I had smelled.

Uncle Tom said, 'Hello Pippa. I hear that everyone is enjoying their new instruments, thanks to your father.'

I didn't know what to say, and felt embarrassed. I thought that I'd better say something, so I said to Kirsty's father, 'I'm sorry, but what should I call you?'

He smiled and said, 'How about Uncle Jimmy?'

I said, 'I'm very sorry to hear about Kirsty and Kenny's mum going into hospital. My mummy went to hospital because she was very sad and drank too much whisky, but she's much better now. I want to go back to her, but I'm not allowed. But I'm very pleased to be here. I think it's the nicest place in the whole world, but it would be even better if Mummy could be here with me.'

Uncle Jimmy said, 'Thank you, Pippa. I'm glad your mummy's better. We all hope that Màiri will get better too, but she's been in hospital so many times that we are all getting very worried.'

After that, I didn't know what else to say. Uncle Tom said, 'Why don't we ask the children to come outside and give us a wee concert? Pippa, you go inside and tell them all to come out here.'

When I went indoors, everyone was having a rest. Auntie said that she would bring some biscuits and orange squash into the garden for us. The afternoon was getting better and better. We brought chairs from indoors and arranged ourselves in a semi-circle in front of the grown-ups, and played our songs for them. They clapped and shouted 'encore', so we had to play again. Then Uncle Jimmy said it was time to take his children home, because they all wanted to go to the hospital. Mr Griffin offered to take them. I looked at Kenny and Kirsty and they stopped looking delighted, and looked very sad. Uncle Tom said, 'Leave your instruments here, so you will have to come back every day to rehearse your songs, until they are perfect and ready for the kaylee.'

Divided attention

After they left, Jessie was very excited and kept running round and round the garden, and Luna chased after her and barked a lot. I suddenly felt that I had had too much excitement, so I put my concertina carefully back in its box and went upstairs to sit on my bed. I picked up Polish Teddy. It really had been the most extraordinary day. Nicol and I were friends again, we had talked about The Birds and the Bees, and I knew that he really liked me. I had made an exciting new friend, who was a real tomboy, my daddy had sent us the most wonderful presents, and we had played lovely music together. I told Teddy that it was one of the happiest days of my life. I went into a little dream, where Mummy and Muriel were living next door to us, and they were best friends with Auntie Aileen, and Mummy talked to Kirsty's mum and told her all about how to stop drinking alcohol. And I went to the local school and learnt how to be a proper Wee Scottish Lassie. Far away downstairs, the telephone was ringing.

There was a knock on the door and Maggie came in. She said, 'I thought I'd find you in here. Are you having a wee rest after all that excitement?' I said I was, and that I had been having a happy dream about Mummy and Muriel coming to live next door. She said, 'That was Rhona on the phone. She's in a hotel in Sweden, and was just ringing to say that she misses me. I told her all about you, and about the musical instruments. And of course she wants to meet you, and to see your pictures. That will be lovely, won't it?' She had a huge smile on her face.

Then I felt something about Maggie, I saw a fine light-blue cloud surrounding her head and shoulders, billowing around her and then settling like a fine dust in her hair, on her face, then on her shoulders and chest. She looked at me with her enormous smile. I had seen that smile many times before, but I couldn't remember where. Then I knew something. I knew something about Maggie and Rhona.

She said, 'I'm so glad that you and Nicol are friends again.'

I said, 'It was horrible when he wouldn't talk to me. I missed him so much. I don't like to miss people like that. It hurts me here.' I touched the space above my Lovely Place. 'And it hurts me here.' I put my hand on my chest.

Maggie said, 'Welcome to the World of Love.'

I knew it. I asked her, 'If I can't sleep in the night, can I come and see you?'

Maggie smiled, 'Of course. But whatever you do, don't wake Jessie. She's very, very excited, and she needs to calm down, otherwise she'll go off pop, and that is not a pretty sight.' She ran her hands through my hair. 'And talking of pretty sights, will you let me cut your hair one day? I've been looking at you and thinking what I'd love to do.'

That question pleased me, but bothered me at the same time. I knew what it was. It was my mummy's job to talk to me about my hair, and to arrange for me to have it cut. I couldn't decide to have my hair cut without Mummy's permission, and Mummy was far away.

I was about to explain that to Maggie when we heard shouting downstairs. Jessie and Nicol were having an argument about something. Maggie said, 'Time to go. The only way to sort Jessie out is to give her buckets full of attention; otherwise we'll all be in trouble. When she was a toddler, she used to stuff herself with pudding until she was almost sick. Then she would run around the house, screaming and yelling. Our mum used to call it 'Jessie's Big Pudding Moment'. Mum knew not to let Jessie have too much sweet food, but couldn't stop herself from giving it to her. And now she's the same when she plays music with other people. She gets so excited that she can't calm down. She just doesn't know when to stop.'

'But what about Nicol? Doesn't he need your attention as well?' I didn't like to think of him missing out on his big sister's love.

Maggie was just about to leave the room, but turned. There was more shouting. She smiled that big smile again. 'Oh no. After all, he's got you now, and he and his dad are big friends again.'

I was tempted to go downstairs to see what was going on, but decided to stay where I was. I had eaten a lot of emotional pudding too, and was letting it rest in my tummy. I used to be a little girl all on her own, with hours and hours to think, draw, and paint, and with the undivided attention of grown-ups who loved me. Now I was just a small part of a big, noisy, and complicated family. In this family, everyone had to fight for their share of attention and space, or had to wait until they were noticed. I didn't mind that at all. I didn't want to go off on my own, like I used to. If ever I had an empty space in the day, I wanted to share it with Nicol. The arguing downstairs had stopped, and Jessie was playing her accordion again. She really was very talented. I wondered if she was like me with my Art. I heard someone coming up the stairs and Nicol called out, 'Pippa! Where are you, Pippa? Are you hiding from me?' Before I answered him, I decided that I would call my next painting 'Maggie's Loving Smile', and it would have lots of dark blue, and would be like a painting by Marc Chagall.

At bedtime, Jessie made a terrible fuss, and refused to go to bed. Uncle Tom had to get quite cross with her. He said, 'If that's how you're going to behave, then we will have to think very carefully about whether you should have the accordion or not, and whether or not you should go to the kaylee, let alone play at it.'

That stopped Jessie's nonsense straight away. In bed, she asked me, 'Is your dad very rich? Could you ask him to send me a set of bagpipes?' I laughed and asked her what a *kaylee* was. 'Don't you know? It's a big night of music and dancing. Dad and his friends organise one every year, at the end of august. This year some musicians are coming from Ireland. If we are allowed to play, people might just dance to our music!'

She was getting excited again. I asked her to come into bed with me, and I stroked her hair, to calm her down. I asked her why the dance was called a kaylee. She said, 'It's Scottish. Do you know how to spell it?'

I told her that I thought it was K-A-Y-L-E-E. She laughed and said that most people thought that, but she knew its proper spelling. She wouldn't tell me what it was, so we spent a few minutes playing a guessing game. Who'd have thought that the right answer was *CEILIDH*? I liked the idea of being half-Scottish. Jessie was fast asleep, in my arms.

○ ○ ○ ○ ○ ○

30th November 1976

What are dreams? Some people say it's just your brain working while you are asleep. It's just all the little chemicals and nerves ticking away while your body rests. Others think it is all the unresolved conflicts of the day, coming back to you and annoying you, so you wake up in the morning feeling a bit anxious about what the day will bring. For others, it's a surge of symbols, bubbling up from your subconscious, telling you what is really going on in your world, but which you have chosen to ignore or push down during the day (some people will tell you that those problems are usually about sex). People around here, who refuse to think about S-E-X, tell me that dreams are glimmers from a past life, or premonitions of the future, or what will happen in your next life. They tell me that Clairvoyants and Initiates and those who have eyes to see are the true Seers, who can interpret your dreams, so that you can be set on the right path to achieve your Manifest Destiny. Quite frankly, I think that's complete and utter bollocks. I've always been a big dreamer. For me, it's my subconscious reminding me about my unresolved conflicts (some of which involve sex, and some that don't.)

○ ○ ○ ○ ○ ○

That night, I knew I would have a Big Dream. I woke up with Jessie in my bed, wrapped around me and purring like a cat. Fortunately, she had remembered to brush her teeth, because she was breathing all over me and dribbling. I had just had a Very Big Dream. In my dream, Kirsty and her mother were standing on a cliff, looking far out to sea. The Lang Stane was jutting out of the sea, like a lighthouse, and the waves were crashing all round it. Kirsty said, 'Listen Mummy, listen to the wind!' The wind was singing, and the tune was Black Jack David. We had played and sung that song so many times, but I had never really thought about the words. But now they came clear to me in my dream. It wasn't a nice story at all. A young girl who is only fifteen is charmed by a dark man who lives in the forest. In the night she rides off with him, and her father wakes up in the morning and finds her gone. He searches and searches, but never finds her, because she is far away in the forest, sleeping with Black Jack David.

Then Kirsty's mother turned to Kirsty and started moaning, 'The Goblins are coming. Don't let me eat the fruit, don't let me eat the fruit!'

Kirsty screamed and screamed and the mother threw herself off the cliff. She plummeted towards the waves, but at the last minute swooped upwards like an angel, and landed next to Kirsty. She said to Kirsty, 'Jump Kirsty! Jump!' But Kirsty refused.

I don't know why Kenny wasn't in the dream. He was such a quiet boy, the opposite of his twin sister, and they went everywhere together. But if you had been in a room with them, afterwards you could never quite remember if Kenny had been there. He was a bit like his sister's shadow.

I got up and went towards Maggie's room. Her door was very slightly open, and as usual, a faint light was shining from underneath it. I heard a sigh, then everything was still. I knocked very quietly, but there was no answer. I pushed the door open, very gently. Maggie was lying on her back, but her eyes were closed. I wasn't sure what to do, so sat on her bed. Her bedside light was switched off, but on her desk, under Rhona's poster, was something very beautiful. It was a bottle, shaped just like the lime juice cordial bottle I had had in hospital. It was on a little silver stand that had a light in it. The bottle was full of a clear liquid, with red shapes like squidgy balloons that rose up from the bottom and made lovely curvy shapes, before slowly bumping into each other. But instead of bursting, the shapes seemed to melt and form one big balloon, which was so heavy it slowly sank down to the bottom again. As it sank, it stretched out, like when you pull bubble gum out of your mouth, then broke apart and then formed a big blob at the bottom, where it lay for a few seconds before rising again. It was like magic.

I felt an arm round my waist and Maggie said, 'I wasn't sleeping. I was just resting my eyes.'

I didn't say anything. I was mesmerised by the lamp. Maggie sat up and gave me a kiss. 'Do you like my lava lamp? Rhona bought it for me in America. We usually keep it up at the cottage, but I thought I'd bring it down here.'

All I could say was 'Mmm.'

We sat and watched it together. She said, 'I thought you'd come. What is it, my little fairy? Come into bed and tell Maggie all about it.' She lifted the covers, and the warmth and Maggie's smell came up to my face. She was wearing her pyjama bottoms, and Rhona's T-shirt.

I told her all about my dream, and it felt to me as if I was talking to Muriel. I finished talking and looked at Maggie. She was fast asleep. I didn't feel sleepy anymore. I lay on my back and looked up at the ceiling. It was covered with a moving red light. Then I remembered something. Nicol had told me that his mother had died while giving birth to Jessie, but Maggie said that she was still alive when Jessie was a toddler. I pushed Maggie, to try to get her to wake up, but she was deeply asleep. I whispered in her ear, 'Maggie, Maggie, please wake up! I need to ask you something.'

She mumbled, 'I want to cut your hair.' I think she was dreaming. Then she said, 'What is it? Oh! I thought you were Rhona.'

I told her about what Nicol had said about their mother. She was a bit more awake now.

She said, 'He used to say that to other children who didn't know him, whenever they asked him where his mum was. Sometimes you can tell other people stories so many times, that after a while you believe them yourself.'

I said, 'Muriel, how did your mum die?'

'Nobody knows for sure exactly what happened, but she drowned, in the sea.'

'Oh.'

'And do you know that you just called me Muriel?'

That wasn't so much of a surprise. Being so warm and close to Maggie in bed, and sharing our deepest thoughts and secrets, reminded me of Muriel. I said, 'You are like Muriel.'

Maggie let out a small sigh. 'What is she like, this Muriel? I know what she looks like. But how did she and your mummy meet?'

I told the story about Muriel falling over on the underground platform, and the taxi, and going to see Max, and Mummy and Muriel not being able to say goodbye to each other.

Maggie sighed again. 'How wonderfully romantic. It was a *coup de foudre*. Love at first sight.'

'Yes it was. And for me too. Muriel saved Mummy. She saved me as well.'

'Saved you? From what?'

I told her about Daddy, and the photographs of Mummy, me and the naked lady in the swimming pool in Malaysia, and Mummy being an alcoholic. And for some strange reason, I told her about when Muriel had worn the nurse's uniform on the train and a man had pinched her bottom, and how I had seen her and Mummy being tender in the changing room, and how the painting I did of that moment led to my parents getting divorced.

Maggie said, 'Goodness gracious!' and held me very tight. I think I fell asleep, straight away, in her arms.

I really don't understand

I woke up in the morning, back in my own bed, and wondered if I had dreamed about being with Maggie. I wanted to see her, so tapped on her door, and peeped inside her room. She had gone, but the lava lamp was on the desk, so I knew I hadn't been dreaming. I really had talked to her, and got everything off my chest. Jessie and Nicol were still asleep, so I went downstairs. Uncle Tom and Auntie were eating breakfast together. Auntie kissed me and asked me if I had slept well, so I said exactly what was on my mind. 'Nicol told me that his mum died when Jessie was being born, but Maggie told me that she was still alive when Jessie was a toddler. Is someone lying to me? I really don't understand at all. Should I just mind my own business and not talk about it?'

Auntie sighed. She said, 'Maggie has just told us about this. She said that you had talked to her in the night.' She said to Uncle Tom, 'Tom, this all has to come out, doesn't it?'

He said, 'Yes, I agree, but what's the best way to go about it?'

Auntie said to me, 'Pippa, I wish we had all been as lucky as you, and gone to an art therapist. Then perhaps we could all talk about some of the complicated things that have happened in our lives. I didn't know that Nicol had said that to you about his mother. She didn't die when Jessie was a baby. She died when Jessie was two years old. I don't think Nicol was lying. I think sometimes you tell yourself something is true so many times that you end up believing it.'

'That's what Maggie said.'

Uncle Tom said, 'Maggie is a very clever girl. She's still young, but she's very wise. I think spending time with Rhona has been very good for her.'

Auntie said to Uncle Tom, 'So what shall we do?'

Then we heard Jessie come down the stairs, followed by Nicol. They were both wearing their pyjamas. Nicol complained that Jessie had come into his bedroom, bounced on his bed, and woken him up, but he looked very pleased. Uncle Tom said to them, 'Help yourselves to breakfast. I'm just going to have a wee chat with Aileen in the garden.' Nicol looked very worried. As soon as they went out, Nicol asked me if something bad had happened. I didn't know what to say.

Nicol said, 'Has something happened to Maggie? Where's Maggie?' I told him that I had seen Maggie in the night. Nicol relaxed. 'I expect she's gone up to the cottage again.'

Jessie said, 'She can't keep away from that place. Dad says that Maggie and Rhona are bosom friends. That sounds a bit rude to me, like they are always showing each other their bosoms.'

Nicol looked like he was going to say something nasty to Jessie, but didn't. We went to the window and looked out. We saw Uncle Tom's pipe smoke rising up in the morning sunlight.

We finished our breakfast in silence. For once, Jessie didn't have anything to say. You could look at Nicol and guess what he was thinking, but you never knew what was going on in Jessie's head. I used to think that all she ever thought about was how she could cause trouble in other people's lives. But after yesterday's concert, I wondered if she was actually more like me than I had realised. Maybe she spent a lot of time thinking about music, just like me and my Art. Nicol looked worried. Jessie was reading the back of the Rice Krispies packet.

Auntie Aileen came indoors. Her shoes were covered in grass and dew, but she didn't seem to notice. She said, 'Uncle Tom has gone up to Rhona's to talk to Maggie. Everyone go and get washed. Jessie, your dad is going to spend the day with you, playing music. Nicol and Pippa are coming with me for a walk.'

Jessie said, 'Oh good!'

Nicol didn't say anything. Upstairs I asked him what he thought about going for a walk. He said, 'We only ever go for a walk with Auntie like that if something has happened and she needs to tell us about it.'

'Do you mind?'

'Not really. You're coming, aren't you?'

I think this was his way of saying, 'I'm very pleased that you are coming with me.'

The Lang Stane

Mr Griffin drove Auntie, Nicol, and me up to The Lang Stane. I sat with Nicol in the back of the car. He was very quiet, so I looked out of the window, and saw a lot of interesting stone walls and sheep. I could feel Nicol's leg resting against mine, and I felt warm inside, because even though we were touching, he didn't move away. We came to a wood full of pine trees, and then Mr Griffin stopped the car at the bottom of a hill. He said, 'Here we are. I'm going for a little walk. Just whistle if you want me for anything, or when it's time to go home.'

We walked along the side of the wood, and up a little path that had been worn by lots of feet. Every so often, there was a lump of sheep's poo and rabbit droppings. I told Nicol that I couldn't understand why the animals had to do their business exactly where we wanted to walk, when they had so much space around them. He laughed, but didn't say anything. We reached what I thought would be the top of the hill. I had imagined that the stone would be huge; perhaps the size of a lighthouse, and right on top of the hill. But we weren't at the top at all. We had reached a small ridge, where the ground sloped down in front of us, and we could see a long way ahead. The sky was huge, with massive grey clouds gathering. I could hear crows cawing, but couldn't see them. Nicol said, 'Look Pippa, there's Lang Stane!' He pointed ahead, along the path. There was no massive stone, but a grey thing sticking up. It looked a bit disappointing.

Nicol ran ahead of us, down the path, and Auntie and I stopped and watched him. She said, 'I love that boy. He's so full of ideas and energy and… oh, I love him for so many reasons!' I held her hand. She said, 'You go on. I'll catch you up in a minute.' I knew that one of the reasons Auntie loved Nicol was because he was like my daddy. And I had a feeling that he reminded her of Wee Callum too. I saw Nicol waving and heard him shout, 'Come on Pippa! Come on!' Nicol stopped shouting and suddenly I couldn't see him anymore. I was gripped by a strange fear that perhaps goblins had grabbed him, knocked him out, and dragged him down a deep dark hole, where they would force him to eat fruit. I started panicking, and ran as fast as I could towards the stone. I slipped and fell and banged my knee, but I jumped up again and kept running forwards.

I reached the stone and Nicol jumped out and shouted, 'Boo!' and we both laughed. I was so glad to see him. He pulled my hand and said, 'Come round this side and we can surprise Aileen as well. But what happened to your knee?' I hadn't noticed, but I had scraped it quite badly, and there was dark blood coming out of it, and running down onto my white sock. He took a hanky out of his pocket, and knelt down and dabbed my knee. He was pressing quite hard and it hurt, but I didn't say anything, because I didn't want him to stop. He looked up at me and said, 'I've cut my finger too.' He stood up in front of me and showed me his right hand. He told me that he had been running his fingers along the stone with his eyes closed, and had touched a jagged piece that was sticking out, and it had sliced quite a deep cut into his pointing finger. I was just about to take the hanky to wrap around his finger, but changed my mind. I took his hand, put his finger in my mouth, and sucked. He didn't pull it away. I didn't look at him, but could taste his salty blood in my mouth. I swallowed his blood down, and then took his finger out. We didn't say anything. My heart was beating very fast, and I felt thrilled. I looked in Nicol's eyes, and I knew he was feeling thrilled too. He whispered, 'I can hear Aileen coming.' He wrapped the hanky round his finger. He stepped out from behind the stone and I heard him say, 'We've both cut ourselves, but we're all right.'

I tried to stop my heart from beating fast, because I didn't want Auntie to notice anything. She said, 'Hello you two! Let's see what you've been up to!'

Nicol didn't look at me, but I could feel his excitement. I hoped that Auntie couldn't.

Lang Stane didn't look very special. It was rough and grey, and about twice as high as Nicol. I think four people could have held hands and stood in a circle round it. It looked like a crane had lifted it high up in the air and dropped it on the ground, so that it got stuck there. Someone had plaited a big garland out of willow branches and wild flowers and put it right over the top of the stone, so it was stuck about a third of the way down. There was a smaller, similar garland on top. Both of them were old and the flowers had dried out, so it looked like the stone was wearing a necklace, with a dried out daisy chain on its head.

Auntie touched the stone and said, 'Women still come here if they are having trouble conceiving a baby. For centuries, people have believed that walking round the stone and putting a garland round it will make them fertile.' I put my hand on the stone. It was cold, and covered with patches of dry light green moss. From a distance, it had looked smooth, but really it was very rough, as if it had been hacked with thousands of axes as cavemen dug it out of the ground. Nicol showed us where he had cut his finger. Touching Lang Stane made me shiver and feel horrible inside. I whispered to Nicol that I didn't like it. He said, 'I don't either. It gives me the willies.' He looked me in the eyes. He was smiling one of those smiles that children have during class, when they are trying to make you giggle. *Willy* just seemed like such a funny word, and I couldn't help smiling back.

I looked at Auntie. She just stood there, stroking the stone and looking into the distance. I whispered in Nicol's ear, 'You are a very naught boy, Nicol Pirie.'

He whispered in my ear, 'I don't care.' The vibration of his lips on my ear and his warm breath made me quiver.

Then I thought about Nicol and his dad standing here, talking about how a man puts his willy inside a woman's Lovely Place, and how his seeds go inside her, and somehow this makes a baby. I supposed that Nicol was thinking exactly the same thing. I looked at him. He said, 'Maggie and Rhona don't like this stone very much. They came here with Rhona's lady friends from Edinburgh, and made a secret place in the woods. Can we go there, Aileen?'

Auntie looked like she was just waking up from a dream. She said, 'I'm sorry darling, I was deep in thought. What did you say?' Nicol said he was sorry for interrupting, but Auntie said that she didn't mind, because she didn't want to have those thoughts anymore. We both knew that she was thinking about Wee Callum.

We walked down the path, with Nicol in front and Auntie behind me. I was still quivering. We reached the wood, and Nicol told us to follow him. The trees were all tall pines, growing in neat rows. We followed a little path and had to climb over a few fallen trees, and then in a clearing we saw Rhona and Maggie's special place. It was a circle of small tree trunks and big stones. In the middle was a black patch of earth where someone had once made a fire. We sat down on one of the logs. Auntie had brought a string bag with her, and took out a banana and told Nicol and I to share it. I hadn't realised how hungry I was. Then Auntie took out a Thermos flask and three cups and we had a cup of tea each. Then, to our delight, she produced a Tupperware box with three chocolate bars in. There was a bar of Cadbury's Fruit and Nut, a Walnut Whip and a Bounty. I knew that Nicol loved Walnut Whips. I had never tried one myself, but loved the advert on the TV. This was a real treat, because you could buy two Bounty Bars for the price on one Walnut Whip, so it was a chocolate you would only have on very special occasions, and even then you would probably have to share it.

We often talked about chocolate in this family, and we all knew that Auntie loved Fruit and Nut.

Auntie said, 'Shall we share our chocolate?'

Nicol and I said, both at the same time, 'No!'

Auntie said, 'Good, because I really need all of this chocolate for myself.'

We sat in silence, eating our chocolate and breathing in the smell of the trees and the dead pine needles under our feet. The wood was very quiet, and it seemed as if all the birds had flown away. The tall trees made a ceiling above our heads, and it was quite dark and cold. I was on one side of Auntie and Nicol was on the other, so we couldn't see each other's faces, unless we turned our heads. I could feel my knee throbbing where I had bashed it. I knew that I would have quite a bruise there.

Then Auntie started talking. 'It really is much nicer here. To tell the truth, I'm not too keen on that stone. I'm going to tell you a story. It's a long story. Not long in the telling; but it stretches back a long way. It's about the history of Nicol's mother's family. For as long as people can remember, there's always been someone on her side of the family who has had an illness called depression. It's not an illness like having tonsillitis or measles, or chicken pox, so you don't have a nasty rash or feel sick. You just feel terribly sad. But you don't feel sad all the time. Sometimes you feel very happy, but then suddenly you can wake up with an awful feeling that life is not worth living. Doctors call it depression, because it's as if you have fallen into a huge hole in the ground. It can last for a few days, or weeks, or even months.

'You can go to the doctor and get tablets, but they don't always work. And around here, if people have depression, they often don't bother going to the doctor, but just drink lots of whisky to try to make themselves feel better. They think it will ease the terrible sadness. It might do that for a while, but once the effect of the whisky wears off, they go back to feeling terrible again.'

I said, 'Like Mummy did.'

'Yes, like your mummy did.'

I was thinking about Nicol's mum, who had drowned, and Kirsty and Kenny's mum, who was in hospital. Auntie must have guessed what I was thinking, because she said, 'But there's a difference between your mummy and Kirsty's mum and Nicol's mum. As far as I can see, your mummy started drinking because she hated the life that she was living; all on her own in a cold country, with nobody to help her look after you. Well, the strain of that made her drink, to help her ease her sadness. But with the other ladies, there seemed to be no cause for it. It just came from nowhere. Nothing had happened to them to make them feel so sad.'

Nicol was very quiet, and looked straight ahead.

Auntie said, 'I know how it feels. I felt like that when Wee Callum died. On some days, I just couldn't raise my head from the pillow. But your father helped me enormously. But I wasn't ill. I was grieving. I still have days when I'm gripped by a terrible sadness, but I know I'm not ill. But your mother, Nicol, was ill.'

Nicol said, 'Wwwwas, wwwas...' He was about to hit his leg, but I held his hand. He didn't pull it away. 'Wwwwas Mum so ill that she killed herself? Did she drown herself in the sea?' I really didn't like to hear Nicol stuttering, because I knew that he was unhappy.

Auntie took a deep breath. 'We don't know exactly what happened. All we know is that her body was found in the morning, on the beach. It's a terrible story, and I know you don't like to talk about it, but we must. We must be like Pippa, who went with her mummy and her auntie to talk about all the bad things that had happened, and the secrets in the family, so that they could understand each other better. What do you think about that, Nicol?'

He didn't say anything, so Auntie said, 'Poor wee Jessie never really had a loving relationship with your mother. She rejected Jessie when she was a baby. I'm sure that has a lot to do with why she behaves the way she does. It's not her fault.

'You see, after Jessie was born, your mum's face went very blank. She wasn't full of the great joy that most mothers feel when they have a baby. She was suffering from something

347

called Post Natal Depression. Perhaps if she had got some help, then she might have got better. But the depression took hold of her, and she could never quite shake it off. Sometimes she seemed to be more cheerful, but then there were days when everything was too much for her, and then the smallest little thing that went wrong would make her very angry. She used to go missing, and once your father found her up here.'

I looked up at the trees above us. There was a small patch of grey sky, and it was getting darker in the wood. Nicol said, 'If it's in the family, does that mean that I will get it? And has Jessie already got it?'

Auntie sighed. 'That's a very good question, which nobody can really answer. I think one of the problems is that up here, in this part of Scotland, people don't talk about being depressed. You are just supposed to get on with your life. That's why so many people turn to drink. If only they could talk about their problems.'

'But why does Auntie Màiri have to go to hospital?'

'I think it's because her problems are so severe that just talking doesn't seem to do any good. It's as if she has a storm in her head and can't make it go away. So the doctors give her medicine and other treatments to calm her down.'

'Is that what happened to Mum? Did she have a storm in her head?'

There was a long pause, so I knew that the answer was *yes*. Auntie said, 'It might have been. Yes, it might have been.'

'So did she throw herself in the sea to make the storm go away?'

Auntie put her hand on Nicol's knee and squeezed it. 'Nobody knows, Nicol. Nobody knows what she was doing by the sea that night. She might just have gone for a midnight swim, to try to help her go to sleep. That's quite possible.'

'Maggie once told me that they found her with all her clothes on, and that her body was full of whisky.'

'When did she tell you that?'

'Oh, a long time ago. When she was angry with Dad. I never wanted to believe it.'

348

'No, that wasn't true. She wasn't wearing clothes. She wasn't wearing a bathing suit either. But they think she went into the sea with her glasses on, because they were found washed up a few days later. Your dad told me that she always used to swim with her glasses on, and kept her head above the water. She was as blind as a bat without them. So I like to believe that she just went for a nice swim. That's what I tell myself.'

I said, 'My Mummy was full of whisky once, and was by the river. A policeman found her. It was on the day of my First Holy Communion. And she was so drunk once in the street that she got arrested. And another time she came to school drunk, and another time she left me all alone at night. But she's better now, thanks to the doctors and Auntie Muriel.'

Suddenly I was proud of Mummy. I wasn't ashamed that she had got drunk. She had just been unhappy and ill. I hoped that saying those things would make Nicol feel better. But he was crying, and Auntie was crying too.

Nicol rubbed his eyes. His finger was still bleeding, and it made a smear of blood across his cheek. He sniffed, 'I'm sorry about crying. I know boys aren't supposed to do it, but sometimes I feel so sad, that I just can't help it.' I thought that was a ridiculous thing to say. Anyone can cry if they want to. It's not my fault that I hate doing it, and don't like to see other people cry, except Mummy and Muriel when they cried with happiness.

So I said something that I thought was serious, but as soon as I started talking, I knew I was not being sensible at all. 'My friend Roger is a real boy, and he cries quite a lot. He's madly in love with my friend Lucy, but she doesn't notice. She's too pure and simple to think about things like that. One day, Roger asked some boys at school how he could make Lucy love him. Unfortunately, he asked the naughtiest boy in the school. He told Roger that he must show Lucy his willy. Unfortunately, Roger believed him, and decided to do it. But Roger told the boy that he didn't want Lucy to think he was being rude, so the boy said, "What you have to do is go and play with Lucy in the woods, and then pretend you are bursting for a wee. Go behind a tree, but do it in such a way that Lucy can see your willy. Then she's bound to fall in love with you."

'Silly Roger did just that. But he didn't wait until they were in the woods. They were playing in Lucy's garden, and Roger said he was bursting, and started to wee up Lucy's fence. Lucy was very angry and said that if Roger ever did that again she would stop being his friend. Roger was so upset that he started crying. Lucy straight away put her arms around Roger to comfort him. So after that Roger fell over a lot and cried, and Lucy always hugged him, and once kissed his arm better. Roger told me all that, but made me swear never to tell anyone. But I don't suppose you'll ever meet him, but if you do then please don't mention that I told you about his willy.'

Nicol had stopped crying and Auntie was laughing. She said that was the funniest thing she had heard in a long time. Nicol asked me what Lucy was like. I explained about her word blindness, and how she was a Christian, and not a pickle like me. Auntie asked me if Lucy had every talked about what Roger had done. Lucy had told me that she didn't really mind about Roger weeing on her fence, but she thought she had better get cross with him, in case he did it again and her mum saw him. Then he would really be in trouble, and perhaps Lucy's mum and dad would stop her from playing with Roger. I told Auntie that Lucy never usually talked about things like that, because she was a Christian. But Roger knew I was Jewish, so told me all sorts of rude things. I think he thought that Jewish girls wouldn't mind hearing about some of the things he got up to in boarding school, like having farting competitions, and the boys showing each other their willies.

It was nice to hear them laughing, after we had talked about such serious things. I wondered if eating Bounties made me say rude things, because I found myself telling them how pretty Lucy was, and how all of the boys liked her. I said I loved being her friend, because she was so simple and not a pickle like me. I told them how she had changed the way she did her hair, and how I was thinking how lovely she looked, and that's how I fell over and smashed my arm and face. And how Roger caught his trousers on the railing, and how his mother had whipped off her blouse to stop me from bleeding.

Auntie and Nicol were laughing again. Auntie said, 'Pippa, surely you are making all that up?'
I said, 'I wish I was, because it really hurt.' I showed them the scar on my arm. I told them that when I was a Catholic, I used to think that God was punishing me for thinking about rude things. But now I was Jewish, I didn't care. I said I knew I had fallen over because I wasn't looking where I was going. It was my own fault, because I had been busy admiring Lucy's hair. It wasn't because I was thinking something forbidden. What's wrong with loving the way your best friend has her hair? And what's wrong with feeling love all over for her, because she is such a lovely person?

I told them that I didn't believe in God anymore; only Jesus. Jesus was very busy, so he had lots of angels working for him. All Catholics had a Guardian Angel, and I was lucky, because even though I had become Jewish, mine didn't desert me. If something was very seriously wrong in my life, then my Guardian Angel would talk to Jesus about it, and he would think about what to do. Then he would tell her a story, like in The Bible, and she would have to decide for herself what to tell me. Jesus was always telling stories. They were a bit like fairy tales, pointing you in the right direction when you had a problem, or telling you how to behave, like The Boy Who Cried Wolf. I said I liked The Elves and the Shoemaker, but wasn't sure what the story was trying to tell me.

They stopped laughing and we were quiet. It started to get windy and the trees were moaning. We walked to the edge of the wood. The sky was full of grey-black clouds that were racing along, and it felt like it was going to rain. Auntie gave a long, loud whistle, and Mr Griffin came walking towards us, through the trees.

Cat's Cradle

In the afternoon, Nicol and I went up to Rhona's garden to play with William the cat. Nicol had some string in his pocket and asked me if I wanted to play Cat's Cradle. I had taught Roger, how to do it, but wished I hadn't, because our faces got close together and his breath had smelled awful.

Now I was hoping that Nicol's face and mine would be close together, and I didn't care if he had bad breath. He didn't. We had both had chocolate cake and custard for pudding and he smelled of that. It was my favourite dessert.

Nicol and I did exactly the same sequence of moves in the Cat's Cradle that I had learned in the school playground in Rayners Park. That time seemed like so many years ago. Then he said, 'I'll show you a new one. Rhona showed Maggie, and Maggie showed me. I showed Kirsty and she said it's called *Two Ladies Fighting*. I told Maggie about that, and she told Rhona, and Rhona told Maggie it should be called *Two Women Dancing*. Maggie told me, and I wrote a story about two girls who were always fighting, until they went to a dance and learned to dance with each other. Maggie showed Rhona, and now Rhona has written a song called *Cat's Cradle*. It's about two women who argue a lot, but then dance together, and realise that they are really the best of friends.'

I was thinking of the game called Chinese Whispers, where people sit in a circle and one person whispers something in your ear, then you pass on exactly what you think you have heard. I asked Nicol, 'Does Rhona take all your ideas and turn them into songs?'

'I hope not, because sometimes I tell her things that I don't want anyone else to know about. Secret things.' I was only nine, but already I knew that if someone said something like that to you, then they were desperate to tell you about their secret.

I wasn't sure that I wanted to know Nicol's secret, so I said, 'I was jealous of Rhona. But I don't feel like that now.'

He didn't take any notice of that. He was getting ready to tell me something very important. He asked me, 'Do you like boys?'

'Well I do, sort of. I like playing with them. But most of them are not so interesting to talk to and look at as girls. I love painting girls and ladies.'

I told him about how I had had a bath with Peter and it had been very nice, and I had liked sleeping in bed with him. But seeing Frances with nothing on had made me feel very excited indeed, and I couldn't get the sight of her naked body out of my mind until I had painted her.

Nicol looked really shocked. I said, 'I'm not being rude; honestly I'm not. It's just that I like to draw and paint people, so I have to look at them very closely.'

Nicol didn't look like he was satisfied with that answer, so I tried to explain a bit more. 'You see, I often wonder what I will be like when I'm older. So it's nice to be able to talk to older girls, who can tell you what it's like. And if you look at them, then you can imagine what you will be like. Don't you do that too?'

Nicol was quiet, and I wondered if I had said too much. But then he said, 'If I looked closely at a boy when he had nothing on, then he would call me something nasty, and probably punch me as well! If I am changing, and a nasty older boy sees me, he will probably say something horrible about me. But I like to look at older boys and men in the changing rooms. Some of them hide themselves when they are drying, but some don't. I like to see what they look like, and especially if they are the same age as me. Do you think that's wrong?'

He was very embarrassed about telling me a big secret about himself, but it didn't seem like a secret at all.

I said, 'Well I don't think girls mind so much. We had a swimming pool at my last school and most of the girls weren't shy at all. Lucy didn't mind if other girls saw her, so it must be all right to do it. But Frances and Bernadette did once tell me that they got washed in front of other girls, and one of them called Bernadette a lesbian.'

'What's a lesbian?'

I didn't want to say it, but Nicol said, 'You must tell me, you must!' He knew it was a secret word.

I mumbled, 'It's a lady who loves another lady.' He went very red and we didn't say anything else for a while.

I thought I'd better change the subject, so I said, 'Boys don't know about that sort of thing.'

Nicol frowned, 'What sort of thing?'

'Well, what happens to girls when they are about thirteen or fourteen.'

I was starting to feel embarrassed, and didn't want to say any more. He said, 'What sort of thing do you mean?'

'I don't want to say it.'

'Yes you do. Otherwise you wouldn't have mentioned it in the first place.'

I didn't want to say the word *periods*, so said, 'You know, when they start bleeding. I thought your dad told you about that.'

Nicol looked confused. 'No, he never mentioned girls cutting themselves. What has that got to do with them growing up?'

He didn't know, and I didn't want to tell him. I said, 'You could ask Maggie, I'm sure that she could tell you.'

I thought he was going to get cross, so I told him what I knew about periods. He listened very carefully and said, 'Now I understand.' But he didn't say anything else. I think we were too embarrassed to talk about bodies anymore.

He said, 'I will miss you when you go to school.'

I wanted to cry, but stopped myself. I kissed him instead, on the cheek.

A demon inside you

We sat quietly together, but I was very worried that our talk about periods might get me into trouble. I had forgotten to say to Nicol that I didn't want him to tell anyone that I had told him. It seemed to me that it was OK for older children to know about The Birds and the Bees, and where a man puts his willy, but you mustn't tell people that you know about periods. And you especially mustn't talk about that with boys. I didn't want to talk about periods with Nicol anymore.

He said, 'Pippa, can I tell you something? It's something only Maggie knows.'

I said, 'Oh dear.' I don't think I made a face when I said it, but perhaps I did.

Nicol frowned. 'What? You don't want to hear it?'

'Oh no, not that. It's just that Muriel said that it's not good to have secrets.'

'What then?'

'Well, she used to say, "If you tell it to me, then I might have to tell someone else. Otherwise it could become a huge worry for me." I love Muriel and would never, ever, do something that she thought was a bad idea.'

He looked at the ground and said, 'I don't want to tell anyone else.'

I didn't know what to say. I hated the feeling that I might be disappointing him. I thought that if I said no to something he wanted me to do, then he might not like me anymore. I didn't know what to do. Then I thought to myself, 'What would Muriel do if she were me?'

I remembered that once I had been in the car with Muriel and Mummy, and we were lost. Muriel was driving and Mummy was supposed to have been looking at the map, but she had been dreaming, so we missed our turning. I think we were late to get somewhere, because Mummy started to get annoyed and blamed Muriel for us being lost. I was sitting in the back, and became frightened that they were going to have an argument, like the time when Mummy had yelled at Muriel during their one and only driving lesson together. Muriel said to Mummy, 'Ruth, I really don't like it when you talk to me like that. It makes me feel very uncomfortable. Please talk to me nicely.'

Mummy stopped straight away. She put her hand on Muriel's knee and said, 'I'm sorry Muriel. Thank you for stopping me.'

I don't know if Mummy had forgotten that I was in the back, or perhaps she wanted me to hear. She said, 'It's like I have so many demons inside me. It's easier to rage at other people, and turn them into demons, than it is to confront the demons inside one.'

Muriel said, 'Do you really mind that we are lost?'

Mummy said, 'Not at all. I think my monthly will arrive soon.'

Muriel said, 'I thought as much.'

They both thought that was very funny. I have always had a suspicion that Muriel talked to Mummy like that in front of me, on purpose. She did it to teach me something. And I loved it, because it stopped me from being frightened of Mummy.

Nicol asked me, 'What are you thinking about, Pippa?' I have always loved that question. It's what lovers ask each other. And I knew Nicol really wanted to know. 'Nicol, do you like me?'

'Yes. I like you a lot. You know I do.'

'Would you still like me as much if you asked me to do something, and I said I didn't want to do it?'

'Of course.'

'Are you sure?'

'Yes I'm sure.'

'Well really and truly I don't want to hear your secret. But if you tell it to me, will you promise me that if I can't bear it, you will tell Auntie, or Maggie, or both of them? Otherwise I might get very worried and have nightmares, or not be able to sleep.'

Nicol said, 'Perhaps I should just tell Maggie. Or perhaps Auntie. I don't want to give you nightmares.'

Was I a strange girl, or would anybody else have felt the same as I did then? Suddenly I couldn't bear the thought that Nicol had chosen me to hear his secret, and I had refused him. Or was he playing a trick on me, just like Jessie? No, I don't think he was capable of doing that. He said, 'Yes, I promise.'

And this was his secret. 'I was about six years old and I fell over in the garden and cut my knee. I went in to tell Mum, but she saw that there was a hole in my trousers, and became furious. She found a long and thin piece of wood, and was going to hit me with it, so I ran out into the garden. But she chased after me and grabbed me by my collar, and kept hitting me with the stick. She hit me very hard, so I screamed, and a man living next door heard me and yelled for Mum to stop. But she swore at him and kept hitting me. So the man climbed over the wall and grabbed the stick off her. I don't remember what happened next. But the man went to the police, and a policeman came to the house and talked to Dad. That was when we lived in our old house. Then we moved to where we live now. Soon after we moved, I was playing about in the shed, and saw the piece of wood that Mummy had hit me with. I never talked to her about it, but I knew that she had decided to keep it, in case she ever needed to hit me again. I was terrified of that piece of wood.

'Then Mum did something terrible to Jessie. Jessie used to cry in the night when she was a baby. One night, Mum shook her and shook her, and Jessie was only a small baby, and she stopped crying straight away, and never cried again in the night. I think she was too frightened of Mum to make a sound after that. I asked Dad about it once, after Mum had died. He cried and said that Mum had had lots of inner demons. I didn't know what he meant, and imagined a dragon living inside her, that had kept tormenting her. I think Maggie knows all about it, because I heard her telling Aileen that just before she was bleeding she used to feel tormented by her demon. It frightened me. Now I think I understand a bit better.'

I said, 'Well I know what I would do if it was me. I would talk to Maggie about it.'

'But you don't understand. I can't talk to Maggie about her... her... you know?'

'What? About her demon?'

'No. About her...'

I thought that this was one of the main differences between girls and boys. Girls could talk about their Lovely Places and their periods, but boys couldn't. I didn't think that boys should go around asking girls about those things. And I didn't mean that they should be like Roger and go around boasting about their willies, and how horribly their last poo smelled, or how high they could wee up walls. Roger loved talking about those things to me. But I thought it would be nice if boys could talk sensibly about private things. If they were like that, then I wouldn't mind telling them about things that were very private. So I said, 'Why can't you talk to Maggie about that?'

'Because she's my big sister.'

'Well what about asking Auntie?'

'She's a lady. It's too embarrassing.'

'Then what about your dad?'

'Oh no! That would be even worse!'

Then I had an idea. 'You could talk to Rhona.'

'Yes, I thought about that, but she seems to want to turn everything I write or say into a song, and then make a record out of it. I don't want her singing a song about me wanting to know about what happens to girls down there.' He pointed between his legs. I knew that Nicol was being funny on purpose.

Then the terribleness of what Nicol had just told me about his mother hit me. It was as if a great wind struck me, then blew straight through me and out the other side. I could feel myself trembling all over. I said, 'Nicol, you must talk to Maggie! She's just like Muriel! She understands everything!'

I must have been shouting, because Nicol looked very frightened. I was still only nine. I was too young to know terrible things like that. And I could see Nicol's mum, full of rage, then feeling full of guilt and shame about hitting her children, and throwing herself into the sea.

Nicol said, 'Shh, shh, I'm sorry, Pippa, I'm sorry. I promise I'll tell her! I'll go right now. Please come with me. Please stop shaking! You're making me feel frightened!'

His voice was very far away. I was with Mummy, by the river on the day of my First Holy Communion. It was pouring with rain, and she was shrieking and laughing, and singing a French song, and taking enormous gulps of whisky from a Johnny Walker bottle. Then a policeman came and took us home, but

Mummy was trying to stab me with a kitchen knife and I couldn't run away because I had huge lead boots on, like a deep-sea diver. Then I heard Maggie's voice saying, 'What's the matter? What's wrong with Pippa?'

She bent down and whispered in my ear. 'It's all right Pippa! It's all right. It's Maggie here! Open your eyes! Open your eyes!'

But I couldn't open them. It felt like they were glued shut.

Then Auntie must have come into the garden, because I heard her say, 'Make her lie down, here, on the grass. Put her on her side. I think she's having a fit. Call 999 and ask for an ambulance.'

I stood up and said, 'No. Please don't do that. I'm all right now. I'm not having a fit. I've had one before, and it's not that. I saw a boy having a real fit, and he was shaking all over and frothing at the mouth and Miss Dawson put a ruler between his teeth and he bit it in half. Please can I have a glass of water?'

There was something wrong with me. I didn't know what it was, but I didn't want to go to hospital again. I said, 'I've had too much pudding.'

Maggie laughed and said, 'Come on, Pippa. Come into the cottage, and you can lie on Rhona's bed. And Nicol, you can come as well.'

They led me indoors, as if I was a blind person. They helped me upstairs and put me in Rhona's bed. I lay there on my side, with my thumb firmly stuck in my mouth. Maggie and Nicol sat beside me. I still couldn't open my eyes, so stopped trying.

I wasn't having a fit, but there was something wrong with me. Usually when someone has a fit, you put them in a quiet place, and when it's over you let them sleep. And afterwards, when they wake up, you're supposed to talk to them about what happened, so that they understand. I wasn't asleep, but I must have looked like I was, because Maggie kissed me and said to Nicol, 'Isn't she beautiful?'

He whispered, 'Yes. Is she all right?'

'Oh I think so. She's just had a bit of a shock. Aileen told me all about Pippa reacting like that. She says that Pippa is highly sensitive.'

I could hear everything that they said. Nicol said, 'I think it's my fault. I told her about Mum hitting me, and the policeman coming round. She says that I must talk to you about it, because you are like her Auntie Muriel, so you will understand.'

Maggie said, 'You can tell me then. I won't mind.'

So Nicol told her all about what we had said about demons and periods, and asked if that had something to do with their mum drowning in the sea. Maggie said, 'I think Mum was ill in her mind, and she was one of those people who couldn't cope when things went wrong. She needed to have a quiet life, but having three children was too much for her.'

'So was it our fault then? Was it because she had us that she went mad?'

'Oh no! I have never thought that! I think she wasn't very strong in her mind, and needed lots of help and time on her own. That's why she went swimming all the time. But one night she swam far out, but something went wrong, and she drowned. I've never thought it was our fault, so please put that idea out of your mind.'

Nicol sighed. 'I'll try.'

Maggie said, 'You are a very lucky boy. Come here.' I felt her put him on her knee and heard her give him a kiss. She said, 'You are such a lovely, sensitive little brother. I think that what upset Pippa was hearing about Mum and her violent moods. You see, her mum was exactly the same. And Auntie Màiri is the same as Mum was. That's what's upset Pippa.'

I heard Nicol sniffing. He was trying to stop himself from crying. Maggie said, 'Shh. Shh. It's all right. It's good that you told her about it. I suppose Auntie must have known that talking about these things up at Lang Stane would bring all of the nasty thoughts out into the open. I used to hate Dad, until he told me the truth. It took me a long time to understand what

360

happened to Mum, but I do now, and I don't feel half as bad. And I have Rhona to talk to.'

'What is the truth? What did Dad tell you?'

'Well the truth is that after you were born, Dad didn't want Mum to have any more babies. She was very depressed and couldn't look after you properly. She got better after a while, but then used to get depressed every month. It was always when she had her period. She would scream and yell and throw things, and get into a terrible rage. Then afterwards she would act as if nothing had happened.

'She pestered and pestered Dad to make another baby with her, and she would be very nasty if he said that he didn't want to. So then they did have a baby, and Dad had been right. It was the worst thing that could have happened. She couldn't look after Jessie. She became obsessed with the sea. She would go out and swim all the time.'

'Do you think that Mum killed herself?'

'No, I don't.'

'But she took all her clothes off and left them in a pile on the beach. If she wanted just to have a swim, then she would have put on a swimming costume.'

'Oh no, Mum didn't like them. She used to go out at midnight and swim with nothing on.'

'How do you know?'

'I used to follow her and watch her do it.'

'And did you see her on the night that she drowned?'

'No. I didn't do that. I used to wish that I had, but now I don't think I could have saved her. It's very dangerous out there, and she used to go very far out.'

I heard Maggie kiss Nicol and whisper, 'You're a very good boy, and a lovely little brother. I'm so lucky to have you. Now let's leave Pippa to sleep, and when she wakes up, you can tell her all about what happened.' I thought they had finished talking, but Maggie said, 'I'll tell you something else that I've just noticed. All the time that we've been talking, you haven't stuttered once. Why do you think that is?'

361

'I don't know.'

'Well I think I know. It's because you have been talking with Dad and Auntie and me, about all these difficult things. And being with Pippa has made you feel more relaxed. You're not so tensed up and unhappy. It's wonderful.'

He said, 'I know. I want to talk to Pippa all the time. Do you think she does it on purpose? Do you think she spends time with me because she feels sorry for me?'

There was a pause, then Maggie said; 'That is the silliest question I have ever heard in my whole life! She's just a very nice wee girl, and you feel comfortable with her. She likes being with you because you are such a nice person. Have you noticed how carefully she listens to everybody? She never interrupts, and you always think that she's trying her best to understand what you're saying to her. She's lovely with Jessie. She's still only very young, but seems so grown up, somehow. Perhaps it's because of all the things she has suffered, and all the help she has had, that have made her into such a lovely person. Or perhaps she was just like that anyway. I love her.'

Nicol sighed. Maggie said, 'And maybe being with Pippa makes you feel happier inside yourself, and this makes the words come out easier.'

Then Maggie kissed me and whispered, 'Sleep well little girl' and they both left the room. I heard them next door, playing the piano and singing.

A lovely month

And after that, everybody seemed to settle down. I thought that we would have weeks and weeks to play together, but Nicol explained that Scottish children went back to school on the 15th of August. That was a bit of a shock, because my boarding school didn't start back until September the 4th. That meant I would have nearly three weeks on my own during the day in Stranhaven, while Nicol and Jessie would be in school. So our days together became very precious, and we spent a lot of time playing up at the recreation ground with Kirsty and Kenny. There was a children's playground in the recreation ground, and like most playgrounds I had been to in England, it had swings, a slide, a seesaw, a roundabout, a rocking horse and a Witch's Hat. I wasn't at all surprised to discover that nearly everything was rusty, and our hands and clothes ware always covered in orange stains. The Witch's Hat was our favourite piece of playground equipment, and as soon as we arrived every day, we would jump, swing, and climb all over it, and do the most dangerous things. Jessie surprised me, and wasn't keen to do anything where there was the slightest risk that she might get hurt. I thought at first that she was being her usual self, and making a fuss to get as much attention as possible, but one morning she fell over and scraped her knee, and cried so much that Nicol had to take her home. Then for the rest of the day she stayed in the garden and refused to go back up to the playground. I asked Kirsty if Jessie was just trying to make us feel sorry for her, or perhaps it was her way of ruining our fun. She said that Jessie had always been afraid of hurting herself, and hated the sight of blood. I really didn't understand her at all.

Kirsty always brought her football, and she was very keen to teach me how to kick a ball properly. Unfortunately, Jessie would always spoil the game by pretending to be hurt, or moaning that nobody passed the ball to her, but when they did, she would pick the ball up, or deliberately pass the ball to the wrong person. Then Nicol would get cross with her, and the game would be ruined. Of course, that was always Jessie's intention. So to make everyone feel better, I decided to take my sketchpad up to the playground and sit with Jessie on the Witch's Hat, and show her how to sketch people moving. She used to complain that she was no good at drawing, and couldn't understand how I was able to draw without ever thinking about it. She said, 'Your pencil is like a part of your hand', which was true. So I told her that I wasn't very good at playing music, and that any instrument was like part of her hands. She liked that, so we decided to bring our concertinas with us, and we passed many happy hours together, chatting, drawing, playing music and singing together.

Like all children, we loved to play board games together, but Jessie usually made things complicated. She was very competitive, and Nicol told me that he didn't like to play with her, because they always ended up fighting. I soon discovered why, because Jessie was a terrible cheat, and if she saw that she was going to lose, she would knock pieces over on purpose, or accuse other people of cheating. Our favourite games were Monopoly and a funny game called Millionaire. I was good at Monopoly, but nobody else would play with Jessie, so we ended up always playing together, and I did my best to make sure that she won. I gave her lots of advice about what properties to buy, and that reminded me of Mummy, and how she used to give advice to men who were good at their jobs, but didn't understand about money, or weren't very good at doing their accounts.

Millionaire was a funny dice game, where the first person to win a million pounds was the winner. You could earn a lot of money, but it was very easy to suddenly lose it all. One day I was playing with Jessie and Uncle Tom, and he lost all his money. Jessie said to me, 'Pippa, your dad's very rich. But do you think that one day he might lose all his money, and then you will be poor?' That thought had never occurred to me, and for a few days afterwards I imagined Daddy having to live in a little house in England, and maybe working in a factory, or a shop. Then he wouldn't be able to pay for me to go to boarding school, so I would have to go to a normal school in Stranhaven, or even back in Ashbourne. I asked Uncle Tom about that and he smiled and said, 'I don't think that will ever happen. Your father owns so much land, and so many properties, and works of art, that if he needed to, he could sell them to pay his debts, and still have lots of money left over.' That thought pleased me and bothered me at the same time, and I couldn't understand why. In the back of my mind, I was sure that Daddy's money was the cause of so many of our problems. And, just like with Peter, I could only play board games with Nicol that involved dice, like Snakes and Ladders or Ludo, because I couldn't bear the thought of competing against him. I explained this to Nicol and he said, 'I'm the same, but I wasn't sure why I'm like that. Now I know.'

A Selkie

The one thing we didn't do was walk on the beach. Auntie did this every day with Luna, but I knew she liked to go on her own, so I never asked her if I could join her. Stranhaven had a harbour too, but we never went there either, which was a shame, because I knew there were lots of fishing boats that sailed in and out and stayed there, and I was very keen to paint them. Once I asked Nicol if we could go down to the beach together, and look at the harbour. He frowned and said, 'It's not somewhere I like to go.'

Without thinking, I said, 'But I do. I love the seaside, and I'd love to see the boats in the harbour.'

Nicol looked very uncomfortable, and I couldn't understand why. He was just about to say something, but then I understood. I said, 'It's OK. Silly me.'

I didn't want to say anything else about it, but Nicol said, 'It's because of Mum. I've been there once or twice, but I had to come back straight away, but if you really want to go with me to the beach, then we should go. I'll just have to stop being silly about it.'

I put my hand on his arm. 'I don't think you're silly. Please don't say that. Anyway, there are lots of other things to do. I can always go there with Auntie; perhaps after you have gone back to school.'

A few hours later, we were sitting in Nicol's garden, and Jessie wasn't around. Nicol said that he'd like to tell me about his mum. I had two feelings. I felt special, because he had chosen me to talk to about his mother, but I didn't want to hear any horrible details about her dead body, and how upset everyone had been. But he didn't do that, but instead told me a strange story. He said that people in his part of Scotland used to believe in a strange creature called a Selkie. A Selkie was a woman who for some reason had turned into a seal. She was like a mermaid, except that her body was completely inside the seal's skin. Every so often, (Nicol supposed it was at full moon), the seal would come ashore Then she would shed her sealskin and walk around naked on the beach. Nicol wasn't sure why she did that, and if he ever wrote a story like that he'd change that bit so that the lady found a pile of clothes and put them on. There was an old story about a Selkie who did that one night, but a man hid her sealskin and tricked her into marrying him. They had children, but the Selkie spent all her time thinking about going back out to sea. One night, when there was a full moon, she discovered her sealskin, put it on, and swam back out to sea, and was never seen again. Nicol said that he didn't like that ending, so used to imagine that whenever the children were on the beach, they would call to their mother and she would reappear in the form of a seal.

I thought that was a lovely story, and Nicol told me that when he was little, he used to believe that his mother had turned into a seal and was still out at sea. He believed this, even though he knew that her body was in a grave. He used to stand at his mother's grave and call out to sea, and sometimes he was sure that he could see a seal bobbing up and down on the waves, and hear her calling his name. He didn't do that now, because he knew that his mother was well and truly dead, and he didn't want people to think he was a daftie. So when he went to her grave now, he would just look out to sea and imagine his mum swimming there, and looking in his direction.

Nicol and Jessie go back to school.

The time seemed to fly by, and in no time at all, my cousins' school holiday came to an end. On the evening before going back to school, Jessie and Nicol put on their school uniforms. They both looked completely different, and much more grown up. I wasn't sure I liked Nicol in his uniform, because he said how much it annoyed him, and he was quite shy about me seeing him in it. Jessie, on the other hand, was proud of her school clothes, which Auntie had bought a few days previously, and were nice and new. We walked over to see Kirsty and Kenny, and they were sitting in the garden with their school uniforms on. Kirsty was wearing a skirt and tights and a white shirt and tie. It was the first time I had seen her wearing a skirt, and I tried to hide what I was thinking. I wasn't sure what to say but she said, 'I know what you're thinking: I look just like a boy dressed up as a girl. Everyone says that, and I don't care.' But the way she said it made me sure that she did care.

I was a bit nervous about going to the twins' house, because I had never met their mother. Jessie said that she didn't like her Auntie Màiri, but wouldn't say why. Suddenly a lady came out of the house and stood near us. I got a real shock when I saw her, because I had imagined that she would look a bit like the twins, but instead she looked just like an older version of Jessie. Her hair was the same colour, and she had the same smile, and the way that she walked and moved her hands was just like Jessie. She seemed quite normal, and not like someone who drank a lot of whisky and had spent a lot of time in hospital. Then I reminded myself that Mummy was quite all right now. The only thing that was different about Auntie Màiri was that her eyes looked strange, and when Kenny was talking to her, she seemed not to listen.

When we got home, Nicol asked me what I thought about Auntie Màiri. I didn't want to say anything, but he said, 'Her eyes look a bit funny, and it's like her mind is far away. She wasn't like that before she went into hospital. And did you notice that she didn't say hello, or say anything to you all the time that we were there?' I had noticed all those things. Nicol explained that Uncle Jimmy had told him that the doctors had given her very strong medicine, to calm her down. Nicol said that she didn't shout at the twins or her husband anymore, but she seemed very dreamy.

There was something else on my mind, and I didn't dare ask Nicol. In the evening, when I was on my own with Auntie, helping her do the washing up, I asked her why Jessie didn't like Auntie Màiri. Auntie asked me, 'Why do you think?'

I answered, 'Because she and Jessie's mum were sisters, and they probably looked like each other.'

Auntie stopped washing up and said, 'They were exactly alike; almost like twins.'

I told her that I thought that if I were Nicol, then I would be a bit bothered by that. Auntie said, 'Yes, I'm sure that he is bothered by it, but never says anything about it.'

I wasn't going to ask Nicol, but I felt sure that one day he would tell me how he felt about having someone living across the road who looked just like his dead mother. It would be like looking at a ghost. Then I thought about Mummy. She knew nothing about her family, and supposed that they had all been killed in The War. It made me wonder if she had a big brother or sister, or perhaps cousins, who might still be alive.

Nicol and Jessie went back to school the next day, and after they left the house, I felt quite lost. Maggie was upstairs, typing away, and I knocked on her bedroom door. She said that she was very busy, typing up one of her dad's short stories, but I could sit on her bed until Auntie came back from taking Jessie to school. Then she said, 'Oh, I almost forgot. Jessie gave me this to give to you.' She handed me a piece of paper. Jessie had written,

Dear Pippa
Don't forget to play your concertina.
I will test you when I come back from school.
We have to make the music perfect for the ceilidh
I love you
From your best cousin Jessie

She had drawn a picture of the two of us sitting on the Witch's Hat, playing our concertinas together. I know that sometimes she was an awful pain in the neck, but my heart suddenly filled with love for her, and I realised how much I missed her, and I couldn't wait for her to come back from school.

I thought that I would be terribly bored when my cousins were at school, but I was very surprised to discover that life was full of excitement and pleasure. Every morning I went with Auntie and Luna to take Jessie to school, then we walked on the beach and around the harbour. If the weather was bad, we would sit by the window in a café on the quayside, and Auntie would drink a cup of coffee and read her newspaper, while I sat stroking Luna and looked out onto the harbour. Then we walked back home and Auntie would do some cleaning and cooking. I always offered to help her, but on most mornings she told me that I should concentrate on my Art and practice my concertina. Of course, I painted scenes from the beach and the harbour, but was careful not to leave them lying around for Nicol or Jessie to see.

One afternoon, I was helping Auntie to make an apple pie. That was one of my favourite things to cook, because of the pastry. I especially liked using a knife to trim the pastry round the rim of the pie dish, then using the trimmings to make fancy patterns on top of the pie. Auntie kept all her flour, sugar and other dry ingredients in big jars made of thick glass, which had *Kilner* written on them. She said she had to keep everything in jars because there was so much damp, and to keep the wee beasties out. One was empty, so she asked me to wash and dry it carefully. The sun was shining through the kitchen door, and I put the jar on the table. Most of Auntie's small jam jars had clear glass, but the Kilner jars were made of thick glass that wasn't exactly clear, so when sunlight shone through it, everything was slightly distorted. This jar excited me, and I had to sit down and give it my full attention. Auntie said that I sat for fifteen minutes, staring at the jar, and occasionally moving my head, to look at it from slightly different angles. She carried on cooking, while I was lost in concentration. She got my art pad and watercolours for me, and I painted the first of a series of paintings that I called *Jars*. Uncle Tom saw it, and went into the shed and came back with a box of jars and bottles including Kilner jars.

For the next few days, all I did was experiment with my jars; looking closely at the way the jar distorted whatever was in the background. Then I filled them with water and dropped paint into them, and put them in rows in different parts of the house and garden, to see how the colours changed with the light. Then, of course, I'd have to paint my arrangements.

Jessie became fascinated with my jars, and as soon as she came home from school, would look at them and at my paintings, and ask if she could help me make a new arrangement, and do some painting herself. It made me feel as if I was getting close to her, and that finally we might be becoming good friends. Then one evening I went for a walk with Nicol and Luna, and when I came back, Jessie had mixed up all the colours, so that they all looked a dirty purple-brown, just like the water in the jar for rinsing your brush, when you have cleaned your brush about ten times, and need to get fresh water. I was really quite cross, but then realised that Jessie had made a mess on purpose, to make me angry, so I pretended that I didn't care. I've never been able to understand why she behaved like that.

My landlord's beautiful daughter
In the last week of my holiday, Rhona and the musicians came back. Maggie went to meet them up at the cottages, but told us that they were all worn out, and would be spending most of their time sleeping, so we couldn't go to see them just yet. Nicol was very disappointed. I had two feelings; I wanted to meet them, then I didn't.

Around about the same time that the Musicians came back, Auntie decided that she needed to clean the house from top to bottom, so on Monday morning we didn't go for our walk on the beach, and Maggie took Luna up to the cottages. After a few hours, Auntie sat down in the kitchen with Uncle Tom, and I went upstairs to go to the toilet. When I was at the bottom of the stairs I heard Auntie say, 'This is silly. It'll take weeks to get rid of all the grime and put everything in order, and then it'll only get messy again.'

Uncle Tom said, 'Aye, and it's not as if your man will notice, or anyone else for that matter.'

In the evening, Auntie said that I had to have a bath, and that Maggie would help me wash and dry my hair. My hair was getting quite long and curly, and I liked it like that, but Maggie often said that she'd love to cut it.

The next morning, I had breakfast with Nicol and Jessie before they went to school. Maggie joined us, and said that she was going to take Jessie to school. Jessie said that she didn't want to go, because she had a tummy ache, but she was smiling and looked at me in a funny way. Uncle Tom said, 'Will you take a look at that dreich! The rest of the country is probably basking in glorious sunshine, but the northeast of Scotland has been plunged into winter! We call it 'dreich'; when there's that fine rain that soaks you through, and it's damp and grey, and cold and miserable.'

Jessie said, 'I'm not miserable. I'm not miserable at all. I have a feeling that something nice is going to happen today.' Auntie gave Jessie a stern look. Jessie said, 'Sorry, Mummy.'

I asked if I could go with Maggie and Jessie, but Auntie said I had to stay with her. Maggie came back in the middle of the morning, and had someone with her. It was a young lady with long dark hair, and wearing a dark brown coat, a long purple velvet skirt, an orange jumper, and a light brown woolly hat.

I knew straight away that it was Rhona. She said, 'Good morning everybody. I hope I'm not interrupting. We've just been for a walk by the sea, and I thought I'd pop in and say hello. I hope you don't mind. If I'm in the way, then I can come back another time.'

Auntie smiled and said, 'Oh that's all right. The more the merrier as far as I'm concerned. What do you think, Tom?' Uncle Tom said that he liked visitors, and was delighted that Rhona had come.

Rhona shook hands with Uncle Tom and kissed Auntie. She looked at me and said, 'And you must be Pippa. It's so nice to meet you, finally.' She leaned forward and kissed me on the cheek. She had the same patchouli oil smell as Maggie, though much stronger. She took her hat off. Actually, it was more liked she peeled it off, and with one movement shook her head, so her long hair fell and settled across her shoulders, like a waterfall. She had very thick, dark eyebrows, and her lips were dark red, though I didn't think she was wearing any lipstick. When she smiled, her top lip curled up slightly, which showed her teeth. And her eyes were big, and a very deep brown. Whenever she leaned her head forward, her hair fell over her face. She put the fingers of both hands to her forehead, where her hair was parted in the middle, and then, with one movement, tucked her hair behind her ears. I wished that she would do it again, and again, just so that I could see her do it.

I smiled, but didn't know what to say. She smiled back at me and sat next to Maggie. I found it very difficult not to stare at her, and she probably thought that I was being quite rude. There were some very surprising things about her. I had imagined that she would be Scottish, but she spoke with an American accent. And not only that, but she was very quiet. She hardly said anything, except to say that she'd love some coffee and that she didn't want anything to eat. And when she said those things, her voice was so quiet that you could hardly hear what she was saying.

I had expected her to be big, with a very loud voice, and to be someone who talked a lot, but Rhona was the exact opposite. Uncle Tom asked her if she had recovered from her concert tour, and her face went a little pink, and she smiled and said, 'I'm fine now, thank you,' then looked at her coffee cup.

She was like a new girl in school, and I couldn't understand how someone like that could be the star of a show. I looked around the table, and everyone was smiling at Rhona. Then I smiled, because it was obvious that everyone liked her.

Then Rhona said to me, 'So you are Pippa. I've heard all about you from Maggie. You have the most beautiful eyes and skin and hair. I think you're like me. My father is Jewish and my mom is Scottish.'

I put my head down and mumbled, 'I'm the other way round.' I was feeling shy and embarrassed. I was shy because she was talking to me, and embarrassed because this was the first time that anyone had mentioned that I was Jewish. I wasn't ashamed of that; I just didn't want anyone in Stranhaven to know.

She said, 'I'm sorry, I didn't mean to embarrass you.' That made me feel even more embarrassed, but I didn't want her to stop talking.

She said, 'I expect you know this already, but your father owns our cottages, and we rent them from him. The cottages are on the edge of his estate, and if you walk from our back garden, you'll eventually come to his very big house. And he owns the hill and the forests around here too. And he owns every house in this town with light blue window frames. He's my landlord, and you're his daughter, and I think you're beautiful. Very beautiful. So I think of you as my landlord's beautiful daughter. Maggie has been telling me all about you, and your family, and your paintings.'

That was a big surprise. Nobody had mentioned anything about my father having a big house on a huge estate. Then I wasn't surprised anymore. It seemed that Daddy owned everything.

Uncle Tom changed the subject, and asked Rhona about her new record. A few wisps of hair had fallen across her face, so she tucked them behind her ear. She said, 'Well, it's still in its early stages, really. I have most of the songs ready, and the musicians I want to record with have all agreed to join us in London, but I think there could be a few problems looming on the horizon. You see, the boys and Etsy are not very keen on me making my own record. They think that it should be enough for me to have one of my songs on the group's next record. But I have written enough songs now to make an LP of my own. And I have an idea how I want it to be produced, and the order that the songs should go in, but I still don't know what the LP cover should look like.'

Uncle Tom scratched his beard. He seemed very interested in everything that Rhona had to say. He said, 'I can imagine that doing something on your own like that could make the others feel a bit... what would you say, Pippa?'

I wasn't expecting anyone to talk to me, so I blurted out, 'Annoyed... and jealous.... and a bit afraid that you might leave the group.'

Rhona smiled at me, then frowned, then tucked her hair behind her ears. I wondered what she would do with her hands if Maggie ever cut her hair short. I hoped that she would change her mind about having short hair. She said, 'It's quite complicated, Pippa. Jealousy is just one of the feelings that they have.' Everyone listened to Rhona. 'You see, before I joined the group, I used to sing on my own. But it was a lonely life, travelling from one folk club to another. It was just me and my guitar, sitting in lonely railway stations after the show and riding on freezing cold trains. But I could choose what I wanted to sing. But now everything is very noisy and I'm only a small part of quite a big operation. It's like being in a travelling circus sometimes. And in pop groups, often the loudest person gets to make all the decisions. And I'm a very quiet person. I suppose I'm a bit shy, and not very good about talking about my feelings. So I write poems; and these poems become songs, and then I enjoy singing them. I just get terrified when people are watching me. It was all right in the folk clubs, because if people liked you then they would throw money in a hat afterwards. Sometimes, before I go onstage, I feel terrified that I might disappoint the people who have paid to come and see us. So the nice thing about being in a group is that I feel that perhaps people in the audience aren't looking at me so much. Do you know what I mean?' She paused, then said, 'Actually, Etsy and the boys are all a bit cross with me, so have gone to Edinburgh for a few days. I'm quite glad, because there was a bit of a bad atmosphere on the tour. They all think I'm going to leave, when really I just want to make my own record. I've been tired out, but I think I've got my energy back now.'

Rhona was a grown-up, but had just taken time to explain her feelings to almost ten year-old me. Then Rhona looked down at her plate, just like me when I thought I had said too much. Her hair fell over her face, so she tucked it behind her ears again. Maggie nudged her with her elbow and they both looked at each other and smiled.

Then I knew why she was the star of the show. It was because she was so lovely, and shy, so when she did say something, everyone listened. I wanted to hear her singing. I imagined that her songs were all about her feelings.

More visitors

There was another knock at the front door, and this time Auntie went to see who it was. I heard her talking to a man in the hallway. Maggie looked at me and smiled. Then Mr Macmillan came in. He said, 'I'm awfully sorry, I thought I was late, but it seems I'm early.'

Auntie introduced him to everyone, and he shook everyone's hand. He took my hands in both of his and said, 'Well, Pippa, I'm very happy to see you here. You look very well. You're completely rested now, by the looks of things. Well done Mr and Mrs Pirie, for doing such an excellent job of caring for young Pippa.'

There wasn't much space round the table now, so Auntie said, 'Pippa, why don't you come into the front room with me? I had a terrible feeling that something awful was going to happen. Mr Macmillan was here, and nobody had told me that he was coming. We went into the front room and Auntie was just about to say something, when I saw the shadow of someone walking into the porch, and I heard a knock on the door. I knew who it was. I ran out of the room and opened the front door. It was Mummy!

I don't think I had ever been so excited in all my life. I threw myself at Mummy and she held me very tight. I shouted, 'I knew you'd come to see me. I knew you'd come to see me one day!'

All Mummy said was 'Oh.'

I felt Auntie's hand on my shoulder. She said, 'Hello Ruth. I'm delighted to meet you, at last.'

Mummy said, 'Me likewise. Thank you so much… thank you so much for… oh it's no good. I promised myself I wouldn't cry, but…' I felt her whole body shaking and Auntie said, 'Come inside. I'm afraid that there are a lot of people here, but I can ask them all to disappear, if you like.'

Mummy was still crying, but she was laughing as well, as she sometimes did when she was crying with happiness. She said, 'Oh no. I've heard so much about everyone. I'm very keen to meet them, but please can I just have a few minutes on my own with my baby?'

But it was too late, because Maggie came into the hall. She hugged Mummy and said, 'It's so exciting to meet you at last! You have such a wonderful daughter. Everyone loves her!'

Auntie said, 'Now Pippa and Ruth need to have a little time together in the front room.' She looked at Mummy, 'You are staying for lunch, Ruth, aren't you?'

Mummy said, 'I'm not exactly sure what the plan is, but yes, we'd love to. I mean, I'd love to, if it's not too much trouble?'

Auntie said that it was no trouble at all, as long as Mummy didn't mind having very plain food. Mummy smiled and said, 'That would be lovely. But do you mind most awfully if I use your lavatory?'

Auntie said, 'Pardon?'

Mummy laughed, 'It's just a little joke that Pippa and I have. Please may I use your toilet?' I didn't want to let Mummy out of my sight, and she knew it. She said, 'Don't worry, Pippa. I'll only be a few minutes, I promise.'

Auntie took me into the front room, and Mr Macmillan joined us.

All the time that Mummy was upstairs, I thought it wasn't true. I thought I was still asleep and dreaming. I pinched my arm and it hurt. Mr Macmillan asked me what I was doing, and when I told him, he smiled. Then Mummy came in and sat on the sofa next to me. I jumped on her knee. She put her arms around me and we just sat there, as she gently rocked me. She had taken her hat and coat and gloves off, and I could smell her. It was as if all my life I had never really thought about her smell. But now I was breathing it in, so that it would become part of me; filling my lungs and then soaking into my blood, and even going into my bones.

After a while Mummy said, 'We've bought you some presents. Would you like to look at them?'
There it was again; that word, *we*. I said, 'Yes please, that's very kind of you. But where's Muriel?'
I felt Mummy look at Mr Macmillan. He nodded his head. Mummy said, 'Muriel came with me on the train. It's such a long way away! She's here, somewhere nearby, but she's not allowed to see you, I'm afraid. That nice Mr Griffin met us at the station and he gave us a lift here. I'm not sure exactly where he's gone with Muriel.'
I sat quietly. I didn't know what to say about Muriel. I said, 'Mummy, why didn't you tell me that you were coming? It's a lovely surprise; the best surprise in the world, really. But if I had known, then perhaps I could have made you a present to take back with you to England.'
'We all thought it best not to tell you. We know what you're like; you get very excited, and we weren't sure until a few days ago that we could come. And then, who knows, something might have happened and we might have... we might have... oh, I can't say it!' She began weeping.
She said, in between her sobs, 'I'm so sorry Pippa. I've tried my best not to be upset. I don't want to upset you, but I just can't help myself!'

Auntie put her arm round Mummy and said, 'There, there. You're here now, Ruth. That's all that matters.'

Mummy almost shouted, 'I have tried so hard not to break down and cry. But the injustice of it! I can't bear it. I have four visits a year. Four! But for Muriel it's just... it's just insupportable. She loves Pippa like nobody else on Earth. And just because we are... just because we love each other, they have banned her from seeing Pippa. It's inhumane!'

Mummy blew her nose in her hanky, and then held me even tighter. I said, 'Mummy, you're squashing me!'

She stopped crying and laughed a very small laugh. 'I'm sorry my love. I've been holding it in for so long. I won't cry like that anymore. I don't want to spoil our day together. I wanted to pretend to you that I'm happy and that everything is all right, but I just can't do it.'

I wasn't shocked at Mummy weeping and being angry. After all, I had seen her like that many times before. She often wept when she talked about her feelings to Muriel and Stephen Hunter. I didn't like it, but at the same time it felt... it felt what? It felt right. It was the right thing for her to have done. It showed me that Mummy loved me; that Mummy cared. But there was a feeling stirring up inside me, starting in my tummy. I pictured The Judge telling my father that he had won. My father had beaten Mummy in The Court, and she was forced to give me up. He had decided that Mummy could only see me four times a year, and each time she saw me, we would never be allowed to be anywhere together on our own. And I saw The Judge telling Mummy that never again must that woman Muriel Standish be allowed to talk to me, or even write to me. And I saw The Judge shaking my father's hand, and the two of them smoking cigars and smiling at each other. The looks on their faces were the same as the people who watched my grandfather being beaten to death in the street. That feeling I had in my tummy was hatred. I hated my father.

Mummy said, 'Pippa, tell me all about what you have been doing. But first, can I see your appendix scar?' It seemed strange that she should ask me. As far back as I could remember, Mummy would always look at my body without asking. She would have said, 'Let me see your scar.'

She said to Mr Macmillan, 'Is that all right? Am I allowed to do that?'

I stood in front of her and pulled up my dress and she pulled my knickers aside and looked at my scar. Mr Macmillan said, 'Yes, yes of course. I'll just pop outside for a wee while. Aileen, would you mind if I use your telephone? I'll be as brief as possible.'

Mummy said, 'They've done a very good job. It's healing nicely. Soon it will look just like Muriel's.' That was the nicest thing that anyone could have said about it. She said, 'Do you mind if I touch it?'

I said, 'Please touch it, Mummy. It doesn't hurt anymore.'

She ran her finger along it. It felt as if she were a nurse. Then she bent down and kissed it. She said, 'Muriel asked me to do that for her, to kiss it better.'

I felt myself quiver all over. It was a feeling of pure joy.

I didn't know if Mummy knew about The Lodge, or how I had got appendicitis in the first place. I decided not to mention it. Instead, I said, 'I hate Daddy. I hate him more than anyone in the whole world. He's just like the men who killed Grandpa in the street.'

Mummy looked terribly shocked. If I'm honest, I wanted to say to her, 'And I think he's a stupid fucking bastard as well.' But I didn't. The effort of not saying it made me bite my bottom lip, and I tasted blood in my mouth.

I couldn't bear the thought that my father had kept me from Muriel, and I wanted to hit him, just like I had punched the nasty boy in the car park. But I pushed that feeling down and closed my mouth, and decided not to say anything else about my father.

I was still standing in front of Mummy, holding my dress up. She straightened the front of my dress, took my hands in hers, and said, 'Look at me Pippa.' I looked in her eyes. They were red from where she had been crying. I thought that she must have been crying a lot. Her pupils were a very deep brown. Her face was very close to mine, and her breath smelled of Polo mints.

She said, 'Listen to me, Pippa. Listen very carefully. Please try not to hate Daddy. I used to hate him, after he made us come to England. I hated and hated him, as I sat in that freezing cold house. But it didn't do me any good. It didn't do you any good either. It didn't do anyone any good. I can't explain how, but hating him made me hate myself. I know that now. I don't hate him anymore. I don't like what he has done. I don't like that he has forced us apart, and when they took you away from us, I raged and raged against him. But really I was raging against myself.

'Please don't hate him. You can dislike what he has done. But he has made a mistake, and one day he will come to realise that. The men who killed my father were full of hate, and it made them do terrible things. But hating them back won't make anything better. We have to show them that we are better than they are; that we don't hate. Your father isn't full of hate. He really thinks that he has done the right thing for you, for his daughter. So I'm not going to hate him, and neither is Muriel.'

Mummy's face looked very pale, and I could see that she had lines around her eyes. There were lines on her forehead, and there was a vertical line between her eyes, like a scar. It was from holding her face in a frown for so many years. She held my hands tighter. 'I don't hate your father. He's really a very lonely man. I don't suppose he has many friends, or people he can trust. Rich men like that must always be thinking, "Does that person really like me, or are they just pretending to be friendly, because I have so much money and power?" '

I said, 'Sorry, Mummy. I'll do my best.'

She gave my hands a squeeze and told me I was a good girl. I wanted to climb back onto her lap, but she held me there, in front of her. She swallowed. She asked me, 'Do you know who made me change my mind about hating your father?'

'Jesus?'

'No. Guess again.'

'Chris the Vicar?'

'No.'

'The Holy Ghost?' That was a wild guess. I have never quite understood who The Holy Ghost is. Mummy smiled. 'I know, was it Shakespeare?' I knew he was famous, and that Muriel was always quoting lines from his plays and poems.

'No Pippa. It was Muriel. It was Muriel who helped me understand that I must try to be friends with Daddy. Isn't that funny? Because Muriel has suffered just as much as I have. That shows how much of a good person Muriel is.'

I was desperate to see Muriel. She was somewhere nearby, but not allowed to see me. The horrible feeling of hatred was rising in me again, but I pushed it down. Mummy said, 'And it was Muriel's idea for me to get you something very special. We couldn't get exactly what we wanted in Gamages, so Muriel suggested I ask Daddy to help us, and he did. I spent a long time talking to Daddy on the telephone, and halfway through I was surprised to find that we were having a nice chat together. I think he was surprised too. He was on the other side of the world, but he still managed to get exactly the present that we wanted, which Muriel and I both agreed was very kind of him.'

Mummy gave me a big paper bag, and inside was a new duffel coat, exactly the same colour as the one that Mummy and Muriel had bought me in Gamages. I tried it on, but it was quite big. I didn't care. Mummy said, 'Daddy helped us find that coat, and he insisted on paying for it as well. So it's a present from all three of us. Muriel thinks that's very funny. We got it a few sizes too big, because girls your age often shoot up.'

I sat in between Mummy and Auntie, with my coat on, thinking about Mummy and Daddy being friendly. I just wished that Daddy could like Muriel as much as everyone else did. And I thought about me shooting up, and Mummy not being with me when it happened. Roger told me that his big sister had shot up while she was away at boarding school, and she had rung her mum up, and was very upset because she was changing shape and didn't know what to do. Roger's mum was upset too. She told Roger that she was upset because she was apart from her daughter, at a time in a girl's life when she most needs her mother to be near her.

Mr Macmillan came in and stood by the door. Mummy said that she had a very important question to ask me. She said, 'Tell me Pippa. Do you remember that day when we first met Muriel? When she fell over in front of us in the station, and then I nearly fainted? Do you ever wonder what might have happened if we had got on an earlier train? Do you ever think about what might have happened then?'

'No Mummy, I have never thought about that. It's a horrible thought. Because then we would have never met Muriel.' This was too awful to think about. I wanted her to stop talking, but I didn't know how to change the subject.

Mr Macmillan frowned. Mummy said, 'I know Pippa. It's a horrible thought. But I have never once regretted meeting Muriel, even though it has caused us all so much pain. But Muriel once said that perhaps it would have been better if we had never met, because then you and I would still be together. I told her that it was a terrible thing to say, and I felt sure that you have never regretted it either. I just have to ask you, so that I can tell Muriel what you think. It's a thought that keeps eating away at her, and it stops her from sleeping. She feels terribly guilty that she has caused us - you and me - so many problems.'

Mummy was frowning and her forehead was wrinkling, as if she had a headache or a pain in her tummy. I could feel myself panicking, and I began to feel as if I was going to get out of control. I said, 'No, no, no! I have never thought that. Muriel saved us. We were both terribly unhappy. And then we met her, and then we were both terribly happy. I can't imagine my life without Muriel. I love her, and it breaks my heart that I can't see her!'

I was shouting. Mummy said, 'It's all right, Pippa. I didn't mean to upset you. It's just something important that I can tell Muriel, to put her mind at rest.' Then she said, 'Tell me about being in hospital.'

'Oh Mummy, it was such a long time ago. I've forgotten about it, really I have. I'm better now, really I am.'

She smiled, but the look in her eyes made me think that her thoughts were now far away. 'I'm glad. And I'm so glad that you have met Aileen and Tom and their lovely family.' She turned to Aileen and patted her hand. 'And thank you, Aileen, for loving my daughter, and allowing her to stay with you. After all the terrible things that have happened, some good has come out of it, after all. I keep telling myself that, and it's a great comfort.'

Aileen said, 'Pippa is like a part of our family. We all love her and she's been marvellous for Nicol and Jessie. The pair of them have calmed down so much since Pippa came to stay with us. It used to be like World War Three here sometimes!'

Mummy smiled. Auntie asked, 'Would you like to see Pippa's room, and Pippa, would you like to show Mummy your paintings?'

Mr Macmillan said, 'I'll stay downstairs. I'm waiting for someone to return my call.'

I didn't want to let go of Mummy, so held her hand as we walked upstairs. Mummy saw Polish Teddy in my bed, and the photograph on my bedside table. She said, 'How lovely! I'm so glad that you still have your teddy bear.' She picked up the photo. I told her that Auntie had framed it, so that I could have it near me in hospital.

Mummy sat on my bed, and I sat next to her. Auntie sat on Jessie's bed. Mummy said, 'Pippa, I'm so glad that you're having a nice time. I hope you have lots more fun and interesting times. And I hope... I know, that when you go to school, you will have more adventures. I feel sure that you will make lots of lovely friends. That is really the most important thing in life.'

She took a few deep breaths and then let out a sigh. I knew that she was trying to be brave. 'Muriel and I went to visit your school yesterday. A very nice nun called Sister Anne showed us round. She told us that she had met you, and was looking forward to seeing you again. You can't imagine how pleased we were about that!'

My words came out in a rush, 'Did she show you the bed that I will to sleep in? And where I will have a wash? And are there any baths there? And can I have a bath every night, like I used to do at home?'

Mummy sighed, 'I don't know darling. We only saw some of the classrooms. All the children were at home, and there were lots of nuns cleaning everywhere, making it all very shiny.'

I felt a terrible feeling of dread rising up through me, but I forced it down and changed the subject. I asked about Lucy and Roger, and Mummy told me that they were always asking about me. It had been very difficult for Mummy to make them understand why I wasn't allowed to live with her and Muriel anymore. They were very excited that Mummy was finally coming to see me, and they had both written me a letter. Mummy took an envelope out of her handbag and gave it to me.

On the front of the envelope, Lucy had written *Pippa* in very large letters. My hands were shaking with excitement, so Mummy had to help me open it. Lucy had written

> Di Pippa.
> I ms u or the tm.
> I hepe u ar hvn a nse tm.
> I cred a lt wn u lft.
> I hv arst Mum and dad to tk me to skotld so I cn se u.
> I hepe u rmbe me.
> I love u
> Lucy xxxxxxxxx
> I pra fr u evri nit

Roger had written underneath

Dear Pippa,

I had to put my arm round Lucy, to stop her from crying.

We all miss you very much. It's not fair that you were taken away.

I hope you will come back soon. I hope we can still be best friends again.

I know Lucy is not a very good speller, but she spent ages writing to you and wouldn't let me help her.

Of coarse, I am still trying to get her to be my girlfriend, but she's just not intrested.

I wish you were here with us now.

Lots of love from Roger

I showed Mummy, and she passed the letter to Auntie. Mummy said that girls like me would always make lots of nice friends. Then she said that she had something else to show me. It was a photograph of all the children from my class, sitting in rows and smiling at the camera. My lovely teacher was standing at the side of them. Right in the middle was lovely Lucy, smiling away.

I said, 'Mummy, can I tell you something? I'm having a lovely time, really I am. But I think I shouldn't. If I laugh and am happy, then that makes me think… I can't think of the word. It just doesn't seem right.'

'I know what you mean, my darling. I feel exactly the same. I want to be happy. We went to the cinema to try to cheer ourselves up, but we left halfway through, because it didn't seem right to be trying to enjoy ourselves without you there.'

'What was the film?'

'*Ben Hur*. We didn't really like it, because it was full of men killing each other.'

'Well that's all right, because I don't like that sort of film either. Next time, can you go and see something that you know I'll like? Maybe a film with The Beatles, *or* about Sooty and Sweep?'

Auntie thought that was very funny, and Mummy smiled, just like I hoped she would. Mummy said, 'You really are a funny girl. We still laugh about some of the funny things you've said.'

I told her about my special time of thinking about her and Muriel, but that I was always too busy to remember. Mummy smiled and said, 'Perhaps you should start saying prayers before bedtime again. Muriel and I say prayers together every night, and we send our prayers off to you. I don't know if you ever feel them, but they are up their somewhere, just floating around, and waiting for you to hear them.'

I said, 'Perhaps Ursula has them;'

'Oh, do you still get visits from Ursula?'

'Only when I am terribly upset or in trouble.' Mummy frowned, so I added, 'But I haven't seen her for a long time. I'm sure she has remembered all your prayers, and will tell them to me one day.'

Mummy frowned again, so I said, 'But you know, I can always ask her to come and see me when I'm happy, otherwise she will find me terribly hard work. And I don't think I'm going to be unhappy anymore.'

I knew that Mummy knew that I was lying, to try to make her stop frowning.

Then the telephone rang downstairs and we heard Mr Macmillan say, 'Macmillan here. Yes, I'll go and get her.' He came upstairs and whispered to Mummy, 'Ruth, I'll just pop down with Pippa. You stay here and look at her artwork.'

I held Mummy's hand tightly, but she said, 'No Pippa, you go downstairs. Everything will be all right; I know it will.

I reluctantly let go of Mummy's hand and held Mr Macmillan's as he led me downstairs. Mr Macmillan picked up the receiver and whispered to me, 'Pippa, it's your father. He wants to speak to you.'

I started backing away, but bumped into Auntie. She whispered in my ear, 'Go on, you talk to your daddy. Tell him exactly how you feel.'

I took the receiver from Mr Macmillan. I was standing up and he sat on a little stool next to me. I said, 'Hello Daddy, is that you?'

He said, 'Hello there, Pippa. Can you hear me all right?'

He sounded a bit faint, so I made my voice very loud. 'Daddy, please can I tell you something? Something very important.'

'Of course you can. What is it?'

'Well, I said a terrible thing just now, and Mummy told me off.'

'Goodness, have you two been arguing?'

'No, not arguing. I would never argue with Mummy. It's just that I said that I hated you, because you won't let me see Muriel. And Mummy said that I mustn't say that ever again. She said it was wrong to hate people. She said it was especially wrong to hate you. She said I might not agree with what you had done, but that's no reason to hate you.'

I thought that perhaps he had gone away, because there was no sound coming into my ear from the receiver. Daddy coughed and said, 'Go on.'

'Well I'm very sorry. I don't hate you. It's just something that I felt, but it's gone now. That's all I wanted to say, really.'

He cleared his throat. 'Well thank you for telling me that, Pippa. I'm glad that you don't hate me. Mummy is quite right to say that. I agree with her entirely.'

'Actually Daddy, it was Muriel who taught her that.'

'Really?'

'Yes. You see, Mummy was in a terrible rage with you after they came to take me away from my happy life. But Muriel told her that she should calm down, and that Mummy was allowed to disagree with you, but she mustn't hate you. And I wish I had seen Muriel this morning, and then I would never have felt that terrible thing, and said it. I feel very ashamed of myself. And I don't mind going to a Catholic boarding school: really I don't. Mummy says it's going to be an adventure, and I will make lots of new friends, and you are allowed to wear a different colour coat and hat if you go to Mass. So of course I'm going to go to Mass every day. And I will pray for you every day.'

He laughed at that. 'Thank you Pippa. And do you like your new coat?'

'Oh yes, I love it!'

'And have you worn it yet?'

'I've got it on right now. It's a bit big, but Mummy said I will shoot up soon, and then it will fit me. But it's raining today and I don't want to go outside in it, in case I spoil it.'

He chuckled. 'I had the same thoughts at your age when I had a new coat. But if it's a good coat, then it is just the right thing to wear in the rain. But can I say something now, please?'

He said, very slowly and carefully, 'It wasn't me who made that decision about Muriel. It was The Judge, in The Court.'

'But couldn't you ask him to change his mind? It's making me desperately unhappy.'

He didn't say *yes*, and he didn't say *no*. He just said, 'Pippa, it's been lovely talking to you, but I really must stop now. But please can you ask Mr Macmillan to talk to me for a few minutes, about something very important?'

That frightened me. 'Are you going to tell him off? Has he done something wrong? And before I go, what is the weather like in Africa? Is it very hot, and have you seen an elephant?'

He chuckled again. I liked hearing him chuckle. 'I'm not in South Africa anymore. I'm in Germany, and the only elephants here are in the zoo.'

'It was lovely to talk to you, Daddy. I'm sorry if I hated you.'

'Good. I'm very pleased about that. You're a good girl, Pippa. Byebye now.'

I was feeling desperate. 'Daddy, there's just one more thing I wanted to say. You know, Daddy, I hardly know you at all. You're a bit of a stranger to me, and I feel sad about that. Please can you come and see me in school?'

'That is a very nice idea. Now…'

'Or perhaps I could come on holiday with you one day?'

He said, 'Byebye Pippa. Now get Mr Macmillan, please.' He said the word *please* very firmly, like an annoyed teacher.

I put the phone back on its cradle. Mr Macmillan said, 'Whoops! You've just cut your Daddy off. I hope he'll ring back.'

I felt a sinking feeling. I had been prepared to offer Daddy anything, and now I thought I had spoiled everything. But the phone rang again. Mr Macmillan said, 'Stranhaven 4512? Yes,

I can take the call. Yes, Mr Dunbar. Macmillan here. How can I help?'

I felt as if I was filling up with something. I wasn't getting over-excited, but I started to feel very uncomfortable in my tummy and in my head. I felt like I wanted to lie down with my eyes closed, next to Mummy. I didn't want to hear what Mr Macmillan and Daddy were talking about. I put my hands over my ears and ran upstairs, past Auntie Aileen. But my foot slipped and I wasn't able to stop myself in time, and I banged my head on the bannister rails and went tumbling back down the stairs.

Mr Macmillan said, 'Just a moment,' and put the telephone receiver down and came over to me. I tried not to make a noise, but I was crying quite loudly. I didn't want to make a fuss, and I especially didn't want my father to hear me crying, while he was far away in Germany. I didn't want him to think that I wasn't being looked after properly. Mummy came down the stairs and picked me up. She said, 'It's all right, darling, Mummy's here,' and helped me to stand up.
Mr Macmillan picked up the receiver and said, 'Pippa's just tripped on the stairs and is a bit shaken up, but no bones broken.'
He made a gesture to Mummy, for her to stay by the phone. Auntie tried to take me back upstairs, but I held onto Mummy's hand. Mummy whispered to me, 'No, Pippa, you go along with Aileen, and I'll come to you as soon as I can. This is very important.'
I thought I was going to cry. When you have been ripped apart from your mother, like I had been, then every second with her counts. But I did as I was told. I knew, of course, that Mummy was feeling the same as me.

Auntie took me back upstairs and shut the bedroom door. I knew that Daddy and Mummy were going to talk about something very important. I could hear Mr Macmillan talking for a bit longer and then Mummy spoke to Daddy, but I couldn't hear her words.

My paintings and drawings were spread out on my bed. Auntie said, 'We are all having a very emotional day. It's not surprising really. You stay here with me, and let's choose the pictures that you'd like to show Mummy. I'm sure there's a story behind each one.'

It seemed like Mummy and Daddy were talking for ages. I didn't want to look at my paintings, so Auntie asked me to come with her into the kitchen and help her make lunch. I agreed, but really I didn't want to go. We walked past Mummy and she waved at me and blew me a kiss. I heard her say, 'Quite. I agree. We met Sister Anne, and were very reassured.' Auntie asked me to help spread butter on some sandwiches, but I couldn't get my hands to do what they were supposed to. Then the phone made a *ding* sound, which meant that Mummy had finished talking to Daddy, and had put the receiver back on its cradle. She came into the kitchen, ran her fingers through my hair, and scratched my scalp at the same time. That was a strange thing to do, because it was the first time in my whole life that she had done it. It was what Muriel used to do to me when I sat on her lap, or needed calming down.

Mummy helped me get lunch ready, and having her beside me made my hands work again. She hummed to herself. Then Uncle Tom came in .He looked at me and I knew that he wasn't sure what to say. Mummy said, 'I've just spoken to Andrew, and he says that he's happy *in principle*, so I have my fingers crossed.'

Uncle Tom said, 'Ah.' This made me think that I wasn't supposed to know something, and that maybe Mummy had come to take me home.

Mummy sat next to me at lunch, but I couldn't eat anything. I didn't really know what to do with myself. My hands were shaking, and I didn't know what to say to anyone. Mummy held my hand very tightly under the table. Mr

Macmillan had eaten a sandwich very quickly, then gone outside to talk to Mr Griffin. Then Mummy said, 'I almost forgot! I have a present for each of the children. She got up, and I had to go with her. In the front room, she showed me a big white paper bag with *Pearson's* written on it in big blue letters. Mummy looked inside and took out a woolly hat. She gave it to me and said, 'This, my love, is no ordinary hat. It's a Fairisle woollen hat. They are probably the warmest hat you can ever wear. Muriel chose this one for you.'

I practically grabbed it off her. It was made of light and dark brown wool, and had a big pompom. It smelled as if the wool had just been taken off a sheep's back. Mummy said that I looked lovely. Then a thought occurred to me, 'Did you ask the manager to put the hat on the Dunbar account?'

Mummy smiled a big smile, so I could see her teeth. 'Of course. So it's a present from your daddy as well, which we both thought was a jolly good idea! And we bought hats for Nicol and Jessie as well, but paid for those ourselves.'

We went back into the dining room, carrying the paper bag, and I was still wearing my hat. Mummy said that I had to guess which hat was for Nicol, and which one for Jessie. It was obvious. Nicol's had a pointy top with flaps to go down over his ears, and Jessie's had a pattern of red, white, and grey stars and lines, and a long tail with a small multi-coloured pompom. The tail was so long that it would reach almost to her shoulders.

Mr Macmillan came in, and at the same time, the phone rang again. He said, 'That will be for me,' and went back into the hall. We heard him say, 'Right. Thank you,' and then the *ding* noise, and he came in quickly and said to Mummy, 'Good news. No time to lose. Can we go now?' I jumped up from my chair. Mummy said, 'No, Pippa. I'm not leaving you on your own, but you must come with me now.' She looked very excited.

Mr Griffin was waiting in the car, with its engine running. Mummy and I sat in the back and Mr Macmillan sat in the front. He said, 'OK. Let's get going up to The Estate. They will be waiting for us there.'

I said, 'What's happening Mummy? Am I going home with you?'

Mummy smiled, squeezed my hand, and whispered, 'No, I'm afraid not, my love, but we have a very special surprise for you.'

Under the pine trees

We drove past Rhona's cottages. I had never been that far up the road and we seemed to drive a very long way. All along our right hand side was a high wall, and the road sloped gradually upwards. Mr Griffin stopped the car at a very high metal gate. It wasn't rusty, but painted light blue. A man with a beard was standing there, with the gate open. He didn't say anything, but waved us through. We drove past him and under the arch of a large gatehouse; with light blue window frames. We drove along a narrow road, with fields of long grass on either side, waving in the wind. In one of the fields, a herd of very grumpy-looking highland cattle stood, looking at us. Mr Griffin slowed the car right down, because we were on the crest of a small hill. The land dropped down in front and to either side of us, so we could see into a long valley. Across the valley, the long grass had been mown, and was lying in great lines that stretched as far as my eyes could see.

The road wound around and down, towards an enormous grey stone house. It looked like one big house with lots of little houses stuck onto the side of it, and there were even two turrets with cone roofs, just like the sort of place where Rapunzel might have been imprisoned. There was another small house built onto the front, with two more cone turrets on either side, and an enormous wooden front door. In front of the house was a stone terrace with wide steps leading down to a wide gravel driveway in front. I didn't notice any trees, except for about eight huge twisted pines growing close together, to the left of the road, about fifty yards from the front of the house.

Then three figures came out of the front door and walked across the terrace. One of them was wearing a white coat and a navy blue hat and began waving at us. Suddenly it started to pour with rain. It was lashing down, and I saw two of the figures run back towards the house. But the person in the white coat didn't go back indoors; but ran down the steps and towards the pine trees. Mr Griffin had to slow down because the rain was hammering on his windscreen and it had suddenly become misted over. He wiped the inside of the windscreen and put the wipers on full blast, but it was still impossible to see anything. He stopped the car.

I flung my door open and raced as fast as I could down the road. I heard Mr Griffin shout, 'Wait a moment!' but I didn't take any notice of him. The rain hit me in the face and went in my eyes and nose, as if I was underwater. I saw the pine trees in front of me and ran off the road and onto the grass. I couldn't see anything except the shape of the trees ahead. The wind was making a rushing sound in my ears, and my feet and legs were soaking. But I didn't care; I had to reach the pine trees. I heard someone calling from near the trees, 'Pippa! Pippa! Come here!' The person in the white coat was running towards me, then stopped and leaned against a huge pine and held out her arms and I jumped towards her and practically knocked her over. Of course, it was Muriel.

She grabbed me and pulled me towards her, and held me so tight that I thought she was going to crush me. I shouted, 'I never had the chance to say goodbye to you properly! I knew something was wrong when you left me at school. I knew you wouldn't come and collect me. I hoped that one day I might see you again. I can't tell you how happy I am to be with you! And I couldn't talk to you or even write to you. And a cruel, wicked lady kept me prisoner in a room, and starved me, and I didn't do a poo for days and then a doctor put his thumb up my bottom without asking me, and he took my appendix out and now I have a scar just like yours!' I turned round so I was facing away from her. I opened my coat and lifted up my skirt.

I grabbed Muriel's hand and made her put it in my knickers. I shouted, 'Feel it Muriel! Feel it! Is it just like yours?'
She said, 'Yes my darling. It's just like mine.'

She tried to take her hand away, but I held it there. I closed my eyes and heard the trees raging above us and felt huge drops of rain splattering on my hat and shoulders. Then I heard a man's voice shouting, 'Is everything all right there?' He had a big red beard and a long coat that was dripping wet. He was holding a lead, with a large black dog on the end of it.
Muriel shouted, 'We're all right thank you!'
The man looked at us. Muriel shouted, 'Don't worry, I'm just feeling her appendix scar!' The man kept looking. Muriel shouted, 'It's quite all right, I'm a nurse.'
The man smiled and was about to walk away when Mr Griffin appeared, carrying a huge umbrella. He said something to the bearded man and then walked towards us. He folded his umbrella, put it by a tree next to us, and said, 'Everyone is waiting in the house.' He pointed to the tree furthest away from us. 'I'll be just over there. Don't be too long, because you're both soaked through.'
Muriel thanked him, and he smiled and walked away.

Muriel touched my scar with her middle finger. She moved it in little circles, beginning from the left and over to the right and then back again. She said, 'Does that feel nice? Does that make you feel better?'
I couldn't speak, so I nodded. It felt like all the horror and pain in my life was passing from the space above my Lovely Place, out through my scar, and away through Muriel's finger.
She said, 'I can feel that it's still quite new, but I'm sure that one day it will be just like mine.' She took her hand away and said, 'Now let me help you do up your lovely new coat.' Her hands were shaking and she couldn't manage to do up the toggles.
I said, 'Let me help you.' Her coat was open and she pulled me towards her and wrapped her coat around me, and I could smell her beautiful Muriel smell of sweat and perfume mixed

together. She was shaking all over. I said, 'Are you cold Muriel?'

She said, 'No, not cold. I'm just...' I couldn't hear what she was saying, but I knew she was crying. I could feel her chest against my face, moving in and out, as she took in great gulps of air.

She said, 'I've never known such pain! And such joy!'

Then she crouched down, so her face was next to mine. It was the first time I had seen her face for a long time. Her hair was soaking wet, but I could see that it was shorter than when I had last seen her. The whites of her eyes were a strange yellow colour, and she had black bags under her eyes. Her face looked thin, and her skin was a strange light blue that was almost grey, with a hint of yellow, like old china. It reminded me of the colour of Jesus' skin, as He was being taken down from The Cross. She scraped her hair away from her face, and I saw how bony her fingers were.

She said, 'You look so strong and healthy and happy, but I am... I'm so weak. Listen carefully, Pippa. Your daddy is not a bad man. You must believe that. He has been very nice to us. He was very upset by The Judge's decision. He was even more upset about what happened to you when you first came to Scotland. He wants to make it all better. Try to love your daddy. Please try. It's what Mummy wants you to do. And I want it too, more than anything.'

I wanted to say, 'Well, he could make it better by letting me live with the people who I love most of all in the whole world, and he could stop me from going to a Catholic boarding school'. But I didn't say that. Something stopped me. It was looking in Muriel's face, and seeing how tired and ill she looked. I said, 'Yes Muriel. I will try, because you have asked me. I love you and Mummy more than anybody in the whole world. I'm lucky, because I have Auntie Aileen and Nicol now.'

I almost said, 'But my heart is broken because I can't be with you,' but I stopped myself, because Muriel leaned forward and kissed me, on the lips.

She said, 'Pippa, listen to me. I'm not very well. I've been bleeding far too much, and I have a terrible pain in my tummy.'
'In your tummy?'
'No, you're quite right. Not in my tummy. It's in my womb. In the place where babies are supposed to grow. I don't want you to worry, but I think I might have to go to hospital, to have an operation.'

I wanted to cry, and to shout and to scream, but I didn't. I said, 'Oh dear. Will you be all right?'
Muriel held both my hands tight. 'Yes, I'm sure, but I'll have to rest for a long time afterwards. Of course, Mummy will look after me.'
For some reason, that information stopped me from wanting to shriek. I pictured the two of them in bed, cuddling each other, and eating toast and drinking soothing cups of tea.
Muriel smiled. I saw her lovely teeth, but her eyes looked full of sadness. She looked over my shoulder, and I turned round. A crowd of people were standing looking at us. Mummy was there, and Auntie Aileen and Uncle Tom. Maggie was standing next to Rhona, and they were holding hands.

Muriel kissed me again, but on the cheek this time. She said, 'All these people love you and will look after you. You are a very lucky girl.' Then she laughed and said, 'Let's go and see the other love of my life.'
I shouted, 'No! Please! Can we stay here just a little bit longer? I want to tell you something.'
'Just for a few seconds, my darling girl.'
I took a deep breath. 'Muriel, I think the day that you fell over in front of us in the station was the best day in my whole life! I'm so glad to have met you. I don't care about anything else!'
'But I've caused so much trouble!'
'I don't care! I don't care! I don't care!'
She smiled and said, 'Bless you! I have been so lucky to have loved you.'
Then she tried to get up, but let out a sigh and fell backwards against the tree. Mummy and Mr Griffin rushed forward.

Muriel was sitting, slumped at the base of the tree. She was smiling and her eyelids were fluttering, and then she toppled over and landed on her side. I could see a patch of dark blood on the back of her coat. Then Mr Griffin picked her up and said to Mummy, 'Take the umbrella and come with me back to the house,'

He shouted to Uncle Tom, 'Run to the house and tell Murdo to call a doctor immediately!'

Inside Daddy's house

I felt someone take my hand. It was Rhona. She said, 'Maggie and Aileen are going home, but you will come with me.' She was holding an umbrella, but the wind was catching it and stopping us from moving forward. She said, 'Stupid thing!' and threw it down. It blew in front of us, tumbling and turning towards the house. Mr Griffin was up ahead, carrying Muriel. Her head was drooping backwards and one of her arms was hanging outspread. It bumped up and down as Mr Griffin marched at full speed towards the front door. Mummy was doing her best to keep up with him, trying to hold her umbrella steady, to keep the rain off Muriel's face. Rhona and I ran as fast as we could to try to catch up with Mr Griffin, but he was already by the front door. Uncle Tom opened it and we heard Mr Griffin say, 'She's as light as a feather.'

I have no recollection of what the inside of the house looked like. The only thing I can remember is that Mr Griffin laid Muriel down on top of a type of sofa that I now know is called a *chaise longue*. Mummy knelt beside Muriel and said, 'Muriel, are you all right? Say something.' But Muriel didn't say anything. She leaned her head sideways towards Mummy and I saw that she had dribble on the side of her mouth.

A lady came in with some towels and a blanket. Mummy said, 'Put one under her, please. She's bleeding.'

Mummy put her hands under Muriel's thighs and bottom, and lifted her up so that the lady could slide the towel underneath her. Then Mummy took Muriel's boots off and rubbed her feet, while the lady covered her with a blanket.

Muriel whispered, 'What happened? Did I get up too quickly? Everything went black. Where's Pippa?'

I had been watching everything in front of me as if it was something happening on a TV programme. But Muriel saying my name made me snap back into reality. I knelt by her and said, 'I'm here Muriel. You just sort of fell over.' She held out her hand and I squeezed it. It was very thin, like an old lady's hand. She still had her eyes closed, but said, 'I'm not very well, Pippa. I think the journey here has worn me out. But I had to be near you. It was the most important thing in the whole world.'

Uncle Tom came in and told us that the doctor was on his way. He arrived about ten minutes later and 'Men and children out of the room please.' I stood up, but Mr Griffin came over to me and said to the doctor, 'I'm Mr Dunbar's personal assistant, and this is his daughter. We'll sit over there, out of the way.' He held my hand and led me to a cushion seat by a big window. We could see the back of the chaise longue and the top of the doctor's and Mummy's heads as they knelt next to Muriel. The lady who had brought in the towels stood by the door, and Uncle Tom left the room.

I supposed that the doctor examined Muriel, because I saw his stethoscope and then he must have been looking at where the blood was coming from, because he said to the lady by the door, 'Mrs Mackie, bring me some warm water and soap and a towel, and some sanitary protection, if you have any.'

Mrs Mackie went red and said, 'I'll see what I can find.'

She was just leaving when the doctor said, 'Oh, and a newspaper please.'

Mrs Mackie looked very surprised and asked, 'Any particular paper? I think we may have yesterday's Scotsman.'

The doctor said, 'I'm not going to read it! It's to put something soiled in.'

Mummy said, 'Muriel should have some in her bag. She always carries them with her these days.'

The doctor asked Mummy where Muriel's bag was. Muriel said, very faintly, 'I left it at Rhona's house, by mistake.'

Mrs Mackie came back in, carrying a bowl of water and with a towel over her wrist and a newspaper tucked under her arm. She had something white in her hand. She dropped it on the floor by accident, but Mummy picked it up and thanked her. Mrs Mackie looked at me and Mr Griffin, and went red again. She said to Mummy, 'I only have the one.'

Mummy smiled and touched her arm; 'That's very kind of you.' Mummy's voice was very wobbly.

Mrs Mackie gave the newspaper to the doctor and said, 'I'm afraid that all I could find was *The Daily Sketch*. It was in the kitchen.'

The doctor smiled and said, 'Best thing to do with it.'

Mrs Mackie didn't smile, 'Shall I make us all a nice cup of tea? With some nice shortbread biscuits for the wee lassie?'

The doctor said, 'Good idea, but nothing for the patient, just in case.'

Mummy looked worried, 'In case of what?' He turned so I couldn't see him, and mumbled something. Mummy said, 'Oh!'

I wanted to run to her, but Mr Griffin held my hand. He said, 'In a minute, sweetheart. Stay over here with me for now.'

The doctor thanked Mrs Mackie, and we heard him put his hands in the water. Mummy said, 'I'd like to do that, if you don't mind.'

The doctor sounded surprised. 'Very well, but do you know what you're doing?'

Mummy said, 'Doctor, please don't be ridiculous.'

There was a lot of splashing and the doctor stood up and looked at me. Then he knelt down again and I heard him say, 'This is more than fibroids, you know.'

Mummy said, 'What shall we do, doctor?'

He said to Mrs Mackie, 'I've finished my examination. Some clean water please, for us to wash our hands.'

Mummy said, 'I think she's asleep.'

Mrs Mackie came back, and the doctor and Mummy washed and dried their hands. The doctor beckoned me over. I walked to him, but my knees were shaking, because I didn't know what

I was going to see. He stood up as I reached the front of the chaise longue, just as he handed Mrs Mackie something wrapped up in newspaper. There was blood on it, like a package you might buy from the butcher. He said, 'Talk to your mummy and keep your auntie company. She's fast asleep.' Then he walked over to Mr Griffin.

We both knelt down next to Muriel, and Mummy put her arm around me. Muriel was lying on her side and her mouth was open. She was dribbling.

The doctor called Mummy over to the window, while I stayed with Muriel and held her hand. She closed her mouth and opened it again, and let out a sigh. I heard the doctor say, 'More serious... more investigations... quite urgent... a question of where? We could begin with Stranhaven and then transfer to Aberdeen for tests, but London would be best...'

Mr Griffin said, 'I could make a phone call and everything would be arranged very quickly.'

Mummy started to cry. The doctor said, 'It's her colour, and some other signs.'

Mummy sighed very loudly and looked at me. After that, the grown-ups didn't say anything else to each other.

Mrs Mackie came in with the tea and biscuits. I wanted to ask why Muriel wasn't allowed anything to eat or drink. After all, she might have fainted because she was very hungry. But I knew that Muriel hadn't just fainted, and that something terrible was wrong with her. I didn't want to leave her side. I felt someone kneel next to me and put their arm round me. It was Rhona. I hadn't noticed that she had been in the room all the time.

She said, 'Muriel is very ill now, but I'm sure she'll get better.'

I whispered, 'How do you know?'

'We had a good chat today, and she explained that she is the opposite of your Mummy. When your Mummy was terribly unhappy once, she had a nervous breakdown. That means that her mind sort of collapsed. Muriel said that all the terrible stress and strain of being without you has made her have a

400

physical breakdown. Her mind is strong, but her body has just given in. It's telling her to stop and rest, and to work hard at looking after herself. She said that all her life she has been looking after other people, but now she needs someone to look after her. I know that your Mummy will take care of her.' Rhona kissed the side of my head. 'And she told us that she is so happy that you are being loved and cared for here. She thinks it's the best place for you.'

I tried to pull away from Rhona. That seemed like such an awful thing to say. The best place for me was to be with Muriel and Mummy. Rhona must have sensed this, because she held onto me, so I relaxed. 'What she meant is that, of course, she and Mummy want you to live with them. But the next best place for you is to be here, with your Auntie and Uncle Tom and their family.'
'But I'm being sent away to school! I don't understand.'
'That's true. But Muriel said that she wants you to try to enjoy yourself as much as possible. And she said that your daddy has been talking to your mummy a lot on the phone, and that makes Muriel very pleased. She wanted you to know how important that is for her; that your daddy and mummy are trying to be friends again.'

I was looking at Muriel while we were talking. I wanted to cry, but stopped myself. Rhona said, 'Muriel is a very special person. I can see why your mummy loves her so much. But Muriel is very strong, and I'm sure that she'll get better.'
I didn't know what to say. Mummy and the doctor and Mr Griffin had started talking quietly again. Someone knocked at the door. It was Mr Macmillan. I had forgotten all about him. He signalled for the grown-ups to come with him, outside the room. Rhona and I stayed kneeling next to Muriel, but we didn't say anything else. I could hear the grown-ups' voices outside the door, but couldn't hear what they were saying.
Rhona bent down and kissed Muriel on the cheek. She said, 'Thank you Muriel. You are a true inspiration.' I kissed Muriel as well, and told her that she was the loveliest person in the

world, as well as Mummy, and that she absolutely had to get better.

Then Mummy came in and knelt down with us. She said that everyone had been discussing what to do next. Mr Griffin had been talking on the phone to Mr Shepherd, and they had agreed on a plan. Muriel was going to Stranhaven hospital for the night, and then she would go with Mummy on a plane to London, where she would stay in a special hospital, where expert doctors would examine her and find out exactly what was wrong her. The very surprising news was that Mr Shepherd had said that Daddy would pay for everything. Mummy thought that was a very good idea, because she loved Muriel so much and was desperate for her to get better. She said that she and Daddy were getting on much better now, and though she didn't like to accept his money, she would do anything to make Muriel well again.

She was trying to be brave and not to cry as she said this, but Rhona hugged her, and Mummy thanked her for being so kind.

Then Mummy looked at me and said, 'And there's some very good news, my darling. I'm going to stay another night here in Scotland, so I can be with you for a little bit longer than I had hoped.'

I couldn't help myself. I jumped up and down and started squealing with excitement. This woke Muriel up, so I stopped bouncing up and down, but still felt hugely excited.

Muriel said, 'What's the matter? What's going on?' We all knelt next to her and Mummy explained the plan. Muriel said, 'Was I bleeding horribly? Was there a mess?'

Mummy said, 'Don't worry about anything, my love. We are going to move you soon. An ambulance is coming.'

I don't know why, but up to that point, everything had seemed very unreal. Suddenly the mention of the word *ambulance* made me realise just how seriously ill Muriel was. I held onto Rhona. She could feel that I was panicking. She said, 'Don't worry, Pippa, everything will be all right.'

I didn't know how she knew that, but I wanted to believe her.

402

We sat at a table by the window, and drank our tea and ate our biscuits, and waited for the ambulance to arrive. Auntie Aileen came in and talked to Mummy and me. Mummy explained what the doctor had said, and she used a word I had never heard before - *jaundice*. This explained why Muriel's face was yellow. Mummy said that you don't turn yellow if you have problems with your womb, so the doctors in the hospital needed to look at Muriel very closely, to find out exactly what else was wrong with her. I hoped that they didn't need to stick their thumbs up Muriel's bottom.

Auntie said that Mummy could stay in Uncle Tom's house tonight. Mummy said that she couldn't possibly, and that she would find a hotel in the town. Auntie said, 'I absolutely insist. You can sleep in Maggie's room. I'm sure if we ask Rhona nicely, she will let Maggie sleep in her house tonight.'

Mummy and Auntie looked at Rhona. Rhona's cheeks went pink. She said, 'Yes, of course. There's plenty of space for her in the other cottages, now that the rest of the group have gone.'

Mummy and Auntie smiled at Rhona again, and her face turned red.

Then Auntie said to me, 'And Pippa, I'm sure you'd like to sleep with Mummy tonight. Wouldn't you?'

Mummy said, 'I'm not sure that's allowed.'

Auntie said, 'Allowed? Of course it's allowed!'

Mummy said, 'There's nothing more I'd love in the world than to be back with my baby.'

Suddenly everything became too much for me. I could feel myself getting very hot. It started in my legs and rushed up through my tummy and towards my head. I felt hot all over and I began to feel dizzy. I didn't want to faint or be sick. I didn't want anybody to think about me. I wanted them to concentrate on Muriel, and how to make her better as quickly as possible. I didn't want to talk about my feelings. I didn't want to have any feelings. I wanted to be pure and simple, like Lucy. And to tell the absolute truth, I felt cross. I was cross that Mummy and Muriel had come to see me, and everything had gone horribly wrong. I was cross that my life in Stranhaven, which seemed to be getting easier for me to live with, was now suddenly very complicated. I was cross, because I was sure that Nicol and Jessie would be very upset when they found out about what had happened today. That feeling of crossness seemed to come from nowhere. It terrified me, because I knew that I was disappointed. I was disappointed, because the moment I had longed for, ever since I had been taken away from school in the shiny green car; the moment of being reunited with Mummy and Muriel, it was nothing like I had imagined. I longed for them to sit on a big sofa with me and tell me that they were taking me home.

I felt liquid in my mouth, and the taste of lunch and the biscuit and cup of tea mixed in with it, and suddenly it all rushed up from my tummy.

How did Mummy know? She stood up and said, 'It's all right Pippa,' and I felt her hold me under the arms and push me towards the table, where I was sick all over the tablecloth. She wiped my mouth with a napkin and suddenly all my crossness and disappointment disappeared. I think it had been swept up in my body and washed away with the sick, never to return.

I said, 'Oh Mummy. I missed you so much. I've suffered terribly and tried to hide it. I've tried to be a good girl, really I have. And this is all my fault. I'm sorry about that. But I feel so much better now. Thank you for coming to see me.'

Mummy said, 'Of course you are a good girl. Everyone thinks that.' She sounded very shocked. 'And nothing is your fault. You mustn't think that; you absolutely mustn't think that!'

She was about to say something else, but we heard the sound of a siren. The ambulance was coming.

Mummy said, very quickly, 'Listen Pippa, I know you must feel terribly disappointed that our visit is going all wrong. I expect that you feel quite cross with us too, and upset about Muriel. I'm upset too, and I'm trying to be very brave. But I'm going to come back and see you as soon as Muriel is comfortable in hospital, and I'm going to ask the doctors... no, I'm going to *tell* the doctors, that you absolutely must come and visit her. Then you can both have a proper chat. And I'm going to be with you tonight, and you can tell me all about what you've been doing, and I want to have a proper look at all your lovely paintings. And I'm sure you want to be with Nicol and Jessie. And I hear they have some lovely cousins who are twins. You are so lucky to have so many nice friends.'

I said, 'How did you know, Mummy. How did you know what I was feeling?'

She smiled. 'You're Mummy's girl. You are just like me, in so many ways.'

Then there was a lot of noise outside the door, and two men came in, dressed in navy blue uniforms and with coats on that were soaking wet with rain. The men's boots left wet patches on the carpet, and that's when I realised that my own shoes were wet and filthy from running through the wet grass. Mummy went over to talk to the men, while Auntie and Rhona stayed with me, and we watched the men bring in a stretcher and put Muriel on it. Just as they were carrying Muriel out of the door, I ran over to her. One of the men said, 'Out of the way please, young lady.'

Muriel said, very faintly, 'Is that Pippa? Tell her I'll see her tonight.'

Then Mummy kissed me, and went with the men and Muriel out of the huge front door. Rhona put her hand on my shoulder and Auntie held my hand. The rain was still pouring down, and Mummy stood with an umbrella over Muriel, to stop her from getting wet. We watched the men put Muriel into the back of the ambulance, and Mummy climbed in after her and blew me a kiss.

Mrs Mackie came out of the room, carrying the dirty tablecloth. I said, 'I'm very sorry for being sick on your table.'

She smiled and said, 'Never you mind. I hope you feel better now, and that your auntie soon gets well. Come and see us again when you can. It's awful lonely here sometimes, and it would be lovely to have some children playing in the garden.'

Mr Griffin took us back home in his car

I had known it all along

As I walked through Auntie's front door, Jessie and Nicol had just come in from school. Auntie had told them all about Rhona and Mummy being here, and Muriel being ill. Jessie threw her arms around me and cried. She said that she was terribly upset to find out that Muriel had gone to hospital. Nicol didn't say anything, but looked in my eyes and looked away. I was sure that he was thinking, 'I'm a big boy now, and I'm trying very hard not to show I am upset.' I wanted him to throw his arms around me and kiss me, but instead he went into the kitchen, to be on his own.

Auntie went over to Uncle Jimmy's house, to explain what was going on, and to ask Uncle Jimmy to give her a lift to the hospital. Maggie had made us all my favourite tea of fish fingers, mashed potatoes and peas, but I didn't feel hungry. Nicol said that if I didn't eat my fish fingers, then he would be forced to have them. That was such a silly thing to say, but it made me smile, and suddenly I felt so much better.

Jessie was very excited that Mummy was going to sleep in our house. She promised to be on her best behaviour, and to try to go up to bed as soon as Auntie told her to. Nicol laughed at that, because there was usually a major struggle to get Jessie ready for bed.

Then I realised just how much my life had changed in such a short time. I loved living in a house with other children, and having friends who lived nearby. But then I told myself that really I was just having a holiday here in Stranhaven. I began to feel cross with myself for forgetting that Mummy and Muriel were my real family. Then I became frightened, because perhaps what was really happening to Muriel was that she was going to die. Her skin did look as pale as Jesus when he was dead on The Cross. All these ideas were flashing through my mind while Jessie was asking me if I wanted to listen to a new tune she had made up.

Nicol asked me what I was thinking about. Instead of saying,' Oh, nothing much', which is what you are supposed to say if your boyfriend asks you that when other people are listening, I told him. I told him I was very confused. I wanted to go home with Mummy, but I liked being in Stranhaven as well.

Maggie said it was quite normal to have feelings like that, in a very difficult situation that I was going through in my life. She said that she knew exactly how I felt.

Jessie said, 'Then you are like me. My feelings are always all over the place.' This made me laugh, but then I burst into tears.

Maggie put me on her knee. Nicol started to tell Jessie off for upsetting me, and she started to get angry with him. Maggie told them both to calm down, and Jessie said she was sorry, but Nicol still looked cross. I supposed that all our feelings were all over the place. Then I reminded myself that sometimes it was nice to be a girl who didn't have any brothers and sisters.

Maggie jiggled me on her knee and said, 'Are you sure you wouldn't like to change your mind about how lovely it is to live in a house with other children?'

That really was another surprise. I said, 'You are just like Mummy and Muriel. They know exactly what I'm thinking.'

Jessie said, 'Maggie is like Aileen. She's a mind reader.'

Maggie said, 'Well, not really. Perhaps it's about being tuned into your own feelings and other people's.'

Jessie said, 'Did Rhona tell you that?' Maggie hesitated. Jessie said, 'I thought so. She's always talking about feelings.' Then Jessie asked Maggie, 'Are you and Rhona in love with each other?' There was a silence. Maggie's face and her neck and the top part of her chest were bright red. She said, 'Yes, I love Rhona, and I'm pleased that she loves me. We are just like sisters… twins really. There's nothing wrong with that. In fact, I'm very proud of it. I'm lucky to know Rhona. So yes, I am in love with her!'

Nicol said, 'I think that's very nice.'

Jessie said, 'So do I. I was only being friendly. So are your feelings all over the place as well?'

Maggie said, 'Yes they are. Everyone's are.'

I jumped off Maggie's lap and sat next to Nicol. He looked very pleased. I nudged Jessie and nodded towards Maggie. Maggie opened her arms and said, 'Come here Jessie!' Jessie jumped on her lap and Maggie let out a big *oomph!* because Jessie had knocked all the wind out of her. Nicol held my hand under the table, and I looked at him and he was crying. Maggie and Jessie were crying too. I knew that they were crying about their mum.

I ate my fish fingers. They were cold, but still crunchy and delicious; as only *Birds Eye* fish fingers can be.

I offered one to Nicol, but he laughed through his tears and shook his head.

Perhaps I was a bit of a mind reader too. I had known all along about Maggie and Rhona being in love. They were more than sisters. They were like Mummy and Muriel. It was as plain as the nose on your face.

And looking at Jessie sitting on Maggie's knee was like looking in the mirror; a little pickle being loved, and that love healing all her wounds. But the love that passed between them was healing Maggie's wounds too. I felt a powerful urge to paint. It would be something with orange and lilac, and a kind of pink that would be intense and creamy at the same time. But then the feeling disappeared, because the phone rang. Jessie jumped up and answered it, and told me very seriously that it was Mummy ringing from the hospital, and she had an important message for me. I was filled with delight and then dread; delight because I could talk to my Mummy, and dread because she might have some terrible news.

But it was good news. She told me that Mr Griffin was on his way to collect me in his car, because it would soon be Visiting Time at the hospital, and we were allowed one hour to talk to Muriel. When I explained that to Maggie, she said that she would take Nicol and Jessie up to Rhona's house, and as a special treat they could bring their new instruments. Jessie jumped up and down and asked if she could play Rhona her new tune. Maggie said she thought that would be a lovely idea.

Nicol didn't say anything, so I whispered, 'Don't you want to go?'

He whispered back, 'Of course I do but…'Maggie was listening. She said, 'But really you'd like to go with Pippa to the hospital?'

Nicol smiled. 'How did you know?'

'I'm a mind reader! Actually I'm your big sister, so I can read you like a book.'

Nicol smiled. 'So can I go?'

'You had better ask Pippa. It's her visit, and her time with her mummy and Muriel. Maybe she would rather spend that precious time with them on her own. She can always tell you about it later.'

I looked at Nicol's face. He wouldn't look at me. I said, 'I would love Nicol to come.' Tats was true, and not true, both at the same time. I wanted to be with him, but I wasn't sure what Mummy, Muriel and Auntie might think. He looked very pleased, and we rushed to put on our coats. Jessie had already run to get her accordion ready. Maggie grabbed Nicol's hand and said, 'Come here Nicol. Have you got a kiss for your big sister?'

He said, 'Don't be silly.'

Maggie said, 'I mean it,' and she pulled him towards her and held him very tight. She said, 'You will never be too big for me to kiss you. Do you understand? Even if you grow up to be six feet tall, I will still be your big sister, and I will expect you to kiss me.'

Her voice sounded playful, but her face looked serious. Nicol smiled and let her kiss him on the cheek. She said, 'Now you must kiss me.' He did.

Then we heard Mr Griffin honk his horn, and we ran outside to see him. When Mr Griffin saw Nicol, he frowned and said, 'I've got orders to collect only one passenger.'

I said, 'Please Mr Griffin, I'd really like Nicol to come. If it's not all right, then perhaps you might you be able to bring him straight back?'

Mr Griffin smiled, but said, 'It won't be possible. When you get to the hospital, then you can ask your mother about him coming next time, but right now, orders are orders.'

Nicol frowned, and I wondered if he was going to argue with Mr Griffin. But instead he said, 'It's OK. I'll go up to Rhona's cottage. You can tell me all about it when you come back.' Before I could say anything, he got out of the car and waved goodbye.

Mr Griffin said, 'Sorry about that, Pippa, but it's a very difficult time for everyone, and we have to keep things as simple as possible.' He was a cheerful man, and seemed quite friendly, but he had killed people in The War, and the nasty boys were absolutely terrified of him.

Muriel's present

Muriel was sitting in bed, and told us that she was feeling much better. I didn't really believe her, because she looked more yellow. She was wearing a nightie that she used to wear at home, and seeing it made my legs feel wobbly. Muriel told me to climb up onto her bed. She held me tight and kissed me, and told me to get comfortable, because she wanted to talk to me.

She said, 'I've been thinking of this moment for a long time. You know, what I would say to you when I saw you again. If I'm honest with you Pippa, sometimes, in my darkest moments, I have wondered if I would ever see you again. And here we are, and I've forgotten what I wanted to say! Isn't that silly of me?'

I said, 'I talk to you all the time in my head, and sometimes out loud. I hope you might hear me, or feel me thinking about you.'

Muriel smiled and said, 'And Mummy and I do exactly the same thing, don't we, Ruth?'

I feel a bit ashamed when I think about it now, but I had almost completely forgotten that Mummy was there. I looked at her and she was smiling. Then I felt sure that she didn't mind at all. She knew that my love for Muriel was precious, and I knew that thought made her feel very happy.

Muriel said, 'I remember now. I've got something for you. But before I give it to you, I want to tell you all about it, and why it's so important for me. You see, when I was a little girl and too young to go to school, all I ever wanted was to have a satchel. All the big girls had them. There was one girl in particular who I liked to look at. Her name was Maud. I would look at her with envy as she walked past our house on her way to school, with her satchel strap proudly placed over one shoulder and across her chest and her satchel swinging on her hip. In her satchel she had her pen and pencil, a bottle of ink, a jotter, her homework, and her sandwiches. I loved to look at Maud, and to me her satchel was a symbol of growing up and learning.

'I desperately wanted a satchel. But when I went to school, my grandmother gave me a cloth bag to put my things in. I was very disappointed, but didn't dare say so. My grandma was a bit fierce and, to tell the truth, I was never sure if she liked me or not. Well, after a year, my cloth bag was practically worn out and full of holes, so Grandma said I could use my Grandpa's old gas mask bag instead. And all through my infant and junior school days, I never did have a satchel. But a few days before I went to boarding school, aged eleven, my grandpa asked me if he could buy me something special: a little treat to remember him by. I whispered in his ear, "A satchel please. A light brown leather satchel, for me to put my school things in."

Grandpa was a bit deaf and shouted, "A sandwich? All you want is a sandwich?" So I had to tell him, loudly, about the satchel.

Grandma said, "Whatever do you want one of those for? In your new posh school, it will only be a hop skip and a jump from where you sleep to where you do your lessons. You'll have no need for a fancy school bag! Tell your grandpa that you'd like a nice pen instead, or a hairbrush."

Grandpa took no notice of her, and winked at me and tapped the side of his nose with his forefinger, so I didn't quite know what to think.

'Well, imagine my surprise, and sheer joy when, just before I went to the station, to catch the train to go to boarding school for the first time, Grandpa gave me what I had asked for. And inside was a lovely fountain pen, and a hairbrush! And Grandma had been right; none of the other girls had a satchel like mine, because you kept all your belongings in your bedside cabinet or in your desk, so really you didn't need a bag. But I carried my satchel everywhere, and in it I kept a notebook and a pen and a hairbrush, and when I was older I kept all sorts of useful things in there, like hairgrips and my purse.' She looked at me and winked. 'And the sorts of things that older girls use, because they never quite know when they might need them.'

Muriel gave me a squeeze. 'So why am I telling you this, Pippa? Why is it such an important thing for me to tell you?' She didn't give me a chance to answer. 'You see, my little Pipsqueak, in that moment I knew that my Grandpa really loved me. He never said so. And he never kissed me, or said how much he would miss me while I was away in my boarding school. But when he gave me that satchel, which must have cost him a lot of money, I knew that he really did love me. So every time I put my satchel over my shoulder, or unscrewed the lid of my pen, or brushed my hair, I remembered that I had been loved. And that knowledge, that lovely feeling that I had been loved, kept me going all the way through school. And sometimes when I felt sad, or lonely, or bored, or when I was ill, or when my time of the month came and I felt prickly and irritable, I would open up my satchel and brush my hair, and then I always felt better.'

She nodded to Mummy, who picked up a big Pearson's paper bag from behind her chair, and passed it to Muriel. Muriel said to me, 'This is for you Pippa. I think about you all the time, and I hope this will help you think of me and Mummy, and remember how much we…' She began to cry.

I had been lying by Muriel's side, with my head against her chest. Muriel's heart was beating very fast, as if she had been running. Mummy helped me get off the bed, so that I could stand up and open my present. I looked at Muriel. Her hair wasn't wet and straggly anymore. It had been washed and brushed. But it didn't look shiny and lovely, like I used to remember it. Her hair used to be just like Lucy's; something soft and bouncy and thick. While Lucy's hair was always tidy, Muriel's always seemed a bit uncontrollable and had a life of its own. I had loved to touch and smell her hair, and I thought about it a lot, so that the colour of it appeared in nearly all my paintings. But now there was no shine and life in Muriel's hair at all. It was like something that just grew out of her head. I knew that this as because she was very ill.

She saw me looking at her, and said, 'You're so full of life, and healthy and strong. I'm so glad. I'm so full of joy, because you are being so well looked after and loved. I'm afraid that I've gone in the opposite direction recently. But I will get better. I'm going to make myself get better.' She squeezed Mummy's hand, 'Aren't I, Ruth?'

I didn't dare look at Mummy's face. She said, 'Of course you are. You just need to rest, that's all.'

Muriel said to me, 'Come on Pippa! Open your present. Don't keep everyone in suspense!'

Inside the bag was something large, wrapped up in beautiful wrapping paper with drawings of Scottish wild flowers on it. Inside was a beautiful light-brown leather satchel. Muriel said, 'The manager asked me if I wanted to put it on the Dunbar account, but I told him that I wanted to pay for it with my own money.' I could feel myself starting to cry, but stopped myself. She said, 'Open it. There are other things inside. Can you guess what they are?'

I whispered in her ear. She said, 'That's right, you clever sausage.'

There was a hairbrush, and a notebook and the very smart gold fountain pen that the lawyer lady had given me, on that day when she had arrived at our house as our enemy, but left as our friend. I didn't want to put my hand in again, in case there was a packet of things that I might need for my time of the month. Muriel laughed, and I went red, because she must have known what I was thinking. She said, 'There are three more things, and none of them are what you are imagining!'

I looked at Mummy. She thought that was very funny. It was the first time I had really seen her smile properly since she had been to see me. I saw her teeth, and felt the space below my tummy fill up with love for her. But I didn't want to leave Muriel. I pushed myself even further back into her, and I knew I was squashing her, but I didn't care. Muriel was used to me squashing her. I used to do it at the weekends, first thing in the morning, when I would run into their bedroom and jump on the bed, and get under the covers with her. Then I would push against her and feel her breasts on my back. Today I couldn't feel any breasts at all.

I put my hand into the satchel again and felt some tissue paper with something soft inside. It was Muriel's scarf. She said, 'That's a special present. You can wear it in the winter, with your lovely coat and hat.' I couldn't stop myself from smelling it, and breathing in that delicious smell of sweat and perfume mixed together. She hadn't washed it, on purpose. I knew exactly what I was going to do with that. It was going to stay under my pillow at boarding school. I put my hand in again and there was a tennis ball. Muriel said, 'It's always nice to have a ball to play with, don't you think?'

The last present was a small book. It had an old burgundy leather cover, which was beginning to fade. Inside the front cover was a piece of paper glued into place. It had a shield on it that said *Walmsley School for Girls,* with some Latin written underneath it. And underneath someone had written, in dark blue ink that was also fading, *To Muriel Standish: First Prize*

*in Seniors Essay Writing, for her outstanding essay 'Tennyson,
Browning and the Growth of Love'.'*

The book was called *In Memorium* and was by Alfred, Lord
Tennyson. I knew all about him, because he was Muriel's
favourite poet. Muriel had once taken Mummy and me to
Tennyson Down on the Isle of Wight. We sat on top of the hill,
under the memorial cross, and had a delicious picnic of cheese
and tomato sandwiches, where the white bread had gone all
soft with the tomato juice, and we drank dandelion and
burdock that Mummy had bought in a shop in Ryde. And
Muriel quoted Tennyson to Mummy while I picked daisies, to
make daisy chains to put in her and Mummy's hair, and I saw a
rabbit and I got a bit over-excited.

I asked her, 'Do you remember when we were in the
changing room in the swimming pool, and you and Mummy
were drying each other, and the little boy was crying and
Mummy picked him up, and Mummy's towel fell down? And
the baby's mummy said that the world needed more people to
be tender with each other? And she said that you and Mummy
were just like her and her friend at boarding school?'

'Yes, I remember. How could I ever forget it?'

'Well, you know I painted a picture of that?'

'Oh yes, I love that picture.'

'Well that was one of the pictures that caused all the problems.
If Daddy hadn't seen it, then perhaps he wouldn't have been so
angry, and perhaps he wouldn't have gone to The Court. I think
about that a lot. I think it was all my fault.'

'And I think it was my fault, and Mummy thinks it's her fault
too. But it's nobody's fault. The truth is, Pippa, that The Law
didn't allow people to love each other in the way that Mummy
and I do. Well now it does, but it doesn't allow ladies like
Mummy and me to look after children. It's cruel. But that's The
Law.'

As Muriel was talking, I pushed even further backwards
into her. She had her arm tight around me and I could feel her
bony chest against my back. She massaged the top of my head

with her fingers, in her usual way that I loved so much. As she did that, I felt both of us melting. My back and her chest became very soft, and soon we were one person, with one heart beating fast, and one pair of lungs, breathing in and out, and one person looking out at Mummy and Auntie.

I was about to say something, but Muriel said that she wanted me to listen very carefully, because she had something very important to tell me. She took a deep breath. 'Until I met you and Mummy, I had only ever been in love with one other person. Of course, I must have loved my parents when they were alive, but I don't remember that. But the love I have for you and Mummy: well it's so strong. I don't think that anything or anybody could change how I feel for you both. I'm a very lucky person.

'You see, when I was at school, none of the girls stayed very long. They were there because their fathers had been killed or badly wounded in The War, and their families had fallen on hard times. But as soon as their mothers remarried, or their fathers were able to work again, they took their daughters away from boarding school, and brought them back into the bosom of their families. But I knew that I would be there for a long time. I wasn't going back to stay in the bosom of my family, because my family didn't have a bosom, if you see what I mean.' I wasn't sure about she was talking about, but Muriel couldn't see my confused face, so carried on. 'So I thought to myself ,"Muriel Standish, don't you ever make a close friend, because sooner or later they will leave you." So that's what I did. But I regret that now. I didn't really know what love was. The girls used to call me *Muriel Stand-offish*, because I was so aloof. I used to watch the other girls in their little groups of friends. Some of these friendships would become very intense, and turned into passionate love affairs, as they can in boarding schools. But then suddenly something would happen and then the two girls would split up and become deadly enemies. Then everyone would get very excited and spend all their time gossiping about what might have happened, and take sides with one girl or the other. Then for a

416

while it would seem like the whole of your dormitory or your form was in a state of civil war. I thought to myself, "If that's what love is, then I really don't want to know."

'I was quite lonely, but then one day a new girl arrived and there was something about her that I found hugely attractive. She was funny and quietly rebellious, and in many ways just like me. Her name was Alice Fisher. So I broke my rule. I couldn't resist love any longer. We spent all our time together, and suddenly I began to enjoy being at school. But then she left, just like all the others. I was very upset, which made me more determined than ever never to fall in love again.'

Muriel stopped. I could tell from her breathing and the way her heart was beating that she was getting ready to say something else, something very important. I was listening so hard, I thought that my ears might burst.

'For as long as I can remember, I have dreamed about water. Often I would dream about drowning, and wake up in an awful panic. Or I dreamed I had a brother and sister who had fallen into a huge dark lake, and I dived in to try and save them, but the water was pitch black, and I couldn't see them anywhere. Or I would dream about diving into a beautiful pool of clear water, only to discover that there was a whirlpool that dragged me down.'

She closed her eyes. Everyone was looking at her. I felt the space above my Lovely Place fill with sadness and longing for Muriel. I knew that she was with me now, but she had been on her own, suffering, and soon she would be without me, and her pain would begin all over again. But she didn't stop talking. 'It's not surprising that I dreamt about swimming, because I was obsessed with it. Our school was by the sea, and there was an open-air swimming baths in the town, so I would swim as often as I could. Diving was my passion. I didn't care how cold it was. And Alice would come with me, because she loved swimming as much as I did.

'There was a teacher who liked me. She was an English teacher and she loved poetry. I suppose she saw something in me, because she encouraged me to write. Not stories, but about things I thought, and about what I saw, and about things that had happened to me in my life. She said that I was a very lonely girl. She told me that my problem was that most of the other girls came from middle-class families, whereas I was from a family that was essentially working class. She said that this made me like a fish out of water. It would be very difficult for me to fit in with the other girls, because our family backgrounds were very different. It was strange to feel so lonely, when I was surrounded by so many other people all the time. But Alice wasn't working class. She was quite posh, but our love of swimming brought us together. It was something that we could understand and talk about. And she loved literature and poetry as much as I did. I used to write for her; short stories about two girls and their families. She liked them very much. And I wrote about swimming with her. I suppose they were love letters, in disguise. So when Alice left and I was terribly, terribly upset, the English teacher gave me lots of love poems to read. She said that I should especially read Shakespeare's Sonnets and *In Memoriam* by Lord Tennyson. I had the distinct impression that my teacher had been in love, but then lost it. One day I plucked up the courage to ask her about her own love. She told me that she had been engaged to be married, but her fiancé had been a soldier and was killed in The War.

'She told me that her favourite lines of poetry were by Tennyson; who wrote *In Memorium* after his very close friend had died. They were

I hold it true, whate'er befall;
I feel it when I sorrow most;
'Tis better to have loved and lost
Than never to have loved at all.

'So when I met Alice, I didn't feel lonely anymore, and I realised that I had been waiting to meet someone who was just like me, who shared my passions, and who was just as interested in me as I was in her. And it was just the same in London. It's a huge place, full of people, but you have to struggle to get to know anybody there. I kept myself to myself, but was quite lonely and bored with my life. And then I met you and Mummy, and everything changed. I knew in an instant that Mummy was my new Alice.

And then she grabbed me, and pulled me into the taxi, and took me to meet her psychiatrist. But it seemed like such a normal thing to do! But what surprised me so much was that I had not fallen for a man, as I had expected, but for a woman. You aren't supposed to do that. It wasn't supposed to be in my life story.

'And there was this beautiful child, so calm and patient and gifted and loving. Of course, I fell in love with her too. And the thought of living with these two people; well it took my breath away.' I heard, from quite far away, the sound of Mummy coughing, and blowing her nose. Muriel asked me, 'Do you remember Albie, Naomi and Saul's daddy? He gave us lots of advice about the court case. Once, he asked me what I would say in Court, if I was ever asked to explain myself; to explain why I chose to live the way I live. I told him what I've just told you. He said that he understood how I felt, but that the Judge wouldn't be impressed. In the end, I wasn't invited to go to the Court. I had to wait outside to discover what had happened. It was too awful for words.'

I heard myself say, 'Mummy, please can you shut the curtains? There is a very strong light and it's hurting my eyes.' I saw her get up, and as she pulled the curtains together there was a loud fluttering sound next to my ear. I couldn't see Ursula, but I knew that she was there. Ursula said, 'I know that you want to see me, but I'm in a bit of a hurry, so tell me quickly what it is that you want me to do.'

I told her that I wanted Muriel to have a Guardian Angel, to protect her. Ursula said, 'I knew that already, and have got someone who will be just right for the job. Open your eyes and you will see him.'

I said, 'Him? But I think Muriel will want a lady Angel. She's not so keen on men.'

Ursula laughed, 'Well, he is just the right person. He's very experienced. He's already been a Guardian Angel for nine people and they have all been delighted with him.'

'So where are all the people now? Does he look after lots of people at the same time?'

'Oh no. They have all gone to Heaven. So, you can see that he has been very successful already!'

'So when someone dies, their Guardian Angel gets a job looking after someone else?'

'That's right, and Jesus was very definite that he wanted Barry to do just one more job before he retires.'

'So you spoke to Jesus?'

'Not quite. Jesus was sitting on a big stone, just like in the picture in your *Children's Illustrated Bible*. There was a great big crowd of us, waiting to ask him questions. I knew you were in a hurry and tried to push in, But Doubting Thomas saw me and said I would have to wait my turn. I explained what the problem was and that it was urgent. Doubting Thomas wasn't sure that Jesus would speak to him, but he did. Jesus said that Barry was just the person for the job.'

I tried to open my eyes, but my eyelids kept fluttering and I couldn't see properly, so I closed them again. Ursula kissed me on the cheek and told me I didn't have to worry about Muriel anymore, because, just like me, she had an angel to protect her, and who would make sure that she went to Heaven one day. And of course, I would see Muriel there, and I would never have to worry about her anymore.

I just had to ask one more thing. 'What about Mummy? Can she have an Angel too? Does it matter that she's Jewish?'

Ursula laughed. 'I'll need to ask Jesus, and that means I'll have to join the back of the queue again, so I'll let you know when I see you next.'

'When will that be?'

'When you're at Boarding School, of course. They all have Guardian Angels there, though I wonder if anyone else can see theirs.'

I heard someone say, 'She's exhausted. Let's leave her and let her sleep.'

Mummy said, 'Come on Sleepy Head. Say goodbye to Muriel, because it's time for you to go home'

'Home? With you?'

'I'm afraid not to our home, but to your Scottish home.'

I kissed Muriel and whispered in her ear, 'Thank you for my lovely presents'. She smiled, and her eyelids fluttered. I supposed that she was dreaming, or perhaps having her first chat with Barry McAngel.

When we were outside the hospital, Mummy asked me if we could walk home together. It had stopped raining, but it was cold, and a strong wind was blowing. Mummy held my hand, and Auntie and Mummy walked arm in arm together. We walked past the playground, and I showed Mummy the slide and the swings and the roundabout and the rocking horse, and the Witch's Hat that we especially loved to play on. Mummy said that I was a lucky girl, to have everything I wanted so close to my house.

It was nearly dark when we got home. Maggie, Rhona and Nicol were sitting by the fire with Jessie, and Rhona was reading Pippi Longstocking, which Jessie and I loved.

Rhona read to the end of the chapter, then asked about Muriel.

Jessie asked Mummy, 'Is Muriel going to die?'

Maggie looked shocked. She hissed, 'Jessie! How could you?'

Jessie said, 'I'm just asking the question. I'm sure everyone else wants to know.'

Maggie said, 'But Pippa's here! Of course Muriel's not going to die.'

Jessie said to me, 'I'm sorry, Pippi. I didn't mean it.'

That made me smile. I liked her thinking I was like Pippi Longstocking. I said, 'It's all right.'

I meant it. I had been asking myself the same question all the time that I had been with Muriel.

In the night

Jessie went up to bed without a fuss, and Maggie and Rhona got ready to go to Rhona's cottage. They kissed Mummy goodbye and said how lovely and inspiring it had been to meet her and Muriel, and they were both sure that Muriel would get better very soon. Mummy said, 'I hope so.' Then she looked at me and said, 'What am I saying? Of course she will.'

Maggie had tidied her room and put her lava lamp on, so her room looked extra-specially cosy. Mummy got me undressed, to get me ready for bed. I was old enough to do that myself, but I let her. I knew that she wanted to look me all over. Mummy said that I had grown a lot, and poked me in the tummy and said, 'Especially there.' I loved people doing that. She said she would lie with me until I was asleep, then she would go downstairs and talk to Auntie for a while, and then come back and sleep with me.

She got undressed. She said, 'Goodness, Scotland is such a cold place!' I could tell that she was cold, before she even said that. She saw me looking at her and smiled. She put on her nightie, then pulled the bed covers back and got quickly into bed. She opened her arms towards me and I went to her. I thought my heart was going to burst with joy.

I lay on my side and Mummy cuddled me from behind. She put her nose into my hair and took a deep breath. She said, 'That's always been one of my favourite smells, right from when you were tiny.'

The lava lamp was casting a moving red glow everywhere. I asked her, 'Mummy, what's happened to Muriel's breasts? Have they disappeared? And is she now…?'

'Is she now like me? As flat as a pancake?' Mummy laughed, and then she sighed. 'That happens sometimes, when ladies get very thin. Their breasts get very small and a bit saggy. But they get their shape back as soon as the lady gets better, and starts eating well again.'

'Is Muriel going to die?' That just came out.

'No. She's not going to die. She is not at all well, but once she has her operation she will bounce back and be her usual self again. Including having lovely breasts.'

'Then why did she say all those things to me in the hospital? It was like she was never going to see me again.'

'Muriel is frightened. When someone becomes very ill, their whole world feels like it has been turned upside down, and you have to allow other people to look after you. Muriel's not used to that. She's used to caring for everybody else, and helping them to get better. And now it's her turn to be looked after, and she really doesn't like it. Plus, she has been terribly upset about being apart from you.'

'But Daddy could change all that. He could make The Judge allow me to live with you both, and to go to a school near where we live. Why won't he do that?'

Mummy sighed again. She replied very slowly, so I knew that she was choosing her words very carefully. 'Daddy has changed a lot. He feels terribly guilty. But there is something that is very important to him. It's what he calls his moral responsibility as a parent, and as a Roman Catholic.'

I thought about that, but couldn't quite understand what Mummy meant. I said, 'I won't be sad at boarding school. I'm going to make lots of friends, and have adventures. I know that's what you and Muriel want me to do. So if I do that, then you will both feel happy, and then you won't need to worry about me.'

Mummy made a little laughing sound. 'A mother never stops worrying about her children. I suppose it's part of her job.'

'You are doing a very good job.'

'I've tried my best.'

We were quiet for a while. Mummy rubbed her fingers through my hair, so my scalp felt lovely and tingly. I supposed that she was thinking about what we had just said, and about my future. She said, 'When you do go to school, listen very carefully to what Sister Anne tells you. She knows lots of things. She is a very wise lady, even if she is a nun. Muriel told me to tell you that.'

'I will Mummy, I promise.'

'Good girl.'

Mummy's breath was warm on my neck. I lay quietly and listened to what she was saying. She said that she would love Maggie to give me a special haircut before I went to school. She said, 'Muriel and I try to go swimming as often as possible, in Guildford, and then we go to the Wimpy. Of course, we think of you all the time we are there. We go to church every Sunday, and help Chris as much as we can. He has been a great help. He was very upset about what Daddy's barrister said about him in The Court, and he spoke about it in Church. He reminded us that Jesus said, "Let he who is without sin throw the first stone."

A man got up and said, "I'm not going to throw any stones, but I'm going to find a church where the Word of God is preached properly, and not distorted out of all recognition." We see that man in the town sometimes, but he looks the other way and pretends that he hasn't seen us. This makes Muriel laugh, but I know that deep down she feels very hurt. And we see Dorothy, and Lucy's mum and dad, and of course we see Lucy and Roger. The two families spend a lot of time with us. Lucy is very popular at school now, and is getting some special help in her lessons, which she likes very much.'

Then she told me that they had been back to Rayners Park, and went to visit the swimming pool and our favourite café. The café owner remembered them and asked, 'Do you want to have your egg and chips and cup of tea before you've both cried your eyes out, or afterwards?'

They all laughed and neither of them cried once.

Then she asked me about painting. I said, 'Painting is my life.'

She said, 'You have been blessed with a great gift. It's not always easy to be like that.'

Then she asked me if Ursula still came to see me. I said, 'Well I thought that she had stopped coming, but she spoke to me in the hospital, while I was sitting next to Muriel.'

Mummy said, 'I thought so. What did she say?' I told her about Muriel's Guardian Angel and that his name was Barry McAngel. Mummy said, 'Muriel will like that! Can I tell her?'

'Yes please, but I'm sure that she already knows.'

In the morning

I woke up very early and Mummy was still fast asleep beside me. I was bursting to do a wee, but didn't want to leave her, or wake her. In the end, I couldn't hold it any longer, so went to the toilet as quietly as I could. I don't know why, but after that I decided to go downstairs. I looked out of the kitchen window and saw Uncle Tom in the garden, smoking his pipe. Again, I don't know why, but I decided to go and talk to him. He said, 'Hello Pippa. I was just thinking about you.'

I said, 'Mummy's still asleep. I should go back upstairs and be with her.'

He puffed on his pipe and tried to blow a smoke ring, but the wind just took it away before it could form properly. He scratched his beard and said, 'We are very lucky to have you here with us. And it has been so… so… I can't think of the word… so lovely… yes, lovely to have your mother and Muriel here. I'm sure it will be very hard for you to say goodbye to them.'

I said, 'I don't know.' That was true. I supposed I would cry when it was time to say goodbye, but I wouldn't scream and shout, or beg them to take me with them. After all, I had my lovely satchel, and my coat and scarf, and my hat, and my tennis ball, and my book of poetry. They would be enough to keep me strong, and stop me from breaking down in front of everybody.

Uncle Tom smiled. He knocked his pipe against the leg of the table, to get rid of the ash. He put his pipe in his jacket pocket and said, 'Come and help me make your mummy a lovely Scottish breakfast.'

That seemed like a very nice thing to do, even though I was still wearing my pyjamas and dressing gown.

Uncle Tom talked to me while we prepared the porridge. 'As I make the porridge, I always think of my children. I soak the oats in milk overnight, because that's how my children like it. But I always make too much, so there's always enough left over for one more helping. I started doing that after my wife died. At first I didn't know why I always did that, but really it's obvious, don't you think?'

'Was it because you were thinking of her too?'

He smiled. 'That's exactly right. Exactly that. Then the children would fight over who would have her share. In the end Maggie and Nicol got tired of arguing about it, and let Jessie have it, which was very thoughtful of them. But she's always too full to finish it, so we give the leftovers to the dog.'

I said, 'Perhaps I should go back upstairs, so that Mummy doesn't wake up alone, and feel awful because I have left her.'

Uncle Tom smiled; but it was a sad smile. 'You could do that, but why not stay with me, and make her a lovely breakfast? So she wakes up with the smell of porridge and drop scones and butter and jam? That would be just as nice as waking up with her lovely daughter. Imagine her pleasure when she comes downstairs and sees that you have done the cooking!'

When he explained it like that, I just had to agree.

While we were cooking, Uncle Tom explained something very important. What he said has stayed with me, and will be inside me forever. 'You see, Pippa, symbols are very important to me; as a writer and in my life. I think that they're especially important for children. I'm not the kind of man who kisses and cuddles his children a lot, and tells them how much Daddy loves them. But I believe that food is love, and I make these breakfasts with love. These breakfasts are a symbol; something that we don't talk about. It just grew out of the love we have for each other, and our need to be together after my wife died. It's not like a made-up symbol that you find on flags, or in churches. It's not like Our Lord's sacred bleeding heart, or a crucifix. Those symbols were carefully thought out and designed by people in The Church, to make people think and feel in a certain way. These cooked breakfasts, that we can share together, are more like the things that I write without thinking. The ideas come from inside me. Then, once I've scribbled them down, I tidy them all up, ready for people to read. But the symbols, the ideas, come first of all, spontaneously from inside me. That's why I sit still for a long time, or go for long walks with my notebook. And I find that smoking my pipe helps it all come out.' I sort of understood what he was saying, but nodded wisely, because I didn't want him to stop talking.

'I've been watching you paint. You're just like me. You don't think too hard about what you paint - if you think about it at all. The inspiration comes from deep inside you. Of course, from time to time I've seen you thinking deeply about the colours you are going to use, but the symbols come as if from nowhere. I imagine that the prolific artists, like Picasso and Chagall; are like you. They wake up in the morning, and there it all is, clearly set out in their mind. And in no time at all it's on the paper, or constructed out of clay or bits and pieces. And if you were to ask them afterwards, 'What does that mean?' They would probably just laugh and throw the question back at you.'

He winked at me. 'Pippa, I have a wee favour to ask you. Thinking of *In Memorium* has given me an idea. I've almost finished a short story about the Lang Stane. It's not really working as I had imagined, so I'm going to try to turn it into a long narrative poem; a poem that tells a story. Or perhaps Rhona and I can work together on a very long song. And I have an idea that you could really help me.'

He didn't say any more, because we both heard someone crying upstairs. It was my mummy. I raced up the stairs. The crying was coming from Maggie's room. I stopped just before the door, because it was half-open. I looked through the gap between the door and its frame. Mummy and Auntie were standing in the middle of the room, still wearing their nighties. They were hugging each other. Mummy said, between her tears, 'But what is it? What exactly is wrong with her? She's so thin! She eats a sandwich and it fills her up for the rest of the day! I'm so frightened! You saw all that blood, and her skin is so yellow. What if she…? The strain of keeping it from Pippa, and trying to act normally, is too much to bear!' She started weeping again.

Auntie said, 'Pippa is a very strong girl. Do you think she doesn't know how ill Muriel is? And I'm sure that she can read you inside out.'

Mummy almost shouted, 'She's even given Muriel a Guardian Angel, called Barry!'

'Don't keep your feelings from her, Ruth. You know how destructive that can be.'

'But I want to protect her.'

'Of course you do. Every mother wants to do that. But pretending that everything is fine; lying to her, will only make her feel ten times worse. And if something awful does happen…'

Then they were quiet.

For a moment I felt a terrible pain in my tummy. Why didn't I stay upstairs in bed with Mummy, so she would have woken up with her baby beside her? Would she have panicked about Muriel then, and started weeping? I thought that Uncle Tom was stupid for telling me to stay downstairs, and I was stupid for listening to him.

I stepped backwards, away from the door. I didn't want to hear anything else; and I didn't want them to see me. I saw that Nicol's door was slightly open, so I tapped gently on it. Nicol opened it and held my hand, so I went in. Jessie was sitting on Nicol's bed. She whispered, 'We didn't hear anything. Honestly we didn't.'

Nicol hissed, 'Don't lie, Jessie. We heard everything.'

I just said, 'Oh.'

Jessie whispered, 'What's a Guardian Angel? Is it like Maggie's lamp? Could you give me one? But don't call it

428

Barry. How about Esmerelda, or Constantia?' That made me laugh. Jessie looked surprised, then pleased.

Auntie put her head round the door. She looked at us, without saying anything. Then she said to me, 'Mummy's all right. She's just having what I call *a wee wobble*. She's woken up with a feeling of panic about Muriel being ill. Anyone would feel the same, if they were in her shoes. She's over it now. Let's all have breakfast and get these youngsters off to school.'

And Mummy *was* better. As soon as she came to the table, I could see that she had got her courage back. I knew that she was strong enough to be in charge.

We all concentrated on eating our delicious breakfast. Uncle Tom stayed in the kitchen and Auntie served us. Every time that Auntie went into the kitchen, I could hear her and Uncle Tom talking in low voices. I had finished my porridge and was just putting jam on my first drop scone, when Mr Griffin came in. He didn't say hello, but went over to Mummy and said something very quietly in her ear. Mummy got up straight away and went with Mr Griffin into the kitchen. We heard the grown-ups talking. Jessie said, 'Is something wrong?' I knew what she was thinking.

Nicol held my hand. He whispered something in my ear. I could tell that he was trying not to cry.

I went red. I said, 'Thank you Nicol.' He had told me that he liked me very much, and that Muriel was not going to die. He went off to school on his own, and Uncle Tom took Jessie.

Mummy and Auntie came back in. Mummy said to me, 'Pippa, we have to go to the hospital. There is some not very good news and some good news. The not good news is that Muriel is feeling worse. The other news is that they are taking her to a big hospital in Aberdeen, and she is going to have her operation there. They are getting her ready to go in the ambulance, and Mr Griffin is going to drive us there. I mean you and me, and Auntie will come with us too.'

Aberdeen

I sat with Mummy in the back of the car, with my yellow cloth bag on my lap. It had Polish Teddy in it, and the photograph of me and Mummy and Muriel, that gave me so much comfort when I was in hospital. Mummy told me that Aberdeen was a city, and that the hospital there was full of very clever doctors. A doctor had seen Muriel very early in the morning, and had decided that she was too ill to travel all the way to London. She needed to be operated on straight away, and at the same time they needed to find out why she was so thin and yellow. I didn't say anything, but a question was forming in my mind. I didn't dare ask Mummy. She said, 'Of course this means that Muriel will stay in hospital in Aberdeen, so we will be near you for some time, won't we Mr Griffin?'

Mr Griffin said, 'I couldn't possibly say at this stage, but that would seem to be a sensible idea. Yes, a very sensible idea. But Mr Macmillan would be the person to speak to about that, and...'

Mummy finished his sentence for him. 'And my husband? I mean Mr Dunbar.'

A lorry was driving slowly in front of us. Mr Griffin overtook it. He didn't say anything else.

I could hardly breathe, because I was so thrilled.

All I can remember about arriving in Aberdeen was that it was very windy. It was still August, but the wind almost blew my hat off.

We weren't allowed to see Muriel straight away, because doctors were talking to her and getting her ready for her operation. Mummy, Auntie, Mr Griffin and I sat in the main reception area, and a nurse came over and told Mummy that she could go upstairs onto the ward. Mummy asked if I could go up with her. The nurse didn't answer straight away, but looked down at me.

There have been only a few times in my life when I have taken an instant dislike to people, and this was one of them. I have looked in my thesaurus for a definition of how that nurse looked at me. I can't choose between *derision, scorn, or*

430

disdain. Maybe using all three words would describe the force of her dislike for me. She said to Mummy, 'In general we try and discourage parents from bringing children onto the wards.'

Mummy looked surprised, 'And why exactly is that?'

The nurse looked at Mummy as if she was a rude child who had just answered her back. 'Why not? I would have thought that was obvious.'

'Well it's not in the least obvious to me.' I could hear a familiar tone in Mummy's voice. Soon she was going to ask to see the manager.

'Children are noisy and cause a nuisance, and tend to disturb the patients and the smooth running of a ward.'

'Really? Is that a rule?'

'Not a regulation, no, but it's what we prefer.'

'We?'

'The staff. Now, do you want to come upstairs or not?'

Mummy stayed sitting down. The nurse looked at her watch. Mummy said, 'It would be in the patient's best interest if she were able to see her niece.'

'Her niece? I think not then. A daughter or granddaughter perhaps, but a niece is hardly a close relative.'

Mummy stood up. She looked directly into the nurse's eyes. The nurse looked away. Mummy said, 'Let's just get this absolutely clear. You are saying that this child is not allowed onto the ward at this moment.'

'Yes. That's what I'm saying.'

'When is Visiting Time?'

'Oh, she won't be allowed at Visiting Time either. Now we are wasting time here, because your sister will be going into theatre shortly.'

Theatre. That word made me imagine that, at that very moment, a doctor was probably sticking his thumb up Muriel's bottom, without her permission. I wanted to run to Muriel and hold her hand. Instead, I passed Mummy my yellow cloth bag. Mummy said, 'Bless you, darling,' and kissed me on the cheek. Then she went with the nurse up a big flight of stairs.

The three of us sat still for a few minutes, not saying anything. I swung my legs, which is what I always used to do when I was happy. I didn't know how to feel. On the one hand, I was upset because Muriel was suffering, but on the other, I was delighted that I would still be able to be with her and Mummy. I had no doubt that Mummy would be successful in arranging for me to see Muriel at Visiting Time.

I sat there, swinging my legs and hoping that Mummy would still be able to stay in Scotland long enough to be able to take me to school. Nothing else seemed to matter. Auntie held my hand and asked me, 'Are you all right, Pippa?' This is what grown-ups ask children, when they want to know what you are thinking about. I stopped being happy, and started thinking about the nasty nurse, and how she was just like cold and wicked Sister Winifred and Sister Eugenie at my new school. And I asked myself who I would talk to if someone was nasty to me. At my primary school, if one of the other children ever said something horrible, or if a teacher was unfair, or unkind, then I could just tell Muriel when she came to collect me, and on the way home she would tell me what to think, or what to do about it. But in my new school I would be all on my own, with no grown-ups to look after me properly, or to tuck me in and kiss me goodnight. And if I fell over, or a wasp stung me, who would kiss it better?

I said, 'Why was that nurse so horrible? Why doesn't she like children?'
Auntie said, 'I was wondering about that as well, and I'm sure Mr Griffin was too.'
Mr Griffin gave a start. I think he was feeling very tired. He said, 'We call that kind of person a *jobsworth*. They are never really in charge, but feel important when they tell you that you can't do something. They often say things like, "It's more than my job's worth to let you do that." There was always someone like that in the army. It was usually someone who had just got promoted, and felt that they had to stick to the rules. I was at Monte Cassino, in Italy. It was a huge fortified monastery on

432

the top of a hill. The Germans were up there, and we couldn't get past them. The Yanks tried dropping bombs on the place, but that just made it worse, because they blew the monastery to bits, and created piles of rubble for the Jerries to hide in.

'Then we tried lighting lots of fires in the valley, to create smoke, so they couldn't see us coming. But that didn't work either, because the smoke just made us cough and our eyes water. So in the end the British and the Poles had to climb up the mountain and try to hide as best we could from the Germans. Me and my pals and an officer were scrambling through the rubble, when all hell was let loose. The Germans had seen us, and their bullets were raining down all around us, like hailstones. The officer was just as terrified as us. He said, "Right men. As soon as this lot has stopped, we will scramble out of here."
Well, a soldier has to obey orders, but that was clearly a very bad order. My pal said, "Excuse me sir, but might there be an alternative solution?"
The officer yelled back at him, "Orders are orders. And our orders are to climb this hill!"
The Germans must have heard him shouting, because just then a bullet hit him and blew his head clean off.'
Auntie said, 'Really Mr Griffin, is that helpful? Young Pippa here needs to think about nice things, and not blood and gore!'
Mr Griffin said, 'Sorry Mrs Pirie, I was just making a point about the need to be flexible in a crisis.'
He winked at me and I couldn't help laughing. I thought about the horrible nurse who had just been rude to Mummy, and the nasty nuns I had met in Rayners Park, and in my new school. They had been horrible to me for no good reason, except that they seemed to detest children. I thought that they should get the sack for that, or perhaps get moved to a job where they didn't have to be near people. But I didn't think that anyone deserved to have their head shot off. The thought of it made me feel hot and then cold, and a little shaky, and a bit sick.
Auntie smiled and said to Mr Griffin, 'Of course, of course. But at the moment nobody knows what's happening, so

let's just take one hour at a time. Then we can make some plans. Right now, all I'm hoping for is that Muriel's operation will be a success.'

Then she wished she hadn't said that. I stood up and faced her. 'What do you mean, Auntie? Of course it's going to be a success! Isn't it? Isn't it the same as taking out your appendix? You just have to lie still afterwards, and hope that nobody makes you laugh, and then after a long rest you feel better again?'

Auntie said, 'Of course, of course.'

But the damage had been done. I sat down again. My mind started to feel very fuzzy, and I began to think about nasty Sister Carmel at school. I was worried about where I was going to have a wash, and what would happen if I went to the toilet and discovered that all the toilet paper had gone? Who would I ask for some more? And what if I had a bad dream, or couldn't get to sleep, or if all my socks were dirty, or if I was bursting to go to the toilet because I hadn't been at playtime, and the nuns wouldn't let me go? And did they even have playtime in my school? And would I know what to do on my first day? And how was I going to stop myself from crying when Mummy said goodbye to me?

Auntie said, 'I'm sorry, Pippa. I didn't mean to upset you. Of course Muriel will be all right.'

I took a few deep breaths and told myself that I didn't feel upset anymore.

Mr Griffin said, 'In the next hour I'd like to find a nice café and have a cup of coffee and a full English breakfast. Don't get me wrong; I love Scotland, but if I see another bowl of porridge or a drop scone in front of me at breakfast time, I'm going to go off pop.'

I imagined lots of bullets raining down all around us like hailstones, and Mr Griffin keeping us all calm with his stories and little jokes and good ideas, and his smart Ford Cortina, and his huge body protecting us. I wanted him to go up and tell that horrible nurse that all children are lovely, as long as you are

434

nice to them. Instead he said; 'I'll just take a wee walk over there, to have a quiet word in that receptionist's ear. Whistle if you want me.' That made Auntie smile.

She took both of my hands in hers and said, 'Come and sit on my knee.'

I was sitting there, sucking my thumb and with Auntie's arms around me, when Mummy came through the door. She sat down next to us, and explained that Muriel was going to have an operation that afternoon, to take out her womb. The doctors still weren't exactly sure why she was so yellow, but they thought perhaps that she was suffering from something called *acute pancreatitis*. Mummy said, 'Poor Muriel is in agony. She has had this terrible pain in her tummy all night. That's why the doctors think that she may have problems with her pancreas or her gallbladder. They may have to take her gallbladder out, but won't know what to do until they… until they…'

Mummy stopped and took a deep breath. She said to me, 'Come here Pippa. Come to Mummy.' I got off Auntie's knee and sat on Mummy's lap. She held me tight. She said, with her voice trembling, 'Pippa, I can't hide it. I'm terribly frightened. Half of me is sure that Muriel will be all right. They have to stop her terrible pain. But the other half of me is so very worried. I can't be brave anymore. I just can't do it!'

I wanted to ask Mummy what a gallbladder and a pancreas were. To me, *your tummy* consisted of your stomach, where your food went, and then there was a curled up tube that was as long as a cricket pitch, and that was where poo was made. And somewhere near that you had a bladder that held your wee. And ladies had an extra thing called a *womb*, that babies grew in. In the butcher's you could buy liver and kidneys, but I supposed that only animals like pigs and sheep and cows had those. I wondered if Muriel had extra bits growing inside her, and these had to be taken out, like my appendix. It hadn't seemed very serious, but suddenly Mummy had frightened me. Somebody had once told me that their grandad had died because he had been waiting for an operation. I imagined him sitting in a chair outside the operating theatre, but the doctors had been having their lunch; and when they got back they found him dead. I had never heard of anyone dying because an operation had gone wrong.

I wanted to ask Mummy if she would be able to come with me on my first day at school. But Mummy was crying, and Auntie put her arm around her, and told Mr Griffin that we had to leave the hospital now, but that Mummy would be allowed to come back in the evening.

Mr Griffin asked Auntie, 'So shall we go home, or would anyone fancy a bite to eat?'

Mummy said, 'Oh Mr Griffin, could you take us to a Wimpy bar, please? And then I'd like to do some shopping with my daughter.'

Mr Griffin smiled.

The Wimpy is my Temple

We found a Wimpy bar, and Mummy and I thoroughly enjoyed our Wimpy burgers. Auntie said that she wasn't hungry, but liked her cup of coffee. Mr Griffin had gone in search of a greasy spoon café, where he could sit in peace and eat his cooked breakfast, then read his paper, and smoke one of his fancy cigarettes. Mummy said that Wimpy bars always reminded her and Muriel of some of the hundreds of happy times that they had spent together, with me. She said that the last thing that Muriel had said to her that morning was that she wanted to buy me a nice present for my birthday. She wanted me to have a kilt, and I should choose the tartan that I liked best. I didn't want to tell Mummy that I already had a kilt, because I would have to tell her that the nasty lady at The Lodge had bought it for me. I had even forgotten her name.

Strangely, I loved that kilt, and wore it as often as I could. I liked to look at myself in the mirror, and the combination of colours excited me. Wearing it didn't fill me with horrible memories, and anyway, The Lodge seemed so far away, as if it was in another life, or had happened to someone else.

Mummy said, 'Are you in a dream, my love?'

I told her that I was, and that nothing seemed quite real anymore. Mummy said, 'I feel exactly the same, but I'm so glad to be with you.'

Then I thought about Nicol, who had said that he liked me very much. Then a strange idea came into my head, and asked, 'Mummy, do you ever think about the story of when Jesus got lost, and his parents searched for him all day, and in the end they found him in the temple, talking to the wise men?'
'I can't say I do, but like all the stories about Jesus' life, it's there to tell us something important. It's a very interesting story.'
'Well sometimes I feel like that. Not that I have run away or got lost, but that I am so far away from you. And the grown-ups I meet either don't like me at all, or think I am very... not clever exactly, but they like my Art.'
Mummy looked terribly sad. That was the opposite of how I wanted her to react. She looked almost full of hate. 'How dare people treat you badly! It's something that I will not tolerate!'
Auntie looked alarmed, and put her hand on Mummy's. 'I know how you feel, Ruth. I agree with you. We'll all do our best to make sure that Pippa is properly supported and cared for. And let's not forget lovely, sweet Mr Macmillan. He seems very soft and gentle, but as far as I can tell, he's the only person I know of who stands up to Andrew, and tells him exactly what he can and can't do. He won't tolerate any nonsense from anybody.'

Mummy said, 'Pippa, tell me more about Jesus.
'Well, the reason I mention about Jesus was because the other day...' Then I stopped, because Mummy was crying. I held her other hand and said, 'I'm sorry Mummy! I'll stop talking now!' She turned to me and kissed me. It made my cheek wet and salty. 'It's all right, my love. I love it when you talk. Whenever Muriel and I are in the Wimpy, or walking on the Common, or sometimes in the deep end at the swimming pool, we are constantly reminded of all the funny and wise things that you say. Of course I understand what you mean about Jesus in the

temple. You're just trying to understand the complicated things that are going on around you. We miss you so much. It has made Muriel quite ill, I'm afraid.'

Now it was my turn to be upset. 'Oh Mummy, I'm sorry! I didn't mean to make Muriel ill. It's all my fault, I know it is. It was that silly painting I did of you both...'

Tears were still coming out of the sides of Mummy's eyes, but she didn't wipe them away. Her face was red and blotchy. Luckily, we were the only customers in the Wimpy. Mummy said, 'No it was not, Pippa. It absolutely was not your fault. Please try and drive that idea out of your head!'

Auntie asked, 'What painting?'

Mummy said to me, 'Darling Pippa, shall I explain, or do you want to?'

I was feeling a bit tired, and frightened that I might say the wrong thing. I said, 'Mummy, I don't want to make you cry.'

'Oh Pippa. Please understand that we must cry! We are such emotional beings, us three! There's nothing wrong with crying! If one doesn't cry, even if we weep bitter tears, then all the poison of our experiences will build up and destroy us. Look what's happening to Muriel! All her life she's tried to put her bad experiences into little compartments in her mind; all her loves and losses and disappointments. And she's tried to keep them all separate, so that she can live what she calls *a normal life*. A life with no ups and downs. And she used to spend all her time thinking of other people's needs, while completely neglecting her own. I, on the other hand, was completely wrapped up in my own needs, and neglected everyone else's.'

Auntie said, 'Ruth, this won't do. You can't go on attacking yourself. I know that you and I have only talked on the telephone, but I feel that I know you quite well. And really there's nothing I would love more than to spend hours walking on the beach with you and Luna, and Muriel when she is better, so we can share our stories. I feel we have so much in common.'

Mummy smiled. 'Really?'

'Well perhaps there's one large area where we may differ.'
They both thought that was very funny.

Auntie said, 'Well done Ruth, you've finally laughed. You really have the loveliest teeth.'

Mummy smiled again. 'Thank you. Are you sure that we don't share the same…?'

Now it was Auntie's turn to laugh. 'Ruth Herman, stop it. You are really quite a wicked woman!' They both laughed again.

I wondered if, when Jesus was in the Temple, the wise men had made jokes that He didn't understand. That made me think that the Wimpy bar was, for me, just like the Temple.

Aileen turned to Mummy. 'Ruth, one of the things that has been so wonderful about us all getting to know you and Muriel, is the effect it has had on Maggie, and her father.'

Mummy looked at me, then to Auntie, 'Do you mean vis à vis her and Rhona being… having very strong mutual feelings?'

I knew she was using grown-up talk, so that I wouldn't understand. But she was wrong. I knew what she was talking about. Auntie said, 'Well, yes. You see, at first we thought it was just a crush. That's not surprising. Half of the town is in love with Rhona, and particularly the girls and young women. At first, Tom and I didn't realise how well known she was. There are always young people hanging around the Musicians' front gate, hoping to catch a glimpse of them. And whenever Rhona is in the town there will always be someone asking for an autograph, or stopping her to tell her how much they enjoy her singing. Apparently, in America she has a huge following; mainly of women of… of a particular persuasion. Do you know, Rhona once showed us an article written about her. It described her as "The doyen of the bra-burning feminist masses." I had to ask Tom what that meant.'

Mummy smiled. 'And what exactly does it mean?'

'It means that she is very popular among women who are, how can I put it, rather independently-minded.'

'Like Muriel and myself, you mean?'

Auntie looked worried. 'Well I don't know. Some women these days really dislike men.'

439

'I don't dislike men at all. And neither does Muriel. But we do believe that men shouldn't be allowed to make decisions about how we live our lives. Is that what you mean?'

'Yes. And for some reason, Rhona seems to have caught the popular imagination. Of course, she has lots of men fans, including my husband, but she seems to be extremely popular with young women and teenage girls. And Maggie adores Rhona, and Rhona, it would seem, feels exactly the same.'

Mummy smiled. Auntie leaned over and said to her, very quietly. 'Tom found it quite difficult at first. For all his modern ideas and lifestyle, underneath he's still a traditional Highland man. But there is something about Rhona. She is so charming. And it's not something manufactured; it's genuinely how she is. He finds her irresistible, and is always flattered when she tells him how much she likes his writing, and how much he has influenced her. That's helped him get used to the idea that… you know.'

Mummy smiled again and said, 'You can say it, Aileen. You can use that word. We won't mind.'

Auntie looked around her. Auntie didn't say *that* word. Instead she said, 'She's a true poet, you know, just like Tom. She's made up of pure feeling. And she sees that in Nicol too, of course.'

Mummy said, 'I know what you mean. She has a certain quiet *presence*. She's very unusual. And her clothes!'

Auntie laughed. 'Don't talk to me about the young people's clothes! Wait until you meet the rest of the musicians! They're a true bunch of hippies, but nice, all the same.'

Then Auntie looked very serious. 'When I first met Maggie, she was so angry and unhappy. It was very difficult to be in the same room as her. But since she's met Rhona, she's like a new person. She's really grown up, and has become so helpful and understanding of our particular family problems.'

'Do you mean your sister-in-law and her children?'

'Yes. Màiri, Jimmy, Kenny and Kirsty. They are going through hell at the moment. And of course it brings up difficult memories for Tom and his children, because, from what I can

440

gather, Màiri is very similar to Tom's first wife, so goodness know what Tom's children went through.'

Mummy put her hand on Auntie's, and looked in her eyes. 'But Aileen, I'm sure you have been such a good influence on everyone. They all love you.'

Auntie blushed, 'Well I try my best. But really, they are all so easy to love. I never thought I'd have another family, so I have been blessed to have been allowed another chance.'

Mummy took both of Auntie's hands in hers and kissed her on the cheek. Mummy said, 'Thank you for finding a space in your heart for my daughter. You saved her, and you've saved us too. Heaven knows what we would have been like if you hadn't loved Pippa like you do. I will never be able to thank you enough.'

I said, 'Excuse me Mummy, but would you mind most awfully if I go to the lavatory?'

Mummy smiled and Auntie looked confused. Mummy said to her, 'I'll tell you all about that when we have our first walk on the beach.'

Shopping

When I came back, Mr Griffin was there, watching Mummy and Auntie having a friendly argument about who was going to pay the bill. He said that if they didn't hurry up, then he would be forced to pay, and then would have to claim it back on expenses, and that means that Mr Dunbar would pay.

I looked up at Mummy and Auntie and saw a shadow pass over both their faces. Auntie said to Mr Griffin, 'I hope you don't mind me asking, but have you ever met Mr Dunbar, my cousin?'

Mr Griffin smiled, 'Only during The War.'

Mummy asked, 'In what capacity? Were you friends?'

Mr Griffin hesitated. 'Not friends. No, not friends. You don't make friends with your commanding officer.'

Mummy said, 'What then?'

Mr Griffin smiled, 'I couldn't possibly say. My car's parked outside.'

There was a time when the mention of Daddy would have filled me with bad feelings; like fear, horror, or even disgust. I would be so full of those feelings, that I would feel cold and start to shake and feel sick, just like when Mr Griffin described the officer having his head shot off. But recently I hadn't felt like that. I suppose it was because Muriel and Mummy talked about him as if he was a kind friend. And there was something about Auntie calling him *my cousin* that made him feel less hard and threatening, but more real and more human. And he had been so thoughtful, and bought all of us exactly the right presents.

Remembering that moment makes me think of my Catholic school in Rayners Park. There was a nun there who Michelle and I were frightened of. She had a big hairy mole under her chin, and we were convinced that she had a disease, and that if we went near her we would get covered in moles. Michelle told me that as soon as a girl became a nun, then she became holy, and didn't need to go to the toilet anymore. This was because going to the toilet was dirty, like allowing your husband to touch your privates. Nuns were never going to fall in love, except with Jesus, and perhaps a few of the saints. And because of that, they would never need to use their private parts to make babies, or do a wee or a poo. (In Michelle's mind, S-E-X and going to the toilet were connected, because if anyone saw you doing those things then you were being very rude.) So in my mind, nuns weren't human. They were a bit like robots, who had machines for hearts. They were like the Daleks from Doctor Who, who have always terrified me.

But one day we saw the nun with the mole go into the teachers' toilet, next to the staff room. Michelle said that the nun had probably gone in there to see if there was enough toilet paper, or to check whether the teachers had flushed the toilet properly. We hid round the corner, to watch what would happen. But the nun didn't come out, and we could hear the tell-tale sounds that everyone makes when they are doing a

442

poo. After that, I stopped believing everything that Michelle told me. The next day the nun with the mole walked past me and I heard her burp. She laughed and looked at me and said, 'Hello dear. That's my breakfast coming back upstairs to say hello.' And the day after that she stopped me in the corridor and asked me if I was the nice girl who did the lovely paintings. I said I was, and she told me that I was charming.

So it was like that with Daddy; the more people talked about him, and said nice things, the more human he became to me, and the less I feared him. But I still didn't trust him. He had decided to send me to a school run by a nun who had a heart like a machine. This made her the same as the Nasty Nun who had hit me with a stick that she kept hidden in her habit. It made her frightening, and capable of tremendous cruelty; like beating children, or not allowing the boys to have any toilet paper because one or two of them had been silly and stuffed toilet rolls down the toilet. Or, worst of all, the nuns were capable of separating two girls who loved each other, causing one of them to try to kill herself. In my mind, it made nuns just as bad as the people who stood in the street and laughed at the German soldiers beating my grandfather to death.
I used to think that my daddy was a cruel man, but now I was beginning to feel that he was really just a man who didn't understand women, and had made a very bad mistake.

Mummy told Mr Griffin that the best place for us to find all the shopping that we needed would be in a big department store, like Pearson's. Mr Griffin told us all to jump in the car, and he would see if he could find the right kind of shop for us. On the way there, we passed a shop that was full of objects made of tartan. Mr Griffin parked the car, and Auntie said that she wanted to stay with Mr Griffin, and have a wee chat. We went inside and Mummy asked the man behind the counter if there was such a thing as a Dunbar tartan. He said, 'Aye madam, there surely is,' and showed us a big bolt of cloth and told us it was the *Dunbar Ancient Tartan*. There was quite a lot of yellow in it, and its particular shade reminded me of the colour of Muriel's face.

Then I saw a shelf full of teddies, dressed in kilts, and each with a tartan hat and scarf. I was almost ten, but teddies with clothes on still made me feel very excited. They were quite expensive, but I wanted to buy one for Muriel. Mummy said that she and Muriel had been putting half a crown in my Post Office Savings Account every Saturday morning since I had been away. After that, Muriel would buy a Bounty and they would pop into the library, then finish their morning with an egg and chip lunch in the café. It was something that they did, as a special time to think and talk about me.
I thought to myself, 'A bit like going to visit someone's grave and putting flowers on it,' but I didn't say it. I thought of them laughing, as they remembered the time that the librarian had been shocked that Muriel had insisted on letting me take out the book of Modigliani nudes. And how impressed we had both been by the artist's attention to detail when he had painted a lady's hair *down there.*

Mummy said I had enough money in my account to buy several teddies. So I bought one for Muriel. He had a label that said his name was Dougal MacDougall, and had a bright red tartan hat. The man behind the counter told me that this was called a *Tam O'Shanter.* He said that there was a special offer on the bears and that if I bought another one, then it would be half price. He said, 'So why don't you buy one for your daddy?' And that's what I did. Later, Mummy said that this was a sign that I was beginning to warm to him as a parent, and that this was a very good thing. I was pleased that she was pleased with me. But I wasn't in a hurry to give him his teddy. I still didn't feel *that* warm about him.

In the end, we chose a kilt for me that Mummy said looked very jolly, with a mixture of red and blue and a hint of purple. The man went into a back room, to find some nice wrapping paper for the teddies.

Mummy said to me, 'By the way, Daddy is happy for you to call yourself Pippa Herman, not Dunbar.'

I told Mummy I was surprised. She said, 'Yes, I was surprised too, so I asked him to explain why. He was a bit vague, but in the end he said that it's better if people in the school don't know that you are his daughter.' Mummy didn't explain any more. I think she wanted the idea to sink into my mind.

I said, 'Is it because he's the richest man in Britain, and he doesn't want me to have special treatment?'

Mummy smiled and said, 'One of.'

'One of the reasons why?'

'Yes, and he's one of the richest men.'

I feel thoroughly ashamed

I was usually full of energy in the middle of the morning, but I suddenly felt a bit weak in my knees and sleepy. I told Mummy, and she said that we should go home straight away. I didn't complain about that, but I wanted to see Muriel. Actually, that wasn't quite true. Yes, I wanted to spend as much time as possible with her, and I wanted to see her face when she opened her present. But a large part of me didn't want to go back into the hospital, to see her worried yellow face and bony hands. And I didn't want to be with her just after her operation. The doctors might have stuck something up her bottom while she was asleep. So if she was going to mess herself, like I had done, then it would be better to do that with just Mummy and a nurse to reassure her and clean her up.

Then I thought about Muriel being all alone, and away from the people who loved her most in the whole world. Then I remembered that Muriel didn't have any family, so we were the *only* people who loved her. I started to feel ashamed of myself for only wanting to be with her when she was fit and healthy, and looking and smelling lovely. I was going to explain that to Mummy, as we sat in the back of Mr Griffin's car, but Mummy was looking out of the window, and I knew that she was crying quietly, to herself.

When we got back home, the house was very quiet. Uncle Tom was upstairs writing, and Maggie had gone up to Rhona's cottage. I suddenly felt that I should practice playing my concertina. There were only a few days to go before the Ceilidh, and Jessie wanted to practice her song. She had announced at breakfast that her group still needed to practice a lot, so that nobody would make her look silly by making a mistake with their saxophone. Everyone except Jessie had thought that was very funny, including Nicol. He said that Jessie was usually very silly about most things in life, but she had recently become very serious about her music. Jessie said, 'Pippa has painting and drawing, and you have poems and stories, and I have music, so just do as you are told, Nicol.'

Auntie had said that Jessie should try not to be bossy with everyone in the group, because this might annoy them. But Nicol said that Jessie was quite right, because it was true that he hadn't been practicing enough. I hadn't been practicing at all, and that was beginning to bother me. I wasn't afraid of Jessie, but she was behaving like a strict teacher that you wanted to please, by always working hard and trying to get everything right.

Uncle Tom joined us in the kitchen for a cup of tea, and Auntie told him all about our busy morning. Mummy didn't say anything, but kept looking out of the window. I didn't feel sleepy anymore, and was suddenly filled with a great urge to paint something. Mummy said that Mr Griffin was going to take her back to Aberdeen for Visiting Time at five o'clock. She didn't say anything about me going, and I didn't mention it either. Uncle Tom asked Mummy if she was going to see Muriel on her own. Mummy said, 'I think that's best, don't you?' Uncle Tom didn't say anything.

I went upstairs. I sat down on my bed, but suddenly my artistic urge vanished and I was flooded by a terrible feeling of shame. I felt ashamed that I should have even imagined being a minute away from Mummy. Then I wondered what she must be thinking; about her only daughter who would rather be upstairs in her bedroom than sitting on her mother's knee. The shame was mixed with panic. I threw my sketchpad down and shouted, 'Mummy, wait for me!' and raced down the stairs. Mummy was eating a piece of cake and drinking her second cup of tea. I jumped on her lap, and threw my arms round her and said, 'Please forgive me! I'm so ashamed of myself!'

Mummy said, 'Whatever for, Pippa? Have you done something terrible?'

I said I had, and explained that, for only a short while, I hadn't wanted to see Muriel, but now I did, and I didn't care what she looked like, and I wouldn't mind if she messed herself in front of me.

Mummy said that of course I could come with her. Mr Griffin had had very strong words with a doctor in the hospital, who had said that of course I could go onto the ward at Visiting Time. He thought that seeing me would cheer Muriel up no end and help her to make a speedy recovery.

Then Mummy asked me what I meant about people messing themselves. I explained about the doctors sticking something up my bottom while I was asleep, which had made me have a terrible accident, and that Bonnie had seen me. Mummy said, 'Oh my darling. I know you've been in hospital, but I don't really know any of the details. You poor thing!'

Then she asked me who Bonnie was. I said, 'Oh, just a nice girl from my new school.' I wasn't going to say anything else about Bonnie. I didn't want Mummy to know, because I didn't want her to worry about me when I was away from her

Auntie looked at me. I could tell that she knew exactly what I was thinking. I knew that Mummy would ask her to describe every tiny detail about my time in hospital. But I also felt certain that Auntie would do her best to avoid telling her about Bonnie and Émilie.

And it was only then that I realised that the story of Émilie and Bonnie was just like Mummy and Muriel. They had all been punished for falling in love. And at that moment, I wanted to see Muriel more than anyone else in the whole world.

Roger's todger

When it was time to go back to Aberdeen, I sat in the back of the car with Mummy, while Auntie sat in front with Mr Griffin. I told Mummy that my feelings were all over the place. I told her that I had gone upstairs, away from her, because I had wanted to draw a picture of Muriel's Guardian Angel, so she could have it by her bed. I said I was sorry, because I could have just as easily brought my drawing things downstairs, so that Mummy wouldn't have thought that I had left her.

Mummy told me that it had been a lovely idea to draw the angel for Muriel, and she didn't mind in the slightest that I had wanted to go off on my own. She said, 'I understand that you might feel like that, Pippa, but it's perfectly natural to want to do things on your own. And there's nothing wrong with wanting to be with your friends. You are so lucky to have them.'

She smiled, but then she sighed and said, 'Pippa, we decided a long time ago that we are always going to do our best to tell you the truth.'

That made me feel much better, straight away. 'Well can I ask you a very important question then?'

Mummy smiled. 'I knew you were going to ask me something.' She gave my tummy a squeeze.

'Well, I heard you say that you were only allowed to see me four times a year, and Muriel wasn't allowed to see me at all.'

Mummy said, 'And I've seen you much more than four times already, and Muriel has been with you too?'

'That's right. Does that mean that The Judge has changed his mind?'

Mummy didn't say anything straight away. It looked like she was planning very carefully what she was going to say next. She cleared her throat. That usually meant that a grown-up was going to say something very important. 'Well Pippa, The Court hasn't changed its decision. Not yet, anyway. But your Daddy has spoken to his lawyer, and they have decided to behave as if they don't know what we are doing here in

Scotland. You might say that they are *turning a blind eye*. Daddy has felt very guilty about what has happened to you, and he wants to make you feel better. So he said to me, "What the Court doesn't see, the Court won't grieve over." In other words, he thinks it's important that we; that's you and me and Muriel, spend as much time together as we like... but as long as Auntie is with us. He promised me that he wouldn't tell The Court that he has changed his mind. It's strange, because when your Daddy first met Muriel, he said some very unpleasant things about her and was very impolite. Well, now he has changed. I think he realises just how good Muriel has been for you. And he's very upset that Muriel has become ill. I wouldn't be surprised if your Daddy will one day actually become very fond of Muriel. After all, everyone else in the world seems to think that the sun shines out of her.'

I wanted to ask my most important question again, but something stopped me. It was the fear of disappointment. Mummy rubbed my arm. 'I know, Pippa. It's very confusing for you. You are probably asking yourself why Daddy and I don't go back to The Court and make The Judge agree that you can come back to me... to us. And yet it doesn't seem right that Daddy can see you whenever he has time, or feels like it. Is that what you want to know?' I nodded. 'Well I don't think I can ask Daddy for that. Not yet. You see, Daddy needs to find out things for himself. If I ask for too much, then he will just dig his heels in, and refuse point blank to do what I ask. Or he might go back to his original position; that you must never see us at all. So we have to be patient with him.'

Mummy sighed. I said, 'What is it, Mummy? What are you sighing about?' She said that of course my feelings were all over the place. She said that hers were too, and Muriel's as well.
Then she said, 'I have always had very powerful feelings. Perhaps they are a lot stronger than other people's because I had a difficult life when I was very young. But then I lived with a nice family, and that helped me have happy feelings. It's

just that things went badly wrong once I got married. I was too young. But when I met Muriel, my life, and yours, seemed so very happy. Until everything went wrong again. But I think that life will be much better now. Nobody knows exactly what will happen. Who could have known that Muriel would be so ill and have to stay in Scotland until she got better?'

I said, 'How long will that be? Will it be until she is well enough to go home on a train, or will she stay here until she is completely better? She told me that could be six weeks.'

Mummy said that she didn't know the answer to that question.

I said, 'Mummy, please will you take me to my new school?'

She said, 'Yes darling, I'll do my best, but I'll have to ask Mr Macmillan about it first.'

I said, 'Oh.'

As usual, that sound, *oh*, was full of all the things I wanted to say, but didn't know how to, or was afraid of saying. I never liked saying *oh*, because it always came from a feeling that there was so much in my life that I just didn't understand. And worse, there were large parts of my life that I had absolutely no control over. Sometimes I felt like I was standing on top of a hill. I had just climbed up there, and was beginning to look around. It was misty, but the air was cool and fresh, but with a feeling that it would be warm soon. Then the sun finally burst through and the mist evaporated, so I could see all around me and down below; all laid out like a huge patterned carpet, as far as I could see. But suddenly there was a horrible smell, like rotten eggs and tobacco smoke mixed with whisky, and I could feel the ground trembling beneath my feet. Then I knew that I was standing on a volcano, which could erupt at any time, and when I felt like that, my head started to ache.

I closed my eyes and held Mummy's hand tightly. Then a memory came into my mind, of Muriel laughing. I had had a tummy ache, so Mummy kept me off school. It must have been a real illness, because I loved going to school and hated being away from Lucy. It was just after lunch, and Dorothy had popped round for a cup of tea.

I was lying upstairs, with my door open. As usual, I could hear every single word that Dorothy said, and I was listening my hardest, so I could hear what everyone had to say. And, as usual, it didn't take long before Dorothy brought up the subject of bodies. She was always talking about her body, or what her children had been doing with theirs. Apparently, there had been a huge row between Roger and his big sister, Felicity. Dorothy said that Felicity's body was growing faster than a stick of bamboo, and she was past the awkward *army and leggy* stage, and was on the way to being *willowy*. Roger, however, was still an annoying little brother, and had done a very bad thing. The day before, he had received a letter from his friend Nigel, who was still at boarding school. Dorothy said that she was glad that Nigel was no longer anywhere near Roger, because Nigel was a bad egg and a thoroughly bad influence.

That morning, Felicity had come storming down the stairs, because someone had taken her nice wooden ruler into the bathroom, and now it was all wet. At first, Roger denied all knowledge of the ruler, but Little Willy said that he had seen his brother taking it into the bathroom and doing something with it. Roger had demanded to know how Little Willy could possibly have seen what he was doing. It wasn't as if Little Willy was Superman, and could see through doors.

Then Little Willy said some things that nobody could understand. So he mimed looking through the keyhole in the bathroom door, and pointed at Roger. Then he grabbed the ruler out of Felicity's hand, pulled down his trousers, and started showing everyone how Roger had obviously been measuring his own willy. And then Little Willy pulled his willy, to show that Roger had been stretching his own willy, to make it look as long as possible. Roger went red and accused Little Willy of lying.

But Dorothy told Mummy and Muriel that Little Willy was incapable of lying, which was why you must never do anything near him that was a bit naughty or rude, because he would go straight to tell his teacher. Luckily for their family, only Dorothy and Felicity and Roger could understand him.

Roger said that Little Willy was a very bad boy for looking through the keyhole.

This only made things worse for Roger, because Willy said, 'You do it. You look at Felicity when she is in the bath!' Apparently, he had said that sentence as clearly as a bell.

Then all hell was let loose. Felicity jumped up and tried to hit Roger with her ruler. Roger cried and said that it was all Nigel's fault. He had asked Roger to spy on Felicity, and then write to tell him what she looked like with nothing on. And Nigel had boasted in his most recent letter that his *todger* had grown by a whole three inches since Roger had seen it last. Roger wanted to measure his own, to see if it had grown at all. It hadn't.

Dorothy said that boys were always thinking about their willies, and that her husband had been just the same. He used to stick a pair of rugby socks down his trousers, just before he went on parade. He said it increased his standing with the troops. He told her that the generals were no better. One of them was known as 'Hamster Tackle,' because he wasn't very well endowed. That made Mummy roar with laughter, and said that was the most ridiculous thing she had ever heard. But Muriel said that it made perfect sense to her. When she was fourteen, she joined the school Drama Society. Muriel had been a very talented actress, and still looked rather boyish, so she was chosen to play the part of Antony in *Antony and Cleopatra*. Their English teacher helped with the play, and gave the girls lots of advice. She particularly helped Muriel to be more *mannish*. She told Muriel to watch how men walked and moved their hands, and to listen to how they spoke. There weren't many men working at the school, so Muriel decided to spy on the old gardener. Then, in her next rehearsal, she spent most of the time picking her nose and spitting, and scratching her bottom and between her legs.

The English teacher thought that was very funny, but said that the headmistress and parents in the audience would not appreciate one of their nice girls playing Antony as if he were an *old geezer*. So Muriel used a burnt cork to give herself a beard and moustache, and one of the girls suggested that she stick a few pairs of tights down her trousers, to make her look and walk more like a man. Just before the show, Muriel got carried away and stuck four pairs of woolly tights between her legs. She was in a hurry to go onstage, so didn't bother to look at herself in the mirror, and when she walked on stage all of the parents started laughing at the huge bulge in the front of Muriel's trousers. This made Muriel feel self-conscious, and she forgot her lines, which caused even more laughter.

Mummy, Dorothy and Muriel laughed and laughed. Dorothy said, 'But seriously, this is one of the reasons I wake up every morning and wish to God that I had been born a man. Life is easier for them. All they have to think about is the size of their manhood, while we have to worry about all sorts of things that can go wrong with our bits and pieces. Don't ever send Pippa to a boarding school! It's awful that all those boys and girls are locked up together during the most impressionable period in their lives. No wonder half of them grow up batting for the other side!'

There was a long silence after that. Dorothy said, 'I'm sorry Ruth, I'm sorry Muriel. I didn't mean it. I can be so insensitive sometimes.'

Muriel said, 'It's all right Dorothy, you can say whatever you like. You and I have both suffered the horrors of boarding school. Surely it wasn't much different for you?'

Dorothy said, 'I enjoyed the sport, but the lack of privacy drove me mad! And sometimes it was just like being in the *Chalet School* books that Felicity likes so much. All those intense, passionate relationships between the girls, and the strange teachers… and their relationships between each other too!'

Mummy said, 'Pippa will never go to boarding school.'

Muriel said, 'I'd rather die than see that happen.'

Mummy said, 'Muriel, please don't say things like that.'

Barry McAngel

If I'm honest, I wanted Mr Griffin to turn the car around and take me back home again, so I could be with Nicol and Jessie. For the rest of the journey, I wondered if I was brave enough to tell Mummy that I wanted to go home. But when we arrived at the hospital, I knew that I had to see Muriel.

When we got to the ward, the first person we saw was the horrible nurse, standing by Muriel's bed. Mummy whispered to me, 'Oh dear, I'm afraid I'm going to lose my temper with that young lady.'

I had expected Muriel to be sitting up, and that she would smile and welcome us. But she was still asleep, and looked terrible. She was still yellow and her head was lolling to one side, and I wondered if she might be dead. The nurse was putting a pillow behind Muriel's head and trying to make her comfortable. She saw Mummy and looked a bit frightened. Mummy asked, 'How is Muriel?'

The nurse looked down and whispered, 'I'm so glad to see you. I just wanted to apologise for being so rude this morning.'

Mummy said, 'No doubt one of the senior doctors has told you off?'

The nurse still looked down. I could see that she was quite young, and probably no older than Maggie. 'Yes, that's true. I got a severe dressing down from Mr Fraser. But I was going to try to say sorry anyway. I shouldn't have said what I said. It's just that…'

Mummy said, 'Of course. I understand. It's not easy being a nurse.'

The nurse looked in Mummy's eyes. She said, 'That may be a reason, but it's not an excuse for bad manners.'

Mummy smiled. 'Please don't be hard on yourself. Muriel is a nurse, you know.'

The nurse looked up. 'Is she? I'll take extra special care of her then!'

'Thank you. Now please, are you able to tell me how Muriel's operation went?'

The nurse blushed and said, 'Well, the doctor told me to go and get him when you arrived, because he wants to talk to you himself.'

Mummy sat down on a chair. Actually, it was more like she fell onto it. She said, to herself, 'Oh God.'

The nurse said, 'I'll just go and call the doctor. I hope he'll be here soon.'

Then Muriel started to wake up. She opened her eyes and said, 'Hello my love. I'm so glad you've come.' Then her eyeballs slipped to one side in her eye sockets, as if she couldn't control them anymore. Then her head lolled to one side again. Mummy almost jumped off her chair, and practically grabbed Muriel's hand. Muriel moaned, 'Oh, it hurts. It still hurts! I thought that they would have stopped the pain!'

Then she was sick, and Mummy said to me, 'Quick Pippa, go and tell the nurse to come immediately!'

But I was sitting on a chair and couldn't move. I heard a loud flapping of wings and saw Ursula. She looked as lovely as ever, and stood next to Muriel. She had an old man with her. He didn't have long white hair and a beard, like God. He was a bit tubby and had combed his hair over on one side, to try to hide the fact that he was bald on top. I imagined him flying up and down from Heaven with his hair blowing to one side; and flapping behind him in a long strand, and looking ridiculous. Bobby Charlton had looked like that when he played in the World Cup Final. Peter's big sister Bernadette said it was called a 'comb-over', and that men with hair like that looked terrible. That was why she didn't support Manchester United, but preferred West Ham instead, because nobody in West Ham had a comb-over. Mummy once said to Muriel that having a comb-over was a sign of a man's vanity, like a lady we saw once in the changing rooms at the swimming baths, who wore a padded bra, because she thought that her bust was too small. Mummy said that you have to be proud of who you are and what you look like, and just get on with life.

Muriel smiled when Mummy said that. I knew she was thinking about Mummy's bust.

Conversations like that always made me think about what I would look like when I became a lady. Muriel told us that when she was at school, some girls tried to make themselves look bigger by borrowing their friends' bras and putting newspaper inside them. Muriel said that up until the age of fifteen she had always looked like a boy, but suddenly changed, and never needed to worry about using newspaper. She said that when the girls took their bras off you could read yesterday's newspaper headlines in reverse on their flat chests. Mummy said that surely must have been an exaggeration, but she laughed anyway.

Ursula said, 'Pippa, I'd like to introduce you to my colleague, Barry McAngel. He's Scottish, but nice, all the same.' He bowed his head at me and his hair started to flop to one side. He quickly scooped his hair back over his scalp again. He said, 'I'm going a wee bit thin on top.' I tried not to laugh, and this made him smile. He said, 'Pippa, obviously you are very worried about your auntie, but I'm here to take care of her. I know the whole story, so obviously I don't need to ask you any questions, and can start right away.'

I was about to say something, but he added, 'Of course, I've heard all the prayers that Muriel and Mummy have ever said for you. I know they're not Catholics, but Jesus loves everyone, including Jews, and even the people who don't know who He is. Heaven is a very big place, after all.'

I heard a Scottish voice say, 'She's still very ill, and we will almost certainly need to operate on her again.' I opened my eyes and a doctor was standing in front of Muriel's bed, and talking to Mummy, who was helping the nurse to clean Muriel up. Muriel looked very floppy.

The doctor said to me, 'I'm Mr Fraser. I operated on Miss Standish. And you must be her niece?' He shook my hand. He said, 'Of course, it must be very upsetting to see your aunt like this, but we are doing our very best to look after her, and to make sure that she is comfortable.'

Muriel cried out in pain. The doctor said, 'And the first thing we must do is to help her with her pain. We are going to give her a wee injection now, and then I'm going to examine her, so, if you don't mind, I'm going to ask nurse to take you for a wee walk.'

A wee walk

I didn't want to leave Muriel, but suddenly the doctor turned his back on me and the nurse took my hand and led me away. We walked up the ward, past an old lady who was talking to a priest, and another lady sleeping on her back, with her mouth wide open. Her false teeth were on top of her bedside cabinet. We went into an office, and the nurse asked me if I liked sweets. I told her I liked Bounty bars best, and she looked in the cupboard and found a bar of Cadbury's Fruit and Nut. She said that patients were very generous, and often gave the staff boxes of chocolates, but at the moment they didn't have any of those, so instead we could have some chocolate that she had bought to share with the other nurses.

Talking about chocolate always took my mind off problems. It still does. The nurse said, 'You must have thought that I was horrible this morning.'
I had to be honest, so I said, 'I was a bit frightened of you, and a bit cross. You see, I love my auntie more than anyone in the whole world.'
She looked surprised. 'More than your mum?'
I had to think about that. She offered me some chocolate. I explained that there were lots of types of love. You might love your dog or your cat, and then you might love your friends. Then of course you would love your mum, and I was lucky because I could love Muriel as well. The nurse smiled and nodded and said that I was very good at explaining how I felt, then asked me, 'And what about your dad? Don't you love him?'
I said, 'I don't know.'
She looked very surprised. 'Is he dead?'
'No. Mummy and Daddy are divorced.'

457

'Oh, I am sorry to hear that.' She made it sound like that having a father who was divorced was worse than having one who was dead.

When we went back to see Muriel, the doctor had gone. Muriel was asleep and Mummy was holding her hand, and I could tell that Mummy was trying to be brave about something. Polish Teddy and the photograph I had given her were sitting on the cabinet next to Muriel's bed.

Mummy told me that Muriel was very pleased to have seen me, but she was still feeling ill. Muriel had wanted me to take Polish Teddy back with me. In bed next to her was the teddy I had bought her.

Mummy was going to stay at the hospital until the end of Visiting Time, but she wanted me to go home with Auntie and Mr Griffin. I didn't make a fuss about that. Mummy looked very sad. She kissed me goodbye and promised me that we could have a good chat in bed. I asked her if I could kiss Muriel, but Mummy said it would be best if I kissed her hand or blew her a kiss. I blew her a kiss.

On the way home, Auntie explained that Muriel had two things wrong with her. The surgeon had taken out Muriel's womb, so her pains and bleeding would stop. She said, 'It means that she won't have any more...' Then she whispered, 'She won't have a monthly time of feeling unwell.' I wondered why she hadn't just said *periods*. I supposed she did that because Mr Griffin wasn't married, so he wasn't supposed to know about those things. That seemed a bit silly. She said, 'But the bad news is that Muriel won't be able to have a baby either.' When Auntie said that, she gave a big sigh.

I could tell that she didn't want to talk about that anymore. She said, 'But Muriel has another problem, and the doctors haven't been able to sort that out yet. It's about another part of her tummy. It's why she's yellow and has terrible pains.'

I thought of Muriel shouting that she was hurting. That made me want to go back to her, but I also felt like staying away, both at the same time. We didn't say anything more until we got home. Auntie thanked Mr Griffin, who turned the car around and drove back to the hospital.

Auntie said, 'I like Mr Griffin. He's a very kind man.' I thought she was going to say, 'But he works for your daddy, so be careful what you say in front of him.' But she didn't say it. But I knew that she wanted to.

I was very pleased to see Nicol, Jessie and Maggie. They didn't mention Muriel. I think Nicol wanted to say something about her, but Jessie said, 'Thank goodness you're here. We need to practice a wee bit. And then would you like to learn some Scottish dancing?'

And that's what we did, until it was time for bed. I was glad.

In bed with Mummy

I went to bed at the same time as Jessie, and Maggie read us a chapter from Pippi Longstocking. Jessie loved it, but I couldn't concentrate, because I wanted to be with Mummy in bed. I kept thinking about Muriel. Just as I was drifting off to sleep, Mummy came back and took me into Maggie's bedroom, and lay with me, with all her clothes on. I told her that I was worried about something. It was about being a girl. It was something that Dorothy had said, about ladies having more to worry about than men. Did that mean that I would get more illnesses in my life, just because I was a girl, and would one day become a lady? Mummy said, 'You weren't supposed to be listening to things we said with Dorothy!'

I said, 'But she had such a loud voice!'

Mummy explained that Dorothy had meant that because ladies are made to have babies, their insides are more complicated than men's. Because we each have a womb and ovaries and a vagina, this means that there can be different things to think about and look after, and sometimes there can be more things that we need to go to the doctor about. I had never heard Mummy use the word *vagina* before. It was a bit shocking. Then she said, 'But it's a good thing too. Some people think that ladies have... how can I put it... have a nicer time than men.'

My next questions were big ones. 'Why is it so sad that Muriel can't have a baby? And are you sad about it too?' But I didn't let Mummy answer. I wanted to get all my questions out all at once, in case I didn't have the courage to ask them later. 'Isn't it a good thing that Muriel won't have any more periods? Then she won't have to worry about the mess and the inconvenience.'

Mummy said that she couldn't explain that very well. She told me about how she had felt about being pregnant for the first time, and how excited she had been because she was going to be a mother. She said, 'It seemed that my body was happy with me. Does that make sense?' It did. 'But then when I lost it, on the ship, it was a terrible shock to my mind, but my body had an even more terrible reaction; as if for a few months it had been happily heading in one direction, like the boat we were on, then suddenly it hit a rock and I just sank.'

'Like the Titanic?'

'Yes, like the Titanic. And then when I couldn't say goodbye to my baby; that was the biggest shock of all. I know the baby would have been terribly unformed, and there may have been something wrong with him anyway, but he was still my baby, and I was already in love with him. And to have him just dumped over the side of the ship like that. Well, it broke my heart. And it made me dislike your father.

'But when you came along, it made everything right again. It was such a thrill, as if nothing else mattered in my whole life. Of course, I didn't have to go to work, or do any shopping, or cooking, or housework, like most women. I was living a life of luxury. All I had to do was feed you from my breasts and think about when I was going to take you into the swimming pool. And you were such a good baby, always making funny little noises and sleeping so soundly. It was like being in Heaven.

'So I was very lucky to have had that experience. I was a mother, and I was very good at it. I was happy that I had done something right in my life. Unfortunately, the other part of my life, my marriage to your daddy, was busy falling apart.'

'So why is it so sad that Muriel won't be able to have a baby? Can two ladies have a baby?'

'No, they can't.'

'So why is it sad, if she can't do it anyway? She doesn't want to leave us and get married, does she?

''No, she doesn't. Do you mind if I think about it a bit more, Pippa? Perhaps I'll talk to Aileen, and Muriel as well, when she feels better.'

'And the doctor in Guildford who you both see every week? Do you talk to her about those things?'

'Yes. Yes, sometimes we do.'

'Do you think that Rhona might know something about it? Everyone says how wise she is.'

'That's an interesting idea.'

'Perhaps you could go for a walk on the beach with Auntie tomorrow, and I can play with Nicol and Jessie and Kirsty and Kenny, and we can practice our music too. And you can talk to Auntie about it and then tell me, in the night.'

'What a good idea.'

'And can you come to the Ceilidh as well?'

'That's a lovely idea. I hadn't thought about that.'

'Will Muriel be out of hospital by then?'

'I don't know, darling. I really don't know. I hope so, but I think it might take her a long time to be well enough to move around. I'll talk to her about it, and ask the doctors.'

And then I didn't think about Muriel's womb and babies anymore. I lay there with Mummy's arms around me and my thumb in my mouth. I fell asleep, safe in the knowledge that I was still Mummy's baby, and that she loved me just as much now as she had done on the day I had been born. Knowing that, I felt sure I would be able to withstand any storm that lay ahead.

Explaining the Mandala

The next day was Saturday, and very cloudy and spitting with rain, but Uncle Tom said it wasn't quite dreich. Mummy and Auntie went for their walk on the beach anyway, because they said that it would be bracing and would help to blow away their cobwebs. All of us, including Kirsty, Kenny, and Luna, went up to Rhona's house with our instruments. The other musicians still hadn't come back, but Rhona said that they would probably return, finally, that evening. She didn't seem very excited about that.

Maggie and Rhona had tidied up the studio and now there were lots of chairs and cushions to sit on, and a table by the window with a big red plate full of candles on it. On another table, in the middle of the wall, they had propped up the strange painting, so it rested against the wall. At the bottom of the painting they had put a small wooden statue of a little man with a pointy hat on, sitting with his legs crossed. In front of him was a small metal bowl with a chunky candle in, and a little bag made out of green cloth.

Maggie saw me inspecting the painting and statue and candle. She said, 'We knew that you would find it very interesting. We sit in front of it every morning and meditate. Rhona is interested in becoming a Buddhist. She got the paintings and the statue of The Buddha from some Tibetan monks, who live in a big house not far from your new school. Rhona says that if ever she goes there again, we can come and see you. That would be lovely, wouldn't it?'

I said, 'Oh yes, that would be lovely,' but I felt feelings of sadness and dread creeping over me.

Maggie said, 'But let's not think about the future. We have to think about what we're going to do right now, and for the rest of this week. There are so many things to sort out before the Ceilidh.'

She lit the candle in front of the statue, and gave me the little cloth bag. She said, 'We, Rhona and I, bought this for you, to take to school.'

Inside was a large silver safety pin, in the shape of a thistle. Maggie said, 'It's for your kilt. You must keep it very safe, and when you look at it you can think of us, Rhona and me, and all the people here who love you.'

All the dread and sadness disappeared, and instead I felt a nice warm feeling, just above My Lovely Place.

I asked Maggie about the strange picture. It had a navy-blue background, that seemed almost black. This showed up everything else that was painted on top. I think it would take me a long time to describe exactly what I could see, so I'll just write what Maggie told me about it. She said it was a *mandala*, and the flower designs in the middle were lotus flowers, and everything in the painting represented Life. You could turn the painting around and it would still look the same, because it was perfectly symmetrical. Maggie said that Buddhists looked at the mandalas while they were meditating. She said that this meant that they were thinking very deeply, and trying to empty their minds of all their thoughts, except about the true meaning of Life.

She said that looking closely at the mandala made her and Rhona think about themselves, as women.
I said, 'But I thought that you were ladies?'
She asked me what the difference was. I said, 'Well, a lady is someone like Mummy or Auntie Aileen, or Muriel. Someone who might be a housewife, and their husband has a job like a doctor, or an art critic. And they live in a nice house with a garden and probably have a car, and don't need to go on the bus. And perhaps they might go to work sometimes, but they don't do work where they get their hands dirty.'
'And a woman?'
'Oh, that's someone who will have to go to work, like in a sweet shop, or a factory, or perhaps works on a farm. And when she gets old we say they she is an *old woman*, and they are usually quite ugly and don't have nice hair or fingernails. And they might have long hairs growing on their chin. Or they might have a tooth that has fallen out, but they haven't got enough money to pay the dentist to put in false teeth. And they might live in a council house that is a bit dusty, and have old furniture, and only have a small garden, and perhaps they have to go to the toilet in a shed outside.'

Maggie laughed and said, 'Pippa, I'd love to spend lots of time talking about your ideas!' I knew that she thought I was talking a lot of nonsense. So I changed the subject and asked her to tell me more about the mandala.

She said that the outside design, which was made up of straight lines that were white and a strong yellow, was very feminine, because it showed how women, and ladies, protect other people. And the pink and orange flowers in the middle represented Nature, and how women and ladies were very close to Nature and the earth. I thought she meant that they liked digging and planting flowers in the garden, but she said it was more about being in touch with the Planet Earth.

And the light blue, almost turquoise flowers and red star in the centre represented the womb and the blood that all women give to The Earth, and give to their children as they grow inside them. And it was about the roundness of the thing that all women and ladies have, that is very precious.

At first I thought she meant their belly button, but there was something about the way Maggie said *thing* and *precious* that made me know exactly what she was talking about. She looked in my eyes and smiled. I knew that she was in love.

I said, 'I wonder if Muriel would like to look at that mandala? Perhaps I could paint one for her?' Then I thought that might be a bad idea, because it might fill her with sadness, because she didn't have a womb anymore. But Maggie said, 'That's a lovely idea. And can you do one for us as well?'

That was an idea that filled me with excitement, and I began to think about the kind of paint that I might use.

Maggie said that Buddhists didn't believe that you went to Heaven when you died. She said that you came back to life again, but as someone else, and that you had to try to live all your lives as a good person, and then eventually when you die you will go to a place called Nirvana. Then you would never come back again.

I said I liked that idea, because I was worried about Muriel. Maggie said that she understood about that, and that she and Rhona were thinking a lot about me and Mummy and Muriel.

I asked her if she was saying prayers for us, and she said, 'Not exactly. It's was more like lighting a candle in front of the Buddha as soon as we woke up together, and we think positive things about you and Mummy and Muriel, and wish you well.'

I imagined them waking up in bed and kissing each other, and saying, 'Shall we go and meditate?' But then deciding to stay in bed for a bit longer, to have a cosy cuddle.

I said, 'Maggie, can I tell you something?' She said I could, and bent down so that I could whisper in her ear. I said, 'I love you, Maggie. And I know that you and Rhona love each other. I think it is lovely, just like Mummy and Muriel.'

Maggie didn't say anything. She straightened herself up and ran her fingers through my hair. Then she smiled and said, 'Would you like me to cut your hair before you go to school? Perhaps before the Ceilidh?'

I said that I would love that.

Whisky Before Breakfast

All the time that we had been talking, Jessie and the other children had been tuning up, singing, and playing little tunes together. We sat in a circle with our instruments. Rhona came in and said that she had something special to show us. It was a wooden instrument that looked like a narrow decorated box, with strings. She explained that it was an Appalachian Mountain Dulcimer, and the word *dulcimer* meant *sweet sound*. That was certainly true. When she put it on her lap and played it, it seemed to me to be the sweetest sound in the whole world. She played a fast tune and sang the words

Early one morning 'fore the sun could shine
I was walkin' down the street, not feelin' so fine
I saw two old men with a bottle between 'em
And this is the song that I heard them singin'
Lord protect us, Saints preserve us
We been drinkin' whisky 'fore breakfast

It was a song about the three men getting drunk in the street early in the morning and playing their instruments and singing, and the whole town coming to listen to them. It was a jolly song, but I wasn't sure I liked it, so didn't sing along. Rhona said, 'I know it's a happy song, but it's not good to drink whisky like that, all day long. Maybe grown-ups can have one small glass every so often, but not all the time. My daddy used to be like that, and it was horrible for him, and for us.'

Kenny said, 'Our dad drinks a lot of whisky. I don't like it when he's drunk.' Rhona looked at me. I could tell that she knew about Mummy. I supposed that Muriel must have told her.

She said to Maggie, 'That wasn't very sensitive of me, was it?' Maggie said, 'No, Rhona, it wasn't.'

Rhona said, 'Whoops. I wasn't thinking. What shall I do?'

I said, 'Well I don't mind. My Mummy used to drink whisky, and get terribly drunk and be sick all over the place. And once she was drunk in the street, and the police came and took her to the police station. And she left me at home in the night, all on my own, and she used to forget to collect me from school. But then she had lots of help from special doctors, in a clinic, and now she's all right again. Once she told me that she will be an alcoholic all her life, but as long as she doesn't drink any alcohol from now on, then she will be all right. And she told me that she was very sorry, but she had drunk whisky because she had been very sad. And she told me that she loves me, and I am the most precious thing in the whole world, and because of that she will never drink alcohol again for the rest of her life.'

Jessie said, 'Can we get on and practice, please?'

Rhona said, 'Yes, of course, but as long as when we've finished, you'll all let me play and sing you something that I've just finished writing. Actually, I didn't really write it. Most of it just came into my head when I was walking along the beach one day, just after talking to Nicol. So he is really the songwriter. You will be the first people in the whole world to hear it.'

Then we played Black Jack David, with Hit the Road Jack in the middle. Nicol had obviously been practicing, because he enjoyed playing and smiled a lot, and especially when Rhona told him that he was a fast learner. Jessie said, 'What about me? Am I a fast learner too?'

Rhona said that Jessie was just like me. She had the gift of music and I had my Art. We didn't really need to learn anything; it was all there inside us already. That pleased Jessie, and she smiled a huge smile.

I wasn't very happy with my concertina playing, and sometimes if I made a mistake, Jessie frowned at me. That's when I realised that I really was a bit frightened of her.

Rhona said that our song was very good, and we needed only one more rehearsal, just before the Ceilidh. She said that she would have to spend time with the other musicians, sorting things out. She said *sorting things out* in such a way, and with such a worried face, that I thought that perhaps there might be some trouble brewing between them.

I looked at Jessie, and I could tell that she had the same idea, but for once she didn't say what she was thinking.

Màthair: The Call

Rhona said that her song was in five parts, and would take twenty minutes. She said that she planned to put it on her new LP record. If people liked it, then she would prepare a concert with her new songs. And if the concert was a success, then she might go on a tour of Britain, and possibly the Unites States and Canada, where she had quite a lot of fans. But first she would have to go down to London and spend a lot of time in a recording studio with other musicians. She was hoping that everything would be finished in a month, and ready to sell in the shops by the beginning of November.

Maggie told us that Rhona had invited her to go with her to help with the recording, and then go on tour with her, as Rhona's assistant and photographer. Maggie thought that would be a wonderful idea. Nicol looked sad and said, 'Does that mean that you'll leave us?'

Jessie said, 'And have you asked Dad?'

Maggie said, 'I'd only be away for a wee while, perhaps three months or so, so it would be just like a long holiday. And anyway, I'm old enough to make my own decisions about how I want to live my life. But I did ask Dad and Aileen what they thought, and they both said it would be a very exciting opportunity for me.'

Jessie asked her, 'Will you send us postcards and buy me a lava lamp?'

Rhona started playing her dulcimer. She said her song was called 'Màthair: The Call'. *Màthair* was Scottish Gaelic for *mother*, and the whole song was about a child calling for his dead mother, and waiting for her response. I knew it was about Nicol. She started singing, and I looked at the mandala and imagined Maggie and Rhona sitting in front of a lighted candle and thinking nice things about me.

There were no words; just a stream of sounds. Rhona had her eyes closed and moved her arms and hands and fingers as she sang, which made me feel that I could almost see the notes as they gently rose and fell and then soared and hung in the air, before they gradually descended again. The sound reminded me of *Lark Ascending* but the picture in my mind was like a painting by Marc Chagall. I saw Nicol standing on the cliff in front of the castle, calling to his mother in the night, and his mother flying high above the waves, sparkling in the moonlight

It reminded me of a story that Uncle Tom told us about a farm girl in Sweden who called to the cows, and they came walking over to listen to her. She sang in a special way, called *Kullning*. You could make swans come over to you by singing like that too. Jessie had said that once she had wanted a calf to come to her, so she just held out her hand with some long grass in it, and it came running. And to make a swan come, all you had to do was chuck some stale bread in the water in front of you. This had made us all laugh.

When Rhona had finished singing, I told her about what Uncle Tom had said about calling the cows. Rhona said that she had got that idea from him. Jessie said, 'If you want my opinion, it's a little on the slow side.' Rhona thought that was very funny. Jessie looked offended, and said that she was being serious. Rhona said, 'Don't worry, Jessie, I'm not going to perform it at the Ceilidh. That would send everyone to sleep.'

Jessie said, 'I didn't mean it was boring. It's just that I prefer Whisky Before Breakfast and the tune we are going to perform, and the song that I have made up.'

Rhona said, 'You've written your own song?'

'Not written it, but it's in my head.'

'Well I'd love to hear it, but I thought you wanted us to rehearse together?'

I knew exactly what Rhona was doing. She was playing Jessie at her own game. Jessie wanted to be the boss, but really it was Rhona who needed to be in charge.

Jessie said, 'You're quite right, but…'

'But you'd like to share it with us?'

'Only if everyone else wants to hear it.'

Rhona smiled and said, 'That's exactly how we should work in rehearsals, but in our group it's the boys who think that they should make all the decisions.'

Then Jessie played her tune on her accordion. It was brilliant; very fast and jolly and it made me tap my feet and want to dance and sing along, even though there were no words yet. She said she wanted to call it *Cottage Pie*.

Rhona clapped along and was delighted. She said, 'I do believe I might have exactly the words to fit your song… if you wouldn't mind sharing with me, of course?'

Jessie tried to look like she was deciding whether that was a good idea or not, but we could all see that she couldn't resist the chance to have a famous singer put words to her music.

Rhona read the words of her song, which was about a mole who is burrowing in the night and bangs his head against something hard. It's in his way, which makes him very cross, so he spends all night pushing the heavy object to the surface. He isn't at all interested in finding out what's inside, and just breathes a sigh of relief and goes on his way. The next morning a boy is out walking with his dog, and the dog digs up the molehill and finds a beautiful casket. The boy opens it, and discovers something inside that is the most beautiful thing in the world.

Jessie said, 'Not bad, Rhona, not bad at all, but really it should be a girl who finds the treasure, not a boy, seeing as I wrote the tune. And none of it is about a cottage pie, so people will get confused.'

Rhona and Maggie looked at each other and laughed. Nicol looked a bit disappointed. I could feel Jessie building up to an argument. Rhona said, 'Good idea. I think your title is great, but why don't we make up another tune together... just you and me... and call it Cottage Pie? It could be a jig or a reel; something that would get everybody up and dancing! We can call our other song something simple, like *The Mole Song*. Jessie smiled.

Halfway through the rehearsal, Rhona got up to go to the toilet, and I went with her, because I was bursting. I went in first, and when I came out she held my hand and said, 'Really the song is about you, and Nicol, and your mom and Muriel, and Maggie and me. What do you think is inside the casket?'

That took me by surprise. I felt a lovely shiver go right through me. All I could say was, 'I think I know. Can I paint a picture for you?'

She said, 'Wait there, because I want to ask you something.' When she came out she said, 'That's better. Now here's what I want to ask you. Maggie showed me the painting you did of our garden. I love it. It would be wonderful if you could do some more paintings, for the cover of my record.'

Now it was my turn to be delighted. I clapped my hands and jumped up and down, and said, 'I'd love to!' Then I thought about it, and explained about my Marc Chagall painting of her and Rhona and the Lang Stane. Rhona said that sounded perfect.

Then I stopped being delighted. 'You'll have to ask Mummy, and Daddy too. She will almost certainly say yes, but Daddy might say no.'

Rhona kissed me on the cheek. She said, 'Of course. I'll ask them.'

I said, 'How will you ask Daddy?'

She smiled and patted the side of her nose with her finger, twice. She said, 'Oh, I'm sure I'll find a way. Maybe I'll leave a letter for him at his house!'

Calling the cattle home

We all went home for lunch. We brought our instruments with us, so we could play Jessie's song for Mummy and Auntie and Uncle Tom. Rhona said she was embarrassed about always eating at our house, so she had arranged for the shopkeeper at the bottom of the hill to send up a big box of fruit and vegetables and bread and biscuits, and a huge fruit cake.

Mummy and Auntie had had a lovely walk on the beach, and looked worn out. They said that they both needed a rest in the afternoon, and asked us what we wanted to do.

I didn't say anything, because I wanted to be with Nicol and everyone else, but didn't want Mummy to feel that I didn't care about her.

Rhona said that she would love to do an experiment. She said we should all take our instruments and go onto my daddy's estate, to see if we could play for the cows, to try to make them come and listen to us.

Everyone thought that was a very exciting idea. Mummy said that she wasn't worn out anymore, and would love to come with us. She said that she would ask Mr Griffin if he could ring Daddy's house, to get permission, and perhaps he could collect all the instruments and bring them in his car.

Uncle Tom said that would be an excellent idea, and he would like to come too. We all went into the front room and played Jessie's song. Uncle Tom blew his nose very loudly afterwards.

Mummy and Auntie said it was the loveliest thing they had ever heard.

A few hours later, we were all standing by the gate of the big field with the dangerous-looking highland cattle in it. They were sitting at the far end of the field, and didn't seem to notice us. When I say *us*, that included a friend of Uncle Tom's, who was the photographer for the local newspaper. He had rushed over, and was ready with his big camera. He was very interested in Rhona, and asked if she would mind if he interviewed her and took some special photos. Rhona thought that was a wonderful idea. Then she had a quick conversation with Maggie and Mummy, and then the three of them said something to the photographer. Mummy said, 'As long as Pippa's face is not in it.'

It had stopped raining, but the wind was strong, so we all had our coats and woolly hats on. In the valley I could see the big pine trees where Muriel and I had been reunited, and beyond it, Daddy's mansion. We got our instruments out and stood facing the gate. Rhona said that we should play all our songs, including Jessie's song about the mole, but first she wanted to try singing like a Swedish milkmaid. She said that the wind was blowing in the direction of the cows, which should help them hear us.

She sang the first part of the song that we had heard in the morning, about the boy calling his mother. At first, nothing happened. So Rhona sang louder, and a big cow stood up, looked around and then slowly began walking. Rhona stopped singing and the cow stood still. Then Rhona sang again, and all the cows stood up and the big cow moved away from the herd and walked slowly in our direction. Then all the cows followed and stood in a line, looking at us.

Rhona stopped singing, and the cows stood still, but they were still quite far away. Rhona said, 'Quick, quick! Start playing!' We all played Black Jack David and, sure enough, the cows all started walking slowly towards us. By the time we had finished

Jessie's tune, they were all standing in a line right in front of us.

I heard the photographer say, 'Everyone turn and look at me.' But I was too busy looking at the biggest cow.

I heard a few clicks and the photographer said, 'Perfect!' Mummy put her arm round my shoulders and whispered, 'I think he's a bull. Wait until I tell Muriel all about this. She won't believe it!'

She asked me if I wanted to come with her to see Muriel, and I said I did.

Mr Griffin drove Mummy and me and the instruments home, and everyone else walked over to Rhona's house.

Later, Nicol told me that when they got back to the cottages, the other three musicians were there. They all said hello to Auntie Aileen and Uncle Tom and the children, but just ignored Rhona and Maggie. Nicol thought that the group called Trailing Clouds of Glory would soon break up, and have to find another singer. I said I thought that was very sad, but Nicol said that Rhona would be happier on her own, writing her own songs. And anyway, she would have Maggie to keep her company. I asked him if he would miss Maggie. He said, 'Why are my favourite people leaving me?'

I went red and he held my hand.

Mummy and I went to see Muriel, but she was asleep. We held one of her hands each and she woke up and smiled, but all the time we were there she seemed to be fighting going back to sleep. In the car on the way back to Stranhaven, Mummy explained that Muriel was on very powerful medicine, to keep her from feeling pain, but it made her very sleepy. She said I wasn't to worry, because the doctors were very happy about how she was healing after the operation, though they were still deciding what to do about her other problem. That made me cry, and Mummy said I was her poor little lamb. For some reason that made me think about the bull in the field, and I stopped crying. It really had been huge.

A conversation in the night

Mummy got me ready for bed again, and as soon as we were in bed she said, 'Auntie Aileen and I had a long chat on the beach, just as Mummy promised. We don't have the same ideas about what children should know about how babies are made. I think you are old enough to understand, but Aileen says that she would prefer to talk about these things with girls when they are older. She has to be very careful what she says to Jessie, because she is such an unusual child, and gets some very strange ideas. And Jessie is very likely to go around talking about sex to other children, and getting it all wrong, either accidentally or on purpose, and causing a lot of worry in the other children's minds.'

'Is that why Auntie didn't want to talk about periods in front of Mr Griffin?'

'Probably, yes. It's a subject that lots of ladies feel shy about. But I'm not like that. Both Muriel and I think that boys and men should understand about their own bodies, and about ladies' bodies too. Then there wouldn't be so many problems in the world.'

Then Mummy told me a very strange story. It was about a man called John Ruskin, who was an art critic, just like my ex-uncle Eric. Mr Ruskin was very famous for his ideas about art. But when he married his wife, he was horrified to see what she looked like with no clothes on. Apparently, he had never seen a real lady with nothing on. He had only ever seen statues and paintings of naked ladies, and none of them had hair on their Lovely Places or under their arms.

I said, 'But didn't he know about Modigliani?'

'Oh no! He died before Modigliani was born. In those days nobody painted ladies as we really are. Except a French painter called Gustave Courbet, but even now you can't see his painting, because people say it is too vulgar.'

'I don't think that having hair is vulgar. I hope I have some, one day.'

'That's because you know all about it. Anyway, Mr Ruskin was so horrified when he saw his wife's hair, it's called *pubic hair,*

474

that he thought there was something terribly wrong with her. After five years he had their marriage annulled.'

'Just like you and Daddy.'

'That's right.'

'But…'

'I know what you are going to say. Daddy wasn't like Mr Ruskin. But he didn't really understand about periods either, and especially not how my period, my menstrual cycle as I prefer to call it, affected how I felt from one day to the next.'

'So should I tell Nicol all about periods and public hair?'

'Pubic hair. No. I think that's his dad's and Auntie Aileen's job.' I didn't ask any more questions. Mummy said, 'You have, haven't you?' I didn't say anything. Mummy squeezed my tummy. 'Mummy doesn't mind. Did he ask you?'

'Yes. No. I can't remember.' I could feel myself getting very hot. I explained about his walk to the Lang Stane with Uncle Tom, and their talk about his father's seeds. Mummy laughed. I said, 'I wasn't being rude, honestly I wasn't.'

Mummy said, '*Being rude*. That's such a Catholic idea, I'm afraid. There's something very important to understand about Catholic schools. They will teach you that the human body is not nice, and is something to be ashamed of. And that's why they won't talk about important things like girls and their periods. I could never understand that.'

'But Auntie isn't a Catholic.'

'That's true, but lots of grown-ups are shy about talking about sex, because it's a very private thing. But she will talk to Nicol and Jessie about it, when the time is right.'

'And when will the time be right?'

'It's usually when the children start taking an interest and asking questions. And it's very important that children understand things properly, otherwise they get very strange ideas, and can even be a bit frightened.'

We lay still. I whispered, 'Mummy, why is Muriel so upset that she won't have a womb and won't have periods anymore? Isn't that a good thing?'

'A good thing?'

'Well, periods are messy, and hurt, and make you have a bad mood. So if they stop, then surely that must be a good thing?'

'I wish it were that simple.'

There was a much bigger question forming in my mind, but I didn't quite know how to ask it, and I wasn't sure if I wanted to know the answer, so I didn't say anything. Mummy waited, but I still didn't know what to say. She said, 'What is it, Pippa? I know there are some more questions in that mind of yours. You are your mummy's daughter, after all!'

This is what I said. 'Well, I think I know something. I know that only a man and a lady can make a baby.' I didn't want to say the next thing, but knew I had to. 'So if two ladies love each other, in bed, in the night, they won't have a baby, will they?'

'No, Pippa. They won't. It's not possible.'

'So if Muriel can't make a baby, because she's with you... if you see what I mean... then why should she be so sad about not being able to have a baby?'

Mummy was quiet for a while. I felt her chest rising and falling against my back. 'Well, this is the most difficult thing to explain. I asked Auntie to help me, because I knew you would ask. She said that when Wee Callum died, people told her to have another child. And I think she thought that was a good idea too. But to have a baby, you have to have sex. She was so terribly shocked and unhappy, so the last thing she wanted to do was to have sex. She stopped wanting to do it. So even though she was still young enough to have another baby, she didn't. And also, sometimes ladies only have one or two babies, and then something happens and they can't have any more. Nature is like that. So Muriel is worried that if she doesn't have a womb anymore, maybe she won't feel so good about loving me in a physical way. And she's worried that I might stop loving her.'

'Just like Auntie and her husband?'

'Exactly. Exactly that. It doesn't matter how much I tell Muriel that I will always love her, she still feels very worried about it. And about having babies? Well, we have talked about this a lot

476

together, and with the doctor in Guildford. She says that lots of women feel a very strong urge to have a baby, just like I did before I had you. It was an idea that took over my whole mind and body. And Muriel feels like that sometimes, even though she has chosen to live with me, with us, and won't have any babies anyway. It's still a feeling that consumes her. And now that her womb has gone, it might take her a long time to get over the sadness of not being able to have a baby. We don't know yet.'

Then something became very clear to me. Or at least I thought it was clear. I had wanted to talk to Auntie about it, before I went to school, but now I had Mummy all to myself, so I asked her. 'Mummy, can I ask you something about what Auntie told me once.'

'Yes, my dear, you can ask me anything you like, and I will do my best to answer.'

'Well, Auntie told me that when she was married the first time, it took her years to have a baby, even though she and her husband… they tried a lot. But as soon as he got married again, his new wife had three children. Why was that?'

'Why was it so difficult for Auntie to have a baby, and yet it was so easy for her ex-husband's new wife?'

'Exactly. And did Muriel tell me all about S-E-X and periods when I was young, because she knew one day that I would go to a Catholic boarding school, with nuns, and they hate that subject so much that they keep it a secret from the girls?'

'Not exactly. Muriel couldn't have known what would happen to you in the future, but we are both very pleased that we have given you a good education in that subject, even though it got us all into lots of trouble.'

Then she sighed. 'I said, 'Please don't sigh, Mummy. I don't think there's anything to sigh about.'

Mummy said, 'Aileen has told me lots of things about herself. She has become a bit of an expert on periods, and why some women have babies and others don't. She talks about women's *fertility*. What she says is that some women are very fertile, and it's almost as if every time they have sex it causes them to have a baby. But other women are not so fertile, and they may only have one or two babies, or none at all. I think I'm one of those women who are very fertile. I don't know for sure about Muriel, but I have a very strong feeling that she is the same as me. Aileen says that most women hate their periods, and don't really understand that the days when you lose blood are only part of the story of what happens inside us during the month. Auntie hated her period, and to her it was a messy, inconvenient, and uncomfortable disappointment. Someone even told her that her period was her womb crying for the baby that hadn't been conceived. That, in my opinion, is the stupidest thing I have ever heard, and was probably said by a man who has no idea about women at all.'

'Like Daddy?' Mummy laughed, even though I was being serious. I said, 'I don't think Uncle Tom would say something like that.'

'You're quite right, but he couldn't resist inventing a character in one of his novels, a man, who says exactly that!' Anyway, before Auntie became pregnant with Callum, she used to say to herself, "This will surely be the month when I get pregnant." But she was always terribly disappointed when her blood came. The disappointment was driving her into depression, and making her hate herself. A bit like me.

'Luckily, she met a woman who understood all about problems with fertility, and helped Aileen to understand more about her body, and especially her womb. The woman told her all about the influence of the Moon, and how a woman's body changes every day throughout the month, depending on the moon. And these changes in our bodies influence how we feel. She helped Aileen to understand that at certain times of the month she might feel especially creative, and this could happen during her period, or perhaps in the middle of her cycle, when she was most fertile. Aileen was much happier once she understood that, and didn't hate her periods anymore. Then she could relax a bit and enjoy being with her husband, and eventually she had a baby.

'Pippa, I just want to say one more thing about this subject, and it's very important. Really, we would have talked about this when your own periods are about to start, but I want to talk about it now. Is that all right?'

'Yes please, Mummy. I really want to know about it.'

'Well, it's about my own periods, and about Muriel's, and why all women are different. I want to tell you, to put your mind at rest about the future. You see, I have terrible problems with my cycle. Not my periods themselves; I'm always so delighted when they come along. But it's the days leading up to my blood flowing. I become terribly blocked, and I feel in a lot of pain and it sometimes drives me mad.'

'I know, Mummy. I know.'

'Well, I'm unlucky about that, and I'm sure that it is a physical thing. Muriel, on the other hand, only feels a bit uncomfortable during her period. Aileen told me that when she first met Maggie, Maggie used to hate her period, and called it 'The Curse', because she had a lot of discomfort and it stopped her from doing sports and going swimming. So Aileen and Maggie talked about it a lot, and now Maggie understands a lot more about her cycle, and about the Moon, and about creativity. And when Maggie met Rhona, it's something that they talked about a lot together, and Rhona has been very influenced by these ideas, and says that she writes her best songs when she is in the middle of her cycle, which is when she is most fertile, and during her period.'

'So, Mummy, what will I be like? Will I be like you?'

'I don't know. Sometimes these things run in the family. But I don't know anything about my relatives. I like to think that you won't, because the ladies on Daddy's side of the family, as far as I know, don't have my type of problem. But there's one very exciting thing to think about.'

I suddenly knew what it was. 'Do you think that when I have my periods, I will be extra creative? That will be funny, because my mind is always full of ideas, so I just might explode!'

Mummy laughed, quietly. That's exactly what Muriel said!'

I thought about what she had said. I was starting to feel very sleepy. I said, 'But Muriel is so lucky to have you. To have someone who understands. That's how I know that you won't be like Auntie and her first husband. You will always be together.'

And after I said that, I said something that just came into my head. 'And because of that I can be a big strong girl, and not get upset in my boarding school.'

Mummy sighed, 'Pippa, these things that mothers and their daughters talk about; about their bodies and especially about making babies… well, they are very private. It's not something that children your age often talk about, except to say silly things that they don't really understand. And it's something that got us into trouble with your daddy and in The Court. The Judge thought that you are too young to know about how your body works, and especially about how babies are made. And it's not something Catholics like to talk about. The nuns and priests don't like it. It's a pity, but that's how they are. It's how they have been brought up; to believe that our bodies and loving our bodies is somehow wrong.'

'So was The Judge a Catholic?'

'He might have been.'

'And was Mr Ruskin a Catholic?'

'He might have been too. But it's not just Catholic grown-ups who don't talk about babies and periods and how boys and girls change as they get older. Poor Muriel found out about most of those things by accident, which must have been awful for her. We didn't want that to happen to you.'

'Is that why there has been so much trouble about my paintings?'

'Yes, I'm afraid so.'

'I wish I hadn't painted them.'

'I used to think that, but I don't anymore. You see, you are a very honest person. Eric once said that the most important thing about great artists is their honesty. Some people get very upset about what some artists paint, while others love it. And what people think of as great art nowadays would have been

480

condemned as disgraceful in the past. I think of Picasso especially.'

It was very hard work trying to understand everything that Mummy was saying, and I was becoming very sleepy, but the mention of Picasso woke me up immediately. Mummy said, 'Oh dear! That was a mistake, wasn't it? Now you're going to want to stay up all night and talk about painting. Let's try and go to sleep instead.' She held me tight and said, 'I think that Muriel will be all right in the end. But it's going to take her a long time to recover.'

I said, 'I do love you, Mummy. I know you will look after Muriel, just like you are looking after me.'

'I love you too, darling.'

'But who will look after you, now that Muriel is ill?'

'Oh, I'll be all right. I'm strong now, and it's my turn to look after her.'

What I was really asking was, 'Who is going to look after me?'

Mummy put her hand under my pyjama top, ran her hand over my chest and tickled my tummy, just like Muriel used to do. She said, 'You know, Pippa, we really want you to be at home with us, but I'm afraid it's not possible at the moment. I hope you understand that. We want to be the ones who care for you every day. But when you are at school, if anything is bothering you, tell your teacher. She is a new nun, called Sister Isabelle. Sister Anne told us that. She said, "I can't be everywhere, but I have chosen Isabelle to be my eyes and ears for your daughter." It was a bit mysterious, but she smiled and winked at us, and tapped the side of her nose twice with her finger. What do you think that meant?'

I said I didn't know, and asked if Sister Isabelle was nice.

'We didn't see her, but she must be. Isn't that exciting?'

It wasn't. More than ever, I felt that I didn't want to be apart from Mummy, but I couldn't say it, because she had so much on her mind.

Mummy sighed and said, 'I wasn't always a good Mummy, was I?'

'No. But you did your best, and I'm all right now.'

She kissed me on the back of the neck and said, 'You're a good girl, Pippa. And by the way, you should go to the hairdresser before you go to school, just to tidy your hair up a bit.'

'Can Maggie do it?'

'What a good idea!'

I said, 'Mummy, there's just one thing I want to know…' But I could feel myself slipping towards sleep, to that place where you can hear things around you, but nothing seems to make any sense. Mummy was saying something, but it sounded all jumbled up. But the very last thing I heard her say was, 'When your time comes, when your first period starts, I promise that I will be with you. I promise.'

Cutting my hair

The next morning, I went downstairs and saw Maggie fast asleep on the sofa. She heard me, and opened her eyes and called me to her. I sat next to her and she smiled and said that now that the other musicians were back, she wasn't able to sleep up in Rhona's cottage anymore. She made a grumpy face but then smiled again. She said, 'It won't be for long, because Rhona has asked me to go on holiday with her.' She pulled me close to her and whispered, 'But you won't tell anyone just yet, will you? It's supposed to be a secret, and I shouldn't have told you, but it sort of slipped out, because I'm so excited about it. She wants to take me to Greece! Can you imagine? I've never been out of Scotland!'

Then she looked at me closely, and told me to turn round. She said, 'Today's the day for me to cut everyone's hair, to make everyone look smart for the Ceilidh, and I'd love to start with you!'

Maggie's hair was short. She said that it was her *pixie look*, and she had been inspired by seeing Audrey Hepburn's films, and Jean Seberg in a film called *Breathless*.

I thought she had said, breastless, so I said, 'Does she look like Mummy then?' Maggie thought that was very funny. I asked her if she wanted to give Mummy a pixie look, and she thought that would be very exciting. She said that Mummy was very attractive, but needed to look after her hair a bit more. I told her that she would have to ask Muriel first, because Muriel always liked to help Mummy make decisions about her hair and clothes.

I had noticed quite a lot of young ladies in Stranhaven with pixie looks. I suspected that they were Maggie's friends. She asked me if girls at my school could have their hair cut whenever they wanted. I said, 'I don't know, I don't know anything about what happens there. I just know that boys who go to boarding schools get their hair cut in the most awful way.'

I wanted to cry and go back upstairs to Mummy. This was not a good way to start the morning. Maggie said, 'Oh dear. I think I'm upsetting you. Come and make some toast with me, and we can think about hair.'

As we ate our toast, Maggie told me that Rhona wanted to have short hair, but her manager wouldn't let her. Now that Rhona was quite famous, her manager said that she had to be very careful about how she looked. Maggie explained that Rhona liked her manager, but unfortunately he was a typical man, and didn't really understand a woman's needs. One of a woman's needs was to have her hair cut in whatever style she wanted. Rhona thought that she might have to find herself a new manager.

Mummy came downstairs and talked to us about my hair. Maggie said that she wanted to give it a bit of a trim, and then see what happened. Mummy asked me what I'd like to do, and I said I didn't know. I wasn't sure that I wanted a pixie look. I liked my hair being long, because then I could play with it, like Lucy, and have it in a ponytail or bunches, and sometimes a French plait. I wanted to ask Nicol what he thought, but he was still fast asleep.

Mummy said to me, 'And anyway, what does it matter what your hair looks like, as long as it's healthy and strong?'

But it did matter. And it always has done, ever since. My hair is very important to me, and other people too.

Maggie was keen to get started straight away. She said that she would cut my hair first, and then give it a good wash afterwards.

So there we were, in the kitchen, with a towel over my shoulders. Maggie wet my hair and snipped very quickly. I felt a large amount of hair fall onto my shoulders and onto the floor. Mummy gasped and Maggie said to her, 'OK?' and Mummy said, 'There's no turning back now,' and laughed quietly.

I seemed to sit there for a long time, and when Jessie came down she said, 'Goodness gracious! Look at all that hair on the floor!'

Then we were finished, and Maggie said to Mummy, 'Right Ruth, you tidy up and I'll help Pippa to wash and dry her hair in the bathroom, and I'll make a few small adjustments as we go along.'

I looked at Mummy. At first I thought she looked a bit doubtful, but then she smiled. She said, 'I've always wanted to work in a hairdresser's. Can you do my hair next?'

Jessie ran upstairs and woke up Nicol , and the pair of them came into the bathroom. That was a bit rude of them, because I might have been naked. Luckily I wasn't, and anyway, Nicol was used to seeing me with no top on. He used to say that I looked like him, but without the muscles. Then he would flex his arms and show me his biceps, or *eggs* as we used to call them. I used to get great pleasure from seeing and feeling them. I would do the same with my arms and he would feel them and we would laugh.

I looked in the mirror and saw a boy looking back at me. I screamed and said, 'I look awful! What have you done?' I ran into my bedroom and threw myself on my bed. I imagined all the girls in my new school having lovely long hair and looking very girlish, but me being the only one with short hair and looking just like a boy, and being teased for it. And I felt sure that none of them would have heard of Audrey Hepburn or Jean Seberg in Breathless, so they would just think I was a boy, and not like a famous actress. I heard Nicol come in and felt him sit on my bed. He said, 'I think you look lovely. It really suits you. You don't look like a boy at all.' When Nicol said that to me, I wasn't upset about my hair anymore. If he liked it, then that was all that mattered.

I went back to the bathroom and apologised to Maggie. She smiled. 'Och, when you cut someone's hair, you are always taking a risk. My grandfather is as bald as a coot, and says he wouldn't care what his hair looked like, as long as he had some! And anyway, I've cut it so that it'll grow nicely. So every morning when you look in the mirror, you'll see an even prettier girl than today. If you can imagine such a thing being possible.'

Surprisingly, Jessie refused point blank to allow Maggie to cut her hair, and got quite upset when Nicol teased her about it. She was quite a complicated child, I thought. Auntie came to see what was going on and smiled. She said to Maggie, 'So the big haircutting day has begun! Who's next, I wonder?'

I looked at Nicol's face. I thought that if he had had long hair, he might just have looked like a girl. He was lovely.

I wear my school uniform

Mummy said that I looked quite transformed, and that she would love to have a hairstyle just like mine. Then she said that I ought to try on my school uniform, to see what I looked like, and to see if she needed to make any adjustments. I really didn't want to do that. My uniform was in a bag on top of the wardrobe in our bedroom, and every night before I went to sleep I could see a corner of the bag sticking out, reminding me that my life in Stranhaven was just a holiday, and that the real, hard, and lonely life of boarding school was just around the corner. Mummy was very cheerful, and wouldn't listen to me when I said that I would look silly. She said, 'Of course you won't! It's all part of the adventure!'

Really and truly, I was worried about what Nicol would say.

Mummy helped me to get dressed, and when I looked in the big mirror I really didn't look too terrible at all. The only thing that I didn't like was that my blazer was very big and my tights were scratchy. Everything looked nice and new. Even my shoes, which I had remembered as being very clumpy, looked nice, and they were surprisingly comfortable.

Then Mummy reminded me that there were still two new things for me to wear: my straw hat and my satchel. And when I put my straw hat on she gave a sigh and kissed me, and said that I looked lovely with my new uniform on, but with my hat on I looked perfect. I heard her voice wobble, and when I looked at her behind me in the mirror, she was wiping tears from the corners of her eyes with the backs of her hands.

Then Jessie came in and saw us, and immediately ran out to tell everyone, and they all came in to have a look at me. Maggie said that she loved my hat. She said the next time I went to see Muriel I should go with my uniform on, because she was certain that she would love to see me. Mummy said that was an excellent idea, and that we would go that evening.

Then Maggie ran downstairs and rang Rhona. It was still quite early in the morning, but Rhona came over very quickly. Usually she was a late riser, because she liked to stay up late, playing music and talking to Maggie. But that morning she said that now that the other musicians were there she hadn't enjoyed being at the cottage. She loved my hair and my hat. She said, 'It's gorgeous! I want one! And your hair! You look like Jean Seberg!'

Mummy said, 'If you want a hat like Pippa's, then you'll have to go to Pearson's in the town where Pippa's school is.'

Rhona laughed and clapped her hands and said, 'We will, and we'll come and see you straight away afterwards!'

Then I realised that I wouldn't be allowed to wear my straw hat in September. I told Rhona that I would have to wear a beret, and she said that was perfect, because berets were very fashionable. Mummy brought it in and Rhona put it on me. She made me look in the mirror and said, 'See? Did you ever see a more beautiful girl, because I never did! I'm going to buy one of those berets and wear it the next time I go on stage.'

Playing for Muriel

Auntie told Mummy that she wasn't able to come with us to the hospital, because Uncle Tom had gone away, and she couldn't ask Maggie to look after Nicol and Jessie, because Rhona and Maggie were going out for the evening. Auntie said to Mummy, 'Anyway, this whole supervised visits idea is a nonsense. You don't need me to go with you.'

Mummy looked very nervous and said, 'I don't know. I'm torn. I'm desperate to see Muriel, and I want Pippa to come with me, but I don't want to put a foot wrong with her father, or The Court.'

Hearing Mummy mention Daddy and The Court made me feel very frightened, so I told her that she should go on her own.

Mummy said to Auntie, 'This is ridiculous. Aileen, please can you give me Mr Shepherd's telephone number, so can I ring him, to sort this out for myself?'

And that's what Mummy did. She told me to go upstairs and get ready to go out. I was already ready, so I knew that Mummy didn't want me to hear what she was saying. Normally I would have stood at the top of the stairs, where Mummy couldn't see me, so I could listen to what she said, but this evening I ran into my room and sang Help! by The Beatles at the top of my voice, to make sure I couldn't hear what Mummy was talking about. I sang, I Want to Hold Your Hand and was half-way through A Hard Day's Night, when Mummy came in and said, 'Pippa, whatever are you doing?' She looked very pleased with herself, and said, 'Mr Shepherd used to really annoy me, but if you speak to him nicely, he's really quite charming.' I knew that he had agreed that we could go to the hospital together, without Auntie. Mummy said, 'And there's another thing...' but she stopped herself, and said, 'Let's not keep that nice Mr Griffin waiting!'

Mr Griffin was waiting outside, and Mummy told me to get in the back of the car, and she shut the door. She stayed outside with Mr Griffin, and stood very close to him, and started talking. She had her back to me, but I could see Mr Griffin's face very clearly. He looked very surprised, and I could just hear him say, 'Blimey O'Riley! That's the first I've heard of that! I hope you aren't having me on, Mrs Dunbar.'

Mr Griffin was usually quite chatty in the car, but today he didn't say anything.

When we entered Muriel's ward, she was awake and sitting up in bed. She gave me a huge smile and opened her arms and said, in a loud voice, 'Hello Alice! You've come to see me, after all these years!'

I said, 'It's Pippa. I'm Pippa.'

Muriel looked confused and then smiled and said, 'Oh yes, of course you are. Just for a moment I thought perhaps I was in Heaven and you were Alice Fisher. You look just like her. Don't you look smart?"

Mummy looked worried, then smiled. 'But I thought you said that you would like to spend Eternity with Pippa and me.'

Muriel laughed. 'Yes, but it would be nice to bump into my old friend from time to time, while I'm wandering around Heaven waiting for you to join me. I'm sure you'd both get on like a house on fire.'

Then Muriel tried to push herself up in bed, to make herself more comfortable. She winced. I said, 'What's wrong, Muriel?'

'It's the morphine. It stops the pain, but gives one all sorts of strange ideas.' I put my hand in hers. It was cold and sweaty at the same time. She said, 'Let me look at you. Oh how I love your hat! It's perfect. Promise me you'll keep it forever. And your hair! It's so lovely. It suits you down to the ground.'

Mummy said, 'And that's where most of Pippa's hair ended up, by the time Maggie had finished.'

Muriel thought that was funny. She said, 'Oh Ruth, might Maggie cut your hair like that?'

Mummy laughed, 'What, so I'd look like a cross between a young boy and Audrey Hepburn?'

Muriel laughed, then frowned, then smiled. She said to Mummy, 'Do you remember when we sang songs from My Fair Lady and danced all over the kitchen, and Pippa was astonished?' She started to sing, 'All I want is a room somewhere, far away from the cold night air.'

I said, 'Muriel, I've brought my concertina. Would you like me to play you a little tune?'

She looked very pleased, 'I'd love it, but won't it disturb the other patients and their visitors?'

Mummy went to find a nurse. The ex-horrible nurse came over and said, 'Och I'm sure they'd love a wee tune. Everybody loves to hear children sing and play music. It'll do them good, and give them something to talk about.'

I played the chorus of Black Jack David several times, and then the very first song that Auntie had taught me, and finally Captain Pugwash. Muriel sighed, 'Oh, that's the most perfect sight; the most wonderful child in the whole world, transformed into a beautiful schoolgirl and playing the concertina! If I never in my life see anything else, then that is surely something I will remember for Eternity.' Then her eyeballs made that funny sliding movement to one side, and I knew that I had exhausted her. She closed her eyes and we held her hands and Mummy stroked Muriel's arm and she went to sleep. Mummy cried. I said, 'What's the matter, Mummy?'

She said, 'Oh you are so beautiful, outside and in. Sometimes it's so hard to be brave. I'll be all right in a little while. I'm sorry.'

I said, 'Don't be sorry.' That made her cry even more. Mummy was on the other side of the bed, and I wanted to go over and comfort her, but I felt Muriel gripping my hand, and I just couldn't bring myself to let go.

Mummy said, 'What are we going to do, Pippa? What are we going to do?'

I said, 'Could you phone Daddy and ask him to help us?'

She said, 'I've been wanting to tell you all day. Daddy is coming to stay in his big house, and of course, he wants to see you. He wants to have supper with you on Friday evening.'

That was a shock

That was a shock. We were still holding Muriel's hands. She opened her eyes again and said, 'Hello. Are you still here?' Mummy said, 'Of course we are, my dear. We still have some time left.'

'Time left before what?'

'Before the end of Visiting Time.'

'Of course. Of course. I'm a bit confused. Please may I have a drink of water?'

She asked that like a child. She used her adult voice, but she looked just like I might have done when I was in hospital. The whole scene filled me with a terrible sadness. Now I would say that it was pathetic. My lovely, strong, reliable Muriel, who had saved us from disaster, was now a disaster herself. She was like an old lady who had become a little girl again.

Mummy put the glass of water to Muriel's lips and she took a few sips. Mummy said, 'Listen carefully, Muriel. Andrew is coming to Aberdeen this week.'

Muriel frowned. Mummy said, 'Andrew Dunbar, my ex-husband, Pippa's father.'

'Whatever for? To see me? Surely not. I'm not sure I want him to see me looking like this.'

'It's all right. He wants to see Pippa before she goes to school. He wants to come and thank Tom and Aileen for being so kind to Pippa. And while he's here, he wants to stay in his big house. And he wants to visit this hospital, to speak to the people who are going to be building the new wing. He's donated a lot of money, after all.'

Muriel suddenly became very alert. 'What a good idea, don't you think? He'll be so busy that he'll forget about me!'

'But what if he wants to meet you? I think he might. Would you send him away?'

'Not at all. But I've only met him briefly. What could we possibly have to talk about? Does he want to come and look at all the damage he's caused?'

Mummy frowned and looked at me. 'Muriel, please don't say things like that. It upsets me terribly.'

Muriel said, 'I'm sorry, Ruth. Sometimes I have no idea what I'm saying. Yesterday I was sure that I saw a giraffe outside the window! Will you be with me when Andrew comes, in case I say the wrong thing?'

'I'll try, but can't promise.'

'Please try. I miss you both so much!' Then it was Muriel's turn to cry. I sat and watched Mummy hug her. I didn't cry. I didn't even feel any tears coming to my eyes. I just sat there and watched, and listened.

Mummy took a hanky out of her bag, wiped Muriel's tears, and helped her to blow her nose. Muriel said, 'You know, Ruth, I keep thinking about when I was Pippa's age. I think I have painted a rather grim picture of my life at boarding school. I think I had forgotten some of the fun things that we did.'

'Well Pippa is just here, so why don't you tell her yourself?'

Muriel smiled at me. 'Hello darling. Come here. Come to me.'

I wanted to climb on the bed, like I had done before, but this time I was worried that I might squash Muriel, and crack one of her bones. I stood as close to her as I could, and she held onto my arm. She said, 'Don't take any notice of what I've been saying to you recently. I feel as if I've been floating along on a cloud of nonsense. I don't think I've said thank you to you.'

'Thank you for what? What have I done?'

'What have you done? Well, I think about that all the time. Just being with you, knowing you, has been such fun.'

I looked at Mummy. She could see the alarm on my face. She said, 'Muriel, you are going to get better, you know. It won't be long until the doctors know what to do about your second illness. Let's talk about now, and the future!'

Muriel frowned again. 'I'm sorry. I suppose everyone who is ill sometimes gets low and thinks the worst.'

Mummy said, 'Pippa, tell Muriel about something nice.'

I said the first thing that came into my head. 'Muriel, do you remember when you fell over at the station? When we first met you? And do you remember when you used to dive in the swimming pool? And do you remember when you took me to the post office and bought me Bounties? And when we looked at the Modigliani books together? And when we were in the Greek restaurant, and when we found Polish Teddy? And how you used to hold me and make me feel so safe and sound? And when the Nasty Nun beat me and you kissed all my wounds? And how you used to dry me after my bath in a big fluffy towel?'

Muriel smiled a big smile. 'Of course I do. I think of those things all the time. I'm not an old lady who has lost all her marbles, you know. At least not yet, anyway. I'm still the Muriel who did all those things.'

That made me feel much better. 'Well I think of those things all the time too. When I was in trouble, when I first came to Scotland, I remembered all the lovely things that we had done together. Just like Mr Wordsworth and his daffodils. I didn't have anyone to talk to for hours on end, except Ursula, of course. So we talked about you for hours at a time. If I had forgotten something, then she would remind me. It was Ursula who told me to put the colour of your hair in every painting I ever did. And it was Ursula who said that I was such a lucky girl to have met you. Please speak to Daddy. I'm sure that he will be nice to you. I'm going to be nice to him, even if he might be a bit grumpy with me.'

But then I couldn't say anything else, because I couldn't see Muriel anymore. It felt like all the tears I hadn't cried since I had been in Scotland were pouring out of my eyes and down my nose. I didn't want to make a noise. I didn't want to disturb anyone. But I couldn't help it. It felt like I was underwater in the deep end of the swimming pool, and I was sinking. It was as if I had heavy weights attached to my feet and that there were invisible hands dragging me down; It didn't matter how much I tried to kick my legs and swim upwards, towards the light, I couldn't move at all. My heart was hammering and I had a horrible burning sensation in my throat.

Muriel pulled my arm towards her, and Mummy held me from behind. I couldn't hear anything, because I was crying so much. I tried to say, 'Oh Muriel! Please don't die! Please be strong! I don't think I could live without you! All the time I was in that terrible place, I thought about you and Mummy being so happy together. And even when I was starving with hunger and so thirsty, and my tummy was hurting terribly and my head ached, and I was so lonely and frightened, all I had to do was think about you, and then I knew that it didn't matter how horrible people were being to me, I would be all right. You have made Mummy and me into strong people.' I tried to say that, but I think it came out like a stream of Double Dutch, like a baby.

Mummy was holding me tight and Muriel was stroking my face. I heard the nurse say, 'Is everything all right? Of course it's not. What can I do to help? Quick, sit her down and put her head between her legs.' I felt her grab me from behind and put me on a chair, and then try to force my head down. I thought that she was trying to drown me.

I heard Muriel say, 'It's all right Pippa. Just breathe. Take a big breath in and out, in, and out. That's a good girl. Do it for Muriel.'

Mummy said, 'My daughter is very upset. She thinks that her aunt is going to die.'

The nurse said, 'Well, I can tell you that's not going to happen. But shall I see if I can find a doctor to explain what they are going to do?'

I lifted my head up, and my tears cleared, and I saw Muriel crouching beside me. She said, 'That's very kind of you, Connie, but there's really no need.' Muriel said to me, 'Connie and I are very good friends, aren't we, Connie?'

The nurse coughed. She said, 'Oh yes, I've been looking after Muriel. We've had quite a laugh together.'

Muriel said, 'You see, Pippa? Muriel's not going to die. I'm as tough as old boots, just like your mummy.'

Then she leant back on the side of her bed and laughed and said, 'Whoops! Could someone help me get back into bed please?'

That made me stop crying and I smiled. Then Muriel shouted, 'Ow!' and the nurse said, 'Right, everyone out please!' Then I saw why Muriel shouldn't have got out of bed. There was a rubber pipe on the floor and at the end of it was a clear bag with orange-yellow liquid in it. It was Muriel's wee. I supposed the pipe had been attached inside her.

Mummy put her arm around me and led me away from Muriel's bed. I supposed the nurse was going to stick the tube back up inside Muriel. We walked up the ward and out into the corridor. I asked Mummy if it was my fault that Muriel had hurt herself. She said, 'Not at all. Muriel is a grown-up. She decides what she wants to do. Don't go blaming yourself for things that adults do.'

'But if I hadn't cried like a baby then she wouldn't have jumped out of bed and her pipe wouldn't have come out, and she wouldn't have been hurt. So it was my fault!'

'Well Pippa, I have to disagree with you. If I were in hospital, like Muriel is, I would want to see you more than anything. It would make me feel better. I might get upset, but afterwards I would get over it. And I would think to myself, "My darling girl loves me, so I must get better, so I can care for her, as soon as possible." '

I said, 'Well, perhaps that nurse was right. All I did was upset everyone.'

'No you didn't. You didn't upset anyone. What you did was show everyone how you feel. That's not a bad thing. I wish everyone could be like you.'

Then a bell rang to tell us that Visiting Time was over. As we walked back to Muriel's bed, a lady called out that she had

494

enjoyed my little concert, and asked me if I was still upset. I said, 'Thank you very much. I'm all right now, thank you.'

The lady said, 'Good. It's very dull in here. It's nice to see and hear children. God bless you, my dear.'

Mummy said, 'See? What did I tell you?'

Muriel was back in bed. The nurse said to me, 'We were going to take that tube out anyway, so don't you worry about anything.'

Mummy said, again, 'See? What did I tell you?' This made me laugh. It was an important lesson. Mummy wiped my face with her hanky. I looked down at the front of my pinafore dress. It had slobber all over it. Mummy said, 'Don't worry, darling. It won't stain.'

A picture for Daddy

I found it very difficult to get to sleep. I tried very hard, but couldn't stop thinking about Muriel, and about Daddy coming. After about half an hour of Mummy stroking me and lying quietly beside me, she said, 'Right Pippa Herman, this won't do. You're obviously wide-awake. Get your drawing things and let's go downstairs.'

Downstairs, Auntie and Uncle Tom were sitting, reading. Mummy sat down next to Auntie and they began talking quietly about books. I asked Mummy if she would come with me to have supper with Daddy. She said, 'No, darling, I won't. Daddy wants to spend time with you on your own. I'll go and see Muriel.' Then she said, 'And what do you think about that?' I was surprised at Mummy asking me that. Then I realised that it was always Muriel who would ask me, 'How do you feel about that, Pippa?' and 'What do you think about that idea?' or 'How does that make you feel?' And I would think very carefully about what I thought and how I felt, and would thoroughly enjoy telling Muriel all about it. But Mummy rarely asked me what I thought and felt, and I would be very careful before telling her. That was the difference between her and Muriel. I had never in my life been terrified of Muriel. I had never felt the need to be careful with her, or to think before I said anything to her.

I said, 'Really and truly, Mummy, I'm frightened of Daddy. I don't want to be with him on my own. Can Auntie come with me, like she has to be with you when you see me?'

Mummy frowned, 'I'm afraid not, my dear. But there's no need to be frightened of Daddy. I think it's a very good thing that you two will get to know each other better. It should have happened a long time ago.'

'But Mummy, he wasn't very nice to me last time he saw me. He told me off for being disobedient, and took photographs of my paintings, and he was horrible to you and Muriel. I'm worried that I might say the wrong thing, and then he might never let me see you again.'

And then I said something that I didn't even know was in my mind. I frightened myself as I said it, 'What if he tells Mr Griffin to grab me, and tie me up and put me in a sack and take me to South Africa? What would happen then?'

Mummy said, 'Pippa, come and sit on my lap.' I did. She said, 'Listen very carefully to me. Your daddy would never do anything like that. He loves you, even though he might not show it in the same way as other people. Also, he has to do what The Court tells him, and he can't take you anywhere without talking to Mr Macmillan first. And he is certainly won't take you out of the country without permission. Do you think I'd let you go with him, if I thought for one minute that he would do a thing like that?' She didn't give me a chance to answer. 'So I suggest you stop being worried, and think of your time with Daddy as a bit of an adventure. I'm sure he'll show you all over his huge house. You are such a lucky girl. Practically everyone in the town wants to know what it's like in there. I hear there's a lovely garden at the back, and there might even be a swing.'

That worked completely. I loved swings. Then I had an idea. 'Can Nicol and Jessie come with me?' I felt sure that they would love to explore the house as well and run around in the garden.

'Not this time, though it does sound like a good idea for another visit. Now, you go and sit at the table and draw something interesting. Perhaps something to give to Daddy.'

I sat at the table and opened my sketchbook. I had brought down some pastels and a box of charcoal sticks. I loved charcoal. It was so delicate, but produced such fascinating lines and effects. I wondered if it would make me over-excited and not be able to go to sleep. I don't remember what happened next. I suppose I must have fallen asleep at the table.

The next morning when I came downstairs, Nicol and Jessie had already gone to school. I must have slept so deeply that I didn't hear them go. My painting was still on the table, and I have to admit that it looked quite strange. It was of the Lang Stane, with the hazy grey sky and the grey clouds and the stone, and two lovers dressed in white robes, flying high overhead. They had dropped garlands onto the stone and were flying away, hand in hand. The stone and the sky were very indistinct, but I had paid a lot of attention to the garlands. Every flower was different, and were from the Scottish wild flowers wrapping paper that Muriel had given me, which I had spent a lot of time studying. The lovers were surrounded by a blue haze, and I knew where that idea had come from. It was pure Marc Chagall, and was very much like the painting I had done for Maggie. I asked Mummy about it and she explained that yes, they had found me asleep at the table, with the completed picture in front of me. Uncle Tom had carried me up into bed and afterwards the three of them had talked for a long time about my picture. They thought that it was extremely beautiful, but all agreed that it would be best not to show it to Daddy.

A Call for Me

Rhona dropped in at teatime, and Uncle Tom asked me to show her my picture. Her response was a bit surprising. She said, very quietly, 'I feel rapture.' That was all she said. She passed it to Maggie, and Maggie's face went very red.

Uncle Tom said, 'It's extraordinary, isn't it?'

Jessie said, 'Is that you and Maggie flying over the Lang Stane and dropping garlands on it, because you'd both like to have babies?'

I didn't know what to say. Jessie said to me, 'Well, Pippa, you should know. After all, it was you who drew it!' Mummy explained to her how, when I was a little girl, I used to draw in my bedroom just before I went to sleep, and in the morning have no memory of what I had done. I was getting very embarrassed. I looked at Nicol. He smiled at me. I remembered that he was my boyfriend now, and that thought made me not care about what anyone said about me.

Rhona said, 'It's as if Chagall himself had painted it. Please may I have it?' I said yes. And she took it, before anyone could object.

The next day, after breakfast, I sat down and wrote a poem. I was thinking about my time in Stranhaven, and all the exciting things that we had done together. I was thinking most about Nicol and his sisters, and their dead mother. My mummy wasn't dead; she was just living somewhere far away. Nicol's mother had swum out to sea, and drowned, but Nicol believed she was still out at sea, like a Selkie, even though her body had been washed up on the shore, and he knew that she was buried in the ground. And if he called her enough times, she might swim back to dry land, and come and see him in the night, while he was asleep. I thought about the song that Rhona had written about him, and about when we had stood and called to the cows. And most of all, I thought about how Mummy and Muriel had reappeared in my life. In a funny kind of way, I was like Nicol's mother. I had passed into another world, and was living a new life. But instead of me calling to Mummy, she was calling to me, and one day the phone would ring, and I would answer her call

Nicol came in after school and asked me what I had been doing. I said, 'I've written a poem. You can read it out loud, or

498

perhaps sing it as a song. It just came into my head. It's about us.'

'About you and me?'

'It's about all of us here, and people living far away. It's called 'A Call for Me'. I read it to Nicol.

'Everyone is calling, calling, calling.

The big sister calling on her best friend, just back from Germany,

The brother calls for his mother, out beyond the sea,

The little sister calls to the cows, eating grass upon the lea,

We're all calling out to someone, including the bird up in the tree,

And when I hear the phone ring

I hope it's a call for me.'

Nicol smiled. He said, 'If you show it to Rhona, I'm sure she'll make a song out of it.'

Supper with Daddy

For the next few days, I wasn't really able to concentrate on anything very well. Mummy went for a walk with Auntie Aileen every morning, and then Rhona came down to our house and she and Maggie would have a chat with Mummy. Then Mummy went with Mr Griffin to Aberdeen every afternoon, while I stayed behind in Stranhaven. When my cousins came home from school, we practiced our songs, but I kept making mistakes. On Thursday, while rehearsing with Nicol and Jessie, I made more mistakes than ever. Jessie tutted at me and rolled her eyes, which made me feel like crying. Nicol told Jessie off, and she said she was sorry, and we went to knock for Kirsty and Kenny, and went to the playground. Kenny said that their dad had got drunk in the night, and that they had both been frightened.

I told him about me getting upset in the hospital, and Muriel jumping out of bed, and how I had seen the long tube and the bag of her wee. This story seemed to cheer Kirsty and Kenny up straight away.

Nicol said, 'You poor thing.' That was a very grown up thing for him to say, and I was pleased with myself for choosing such a kind and grown up boyfriend. Then Kenny farted very loudly and Nicol laughed his head off, and that made me realise that he was still a very silly boy after all.

Kirsty asked me, 'Is your daddy really very rich?' I told her that he was, but I didn't know him very well. She said, 'No wonder you're a bit quiet today.'

I told her I was a bit worried that I might say the wrong thing and get Mummy into trouble. Kirsty said, 'Yes, that's what I would feel as well.'

We sat quietly on the bench and watched Nicol and Kenny take turns to push Jessie higher and higher, on the swing, to make her scream. Kirsty said, 'I have a good idea. It always works with my mum when she's feeling a bit funny, and we don't really know what to say to her. Ask him what he likes to pray about.'

The next day, after lunch, Mummy got my clothes ready to wear in the evening, because she had to take the train to Aberdeen. She had helped me look smart, and I was wearing my new kilt with Maggie and Rhona's silver kilt pin, and a very nice white blouse. Then at the last minute, Mummy said, 'I've got an idea, Pippa! Why don't you wear your school uniform? I'm sure Daddy would love to see you wearing that.'

This was the very first time that Mummy had ever changed her mind like that. And it was the first time that I told her exactly what I thought about one of her ideas. 'No, Mummy. I don't like that idea at all. If Daddy wants to see me in my uniform, then he can wait to see my school photograph!'

Mummy looked very surprised, so I said, 'And really and truly, I might spill food on my nice new pinafore dress.'

Mummy smiled, then frowned, then smiled again. That told me that she was nervous. I said, 'Don't worry, Mummy, I'll be all right. I'll have a nice time with Daddy. I'll be on my best behaviour.'

Mummy said, 'Of course you will. You're such a good girl. When have you ever behaved badly? I have no worries about you at all.'

I shouldn't have said what I said next. 'So Mummy, why are you frowning?'

Mummy looked in my eyes. She said, 'Pippa, you really are growing up, aren't you? You'd have never spoken to me like that before.' I thought she was telling me off. I must have looked frightened, but she smiled that smile of hers that I sometimes saw, with all the sadness of her life behind it. 'I'm thinking about Muriel. I can't hide it from you. I'm very worried about her. She's not at all well.'

'Oh, Mummy!'

'I know, Pippa. I don't know why I'm so worried. The doctor told me that she is doing as well as can be expected. But until they know what is exactly wrong with her, all they can do is give her injections of very strong medicine, to help take her terrible pain away. And she's so thin!'

I didn't know what to say. Mummy said, 'I'm sorry, darling. I told myself I wouldn't say anything to you. But Muriel always tells me that telling someone the truth is more important than hiding it.'

Mummy smiled, but the sadness was still there. She kissed me. 'You are such a dear child. Everyone says so. I'm so lucky to have you.' I was about to say something, but she put her finger on my lips. 'And your daddy; who hardly knows you at all, will have the pleasure of discovering what a delightful daughter he has.'

Soon after that, Mummy left the house. When Nicol came home from school, I sat with him and had a very deep think. He knew that I was a bit upset, so he just read a book, which was very nice of him. I thought about Nicol, whose mother had possibly drowned herself. Whatever the true story was, she had left her children behind. I thought about Kirsty and Kenny, and their mother in the special clinic, and their father who drank too much whisky and frightened them in the night. Thinking about them made me realise that my own life wasn't so bad after all. But the one person I couldn't bring myself to think about was Muriel. If I did, I kept seeing the long tube that had been up inside her, and the bag of her yellow-orange wee.

I think I must have started to cry, because Nicol asked me if I was all right. I told him what I was thinking, except for the bit about his mother. He said, 'If I gave you a kiss, would that make you feel better?'

I said, 'Yes please.' We both laughed at that and he kissed me on the cheek and suddenly all my fear of Daddy vanished.

At a quarter to six, Mr Griffin came to collect me. He had washed his car and was wearing a very smart suit and tie. We drove through the big gates again, and as soon as the big house came into view, I saw a tall man waiting outside the front door. I knew it was Daddy. The last time I had driven there had been to play music to the cows, and the time before that I had jumped out of the car to run towards Muriel. I didn't jump out of the car this time. Mr Griffin stopped his car at the bottom of the steps, where Daddy was waiting. He got out and left his door open, and shook hands with Daddy. I heard Daddy say, 'Good man, Griffin. You've done sterling work. Thank you for everything.'

Mr Griffin looked very pleased. Then Daddy came over to the car and opened my door. He leaned in and put his hand towards me. I held onto it and he half-pulled, half-helped me out of the car. He said, 'How nice to see you again, Pippa.'

It was windy, and the rain was spitting. He said, 'What would you like to do? Have a quick look around the garden, and then a tour of the house before supper?'

I said, 'Yes please.'

He kept hold of my hand, and we walked along the side of the house. Our shoes crunched on the gravel. I didn't like holding Daddy's hand. It was a very big house and it seemed to take a very long time to get to the back of it. All the way there, I was trying to think of how I could let go of Daddy's hand, without appearing rude. In the end, he let go of it, and lit a cigarette. He was wearing the same coat as when I had first met him. I looked at his shoes. They looked the same too.

He saw me looking at his shoes. He said, 'I like your new coat and shoes. You look very smart, Pippa. When you're growing fast, like you are, one needs to be buying new clothes all the time. But I've stopped growing now, so what I like to do is find the very best clothes, and wear them a lot. That saves me from having to waste time going shopping, and I can put my money to a better use.'

I didn't know what to say. He laughed and said, 'You probably don't know what to say to me. We're almost strangers. But we can have a nice chat over supper, and then we will understand each other much better, don't you think?'

I said, 'Yes, Daddy.'

He asked me if I liked to eat fish and I said, 'Yes I do.' I was going to say, 'Especially Birds Eye fish fingers,' but I thought that would sound silly, so instead I said, 'What a lovely garden. Please can I come here one day to play with Nicol and Jessie, and perhaps Kirsty and Kenny?'

Daddy laughed. He said, 'That will make a change for Mrs Mackie. She's usually here all on her own!'

The garden actually wasn't very special, and there were no swings, but the lawn was huge and very soft. It was like walking on a firm sponge. I thought it would be wonderful to run around on with bare feet, and do cartwheels. Daddy said, 'Your nice new shoes are getting all wet. Let's go inside.'

He held my hand again, and this time I didn't mind quite so much. He hummed a tune to himself as we walked. As soon as we got inside the front door, Daddy took his shoes off, and asked me to do the same. Then he changed his mind. He said, 'Do you know what? Let's give our shoes a jolly good wipe on the mat, and I'm sure we won't leave a mess.'

He took my shoes over to the huge mat in front of the door. He knelt down and gave each of them a good, hard wipe. He inspected them closely and passed them to me. Then he wiped his own shoes. Mrs Mackie appeared from around the corner.

She saw us kneeling on the mat and said, 'Goodness, sir! I can do that for you!'

Daddy said, 'No problem at all. I prefer to do things for myself, and I'm sure Pippa's the same.'

Mrs Mackie smiled at me. I felt sure that she wanted to say something nice to me, and perhaps even ask how Muriel was. But instead she just winked and said nothing. I tried to wink back, but it must have looked like I was just closing and opening both of my eyes.

Daddy said, 'We're going on a tour of the house. How long shall we take, Pippa? Are you very hungry? If so, it can be just a short trip, but if you'd prefer to wait, then we can take a lot longer.'

He seemed to be asking me a lot of questions all at once, and I wasn't sure how to answer, so I just replied, 'Yes, Daddy.'

He said, 'Yes to what? What would you like to do?'

I said, 'Whatever you like.'

He said, 'Then let's go for the middle. Let's say supper in half an hour. Is that possible Mrs Mackie?'

She said, 'Yes, of course, sir.'

Daddy said, 'Jolly good,' then held my hand again.

He said, 'I know you love Art, so let's have a little explore, and you can count how many pictures you see. I have one original painting by a very famous artist, and I wonder if you can spot it.'

Suddenly I forgot to be quiet and on my best behaviour. I almost shouted, 'How wonderful! Please can you give me a clue?'

He laughed and said, 'Come on. You can ask me questions about the artist as we go along.'

I said, 'Daddy, I don't know if you know this, but sometimes I can get a bit too excited about Art. What if it's a painting by Marc Chagall, or Wassily Kandinsky or Franz Marc, or even a sketch by Mr Henry Moore? I might not be able to breathe for a little while, and I might go off into a dream. But don't be frightened, because I always calm down.'

504

Daddy looked at me. He smoothed his moustache and smiled. 'Well, luckily it's not any of those, though I am a great admirer of their work.'

We walked up a very wide staircase. There were very large paintings on the wall all the way up, but they seemed a bit old and dark and not very interesting. Daddy took me along a long corridor with lots of doors. I think I had been expecting to see lots of suits of armour, and stuffed animal heads on the walls. But most of the walls were blank, apart from one or two paintings here and there. They didn't really interest me very much.

Daddy said, 'Right, let's see if you can guess who painted the most valuable painting in this house, and then we can go and find it.' All fear of my father completely vanished. It was an extraordinary feeling. I asked, 'Is it a man or a lady?

Daddy said, 'A man, of course. How many lady artists do you know of? I mentioned six of them, including Lady Celia. Daddy rubbed his chin and said, 'I see that you have had a very thorough art education already. But then I've known that for a while.'

I asked my other questions, and Daddy answered with only one word.

Is he dead? Yes.

Was he British? Yes.

Were his paintings of real things, or imaginary? Real

Are they exact, like photographs, or impressions? Impressions.

Did he live in this century? No.

Did he paint the sea? Yes.

Did he paint a picture about a shipwreck? Yes.

With each question, I was getting more and more excited. At first I wondered if it might be William Blake, or perhaps Constable. But once I asked about the shipwreck, I was certain. I could feel myself filling up with excitement, like a balloon. I had once seen a photograph of his painting, Wreckers: Coast of Northumberland, with a Steamboat Assisting. Having lived in Northumberland, and loving the sea and this man's work in

505

general, this painting has always fascinated me. I said, 'Daddy, it's surely not a painting by Mr JMW Turner, is it?'

Daddy clapped his hands. 'Well done! What a clever girl you are! And you're still only nine years old. That's quite extraordinary!'

I said, 'Mummy... and Muriel, have been very careful to help me find out all I want to know about Art.'

There it was, out in the open; I had mentioned Muriel's name. Daddy didn't seem to mind. I said, 'And really and truly, Lady Celia has been my biggest inspiration.'

That might have been a mistake. He didn't seem very pleased about hearing her name. He said, 'Yes, so I'm told.' I wasn't sure what he meant by that. I thought that from now on I'd have to be very careful about what I said.

Daddy put his hand on my back, between my shoulders. 'Come, my little artist. Let's go off in search of our very own Turner!' We went back downstairs, and to my horror, he took me to the room where Muriel had been ill on the sofa, and where I had been sick on the table. Mrs Mackie was in there, getting the table ready for our supper. She stood up straight when we came in. She said, 'I'm sorry sir, I'm not quite ready. I was going to call you shortly.'

Daddy said, 'Oh, that's all right. Don't worry about us. We're just going to have a look at the paintings in the room next door. Please carry on.'

She didn't carry on, but just stood looking at Daddy. She seemed to be a bit frightened of him, as if he were a king or something. I wondered if she had told Daddy about Muriel bleeding on the sofa and me vomiting on his table. I hoped not.

We went through two open doors and into the next room. It had three very big windows, so there was quite a lot of light in there. There were a few paintings on each wall, and at first I couldn't see anything that looked like a painting by Turner. I wondered if Daddy had been teasing me. But then I saw it. The reason why I hadn't spotted it straight away was because I had only ever seen very large Turners, but had missed this one

506

because it was very small, and too high up for me to see it properly.

Daddy was very pleased with me. He said, 'Let's get a chair so you can stand on it and take a good look.'

He brought over a very fancy chair and helped me to stand on it. Even when I was standing on the chair, Daddy was still taller than me.

He explained that the painting was called The Dark Rigi, and that Turner loved the small Swiss town of Lausanne. He painted three paintings of the mountain called The Rigi. The other two were in museums, but Daddy had bought this one at an auction in London, and was very pleased with it. He said he loved Turner's work, but also knew that paintings become more valuable with time, so it was what he called a good investment.

I was only half-listening to what he was saying, because I was looking very closely at the yellow of the sky and how Turner had used blue, black and white to create the mountain, and how the light on the shore made it look so slippery. I heard Daddy say, 'Whoops, I've got you!' and I felt him hold me up. I must have slipped into My Colour Dream and lost my balance.

I was suddenly wide-awake. Daddy lifted me under the arms, and put me on my feet on the ground. He said, 'So finally I've witnessed your famous trance state! I've heard about you doing that, but never really believed it. What happened?' I was a bit embarrassed and still not fully back with him, so couldn't say anything. He said, 'What a funny, intense little girl you are. And to think that Muriel took you to the National Gallery, and a very nice attendant gave you a set of opera glasses, so that you could look at a painting properly!'

I wasn't sure what he was talking about, but then I remembered seeing Van Gogh's A Wheatfield, with Cypresses for the first time. Daddy smiled at me, 'It was just like you were talking in your sleep. It's obvious that Muriel has had a huge influence on your artistic tastes.'

I started to feel panic rising in me. What else had I told him while I was in My Colour Dream? Then I realised that I needed to do a wee, urgently. I said, 'Excuse me Daddy, but is there a lavatory near here, because I'm bursting!'

Daddy laughed. He said, 'Everything in this big house is far away. Quick, let's go next door and Mrs Mackie can take you.'

And that's what she did. We practically ran out of the room, across the hallway, and down a long corridor. To my surprise, and great pleasure, we passed a coat of armour standing up straight, with a sword and a spear. Then we took a few more turnings and went up a small flight of stairs.

We got to the toilet just in time. Mrs Mackie said that she had to go off to finish getting the supper ready, and would I be able to find my own way back? I was in such a hurry to get into the toilet that I quickly said I would be all right. When I came outside, Mrs Mackie had gone, and I wasn't all right at all. I couldn't remember exactly how I had got to the toilet. I went down the stairs and turned right. I turned right again and came to a long corridor. I walked along it and supposed that I would see the suit of armour. But this corridor wasn't very bright, and it looked like the carpet hadn't been cleaned for a long time. Someone had torn off great strips of wallpaper and left them in a heap on the floor, near a ladder and a bucket, and there were lots of old white sheets everywhere. I was in a part of the house that was being decorated. And I knew I was lost.

What would you have done if you were me? Would you have screamed? Probably not, but that's what I did. I screamed and yelled Daddy! as loudly as I could. Nothing happened, so I screamed and yelled even louder. Then I became very frightened. I had an idea that someone would come out of one of the rooms and tie me up with a rope, and put a gag over my mouth and kidnap me, just like in TinTin. I was getting ready to scream even louder when I heard someone calling my name. I yelled, 'Daddy! Daddy!'

And suddenly he was there, smiling and laughing. He knelt down beside me and said, 'No need to shout. Daddy's here. I thought you'd get lost, so came looking for you. Mrs Mackie's all in a lather, and thinks I'm going to give her the sack for losing you! Of course I won't do that. It wasn't anyone's fault. These things happen.'

All the time he was talking to me, I was trying to calm myself down, by taking big breaths. I think I must have breathed in too deeply, because I felt myself feeling dizzy. For a second time I heard Daddy say, 'I've got you.' But this time he picked me up and carried me until we came to a chair, and he sat me on it.

He knelt in front of me and said, 'Take some breaths, but not very deep ones, otherwise you'll hyper-ventilate.' I did that, and felt better. Daddy said, 'Is being with you always such an adventure?'

I thought he was telling me off, but I looked in his face and he was smiling. I think he was enjoying himself.

I said, 'I'm sorry, Daddy. I get very excited about Art. People think I'm having a fit, or something like that, but really I'm just drinking in all the details, and when I saw that it was a real painting by Turner, and not just a copy, well that was a bit too much for me. Do you think that's silly? Should I try to stop doing it?'

Daddy scratched his chin. 'Well, I think that's very interesting. But I suppose it could be a bit of a problem for the teachers in school; especially if they don't know you.'

Then he smiled again, 'Or for your Daddy, who is getting to know your funny little ways. Let's go and have our supper.'

He held my hand and we walked back to the dining room. On the way, we came to the suit of armour. As we walked past it, I hesitated slightly. Daddy must have felt that, because he said, 'No you don't! Our supper will be getting cold. You can look at it another time.'

He thought that was very funny.

Talking with Daddy

I had told Daddy that I liked to eat fish, but the fish on my plate was covered in a white sauce with little bits of green in it, and it didn't smell very nice. There was some mashed potato and some lovely-looking green peas. I ate all the mashed potato and peas and then took a mouthful of the fish. I think if I had been with Muriel or Mummy, or even Auntie Aileen, I could have carefully taken the fish out of my mouth and put it carefully on the side of my plate. Then they would have known that I didn't like it. They wouldn't have made a fuss, but would have said, 'Oh dear, is it a bit strong? Don't worry, leave it and one of us will eat it.'

But I didn't know what Daddy thought about wasting food. For all I knew, he might have turned nasty, and said something like, 'You can sit here until you've eaten every last mouthful.'

So I asked him, 'Do you say your prayers every night Daddy, before you go to sleep?'

He looked very surprised. He said, 'I do, most of the time.'

'What do you pray for?'

'I ask God to grant us peace in the world, and freedom from poverty and hunger.'

He didn't say that he prayed for me. Instead he had said hunger. I felt certain that he was going to tell me that I was a bad girl for wasting my food, and that I should think about all the starving people in Africa who would love to eat my fish.

But he didn't say any of that. Instead, he carried on talking about himself. He said, 'In many ways, my work is a kind of living prayer. When I buy property or a business, or use my money to build a factory, or help rebuild a country after a terrible war, it's a way of giving people work. In South Africa, I use my money to build mines, and they are full of people working. Without the mine to work in, what would the poor Africans do? They would probably starve. But now they have money to buy food to feed their families. And I always arrange for a church, a Roman Catholic church, to be built. And I help the priests and the nuns who will minister to the people there.'

I said, 'Is that so that they can know God? And even though they might be a bit hungry, they won't suffer?'

Daddy looked at me. 'Yes, that's right. Did you learn about that in school?'

'Yes, in my first school we had to colour in a Black Baby, and give a penny for every part we coloured in.'

Daddy smiled at that. I didn't tell him that Mummy had refused to give any money, and that the African nun who fixed my broken wrist had thought the Black Babies was a ridiculous idea.

I was getting used to talking to Daddy, but still thought that he might be testing me, or setting a trap so that he could blame Mummy and Muriel for something that they had done wrong. I asked him, 'Daddy, is it true that you own Pearson's? I liked it there, and the staff are very helpful and friendly.'

He said, 'Yes. I like that shop very much. It's one of the first businesses I bought in Scotland.'

'And will you give money to my school?'

He paused and looked at my plate. 'I don't believe in giving money. But I use my money to help people build useful places, like the new wing on the hospital in Aberdeen. You don't really like your fish, do you?'

I looked at my plate. But the way he had asked me told me that he didn't mind. I said, 'Not really, no. If I'm honest about it.'

He said, 'I don't like waste. It's something that my parents taught me. They used to say, "Waste not, want not." I've always believed in that.'

I said, 'I'm sorry, Daddy. I hope you don't mind.'

He laughed. 'Not at all. Give it to me and I'll help you finish it.'

He asked me, 'Pippa, what do you like to eat?'

'Well, really and truly, I love fish fingers.'

He smiled. 'And what would you like for pudding?'

'Well, what is there?'

'Oh, lots of things, I'm sure. You tell me, and I'll ask Mrs Mackie if we've got it.'

'Well, I like ice cream.'

'Who doesn't? What flavour?'

'I think strawberry is my favourite. Have you heard of an ice cream called sorbet?'

'It's my favourite ice cream.'

'Really? I used to have it with Mummy when we went shopping in Romford.'

'How funny! It was me that introduced her to it.'

'It was Muriel's favourite too.' There. I had said Muriel's name again. I looked out of the window. I didn't want to look at Daddy's face, because I didn't want to see his reaction.

He said, 'I'm sure it still is her favourite ice cream' I didn't say anything. He said, 'You said it was her favourite. Has she changed her mind and found something else?'

I didn't want to talk about Muriel, but Daddy clearly did. 'Pippa, I want to talk about Muriel. She is very unwell. We all know that. The doctors aren't sure what to do with her. I know that you are very... very fond of her, and it must be very upsetting for you to know that she is so ill.'

I thought there was a wolf sitting in front of me. One false move and he would leap off his chair and devour me. I didn't say anything. I looked at the tablemat in front of me. There were Scottish wild flowers on it, including my favourite, the grass of Parnassus.

He said, 'I know it's not easy for you. I imagine that you hate me for what I did. But believe me, I want what's best for you.'

I said, 'It's all right Daddy. I know you do. I don't mind anymore. Really I don't.'

Daddy didn't take any notice of that. He said, 'Your mummy and I have been talking a lot recently. And I went to see Muriel today.'

Mrs Mackie came in and asked us if we'd finished. At least I supposed that was what she said. I could feel a ringing in my ears and it seemed that all the blood in my body was rising to my head. Daddy said, 'Are you all right, Pippa?'

I whispered, 'Yes. I think so. No, I'm not. Please may I have a drink of water?'

Daddy poured it for me. The water sounded like it was rushing, full blast, from a tap into a bath. He took his cigarettes and lighter out of his pocket and lit a cigarette. Then he looked at me. I looked away. He said, 'Pippa, please look at me. I want to say something very important.' I looked at him. He wasn't smiling, but he didn't look like a wolf about to pounce on me either. 'Pippa, you might think that I have been very unkind to your mother and Muriel. Perhaps I have. But I went to see Muriel this afternoon, to find out if there is anything I can do to help her. I must admit, I was quite worried that she might not want to see me. But do you know what happened? She smiled at me, and shook my hand, and said that she was delighted to see me. I didn't stay for very long, but she said that she wanted me to know that she didn't bear me any malice. She said that any father would want to do the best for his child.'

I didn't know what to say. I said, 'Daddy, I don't really know what to say about that. Please can we talk about something else?'

Daddy looked at me. He picked his lighter up and started turning it in his fingers. 'Well I know what to say. I just want to say one more thing about Muriel, if you don't mind?' I didn't say anything. Daddy said, 'I don't know Muriel at all, really. But I do know that she is a charming young woman and a decent person. And I know that she cares for you very much. That's all I want to say.'

I looked at Daddy. He kept playing with his lighter. I said, 'Daddy, please can I go back to living with Mummy? I think it would be best for me. I could still go to boarding school. I know it would be a long way to go on the train, but I really wouldn't mind.'

Daddy stopped playing with the lighter and looked at me. 'But what about your new family in Stranhaven? Wouldn't you miss them?'

'Yes, you're right. I would miss them. But a girl needs her Mummy. I will need her a lot as I get older, to help me with things.'

'But your Auntie can help you.'

I knew that the subject was closed. I said, 'That's all right. I just thought I'd ask, that's all.'

He said, 'Doesn't a girl need her daddy as well?'

I didn't want him anymore, even if he did own a painting by Turner. I said, 'Of course, Daddy. Of course I need you.'

He smoothed his moustache and smiled. He said, 'Good. I'm very glad to hear it.'

Mrs Mackie brought us our pudding. It was the most delicious strawberry sorbet. Daddy said, 'Your Mummy told me it was your favourite, so I got Mrs Mackie to order some especially for you.'

I smiled at him. 'Thank you, Daddy, you are a very kind and thoughtful man.'

I wondered if he could see all the sadness of my life behind that smile of mine. If he did, he didn't show it. He asked me, 'What have you been painting recently?'

That was a dangerous subject. 'To tell the truth, Daddy, I've hardly painted anything since I've been in Scotland. I've been too busy playing with my cousins.'

I didn't want to talk about The Lodge and I had a feeling that he didn't want to either. I wondered if he had seen my painting of half-naked Ursula. I asked him, 'Daddy, why am I good at Art?'

He said, 'Let me think about that.' He lit a cigarette and said, 'Why is Jessie good at playing musical instruments? It's a God-given gift. You should use it for the glory of God. As a way of thanking Him, and to continue the good works of The Lord.'

I thought, 'I don't want to talk about Ursula. She does God's good works, but comes to me with next to nothing on, so I can see how much she is growing. I think she's proud of how she looks. Pride is supposed to be a sin, but Ursula doesn't care, and she talks to angels and saints and sometimes Jesus. But if I paint Barry, with his tubby belly and comb-over, people won't be very interested in looking at him. Perhaps it would be better if I painted pictures of Jesus when he was young, and of his mother as well. People like looking at her when she was young.

But people like looking at Jesus when he was suffering terribly, with just a piece of cloth to cover his privates, and blood coming out of his side where a soldier had stabbed him with a spear, to see if Jesus was still alive or not. And he had blood

dripping from the nasty gashes on his head, where the horrible
Roman soldiers had pressed the crown of thorns hard into his
skull, just so that they could hurt him even more, and to make
him bleed. And his back was covered in horrible cuts where
they had whipped him. And his hands and feet had bloody
holes in them, from where a man had banged nails to fix him to
the cross. And the Romans left Him in the blazing sun for
hours on end, and all he had to drink was vinegar dipped in a
sponge and raised up to his mouth on a stick, so he could suck
on it. People like looking at pictures of that. But how is that for
the glory of God?'

I wanted to ask Daddy about that, but knew not to.

Daddy said, 'Gosh, Pippa, that must have been a very
interesting thing that I just said. Are you still thinking about it?'
I snapped out of my deep thought. I said, 'Sorry Daddy, I just
can't help thinking deep thoughts.'

He smiled. 'Well I think that's a very good thing. But people
usually do that when they are in Mass and listening to the
priest. It's not so common for children to do it at the dinner
table.'

I looked down at my empty pudding bowl. Daddy laughed.
'I'm only teasing you. I think it's very sweet. But I think it will
be very important for Mummy and Auntie to explain that side
of you to your new teachers. Otherwise they might think that
you are a bit of an idle dreamer.'

That made me come right back to reality. 'Are they both going
to take me to school?'

'Yes they are. It's been agreed. What do you think about that?'
I clapped my hands. 'Oh thank you, Daddy! You are such a
kind and thoughtful man!'

Daddy looked pleased.

I thought I'd talk about God, because it seemed to be
Daddy's favourite subject. 'Daddy, if I want to find out about
God in school, who would be the best person to talk to? Should
I go to Confession and ask the priest questions?'

'I think he might be a bit busy in the Confessional, but perhaps you could ask him afterwards.'

'Should I ask Sister Anne?'

'Yes, Pippa. That would be a very good idea. A very good idea indeed.' He looked at me for a while and smoothed his moustache. 'But what is it that you want to know?'

'I think if I asked you, it might take a long time to explain.'

'Try.' I wanted to ask him about Jesus when he had been a little boy and had got lost, but suddenly everything I wanted to say just disappeared out of my head.

Daddy said, 'Let's go for a wee walk. I'd like to show you something.'

We climbed up the stairs again and along the corridor. We came to a door and Daddy took a key out of his pocket and unlocked it. It was a small bedroom. Daddy said, 'This is where I sleep, on the very rare occasions when I come here. What do you think?'

'Well Daddy, I'm a bit surprised. It's very small and...'

'Yes?'

'A bit pokey.'

'Pokey?'

'Yes. I'm not being rude, but if you have enough money to buy a very expensive painting by Turner, and you own this huge house and lots of other buildings around the world, well, why don't you have the nicest and biggest bedroom in the house?'

Daddy didn't answer that question. He sat on the bed and asked me to sit next to him. His small suitcase was on the floor. He opened it and gave me a big envelope. He said, 'Look in there.'

It was my painting of Ursula that I had painted for Daddy while we had been living in Canada.

He said, 'I take it with me everywhere I go, and put it on my bedside table. It reminds me of you. It reminds me that I am a daddy. Now, tell me about Ursula.'

'I worry about painting her.'

'Why?'

I didn't want to explain why. I was sure that he knew. 'I just do. I don't like to talk about her. I think that people might not understand.'

516

'But you will be in a Catholic school very soon. On Sunday, in fact. The nuns there will understand.'

He paused. I looked down. 'Just make sure that when you draw or paint Ursula, you paint her with lots of clothes on, or perhaps a nice thick suit of armour.'

I heard the laugh in his voice, but his words still upset me. 'Oh Daddy! I'm so sorry! I didn't mean to cause trouble; really I didn't! All I want to do is paint. I can't really control it.'

'It makes me think of Mozart.'

'Was he a painter?'

'No. He was probably the greatest musician and composer who ever lived. He used to hear music in his head and just write it down, and there it was, a perfect piece of music.'

'Am I like that?'

'Well perhaps not as great a genius as that, but you certainly have a powerful gift. Matthew McCusker told me about meeting you in the Tate Gallery.'

That was a shock. 'How do you know him?'

'Oh, you might say that I was a patron of his, in his early days. Henry Moore introduced us. I have several of Matthew's paintings. They're not exactly to my taste...'

'But they're a good investment.'

'Exactly. I was at an exhibition of his, and he told me that he had bumped into an extraordinary girl at the Tate Gallery. I knew it was you, straight away. He told me about how you had transformed the Henry Moore sculpture into a sketch of a mother and child. It quite took his breath away;'

'And he took my sketch away, without asking me!'

Daddy laughed out loud. 'You are a very funny girl!'

I couldn't resist asking, 'Funny ha-ha, or funny peculiar?'

'Oh, both! But I mean it in the nicest possible way.'

I was pleased, but wasn't sure I liked him teasing me.

I could feel Daddy looking at me. He said, 'Would you like your sketch back? I'm sure he's shown it to Henry by now.'

'No. It's all right. I can always do another one.'

'So you remember it?'

'Yes. I can't forget anything.'

'So could you do one for me?'

'No.'

'Why not?'

'I don't want to say.' It was because the mother and child were naked.

Daddy said, 'I think I know why not.'

'Well then, you will know it's not a good idea.'

That was terribly cheeky of me, but Daddy didn't seem to mind. He just smoothed his moustache with his fingers and smiled. But, like Mummy, I knew that he was trying to hide something behind his smile. He said, 'I think I understand something.'

I wanted to ask him, 'What is it that you understand?' I wanted to shout the question at him. Instead, he said, 'Let's go back downstairs again.'

We went into the dining room. Mrs Mackie had cleared the table. Daddy said, 'Have you seen a piano anywhere?' I hadn't. He said, 'Well that just shows how much your mind is dominated by Art. Come with me.' We went through to the room where the Turner painting was. He said, 'How could you have missed it?'

It was true. In the middle of the room was a huge piano. I had never seen anything like it. I now know that it was a grand piano. Daddy said, 'Can I play you a tune?' He seemed a bit shy.

'Oh, yes please, that would be wonderful.'

We sat on the piano stool together. He opened the lid and ran his fingers up and down the keys. He said, 'When I was a little boy, I learned to play the piano. Actually, now I think of it, I was quite good. But it's been a little while since I played.'

He played something very slow. It was lovely. I could tell that he was making a few mistakes, but it sounded just beautiful. He told me it was the beginning of the The Moonlight Sonata by Beethoven. When he finished, I clapped and he went straight on to playing another tune. It was just slightly faster. He sang

'You must remember this
A kiss is just a kiss,
A sigh is just a sigh...'

He stopped singing, but kept playing. He said, 'Pippa, it's a song from my favourite film, called Casablanca.'

When he stopped playing, I asked him if he liked The Beatles. He said, 'Of course, I've heard of them, but they're not really my cup of tea.'

'What about football? Do you like football? I know about West Ham the most.'

'I used to play football at my boarding school. And rugby.'

'And did you like school?'

'Not at first. But as I grew up, I enjoyed it enormously. I learned such a lot. You could say it gave me my values.'

'Values? Is that about money?'

'Not really. It's about what one believes in.'

'And what do you believe in?'

'God, The Catholic Church, and hard work. And using your hard work for the glory of God and The Church.'

I said, 'I love the stories that Jesus told.'

Daddy smiled, 'So do I, and I particularly like the story of the Talents. The Talents, and the one about never hiding your light under a bushel.'

'What's a bushel?'

He said, 'If you don't know, then I'm sure you'll find out all about it at school.'

I didn't want to talk anymore. I'd had enough of talking about God. My bottom was feeling uncomfortable, from sitting next to Daddy on a hard piano stool. I asked him, 'Daddy, would you mind most awfully if I sat on your lap for a little while. And would you think I was a terrible baby if I sucked my thumb? You see, suddenly I feel very, very tired. But if you don't mind, I really don't want to go home just yet.'

What happened next?

I didn't know what happened next. Well, not at the time, anyway. But the next morning Maggie told me all about it. After Mummy came back from the hospital, Auntie, Mummy and Uncle Tom went down the road to see Uncle Jimmy. Nicol and Jessie were in bed, but Maggie had strict instructions to ring Uncle Jimmy's house as soon as I got back, so that Mummy could see me before I went to bed. But Maggie didn't do that; at least not straight away. She told me that she and Rhona were in the back garden, smoking and drinking beer. They heard a car pull up, and Mr Griffin appeared at the back gate. He told them that Mr Dunbar was in the car, and had me fast asleep with him. I think Maggie had been drinking a lot of beer, because she didn't quite understand what Mr Griffin was talking about. He whispered, 'It's Pippa's father, you silly girl. Put the beer away and hide that smelly cigarette. He wants to come in!'

Maggie laughed when she told me that, but said that at the time she had been terrified.

Daddy carried me upstairs to bed, and Maggie started to take my clothes off. Daddy had wanted to leave the room, but Maggie said, 'Please stay, Mr Dunbar. She is your daughter, after all.' So between them they got me ready for bed and took me to the toilet, and put me into bed, and then tucked me in and gave me a kiss goodnight.

Daddy whispered, 'She's such a sweet girl, but I'm a complete stranger to her.'

Then they went down to the garden, and Daddy stayed to talk to Maggie and Rhona. Daddy seemed to be very interested in Rhona, and asked her all sorts of questions, including what she thought about The Beatles. He asked her if she liked the cottages, and wanted to know about her music. Rhona told him that the cottages were very nice, and just what they needed. Despite local rumours, all the group members lived separately in each cottage, and only got together to cook and eat, and play music. Then Daddy said, 'I have some investments in music. Not so much in the musicians themselves. If they are good, then the success will come to them. I'm more interested in supporting studios where they make their music, and I support orchestras. I suppose you could say that I'm a patron of the Arts, but I prefer to be anonymous.'

Then he asked Maggie to go down to Uncle Jimmy's house; and tell Mummy that he was there. While Maggie was away, Rhona asked Daddy a special favour. 'Mr Dunbar, I had a photo taken last week, and Pippa is in one it. I would like to use it on the cover of my next record. And I love her art so much. I'd like to have one of her paintings on the cover as well.'

Unfortunately, Daddy didn't like this idea at all. He said, 'It's a very nice idea, but I can't allow people to know about my daughter. It's a question of her safety.'

Rhona had once told Maggie that, as an American, it was not in her nature to take no for an answer. She didn't argue with Daddy, but said, 'I understand. What about if her face couldn't be seen in the photo, and we don't credit her as the artist?'

Daddy smiled at that. He said, 'You've thought this all out in advance, haven't you?'

Rhona said, 'Not really. You see, I asked Pippa's mother, and she refused, for exactly the same reason.'

This surprised Daddy, and he said, 'That's interesting. You can use the photograph, as long as nobody can see Pippa's face, and you must credit Pippa as the artist, but you must call her Philippa Herman. That's very important.'

Then Daddy asked Rhona if he had met Muriel. Rhona said she had, but didn't say anything else.

So Daddy asked her what she thought of Muriel. Rhona said, 'I think she's a very good influence on your daughter. It sounds like she has rescued Ruth from depression and alcoholism and possible disaster, and that Pippa has blossomed under her care.'

Daddy said, 'That's what everyone seems to say about her.'

Then Maggie, Mummy, Uncle Tom and Auntie Aileen came back, and they spent a few hours together, talking in the garden. I never did find out what they talked about, because Rhona and Maggie said goodnight and went up to Rhona's cottage. But Maggie did tell me that when they arrived, Daddy had tried to shake everyone's hand, but Auntie and Mummy had kissed him on the cheek, and he had been embarrassed, but smiled and looked very pleased, all the same.

I didn't see Daddy after that. Mummy told me that he had to meet people at his house in the morning, and then he was going to travel back to London, and then fly to a foreign country. I forget which one.

Muriel says goodbye

The next day was Saturday. It was the day of the Ceilidh, and my very last day in Stranhaven. Mummy told me that the hospital doctors had given us special permission to see Muriel before lunchtime, so I would be able to spend the afternoon getting ready for the Ceilidh. It was going to start at seven o'clock and go on for most of the night, but I would have to leave soon after we had played our tune, so I wouldn't be too tired.

Muriel didn't look any better. In fact, she looked a lot worse. The bags under her eyes were bigger and darker, and her skin had turned even more yellow. We held her hands, as usual, and Muriel smiled. When she looked at me, it seemed like she thought I was on the other side of the room. Then she realised that I was right next to her and said, 'Oh! There you are!' Her eyes looked sleepy and, if I'm absolutely honest, they seemed a bit dead. I hoped it was the strong medicine that was making her like that. Straight away, she said to me, 'Pippa. I've been thinking a lot about you. Well, really and truly, I think about you and Mummy all the time. Sometimes I feel terribly sad, because I'm away from you. But most of the time I think of all the lovely things that we've done together, and all the things we've talked about and, above all, what a lovely, special person you are. And when I'm feeling very sad, then I tell myself how lucky I am to have met you. I can't imagine my life without you and Mummy in it.'

She stopped talking, and Mummy gave her a drink of water. Then she said, 'Come closer to me, Pippa. I want you right next to me.' I pulled my chair as close as it would go, but

I still felt far away. I stood up, but I still didn't feel close enough. She moved herself so that she was as close to the side of the bed as possible, without falling out. I could smell her breath. It smelled old.

She whispered, 'Listen Pippa. None of this was your fault, or Mummy's fault. Some people might say that your daddy made me ill, but that's just not true. I saw him yesterday. He's a very nice man. But he just made a mistake. That's all. I'm sure he knows that. And I'm sure that one day he will try to put it all right. But I want you to promise me something.'

She pulled me towards her. I tried not to smell her breath. 'Promise me that you'll try not to blame him. He is your daddy, after all, and he has only tried to do what he thinks is best for his daughter. I know that you may not agree with him, but he has done his best, and that makes him a good daddy. And try to make friends with your daddy. You don't know each other, but I'm sure with time you will become very close. I know that Daddy wants that, it's just that he doesn't know how to tell you, because he doesn't really know how to talk to children.'

Mummy gave her another sip of water. Muriel said, 'Pippa, make friends with your Daddy. Teach him to love you. He is the key to your happiness.'

She turned her head towards Mummy. 'What do you think, Ruth? Am I right?'

Mummy whispered, 'Yes, Muriel, of course. Of course you are right.'

I looked at Mummy, but I wished I hadn't, because I had never seen her look so sad in all my life.

Muriel's eyeballs slid to one side and her eyelids closed. She frowned and I knew that she must have been in pain.

Then a nurse came and asked us how Muriel was. I thought, 'Why don't you ask her yourself?' But when I looked at Muriel, she had gone to sleep. Mummy said to the nurse, 'Well, it seems to me that she's not getting any better.'

The nurse looked at me. She said, 'We have increased the amount of care we're giving her, to make sure that she's comfortable.'

Mummy said, 'What happens next? '

The nurse looked at me again. 'If you like, I can ask a doctor to talk to you.'

Mummy looked at me. She said, 'Well, perhaps it might be easier if I could speak to someone on the telephone? Perhaps this afternoon?'

The nurse went away. I said to Mummy, 'Mummy, I don't mind if you want to go away and leave me here with Muriel. Then you can have your chat and come back.'

Mummy smiled her sad smile. 'It's very kind of you, but I want to be with you, because this is your last visit before... your last visit... your last visit before... oh dear!'

She sat down and put her head in her hands. I let go of Muriel's hand and put my arms around Mummy.

The nurse came back, and had a doctor with her. They stood and looked at Mummy crying. Mummy wiped her tears with her hanky and blew her nose. She said, 'I'm awfully sorry. Crying isn't helping, is it?'

The doctor said, 'Let's go and talk. Nurse will stay here with your daughter.'

Mummy looked at me. I said, 'Don't worry, Mummy, I'll be all right.'

Mummy went with the doctor, and the nurse sat down on Mummy's chair. She picked up the photo on Muriel's bedside cabinet and said, 'What a lovely photo. And you've grown so much!'

I looked at Muriel in the photo. She was obviously delighted to be with Mummy and me. She was smiling such a wide smile that you could see her teeth. And the thing that caught my eye, and I supposed anyone who looked at it, was Muriel's décolletage. Mummy was always reminding Muriel not to show too much cleavage, and Roger's mother said that Muriel was one of the prettiest women she had ever met. Mummy had said, 'Dorothy, should I be feeling jealous?' But Dorothy

laughed and said that Mummy and Muriel were so lucky to
have each other, and yes, to tell the truth, she would give
anything to feel how Mummy and Muriel felt about each other.
Now Muriel looked tired and a lot older. And there wasn't
much of her cleavage left.

Then the nurse started to admire Muriel's teddy, but I
wasn't really listening. I held Muriel's hand and heard a
rushing of wings in my ears. It was Barry. He stood next to
Muriel and said to me, 'Don't worry Pippa, Jesus loves Muriel.
We'll look after her.' He bowed his head, as if he was saying a
prayer. His hair fell over to one side of his face. He put his
head up and at the same time said, 'Whoops!' and scooped his
hair back into place. That made me laugh.
Muriel's eyelids fluttered and she looked at me. She said, 'Oh
good. You're still here. Was someone laughing, or was it my
imagination?' I told her I was thinking of something funny. She
said 'That's nice. What was it?'
I said, 'Just a silly thing really.' I didn't want to tell her about
Barry.
She said, 'Pippa, please tell me.' She sounded as if she wanted
to hear about the most important thing in the world.
I said, 'Muriel, you know about Ursula?' Muriel nodded. 'Well
she has always looked after me, and especially when I've been
very unhappy, or in trouble.'
Muriel frowned. 'I don't like to think about my lovely Pippa
being unhappy and in trouble.'
'It's all right, Muriel, because I always seem to be all right in
the end. Like TinTin.'
Muriel smiled. 'I remember how much you loved TinTin, and
how you used to get so excited and frightened every time he
was in trouble.'
'I still do. Well, do you have someone to look after you?'
'Of course I do. I have your mummy.'
'I know, but I mean someone like Ursula?'
Muriel smiled. 'It's a lovely idea.'
'Well, you have got one.'
'Really? What's she like?'

'Oh no. It's a man.'

Muriel opened her eyes as much as she could. 'A man? I thought they were all pretty girls like Ursula.'

'Oh no. Most of them are men. I know because I've seen pictures of them, and Ursula told me.'

'What's he like?'

'Well that's just it. I thought he would be very young, and have long hair, and maybe a suit of armour and a sword.'

'But?'

'Well he's a bit…' I looked around, but Barry had gone. I could only see the nurse, who was pretending that she wasn't listening. 'It's a bit odd. He's quite old, and he's a bit bald.' I told Muriel about Barry's comb-over.

'And what's his name? Don't tell me it's Cuthbert, or Reginald, because those are my least favourite names.'

'It's Barry. He may look a bit old, but Ursula told me that he's looked after lots of people, and you're his last one before he retires.'

Muriel smiled. I saw her teeth. It was the first time I had seen her smile like that for a long time. She didn't look old anymore. She said, 'Well you can tell Barry that he's going to be working for a long time yet. I have no intention of going with him up to Heaven for a very long time!'

Then she laughed again. She frowned and said, 'Oh!' and I supposed that she was feeling another pain in her tummy.

Mummy came back on her own. Muriel said, 'Pippa's been telling me a very funny story. Do you want to hear it?'

Mummy said, 'Let's save it for my next visit. I'm afraid it's almost time for us to go.'

Muriel stopped smiling. She asked Mummy when I was going to school, but Mummy couldn't say it. Muriel said, 'Don't cry, my love. Come here.' Mummy went up close to Muriel and Muriel put her arm around Mummy's neck.

Mummy said, 'Say goodbye to Pippa.'

I went very close to Muriel, and she held my hand. She said, 'It's been lovely seeing you again Pippa. You're my little Pipsqueak. You put all the colour back into my life.'

I wanted to say something, but nothing would come out. My sight went blurry and I felt a very big tear run out of the side of each of my eyes and down my cheeks. Muriel said, 'You're a big strong girl, Pippa. I've always thought that. You look after yourself, and make lots of nice friends. Will you promise me that you'll do that?'

I said, 'I promise, Muriel, I promise.' But I had to look away, because she was crying too, and I knew that it was hurting her.

She said, 'Come here, Pippa. Let me hold you.' I stood by her and leaned as close as I could to her. She put her arm round my shoulder. She said, 'You are such a big girl now.'

Mummy said, 'Muriel, I won't see you tomorrow, because I'm taking Pippa to school, but I'll see you on Monday and will tell you all about it.'

Muriel smiled and let go of me. Then her eyes closed again.

As we left the ward, a nurse came in, pushing a trolley with the patients' lunch. She smiled at me. I tried to smile back, but the muscles in my face just didn't want to do it.

The graveyard

In the car, I told Mummy that I didn't want to go to the Ceilidh. And I told her I didn't want any lunch either. Mummy said, 'Of course you do. Muriel wants you to do both those things.'

'Does she?'

'Of course she does. She told you to look after yourself, and that means enjoying yourself with other children, and doing fun things that will make you happy.'

Mr Griffin took us to the Wimpy Bar and we had a delicious lunch. Mummy didn't say very much, so neither did I. When we had finished, Mummy asked me to tell her what I had said to Muriel that she found so funny. I told her about Barry. She smiled her sad smile and said, 'That's a lovely story.'

When we got back to Stranhaven, Nicol was waiting for me outside the house. He said that he and Jessie had had an argument and that she was up in her room, sulking and refusing to come out. He said that it was her nerves, and that she was very worried about the Ceilidh. I didn't want to think about Jessie being in a sulk. I wanted to sit quietly and think about Muriel. Mummy said, 'Why not leave Jessie for a little while, and you and Nicol can sit and have a chat? You can tell him all about Muriel. Then perhaps everyone will feel better.' Mummy left the room in a hurry, and I knew that she was getting upset.

Nicol sat with me in the garden, and I explained how Muriel had looked terrible, but I had made her laugh, and that we had all cried when it was time to say goodbye.

Nicol said, 'I don't like to say goodbye to people. I wish we didn't have to go tonight.'

I said, 'But it will be fun! Let's go and sort Jessie out.'

We went upstairs and Nicol went into his room. I knocked on my bedroom door. Jessie said, 'Go away! You're horrible. I don't want to go tonight.'

I said, 'Of course you do, Jessie. What would we do without you?'

She opened the door and said, 'I thought you were Nicol.'

I said, 'Let's go and play our tunes and then we can get dressed in our nicest clothes, because soon it will be time to go.'

I went into the kitchen with Jessie and saw Mummy and Auntie Aileen sitting together. Auntie was holding both of Mummy's hands. They stopped talking as soon as we came in. I knew that they had been talking about Muriel.

The Ceilidh was in a village about ten miles away from Stranhaven, by the sea. Nicol had told me that his mother was buried in the churchyard there, and that if there was time, we could visit her grave. I didn't want to do that, but I didn't say anything.

Mr Griffin took Mummy and me to the village, with all our instruments in the boot of his car, while Auntie and the other four children went in Uncle Jimmy's car. Maggie had already gone with Uncle Tom, to help get the village hall ready.

Mr Griffin drove us up the hill to the church. Mummy and I went into the graveyard, to see if we could find the grave.

There were lots of graves there, and some of them were so old that you couldn't read the writing anymore. Some of them had a skull and crossbones on, and even though I knew there weren't pirates buried under there, they frightened me anyway. Then we found Nicol's mother's grave. What Nicol had said was true, because there were rabbit droppings on the grass in front of her headstone, and the beginnings of some rabbit holes. It was a lovely place to be buried, because as we stood in front of the grave we could see the sea, where it met the sky.

Then Auntie, Nicol, and Jessie arrived. They had a bunch of flowers each and they put them in front of their mother's headstone. Nicol said, 'Hello Mummy. We're going to have a great time tonight. I wish you were here to enjoy it.'
Everybody just stood there. I wanted to get away as quickly as possible, but it was obvious that Nicol didn't want to leave. Jessie told Auntie that she needed to do a wee, so Auntie said, 'Come on everybody, let's go back down to the hall.'
Nicol whispered to Jessie, 'You always do that.'
She whispered back, 'It's not my fault.' I wondered what their mother would have said if she had heard them starting an argument in front of her grave.

There were lots of people at the hall, carrying things inside and getting the stage and chairs ready. A man with a very fat belly and a comb-over walked towards us and said that he was Dougie, and that he was in charge. Auntie said, 'Really? I thought Tom was organising everything.'
Dougie winked at her. 'He's in charge of the music and the dancing, but I'm the most important person here.'
Auntie laughed, 'Is that because you run the bar?'
Dougie laughed and patted his belly. 'Quite right! But seriously folks, we need to be on our best behaviour, because we have our musicians from Ireland with us, and some very special guests.'
He looked over his shoulder and we saw Rhona and Maggie. They were talking to two men with very long hair and beards, and a lady with a tooth missing. They were all dressed in

various bright colours and had on long coats. I knew that they must be the other musicians from Trailing Clouds of Glory.

Dougie said, 'We're still waiting for the Irish, but they had a very late night last night, so they'll probably turn up at the last minute.'

A man carrying a crate of beer bottles asked Dougie where he wanted it to go. Dougie asked to be excused, and walked away.

Then Rhona and Maggie came over and kissed us all. Rhona gave Mummy a very big hug and whispered something in her ear. Mummy whispered back, 'It's not good, I'm afraid, but we are going to do our best to stay cheerful.'

Rhona kissed Mummy on the cheek and said, 'I understand. Come and meet the rest of the group.'

Nicol and Jessie had already gone over to talk to them, and suddenly I became very shy. And with that shyness came a terrible rush of feelings. It was as if everything that I had pushed away and tried not to feel - about meeting Daddy, about Muriel, about saying goodbye to Mummy, about going to school, about having to leave Stranhaven and the people who loved me - as if all those feelings were swirling around my body and taking over my mind.

Mummy must have noticed that something strange was happening to me, because she said to Auntie, 'I'll just take Pippa out for a little while.'

We sat on a bench outside the hall. We could hear the musicians inside, tuning up their instruments. Mummy held my hand and said, 'You're going to miss all this, aren't you?' I nodded. She said, 'I've got an idea. Why don't we go back up to the graveyard and have a proper look at Nicol's mother's grave? Would you like that?'

At first, that didn't seem like a good idea, so I didn't say anything. Then I thought it would be a very nice to go back with Nicol, and perhaps Maggie, but definitely not Jessie.

Mummy said, 'Why don't I ask Nicol to come? I think he might have liked to have spent a bit longer there, but it was obvious that his little sister didn't like it, or was desperate to be with the musicians.'

How did she know that that was exactly what I was thinking? She said, 'Were you thinking the same thing?'

I said, 'Yes, Mummy, I was.'

She squeezed my hand and smiled. Then she went into the hall. I imagine that she had only left me for two minutes, but it was if Mummy had walked out of my life forever, and Muriel was someone who didn't exist anymore. I felt a kind of overwhelming sickness, not caused by being ill, but by being snatched away from everything I loved, and dropped into a strange and uncertain future. I didn't know it then, but I was already feeling homesick.

But then the feeling vanished, because Mummy came out with Nicol and Maggie, but not Jessie. Mr Griffin drove us back up to the graveyard and we stayed for about an hour, tidying up the grave as best we could. Nicol had left a collection of stones and shells there, but the animals had scattered them all, so I went off with him to find some nice leaves and berries to make a new pattern with the shells and stones, and to look at all the graves. Mummy stayed and chatted with Maggie.

Nicol asked me, 'Will you come back and stay with us for Christmas?'

I wanted to be with Mummy and Muriel at Christmas, but being back in Stranhaven would have been my second choice. I didn't tell Nicol that. I just said, 'I don't know.'

He said, 'Will you ever come back?'

I said, 'Of course I will!' But really I had no idea what would happen to me in the future.

Nicol said, 'In ten years' time you'll be nineteen, and I will be twenty-two.'

I tried to imagine Nicol as a man. 'Will you have a beard, like your dad? And will you have long hair, like a hippie?'

He said, 'I'm never going to grow a beard, or smoke a pipe! That will be in 1977. And I suppose you will be tall, like your dad. And I suppose you will have...' He stopped himself. I knew what he was thinking.

I said, 'No I won't. I'm going to look just like Mummy. I'm sure of that.'

The Ceilidh

You will often hear people saying, 'Oh, but it was marvellous!' or, 'It was wonderful!' or even, 'It was absolutely fantastic!' But really what they mean is, 'It was nice, and we enjoyed ourselves.' But the Ceilidh was absolutely, marvellously, wonderfully fantastic. The hall had seemed quite big when it was empty, but by the time we got back it was almost full, and seemed quite small. There were cars parked all the way up the hill, and people were getting out of them and making their way down to the hall. Everyone was wearing their best clothes, as if they were going to Church, and children seemed to be running around everywhere.

Rhona and the musicians were outside the hall, holding their instruments, and having their photograph taken by the man from the newspaper. Rhona was wearing a navy blue beret, just like mine. When the photographer had finished, Rhona took my hand and introduced me to the musicians. One of them asked me if I was going to play with them tonight. I wasn't shy anymore. I said, 'Well, if you like.'

He smiled and said, 'Oh, I'd like that very much. Jessie's already told us that you play the concertina and are a wonderful painter.'

Then I became shy again. I said, 'I do my best.'

Then Etsy gave me a kiss and said, 'Yes my dear, you do your best.'

She smelled of cigarettes, and I saw the big gap where her front tooth was missing.

Ten minutes later, the hall was completely full, with adults sitting on chairs and standing at the back, and at the sides, and the children sitting on the floor right up to the front of the stage. We stood by the side of the stage, with our instruments ready. Uncle Tom climbed up and said how pleased he was that everyone had come, but had anyone seen the Irish? There was lots of laughter at that. He said he was delighted to welcome some young musicians who had just returned from a big tour of Europe, where they had been playing to audiences ten times bigger than here. Someone shouted, 'Hundreds of times bigger!' and then people laughed and clapped. Then Uncle Tom said, 'And we're still hoping that our Irish friends will arrive shortly, and then we can get on with the serious business of dancing the night away;'

Someone shouted, and 'What about drinking the night away?' And there was more laughing and clapping.

Then Rhona led Jessie, Nicol, Kirsty, Kenny and me onto the stage, and we sat on our chairs, while Trailing Clouds of Glory and Maggie stood behind us. Everyone clapped and then grew quiet. Jessie tried to put her accordion on by herself, but it was too heavy, so Maggie had to help her, and lots of people laughed. Jessie looked very cross and that made people laugh even more. I looked for Mummy and I saw her sitting in the middle of the audience, and she waved and smiled at me and blew me a kiss. Uncle Tom came back onto the stage and said, 'Ladies and gentlemen, for one night only, here are the wonderfully talented group of musicians who go by the name of...' he looked at Jessie, but she looked confused. I don't know why, but I shouted out, 'Cottage Pie! We're called Cottage Pie!' Everyone laughed, except Jessie, who scowled at me, and shouted, 'No we're not!' and this made people laugh even more.

Then Jessie started to play the introduction to Black Jack David, and we were off. I hadn't done any rehearsing with the musicians, but it must have been one of their favourite songs, because all of them fitted in perfectly with our music and singing. Half way through, Nicol stood up and played Hit the Road Jack on his saxophone, with Maggie on harmonica. Then one of the musicians took up the tune with the fiddle and Etsy and Rhona started singing. Nicol wasn't expecting that and started to get his notes wrong, but Maggie told him just to keep on playing until Jessie came in with the accordion. The song seemed to go on for ten times longer that we had rehearsed, and the audience were singing along. Then Maggie nudged Jessie and she started playing, and then everyone sang along to Black Jack David until we had finished. Everyone clapped and cheered, and we had to play the song all over again, and the children got up and clapped and stamped and danced around.

Then it was time for us to stop and leave the stage. Uncle Tom came up and said something, but nobody in the audience was really listening. Mummy and Auntie came to the front of the stage and said we were all wonderful, and we were all very pleased with ourselves. Then lots of children and adults crowded around us and said how fantastic we were. A big girl with red hair said to Nicol, 'Wow Nicol! I didn't know you could play an instrument!' He smiled, then looked at me and stopped smiling. I supposed that she was one of the girls from his school, who liked him so much.

Then suddenly a crowd formed around Rhona and the musicians, and all I could see was a big circle of adult backs, with purple skirts and jeans and boots and long coats. I supposed that they were hippie fans of the group.

Then someone shouted, 'The Irish are here!' and everyone went back to their seats and we sat with the children on the floor. There were five musicians, all dressed in black, and they sat down on the chairs that we had been sitting on. One of them said, 'Hello there, we're from Dublin!'

There was a great big cheer, and the band started tuning up their instruments. There was a man with a set of small bagpipes, another with a drum and a small stick, a lady with a fiddle, and a man with a guitar, a banjo, and a mandolin. The man with the bagpipes said, 'We're real sorry for being so late, but the thing is, we had a bit of a late night last night and you know... Jeez but sure we can't play and sing without a wee drop of some of that local stuff to wet our whistles. And why was everyone clapping just as we were coming in? Are there some other musicians in here?'

Someone shouted, 'Get the bairns and Trailing Clouds of Glory back on!'

The man with the guitar said, 'Sure, bring them all up and we can do something together.'

Everyone started clapping and shouting and stamping their feet. Jessie jumped up on the stage. Nicol climbed up and tried to pull her back down again, but this just made people shout and clap even louder.

So Maggie came forward with Rhona, and then the other musicians. There was another cheer and they were all on the stage. A girl behind me said, 'Go on! You go on!' She pulled me to stand up and took me to the stage and Maggie pulled me up. Mr Griffin had packed away all our instruments in his car, but he went out to get them, and Dougie and Uncle Tom brought them to us. While all this was going on, the Irish group and Trailing Clouds of Glory were talking about what to play. They all agreed that we should play Captain Pugwash and see if we could make it get faster and faster, until we had to stop.

I looked at Nicol. He showed me his tin whistle. We knew that there would be so much noise that nobody would hear him, but he was smiling. I knew that he liked being on stage in front of all those people. Jessie and I had our concertinas and Maggie had her harmonica, and Kirsty her fiddle and Kenny his guitar. Maggie said to us, 'Just imagine that you are in our front room, playing together, but keep looking at the Irishman with the mandolin.'

Then the man with the mandolin nodded to Jessie and me and we began playing, slowly and normally. There was a big cheer and some of the children got up and danced around. Then, one by one, the other instruments joined in, until we were all playing together. More people got up to dance and then the mandolin man nodded and we got faster and faster, until I couldn't get my fingers to go where they were supposed to, so I just pretended to play and moved my concertina in and out. Nicol had stopped playing, and soon only the adults and Jessie could keep up the pace. Then the man nodded to her, and the tune came to a sudden stop and everyone clapped and cheered.

Then Rhona stepped to the front of the stage and tried to speak, but there was so much noise that nobody could hear her. Then a lot of people began to tell each other to shush, and eventually there was quiet. Rhona said, 'It's wonderful to be here. It's true, we have been very lucky to have played in front of some big audiences recently, but this has surely been the best crowd we have ever had.' There were cheers at that. 'But now we'd like to play one more song and then leave the stage to our Irish friends. I'm sure you'll all know this song. I'm an American, as I'm sure you've all noticed, but half of me is Scottish, and I love this song, and I hope you will too. It's *The Flowers of the Forest*.'

Then she turned to Etsy and called her to join her at the front of the stage. They held hands and the Irish piper started blowing air into his bagpipes. Suddenly the hall changed from being a mad noisy place to being completely silent. Rhona took off her beret and shook her long hair, so it cascaded over her shoulders. She cleared her throat and nodded to the piper. He began playing a slow tune. I could tell immediately that what Rhona was going to sing would be very sad. She sang

I've heard the lilting, at the yowe-milking,
Lassies a-lilting before dawn o' day;
But now they are moaning on ilka green loaning;
The Flooers o' the Forest are a' wede away.

Dool and wae for the order sent oor lads tae the Border!
The English for ance, by guile wan the day,
The Flooers o' the Forest, that fought aye the foremost,
The pride o' oor land lie cauld in the clay.

We all thought that Etsy was going to sing, but she just stood there, holding Rhona's hand. I didn't know what any of the words meant, but it was obvious that it was a terribly sad song. I looked out over the audience. Some of the older ladies were reaching for their hankies, and dabbing their eyes. The men were standing there, totally still, and each one of them was looking at Rhona. Even the children had stopped fidgeting and chatting. Rhona's voice was strong and beautiful, and powerful, and seemed to fill the whole hall.

○ ○ ○ ○ ○ ○

1st December 1976

At the time, I didn't have the words to describe that song, and the effect that it had on everybody who heard Rhona singing it. Afterwards, someone said that they had been moved. I think I was moved. But it wasn't just the sadness that took over my whole mind and body. It was something moving in me and over me, which was much more than sadness. Even now, I can't find a word for it. As I grew older, whenever someone sang that song, or I heard it on a record, I could feel something rushing through me, like a wind or a river, and then settling behind my eyes, where my tears would break. In that river were my grandparents, and all my murdered Jewish relatives. And Mummy and Muriel were there too, when they were small, not knowing or understanding what had gone before them, or what would be their futures. And the millions of Jews and Polish people who had been swept away by the Nazis, killed on the streets or in their villages, or dragged away to be exterminated in camps, with nobody ever knowing what had happened to them. And then I would cry for myself, Pippa Herman, growing up far away from home.

And I sing that song to myself now, in my lonely little caravan, far away from anyone who loves me. And I'm separated from the one person I wish, above all others, would love me again. And I become overwhelmed with a feeling of... of what? A sense of the pointless devastation of millions of lives. The death of young men, living in harmony with Nature and suddenly slaughtered by brutal men who hate them. Young men, with young wives and little children, all killed because of the greed and blind, ignorant and brutal hatred of other men,

537

who believe that anyone different must be an enemy. And the killing might be over in seconds, or minutes, or perhaps they are humiliated before they are tortured, or starved to death. But once they finally die, the impact on those left behind rolls on, to blight the lives of generations to come.

And that song reminds me that my heart has been completely broken.

○ ○ ○ ○ ○ ○

I looked for Mummy again, and saw her with her cheeks wet with tears. She got up to leave, and Auntie went with her. Suddenly I was terrified; terrified that Mummy was leaving me. I wanted to get up and shout for her to come back, but Rhona was still singing and the piper was still playing, and I just had to sit there. Rhona stopped singing, and the piper played on for a minute or so, and then stopped. There was a moment of silence and then a huge roar of clapping and cheering. I tried to leave the stage, by walking down the steps at the side, but Jessie and Kenny were in my way. I turned to Maggie and shouted, 'Mummy has gone without me!'

She took my concertina and lowered me off the stage. The children were milling around in front of me, and I knocked into a big boy by accident and he said, 'Hey, watch out will you!' Then he saw it was me, and laughed and said, 'Hello gorgeous. You're a great player. Will you have a wee dance with me later?'

I pushed my way to the back of the hall and ran outside. Mummy was sitting on the bench with Auntie. She was still crying. I went to her and she said, 'I'm sorry Pippa. It was lovely to see you up on the stage, but Rhona's singing was so beautiful that it almost broke my heart in two.'

I said, 'Can we go home now?'

Mummy looked at Auntie. Auntie said, 'Do you not want to stay and listen to the band and have a wee dance?' I did, but more than anything I wanted to spend every possible minute with Mummy.

Mummy said, 'Let's get your concertina and then Mr Griffin can take us home, if you don't mind. I feel so exhausted.'

We stayed outside in the cold, and Auntie went in to get our coats and my concertina. After a few minutes, she came out, and brought the whole family with her. They all crowded round us and said goodbye. I knew that I wouldn't see Kirsty and Kenny for a long time. They both looked very sad. Kirsty kissed me and wished me good luck in my new school. Kenny tried to shake my hand, but I kissed him on the cheek and he looked very pleased. Then Rhona came out and we all said how wonderful her singing had been. Mummy said, 'I'm sorry, but I just had to go out. My crying would have made everyone stop listening to you.'

Rhona didn't say anything. She gave Mummy a hug and we all saw that Rhona was crying now. She kissed me and hugged me, and she promised that she and Maggie would come and see me one day in school, and we would all go to Pearson's and buy lovely straw hats. Then she said, 'Goodness! I almost forgot!' She took off her beret and said, 'Pippa, I hope you don't mind, but we didn't have time to buy a beret, so Maggie said that she was sure that you wouldn't mind if I borrowed yours.'.

I could tell that Jessie was desperate to get back indoors. She pulled Nicol's hand and said to him, 'Come on Nicol, let's have a dance.' He suddenly looked furious, and I thought that he was going to hit her. But he stopped himself and looked at me and smiled. Then he waved at me and went inside with his little sister. I loved him more than anything for doing that, but I couldn't understand why. I do now. He was someone who could never put himself first. Just like me.

And then Mr Griffin walked over, and we went with him to his car, and he took us home.

Feeling protected

My school suitcase was at the bottom of the stairs. In Maggie's bedroom, someone had folded my school clothes and put them on the chair. We both undressed and got into bed as quickly as we could. Mummy said, 'Pippa, do you think I would be a bad mother if I took your school uniform out of here and put it downstairs?' I had been thinking exactly the same thing.

Just before I went to sleep, Mummy asked me what it had been like to be on the stage, in front of all those people. She asked me if I had been nervous at all. I said, 'Well, really I didn't have any time to get nervous. So many things were happening to me, so I didn't really think about it. And you were in the audience, so I just played for you. And I thought about Muriel, and how much she would have liked to have seen me there. And now you can tell her all about it.'

In the night, Mummy kept sighing and turning over and over in bed. Once, I asked her what was the matter. She said, 'I'm thinking about Muriel, and about you going to school.'

I said, 'Well, why doesn't Auntie take me to school, and you stay here? Then you could visit Muriel.'

Mummy seemed shocked. 'No. I couldn't possibly do that!'

'But what if something terrible happened to Muriel, and you hadn't seen her?'

Mummy whispered, 'What sort of terrible thing, Pippa? What are you thinking about?'

I didn't want to say it. Mummy held me tight. After a while I said, 'Well, what if Muriel dies?'

I could feel Mummy tightening up, and she held me a bit tighter. It felt like she was frightened, and trying to protect me from something horrible or dangerous. It felt uncomfortable.

'Pippa, listen to me. Muriel is very unwell, but the doctors are going to make her better. You have to believe that.'

I wanted to believe it. I said, 'Yes Mummy, I know.'

'Good. Good girl.' She kissed the back of my head.

But I couldn't let go of the idea of Muriel being without Mummy. I said, 'But I like it when you go to see Muriel. It makes me feel better.'

'Better?'

'Yes. It makes me feel that everything is going to be all right for her. I hate thinking of her being on her own, with nobody to look after her properly.'

'But the doctors and nurses are there. They know what to do.'

'But they don't love her like you do.'

I didn't really think about what I was saying. But, over the years, I've thought about that moment a lot. I didn't want Mummy to become terribly upset when she said goodbye to me at school. I wanted to protect her from that. And I didn't want to see her being upset. I wanted to protect myself from that.

Mummy was quiet for a long time. I fell asleep again. Then I was woken up by a noise downstairs and outside our room. Mummy was awake too. She said, 'I don't want to leave you, Pippa.'

I thought perhaps she wanted to go downstairs, to see what was going on. I said, 'That's all right Mummy. I know you will come back.'

○ ○ ○ ○ ○ ○

2nd December 1976

That moment, in bed with Mummy, will stay with me forever. It felt like I had suddenly grown up. Several years later, I saw a terrible photograph. I think it is the most awful thing I have seen in my whole life. I didn't want to look at it, but some horrible girl found out that I was Jewish, and showed it to me. I shivered and shook, and thought I was going to break into pieces, because it was so awful. It was of a German soldier. About ten yards away from him is a young woman. She is holding a baby. The soldier has a rifle, and is taking aim at the mother. She has turned her back on the soldier, to try to protect her baby. But we all know that even if the baby isn't killed, the soldier will shoot it, or leave it in the mud to die.

Why do I think of that awful scene, while at the same time thinking of Mummy hugging me in bed? I was her baby, and she was trying to protect me. She wasn't shielding me from a bullet, but from my future. She hadn't always been able to be a good mother, but she was doing her best now. But she knew, and I knew, that soon I would be on my own, and that we had been forced apart because she was different. And because of that, I would have to learn to fend for myself, and protect myself as best as I could.

○ ○ ○ ○ ○ ○

The train journey to the town

When we woke up, the first thing that Mummy said to me was, 'Pippa, I have decided. I will go with Auntie Aileen to take you to school, and then, if there is time, I will come back and see Muriel. And that's final.'

We went downstairs and Auntie was at the table, busy making our sandwiches. The house was quiet, and I supposed that everyone else was still fast asleep. Mummy went into the kitchen to make a pot of tea, and Auntie stayed at the table with me. I whispered to her, 'I feel like Bonnie. When she left the hospital, she looked like she was being taken to prison.'

Auntie said, 'Pippa, if you let yourself feel like that all the time, it might work like a poison inside you. Enjoy every little thing that you do, and the friends that you have. You aren't going to prison. You will be in a school. And you aren't being punished. Have fun whenever you can. We will all be thinking of you. And if you write letters to Nicol and Jessie, and draw them pictures and write them little stories, I will make sure that they write back.'

Mummy came back in and we had our breakfast in silence. Then Mummy ran me a bath and I had to be very quick, just in case anyone woke up and needed the bathroom. Mummy insisted on staying in the bathroom with me and drying me all over. I cleaned my teeth and then Mummy helped me put on my school uniform. I looked at myself in Maggie's mirror. I looked like a Roman Catholic schoolgirl. Mummy came up behind me and kissed me, and put my beret on my head and said, 'There. You look perfect. I'm very proud of you.'

542

I looked perfect and Mummy was proud of me. I had to smile. I had to admit that my beret looked nice. It smelled of Rhona's patchouli oil and somebody's cigarettes.

Underneath my uniform, my skin was brown and bruised and scratched, and I was fit and healthy, and stronger. Inside myself I was happier. Was I ready to go? I felt like my life had been heading in one direction, up in the north of Scotland, where I could play out in the open, with a family and cousins, and a boyfriend who said he liked me very much, and with musicians and writers, and the sea, and an open air swimming pool, and a standing stone, and freedom, and choices, and a huge house that my father owned, with a real Turner painting in it. And where was I going? Down South, to a boarding school where everyone wore grey, with nuns, and Mass, and rules, and walls, and only girls, and where nobody must know that I am a half a Dunbar, and half-Jewish, and where a girl had fallen in love with a French girl, and felt such despair that she had thrown herself off a roof.

Mr Griffin drove us down to the station and left very quickly. It was raining and Mummy said that we should sit in the waiting room. Then I got a very big surprise. There was something very important that I had completely forgotten. Mummy said, 'Happy birthday, my darling girl.' It was the third of September, 1967, and it was my tenth birthday. I had been so busy thinking about leaving that I hadn't thought about that at all. Mummy kissed me and held me tight. Then she let go of me and took a small package out of her coat pocket. She said, 'We can look at it together on the train. '
Then there was a commotion outside, and Nicol, Maggie, Rhona, Jessie and Mr Griffin came in. They all sang Happy Birthday to You, and Jessie gave me a present, wrapped up in pretty green wrapping paper and tied with gold string. I wanted to open it, but a man announced that the train would be arriving in two minutes. Mr Griffin picked up my case, and then I realised that I didn't have my concertina with me.

Mummy said, 'It's probably best to leave it here. I don't know if you will be allowed to play it at school.' My heart sank. But Mummy said, 'But never mind, your case is full of painting and drawing equipment, and that should keep you busy and out of mischief for a long time.'

I smiled at the thought of me being mischievous and doing lots of painting. My heart lifted again.

Then the train arrived and Mr Griffin climbed on with my suitcase. Everybody seemed to be hugging and kissing me and saying things to me, all at the same time. Then a man wearing a uniform told us that we had to hurry up, because the train was about to leave. I climbed into the carriage and Mummy shut the door behind us. She pulled the window down so that I could look out and wave. Everyone was down below with Mr Griffin; waving at me and blowing me kisses. But Nicol wasn't there. He wasn't with the others. Then I saw him. He had moved away from everyone else and was standing by a pillar. His face was very red and he was crying. He wasn't just sniffing, like Maggie and Rhona and Jessie were doing. He was weeping very big tears, and trying his best not to make a noise, because he didn't want anybody to see him.

And he wasn't looking at me, because I knew that he didn't want me to see that he was upset. What a silly boy!

The train was moving and I shouted, 'Nicol! Nicol!' He looked up and wiped his face on his coat sleeve. There must have been snot on his sleeve, because he looked at it and said, 'Urgh!' And then he saw that I was looking at him doing it, and he laughed and waved at me.

I didn't cry. I sat next to Mummy and she held my hand. Auntie sat opposite me and nobody spoke for a while. Then I said to Auntie, 'Do you think Nicol will be all right without me?'

And then I cried. I tried not to make too much noise, because there was a mother with a baby sitting nearby, and the baby was fast asleep in her arms. But the more I tried not to make a noise, the worse I felt, until I thought I was going to explode.

Then I couldn't hold it in anymore and I heard myself make a horrible noise, just like a wailing baby. Mummy held me tight and said, 'Shh. There, there. You'll be all right. Everything will be all right.'

That stopped me from making a noise, but I couldn't stop my tears from running down my face in big streams. My crying seemed to go on forever, but it was probably only five minutes. I sniffed and wiped my eyes with Mummy's hanky. I looked at the mother with the baby. The baby was still fast asleep, but the mother looked very worried. She said to me, 'Are you all right pet? Whatever is the matter?'

I couldn't speak. Mummy said, 'I'm sorry. We're taking her to boarding school.'

The mother looked shocked. She said, 'Whatever for? Aren't there any good schools in Stranhaven?'

Mummy said, 'It's not my idea. It's her father who wants her to go.'

The mother didn't say anything after that, and looked out of the window.

Mummy suggested that we open my presents. She had given me a watch! I couldn't believe what I was seeing. It was a lovely Timex girl's watch, with a round face and a light blue strap. Mummy said, 'It was Muriel's idea. We bought it in the jewellers in Ashbourne on the day before we came up to see you. We showed it to Lucy, and she kissed it and said how much she missed you and that she loved you.'

'She loved me? Not just liked me?'

'No. She was very definite. She said that she had woken up one morning and felt there was a huge hole in her life, that would never be filled until you came back to see her again. She wanted to write you a letter, but you know how long that would have taken her, and we were in a bit of a hurry. But she did give you this.'

She handed me an envelope. Inside was a school photograph of Lucy, in her school uniform. She looked as lovely as ever. Mummy showed me how to set the hands on my watch to the right time, and how to it wind it properly, then helped me put it on my wrist. I was very proud of it.

Then we opened the present that Jessie had given me. There was a box, with four small packages inside. Auntie said, 'You can put those in your satchel and open them when you get to school, and perhaps there will be something in your case that you can share with your new friends, and Émilie; of course.'
There was an envelope in the bottom of the box, and Auntie said that I could open that. There was a lovely birthday card with a kitten on it, and my cousins had written nice messages inside.
There was a piece of paper and someone had typed a poem on it.
I read it to myself and then passed it to Mummy to look at. She read it and passed it to Auntie, then took a hanky from her handbag and dabbed her eyes. Auntie said, 'I think it's about his mother.'
Mummy said, 'Are you sure?'

We were going to Edinburgh, where we had to change trains. It was a slow train, which suited me just fine. I hoped it would break down in the middle of nowhere and stop for several hours. I kept looking at my watch. Mummy smiled at me and said that if I kept looking at it then time would seem to slow down. But the truth was that I wanted time to stop. But the more I wanted it to stop, the faster it seemed to run away from me. It was a horrible feeling, and I realised that I was becoming upset again. I tried to push my bad feeling down, but it kept popping up again, like sick. I looked out of the window and saw a beautiful white horse, standing in a field and shaking his head. I thought, 'If only I could be that horse. I could run around, and eat grass, and watch the trains go by all day long, full of little girls on their way to boarding school.'
Mummy said, 'Good heavens, I almost forgot!' She put her hand in her handbag and told me to guess what she had in there, and that it was a present from Muriel. Of course, I knew exactly what it was. It was a Bounty. There were two pieces, as

usual, and I took a bite out of one and gave the other to Mummy. Then there was a little argument between her and Auntie about which of them should have it, and in the end they agreed to have a bite each. And then my upset disappeared. At Edinburgh station, we saw several Convent girls, and they got on our train. The older ones, without their parents, were laughing and chatting noisily to each other. The younger girls with their parents were very quiet and looked sad.

The first moments

When we finally arrived at our town, I was feeling very tired and quite nervous. I held on tightly to Mummy, and didn't want to look around me. But I couldn't stop myself from being curious. The train had to wait at the station, while men unloaded trunks from the guard's van and put them onto a big wooden trolley. There were about twenty girls of all shapes and sizes standing on the platform. Some of them were like me, with brand new uniforms and blazers that were much too big for them, while others looked smart, but wearing clothes that were obviously not new. One girl looked quite untidy, which surprised me. I supposed that she had travelled for a long time and must have fallen asleep, because her hair was all over the place and she had just plonked her beret on her head any old how. She was laughing and making quite a lot of noise, so it was impossible to ignore her. I heard her say, 'Back to the old prison again!'

Then Mummy said to Auntie, 'Aileen, I've just realised that I have absolutely no idea what to do! I don't even know where the school is, or how to get there!' There was something in Mummy's voice that bothered me. She was starting to panic.

Auntie said, 'It's all right, Ruth. Try and relax.'

Mummy said, 'I've been trying that all through the journey, but something's happening. I can't control it. I can't do this. I can't!'

Auntie said, 'You must, Ruth, for Pippa's sake.'

Mummy took in a deep breath, and let it out again. She squeezed my hand, bent down towards me said, 'I'm sorry, Pippa. I'm trying not to be upset, but this is a terrible ordeal for me. I just want to grab you and run away from here, and to hell with the consequences!' Auntie was behind Mummy, and I saw the worried look on her face. Mummy straightened up and took in another deep breath. She said, 'I'm sorry, Pippa. I'm sorry. I'm all right now. I know what to do.'

The girl with the untidy hair was just walking past us and Mummy stopped her and said, 'Excuse me, my dear, but we are new here. How do we get to the Convent?'

The girl smiled and said, 'Well, you can take a taxi, like us.' She pointed to another girl who was dragging a big case. I'm Mary, and this is Grazia. There are so many Marys in our school, so everyone calls me Unholy Mary, because I'm such an unholy mess! Why don't you come in our taxi? My parents ordered it, so we can all squeeze in.'

Auntie said, 'That's very kind of you, Mary, but we'll follow you, and see if we can get our own taxi.' Mary looked disappointed, and we walked with her out of the station lobby and into the street, where a large taxi was waiting. Mary said to the driver, 'I'm Mary Forsythe. Did my father order a taxi to take me to the Convent? And might there be room for all of us?' The driver laughed and we all got in the taxi. Mummy nudged me and whispered 'Who does Mary remind you of?'

I whispered back, 'Dorothy.' We both smiled at each other, and I knew that Mummy's wobble was over.

In the taxi, I closed my eyes, until it stopped and we were at the front of the big school building. We all climbed the steps and there was a nun standing by the front door. She shook hands with Mummy and Auntie, but ignored the girls. Just as we were walking through the door the nun called after us, 'Now remember girls, this is the only time you may use the front door.'

A nun was standing at the bottom of the stairs. Mummy said to her, 'My daughter is new here. She's in the Junior Division. Where do we take her?

The he nun didn't smile. She said, 'Parents don't go upstairs. You can say goodbye to your daughter here.'

Mummy took in a sudden, sharp breath. Mary was standing behind us, and the nun said to her, 'Forsythe, help this girl carry her case up to the Juniors' dormitory.' She looked at me and said, 'It's at the top of the stairs. Say goodbye, and follow Forsythe.'

Mummy said, 'It's quite all right, Mary. If you could carry Pippa's case up to her dormitory, that would be very kind of you, but we are just going to pop outside for a quick breath of fresh air.' Mummy ignored the nun, but I looked at her, and she was scowling at Mummy.

We walked through a small door, into the space at the back of the building. There was a lovely big lawn, and beyond it a brown, ugly-looking church. We walked onto the lawn, and Mummy said, 'Let's sit down here for a little while.' The sun was shining and there was only a very slight wind. I felt very hot with my coat on, so Mummy helped me take it off, and we sat on the grass.

Auntie said to Mummy, 'I feel that you are back in control now, Ruth.'

Mummy said, 'Thank you, Aileen, but I'm so glad that you're here. I couldn't do this without you. Everything just came flooding back to me, from all those years ago. It's like history repeating itself.'

Auntie Aileen smiled, 'But Pippa is older than you were, and she has you still, and Muriel, and me, and all of us. And she has her father too.'

Mummy frowned, and then she smiled. 'Of course, Andrew is doing his best. He's a good man. I know he is.'

Auntie said, 'Yes, he's a good man.'

I knew that they were saying all of those things for me to think about.

Then a car stopped in front of us and a man got out. The back door opened and a girl in a brand new uniform got out. The man opened the car boot, took out a big case, and put it down next to the girl. He said to her, 'Right. I'd best be off then. I'm sure you'll be fine on your own.' The girl looked a bit shocked, but didn't say anything. The man got back into his car and drove off. The girl put her hands to the sides of her head and let out an almighty wail. Mummy said, 'Goodness gracious,' and rushed over to the girl and crouched down beside her, and tried to stop her from crying. She tried to hold the girl's hand, but she moved away from Mummy. I supposed that she was very frightened. Mummy said, 'It's all right. Come and sit with us. My daughter is new too.' Mummy put out her hand again, and this time the girl took it and came and stood next to us, but was still crying loudly. Mummy crouched down again and asked the girl what her name was.

She said it was Antonia. Her crying became a bit quieter, but she was taking in big gulps of air, and I thought she was going to make herself choke.

Mummy said to her, 'This is Pippa. She's a lovely girl. Pippa, will you and Antonia look after each other?'

I said, 'Yes please!'

Auntie laughed and Antonia stopped crying. But then she put her hand in her blazer pocket and felt for something, and started crying again. Mummy asked her what was wrong, and Antonia whimpered, 'I can't find my hanky. I don't know where anything is. I wish my mummy and daddy were here.'

I said, 'But I thought that was your daddy. Where are your parents?'

Antonia stopped crying. She looked at me. Her skin was very tanned, but I could see that she had freckles on her face. Her hair was in two neat plaits, tied with red ribbons. She reminded me of Pippi Longstocking. I smiled at her and put out my hand. She took it, and I pulled at her, to try to make her sit next to me. She said, 'Mummy and Daddy live in Brazil. My grannie lives about thirty miles away from here. I've been staying with her for a few days, and she was supposed to bring me today, in a taxi. But she's ill, so she asked the taxi driver to bring me on my own.'

I said, 'I thought he was your daddy.'

550

Antonia said, 'Good heavens, no! My daddy would have given me a hug and a kiss, and cried his eyes out! He's always telling me I'm his favourite daughter!'

'So do you have a sister?'

'Not at all. It's just one of Daddy's silly jokes.' She started to cry again. Mummy looked at Auntie. I felt certain that they were thinking the same as me; 'If the daddy loves his daughter so much, why did he send her half-way across the world, to go to a school in a freezing cold country?' I wondered if Antonia was thinking the same thing, and that's what was really making her cry.

A nun walked by, but didn't take any notice of us. Mummy stood up and called out, 'Excuse me!'

The nun carried on walking, so Mummy called out again, but this time twice as loud. 'Excuse me. This child is very distressed. Is there anyone who can help her?'

The nun turned round. She looked like she didn't understand, and I wondered if she was foreign, or perhaps deaf. She said to Mummy, 'What's the child's name and how old is she?'

Mummy asked Antonia, 'What's your name Antonia, and how old are you?'

Antonia looked at her shoes. They were just like mine. 'Antonia McLeish. I'm ten.'

The nun said, 'Tell her to find an older girl who will show her where she should go. There will be a nun there who will see to her.'

Mummy said, 'See to her?'

The nun stared at Mummy. 'That's right. See to her.' She walked away. Then she turned round and said to Mummy, 'And by the way, girls are not allowed on the lawn.'

Then we saw Sister Anne walking across the lawn towards us. She smiled at me and said, 'Hello Pippa! So you came here after all! I spent a few sleepless nights, thinking that you might not like us, and would decide to go somewhere else! But I prayed to the Lord, and here you are!' She looked at Antonia.

'And have you made a friend already? How nice. What's your name, my dear?'

Antonia went bright red and started wailing again. Sister Anne opened her arms and said to Antonia, 'Come here.' Antonia went to her, and Sister Anne held her hand. She said, 'Now look at me. Don't be frightened.'

Sister Anne looked at Mummy and Auntie. I'm sure that she winked at them. Mummy smiled. Antonia said, 'My mummy and daddy are in Brazil.'

Sister Anne looked very surprised. 'Really? As far away as that? So can you speak Brazilian? But what a lovely Scottish accent you have! Actually, now I think about it, people in Brazil speak Portuguese. That gives me an idea. I'm going to introduce you to Maria, who is the lady who does all our sewing. She's from Portugal, and I'm sure she will be delighted to speak Portuguese with you.'

Antonia smiled. Sister Anne said, 'What a lovely smile. But have you been shown where everything is? I always think that the first thing to find out about in a new place is where the toilets are.'

A big girl walked by in front of the lawn. She looked like she had been crying. Sister Anne said to her, 'Excuse me, Rebecca...' then she saw the girl's face. 'Oh dear, what's the matter?'

Rebecca said, 'I've just said goodbye to my parents, so I'm a bit upset.'

Sister Anne smiled at her. 'Of course you are. Come here and give me a hug.' Rebecca walked onto the lawn, but Sister Anne couldn't hug her properly, because Antonia wouldn't let go of her hand. This made everyone laugh. Sister Anne said, 'When these two charming girls are ready to say goodbye, would you be so kind as to take them to the toilets? And then show them where they have to go to meet Sister Carmel, in the Junior dormitory?'

Rebecca said, 'Oh yes, Sister, I'd love to. But first, I must go to the toilet myself. I'm absolutely busting.'

'Sister Anne laughed. 'It's bursting, my dear, bursting.'

552

Rebecca ran into the building. We hadn't noticed another nun standing by the door. It was Sister Winifred, the nasty nun in charge of the school. She said to Rebecca, 'Walk, child. Walk.'

The nun stared at us, then went indoors again. Sister Anne said to Mummy. 'That's Sister Winifred. She has a lot on her mind. So much responsibility. And what with the new building work soon to start, it's all a bit much for her. But I'm so glad that you are here. But where is that delightful young woman who came with you the last time we met?'

Mummy explained that Muriel was in hospital in Aberdeen, waiting for an operation. Sister Anne said, 'But that's terrible! You must be so worried.' She looked at me. 'And how must young Pippa be feeling?' I wanted to look down at my shoes, but there was something about Sister Anne, some force, that made me look into her eyes. But I couldn't say anything. Sister Anne said, 'Of course, my dear. I do understand. Now, I must be going, but if there's anything that you think I need to know, about good things as well as the occasional wee problem, you know what to do, don't you?' She tapped the side of her nose with her pointing finger. I nodded. Then she shook Mummy and Auntie's hands and whispered something in Mummy's ear. Mummy smiled and said, 'Thank you Sister Anne. Oh, thank you.'

Sister Anne said, 'God bless you. God bless you both,' then walked into the building.

Mummy said, 'Pippa, we really have to get back to the station, otherwise we will miss our train.' I had been preparing myself for this terrible moment, ever since Mummy told me that she would be able to take me to school. She crouched down in front of me. She said, 'Daddy and Muriel were right. You are going to make lots of nice friends. Look, you already have one.' Antonia held my hand. 'And you can go with Antonia and that nice big girl. And when you are ready, you can open your birthday presents. And there's something in your suitcase that you can share.'

Mummy's voice was becoming very wobbly. I wanted her to stop talking, but she wouldn't. She said, 'You know that I love you, and this is not what I would have ever chosen for you. But I know... I know that you will do your best to... to make the most of it!' She held me tight and I could feel her whole body shaking.

Auntie said, 'It's all right, Ruth. Pippa will be all right.'

I said to Mummy, 'Yes, Mummy. I will be all right. I'm a big strong girl. Please don't miss your train.' But I desperately wanted her to miss her train, so she would have to stay in the town in a hotel, and come and see me again.

She said, 'Yes, darling. You're quite right. We must go now.' She kissed me on both cheeks and stood up. Auntie kissed me too, but didn't say anything. I think she was trying not to cry too.

Then Mummy said, 'Whatever am I thinking of? Antonia must think I am the rudest person in the world! Come here and let me kiss you too. You will look after Pippa for me, won't you? She's my favourite daughter, after all!'

That made me smile.

Then they both walked away, and through the door into the building.

Antonia and I were now on our own, standing on the lawn. I moved to walk off it, onto the tarmac, but Antonia said, 'Where are you going?'

'But we're not allowed on the grass.'

'Well, I'm new, and I don't know that.'

'Yes you do. That horrible nun told you.'

'She didn't tell me. She just said it to your mother.'

I went back onto the grass. I said, 'I already know some of the big girls here. I met them when I was in hospital in this town. They're very nice, and promised to look after me, so I'll tell them to look after you too. One of them is French and is called Émilie, and she has the most fascinating accent.'

Antonia looked like she was going to cry again. She said, 'Pippa, will you be my friend? I'm frightened, and don't want to be on my own.'

'Yes, of course. I'm frightened too, but I'm not going to show it.' Antonia smiled. I said, 'Do you know, Antonia, that today is my birthday? And I haven't opened all my presents yet. And Mummy says there's something in my case that I can share with my new friends, and I hope she means that she's made me a birthday cake. And because you're my first new friend, you can have an extra-large piece.'

Antonia looked very impressed and said, 'I knew as soon as I saw you that we would be friends.'

I didn't want that big girl called Rebecca to come back. I didn't want her to take us upstairs to be seen to by Sister Carmel. I wanted to sit there for as long as possible, and make friends with this girl from Brazil, with freckles and two lovely light brown French plaits. I told Antonia about the way that Émilie wore her beret, and how it made me pleased to think that I might look like her. We adjusted our berets, and Antonia said that I looked very French. She admired my satchel, and said that she would love to have one just like it. I opened it and took out Nicol's poem. I told Antonia that my cousin had written it, and that it was about his mother. Antonia read it very carefully and said, 'Are you Pippa Dunbar?'

I said, 'I'm Herman really, but some people know me as Pippa Dunbar. How do you know?'

'This poem is about you.' I read Nicol's poem again.

> Please swim with me
> In the deep dark sea
> Please dive down, holding my hand.
> Promise me that one day you will come back,
> And never leave me again.

> Diving deep down,
> Under the foam and the waves,
> Never looking above or below; just straight ahead, knowing that
> Behind us everyone will
> Always be near us, and they will
> Remember that you loved us, once.

Then Antonia said, 'I'm busting to do a wee.'
I said, 'Bursting, my dear. Bursting.' We both laughed at that. I said, 'Me too. Let's go and find a toilet.' Antonia held my hand, but I stood still. Antonia said, 'Come on. Take a deep breath. One two, three... Go!' and we rushed into the building.

○ ○ ○ ○ ○ ○

3rd December 1976

All day yesterday, my head was full of thoughts of Muriel, and I've just woken up from a horrible dream. I dreamed I was in London, opposite the Houses of Parliament, leaning on a wall and looking down onto the River Thames. It was a hot, sunny day, and the tide was out, and I could see an ugly little beach of mud and pebbles. There were lots of small pleasure boats and rowing boats on the river, full of happy families. Two boats caught my eye. One had six young boys in it, and the other had a group of adults. I wondered why the children weren't in the same boat as the adults. Then I realised that the adults weren't their parents.

Suddenly, from the opposite direction, a big speedboat came rushing towards the pleasure boats, and just missed them. It created a huge swell, and all the boats were bobbing up and down, and people inside them were laughing. But the boys weren't laughing, because the swell had made a wave of water swamp their boat, and gradually it started to sink. I watched in horror, as the boys tried desperately to save their boat from sinking. But they couldn't, and one by one, they fell into the water and tried to swim towards the muddy shore, just below me. I jumped over the wall and landed in thick mud. I managed to wade through the mud, towards where the boys had swum. But none of them had been able to reach the beach, so in a frenzy of panic, I dived below the surface. I held out my hand and felt one of the boys grab my arm. I pulled him towards me and up to the surface. Gasping for breath, he scrambled onto the beach. I did this three more times, and each time a desperate child grabbed me. But I knew that there were still some more children under the water, and that they had been there for a long time. If I didn't find them soon, then they would certainly drown.

I was almost overcome with panic and exhaustion. I waded in the muddy water up to my waist, and trod on a child. I dragged him to the surface and threw him onto the beach. I had no idea if he were dead or alive. Then my panic overcame me, because I couldn't remember how many boys there had been in the boat. Was it six? Or seven? I looked across the river and saw that the adults who had been looking after the children were just sitting in their boat, watching. I yelled and screamed at them, 'How many children were there? How many have I saved? And is there one more under the water?'
But the adults didn't say anything. I screamed again, 'Call the police! Get the police!'
Then I noticed, to my horror, that the adults in the other boats were laughing. To them it was a great piece of entertainment. It was like some sort of terrible sport. One of them, a man, laughed a horrible laugh, and sneered, 'Why waste your time trying to save them? They're all going to die anyway.'

I looked at the children I had saved. They were all sitting there, on the bank, glistening and shiny with water. They looked like sleek little otters, or baby guinea pigs. Then I realised that they weren't boys at all. They were all girls, at that stage in their lives when they are androgynous, just like I was when I started school. And I knew that there was one more girl under the water, in the mud, and that she was almost certainly dead.

I shouldn't think about Muriel as much as I do. It's not good for me. But I get such comfort from reminding myself of the times when I was truly loved. But then I feel an awful sense of despair, which I can't shake off. It's then that I know how Mummy felt when Daddy forced her to go back to England, and to take me with her. She drank whisky to stop herself from going mad. And when she left me at the Convent, I know what was going through her mind, body, and soul. She was trying so hard to control herself, for my sake. She was remembering, reliving, the dreadful moment when her parents handed her over to strangers, and to an uncertain future, rather than risk her being murdered by heartless Nazis. And now she had to hand me over, her only child, against her will and better judgement, to a bunch of heartless nuns. What saved her from going completely mad? Auntie Aileen, surely, but really it was Muriel. Muriel saved us both. But Muriel was lying alone in a hospital in Aberdeen. So I was split in two; half of me desperately wanted Mummy to stay, while the other half wanted her to rush away and get back to Muriel. I had to be all right. If I wasn't all right, then Mummy would crumble, completely. Thank God I had Antonia, lovely Antonia.

Did Vincent Van Gogh know that he was mad? Someone once told me that the difference between a mad person and a sane person is this: 'A sane person knows that she is sane, even though she might feel sometimes like she is going mad. A mad person has no doubt that she is sane, and never feels that she has gone mad.'

So where does that leave me?

The sky has been so grey recently. I long for some Van Gogh Blue.

Lightning Source UK Ltd.
Milton Keynes UK
UKHW010631050422
401124UK00002B/278